Robert Elsmere

by

Mary Augusta Ward

edited with an introduction and notes by Miriam Elizabeth Burstein

Victorian Secrets 2018

Published by

Victorian Secrets Limited
32 Hanover Terrace
Brighton BN2 9SN

www.victoriansecrets.co.uk

Robert Elsmere by Mary Augusta Ward
First published in 1888
First published by Victorian Secrets in 2013.
This 2nd edition published in 2018.

Introduction and notes © 2018 by Miriam Elizabeth Burstein

Composition and design by Catherine Pope
Cover image © iStockPhoto/duncan1890

A catalogue record for this book is available from the British Library.

ISBN 978-1-906469-61-0

CONTENTS

INTRODUCTION

Reflecting on the belated French proposal to translate *Robert Elsmere*, Mary Ward proudly concludes, "it had seemed to show that with all its many faults—and who knew them better than I?—my book had yet possessed a certain representative and pioneering force; and that, to some extent at least, the generation in which it appeared had spoken through it."[1] At first glance, Ward's assessment of her own achievement ties the novel tightly to its historical time and place: a country with an established church, with all the rights and privileges that entailed; orthodox Christians dealing with the fallout from the new German Biblical criticism, the shifting civic roles of skeptics, Catholics, and Jews, and post-Darwinian biology; and liberal Christians wondering where, exactly, their place was in late-nineteenth-century Anglicanism. And yet, the United States, with no state church and an even unrulier state of religious affairs, embraced the book wholeheartedly— in part because Ward had inadvertently tapped into an entirely different and thoroughly American genre, the social gospel novel, with its this-worldly emphasis on practical Christianity and social amelioration.[2] *Robert Elsmere's* bestsellerdom is now legendary: "[b]y March 1889 it was said that between 30,000 and 40,000 copies had been sold in England and 200,000 copies in the United States."[3] It was reviewed in all the best journals (by William Gladstone, the Prime Minister, no less), spawned fictional and nonfictional responses, and eventually wound up on stage. Nevertheless, twentieth- and twenty-first century scholars have found themselves in something of a rut, repeatedly apologizing for studying a novel so relentlessly out of fashion. *Robert Elsmere* "has for too long been underrated—and virtually unread by any except specialists," sighs William Peterson in 1976; things are no better in 2007, when Erin A. Smith observes that "almost nobody besides Victorian

---

1   Mrs. [Mary Augusta] Humphry Ward, *A Writer's Recollections* (London: W. Collins Sons and Co., 1918), 254.
2   For a reading of the novel in this American context, see Erin A. Smith, "What Would Jesus Do? The Social Gospel and the Literary Marketplace," *Book History* 10 (2007): 195-99.
3   William S. Peterson, *Victorian Heretic: Mrs Humphry Ward's* Robert Elsmere (Leicester: Leicester University Press, 1976), 159.

novel scholars reads *Robert Elsmere*…"[4] Why, then, bring the novel back into print?

Well, to begin with, *Robert Elsmere*'s reputation for theological clunkiness bears little relationship to the actual novel, which is both absorbing and an exceptionally ambitious literary undertaking. (For true theological clunkiness, alas, one must turn to *Robert Elsmere*'s direct sequel, *The Case of Richard Meynell* [1911].) Granted, Mary Ward's religious project is deeply serious: in chronicling Robert Elsmere's transformation from orthodox Christian clergyman to the preacher of a new, liberalized and humanized religion—one that preaches "the duties of applied altruism rather than personal piety," as Melvin Richter puts it[5]—Ward charts what, at this point in her intellectual development, she believed to be the only honest response to doubts about such canonical points of Christian faith as the divinity of Christ and the possibility of miracles. Indeed, Ward would attempt to put Robert Elsmere's social (albeit not Socialist) advocacy into practice with the Passmore Edwards Settlement, founded in 1897, which combined working-class outreach with pioneering efforts toward the education of disabled children.[6] But although Robert's spiritual journey is a bookish one, as we will discuss in just a moment, it primarily unfolds through a series of intense conflicts with those closest to him: Langham, Robert's world-weary and self-defeating tutor at Oxford; Squire Wendover, the dour skeptic with a magnificent library; and, above all, Robert's orthodox wife Catherine, whose growing disappointment in and alienation from her husband owes something to Dorothea Brooke's experiences with Casaubon in George Eliot's *Middlemarch*.

Although Ward did not begin writing *Robert Elsmere* until 1885, she first explored its central narrative about the painful process of faith's loss and rebirth in *Sin and Unbelief* (reprinted in the *North American Review* in 1889), her pamphlet against John Wordsworth's lecture *The One Religion: Truth, Holiness, and Peace Desired by the Nations, and Revealed by Jesus Christ* (1881). Wordsworth had warned against a world defined by Arnoldian "culture," which could only ever lead to sin and falling away. By contrast, Ward traced out two potential life courses for young men experiencing the effects of an Oxford education, one leading to a renovated faith and one to the

---

4   Peterson, 14; Smith, 214.

5   Melvin Richter, *The Politics of Conscience: T. H. Green and His Age* (Cambridge, MA: Harvard University Press, 1964), 29.

6   The frequently conflicted history of the Passmore Edwards Settlement, which emerged from a less-successful and more religiously-oriented project, University Hall, is discussed in John Sutherland, *Mrs Humphry Ward: Eminent Victorian, Pre-Eminent Edwardian* (Oxford: Oxford University Press, 1990), 215-29.

etiolated conservatism of Wordsworth, as it were. *Robert Elsmere* works out in novelistic form *Sin and Unbelief*'s hypothetical tale of the young Christian turned religious liberal: he arrives at the University and finds that his reading slowly but surely puts him at odds with everything he once believed. Whether he wishes or no, this earnest student undergoes an intellectual conversion experience of a much more frightening sort than the Christian variety, a "bewildering and terrible light breaking upon life," after which he realizes that Christianity is "the product of human needs and human skill."[7] Out of this initially bleak conversion, however, eventually comes the Idealist discovery of a God who transcends all purely human modes of inquiry (172). This life plot foreshadows both Robert's far more detailed conversion experience and how heavily the novel will rely on books as the primary agents of religious change. But it also suggests how invested Ward is in storytelling—fictional or not—as a mode of argumentation.

Mary Ward knew more than she wanted to about how a sea-change in religious views could upset an entire family. Her father, Thomas Arnold—son of the great educational reformer and man of letters, Thomas Arnold; brother of the legendary poet and cultural critic, Matthew Arnold—seesawed back and forth between Anglican and Roman Catholic allegiances, each time upending the family's finances and exasperating friends on all sides of the question. Thomas' spiritual quest destroyed his marriage, although Ward remained close to her father despite her strong misgivings about orthodox Roman Catholicism (later explored in one of her most powerful novels, *Helbeck of Bannisdale* [1898]).[8] Her own fraught spiritual journey took place in the context of the liberal religious atmosphere of mid-to-late Victorian Oxford, after the Tractarian or Oxford movement—which sought to rejuvenate the Church of England by calling it back to its pre-Reformation liturgical roots—stumbled in the wake of John Henry Newman's conversion to Catholicism. As a result, the novel's core theological crises at times seem to be rather out of date, owing more to the dust-up over the Oxford Movement than to what was actually happening in 1880s theology[9] Ward's close friends in Oxford included such intellectuals as Mark Pattison, the Rector of Lincoln College and one of the models for both Langham and Wendover, whose failed marriage to the much younger Emily Francis Strong worked its way into several late-Victorian novels; Benjamin Jowett, the Master of Balliol, whose

---

7   Mary A. Ward, "Sin and Unbelief," *North American Review* 148.387 (Mar. 1889): 170.

8   Bernard Bergonzi chronicles Thomas' career in *A Victorian Wanderer: The Life of Thomas Arnold the Younger* (New York: Oxford University Press, 2003).

9   A point made by Peterson, 132-33.

religious liberalism both inspired and angered many of his contemporaries; and Walter Pater (another inspiration for Langham), the novelist and art critic most notorious for *The Renaissance*. Perhaps most importantly of all for *Robert Elsmere*, Ward also befriended Thomas Hill Green, the Idealist thinker whose "emphasis on the necessity for moral seriousness, even when it was a seriousness that could no longer rest on doctrines concerning the Christian God" inspired many late-Victorian politicians and social reformers who yearned to better the world but could no longer accept orthodox dogmas.[10] And then, of course, there was her uncle, Matthew Arnold, whose own critique of dogmatic theology—"a separable accretion, which never had any business to be attached to Christianity, never did it any good, and now does it great harm, and thickens an hundredfold the religious confusion in which we live"—recognizably underpins Robert Elsmere's attempts to jettison dogmatic statements in favor of what Arnold called a "reconstruction" of religion, grounded in a careful attention to the Bible itself.[11]

As Ward's introduction to the "Library Edition" of *Robert Elsmere* details, the novel's autobiographical roots extend to its bookish*ness*. Robert's historical studies and the increasing theological problems they pose, most notably when it comes to historical testimony, derive from Ward's own experience working on the Spanish articles for the *Dictionary of Christian Biography*.[12] In the wake of the German Higher Criticism, initially mediated to Robert through Squire Wendover, it becomes harder and harder to read the Gospel narratives as anything but products of minds circumscribed by the specifics of their time, place, and culture. But Ward also loads the novel with quotations from poetry (with William Wordsworth, Matthew Arnold, and Arthur Hugh Clough playing important roles), contemporary fiction, Shakespeare, and, perhaps most frequently, the Bible. Allusions veer from *The Three Musketeers* one instant to the theology of Ernest Renan the next. The novel itself mixes and matches different literary genres with glee, behaving like a novel of religious

---

10 Timothy Maxwell Gouldstone, *The Rise and Decline of Anglican Idealism in the Nineteenth Century* (Houndmills, UK: Palgrave Macmillan, 2005), 49. Leigh Dale has recently suggested a much more negative assessment of Green's representation in *Robert Elsmere*, describing him as "the insidiously influential Mr. Grey, whose liberalism and skepticism have tragic consequences." "T. H. Green and the Modern Novel: English at Oxford," *Modern Language Quarterly* 75.2 (June 2014): 244.

11 Matthew Arnold, *Literature and Dogma*, in *Dissent and Dogma*, ed. R. H. Super (Ann Arbor, MI: University of Michigan Press, 1968), 382-83, 380.

12 Mrs. [Mary Augusta] Humphry Ward, "Introduction," *The Writings of Mrs. Humphry Ward, Vol. I: Robert Elsmere* (Boston and New York: Houghton Mifflin Company, 1911), xvii.

controversy at one moment, like a Gothic a few pages later.[13] Characters think and talk in snippets of other texts; their reading becomes, in a way, their inner being. Ruth Clayton Windscheffel astutely points out that Ward dwells on the moral and ethical implications of what characters read, where they read it, and what they do with this reading.[14] It is important, for example, that Catherine appears to have no acquaintance with modern languages, which cuts her off from the Continental theological and literary upheavals that so exercise the other characters, but it is just as important that "when he [Robert] quoted a very well-known line of Shelley's she asked him where it came from" (57). Catherine's education, that is, does not extend to an atheist, radical poet. Her limited range of literary references—she most frequently quotes the Bible—denotes both the intensity of her faith and the strict boundaries of her religious horizon. Similarly, Squire Wendover's magnificent library, which embodies in miniature the history of English thought, generates little in the way of new knowledge; the Squire has "severed his scholarly appetites from the broader human passions and from immediate contexts that alone could give them significance," consuming texts *selfishly*, as it were.[15] Like George Eliot's Casaubon, who never finishes his unfinishable *Key to All Mythologies*, Wendover toils forever at his "History of Testimony," which (also like Casaubon) he leaves in manuscript at the end, hoping that Robert will finish it. Similarly, Edward Langham's once-promising intellectual career repeatedly implodes under the sheer force of his unwillingness to engage with anyone or anything for very long; his self-destructing attempt to woo Catherine's sister Rose Leyburn finally falls apart permanently once his "endangered habits and threatened individuality" (507) come back to the fore.

By contrast, Robert transforms Christianity through what, at first glance, seems an utterly unrelated practice: by performing tales from classic literary texts for his working-class parishioners. Early on, he tries to explain his "story-telling" to an initially bemused Langham:

---

13 Or, as Judith Wilt puts it, "Robert Elsmere himself enters the provincial section of the novel thinking he's in a Jane Austen comedy of manners [...], then finds himself in the world of late Charlotte Brontë novels, and dies holding hard to both marriage and God against the bleak pull of Hardyesque modernity." *Behind Her Times: Transition England in the Novels of Mary Arnold Ward* (Charlottesville and London: University of Virginia Press, 2005), 48.

14 Ruth Clayton Windscheffel, *Reading Gladstone* (Houndmills: Palgrave Macmillan, 2008), 140. For a more general overview, see Michael Wheeler, *The Art of Allusion in Victorian Fiction* (London: Macmillan, 1979), 116-36.

15 Daniel Cook, "Bodies of Scholarship: Witnessing the Library in Late-Victorian Fiction," *Victorian Literature and Culture* 39 (2011): 117.

> "My story-telling is the simplest thing in the world. I began it
> in the winter with the object of somehow or other getting at the
> *imagination* of these rustics. Force them for only half an hour
> to live someone else's life—it is the one thing worth doing with
> them. That's what I have been aiming at. I *told* my stories all the
> winter—Shakespeare, Don Quixote, Dumas—Heaven knows
> what! And on the whole it answers best." (212)

Robert's early storytelling practice, begun before he has consciously
abandoned his orthodoxy, cultivates "imagination" as the foundation for
empathy. To "live someone else's life" becomes a gateway drug of sorts to a
more capacious morality: escape the narrow bounds of subjectivity and enter
into the minds of others, *any* others, in order to realize the larger claims
of social obligation. Unlike the singularly unproductive Squire Wendover
and Langham, Robert translates his intellectual baggage into new, more
productive forms. But his initial discovery of storytelling's power recurs later
in his new understanding of the Bible as itself a collection of powerful stories,
characterized by "'poetical truth'" (446) instead of historical. When, near
the novel's end, Robert confronts a group of working-class freethinkers, he
challenges their blasphemy by retelling the Gospels: "The dramatic force, the
tender passionate insight, the fearless modernness with which the story was
told, made it almost unbearable. Those listening saw the trial, the streets of
Jerusalem, that desolate place outside the northern gate; they were spectators
of the torture, they heard the last cry. No one present had ever so seen, so
heard before" (544). Robert's effect on his listeners is reminiscent of Charles
Dickens in one of his famous live readings. The old story, translated into the
language of "modern" England, transports its auditors to Christ's Passion;
Robert's novelistic transformation of the Gospel—an oral retelling that
apparently outdoes even the most intense of the "Lives of Jesus" so popular in
the nineteenth century[16]—momentarily shatters the boundaries of time and
space to make narrative into an act of spiritual communion. All distinctions
of class, age, and gender briefly coalesce into the unified "they," undergoing
not the Passion itself, but rather the agonizing experience of Christ's first
followers as they watch his sufferings. Here, then, is the novel's dream of a
new Christianity, to be called into being by identifying fully with the founders
of the old.

---

16 On the use of highly-evocative fictional technique in nineteenth-century biog-
raphies of Jesus by Ernest Renan and F. W. Farrar in particular, see Jennifer Stevens,
The Historical Jesus and the Literary Imagination, 1860-1920 (Liverpool: Liverpool
University Press, 2010), 42-49, 56-62.

But speaking of "the modern," one irresolvable tension in the novel for twenty-first century readers is its attitude to its female characters. It is always dangerous to assume that religious liberalism predicts political liberalism (the outspoken agnostic and equally outspoken anti-feminist Eliza Lynn Linton, whose *True History of Joshua Davidson, Communist* [1872] anticipates *Robert Elsmere*'s fully-humanized Jesus, is another case in point). *Robert Elsmere*'s "religious explorations were daring and progressive in their time," but "the social universe in which she [Ward] envisions them is profoundly retrograde in its gender relations."[17] Within the Elsmere marriage, it is Robert who willingly (if with considerable agony) pursues new routes to faith opened up by modern history, philosophy, and science, while Catherine represents a conservative, evangelical counter-movement rooted in traditional attitudes to both the Bible and religious practice. Ward, Ilana Blumberg has recently argued, identifies Catherine's religious conservatism with a "[p]rideful and self-asserting" mode of "self-sacrifice" that "breaks down social ties."[18] This conservatism becomes most obvious in the case of *Robert Elsmere*'s prominent subplot about Catherine's sister Rose, courted by both Langham and the aristocratic, somewhat dilettantish Hugh Flaxman. The rebellious Rose is, by all appearances, a true artist, an aspiring concert violinist whose performances ravish her hearers. "Where had a little provincial maiden learned to play with this intelligence, this force, this delicate command of her instrument?" a stunned Robert asks himself when he first listens to her play (61). Later, an overwhelmed Langham muses, "What magic and mastery in the girl's touch! What power of divination, and of rendering!" (208) Although Ward gently mocks Rose's penchant for Pre-Raphaelite aestheticism and contemporary design fads—the Japanese pots, the hair, the wild clothes—she nevertheless makes clear that Rose moves steadily up the ladder of a serious musical career. Rose goes to Manchester, one of the centers of late-Victorian musical culture; she studies with the best violinists. But the true drama of her plot turns out to reside in her discovery of love and a yearning for marriage, first with Langham (who, as terrified as Squire Wendover of loving connections, brutally throws her over) and, finally, with Flaxman. In this relationship, we, like Flaxman, see the stirrings of her transformation from "fanciful enchantress" to "wife that was to be" (620), from bohemian *artiste* to budding companion and mother. The reader wondering if Rose will be able to maintain her musical

17 Marty Hipsky, "Romancing Bourdieu: A Case Study in Gender Politics in the Literary Field," *Pierre Bourdieu: Fieldwork in Culture*, ed. Nicholas Brown and Imre Szeman (Boston: Rowman & Littlefield, 2000), 198.

18 Ilana M. Blumberg, *Victorian Sacrifice: Ethics and Economics in Mid-Century Novels* (Columbus: Ohio State University Press, 2013), 210.

career after marriage will discover, if they turn to *The Case of Richard Meynell*, that Rose has settled down into a gossipy, rather bossy mother, whose musical impulses are now fulfilled entirely by listening instead of playing.

In *The Case of Richard Meynell*, Ward symbolically and literally hands Robert Elsmere's project on to the next generation, only to dismantle it. By 1911, Ward had become intrigued by the Modernist movement in Roman Catholicism, which sought to integrate the new Biblical scholarship into Catholic teaching. She took Modernism as her model for a revived Anglicanism. Instead of Robert's resolute journey outside the Church to develop a new mode of Christian faith, Richard Meynell's "case"—literally, as he is on trial for his heterodox beliefs—rests firmly within the Church of England. Although Meynell's fate remains uncertain, he is nevertheless a full-blown saint rewarded with marriage to Robert's daughter; the novel ends with Catherine's quiet death, with "the vision of an opening glory—a heavenly throng!"[19] Catherine's final apotheosis revises Robert's own death, in which his "ecstasy of joy" (658) derives not from a vision of heaven, but of earthly happiness: the birth of his child. And yet, both dying visions are utterly appropriate for the characters' religious beliefs—Catherine's yearning for God in the world beyond, Robert's for God in this. The truth they see at death, that is, is "poetic," as much a creation of one human mind's understanding and needs as the Gospels.[20] Even as Catherine's death heralds the figurative end of an old Anglicanism, it also calls back to the capaciousness of Robert's dream for a new Christianity.

---

19 Mrs. [Mary Augusta] Humphry Ward, *The Case of Richard Meynell* (Garden City and New York: Doubleday, Page & Company, 1911), 630.

20 Norman Vance has suggested that at Robert's death, Catherine experiences a "version of miracle, a trance or hallucination conveying a sense of the transcendent"; this is orthodox miracle psychologized, in other words. *Bible & Novel: Narrative Authority & the Death of God* (Oxford: Oxford University Press, 2013), 153.

SELECT BIBLIOGRAPHY

Gouldstone, Timothy Maxwell. *The Rise and Decline of Anglican Idealism in the Nineteenth Century.* Houndmills: Palgrave Macmillan, 2005.

Perkin, J. Russell. *Theology and the Victorian Novel.* Montréal: McGill-Queen's University Press, 2010.

Peterson, William S. *Victorian Heretic: Mrs. Humphry Ward's* Robert Elsmere. Leicester: Leicester University Press, 1976.

Richter, Melvin. *The Politics of Conscience: T. H. Green and His Age.* Cambridge, MA: Harvard University Press, 1964.

Sutherland, John. *Mrs. Humphry Ward: Eminent Victorian, Pre-Eminent Edwardian.* Oxford: Oxford University Press, 1990.

Wheeler, Michael. *The Art of Allusion in Victorian Fiction.* London and Basingstoke: Macmillan, 1979.

Wilt, Judith. *Behind Her Times: Transition England in the Novels of Mary Arnold Ward.* Charlottesville, VA: University of Virginia Press, 2005.

Wolff, Robert Lee. *Gains and Losses: Novels of Faith and Doubt in Victorian England.* New York: Garland, 1977.

A NOTE ON THE TEXT

In 1888, Smith, Elder released *Robert Elsmere* in three volumes, a one volume "cheap" edition, and finally a two-volume "Library Edition." Macmillan also brought out both one- and two-volume authorized editions for "colonial" and US distribution in 1888; the two-volume edition provided the plates for Smith, Elder's Library Edition, not *vice-versa*.[1] That same year, Bernard Tauchnitz brought out a three-volume edition for his "English Authors" library. A two-volume edition of *Robert Elsmere* was issued by Houghton Mifflin (USA) and Smith, Elder as part of the "Westmoreland Edition" of Ward's collected *Writings* (1911-1912), for which Ward wrote a new introduction. The surviving manuscript material, housed at the Claremont Colleges Library, includes most of the handwritten foul copy, as well as some proof pages for the final chapters. Clyde de L. Ryals' Nebraska edition (1967) is a facsimile of the one-volume Macmillan edition; Rosemary Ashton's Oxford World's Classics edition (1987) is based on a 1907 reprint of the Smith, Elder one-volume edition.

Ward did not revise the language or structure of *Robert Elsmere* at any point after it was published. However, in all editions, the accidentals are inconsistent and sometimes idiosyncratic; some of the discrepancies possibly derive from Ward's extensive, last-minute revisions at the proof stage, which may have inadvertently introduced errors in the process of correcting others. More seriously, although the authorized editions of 1888 are *largely* consistent, there are multiple instances in which accidentals and orthography are inconsistent *across* editions, with no two identical. The Westmoreland edition is, again, not identical to any preceding authorized edition, although it accepts many of the changes from the earlier ones. It regularizes or restores some orthographical inconsistencies (e.g., "connection" to "connexion") and alters, adds, or restores some capitalization, hyphenation, and commas. It is unclear how much effort Ward put into reading the proofs; editor Roger L. Scaife certainly had not anticipated that she would be particularly involved in that aspect of production.[2] It is therefore difficult to determine with whom responsibility for the Westmoreland edition's punctuation actually rests.

We have therefore followed precedent in using the best-selling one-volume Macmillan edition, but have very sparingly incorporated variants from the

---

1 George Smith to Mrs. Humphry Ward, 27 November 1888, Box 1, Folder 8, Mrs. Humphry Ward Collection, Special Collections, The Claremont Colleges Library.
2 Roger L. Scaife to Mrs. Humphry Ward, 13 April 1910, Box 6, Folder 20, Mrs. Humphry Ward Collection, Special Collections, The Claremont Colleges Library.

first edition (*SE*), one-volume Smith, Elder edition (*SE[1]*), or Westmoreland edition (*W*) when they a) correct typographical or grammatical errors, b) clarify the sense, and/or c) are more consistent with the text's most common usage. I have prioritized variants that appear in multiple editions. Emendations and their sources are identified in the footnotes; more obvious typographical errors (such as inconsistent italics) have been silently corrected.

ABOUT THE EDITOR

Miriam Elizabeth Burstein is Professor of English at the State University of New York, College at Brockport, specializing in nineteenth-century literature. She is the author of *Narrating Women's History in Britain, 1770-1902* (2004) and *Victorian Reformations: Historical Fiction and Religious Controversy, 1820-1900* (Notre Dame, 2013).

ACKNOWLEDGEMENTS

My thanks to publisher and editor Catherine Pope, who graciously invited me onboard for this edition, and just as graciously provided the transcribed text. Thanks also to Kaite Welsh, who assisted with the text preparation. For the second edition, Teresa Lehr proofread the text. I am indebted to the work of Robert Elsmere's previous editors, Clyde de L. Ryals (University of Nebraska Press, 1967) and Rosemary Ashton (Oxford University Press, 1987). In this digital age, I am also indebted to the legions of workers who have scanned texts into such repositories as Google Books, HathiTrust, and the Internet Archive; their work has made identifying some previously impossible allusions possible. Daniel Cook offered a number of thoughtful insights about the implications of Squire Wendover's library. And Stanley M. Burstein helped me track down some particularly wayward classical references.

Robert Elsmere

Dedicated to the Memory

OF

MY TWO FRIENDS,

SEPARATED, IN MY THOUGHT OF THEM, BY MUCH DIVERSITY

OF

CIRCUMSTANCE AND OPINION;

LINKED, IN MY FAITH ABOUT THEM, TO EACH OTHER,

AND TO ALL THE SHINING ONES OF THE PAST,

BY THE LOVE OF GOD AND THE

SERVICE OF MAN:

THOMAS HILL GREEN

(LATE PROFESSOR OF MORAL PHILOSOPHY IN THE

UNIVERSITY OF OXFORD),

Died 26th March 1882;

AND

LAURA OCTAVIA MARY LYTTELTON,

Died Easter Eve 1886.

NOTE

The quotations given in the present book on pp. 58, 330, and 536, are either literally or substantially taken from a volume of Lay Sermons, called *The Witness of God*, by the late Professor T. H. Green.[1]

---

1 Ward's original note. In this edition, the quotations appear on pp. 81, 372, and 587.

BOOK I - WESTMORELAND

CHAPTER I

It was a brilliant afternoon towards the end of May. The spring had been unusually cold and late, and it was evident from the general aspect of the lonely Westmoreland valley of Long Whindale that warmth and sunshine had only just penetrated to its bare green recesses, where the few scattered trees were fast rushing into their full summer dress, while at their feet, and along the bank of the stream, the flowers of March and April still lingered, as though they found it impossible to believe that their rough brother, the east wind, had at last deserted them. The narrow road, which was the only link between the farmhouses sheltered by the crags at the head of the valley and those far-away regions of town and civilisation suggested by the smoke wreaths of Whinborough on the southern horizon, was lined with masses of the white heckberry or bird-cherry, and ran, an arrowy line of white, through the greenness of the sloping pastures. The sides of some of the little becks running down into the main river and many of the plantations round the farms were gay with the same tree, so that the farmhouses, gray-roofed and gray-walled, standing in the hollows of the fells, seemed here and there to have been robbed of all their natural austerity of aspect, and to be masquerading in a dainty garb of white and green imposed upon them by the caprice of the spring.

During the greater part of its course the valley of Long Whindale is tame and featureless. The hills at the lower part are low and rounded, and the sheep and cattle pasture over slopes unbroken either by wood or rock. The fields are bare and close shaven by the flocks which feed on them; the walls run either perpendicularly in many places up the fells or horizontally along them, so that, save for the wooded course of the tumbling river and the bush-grown hedges of the road, the whole valley looks like a green map divided by regular lines of grayish black. But as the walker penetrates farther, beyond a certain bend which the stream makes half way from the head of the dale, the hills grow steeper, the breadth between them contracts, the enclosure lines are broken and deflected by rocks and patches of plantation, and the few farms stand more boldly and conspicuously forward, each on its spur of land, looking up to or away from the great masses of frowning crag which close in the head of the valley, and which from the moment they come into sight give it dignity and a wild beauty.

On one of these solitary houses, the afternoon sun, about to descend before very long behind the hills dividing Long Whindale from Shanmoor, was still lingering on this May afternoon we are describing, bringing out the whitewashed porch and the broad bands of white edging the windows into relief against the gray stone of the main fabric, the gray roof overhanging it, and the group of sycamores and Scotch firs which protected it from the cold east and north. The western light struck full on a copper beech, which made a welcome patch of warm colour in front of a long gray line of outhouses standing level with the house, and touched the heckberry blossom which marked the upward course of the little lane connecting the old farm with the road; above it rose the green fell, broken here and there by jutting crags, and below it the ground sank rapidly through a piece of young hazel plantation, at this present moment a sheet of bluebells, towards the level of the river. There was a dainty and yet sober brightness about the whole picture. Summer in the North is for Nature a time of expansion and of joy as it is elsewhere, but there is none of that opulence, that sudden splendour and superabundance, which mark it in the South. In these bare green valleys there is a sort of delicate austerity even in the summer; the memory of winter seems to be still lingering about these wind-swept fells, about the farmhouses, with their rough serviceable walls, of the same stone as the crags behind them, and the ravines, in which the shrunken becks trickle musically down through the *débris* of innumerable Decembers. The country is blithe, but soberly blithe. Nature shows herself delightful to man, but there is nothing absorbing or intoxicating about her. Man is still well able to defend himself against her, to live his own independent life of labour and of will, and to develop the tenacity of hidden feeling, that slowly growing intensity of purpose, which is so often wiled out of him by the spells of the South.

The distant aspect of Burwood Farm differed in nothing from that of the few other farmhouses which dotted the fells or clustered beside the river between it and the rocky end of the valley. But as one came nearer, certain signs of difference became visible. The garden, instead of being the old-fashioned medley of phloxes, lavender bushes, monthly roses, gooseberry trees, herbs, and pampas grass, with which the farmers' wives of Long Whindale loved to fill their little front enclosures, was trimly laid down in turf dotted with

neat flower-beds, full at the moment we are writing of with orderly patches
of scarlet and purple anemones, wallflowers, and pansies. At the side of the
house a new bow window, modest enough in dimensions and make, had been
thrown out on to another close-shaven piece of lawn, and by its suggestion of
a distant sophisticated order of things disturbed the homely impression left
by the untouched ivy-grown walls, the unpretending porch, and wide slate
window-sills of the front. And evidently the line of sheds standing level with
the dwelling-house no longer sheltered the animals, the carts, or the tools
which make the small capital of a Westmoreland farmer. The windows in
them were new, the doors fresh painted and closely shut; curtains of some soft
outlandish make showed themselves in what had once been a stable, and the
turf stretched smoothly up to a narrow gravelled path in front of them, unbroken by a single footmark. No, evidently the old farm, for such it undoubtedly was, had been but lately, or comparatively lately, transformed to new and
softer uses; that rough patriarchal life of which it had once been a symbol and
centre no longer bustled and clattered through it. It had become the shelter
of new ideals, the home of another and a milder race than once possessed it.

In a stranger coming upon the house for the first time, on this particular
evening, the sense of a changing social order and a vanishing past produced
by the slight but significant modifications it had undergone, would have been
greatly quickened by certain sounds which were streaming out on to the evening air from one of the divisions of that long one-storied addition to the main
dwelling we have already described. Some indefatigable musician inside was
practising the violin with surprising energy and vigour, and within the little
garden the distant murmur of the river and the gentle breathing of the west
wind round the fell were entirely conquered and banished by these triumphant shakes and turns, or by the flourishes and the broad *cantabile*[1] passages
of one of Spohr's[2] Andantes. For a while, as the sun sank lower and lower towards the Shanmoor hills, the hidden artist had it all his, or her, own way; the
valley and its green spaces seemed to be possessed by this stream of eddying
sound, and no other sign of life broke the gray quiet of the house. But at last,
just as the golden ball touched the summit of the craggy fell, which makes the
western boundary of the dale at its higher end, the house door opened, and
a young girl, shawled and holding some soft burden in her arms, appeared
on the threshold, and stood there for a moment, as though trying the quality of the air outside. Her pause of inspection seemed to satisfy her, for she
moved forward, leaving the door open behind her, and, stepping across the

---

1 "In a smooth flowing style, such as would be suited for singing" (OED).
2 Louis Spohr (1784–1859), German Romantic composer and violinist.

lawn, settled herself in a wicker chair under an apple-tree, which had only just shed its blossoms on the turf below. She had hardly done so when one of the distant doors opening on the gravel path flew open, and another maiden, a slim creature garbed in æsthetic blue, a mass of reddish brown hair flying back from her face, also stepped out into the garden.[3]

'Agnes!' cried the new-comer, who had the strenuous and dishevelled air natural to one just emerged from a long violin practice. 'Has Catherine come back yet?'

'Not that I know of. Do come here and look at pussie; did you ever see anything so comfortable?'

'You and she look about equally lazy. What have you been doing all the afternoon?'

'We look what we are, my dear. Doing? Why, I have been attending to my domestic duties, arranging the flowers, mending my pink dress for to-morrow night, and helping to keep mamma in good spirits; she is depressed because she has been finding Elizabeth out in some waste or other, and I have been preaching to her to make Elizabeth uncomfortable if she likes, but not to worrit herself. And after all, pussie and I have come out for a rest. We've earned it, haven't we, Chattie? And, as for you, Miss Artistic, I should like to know what you've been doing for the good of your kind since dinner. I suppose you had tea at the vicarage?'

The speaker lifted inquiring eyes to her sister as she spoke, her cheek plunged in the warm fur of a splendid Persian cat, her whole look and voice expressing the very highest degree of quiet, comfort, and self-possession. Agnes Leyburn was not pretty; the lower part of the face was a little heavy in outline and moulding; the teeth were not as they should have been, and the nose was unsatisfactory. But the eyes under their long lashes were shrewdness itself, and there was an individuality in the voice, a cheery even-temperedness in look and tone, which had a pleasing effect on the bystander. Her dress was neat and dainty; every detail of it bespoke a young woman who respected both herself and the fashion.

Her sister, on the other hand, was guiltless of the smallest trace of fashion. Her skirts were cut with the most engaging *naïveté*, she was much adorned with amber beads, and her red brown hair had been tortured and frizzled to look as much like an aureole as possible. But, on the other hand, she was a beauty, though at present you felt her a beauty in disguise, a stage Cinderella as it were, in very becoming rags, waiting for the godmother.

---

3 Rose emulates the floating masses of hair preferred by the Pre-Raphaelite painter Dante Gabriel Rossetti (1828–1882).

'Yes, I had tea at the vicarage,' said this young person, throwing herself on the grass in spite of a murmured protest from Agnes, who had an inherent dislike of anything physically rash, 'and I had the greatest difficulty to get away. Mrs. Thornburgh is in such a flutter about this visit! One would think it was the Bishop and all his Canons, and promotion depending on it, she has baked so many cakes and put out so many dinner napkins! I don't envy the young man. She will have no wits left at all to entertain him with. I actually wound up by administering some sal-volatile to her.'

'Well, and after the sal-volatile did you get anything coherent out of her on the subject of the young man?'

'By degrees,' said the girl, her eyes twinkling; 'if one can only remember the thread between whiles one gets at the facts somehow. In between the death of Mr. Elsmere's father and his going to college, we had, let me see,—the spare room curtains, the making of them and the cleaning of them, Sarah's idiocy in sticking to her black sheep of a young man, the price of tea when she married, Mr. Thornburgh's singular preference of boiled mutton to roast, the poems she had written to her when she was eighteen, and I can't tell you what else besides. But I held fast, and every now and then I brought her up to the point again, gently, but firmly, and now I think I know all I want to know about the interesting stranger.'

'My ideas about him are not many,' said Agnes, rubbing her cheek gently up and down the purring cat, 'and there doesn't seem to be much order in them. He is very accomplished—a teetotaller—he has been to the Holy Land, and his hair has been cut close after a fever. It sounds odd, but I am not curious. I can very well wait till to-morrow evening.'[4]

'Oh, well, as to ideas about a person, one doesn't get that sort of thing from Mrs. Thornburgh. But I know how old he is, where he went to college, where his mother lives, a certain number of his mother's peculiarities, which seem to be Irish and curious, where his living is, how much it is worth, likewise the colour of his eyes, as near as Mrs. Thornburgh can get.'

'What a start you have been getting!' said Agnes lazily. 'But what is it makes the poor old thing so excited?'

Rose sat up and began to fling the fir cones lying about her at a distant mark with an energy worthy of her physical perfections and the æsthetic

---

4 Elsmere sympathizes with the temperance movement in its strictest sense, full abstention from alcohol, and has taken one of the tours of what was then known as Palestine, which, thanks to the efforts of Thomas Cook, became increasingly easy and popular in the second half of the nineteenth century. See Timothy Larsen, "Spiritual Exploration: Thomas Cook, Victorian Tourists, and the Holy Land," *Contested Christianity* (Waco, TX: Baylor University Press, 2004), 29–39.

freedom of her attire.

'Because, my dear, Mrs. Thornburgh at the present moment is always seeing herself as the conspirator sitting match in hand before a mine. Mr. Elsmere is the match—we are the mine!'

Agnes looked at her sister, and they both laughed, the bright rippling laugh of young women perfectly aware of their own value, and in no hurry to force an estimate of it on the male world.

'Well,' said Rose deliberately, her delicate cheek flushed with her gymnastics, her eyes sparkling, 'there is no saying. "Propinquity does it"—as Mrs. Thornburgh is always reminding us.—But where *can* Catherine be? She went out directly after lunch.'

'She has gone out to see that youth who hurt his back at the Tysons—at least I heard her talking to mamma about him, and she went out with a basket that looked like beef-tea.'

Rose frowned a little.

'And I suppose I ought to have been to the school or to see Mrs. Robson, instead of fiddling all the afternoon. I daresay I ought—only, unfortunately, I like my fiddle, and I don't like stuffy cottages; and as for the goody books, I read them so badly that the old women themselves come down upon me.'

'I seem to have been making the best of both worlds,' said Agnes placidly. 'I haven't been doing anything I don't like, but I got hold of that dress she brought home to make for little Emma Payne and nearly finished the skirt, so that I feel as good as one when one has been twice to church on a wet Sunday. Ah, there is Catherine. I heard the gate.'

As she spoke steps were heard approaching through the clump of trees which sheltered the little entrance gate, and as Rose sprang to her feet a tall figure in white and gray appeared against the background of the sycamores, and came quickly towards the sisters.

'Dears, I am so sorry; I am afraid you have been waiting for me. But poor Mrs. Tyson wanted me so badly that I could not leave her. She had no one else to help her or to be with her till that eldest girl of hers came home from work.'

'It doesn't matter,' said Rose, as Catherine put her arm round her shoulder; 'mamma hasn't been fidgeting, and as for Agnes, she looks as if she never wanted to move again.'

Catherine's clear eyes, which at the moment seemed to be full of inward light, kindled in them by some foregoing experience, rested kindly, but only half consciously, on her younger sister, as Agnes softly nodded and smiled to her. Evidently she was a good deal older than the other two—she looked about six-and-twenty, a young and vigorous woman in the prime of health and strength. The lines of the form were rather thin and spare, but they were softened by the loose bodice and long full skirt of her dress, and by the folds of a large white muslin handkerchief which was crossed over her breast. The face, sheltered by the plain shady hat, was also a little spoilt from the point of view of beauty by the sharpness of the lines about the chin and mouth, and by a slight prominence of the cheekbones, but the eyes, of a dark bluish gray, were fine, the nose delicately cut, the brow smooth and beautiful, while the complexion had caught the freshness and purity of Westmoreland air and Westmoreland streams. About face and figure there was a delicate austere charm, something which harmonised with the bare stretches and lonely crags of the fells, something which seemed to make her a true daughter of the mountains, partaker at once of their gentleness and their severity. *She* was in her place here, beside the homely Westmoreland house and under the shelter of the fells. When you first saw the other sisters you wondered what strange chance had brought them into that remote sparely-peopled valley; they were plainly exiles, and conscious exiles, from the movement and exhilarations of a fuller social life. But Catherine impressed you as only a refined variety of the local type; you could have found many like her, in a sense, among the sweet-faced serious women of the neighbouring farms.

Now, as she and Rose stood together, her hand still resting lightly on the other's shoulder, a question from Agnes banished the faint smile on her lips, and left only the look of inward illumination, the expression of one who had just passed, as it were, through a strenuous and heroic moment of life, and was still living in the exaltation of memory.

'So the poor fellow is worse?'

'Yes. Doctor Baker, whom they have got to-day, says the spine is hopelessly injured. He may live on paralysed for a few months or longer, but there is no hope of cure.'

Both girls uttered a shocked exclamation. 'That fine strong young man!' said Rose under her breath. 'Does he know?'

'Yes; when I got there the doctor had just gone, and Mrs. Tyson, who was quite unprepared for anything so dreadful, seemed to have almost lost her wits, poor thing! I found her in the front kitchen with her apron over her head, rocking to and fro, and poor Arthur in the inner room—all alone— waiting in suspense.'

'And who told him? He has been so hopeful.'

'I did,' said Catherine gently; 'they made me. He *would* know, and she couldn't—she ran out of the room. I never saw anything so pitiful.'

'Oh, Catherine!' exclaimed Rose's moved voice, while Agnes got up, and Chattie jumped softly down from her lap, unheeded.

'How did he bear it?'

'Don't ask me,' said Catherine, while the quiet tears filled her eyes and her voice broke, as the hidden feeling would have its way. 'It was terrible! I don't know how we got through that half-hour—his mother and I. It was like wrestling with some one in agony. At last he was exhausted—he let me say the Lord's Prayer; I think it soothed him, but one couldn't tell. He seemed half asleep when I left. Oh!' she cried, laying her hand in a close grasp on Rose's arm, 'if you had seen his eyes, and his poor hands—there was such despair in them! They say, though he was so young, he was thinking of getting married; and he was so steady, such a good son!'

A silence fell upon the three. Catherine stood looking out across the valley towards the sunset. Now that the demand upon her for calmness and fortitude was removed, and that the religious exaltation in which she had gone through the last three hours was becoming less intense, the pure human pity of the scene she had just witnessed seemed to be gaining upon her. Her lip trembled, and two or three tears silently overflowed. Rose turned and gently kissed her cheek, and Agnes touched her hand caressingly. She smiled at them, for it was not in her nature to let any sign of love pass unheeded, and in a few more seconds she had mastered herself.

'Dears, we must go in. Is mother in her room? Oh, Rose! in that thin dress on the grass; I oughtn't to have kept you out. It is quite cold by now.'

And she hurried them in, leaving them to superintend the preparations for supper downstairs while she ran up to her mother.

A quarter of an hour afterwards they were all gathered round the supper-table, the windows open to the garden and the May twilight. At Catherine's right hand sat Mrs. Leyburn, a tall delicate-looking woman, wrapped in a white shawl, about whom there were only three things to be noticed—an amiable temper, a sufficient amount of weak health to excuse her all the more tiresome duties of life, and an incorrigible tendency to sing the praises of her daughters at all times and to all people. The daughters winced under it: Catherine, because it was a positive pain to her to hear herself brought forward and talked about; the others, because youth infinitely prefers to make its own points in its own way. Nothing, however, could mend this defect of Mrs. Leyburn's. Catherine's strength of will could keep it in check sometimes, but in general it had to be borne with. A sharp word would have silenced the mother's well-meant chatter at any time—for she was a fragile, nervous woman, entirely dependent on her surroundings—but none of them were capable of it, and their mere refractoriness counted for nothing.

The dining-room in which they were gathered had a good deal of home-ly dignity, and was to the Leyburns full of associations. The oak settle near the fire, the oak sideboard running along one side of the room, the black oak table with carved legs at which they sat, were genuine pieces of old Westmoreland work, which had belonged to their grandfather. The heavy carpet covering the stone floor of what twenty years before had been the kitchen of the farmhouse was a survival from a south-country home, which had sheltered their lives for eight happy years. Over the mantelpiece hung the portrait of the girls' father, a long serious face, not unlike Wordsworth's face in outline, and bearing a strong resemblance to Catherine; a line of sil-houettes adorned the mantelpiece; on the walls were prints of Winchester and Worcester Cathedrals, photographs of Greece, and two old-fashioned engravings of Dante and Milton; while a bookcase, filled apparently with the father's college books and college prizes and the favourite authors—mostly poets, philosophers, and theologians—of his later years, gave a final touch of habitableness to the room. The little meal and its appointments—the eggs, the home-made bread and preserves, the tempting butter and old-fashioned silver gleaming among the flowers which Rose arranged with fanciful skill in Japanese pots of her own providing—suggested the same family qualities as the room.[5] Frugality, a dainty personal self-respect, a family consciousness, tenacious of its memories and tenderly careful of all the little material objects which were to it the symbols of those memories—clearly all these elements entered into the Leyburn tradition.

And of this tradition, with its implied assertions and denials, clearly Catherine Leyburn, the elder sister, was, of all the persons gathered in this lit-tle room, the most pronounced embodiment. She sat at the head of the table, the little basket of her own and her mother's keys beside her. Her dress was a soft black brocade, with lace collar and cuff, which had once belonged to an aunt of her mother's. It was too old for her both in fashion and material, but it gave her a gentle, almost matronly dignity, which became her. Her long thin hands, full of character and delicacy, moved nimbly among the cups; all her ways were quiet and yet decided. It was evident that among this little party she, and not the plaintive mother, was really in authority. To-night, however, her looks were specially soft. The scene she had gone through in the afternoon had left her pale, with traces of patient fatigue round the eyes and

5 Although the English became newly interested in Japanese art and aesthetics af-ter the Japanese reopened trade relations with the West in the 1850s, Japanese or Japanese-style products were especially fashionable in the 1880s, which saw, among other things, the debut of Gilbert and Sullivan's *The Mikado* (1885).

mouth, but all her emotion was gone, and she was devoting herself to the others, responding with quick interest and ready smiles to all they had to say, and contributing the little experiences of her own day in return.

Rose sat on her left hand in yet another gown of strange tint and archaic outline. Rose's gowns were legion. They were manufactured by a farmer's daughter across the valley, under her strict and precise supervision. She was accustomed, as she boldly avowed, to shut herself up at the beginning of each season of the year for two days' meditation on the subject. And now, thanks to the spring warmth, she was entering at last with infinite zest on the results of her April vigils.

Catherine had surveyed her as she entered the room with a smile, but a smile not altogether to Rose's taste.

'What, another, Röschen?' she had said, with the slightest lifting of the eyebrows. 'You never confided that to me. Did you think I was unworthy of anything so artistic?'

'Not at all,' said Rose calmly, seating herself. 'I thought you were better employed.'

But a flush flew over her transparent cheek, and she presently threw an irritated look at Agnes, who had been looking from her to Catherine with amused eyes.

'I met Mr. Thornburgh and Mr. Elsmere driving from the station,' Catherine announced presently; 'at least there was a gentleman in a clerical wideawake, with a portmanteau behind, so I imagine it must have been he.'

'Did he look promising?' inquired Agnes.

'I don't think I noticed,' said Catherine simply, but with a momentary change of expression. The sisters, remembering how she had come in upon them with that look of one 'lifted up,' understood why she had not noticed, and refrained from further questions.

'Well, it is to be hoped the young man is recovered enough to stand Long Whindale festivities,' said Rose. 'Mrs. Thornburgh means to let them loose on his devoted head to-morrow night.'

'Who are coming?' asked Mrs. Leyburn eagerly. The occasional tea parties of the neighbourhood were an unfailing excitement to her, simply because, by dint of the small adornments, natural to the occasion, they showed her daughters to her under slightly new aspects. To see Catherine, who never took any thought for her appearance, forced to submit to a white dress, a line of pearls round the shapely throat, a flower in the brown hair, put there by Rose's imperious fingers; to sit in a corner well out of draughts, watching the effect of Rose's half-fledged beauty, and drinking in the compliments of the neighbourhood on Rose's playing or Agnes's conversation, or Catherine's practical ability—these were Mrs. Leyburn's passions, and a tea party always gratified them to the full.

'Mamma asks as if really she wanted an answer,' remarked Agnes drily. 'Dear mother, can't you by now make up a tea party at the Thornburghs out of your head?'

'The Seatons?' inquired Mrs. Leyburn.

'*Mrs.* Seaton and Miss Barks,' replied Rose. 'The rector won't come. And I needn't say that, having moved heaven and earth to get Mrs. Seaton, Mrs. Thornburgh is now miserable because she has got her. Her ambition is gratified, but she knows that she has spoilt the party. Well, then, Mr. Mayhew, of course, his son, *and* his flute.'

'You to play his accompaniments?' put in Agnes slily. Rose's lip curled.

'Not if Miss Barks knows it,' she said emphatically, 'nor if I know it. The Bakers, of course, ourselves, and the unknown.'

'Dr. Baker is always pleasant,' said Mrs. Leyburn, leaning back and drawing her white shawl languidly round her. 'He told me the other day, Catherine, that if it weren't for you he should have to retire. He regards you as his junior partner. "Marvellous nursing gift your eldest daughter has, Mrs. Leyburn," he said to me the other day. A most agreeable man.'

'I wonder if I shall be able to get any candid opinions out of Mr. Elsmere the day after to-morrow?' said Rose, musing. 'It is difficult to avoid having an opinion of some sort about Mrs. Seaton.'

'Oxford dons don't gossip and are never candid,' remarked Agnes severely.

'Then Oxford dons must be very dull,' cried Rose. 'However,' and her countenance brightened, 'if he stays here four weeks we can teach him.'

Catherine, meanwhile, sat watching the two girls with a soft elder sister's indulgence. Was it in connection with their bright attractive looks that the thought flitted through her head, 'I wonder what the young man will be like?'

'Oh, by the way,' said Rose presently, 'I had nearly forgotten Mrs. Thornburgh's two messages. I informed her, Agnes, that you had given up water-colour and meant to try oils, and she told me to implore you not to, because "water-colour is so *much* more lady-like than oils." And as for you, Catherine, she sent you a most special message. I was to tell you that she just *loved* the way you had taken to plaiting your hair lately—that it was exactly like the picture of Jeanie Deans she has in the drawing-room, and that she would never forgive you if you didn't plait it so to-morrow night.'[6]

---

6 The heroine of Sir Walter Scott's *The Heart of Midlothian* (1818). Jeanie first refuses to lie to save her sister from being convicted of infanticide, then walks to London in

Catherine flushed faintly as she got up from the table.

'Mrs. Thornburgh has eagle-eyes,' she said, moving away to give her arm to her mother, who looked fondly at her, making some remark in praise of Mrs. Thornburgh's taste.

'Rose!' cried Agnes indignantly, when the other two had disappeared, 'you and Mrs. Thornburgh have not the sense you were born with. What on earth did you say that to Catherine for?'

Rose stared; then her face fell a little.

'I suppose it was foolish,' she admitted. Then she leant her head on one hand and drew meditative patterns on the table-cloth with the other. 'You know, Agnes,' she said presently, looking up, 'there are drawbacks to having a St. Elizabeth for a sister.'[7]

Agnes discreetly made no reply, and Rose was left alone. She sat dreaming a few minutes, the corners of the red mouth drooping. Then she sprang up with a long sigh. 'A little life!' she said half-aloud, 'a little *wickedness*!' and she shook her curly head defiantly.

A few minutes later, in the little drawing-room on the other side of the hall, Catherine and Rose stood together by the open window. For the first time in a lingering spring, the air was soft and balmy; a tender grayness lay over the valley; it was not night, though above the clear outlines of the fell the stars were just twinkling in the pale blue. Far away under the crag on the farther side of High Fell a light was shining. As Catherine's eyes caught it there was a quick response in the fine Madonna-like face.

'Any news for me from the Backhouses this afternoon?' she asked Rose.

'No, I heard of none. How is she?'

'Dying,' said Catherine simply, and stood a moment looking out. Rose did not interrupt her. She knew that the house from which the light was shining sheltered a tragedy; she guessed with the vagueness of nineteen that it was a tragedy of passion and sin; but Catherine had not been communicative on the subject, and Rose had for some time past set up a dumb resistance to her

---

order to ask the Queen for a pardon.

7 St. Elizabeth of Hungary (1207–31). For Victorian Protestants, St. Elizabeth was a deeply problematic figure: on the one hand, she was notable for her enthusiastic and extensive charity; on the other, she seemed inappropriately devoted to her ultra-strict confessor, Konrad von Marburg (frequently represented as a stereotypically evil agent of the Inquisition), and the vow of celibacy she took after her husband's death struck many as perverse, even dangerous. Charles Kingsley's verse drama *The Saint's Tragedy* (1848), which used St. Elizabeth's life to launch an anti-Catholic assault on asceticism, suggested that in his self-serving quest to "make" a saint, Konrad forced her to live a celibate marriage and abandon anything that might give her pleasure, including charity.

sister's most characteristic ways of life and thought, which prevented her now from asking questions. She wished nervously to give Catherine's extraordinary moral strength no greater advantage over her than she could help.

Presently, however, Catherine threw her arm round her with a tender protectingness.

'What did you do with yourself all the afternoon, Röschen?'

'I practised for two hours,' said the girl shortly, 'and two hours this morning. My Spohr is nearly perfect.'

'And you didn't look into the school?' asked Catherine, hesitating; 'I know Miss Merry expected you.'

'No, I didn't. When one can play the violin and can't teach, any more than a cockatoo, what's the good of wasting one's time in teaching?'

Catherine did not reply. A minute after Mrs. Leyburn called her, and she went to sit on a stool at her mother's feet, her hands resting on the elder woman's lap, the whole attitude of the tall active figure one of beautiful and childlike abandonment. Mrs. Leyburn wanted to confide in her about a new cap, and Catherine took up the subject with a zest which kept her mother happy till bedtime.

'Why couldn't she take as much interest in my Spohr?' thought Rose.

Late that night, long after she had performed all a maid's offices for her mother, Catherine Leyburn was busy in her own room arranging a large cupboard containing medicines and ordinary medical necessaries, a storehouse whence all the simpler emergencies of their end of the valley were supplied. She had put on a white flannel dressing-gown and moved noiselessly about in it, the very embodiment of order, of purity, of quiet energy. The little white-curtained room was bareness and neatness itself. There were a few book-shelves along the walls, holding the books which her father had given her. Over the bed were two enlarged portraits of her parents, and a line of queer little faded monstrosities, representing Rose and Agnes in different stages of childhood. On the table beside the bed was a pile of well-worn books—Keble, Jeremy Taylor, the Bible—connected in the mind of the mistress of the room with the intensest moments of the spiritual life.[8] There was a strip of carpet by the bed, a plain chair or two, a large press; otherwise no furniture that was not

---

8 John Keble (1792–1866), whose sermon "On National Apostasy" (1833) was one of the primary sparks for the Oxford Movement. Catherine is reading his bestselling *The Christian Year* (1827), which consists of poems written to commemorate the liturgical calendar. Jeremy Taylor (1613-67), leading Anglican clergyman and theologian, likely represented at Catherine's bedside by his influential *The Rule and Exercises of Holy Living* (1650) and *The Rule and Exercises of Holy Dying* (1651), frequently printed together as *Holy Living and Holy Dying*.

absolutely necessary, and no ornaments. And yet, for all its emptiness, the little room in its order and spotlessness had the look and spell of a sanctuary.

When her task was finished Catherine came forward to the infinitesimal dressing-table, and stood a moment before the common cottage looking-glass upon it. The candle behind her showed her the outlines of her head and face in shadow against the white ceiling. Her soft brown hair was plaited high above the broad white brow, giving to it an added stateliness, while it left unmasked the pure lines of the neck. Mrs. Thornburgh and her mother were quite right. Simple as the new arrangement was, it could hardly have been more effective.

But the looking-glass got no smile in return for its information. Catherine Leyburn was young; she was alone; she was being very plainly told that, taken as a whole, she was, or might be at any moment, a beautiful woman. And all her answer was a frown and a quick movement away from the glass. Putting up her hands she began to undo the plaits with haste, almost with impatience; she smoothed the whole mass then set free into the severest order, plaited it closely together, and then, putting out her light, threw herself on her knees beside the window, which was partly open to the starlight and the mountains. The voice of the river far away, wafted from the mist-covered depths of the valley, and the faint rustling of the trees just outside, were for long after the only sounds which broke the silence.

When Catherine appeared at breakfast next morning her hair was plainly gathered into a close knot behind, which had been her way of dressing it since she was thirteen. Agnes threw a quick look at Rose; Mrs. Leyburn, as soon as she had made out through her spectacles what was the matter, broke into warm expostulations.

'It is more comfortable, dear mother, and takes much less time,' said Catherine, reddening.

'Poor Mrs. Thornburgh!' remarked Agnes drily.

'Oh, Rose will make up!' said Catherine, glancing, not without a spark of mischief in her gray eyes, at Rose's tortured locks; 'and mamma's new cap, which will be superb!'

CHAPTER II

About four o'clock on the afternoon of the day which was to be marked in the annals of Long Whindale as that of Mrs. Thornburgh's 'high tea,' that lady was seated in the vicarage garden, her spectacles on her nose, a large *couvre-pied*[9] over her knees, and the Whinborough newspaper on her lap. The neighbourhood of this last enabled her to make an intermittent pretence of reading; but in reality the energies of her housewifely mind were taken up with quite other things. The vicar's wife was plunged in a housekeeping experiment of absorbing interest. All her *solid* preparations for the evening were over, and in her own mind she decided that with them there was no possible fault to be found. The cook, Sarah, had gone about her work in a spirit at once lavish and fastidious, breathed into her by her mistress. No better tongue, no plumper chickens, than those which would grace her board to-night were to be found, so Mrs. Thornburgh was persuaded, in the district. And so with everything else of a substantial kind. On this head the hostess felt no anxieties.

But a 'tea' in the north country depends for distinction, not on its solids or its savouries, but on its sweets. A rural hostess earns her reputation, not by a discriminating eye for butcher's-meat, but by her inventiveness in cakes and custards. And it was just here, with regard to this 'bubble reputation,' that the vicar's wife of Long Whindale was particularly sensitive. Was she not expecting Mrs. Seaton, the wife of the Rector of Whinborough—odious woman— to tea? Was it not incumbent on her to do well, nay, to do brilliantly, in the eyes of this local magnate? And how was it possible to do brilliantly in this matter with a cook whose recipes were hopelessly old-fashioned, and who had an exasperating belief in the sufficiency of buttered 'whigs' and home-made marmalade for all requirements?

Stung by these thoughts, Mrs. Thornburgh had gone prowling about the neighbouring town of Whinborough till the shop window of a certain newly-arrived confectioner had been revealed to her, stored with the most airy and appetising trifles—of a make and colouring quite metropolitan. She had flattened her gray curls against the window for one deliberative moment; had then rushed in; and as soon as the carrier's cart of Long Whindale, which she was now anxiously awaiting, should have arrived, bearing with it the produce of that adventure, Mrs. Thornburgh would be a proud woman, prepared to meet a legion of rectors' wives without flinching. Not, indeed, in all respects a woman at peace with herself and the world. In the country, where every household should be self-contained, a certain discredit attaches in every well-regulated mind to 'getting things in.' Mrs. Thornburgh was also nervous at the thought of the bill. It would have to be met gradually out of the weekly money. For 'William' was to know nothing of the matter, except so far as a few magnificent generalities and the testimony of his own dazzled eyes might

---

9 A quilt or throw.

inform him. But after all, in this as in everything else, one must suffer to be distinguished.

The carrier, however, lingered. And at last the drowsiness of the afternoon overcame even those pleasing expectations we have described, and Mrs. Thornburgh's newspaper dropped unheeded to her feet. The vicarage, under the shade of which she was sitting, was a new gray stone building with wooden gables, occupying the site of what had once been the earlier vicarage house of Long Whindale, the primitive dwelling-house of an incumbent, whose chapelry, after sundry augmentations, amounted to just twenty-seven pounds a year. The modern house, though it only contained sufficient accommodation for Mr. and Mrs. Thornburgh, one guest, and two maids, would have seemed palatial to those rustic clerics of the past from whose ministrations the lonely valley had drawn its spiritual sustenance in times gone by. They, indeed, had belonged to another race—a race sprung from the soil and content to spend the whole of life in very close contact and very homely intercourse with their mother earth. Mr. Thornburgh, who had come to the valley only a few years before from a parish in one of the large manufacturing towns, and who had no inherited interest in the Cumbrian folk and their ways, had only a very faint idea, and that a distinctly depreciatory one, of what these mythical predecessors of his, with their strange social status and unbecoming occupations, might be like. But there were one or two old men still lingering in the dale who could have told him a great deal about them, whose memory went back to the days when the relative social importance of the dale parsons was exactly expressed by the characteristic Westmoreland saying: 'Ef ye'll nobbut send us a gude schulemeaster, a verra' moderate parson 'ull dea!' and whose slow minds, therefore, were filled with a strong inarticulate sense of difference as they saw him pass along the road, and recalled the incumbent of their childhood, dropping in for his 'crack' and his glass of 'yale' at this or that farmhouse on any occasion of local festivity, or driving his sheep to Whinborough market with his own hands like any other peasant of the dale.

Within the last twenty years, however, the few remaining survivors of this primitive clerical order in the Westmoreland and Cumberland valleys have dropped into their quiet unremembered graves, and new men of other ways and other modes of speech reign in their stead. And as at Long Whindale, so almost everywhere, the change has been emphasised by the disappearance of the old parsonage houses with their stone floors, their parlours lustrous with oak carving on chest or dresser, and their encircling farm-buildings and meadows, in favour of an upgrowth of new trim mansions designed to meet the needs, not of peasants, but of gentlefolks.

And naturally the churches too have shared in the process of transformation. The ecclesiastical revival of the last half-century has worked its will even in the remotest corners of the Cumbrian country, and soon not a vestige of the homely worshipping-places of an earlier day will remain.[10] Across the road, in front of the Long Whindale parsonage, for instance, rose a freshly built church, also peaked and gabled, with a spire and two bells, and a painted east window, and Heaven knows what novelties besides.[11] The primitive whitewashed structure it replaced had lasted long, and in the course of many generations time had clothed its moss-grown walls, its slated porch, and tombstones worn with rain in a certain beauty of congruity and association, linking it with the purple distances of the fells, and the brawling river bending round the gray enclosure. But finally, after a period of quiet and gradual decay, the ruin of Long Whindale chapel had become a quick and hurrying ruin that would not be arrested. When the rotten timbers of the roof came dropping on the farmers' heads, and the oak benches beneath offered gaps, the geography of which had to be carefully learnt by the substantial persons who sat on them, lest they should be overtaken by undignified disaster; when the rain poured in on the Communion Table and the wind raged through innumerable mortarless chinks, even the slowly-moving folk of the valley came to the conclusion that 'summat 'ull hev to be deun.' And by the help of the Bishop, and Queen Anne's Bounty, and what not, aided by just as many half-crowns as the valley found itself unable to defend against the encroachments of a new and 'moiderin' parson, 'summat' was done, whereof the results—namely, the new church, vicarage, and schoolhouse—were now conspicuous.[12]

This radical change, however, had not been the work of Mr. Thornburgh, but of his predecessor, a much more pushing and enterprising man, whose successful efforts to improve the church accommodation in Long Whindale had moved such deep and lasting astonishment in the mind of a somewhat lethargic bishop, that promotion had been readily found for him.[13] Mr. Thornburgh was neither capable of the sturdy begging which had raised the

---

10 The combined influences of the Oxford Movement and the Cambridge Camden (or Ecclesiological) Society, which inspired renewed interest in church architecture and restoration. The Cambridge Camden Society in particular was linked to the Gothic Revival.

11 None of these things were "novelties" in the 1880s; the implication is that this is a church in the Gothic mode popularized in the 1840s. The whitewashing may date as far back as the Reformation, which replaced elaborate church decorations with plain white walls.

12 Queen Anne's Bounty was established in 1704 to assist impoverished clergymen.

13 "had not been the work of Mr. Thornburgh, but": comma added as per *SE(1)* and *W*.

church, nor was he likely on other lines to reach preferment. He and his wife, who possessed much more salience of character than he, were accepted in the dale as belonging to the established order of things. Nobody wished them any harm, and the few people they had specially befriended, naturally, thought well of them.

But the old intimacy of relation which had once subsisted between the clergyman of Long Whindale and his parishioners was wholly gone. They had sunk in the scale; the parson had risen. The old statesmen or peasant proprietors of the valley had for the most part succumbed to various destructive influences, some social, some economical, added to a certain amount of corrosion from within; and their place had been taken by leaseholders, less drunken perhaps, and better educated, but also far less shrewd and individual, and lacking in the rude dignity of their predecessors.

And as the land had lost, the church had gained. The place of the dalesmen knew them no more, but the church and parsonage had got themselves rebuilt, the parson had had his income raised, had let off his glebe to a neighbouring farmer, kept two maids, and drank claret when he drank anything. His flock were friendly enough, and paid their commuted tithes without grumbling. But between them and a perfectly well-meaning but rather dull man, who stood on his dignity and wore a black coat all the week, there was no real community. Rejoice in it as we may, in this final passage of Parson Primrose to social regions beyond the ken of Farmer Flamborough, there are some elements of loss as there are in all changes.[14]

Wheels on the road! Mrs. Thornburgh woke up with a start, and stumbling over newspaper and *couvre-pied*, hurried across the lawn as fast as her short squat figure would allow, gray curls and cap-strings flying behind her. She heard a colloquy in the distance in broad Westmoreland dialect, and as she turned the corner of the house she nearly ran into her tall cook, Sarah, whose impassive and saturnine countenance bore traces of unusual excitement.

'Missis, there's naw cakes. They're all left behind on t' counter at Randall's. Mr. Backhouse says as how he told old Jim to go fur 'em, and he niver went, and Mr. Backhouse he niver found oot till he'd got past t' bridge, and than it wur too late to go back.'

Mrs. Thornburgh stood transfixed, something of her fresh pink colour slowly deserting her face as she realised the enormity of the catastrophe. And was it possible that there was the faintest twinkle of grim satisfaction on the

---

14 Two characters from Oliver Goldsmith's sentimental novel *The Vicar of Wakefield* (1766). Primrose, the eponymous vicar, is a well-educated man living in close proximity to Flamborough, a goodnatured but rustic sort.

face of that elderly minx, Sarah?

Mrs. Thornburgh, however, did not stay to explore the recesses of Sarah's mind, but ran with little pattering, undignified steps across the front garden and down the steps to where Mr. Backhouse the carrier stood, bracing himself for self-defence.

'Ya may weel fret, mum,' said Mr. Backhouse, interrupting the flood of her reproaches, with the comparative *sang-froid* of one who knew that, after all, he was the only carrier on the road, and that the vicarage was five miles from the necessaries of life; 'it's a bad job, and I's not goin' to say it isn't. But ya jest look 'ere, mum, what's a man to du wi' a daft thingamy like *that*, as caan't tëak a plain order, and spiles a poor man's business as caan't help hissel'?'

And Mr. Backhouse pointed with withering scorn to a small, shrunken old man, who sat dangling his legs on the shaft of the cart, and whose countenance wore a singular expression of mingled meekness and composure, as his partner flourished an indignant finger towards him.

'Jim,' cried Mrs. Thornburgh reproachfully, 'I did think you would have taken more pains about my order!'

'Yis, mum,' said the old man placidly, 'ya might 'a' thowt it. I's reet sorry, bit ya caan't help these things *sum*times—an' it's naw gud, a hollerin' ower 'em like a mad bull. Aa tuke yur bit paper to Randall's and aa laft it wi' 'em to mek up, an' than, aa, weel, aa went to a frind, an' ee *may* hev giv' me a glass of yale, aa doon't say ee *dud*—but ee may, I ween't sweer. Hawsomiver, aa niver thowt naw mair aboot it, nor mair did John, so *ee* needn't taak—till we wur jest two mile from 'ere. An' ee's a gon' on sence! My! an' a larroping the poor beeast like onything!'

Mrs. Thornburgh stood aghast at the calmness of this audacious recital. As for John, he looked on, surveying his brother's philosophical demeanour at first with speechless wrath, and then with an inscrutable mixture of expressions, in which, however, any one accustomed to his weather-beaten countenance would have probably read a hidden admiration.[15]

'Weel, aa niver!' he exclaimed, when Jim's explanatory remarks had come to an end, swinging himself up on to his seat and gathering up the reins. 'Yur a boald 'un to tell the missus theer to hur feeace as how ya wur 'tossicatit whan yur owt ta been duing yur larful business. Aa've doon wi' yer. Aa aims to please ma coostomers, an' aa caan't abide sek wark. Yur like an oald kneyfe, I can mak' nowt o' ya', nowder back nor edge.'

Mrs. Thornburgh wrung her fat short hands in despair, making little incoherent laments and suggestions as she saw him about to depart, of which

---

15 "he looked on, surveying": comma as per *W*.

John at last gathered the main purport to be that she wished him to go back to Whinborough for her precious parcel.

He shook his head compassionately over the preposterous state of mind betrayed by such a demand, and with a fresh burst of abuse of his brother, and an assurance to the vicar's wife that he meant to 'gie that oald man naw-tice when he got haum; he wasn't goan to hev his bisness spiled for nowt by an oald ijiot wi' a hed as full o' yale as a hayrick's full of mice,' he raised his whip and the clattering vehicle moved forward; Jim meanwhile preserving through all his brother's wrath and Mrs. Thornburgh's wailings the same mild and even countenance, the meditative and friendly aspect of the philosopher letting the world go 'as e'en it will.'

So Mrs. Thornburgh was left gasping, watching the progress of the lumbering cart along the bit of road leading to the hamlet at the head of the valley, with so limp and crestfallen an aspect that even the gaunt and secretly jubilant Sarah was moved to pity.

'Why, missis, we'll do very well. I'll hev some scones in t'oven in naw time, an' theer's finger biscuits, an' wi' buttered toast an' sum o' t' best jams, if they don't hev enuf to eat they ought to.' Then, dropping her voice, she asked with a hurried change of tone, 'Did ye ask un' hoo his daater is?'

Mrs. Thornburgh started. Her pastoral conscience was smitten. She opened the gate and waved violently after the cart. John pulled his horse up, and with a few quick steps she brought herself within speaking, or rather shouting, distance.

'How's your daughter to-day, John?'

The old man's face peering round the oilcloth hood of the cart was darkened by a sudden cloud as he caught the words. His stern lips closed. He muttered something inaudible to Mrs. Thornburgh and whipped up his horse again. The cart started off, and Mrs. Thornburgh was left staring into the receding eyes of 'Jim the Noodle,' who, from his seat on the near shaft, regarded her with a gaze which had passed from benevolence into a preternatural solemnity.

'He's sparin' ov 'is speach is John Backhouse,' said Sarah grimly, as her mistress returned to her. 'Maybe ee's aboot reet. It's a bad business an' ee'll not mend it wi' taakin'.'

Mrs. Thornburgh, however, could not apply herself to the case of Mary Backhouse. At any other moment it would have excited in her breast the shuddering interest which, owing to certain peculiar attendant circumstances, it awakened in every other woman in Long Whindale. But her mind—such are the limitations of even clergymen's wives—was now absorbed by her own misfortune. Her very cap-strings seemed to hang limp with depression, as she followed Sarah dejectedly into the kitchen, and gave what attention she could to those second-best arrangements so depressing to the idealist temper.

Poor soul! All the charm and glitter of her little social adventure was gone. When she once more emerged upon the lawn, and languidly read-justed her spectacles, she was weighed down by the thought that in two hours Mrs. Seaton would be upon her. Nothing of this kind ever happened to Mrs. Seaton. The universe obeyed her nod. No carrier conveying goods to her august door ever got drunk or failed to deliver his consignment. The thing was inconceivable. Mrs. Thornburgh was well aware of it.

Should William be informed? Mrs. Thornburgh had a rooted belief in the brutality of husbands in all domestic crises, and would have preferred not to inform him. But she had also a dismal certainty that the secret would burn a hole in her till it was confessed—bill and all. Besides—frightful thought!—would they have to eat up all those *meringues* next day?

Her reflections at last became so depressing that, with a natural epicurean instinct, she tried violently to turn her mind away from them. Luckily she was assisted by a sudden perception of the roof and chimneys of Burwood, the Leyburns' house, peeping above the trees to the left. At sight of them a smile overspread her plump and gently wrinkled face. She fell gradually into a train of thought, as feminine as that in which she had been just indulging, but infinitely more pleasing.

For, with regard to the Leyburns, at this present moment Mrs. Thornburgh felt herself in the great position of tutelary divinity or guardian angel. At least if divinities and guardian angels do not concern themselves with the questions to which Mrs. Thornburgh's mind was now addressed, it would clearly have been the opinion of the vicar's wife that they ought to do so.

'Who else is there to look after these girls, I should like to know,' Mrs. Thornburgh inquired of herself, 'if I don't do it? As if girls married themselves! People may talk of their independence nowadays as much as they like—it always has to be done for them, one way or another. Mrs. Leyburn, poor lackadaisical thing! is no good whatever. No more is Catherine. They both behave as if husbands tumbled into your mouth for the asking. Catherine's too good for this world—but if she doesn't do it, I must. Why, that girl Rose is a beauty—if they didn't let her wear those ridiculous mustard-coloured things, and do her hair fit to frighten the crows! Agnes too—so lady-like and well-mannered; she'd do credit to any man. Well, we shall see, we shall see!'

And Mrs. Thornburgh gently shook her gray curls from side to side, while her eyes, fixed on the open spare room window, shone with meaning.

'So eligible, too—private means, no encumbrances, and as good as gold.'
She sat lost a moment in a pleasing dream.

'Shall I bring oot the tea to you theer, mum?' called Sarah gruffly, from
the garden door. 'Master and Mr. Elsmere are just coomin' down t' field by t'
stepping-stones.'

Mrs. Thornburgh signalled assent and the tea-table was brought.
Afternoon tea was by no means a regular institution at the vicarage of Long
Whindale, and Sarah never supplied it without signs of protest. But when a
guest was in the house Mrs. Thornburgh insisted upon it; her obstinacy in the
matter, like her dreams of cakes and confections, being all part of her determination to move with the times, in spite of the station to which Providence
had assigned her.

A minute afterwards the vicar, a thick-set gray-haired man of sixty, accompanied by a tall younger man in clerical dress, emerged upon the lawn.

'Welcome sight!' cried Mr. Thornburgh; 'Robert and I have been covet-
ing that tea for the last hour. You guessed very well, Emma, to have it just
ready for us.'

'Oh, that was Sarah. She saw you coming down to the stepping-stones,'
replied his wife, pleased, however, by any mark of appreciation from her mankind, however small. 'Robert, I hope you haven't been walked off your legs?'

'What, in this air, cousin Emma? I could walk from sunrise to sundown.
Let no one call me an invalid any more. Henceforth I am a Hercules.'

And he threw himself on the rug which Mrs. Thornburgh's motherly
providence had spread on the grass for him, with a smile and a look of supreme physical contentment, which did indeed almost efface the signs of
recent illness in the ruddy boyish face.

Mrs. Thornburgh studied him; her eye caught first of all by the stubble
of reddish hair which, as he took off his hat, stood up straight and stiff all
over his head with an odd wildness and aggressiveness.[16] She involuntarily
thought, basing her inward comment on a complexity of reasons—'Dear me,
what a pity; it spoils his appearance!'

'I apologise, I apologise, cousin Emma, once for all,' said the young man,
surprising her glance, and despairingly smoothing down his recalcitrant locks.
'Let us hope that mountain air will quicken the pace of it before it is necessary
for me to present a dignified appearance at Murewell.'

He looked up at her with a merry flash in his gray eyes, and her old face
brightened visibly as she realised afresh that in spite of the grotesqueness
of his cropped hair, her guest was a most attractive creature. Not that he

---

16 "which, as he took off his hat, stood up": commas as per *SE(1)* and *W*.

could boast much in the way of regular good looks: the mouth was large, the nose of no particular outline, and in general the cutting of the face, though strong and characteristic, had a bluntness and *naïveté* like a vigorous unfinished sketch. This bluntness of line, however, was balanced by a great delicacy of tint—the pink and white complexion of a girl, indeed—enhanced by the bright reddish hair, and quick gray eyes.

The figure was also a little out of drawing, so to speak; it was tall and loosely-jointed. The general impression was one of agility and power. But if you looked closer you saw that the shoulders were narrow, the arms inordinately long, and the extremities too small for the general height. Robert Elsmere's hand was the hand of a woman, and few people ever exchanged a first greeting with its very tall owner without a little shock of surprise.

Mr. Thornburgh and his guest had visited a few houses in the course of their walk, and the vicar plunged for a minute or two into some conversation about local matters with his wife. But Mrs. Thornburgh, it was soon evident, was giving him but a scatterbrained attention. Her secret was working in her ample breast. Very soon she could contain it no longer, and breaking in upon her husband's parish news, she tumbled it all out pell-mell, with a mixture of discomfiture and defiance infinitely diverting. She could not keep a secret, but she also could not bear to give William an advantage.

William certainly took his advantage. He did what his wife in her irritation had precisely foreseen that he would do. He first stared, then fell into a guffaw of laughter, and as soon as he had recovered breath, into a series of unfeeling comments which drove Mrs. Thornburgh to desperation.

'If you will set your mind, my dear, on things we plain folks can do perfectly well without'—et cetera, et cetera—the husband's point of view can be imagined. Mrs. Thornburgh could have shaken her good man, especially as there was nothing new to her in his remarks; she had known to a T beforehand exactly what he would say. She took up her knitting in a great hurry, the needles clicking angrily, her gray curls quivering under the energy of her hands and arms, while she launched at her husband various retorts as to his lack of consideration for her efforts and her inconvenience, which were only very slightly modified by the presence of a stranger.

Robert Elsmere meanwhile lay on the grass, his face discreetly turned away, an uncontrollable smile twitching the corners of his mouth. Everything was fresh and piquant up here in this remote corner of the north country, whether the mountain air or the wind-blown streams, or the manners and customs of the inhabitants. His cousin's wife, in spite of her ambitious conventionalities, was really the child of Nature to a refreshing degree. One does not see these types, he said to himself, in the cultivated monotony of Oxford or London. She was like a bit of a bygone world—Miss Austen's or Miss Ferrier's—unearthed for his amusement.[17] He could not for the life of him help taking the scenes of this remote rural existence, which was quite new to him, as though they were the scenes of some comedy of manners.

Presently, however, the vicar became aware that the passage of arms between himself and his spouse was becoming just a little indecorous. He got up with a 'Hem!' intended to put an end to it, and deposited his cup.

'Well, my dear, have it as you please. It all comes of your determination to have Mrs. Seaton. Why couldn't you just ask the Leyburns and let us enjoy ourselves?'

With this final shaft he departed to see that Jane, the little maid whom Sarah ordered about, had not, in cleaning the study for the evening's festivities, put his last sermon into the waste-paper basket. His wife looked after him with eyes that spoke unutterable things.

'You would never think,' she said in an agitated voice to young Elsmere, 'that I had consulted Mr. Thornburgh as to every invitation, that he entirely agreed with me that one *must* be civil to Mrs. Seaton, considering that she can make anybody's life a burden to them about here that isn't; but it's no use.'

And she fell back on her knitting with redoubled energy, her face full of a half-tearful intensity of meaning. Robert Elsmere restrained a strong inclination to laugh, and set himself instead to distract and console her. He expressed sympathy with her difficulties, he talked to her about her party, he got from her the names and histories of the guests. How Miss Austenish it sounded: the managing rector's wife, her still more managing old maid of a sister, the neighbouring clergyman who played the flute, the local doctor, and a pretty daughter just out—'Very pretty,' sighed Mrs. Thornburgh, who was now depressed all round, 'but all flounces and frills and nothing to say'—and last of all, those three sisters, the Leyburns, who seemed to be on a different level, and whom he had heard mentioned so often since his arrival by both husband and wife.

'Tell me about the Miss Leyburns,' he said presently. 'You and cousin William seem to have a great affection for them. Do they live near?'

'Oh, quite close,' cried Mrs. Thornburgh, brightening at last, and like a great general, leaving one scheme in ruins, only the more ardently to take up another. 'There is the house,' and she pointed out Burwood among its trees.

---

17 Jane Austen (1775–1817) and the author considered her Scottish equivalent, Susan Ferrier (1782–1854). Both novelists specialized in often ironic, finely-observed portraits of genteel domestic life.

Then with her eye eagerly fixed upon him, she fell into a more or less incoherent account of her favourites. She laid on her colours thickly, and Elsmere at once assumed extravagance.

'A saint, a beauty, and a wit all to yourselves in these wilds!' he said, laughing. 'What luck! But what on earth brought them here—a widow and three daughters—from the south? It was an odd settlement surely, though you have one of the loveliest valleys and the purest airs in England.'

'Oh, as to lovely valleys,' said Mrs. Thornburgh, sighing, 'I think it very dull; I always have. When one has to depend for everything on a carrier that gets drunk, too! Why, you know they belong here. They're real Westmoreland people.'

'What does that mean exactly?'

'Oh, their grandfather was a farmer, just like one of the common farmers about. Only his land was his own, and theirs isn't.'

'He was one of the last of the statesmen,' interposed Mr. Thornburgh—who, having rescued his sermon from Jane's tender mercies, and put out his modest claret and sherry for the evening, had strolled out again and found himself impelled as usual to put some precision into his wife's statements—'one of the small freeholders who have almost disappeared here as elsewhere. The story of the Leyburns always seems to me typical of many things.'

Robert looked inquiry, and the vicar, sitting down—having first picked up his wife's ball of wool as a peace-offering, which was loftily accepted—launched into a narrative which may be here somewhat condensed.

The Leyburns' grandfather, it appeared, had been a typical north-country peasant—honest, with strong passions both of love and hate, thinking nothing of knocking down his wife with the poker, and frugal in all things save drink. Drink, however, was ultimately his ruin, as it was the ruin of most of the Cumberland statesmen. 'The people about here,' said the vicar, 'say he drank away an acre a year. He had some fifty acres, and it took about thirty years to beggar him.'

Meanwhile, this brutal, rollicking, strong-natured person had sons and daughters—plenty of them. Most of them, even the daughters, were brutal and rollicking too. Of one of the daughters, now dead, it was reported that, having on one occasion discovered her father, then an old infirm man, sitting calmly by the fire beside the prostrate form of his wife, whom he had just felled with his crutch, she had taken off her wooden shoe and given her father a clout on the head, which left his gray hair streaming with blood; after which she had calmly put the horse into the cart, and driven off to fetch the doctor to both her parents. But among this grim and earthy crew there was

one exception, a 'hop out of kin,' of whom all the rest made sport. This was
the second son, Richard, who showed such a persistent tendency to 'book-
larnin',' and such a persistent idiocy in all matters pertaining to the land, that
nothing was left to the father at last but to send him with many oaths to the
grammar school at Whinborough. From the moment the boy got a footing
in the school he hardly cost his father another penny. He got a local bursary
which paid his school expenses, he never missed a remove or failed to gain a
prize, and finally won a close scholarship which carried him triumphantly to
Queen's College.[18]

His family watched his progress with a gaping, half-contemptuous
amazement, till he announced himself as safely installed at Oxford, having
borrowed from a Whinborough patron the modest sum necessary to pay his
college valuation—a sum which wild horses could not have dragged out of his
father, now sunk over head and ears in debt and drink.[19]

From that moment they practically lost sight of him. He sent the class
list which contained his name among the Firsts to his father; in the same way
he communicated the news of his Fellowship at Queen's, his ordination and
his appointment to the headmastership of a south-country grammar school.
None of his communications were ever answered till, in the very last year of
his father's life, the eldest son, who had a shrewder eye all round to the main
chance than the rest, applied to 'Dick' for cash wherewith to meet some of the
family necessities. The money was promptly sent, together with photographs
of Dick's wife and children. These last were not taken much notice of. These
Leyburns were a hard, limited, incurious set, and they no longer regarded
Dick as one of themselves.

'Then came the old man's death,' said Mr. Thornburgh. 'It happened
the year after I took the living. Richard Leyburn was sent for and came. I
never saw such a scene in my life as the funeral supper. It was kept up in
the old style. Three of Leyburn's sons were there: two of them farmers like
himself, one a clerk from Manchester, a daughter married to a tradesman in
Whinborough, a brother of the old man, who was under the table before supper was half over, and so on. Richard Leyburn wrote to ask me to come, and I

---

18 Richard was a scholarship student ("local bursary") at the secondary or grammar school, which by the late nineteenth century supplied young men with both
up-to-date subjects and the classical languages necessary to succeed at Oxford or
Cambridge. Eligibility for a close scholarship was restricted to scholars from specific
schools.

19 Ward may mean the cost of purchasing furniture for college rooms, which is how
the *Student Handbook to the University and Colleges of Oxford*, 9th ed. (1888) consist-
ently uses "valuation," or she may mean the schedule of fees.

went to support his cloth. But I was new to the place,' said the vicar, flushing a little, 'and they belonged to a race that had never been used to pay much respect to parsons. To see that man among the rest! He was thin and dignified; he looked to me as if he had all the learning imaginable, and he had large, absent-looking eyes, which, as George, the eldest brother, said, gave you the impression of some one that "had lost somethin' when he was nobbut a lad, and had gone seekin' it iver sence." He was formidable to me; but between us we couldn't keep the rest of the party in order, so when the orgie had gone on a certain time, we left it and went out into the air. It was an August night. I remember Leyburn threw back his head and drank it in. "I haven't breathed this air for five-and-twenty years," he said. "I thought I hated the place, and in spite of that drunken crew in there, it draws me to it like a magnet. I feel, after all, that I have the fells in my blood." He was a curious man, a refined-looking melancholy creature, with a face that reminded you of Wordsworth, and cold donnish ways, except to his children and the poor. I always thought his life had disappointed him somehow.'

'Yet one would think,' said Robert, opening his eyes, 'that he had made a very considerable success of it!'

'Well, I don't know how it was,' said the vicar, whose analysis of character never went very far. 'Anyhow, next day he went peering about the place and the mountains and the lands his father had lost. And George, the eldest brother, who had inherited the farm, watched him without a word, in the way these Westmoreland folk have, and at last offered him what remained of the place for a fancy price. I told him it was a preposterous sum, but he wouldn't bargain. "I shall bring my wife and children here in the holidays," he said, "and the money will set George up in California." So he paid through the nose, and got possession of the old house, in which, I should think, he had passed about as miserable a childhood as it was possible to pass. There's no accounting for tastes.'

'And then the next summer they all came down,' interrupted Mrs. Thornburgh. She disliked a long story as she disliked being read aloud to. 'Catherine was fifteen, not a bit like a child. You used to see her everywhere with her father. To my mind he was always exciting her brain too much, but he was a man you could not say a word to. I don't care what William says about his being like Wordsworth; he just gave you the blues to look at.'

'It was so strange,' said the vicar meditatively, 'to see them in that house. If you knew the things that used to go on there in old days—the savages that lived there. And then to see those three delicately brought-up children going in and out of the parlour where old Leyburn used to sit smoking and drinking; and Dick Leyburn walking about in a white tie, and the same men touching their hats to him who had belaboured him when he was a boy at the village school—it was queer.'

'A curious little bit of social history,' said Elsmere. 'Well, and then he died and the family lived on?'

'Yes, he died the year after he bought the place. And perhaps the most interesting thing of all has been the development of his eldest daughter. She has watched over her mother, she has brought up her sisters; but much more than that: she has become a sort of Deborah in these valleys,' said the vicar, smiling. 'I don't count for much, she counts for a great deal.[20] I can't get the people to tell me their secrets, she can. There is a sort of natural sympathy between them and her. She nurses them, she scolds them, she preaches to them, and they take it from her when they won't take it from us. Perhaps it is the feeling of blood. Perhaps they think it as mysterious a dispensation of Providence as I do that that brutal, swearing, whisky-drinking stock should have ended in anything so saintly and so beautiful as Catherine Leyburn.'

The quiet, commonplace clergyman spoke with a sudden tremor of feeling. His wife, however, looked at him with a dissatisfied expression.

'You always talk,' she said, 'as if there were no one but Catherine. People generally like the other two much better. Catherine is so stand-off.'

'Oh, the other two are very well,' said the vicar, but in a different tone.

Robert sat ruminating. Presently his host and hostess went in, and the young man went sauntering up the climbing garden-path to the point where only a railing divided it from the fell-side. From here his eye commanded the whole of the upper end of the valley—a bare, desolate recess filled with evening shadow, and walled round by masses of gray and purple crag, except in one spot, where a green intervening fell marked the course of the pass connecting the dale with the Ullswater district. Below him were church and parsonage; beyond, the stone-filled babbling river, edged by intensely green fields, which melted imperceptibly into the browner stretches of the opposite mountain. Most of the scene, except where the hills at the end rose highest and shut out the sun, was bathed in quiet light. The white patches on the farmhouses, the heckberry trees along the river and the road, caught and emphasised the golden rays which were flooding into the lower valley as into a broad green cup. Close by, in the little vicarage orchard, were fruit trees in blossom; the air was mild and fragrant, though to the young man from the warmer south there was still a bracing quality in the soft western breeze which blew about him.

---

20 Deborah, the female judge and prophet who appears in the Book of Judges 4-5.

He stood there bathed in silent enchantment, an eager nature going out to meet and absorb into itself the beauty and peace of the scene. Lines of Wordsworth were on his lips; the little well-worn volume was in his pocket, but he did not need to bring it out; and his voice had all a poet's intensity of emphasis as he strolled along, reciting under his breath—

'It is a beauteous evening, calm and free,
The holy time is quiet as a nun
Breathless with adoration!'[21]

Presently his eye was once more caught by the roof of Burwood, lying beneath him on its promontory of land, in the quiet shelter of its protecting trees. He stopped, and a delicate sense of harmonious association awoke in him. That girl, atoning as it were by her one white life for all the crimes and coarseness of her ancestry: the idea of her seemed to steal into the solemn golden evening and give it added poetry and meaning. The young man felt a sudden strong curiosity to see her.

CHAPTER III

The festal tea had begun, and Mrs. Thornburgh was presiding. Opposite to her, on the vicar's left, sat the formidable rector's wife. Poor Mrs. Thornburgh had said to herself as she entered the room on the arm of Mr. Mayhew, the incumbent of the neighbouring valley of Shanmoor, that the first *coup d'œil* was good. The flowers had been arranged in the afternoon by Rose; Sarah's exertions had made the silver shine again; a pleasing odour of good food underlay the scent of the bluebells and fern; and what with the snowy table-linen, and the pretty dresses and bright faces of the younger people, the room seemed to be full of an incessant play of crisp and delicate colour.

But just as the vicar's wife was sinking into her seat with a little sigh of wearied satisfaction, she caught sight suddenly of an eye-glass at the other end of the table slowly revolving in a large and jewelled hand. The judicial eye behind the eye-glass travelled round the table, lingering, as it seemed to Mrs. Thornburgh's excited consciousness, on every spot where cream or jelly or *meringue* should have been and was not. When it dropped with a harsh little click, the hostess, unable to restrain herself, rushed into desperate conversation with Mr. Mayhew, giving vent to incoherencies in the course of the first

---

21 The opening lines of William Wordsworth's "It is a beauteous evening, calm and free" (1807).

act of the meal which did but confirm her neighbour—a grim, uncommu-
nicative person—in his own devotion to a policy of silence. Meanwhile the
vicar was grappling on very unequal terms with Mrs. Seaton. Mrs. Leyburn
had fallen to young Elsmere. Catherine Leyburn was paired off with Dr.
Baker, Agnes with Mr. Mayhew's awkward son—a tongue-tied youth, lately
an unattached student at Oxford, but now relegated, owing to an invincible
antipathy to Greek verbs, to his native air, till some other opening into the
great world should be discovered for him.[22]

Rose was on Robert Elsmere's right. Agnes had coaxed her into a white
dress as being the least startling garment she possessed, and she was like a
Stothard picture with her high waist, her blue sash ribbon, her slender
neck and brilliant head.[23] She had already cast many curious glances at the
Thornburghs' guest. 'Not a prig, at any rate,' she thought to herself with satisfaction, 'so Agnes is quite wrong.'

As for the young man, who was, to begin with, in that state which so often follows on the long confinement of illness, when the light seems brighter
and scents keener and experience sharper than at other times, he was inwardly
confessing that Mrs. Thornburgh had not been romancing. The vivid creature
at his elbow, with her still unsoftened angles and movements, was in the first
dawn of an exceptional beauty; the plain sister had struck him before supper
in the course of twenty minutes' conversation as above the average in point of
manners and talk. As to Miss Leyburn, he had so far only exchanged a bow
with her, but he was watching her now, as he sat opposite to her, out of his
quick observant eyes.

She, too, was in white. As she turned to speak to the youth at her side,
Elsmere caught the fine outline of the head, the unusually clear and perfect
moulding of the brow, nose, and upper lip. The hollows in the cheeks struck
him, and the way in which the breadth of the forehead somewhat overbal-
anced the delicacy of the mouth and chin. The face, though still quite young,
and expressing a perfect physical health, had the look of having been polished
and refined away to its foundations. There was not an ounce of superfluous
flesh on it, and not a vestige of Rose's peach-like bloom. Her profile, as he
saw it now, had the firmness, the clear whiteness, of a profile on a Greek gem.

She was actually making that silent, awkward lad talk! Robert, who, out
of his four years' experience as an Oxford tutor, had an abundant compassion

22 Unlike Elsmere, Mr. Mayhew's "awkward son" matriculated at Oxford without
joining any one of its colleges or halls. However, to receive a B.A., he would have
had to pass the first examination, Responsions, which required both Greek and Latin
grammar as one of the subjects.
23 Thomas Stothard (1755–1834), painter, illustrator, and engraver.

for and understanding of such beings as young Mayhew, watched her with a pleased amusement, wondering how she did it. What? Had she got him on carpentering, engineering—discovered his weak point? Water-wheels, inventors, steam-engines—and the lumpish lad all in a glow, talking away nineteen to the dozen. What tact, what kindness in her gray-blue eyes!

But he was interrupted by Mrs. Seaton, who was perfectly well aware that she had beside her a stranger of some prestige, an Oxford man, and a member, besides, of a well-known Sussex county family. She was a large and commanding person, clad in black *moiré* silk. She wore a velvet diadem, Honiton lace lappets,[24] and a variety of chains, beads, and bangles bestrewn about her that made a tinkling as she moved. Fixing her neighbour with a bland majesty of eye, she inquired of him if he were 'any relation of Sir Mowbray Elsmere?' Robert replied that Sir Mowbray Elsmere was his father's cousin, and the patron of the living to which he had just been appointed. Mrs. Seaton then graciously informed him that long ago—'when I was a girl in my native Hampshire'—her family and Sir Mowbray Elsmere had been on intimate terms. Her father had been devoted to Sir Mowbray. 'And I,' she added, with an evident though lofty desire to please, 'retain an inherited respect, sir, for your name.'

Robert bowed, but it was not clear from his look that the rector's wife had made an impression. His general conception of his relative and patron Sir Mowbray—who had been for many years the family black sheep—was, indeed, so far removed from any notions of 'respect,' that he had some difficulty in keeping his countenance under the lady's look and pose. He would have been still more entertained had he known the nature of the intimacy to which she referred. Mrs. Seaton's father, in his capacity of solicitor in a small country town, had acted as electioneering agent for Sir Mowbray (then plain Mr.) Elsmere on two occasions—in 18—, when his client had been triumphantly returned at a bye-election; and two years later, when a repetition of the tactics, so successful in the previous contest, led to a petition, and to the disappearance of the heir to the Elsmere property from parliamentary life.

Of these matters, however, he was ignorant, and Mrs. Seaton did not enlighten him. Drawing herself up a little, and proceeding in a more neutral tone than before, she proceeded to put him through a catechism on Oxford, alternately cross-examining him and expounding to him her own views and her husband's on the functions of Universities. She and the Archdeacon conceived that the Oxford authorities were mainly occupied in ruining the young men's health by over-examination, and poisoning their minds by free-thinking

---

24 A loose part of a garment.

opinions. In her belief, if it went on, the mothers of England would refuse to send their sons to these ancient but deadly resorts. She looked at him sternly as she spoke, as though defying him to be flippant in return. And he, indeed, did his polite best to be serious.

But it somewhat disconcerted him in the middle to find Miss Leyburn's eyes upon him. And undeniably there was a spark of laughter in them, quenched, as soon as his glance crossed hers, under long lashes. How that spark had lit up the grave, pale face! He longed to provoke it again, to cross over to her and say, 'What amused you? Do you think me very young and simple? Tell me about these people.'

But, instead, he made friends with Rose. Mrs. Seaton was soon engaged in giving the vicar advice on his parochial affairs, an experience which generally ended by the appearance of certain truculent elements in one of the mildest of men. So Robert was free to turn to his girl neighbour and ask her what people meant by calling the Lakes rainy.

'I understand it is pouring at Oxford. To-day your sky here has been without a cloud, and your rivers are running dry.'

'And you have mastered our climate in twenty-four hours, like the tourists—isn't it?—that do the Irish question in three weeks?'[25]

'Not the answer of a bread-and-butter miss,' he thought to himself, amused, 'and yet what a child it looks.'

He threw himself into a war of words with her, and enjoyed it extremely. Her brilliant colouring, her gestures as fresh and untamed as the movements of the leaping river outside, the mixture in her of girlish pertness and ignorance with the promise of a remarkable general capacity, made her a most taking, provoking creature. Mrs. Thornburgh—much recovered in mind since Dr. Baker had praised the pancakes by which Sarah had sought to prove to her mistress the superfluity of naughtiness involved in her recourse to foreign cooks—watched the young man and maiden with a face which grew more and more radiant. The conversation in the garden had not pleased her. Why should people always talk of Catherine; Mrs. Thornburgh stood in awe of Catherine and had given her up in despair. It was the other two whose fortunes, as possibly directed by her, filled her maternal heart with sympathetic emotion.

Suddenly in the midst of her satisfaction she had a rude shock. What on

---

25 By the 1880s, the "Irish question" referred to the struggles over Home Rule (which would restore an Irish legislature and some additional degree of independence from the rest of Great Britain, although how much was a matter of heated debate) vs. Unionism (which advocated maintaining Ireland's current relationship with Great Britain).

earth was the vicar doing? After they had got through better than any one could have hoped, thanks to a discreet silence and Sarah's makeshifts, there was the master of the house pouring the whole tale of his wife's aspirations and disappointment into Mrs. Seaton's ear! If it were ever allowable to rush upon your husband at table and stop his mouth with a dinner napkin, Mrs. Thornburgh could at this moment have performed such a feat. She nodded and coughed and fidgeted in vain!

The vicar's confidences were the result of a fit of nervous exasperation. Mrs. Seaton had just embarked upon an account of 'our charming time with Lord Fleckwood.' Now Lord Fleckwood was a distant cousin of Archdeacon Seaton, and the great magnate of the neighbourhood, not, however, a very respectable magnate. Mr. Thornburgh had heard accounts of Lupton Castle from Mrs. Seaton on at least half a dozen different occasions. Privately he believed them all to refer to one visit, an event of immemorial antiquity periodically brought up to date by Mrs. Seaton's imagination. But the vicar was a timid man, without the courage of his opinions, and in his eagerness to stop the flow of his neighbour's eloquence he could think of no better device, or more suitable rival subject, than to plunge into the story of the drunken carrier, and the pastry still reposing on the counter at Randall's.

He blushed, good man, when he was well in it. His wife's horrified countenance embarrassed him. But anything was better than Lord Fleckwood. Mrs. Seaton listened to him with the slightest smile on her formidable lip. The story was pleasing to her.

'At least, my dear sir,' she said when he paused, nodding her diademed head with stately emphasis, 'Mrs. Thornburgh's inconvenience may have one good result. You can now make an example of the carrier. It is our special business, as my husband always says, who are in authority, to bring their low vices home to these people.'

The vicar fidgeted in his chair. What ineptitude had he been guilty of now! By way of avoiding Lord Fleckwood he might have started Mrs. Seaton on teetotalism. Now if there was one topic on which this awe-inspiring woman was more awe-inspiring than another it was on the topic of teetotalism. The vicar had already felt himself a criminal as he drank his modest glass of claret under her eye.

'Oh, the drunkenness about here is pretty bad,' said Dr. Baker, from the other end of the table. 'But there are plenty of worse things in these valleys. Besides, what person in his senses would think of trying to disestablish John Backhouse? He and his queer brother are as much a feature of the valley as High Fell. We have too few originals left to be so very particular about trifles.'

'Trifles?' repeated Mrs. Seaton in a deep voice, throwing up her eyes. But she would not venture an argument with Dr. Baker. He had all the cheery self-confidence of the old established local doctor, who knows himself to be a power, and neither Mrs. Seaton nor her restless intriguing little husband had ever yet succeeded in putting him down.

'You must see these two old characters,' said Dr. Baker to Elsmere across the table. 'They are relics of a Westmoreland which will soon have disappeared. Old John, who is going on for seventy, is as tough an old dalesman as ever you saw. He doesn't measure his cups, but he would scorn to be floored by them. I don't believe he does drink much, but if he does there is probably no amount of whisky that he couldn't carry. Jim, the other brother, is about five years older. He is a kind of softie—all alive on one side of his brain, and a noodle on the other. A single glass of rum and water puts him under the table. And as he never can refuse this glass, and as the temptation generally seizes him when they are on their rounds, he is always getting John into disgrace. John swears at him and slangs him. No use. Jim sits still, looks—well, nohow. I never saw an old creature with a more singular gift of denuding his face of all expression. John vows he shall go to the "house"; he has no legal share in the business; the house and the horse and cart are John's.[26] Next day you see them on the cart again just as usual. In reality neither brother can do without the other. And three days after, the play begins again.'

'An improving spectacle for the valley,' said Mrs. Seaton drily.

'Oh, my dear madam,' said the doctor, shrugging his shoulders, 'we can't all be so virtuous. If old Jim is a drunkard, he has got a heart of his own somewhere, and can nurse a dying niece like a woman. Miss Leyburn can tell us something about that.'

And he turned round to his neighbour with a complete change of expression, and a voice that had a new note in it of affectionate respect. Catherine coloured as if she did not like being addressed on the subject, and just nodded a little with gentle affirmative eyes.

'A strange case,' said Dr. Baker, again looking at Elsmere. 'It is a family that is original and old-world even in its ways of dying. I have been a doctor in these parts for five-and-twenty years. I have seen what you may call old Westmoreland die out—costume, dialect, superstitions. At least, as to dialect, the people have become bi-lingual. I sometimes think they talk it to each other as much as ever, but some of them won't talk it to you and me at all. And as to superstitions, the only ghost story I know that still has some hold on popular belief is the one which attaches to this mountain here, High Fell,

---

26 "House": the workhouse.

at the end of this valley.'

He paused a moment. A salutary sense has begun to penetrate even modern provincial society, that no man may tell a ghost story without leave. Rose threw a merry glance at him. They two were very old friends. Dr. Baker had pulled out her first teeth and given her a sixpence afterwards for each operation. The pull was soon forgotten; the sixpence lived on gratefully in a child's warm memory.

'Tell it,' she said; 'we give you leave. We won't interrupt you unless you put in too many inventions.'

'You invite me to break the first law of story-telling, Miss Rose,' said the doctor, lifting a finger at her. 'Every man is bound to leave a story better than he found it. However, I couldn't tell it if I would. I don't know what makes the poor ghost walk; and if you do, I shall say you invent. But at any rate there is a ghost, and she walks along the side of High Fell at midnight every Midsummer day. If you see her and she passes you in silence, why you only get a fright for your pains. But if she speaks to you, you die within the year. Old John Backhouse is a widower with one daughter. This girl saw the ghost last Midsummer day, and Miss Leyburn and I are now doing our best to keep her alive over the next; but with very small prospect of success.'

'What is the girl dying of?—fright?' asked Mrs. Seaton harshly.

'Oh no!' said the doctor hastily, 'not precisely. A sad story; better not inquire into it. But at the present moment the time of her death seems likely to be determined by the strength of her own and other people's belief in the ghost's summons.'

Mrs. Seaton's grim mouth relaxed into an ungenial smile. She put up her eye-glass and looked at Catherine. 'An unpleasant household, I should imagine,' she said shortly, 'for a young lady to visit.'

Doctor Baker looked at the rector's wife, and a kind of flame came into his eyes. He and Mrs. Seaton were old enemies, and he was a quick-tempered mercurial sort of man.

'I presume that one's guardian angel may have to follow one sometimes into unpleasant quarters,' he said hotly. 'If this girl lives, it will be Miss Leyburn's doing; if she dies, saved and comforted, instead of lost in this world and the next, it will be Miss Leyburn's doing too. Ah, my dear young lady, let me alone! You tie my tongue always, and I won't have it.'

And the doctor turned his weather-beaten elderly face upon her with a look which was half defiance and half apology. She, on her side, had flushed painfully, laying her white finger-tips imploringly on his arm. Mrs. Seaton turned away with a little dry cough, so did her spectacled sister at the other end of the table. Mrs. Leyburn, on the other hand, sat in a little ecstasy, looking at Catherine and Dr. Baker, something glistening in her eyes. Robert Elsmere alone showed presence of mind. Bending across to Dr. Baker, he asked him a sudden question as to the history of a certain strange green mound or barrow that rose out of a flat field not far from the vicarage windows. Dr. Baker grasped his whiskers, threw the young man a queer glance, and replied. Thenceforward he and Robert kept up a lively antiquarian talk on the traces of Norse settlement in the Cumbrian valleys, which lasted till the ladies left the dining-room.

As Catherine Leyburn went out Elsmere stood holding the door open. She could not help raising her eyes upon him, eyes full of a half-timid, half-grateful friendliness. His own returned her look with interest.

"'A spirit, but a woman too,'" he thought to himself with a new-born thrill of sympathy, as he went back to his seat. She had not yet said a direct word to him, and yet he was curiously convinced that here was one of the most interesting persons, and one of the persons most interesting to *him*, that he had ever met. What mingled delicacy and strength in the hand that had lain beside her on the dinner-table—what potential depths of feeling in the full dark-fringed eye!

Half an hour later, when Elsmere re-entered the drawing-room, he found Catherine Leyburn sitting by an open French window that looked out on the lawn, and on the dim rocky face of the fell. Adeline Baker, a stooping red-armed maiden, with a pretty face, set off, as she imagined, by a vast amount of cheap finery, was sitting beside her, studying her with a timid adoration. The doctor's daughter regarded Catherine Leyburn, who during the last five years had made herself almost as distinct a figure in the popular imagination of a few Westmoreland valleys as Sister Dora among her Walsall miners, as a being of a totally different order from herself.[27] She was glued to the side of her idol, but her shy and awkward tongue could find hardly anything to say to her. Catherine, however, talked away, gently stroking the while the girl's rough hand which lay on her knee, to the mingled pain and bliss of its owner, who was outraged by the contrast between her own ungainly member and Miss Leyburn's delicate fingers.

Mrs. Seaton was on the sofa beside Mrs. Thornburgh, amply avenging herself on the vicar's wife for any checks she might have received at tea. Miss Barks, her sister, an old maid with a face that seemed to be perpetually

---

27 Dorothy Pattison (1832–78), renowned mid-Victorian nursing sister. After joining the Anglican Sisterhood of the Good Samaritans in 1864, she became famous for indefatigably nursing the working classes in Walsall, Staffordshire. Sister Dora was Mark Pattison's sister.

peering forward, light colourless hair surmounted by a cap adorned with artificial nasturtiums, and white-lashed eyes armed with spectacles, was having her way with Mrs. Leyburn, inquiring into the household arrangements of Burwood with a cross-examining power which made the mild widow as pulp before her.

When the gentlemen entered, Mrs. Thornburgh looked round hastily. She herself had opened that door into the garden. A garden on a warm summer night offers opportunities no schemer should neglect. Agnes and Rose were chattering and laughing on the gravel path just outside it, their white girlish figures showing temptingly against the dusky background of garden and fell. It somewhat disappointed the vicar's wife to see her tall guest take a chair and draw it beside Catherine—while Adeline Baker awkwardly got up and disappeared into the garden.

Elsmere felt it an unusually interesting moment, so strong had been his sense of attraction at tea; but like the rest of us he could find nothing more telling to start with than a remark about the weather. Catherine in her reply asked him if he were quite recovered from the attack of low fever he was understood to have been suffering from.[28]

'Oh yes,' he said brightly, 'I am very nearly as fit as I ever was, and more eager than I ever was to get to work. The idling of it is the worst part of illness. However, in a month from now I must be at my living, and I can only hope it will give me enough to do.'

Catherine looked up at him with a quick impulse of liking. What an eager face it was! Eagerness, indeed, seemed to be the note of the whole man, of the quick eyes and mouth, the flexible hands and energetic movements. Even the straight, stubbly hair, its owner's passing torment, standing up round the high open brow, seemed to help the general impression of alertness and vigour.

'Your mother, I hear, is already there?' said Catherine.

'Yes. My poor mother!' and the young man smiled half sadly. 'It is a curious situation for both of us. This living which has just been bestowed on me is my father's old living. It is in the gift of my cousin, Sir Mowbray Elsmere. My great-uncle'—he drew himself together suddenly. 'But I don't know why I should imagine that these things interest other people,' he said, with a little quick, almost comical, accent of self-rebuke.

'Please go on,' cried Catherine hastily. The voice and manner were singularly pleasant to her; she wished he would not interrupt himself for nothing.

'Really? Well then, my great-uncle, old Sir William, wished me to have

28 Typhus.

it when I grew up. I was against it for a long time, took orders; but I wanted something more stirring than a country parish. One has dreams of many things. But one's dreams come to nothing. I got ill at Oxford. The doctors forbade the town work. The old incumbent who had held the living since my father's death died precisely at that moment. I felt myself booked, and gave in to various friends; but it is second best.'

She felt a certain soreness and discomfort in his tone, as though his talk represented a good deal of mental struggle in the past.

'But the country is not idleness,' she said, smiling at him. Her cheek was leaning lightly on her hand, her eyes had an unusual animation; and her long white dress, guiltless of any ornament save a small old-fashioned locket hanging from a thin old chain and a pair of hair bracelets with engraved gold clasps, gave her the nobleness and simplicity of a Romney picture.[29]

'*You* do not find it so, I imagine,' he replied, bending forward to her with a charming gesture of homage. He would have liked her to talk to him of her work and her interests. He, too, mentally compared her to Saint Elizabeth. He could almost have fancied the dark red flowers in her white lap.[30] But his comparison had another basis of feeling than Rose's.

However, she would not talk to him of herself. The way in which she turned the conversation brought home to his own expansive confiding nature a certain austerity and stiffness of fibre in her which for the moment chilled him. But as he got her into talk about the neighbourhood, the people and their ways, the impression vanished again, so far at least as there was anything repellent about it. Austerity, strength, individuality, all these words indeed he was more and more driven to apply to her. She was like no other woman he had ever seen. It was not at all that she was more remarkable intellectually. Every now and then, indeed, as their talk flowed on, he noticed in what she said an absence of a good many interests and attainments which in his ordinary south-country women friends he would have assumed as a matter of course.

'I understand French very little, and I never read any,' she said to him once, quietly, as he fell to comparing some peasant story she had told him with an episode in one of George Sand's Berry novels.[31] It seemed to him that

---

29   George Romney (1734-1802), leading portrait painter of the late eighteenth century.

30   One of the miracles associated with St. Elizabeth. On a trip to succor the poor and ill, she encountered her husband. When he asked to see what she was carrying in her mantle, the food was transformed into red and white roses.

31   Catherine has not been educated in female "accomplishments," which would have included a modern Romance language like French or Italian. The celebrated

she knew her Wordsworth by heart. And her own mountain life, her own rich and meditative soul, had taught her judgments and comments on her favourite poet ·which stirred Elsmere every now and then to enthusiasm—so true they were and pregnant, so full often of a natural magic of expression. On the other hand, when he quoted a very well-known line of Shelley's she asked him where it came from. She seemed to him deeper and simpler at every moment; her very limitations of sympathy and knowledge, and they were evidently many, began to attract him. The thought of her ancestry crossed him now and then, rousing in him now wonder, and now a strange sense of congruity and harmony. Clearly she was the daughter of a primitive unexhausted race. And yet what purity, what refinement, what delicate perception and self-restraint!

Presently they fell on the subject of Oxford.

'Were you ever there?' he asked her.

'Once,' she said. 'I went with my father one summer term. I have only a confused memory of it—of the quadrangles, and a long street, a great building with a dome, and such beautiful trees!'

'Did your father often go back?'

'No; never towards the latter part of his life'—and her clear eyes clouded a little; 'nothing made him so sad as the thought of Oxford.'

She paused, as though she had strayed on to a topic where expression was a little difficult. Then his face and clerical dress seemed somehow to reassure her, and she began again, though reluctantly.

'He used to say that it was all so changed. The young fellows he saw when he went back scorned everything he cared for. Every visit to Oxford was like a stab to him. It seemed to him as if the place was full of men who only wanted to destroy and break down everything that was sacred to him.'

Elsmere reflected that Richard Leyburn must have left Oxford about the beginning of the Liberal reaction, which followed Tractarianism, and in twenty years transformed the University.[32]

'Ah!' he said, smiling gently. 'He should have lived a little longer. There is another turn of the tide since then. The destructive wave has spent itself, and at Oxford now many of us feel ourselves on the upward swell of a religious revival.'

Catherine looked up at him with a sweet sympathetic look. That dim

---

(and scandalous) French novelist Amantine Lucile Aurore Dupin (1804–76), who wrote under the male pseudonym "George Sand," set a number of her novels in the French province of Berry, where she also lived.

32 In particular, the influence of such figures as Benjamin Jowett (1817–93), the Master of Balliol, in the wake of prominent Tractarian conversions to Catholicism, especially that of John Henry Newman in 1845.

vision of Oxford, with its gray, tree-lined walls, lay very near to her heart for her father's sake. And the keen face above her seemed to satisfy and respond to her inner feeling.

'I know the High Church influence is very strong,' she said, hesitating; 'but I don't know whether father would have liked that much better.'

The last words had slipped out of her, and she checked herself suddenly. Robert saw that she was uncertain as to his opinions, and afraid lest she might have said something discourteous.

'It is not only the High Church influence,' he said quickly, 'it is a mixture of influences from all sorts of quarters that has brought about the new state of things. Some of the factors in the change were hardly Christian at all, by name, but they have all helped to make men think, to stir their hearts, to win them back to the old ways.'

His voice had taken to itself a singular magnetism. Evidently the matters they were discussing were matters in which he felt a deep and loving interest. His young boyish face had grown grave; there was a striking dignity and weight in his look and manner, which suddenly roused in Catherine the sense that she was speaking to a man of distinction, accustomed to deal on equal terms with the large things of life. She raised her eyes to him for a moment, and he saw in them a beautiful, mystical light—responsive, lofty, full of soul.

The next moment, it apparently struck her sharply that their conversation was becoming incongruous with its surroundings. Behind them Mrs. Thornburgh was bustling about with candles and music-stools, preparing for a performance on the flute by Mr. Mayhew, the black-browed vicar of Shanmoor, and the room seemed to be pervaded by Mrs. Seaton's strident voice. Her strong natural reserve asserted itself, and her face settled again into the slight rigidity of expression characteristic of it. She rose and prepared to move farther into the room.

'We must listen,' she said to him, smiling, over her shoulder.

And she left him, settling herself by the side of Mrs. Leyburn. He had a momentary sense of rebuff. The man, quick, sensitive, sympathetic, felt in the woman the presence of a strength, a self-sufficingness which was not all attractive. His vanity, if he had cherished any during their conversation, was not flattered by its close. But as he leant against the window-frame waiting for the music to begin, he could hardly keep his eyes from her. He was a man who, by force of temperament, made friends readily with women, though except for a passing fancy or two he had never been in love; and his sense of difficulty with regard to this stiffly-mannered, deep-eyed country girl brought with it an unusual stimulus and excitement.

Miss Barks seated herself deliberately, after much fiddling with bracelets and gloves, and tied back the ends of her cap behind her. Mr. Mayhew took out his flute and lovingly put it together. He was a powerful swarthy man, who said little and was generally alarming to the ladies of the neighbourhood. To propitiate him, they asked him to bring his flute, and nervously praised the fierce music he made on it. Miss Barks enjoyed a monopoly of his accompaniments, and there were many who regarded her assiduity as a covert attack upon the widower's name and position. If so, it was Greek meeting Greek, for with all his taciturnity the vicar of Shanmoor was well able to defend himself.[33]

'Has it begun?' said a hurried whisper at Elsmere's elbow, and turning he saw Rose and Agnes on the step of the window, Rose's cheeks flushed by the night breeze, a shawl thrown lightly round her head.

She was answered by the first notes of the flute, following some powerful chords in which Miss Barks had tested at once the strength of her wrists and the vicarage piano.

The girl made a little *moue* of disgust, and turned as though to fly down the steps again. But Agnes caught her and held her, and the mutinous creature had to submit to be drawn inside while Mrs. Thornburgh, in obedience to complaints of draughts from Mrs. Seaton, motioned to have the window shut. Rose established herself against the wall, her curly head thrown back, her eyes half shut, her mouth expressing an angry endurance. Robert watched her with amusement.

It was certainly a remarkable duet. After an *adagio* opening in which flute and piano were at magnificent cross purposes from the beginning, the two instruments plunged into an *allegro* very long and very fast, which became ultimately a desperate race between the competing performers for the final chord. Mr. Mayhew toiled away, taxing the resources of his whole vast frame to keep his small instrument in a line with the piano, and taxing them in vain. For the shriller and the wilder grew the flute, and the greater the exertion of the dark Hercules performing on it, the fiercer grew the pace of the piano. Rose stamped her little foot.

'Two bars ahead last page,' she murmured, 'three bars this: will no one stop her!'

But the pages flew past, turned assiduously by Agnes, who took a sardonic delight in these performances, and every countenance in the room seemed

---

33 A common misquotation from Nathaniel Lee's (1653-92) tragedy *The Rival Queens, or the Death of Alexander the Great* (1677), 4.1: "When Greeks joyn'd Greeks, then was the tug of War."

to take a look of sharpened anxiety as to how the duet was to end, and who was to be victor.

Nobody knowing Miss Barks need to have been in any doubt as to that! Crash came the last chord, and the poor flute nearly half a page behind was left shrilly hanging in mid-air, forsaken and companionless, an object of derision to gods and men.

'Ah! I took it a little fast!' said the lady, triumphantly looking up at the discomfited clergyman.

'Mr. Elsmere,' said Rose, hiding herself in the window curtain beside him, that she might have her laugh in safety. 'Do they play like that in Oxford, or has Long Whindale a monopoly?'

But before he could answer, Mrs. Thornburgh called to the girl—

'Rose! Rose! Don't go out again! It is your turn next!'

Rose advanced reluctantly, her head in air. Robert, remembering something that Mrs. Thornburgh had said to him as to her musical power, supposed that she felt it an indignity to be asked to play in such company.

Mrs. Thornburgh motioned to him to come and sit by Mrs. Leyburn, a summons which he obeyed with the more alacrity, as it brought him once more within reach of Mrs. Leyburn's eldest daughter.

'Are you fond of music, Mr. Elsmere?' asked Mrs. Leyburn in her little mincing voice, making room for his chair beside them. 'If you are, I am sure my youngest daughter's playing will please you.'

Catherine moved abruptly. Robert, while he made some pleasant answer, divined that the reserved and stately daughter must be often troubled by the mother's expansiveness.

Meanwhile the room was again settling itself to listen. Mrs. Seaton was severely turning over a photograph book. In her opinion the violin was an unbecoming instrument for young women.[34] Miss Barks sat upright with the studiously neutral expression which befits the artist asked to listen to a rival. Mr. Thornburgh sat pensive, one foot drooped over the other. He was very fond of the Leyburn girls, but music seemed to him, good man, one of the least comprehensible of human pleasures. As for Rose, she had at last

34 Mrs. Seaton's disapproval reflects an attitude common well into the nineteenth century, but it was becoming outmoded by the 1880s. Paula Gillett suggests that the deep-seated prejudice against women violinists sprang from two factors, "a strong sense of unfitness that derived from the instrument's ascribed gender [female] and male-defined mode of performance" and "the instrument's close associations with ideas of sin and death, and with Satan, traditionally believed to be the agent who brought both into human history": *Musical Women in England, 1870-1914: "Encroaching on All Men's Privileges"* (New York: St. Martin's Press, 2000), 87.

arranged herself and her accompanist Agnes, after routing out from her music a couple of *Fantasie-Stücke*, which she had wickedly chosen as presenting the most severely classical contrast to the 'rubbish' played by the preceding performers.[35] She stood with her lithe figure in its old-fashioned dress thrown out against the black coats of a group of gentlemen beyond, one slim arched foot advanced, the ends of the blue sash dangling, the hand and arm, beautifully formed, but still wanting the roundness of womanhood, raised high for action, the lightly poised head thrown back with an air. Robert thought her a bewitching, half-grown thing, overflowing with potentialities of future brilliance and empire.

Her music astonished him. Where had a little provincial maiden learned to play with this intelligence, this force, this delicate command of her instrument? He was not a musician, and therefore could not gauge her exactly, but he was more or less familiar with music and its standards, as all people become nowadays who live in a highly cultivated society, and he knew enough at any rate to see that what he was listening to was remarkable, was out of the common range. Still more evident was this, when from the humorous piece with which the sisters led off—a dance of clowns, but clowns of Arcady— they slid into a delicate rippling *chant d'amour*,[36] the long drawn notes of the violin rising and falling on the piano accompaniment with an exquisite plaintiveness. Where did a *fillette*,[37] unformed, inexperienced, win the secret of so much eloquence—only from the natural dreams of a girl's heart as to 'the lovers waiting in the hidden years'?[38]

But when the music ceased, Elsmere, after a hearty clap that set the room applauding likewise, turned not to the musician but the figure beside Mrs. Leyburn, the sister who had sat listening with an impassiveness, a sort of gentle remoteness of look, which had piqued his curiosity. The mother meanwhile was drinking in the compliments of Dr. Baker.

'Excellent!' cried Elsmere. 'How in the name of fortune, Miss Leyburn, if I may ask, has your sister managed to get on so far in this remote place?'

'She goes to Manchester every year to some relations we have there,' said Catherine quietly; 'I believe she has been very well taught.'

'But surely,' he said warmly, 'it is more than teaching—more even than talent—there is something like genius in it?'

She did not answer very readily.

---

35 Fantasy pieces, "short mood pieces" (*Concise Oxford Dictionary of Music*).
36 Love song.
37 Girl.
38 "lovers waiting ...": A misquotation from Fredrick W. H. Myers, "Saint Paul" (1867).

'I don't know,' she said at last. 'Every one says it is very good.'

He would have been repelled by her irresponsiveness but that her last words had in them a note of lingering, of wistfulness, as though the subject were connected with an inner debate not yet solved which troubled her. He was puzzled, but certainly not repelled.

Twenty minutes later everybody was going. The Seatons went first, and the other guests lingered awhile afterwards to enjoy the sense of freedom left by their departure. But at last the Mayhews, father and son, set off on foot to walk home over the moonlit mountains; the doctor tucked himself and his daughter into his high gig, and drove off with a sweeping ironical bow to Rose, who had stood on the steps teasing him to the last; and Robert Elsmere offered to escort the Miss Leyburns and their mother home.

Mrs. Thornburgh was left protesting to the vicar's incredulous ears that never—never as long as she lived—would she have Mrs. Seaton inside her doors again.

'Her manners—' cried the vicar's wife, fuming—'her manners would disgrace a Whinborough shop-girl. She has none—positively none!'

Then suddenly her round comfortable face brightened and broadened out into a beaming smile—

'But, after all, William, say what you will—and you always do say the most unpleasant things you can think of—it was a great success. I know the Leyburns enjoyed it. And as for Robert, I saw him *looking—looking* at that little minx Rose while she was playing as if he couldn't take his eyes off her. What a picture she made, to be sure!'

The vicar, who had been standing with his back to the fireplace and his hands in his pockets, received his wife's remarks first of all with lifted eyebrows, and then with a low chuckle, half scornful, half compassionate, which made her start in her chair.

'Rose?' he said impatiently. 'Rose, my dear, where were your eyes?'

It was very rarely indeed that on her own ground, so to speak, the vicar ventured to take the whip-hand of her like this. Mrs. Thornburgh looked at him in amazement.

'Do you mean to say,' he asked, in raised tones, 'that you didn't notice that from the moment you first introduced Robert to Catherine Leyburn, he had practically no attention for anybody else?'

Mrs. Thornburgh gazed at him—her memory flew back over the evening—and her impulsive contradiction died on her lips. It was now her turn to ejaculate—

'Catherine!' she said feebly. 'Catherine! how absurd!'

But she turned and, with quickened breath, looked out of window after the retreating figures. Mrs. Thornburgh went up to bed that night an inch taller. She had never felt herself more exquisitely indispensable, more of a personage.

CHAPTER IV

Before, however, we go on to chronicle the ultimate success or failure of Mrs. Thornburgh as a match-maker, it may be well to inquire a little more closely into the antecedents of the man who had suddenly roused so much activity in her contriving mind. And, indeed, these antecedents are important to us. For the interest of an uncomplicated story will entirely depend upon the clearness with which the reader may have grasped the general outlines of a quick soul's development. And this development had already made considerable progress before Mrs. Thornburgh set eyes upon her husband's cousin, Robert Elsmere.

Robert Elsmere, then, was well born and fairly well provided with this world's goods; up to a certain moderate point, indeed, a favourite of fortune in all respects. His father belonged to the younger line of an old Sussex family, and owed his pleasant country living to the family instincts of his uncle, Sir William Elsmere, in whom Whig doctrines and Conservative traditions were pretty evenly mixed, with a result of the usual respectable and inconspicuous kind. His virtues had descended mostly to his daughters, while all his various weaknesses and fatuities had blossomed into vices in the person of his eldest son and heir, the Sir Mowbray Elsmere of Mrs. Seaton's early recollections.

Edward Elsmere, rector of Murewell in Surrey, and father of Robert, had died before his uncle and patron; and his widow and son had been left to face the world together. Sir William Elsmere and his nephew's wife had not much in common, and rarely concerned themselves with each other. Mrs. Elsmere was an Irishwoman by birth, with irregular Irish ways, and a passion for strange garments, which made her the dread of the conventional English squire; and, after she left the vicarage with her son, she and her husband's uncle met no more. But when he died it was found that the old man's sense of kinship, acting blindly and irrationally, but with a slow inevitableness and certainty, had stirred in him at the last in behalf of his great-nephew. He left him a money legacy, the interest of which was to be administered by his mother till his majority, and in a letter addressed to his heir he directed that, should the boy on attaining manhood show any disposition to enter the Church, all possible steps were to be taken to endow him with the family living of Murewell, which had been his father's, and which at the time of the old Baronet's death was occupied by another connection of the family, already well stricken in years.[39]

Mowbray Elsmere had been hardly on speaking terms with his cousin Edward, and was neither amiable nor generous, but his father knew that the tenacious Elsmere instinct was to be depended on for the fulfilment of his wishes. And so it proved. No sooner was his father dead than Sir Mowbray curtly communicated his instructions to Mrs. Elsmere, then living at the town of Harden for the sake of the great public school recently transported there. She was to inform him, when the right moment arrived, if it was the boy's wish to enter the Church, and meanwhile he referred her to his lawyers for particulars of such immediate benefits as were secured to her under the late Baronet's will.

At the moment when Sir Mowbray's letter reached her, Mrs. Elsmere was playing a leading part in the small society to which circumstances had consigned her. She was the personal friend of half the masters and their wives, and of at least a quarter of the school, while in the little town which stretched up the hill covered by the new school buildings, she was the helper, gossip, and confidante of half the parish. Her vast hats, strange in fashion and inordinate in brim, her shawls of many colours, hitched now to this side now to that, her swaying gait and looped-up skirts, her spectacles, and the dangling parcels in which her soul delighted, were the outward signs of a personality familiar to all. For under those checked shawls which few women passed without an inward marvel, there beat one of the warmest hearts that ever animated mortal clay, and the prematurely wrinkled face, with its small quick eyes and shrewd indulgent mouth, bespoke a nature as responsive as it was vigorous.

Their owner was constantly in the public eye. Her house, during the hours at any rate in which her boy was at school, was little else than a halting-place between two journeys. Visits to the poor, long watches by the sick; committees, in which her racy breadth of character gave her always an important place; discussions with the vicar, arguments with the curates, a chat with this person and a walk with that—these were the incidents and occupations which filled her day. Life was delightful to her; action, energy, influence, were delightful to her; she could only breathe freely in the very thick of the stirring, many-coloured tumult of existence. Whether it was a pauper in the work-house, or boys from the school, or a girl caught in the tangle of a love-affair, it was all the same to Mrs. Elsmere. Everything moved her, everything appealed

---

39 The Elsmere family has the right to present a clergyman of their choosing to preside at the local church. Such livings were often used to provide for younger sons.

to her. Her life was a perpetual giving forth, and such was the inherent nobility and soundness of the nature, that in spite of her curious Irish fondness for the vehement romantic sides of experience, she did little harm, and much good. Her tongue might be over-ready and her championships indiscreet, but her hands were helpful, and her heart was true. There was something contagious in her enjoyment of life, and with all her strong religious faith, the thought of death, of any final pause and silence in the whirr of the great social machine, was to her a thought of greater chill and horror than to many a less brave and spiritual soul.

Till her boy was twelve years old, however, she had lived for him first and foremost. She had taught him, played with him, learnt with him, communicating to him through all his lessons her own fire and eagerness to a degree which every now and then taxed the physical powers of the child. Whenever the signs of strain appeared, however, the mother would be overtaken by a fit of repentant watchfulness, and for days together Robert would find her the most fascinating playmate, story-teller, and romp, and forget all his precocious interest in history or vulgar fractions. In after years when Robert looked back upon his childhood, he was often reminded of the stories of Goethe's bringing-up.[40] He could recall exactly the same scenes as Goethe describes,— mother and child sitting together in the gloaming, the mother's dark eyes dancing with fun or kindling with dramatic fire, as she carried an imaginary hero or heroine through a series of the raciest adventures; the child all eagerness and sympathy, now clapping his little hands at the fall of the giant, or the defeat of the sorcerer, and now arguing and suggesting in ways which gave perpetually fresh stimulus to the mother's inventiveness. He could see her dressing up with him on wet days, reciting King Henry to his Prince Hal, or Prospero to his Ariel, or simply giving free vent to her own exuberant Irish fun till both he and she would sink exhausted into each other's arms, and end the evening with a long croon, sitting curled up together in a big armchair in front of the fire.[41] He could see himself as a child of many crazes, eager for poetry one week, for natural history the next, now spending all his spare time in strumming, now in drawing, and now forgetting everything but the delights of tree-climbing and bird-nesting.

And through it all he had the quick memory of his mother's

40 Johann Wolfgang von Goethe (1749–1832), German novelist, dramatist, poet, and critic, whose works include *The Sorrows of Young Werther* (1774), *Wilhelm Meister's Apprenticeship* (1795-96), and *Faust, Parts One* (1808) and *Two* (1832). He writes affectionately of his well-educated mother, Catharina Elisabeth, in his autobiography, *Aus Meinem Leben: Dichtung und Wahreit* (1811-33).
41 William Shakespeare's *Henry IV, Parts I and II* and *The Tempest*.

companionship, he could recall her rueful looks whenever the eager inaccurate ways, in which he reflected certain ineradicable tendencies of her own, had lost him a school advantage; he could remember her exhortations, with the dash in them of humorous self-reproach which made them so stirring to the child's affection; and he could realise their old far-off life at Murewell, the joys and the worries of it, and see her now gossiping with the village folk, now wearing herself impetuously to death in their service, and now roaming with him over the Surrey heaths in search of all the dirty delectable things in which a boy-naturalist delights. And through it all he was conscious of the same vivid energetic creature, disposing with some difficulty and *fracas* of its own excess of nervous life.

To return, however, to this same critical moment of Sir Mowbray's offer. Robert at the time was a boy of sixteen, doing very well at school, a favourite both with boys and masters. But as to whether his development would lead him in the direction of taking orders, his mother had not the slightest idea. She was not herself very much tempted by the prospect. There were recollections connected with Murewell, and with the long death in life which her husband had passed through there, which were deeply painful to her; and, moreover, her sympathy with the clergy as a class was by no means strong. Her experience had not been large, but the feeling based on it promised to have all the tenacity of a favourite prejudice. Fortune had handed over the parish of Harden to a ritualist vicar.[42] Mrs. Elsmere's inherited Evangelicalism— she came from an Ulster county—rebelled against his doctrine, but the man himself was too lovable to be disliked.[43] Mrs. Elsmere knew a hero when she saw him. And in his own narrow way, the small-headed emaciated vicar was a hero, and he and Mrs. Elsmere had soon tasted each other's quality, and formed a curious alliance, founded on true similarity in difference.

But the criticism thus warded off the vicar expended itself with all the more force on his subordinates. The Harden curates were the chief crook in Mrs. Elsmere's otherwise tolerable lot.[44] Her parish activities brought her across them perpetually, and she could not away with them. Their cassocks, their pretensions, their stupidities, roused the Irish-woman's sense of humour

---

42 "Ritualist" refers to the Anglo-Catholic practice of reintroducing liturgical elements from pre-Reformation Catholic traditions (e.g., crucifixes, mixing water and wine in the chalice, elevating the Host).

43 Ulster, in Northern Ireland, was and is strongly Protestant in character, both Church of Ireland and Presbyterian. It was the site of a famous religious revival in 1859.

44 The curate worked under the incumbent, a rector or vicar, and received a salary directly from him.

at every turn.[45] The individuals came and went, but the type it seemed to her was always the same; and she made their peculiarities the basis of a pessimist theory as to the future of the English Church, which was a source of constant amusement to the very broad-minded young men who filled up the school staff. She, so ready in general to see all the world's good points, was almost blind when it was a curate's virtues which were in question. So that, in spite of all her persistent church-going, and her love of church performances as an essential part of the busy human spectacle, Mrs. Elsmere had no yearning for a clerical son. The little accidents of a personal experience had led to wide generalisations, as is the way with us mortals, and the position of the young parson in these days of increased parsonic pretensions was, to Mrs. Elsmere, a position in which there was an inherent risk of absurdity. She wished her son to impose upon her when it came to his taking any serious step in life. She asked for nothing better, indeed, than to be able, when the time came, to bow the motherly knee to him in homage, and she felt a little dread lest, in her flat moments, a clerical son might sometimes rouse in her that sharp sense of the ludicrous which is the enemy of all happy illusions.

Still, of course, the Elsmere proposal was one to be seriously considered in its due time and place. Mrs. Elsmere only reflected that it would certainly be better to say nothing of it to Robert until he should be at college. His impressionable temperament, and the power he had occasionally shown of absorbing himself in a subject till it produced in him a fit of intense continuous brooding, unfavourable to health and nervous energy, all warned her not to supply him, at a period of rapid mental and bodily growth, with any fresh stimulus to the sense of responsibility. As a boy, he had always shown himself religiously susceptible to a certain extent, and his mother's religious likes and dislikes had invariably found in him a blind and chivalrous support. He was content to be with her, to worship with her, and to feel that no reluctance or resistance divided his heart from hers. But there had been nothing specially noteworthy or precocious about his religious development, and at sixteen or seventeen, in spite of his affectionate compliance, and his natural reverence for all persons and beliefs in authority, his mother was perfectly aware that many other things in his life were more real to him than religion. And on this point, at any rate, she was certainly not the person to force him.

He was such a schoolboy as a discerning master delights in—keen about everything, bright, docile, popular, excellent at games. He was in the sixth,

45 Cassock: a long black clerical robe, traditionally part of both Roman Catholic and Anglican dress. In nineteenth-century controversies over vestments, evangelicals frequently associated the cassock (along with the surplice, a long-sleeved white garment worn over the cassock) with Anglo-Catholicism.

moreover, as soon as his age allowed: that is to say, as soon as he was sixteen; and his pride in everything connected with the great body in which he had already a marked and important place was unbounded. Very early in his school career the literary instincts, which had always been present in him, and which his mother had largely helped to develop by her own restless imaginative ways of approaching life and the world, made themselves felt with considerable force. Some time before his cousin's letter arrived, he had been taken with a craze for English poetry, and, but for the corrective influence of a favourite tutor would probably have thrown himself into it with the same exclusive passion as he had shown for subject after subject in his eager ebullient childhood. His mother found him at thirteen inditing a letter on the subject of *The Faerie Queene* to a school-friend, in which, with a sincerity which made her forgive the pomposity, he remarked—

'I can truly say with Pope, that this great work has afforded me extraordinary pleasure.'[46]

And about the same time, a master who was much interested in the boy's prospects of getting the school prize for Latin verse, a subject for which he had always shown a special aptitude, asked him anxiously, after an Easter holiday, what he had been reading; the boy ran his hands through his hair, and still keeping his finger between the leaves, shut a book before him from which he had been learning by heart, and which was, alas! neither Ovid nor Virgil.[47]

'I have just finished Belial!' he said, with a sigh of satisfaction, 'and am beginning Beelzebub.'[48]

A craze of this kind was naturally followed by a feverish period of juvenile authorship, when the house was littered over with stanzas from the opening canto of a great poem on Columbus, or with moral essays in the manner of Pope, castigating the vices of the time with an energy which sorely tried the gravity of the mother whenever she was called upon, as she invariably was, to play audience to the young poet.[49] At the same time the classics absorbed in reality their full share of this fast developing power. Virgil and

---

46 Chivalric epic (1590-96) by the poet Edmund Spenser (1552–99). For Pope's comment, see Joseph Spence, *Anecdotes, Observations, and Characters, of Books and Men. Collected from the Conversation of Mr. Pope, and Other Eminent Persons of His Time* …, ed. Samuel Weller Singer (London: W. H. Carpenter, 1820), 296-97.

47 Robert is not devoting himself sufficiently to his Latin poetry. Publius Ovidius Naso (43 BCE–17 CE), author of *The Metamorphoses*, the *Heroides*, and the *Art of Love*; Publius Vergilius Maro (70 BCE–19 BCE), author of the *Aeneid*, the *Eclogues*, and the *Georgics*.

48 i.e., from John Milton's *Paradise Lost* (1667).

49 As the young Robert is imitating other poets, he may be borrowing from Samuel Rogers' *The Voyage of Columbus* (1810), along with Pope's *An Essay on Man* (1734).

Æschylus appealed to the same fibres, the same susceptibilities, as Milton and Shakspeare, and the boy's quick imaginative sense appropriated Greek and Latin life with the same ease which it showed in possessing itself of that bygone English life whence sprung the *Canterbury Tales*, or *As You Like It*.[50] So that his tutor, who was much attached to him, and who made it one of his main objects in life to keep the boy's aspiring nose to the grindstone of grammatical *minutiæ*, began about the time of Sir Mowbray's letter to prophesy very smooth things indeed to his mother as to his future success at college, the possibility of his getting the famous St. Anselm's scholarship, and so on.

Evidently such a youth was not likely to depend for the attainment of a foothold in life on a piece of family privilege. The world was all before him where to choose, Mrs. Elsmere thought proudly to herself, as her mother's fancy wandered rashly through the coming years. And for many reasons she secretly allowed herself to hope that he would find for himself some other post of ministry in a very various world than the vicarage of Murewell.

So she wrote a civil letter of acknowledgment to Sir Mowbray, informing him that the intentions of his great-uncle should be communicated to the boy when he should be of fit age to consider them, and that meanwhile she was obliged to him for pointing out the procedure by which she might lay hands on the legacy bequeathed to her in trust for her son, the income of which would now be doubly welcome in view of his college expenses. There the matter rested, and Mrs. Elsmere, during the two years which followed, thought little more about it. She became more and more absorbed in her boy's immediate prospects, in the care of his health, which was uneven and tried somewhat by the strain of preparation for an attempt on the St. Anselm's scholarship, and in the demands which his ardent nature, oppressed with the weight of its own aspirations, was constantly making upon her support and sympathy.

At last the moment so long expected arrived. Mrs. Elsmere and her son left Harden amid a chorus of good wishes, and settled themselves early in November in Oxford lodgings. Robert was to have a few days' complete holiday before the examination, and he and his mother spent it in exploring the beautiful old town, now shrouded in the 'pensive glooms' of still, gray autumn weather.[51] There was no sun to light up the misty reaches of the

---

50 Aeschylus, fifth-century playwright, who with Euripides and Sophocles is one of the still-extant Greek tragedians; *The Canterbury Tales*, Geoffrey Chaucer's (1343-1400) late fourteenth-century poetic narratives told by a group of pilgrims on their way to Canterbury, and one of the seminal works of English verse; *As You Like It*, Shakespeare's comedy.

51 From the final line of William Wordsworth's sonnet "Wansfell! This Household

river; the trees in the Broad Walk were almost bare; the Virginian creeper no longer shone in patches of delicate crimson on the college walls; the gardens were damp and forsaken. But to Mrs. Elsmere and Robert the place needed neither sun nor summer 'for beauty's heightening.'[52] On both of them it laid its old irresistible spell; the sentiment haunting its quadrangles, its libraries, and its dim melodious chapels, stole into the lad's heart and alternately soothed and stimulated that keen individual consciousness which naturally accompanies the first entrance into manhood. Here, on this soil, steeped in memories, *his* problems, *his* struggles were to be fought out in their turn. 'Take up thy manhood,' said the inward voice, 'and show what is in thee. The hour and the opportunity have come!'

And to this thrill of vague expectation, this young sense of an expanding world, something of pathos and of sacredness was added by the dumb influences of the old streets and weather-beaten stones. How tenacious they were of the past! The dreaming city seemed to be still brooding in the autumn calm over the long succession of her sons. The continuity, the complexity of human experience; the unremitting effort of the race; the stream of purpose running through it all; these were the kind of thoughts which, in more or less inchoate and fragmentary shape, pervaded the boy's sensitive mind as he rambled with his mother from college to college.

Mrs. Elsmere, too, was fascinated by Oxford. But for all her eager interest, the historic beauty of the place aroused in her an under-mood of melancholy, just as it did in Robert. Both had the impressionable Celtic temperament, and both felt that a critical moment was upon them, and that the Oxford air was charged with fate for each of them. For the first time in their lives they were to be parted. The mother's long guardianship was coming to an end. Had she loved him enough? Had she so far fulfilled the trust her dead husband had imposed upon her? Would her boy love her in the new life as he had loved her in the old? And could her poor craving heart bear to see him absorbed by fresh interests and passions, in which her share could be only, at the best, secondary and indirect?

One day—it was on the afternoon preceding the examination—she gave hurried, half-laughing utterance to some of these misgivings of hers. They were walking down the Lime-walk of Trinity Gardens; beneath their feet a yellow fresh-strewn carpet of leaves, brown interlacing branches overhead, and a red misty sun shining through the trunks. Robert understood his mother perfectly, and the way she had of hiding a storm of feeling under these

---

Has a Favoured Lot" (1842).
52 Matthew Arnold, "Thyrsis" (1865), l. 20.

tremulous comedy airs. So that, instead of laughing too, he took her hand and, there being no spectators anywhere to be seen in the damp November garden, he raised it to his lips with a few broken words of affection and gratitude which very nearly overcame the self-command of both of them. She dashed wildly into another subject, and then suddenly it occurred to her impulsive mind that the moment had come to make him acquainted with those dying intentions of his great-uncle which we have already described. The diversion was a welcome one, and the duty seemed clear. So, accordingly, she made him give her all his attention while she told him the story and the terms of Sir Mowbray's letter, forcing herself the while to keep her own opinions and predilections as much as possible out of sight.

Robert listened with interest and astonishment, the sense of a new-found manhood waxing once more strong within him, as his mind admitted the strange picture of himself occupying the place which had been his father's; master of the house and the parish he had wandered over with childish steps, clinging to the finger or the coat of the tall, stooping figure which occupied the dim background of his recollections. 'Poor mother,' he said thoughtfully, when she paused, 'it would be hard upon *you* to go back to Murewell!'

'Oh, you mustn't think of me when the time comes,' said Mrs. Elsmere, sighing. 'I shall be a tiresome old woman, and you will be a young man wanting a wife. There, put it out of your head, Robert. I thought I had better tell you, for, after all, the fact may concern your Oxford life. But you've got a long time yet before you need begin to worry about it.'

The boy drew himself up to his full height, and tossed his tumbling reddish hair back from his eyes. He was nearly six feet already, with a long thin body and head, which amply justified his school nickname of 'the darning-needle.'

'Don't you trouble either, mother,' he said, with a tone of decision: 'I don't feel as if I should ever take orders.'

Mrs. Elsmere was old enough to know what importance to attach to the trenchancy of eighteen, but still the words were pleasant to her.

The next day Robert went up for examination, and after three days of hard work, and phases of alternate hope and depression, in which mother and son excited one another to no useful purpose, there came the anxious crowding round the college gate in the November twilight, and the sudden flight of dispersing messengers bearing the news over Oxford. The scholarship had been won by a precocious Etonian with an extraordinary talent for 'stems,' and all that appertained thereto. But the exhibition fell to Robert, and mother and son were well content.[53]

---

53 An Exhibition might be awarded to the runner-ups in a scholarship election or

The boy was eager to come into residence at once, though he would matriculate too late to keep the term. The college authorities were willing, and on the Saturday following the announcement of his success he was matriculated, saw the Provost, and was informed that rooms would be found for him without delay. His mother and he gaily climbed innumerable stairs to inspect the garrets of which he was soon to take proud possession, sallying forth from them only to enjoy an agitated delightful afternoon among the shops. Expenditure, always charming, becomes under these circumstances a sacred and pontifical act. Never had Mrs. Elsmere bought a teapot for herself with half the fervour which she now threw into the purchase of Robert's; and the young man, accustomed to a rather bare home, and an Irish lack of the little elegancies of life, was overwhelmed when his mother actually dragged him into a printseller's, and added an engraving or two to the enticing miscellaneous mass of which he was already master.

They only just left themselves time to rush back to their lodgings and dress for the solemn function of a dinner with the Provost.[54] The dinner, however, was a great success. The short, shy manner of their white-haired host thawed under the influence of Mrs. Elsmere's racy, unaffected ways, and it was not long before everybody in the room had more or less made friends with her, and forgiven her her marvellous drab poplin, adorned with fresh pink ruchings for the occasion. As for the Provost, Mrs. Elsmere had been told that he was a person of whom she must inevitably stand in awe. But all her life long she had been like the youth in the fairy tale who desired to learn how to shiver and could not attain unto it. Fate had denied her the capacity of standing in awe of anybody, and she rushed at her host as a new type, delighting in the thrill which she felt creeping over her when she found herself on the arm of one who had been the rallying-point of a hundred struggles, and a centre of influence over thousands of English lives.

And then followed the proud moment when Robert, in his exhibitioner's gown, took her to service in the chapel on Sunday.[55] The scores of young faces, the full unison of the hymns, and finally the Provost's sermon, with its strange brusqueries and simplicities of manner and phrase—simplicities so suggestive, so full of a rich and yet disciplined experience, that they haunted her mind for weeks afterwards—completed the general impression made upon her by the Oxford life. She came out, tremulous and shaken, leaning on her son's arm. She, too, like the generations before her, had launched her venture

---

in lieu of a scholarship, and would be held for at least one year.
54   The Provost is based loosely on Benjamin Jowett, the Master of Balliol.
55   Exhibitioner's gown: a knee-length black robe.

into the deep. Her boy was putting out from her into the ocean; henceforth she could but watch him from the shore. Brought into contact with this imposing University organisation, with all its suggestions of virile energies and functions, the mother suddenly felt herself insignificant and forsaken. He had been her all, her own, and now on this training-ground of English youth, it seemed to her that the great human society had claimed him from her.

CHAPTER V

In his Oxford life Robert surrendered himself to the best and most stimulating influences of the place, just as he had done at school. He was a youth of many friends, by virtue of a natural gift of sympathy, which was no doubt often abused, and by no means invariably profitable to its owner, but wherein, at any rate, his power over his fellows, like the power of half the potent men in the world's history, always lay rooted. He had his mother's delight in living. He loved the cricket-field, he loved the river; his athletic instincts and his athletic friends were always fighting in him with his literary instincts and the friends who appealed primarily to the intellectual and moral side of him. He made many mistakes alike in friends and in pursuits; in the freshness of a young and roving curiosity he had great difficulty in submitting himself to the intellectual routine of the University, a difficulty which ultimately cost him much; but at the bottom of the lad, all the time, there was a strength of will, a force and even tyranny of conscience, which kept his charm and pliancy from degenerating into weakness, and made it not only delightful, but profitable to love him. He knew that his mother was bound up in him, and his being was set to satisfy, so far as he could, all her honourable ambitions.

His many undergraduate friends, strong as their influence must have been in the aggregate on a nature so receptive, hardly concern us here. His future life, so far as we can see, was most noticeably affected by two men older than himself, and belonging to the dons—both of them fellows and tutors of St. Anselm's, though on different planes of age.

The first one, Edward Langham, was Robert's tutor, and about seven years older than himself. He was a man about whom, on entering the college, Robert heard more than the usual crop of stories. The healthy young English barbarian has an aversion to the intrusion of more manner into life than is absolutely necessary. Now, Langham was overburdened with manner, though it was manner of the deprecating and not of the arrogant order. Decisions, it seemed, of all sorts were abominable to him. To help a friend he had once

consented to be Pro-proctor.[56] He resigned in a month, and none of his acquaintances ever afterwards dared to allude to the experience. If you could
have got at his inmost mind, it was affirmed, the persons most obnoxious
there would have been found to be the scout,[57] who intrusively asked him
every morning what he would have for breakfast, and the college cook, who,
till such a course was strictly forbidden him, mounted to his room at half-past
nine to inquire whether he would 'dine in.' Being a scholar of considerable
eminence, it pleased him to assume on all questions an exasperating degree of
ignorance; and the wags of the college averred that when asked if it rained, or
if collections took place on such and such a day, it was pain and grief to him
to have to affirm positively, without qualifications, that so it was.

Such a man was not very likely, one would have thought, to captivate
an ardent, impulsive boy like Elsmere. Edward Langham, however, notwithstanding undergraduate tales, was a very remarkable person. In the first place,
he was possessed of exceptional personal beauty. His colouring was vividly
black and white, closely curling jet-black hair, and fine black eyes contrasting
with a pale, clear complexion and even, white teeth. So far he had the charac-
teristics which certain Irishmen share with most Spaniards. But the Celtic or
Iberian brilliance was balanced by a classical delicacy and precision of feature.
He had the brow, the nose, the upper lip, the finely-moulded chin, which
belong to the more severe and spiritual Greek type. Certainly of Greek blitheness and directness there was no trace. The eye was wavering and profoundly
melancholy; all the movements of the tall, finely-built frame were hesitating
and doubtful. It was as though the man were suffering from paralysis of some
moral muscle or other; as if some of the normal springs of action in him had
been profoundly and permanently weakened.

He had a curious history. He was the only child of a doctor in a
Lincolnshire country town. His old parents had brought him up in strict
provincial ways, ignoring the boy's idiosyncrasies as much as possible. They
did not want an exceptional and abnormal son, and they tried to put down
his dreamy, self-conscious habits by forcing him into the common, middle-
class, Evangelical groove. As soon as he got to college, however, the brooding,
gifted nature had a moment of sudden and, as it seemed to the old people
in Gainsborough, most reprehensible expansion. Poems were sent to them,
cut out of one or the other of the leading periodicals, with their son's initials
appended, and articles of philosophical art-criticism, published while the boy
was still an undergraduate—which seemed to the stern father everything that

56 The Pro-proctor helped Examiners and Proctors oversee the examination process.
57 A college servant.

was sophistical and subversive.[58] For they treated Christianity itself as an open question, and showed especially scant respect for the 'Protestantism of the Protestant religion.'[59] The father warned him grimly that he was not going to spend his hard-earned savings on the support of a free-thinking scribbler, and the young man wrote no more till just after he had taken a double first in Greats.[60] Then the publication of an article in one of the leading Reviews on 'The Ideals of Modern Culture' not only brought him a furious letter from home stopping all supplies, but also lost him a probable fellowship. His college was one of the narrowest and most backward in Oxford, and it was made perfectly plain to him before the fellowship examination that he would not be elected.

He left the college, took pupils for a while, then stood for a vacant fellowship at St. Anselm's, the Liberal headquarters, and got it with flying colours.

Thenceforward one would have thought that a brilliant and favourable mental development was secured to him. Not at all. The moment of his quarrel with his father and his college had, in fact, represented a moment of energy, of comparative success, which never recurred. It was as though this outburst of action and liberty had disappointed him, as if some deep-rooted instinct—cold, critical, reflective—had reasserted itself, condemning him and his censors equally. The uselessness of utterance, the futility of enthusiasm, the inaccessibility of the ideal, the practical absurdity of trying to realise any of the mind's inward dreams: these were the kind of considerations which descended upon him, slowly and fatally, crushing down the newly springing growths of action or of passion. It was as though life had demonstrated to him the essential truth of a childish saying of his own which had startled and displeased his Calvinist mother years before. 'Mother,' the delicate, large-eyed child had said to her one day in a fit of physical weariness, 'how is it I dislike the things I dislike so much more than I like the things I like?'

---

58 Langham's intellectual development and later characterization combine the careers of Ward's friend Walter Pater (1839–1894), whose *Studies in the History of the Renaissance* (1873) influenced the Aesthetic and Decadent movements; the Swiss philosopher Henri Frédéric Amiel (1821–1881); and another close friend of Ward's, the rector of Lincoln College, Mark Pattison (1813–1884), author of a monograph on Isaac Casaubon.

59 Originally from Edmund Burke, but later taken up as the slogan of *The Nonconformist*, the newspaper closely associated with the Congregationalist editor Edward Miall (1830–1881). In *Culture and Anarchy* (1869), Matthew Arnold uses the phrase to indict Dissenting intellectual culture, or the lack thereof.

60 Honors were awarded by examination. Langham scored in the first class of the classical school, Literae Humaniores ("Greats"), and also took honors in another school, a rare and prestigious accomplishment.

So he wrote no more, he quarrelled no more, he meddled with the great passionate things of life and expression no more. On his taking up residence in St. Anselm's, indeed, and on his being appointed first lecturer and then tutor, he had a momentary pleasure in the thought of teaching.[61] His mind was a storehouse of thought and fact, and to the man brought up at a dull provincial day-school and never allowed to associate freely with his kind, the bright lads fresh from Eton and Harrow about him were singularly attractive. But a few terms were enough to scatter this illusion too. He could not be simple, he could not be spontaneous; he was tormented by self-consciousness, and it was impossible to him to talk and behave as those talk and behave who have been brought up more or less in the big world from the beginning. So this dream, too, faded, for youth asks, before all things, simplicity and spontaneity in those who would take possession of it. His lectures, which were at first brilliant enough to attract numbers of men from other colleges, became gradually mere dry, ingenious skeletons, without life or feeling. It was possible to learn a great deal from him; it was not possible to catch from him any contagion of that *amor intellectualis* which had flamed at one moment so high within him. He ceased to compose; but as the intellectual faculty must have some employment, he became a translator, a contributor to dictionaries, a microscopic student of texts, not in the interest of anything beyond, but simply as a kind of mental stone-breaking.

The only survival of that moment of glow and colour in his life was his love of music and the theatre. Almost every year he disappeared to France to haunt the Paris theatres for a fortnight; to Berlin or Bayreuth to drink his fill of music.[62] He talked neither of music nor of acting; he made no one sharer of his enjoyment, if he did enjoy. It was simply his way of cheating his creative faculty, which, though it had grown impotent, was still there, still restless. Altogether a melancholy, pitiable man—at once thorough-going sceptic and thorough-going idealist, the victim of that critical sense which says No to every impulse, and is always restlessly, and yet hopelessly, seeking the future through the neglected and outraged present.

And yet the man's instincts, at this period of his life at any rate, were habitually kindly and affectionate. He knew nothing of women, and was not liked by them, but it was not his fault if he made no impression on the youth about him. It seemed to him that he was always seeking in their eyes and faces for some light of sympathy which was always escaping him, and which

---

61 In ascending order, the academic ranks are Lecturer, Tutor, University Reader, and Professor.

62 Berlin … Bayreuth: Berlin was one of Europe's preeminent cities for orchestral music and opera; Bayreuth has hosted Richard Wagner's operas since 1876.

he was powerless to compel. He met it for the first time in Robert Elsmere. The susceptible, poetical boy was struck at some favourable moment by that romantic side of the ineffective tutor—his silence, his melancholy, his personal beauty—which no one else, with perhaps one or two exceptions among the older men, cared to take into account; or touched perhaps by some note in him, surprised in passing, of weariness or shrinking, as compared with the contemptuous tone of the College towards him. He showed his liking impetuously, boyishly, as his way was, and thenceforward during his University career Langham became his slave. He had no ambition for himself; his motto might have been that dismal one—'The small things of life are odious to me, and the habit of them enslaves me; the great things of life are eternally attractive to me, and indolence and fear put them by;' but for the University chances of this lanky, red-haired youth—with his eagerness, his boundless curiosity, his genius for all sorts of lovable mistakes—he disquieted himself greatly. He tried to discipline the roving mind, to infuse into the boy's literary temper the delicacy, the precision, the subtlety of his own. His fastidious, critical habits of work supplied exactly that antidote which Elsmere's main faults of haste and carelessness required. He was always holding up before him the inexhaustible patience and labour involved in all true knowledge; and it was to the germs of critical judgment so implanted in him that Elsmere owed many of the later growths of his development—growths with which we have not yet to concern ourselves.

And in return, the tutor allowed himself rarely, very rarely, a moment of utterance from the depths of his real self. One evening in the summer term following the boy's matriculation, Elsmere brought him an essay after Hall, and they sat on talking afterwards. It was a rainy, cheerless evening; the first contest of the Boats week had been rowed in cold wind and sleet; a dreary blast whistled through the College. Suddenly Langham reached out his hand for an open letter. 'I have had an offer, Elsmere,' he said abruptly.

And he put it into his hand. It was the offer of an important Scotch professorship, coming from the man most influential in assigning it. The last occupant of the post had been a scholar of European eminence. Langham's contributions to a great foreign review, and certain Oxford recommendations, were the basis of the present overture, which, coming from one who was himself a classic of the classics, was couched in terms flattering to any young man's vanity.

Robert looked up with a joyful exclamation when he had finished the letter.

'I congratulate you, sir.'

'I have refused it,' said Langham abruptly.

His companion sat open-mouthed. Young as he was, he knew perfectly well that this particular appointment was one of the blue ribbons of British scholarship.

'Do you think—' said the other in a tone of singular vibration, which had in it a note of almost contemptuous irritation—'do you think *I* am the man to get and keep a hold on a rampagious class of hundreds of Scotch lads? Do you think *I* am the man to carry on what Reid began—Reid, that old fighter, that preacher of all sorts of jubilant dogmas?'[63]

He looked at Elsmere under his straight black brows imperiously. The youth felt the nervous tension in the elder man's voice and manner, was startled by a confidence never before bestowed upon him, close as that unequal bond between them had been growing during the six months of his Oxford life, and plucking up courage hurled at him a number of frank, young expostulations, which really put into friendly shape all that was being said about Langham in his College and in the University. Why was he so self-distrustful, so absurdly diffident of responsibility, so bent on hiding his great gifts under a bushel?

The tutor smiled sadly, and, sitting down, buried his head in his hands and said nothing for a while. Then he looked up and stretched out a hand towards a book which lay on a table near. It was the *Rêveries* of Senancour.[64] 'My answer is written *here*,' he said. 'It will seem to you now, Elsmere, mere Midsummer madness. May it always seem so to you. Forgive me. The pressure of solitude sometimes is too great.'

Elsmere looked up with one of his flashing, affectionate smiles, and took the book from Langham's hand. He found on the open page a marked passage:

'Oh swiftly passing seasons of life! There was a time when men seemed to be sincere; when thought was nourished on friendship, kindness, love; when dawn still kept its brilliance, and the night its peace. *I can*, the soul said to itself, and *I will*; I will do all that is right—all that is natural. But soon resistance, difficulty, unforeseen, coming we know not whence, arrest us, undeceive us, and the human yoke grows heavy on our necks. Thenceforward we become merely sharers in the common woe. Hemmed in on all sides, we feel our faculties only to realise their impotence: we have time and strength to do what we *must*, never what we will. Men go on repeating the words *work*,

---

63 Thomas Reid (1710–96), leading member of the Scottish "common sense" school. Ward may be implying that Langham has been offered the position of Professor of Moral Philosophy at the University of Glasgow.

64 Etienne Pivert de Senancour's (1770–1846) *Rêveries sur la nature primitive de l'homme* (1799).

genius, success. Fools! Will all these resounding projects, though they enable us to cheat ourselves, enable us to cheat the icy fate which rules us and our globe, wandering forsaken through the vast silence of the heavens?'[65]

Robert looked up startled, the book dropping from his hand. The words sent a chill to the heart of one born to hope, to will, to crave.

Suddenly Langham dashed the volume from him, almost with violence.

'Forget that drivel, Elsmere. It was a crime to show it to you. It is not sane; neither perhaps am I. But I am not going to Scotland. They would request me to resign in a week.'

Long after Elsmere, who had stayed talking a while on other things, had gone, Langham sat on brooding over the empty grate.

'Corrupter of youth!' he said to himself once bitterly.[66] And perhaps it was to a certain remorse in the tutor's mind that Elsmere owed an experience of great importance to his after life.

The name of a certain Mr. Grey had for some time before his entry at Oxford been more or less familiar to Robert's ears as that of a person of great influence and consideration at St. Anselm's.[67] His tutor at Harden had spoken of him in the boy's hearing as one of the most remarkable men of the generation, and had several times impressed upon his pupil that nothing could be so desirable for him as to secure the friendship of such a man. It was on the occasion of his first interview with the Provost, after the scholarship examination, that Robert was first brought face to face with Mr. Grey. He could remember a short dark man standing beside the Provost, who had been introduced to him by that name, but the nervousness of the moment had been so great that the boy had been quite incapable of giving him any special attention.

During his first term and a half of residence, Robert occasionally met Mr. Grey in the quadrangle or in the street, and the tutor, remembering the thin, bright-faced youth, would return his salutations kindly, and sometimes stop to speak to him, to ask him if he were comfortably settled in his rooms, or make a remark about the boats. But the acquaintance did not seem likely to progress, for Mr. Grey was a Greats tutor, and Robert naturally had nothing to do with him as far as work was concerned.

---

65 Ward here silently combines quotations from two entirely different places in the text into a new paragraph; see *Rêveries*, 3rd ed. (Paris: Librairie d'Abel Ledoux, 1833), 287, 330.

66 The indictment against the Greek philosopher Socrates (d. 399 BCE).

67 Based on Idealist philosopher Thomas Hill Green (1836-82), the Whyte's Professor of Moral Philosophy, and a strong influence on late Victorian liberal theology. As Ward indicates in her preface, a number of Grey's pronouncements and ideas have been taken directly from Green's work.

However, a day or two after the conversation we have described, Robert, going to Langham's rooms late in the afternoon to return a book which had been lent to him, perceived two figures standing talking on the hearth-rug, and by the western light beating in recognised the thick-set frame and broad brow of Mr. Grey.

'Come in, Elsmere,' said Langham, as he stood hesitating on the threshold. 'You have met Mr. Grey before, I think?'

'We first met at an anxious moment,' said Mr. Grey, smiling and shaking hands with the boy. 'A first interview with the Provost is always formidable. I remember it too well myself. You did very well, I remember, Mr. Elsmere. Well, Langham, I must be off. I shall be late for my meeting as it is. I think we have settled our business. Good-night.'

Langham stood a moment after the door closed, eyeing young Elsmere. There was a curious struggle going on in the tutor's mind.

'Elsmere,' he said at last abruptly, 'would you like to go to-night and hear Grey preach?'

'Preach!' exclaimed the lad. 'I thought he was a layman.'

'So he is. It will be a lay sermon. It was always the custom here with the clerical tutors to address their men once a term before Communion Sunday, and some years ago, when Grey first became tutor, he determined, though he was a layman, to carry on the practice. It was an extraordinary effort, for he is a man to whom words on such a subject are the coining of his heart's blood, and he has repeated it very rarely. It is two years now since his last address.'

'Of course I should like to go,' said Robert with eagerness. 'Is it open?'

'Strictly it is for his Greats pupils, but I can take you in. It is hardly meant for freshmen; but—well, you are far enough on to make it interesting to you.'

'The lad will take to Grey's influence like a fish to water,' thought the tutor to himself when he was alone, not without a strange reluctance. 'Well, no one can say I have not given him his opportunity to be "earnest."'

The sarcasm of the last word was the kind of sarcasm which a man of his type in an earlier generation might have applied to the 'earnestness' of an Arnoldian Rugby.[68]

At eight o'clock that evening Robert found himself crossing the quadrangle with Langham on the way to one of the larger lecture rooms, which was to be the scene of the address. The room when they got in was already

---

68 Thomas Arnold (1795–1841), Ward's grandfather. As head of Rugby School (1828–41), Arnold instituted a reformist regime famous for character-building through both Christian faith and, to a lesser degree, organized sports. Arnold's work at the school was fictionalized in Thomas Hughes' admiring *Tom Brown's Schooldays* (1857).

nearly full, all the working fellows of the college were present, and a body of some thirty men besides, most of them already far on in their University career. A minute or two afterwards Mr. Grey entered. The door opening on to the quadrangle, where the trees, undeterred by east wind, were just bursting into leaf, was shut; and the little assembly knelt, while Mr. Grey's voice with its broad intonation, in which a strong native homeliness lingered under the gentleness of accent, recited the collect 'Lord of all power and might,' a silent pause following the last words.[69] Then the audience settled itself, and Mr. Grey, standing by a small deal table with the gaslight behind him, began his address.

All the main points of the experience which followed stamped themselves on Robert's mind with extraordinary intensity. Nor did he ever lose the memory of the outward scene. In after years, memory could always recall to him at will the face and figure of the speaker, the massive head, the deep eyes sunk under the brows, the Midland accent, the make of limb and feature which seemed to have some suggestion in them of the rude strength and simplicity of a peasant ancestry; and then the nobility, the fire, the spiritual beauty flashing through it all! Here, indeed, was a man on whom his fellows might lean, a man in whom the generation of spiritual force was so strong and continuous that it overflowed of necessity into the poorer, barrener lives around him, kindling and enriching. Robert felt himself seized and penetrated, filled with a fervour and an admiration which he was too young and immature to analyse, but which was to be none the less potent and lasting.

Much of the sermon itself, indeed, was beyond him. It was on the meaning of St. Paul's great conception, 'Death unto sin and a new birth unto righteousness.'[70] What did the Apostle mean by a death to sin and self? What were the precise ideas attached to the words 'risen with Christ'? Are this death and this resurrection necessarily dependent upon certain alleged historical events? Or are they not primarily, and were they not, even in the mind of St. Paul, two aspects of a spiritual process perpetually re-enacted in the soul of man, and constituting the veritable revelation of God? Which is the stable and lasting witness of the Father: the spiritual history of the individual and

---

69 Collect: a brief prayer, the number and content of which vary according to the day in the liturgical calendar. The collect quoted here is used on the seventh Sunday after Trinity.

70 What follows is not, however, a direct quotation from Paul, but from the Church of England catechism concerning the sacrament of baptism. The relevant epistle is Romans 6.1-11. The summary of Grey's speech hews very closely to Green's "Faith," *The Witness of God and Faith: Two Lay Sermons*, ed. Arnold Toynbee (London: Longmans, Green, and Co., 1886), 63.

the world, or the envelope of miracle to which hitherto mankind has attributed so much importance?

Mr. Grey's treatment of these questions was clothed, throughout a large portion of the lecture, in metaphysical language, which no boy fresh from school, however intellectually quick, could be expected to follow with any precision. It was not, therefore, the argument, or the logical structure of the sermon, which so profoundly affected young Elsmere. It was the speaker himself, and the occasional passages in which, addressing himself to the practical needs of his hearers, he put before them the claims and conditions of the higher life with a pregnant simplicity and rugged beauty of phrase. Conceit, selfishness, vice—how, as he spoke of them, they seemed to wither from his presence! How the 'pitiful, earthy self' with its passions and its cravings sank into nothingness beside the 'great ideas' and the 'great causes' for which, as Christians and as men, he claimed their devotion.

To the boy sitting among the crowd at the back of the room, his face supported in his hands and his gleaming eyes fixed on the speaker, it seemed as if all the poetry and history through which a restless curiosity and ideality had carried him so far, took a new meaning from this experience. It was by men like this that the moral progress of the world had been shaped and inspired; he felt brought near to the great primal forces breathing through the divine workshop; and in place of natural disposition and reverent compliance, there sprang up in him suddenly an actual burning certainty of belief. 'Axioms are not axioms,' said poor Keats, 'till they have been proved upon our pulses;' and the old familiar figure of the Divine combat, of the struggle in which man and God are one, was proved once more upon a human pulse on that May night, in the hush of that quiet lecture room.[71]

As the little moving crowd of men dispersed over the main quadrangle to their respective staircases, Langham and Robert stood together a moment in the windy darkness, lit by the occasional glimmering of a cloudy moon.

'Thank you, thank you, sir!' said the lad, eager and yet afraid to speak, lest he should break the spell of memory. 'I should be sorry indeed to have missed that!'

'Yes, it was fine, extraordinarily fine, the best he has ever given, I think. Good-night.'

And Langham turned away, his head sunk on his breast, his hands behind him. Robert went to his room conscious of a momentary check of feeling. But it soon passed, and he sat up late, thinking of the sermon, or pouring out

---

71 A slight misquotation from the poet John Keats' (1795-1821) letter to J. H. Reynolds, 3 May 1818.

in a letter to his mother the new hero-worship of which his mind was full.

A few days later, as it happened, came an invitation to the junior exhi-bitioner to spend an evening at Mr. Grey's house. Elsmere went in a state of curious eagerness and trepidation, and came away with a number of fresh impressions which, when he had put them into order, did but quicken his new-born sense of devotion. The quiet unpretending house with its exqui-site neatness and its abundance of books, the family life, with the heart-hap-piness underneath, and the gentle trust and courtesy on the surface, the little touches of austerity which betrayed themselves here and there in the house-hold ways—all these surroundings stole into the lad's imagination, touched in him responsive fibres of taste and feeling.

But there was some surprise, too, mingled with the charm. He came, still shaken, as it were, by the power of the sermon, expecting to see in the preacher of it the outward and visible signs of a leadership which, as he al-ready knew, was a great force in Oxford life. His mood was that of the disciple only eager to be enrolled. And what he found was a quiet, friendly host, sur-rounded by a group of men talking the ordinary pleasant Oxford chit-chat—the river, the schools, the Union, the football matches, and so on.[72] Every now and then, as Elsmere stood at the edge of the circle listening, the rugged face in the centre of it would break into a smile, or some boyish speaker would elicit the low spontaneous laugh in which there was such a sound of human fellowship, such a genuine note of self-forgetfulness. Sometimes the conversa-tion strayed into politics, and then Mr. Grey, an eager politician, would throw back his head, and talk with more sparkle and rapidity, flashing occasionally into grim humour which seemed to throw light on the innate strength and pugnacity of the peasant and Puritan breed from which he sprang. Nothing could be more unlike the inspired philosopher, the mystic surrounded by an adoring school, whom Robert had been picturing to himself in his walk up to the house, through the soft May twilight.

It was not long before the tutor had learned to take much kindly notice of the ardent and yet modest exhibitioner, in whose future it was impossible not to feel a sympathetic interest.

'You will always find us on Sunday afternoons, before chapel,' he said to him one day as they parted after watching a football match in the damp mists of the Park, and the boy's flush of pleasure showed how much he valued the permission.

For three years those Sunday half-hours were the great charm of Robert

---

72 "quiet, friendly host": incorrect comma between "friendly" and "host" deleted in W.

Elsmere's life. When he came to look back upon them, he could remember
nothing very definite. A few interesting scraps of talk about books; a good
deal of talk about politics, showing in the tutor a living interest in the needs
and training of that broadening democracy on which the future of England
rests; a few graphic sayings about individuals; above all, a constant readiness
on the host's part to listen, to sit quiet, with the slight unconscious look of
fatigue which was so eloquent of a strenuous intellectual life, taking kindly
heed of anything that sincerity, even a stupid awkward sincerity, had got to
say—these were the sort of impressions they had left behind them, reinforced
always, indeed, by the one continuous impression of a great soul speaking
with difficulty and labour, but still clearly, still effectually, through an un-
blemished series of noble acts and efforts.

Term after term passed away. Mrs. Elsmere became more and more
proud of her boy, and more and more assured that her years of intelligent
devotion to him had won her his entire love and confidence, 'so long as they
both should live;' she came up to see him once or twice, making Langham
almost flee the University because she would be grateful to him in public, and
attending the boat-races in festive attire to which she had devoted the most
anxious attention for Robert's sake, and which made her, dear, good, impracticable soul, the observed of all observers. When she came she and Robert
talked all day, so far as lectures allowed, and most of the night, after their own
eager, improvident fashion; and she soon gathered, with that solemn, half-
tragic sense of change which besets a mother's heart at such a moment, that
there were many new forces at work in her boy's mind, deep under-currents
of feeling, stirred in him by the Oxford influences, which must before long
rise powerfully to the surface.

He was passing from a bright buoyant lad into a man, and a man of
ardour and conviction. And the chief instrument in the transformation was
Mr. Grey.

Elsmere got his first in Moderations easily.[73] But the Final Schools were
a different matter.[74] In the first days of his return to Oxford, in the October
of his third year, while he was still making up his lecture list, and taking a
general oversight of the work demanded from him, before plunging definitely

---

73 Moderations is the First Public Examination (a combined written and oral
exam), to be taken after Responsions; in the nineteenth century, students would
be examined on the Bible and one other topic. Robert elected to take the Honors
examination.

74 The Second Public Examination. There were eight options for the Final Honor
Schools; candidates could opt to take more than one examination (hence the possibility of a double first).

into it, he was oppressed with a sense that the two years lying before him constituted a problem which would be harder to solve than any which had yet been set him. It seemed to him in a moment which was one of some slackness and reaction, that he had been growing too fast. He had been making friends besides in far too many camps, and the thought, half attractive, half repellent, of all those midnight discussions over smouldering fires, which Oxford was preparing for him, those fascinating moments of intellectual fence with minds as eager and as crude as his own, and of all the delightful dipping into the very latest literature, which such moments encouraged and involved, seemed to convey a sort of warning to the boy's will that it was not equal to the situation. He was neither dull enough nor great enough for a striking Oxford success. How was he to prevent himself from attempting impossibilities and achieving a final mediocrity? He felt a dismal certainty that he should never be able to control the strayings of will and curiosity, now into this path, now into that; and a still stronger and genuine certainty that it is not by such digression that a man gets up the Ethics or the Annals.[75]

Langham watched him with a half irritable attention. In spite of the paralysis of all natural ambitions in himself, he was illogically keen that Elsmere should win the distinctions of the place. He, the most laborious, the most disinterested of scholars, turned himself almost into a crammer for Elsmere's benefit. He abused the lad's multifarious reading, declared it was no better than dram-drinking, and even preached to him an ingenious variety of mechanical aids to memory and short cuts to knowledge, till Robert would turn round upon him with some triumphant retort drawn from his own utterances at some sincerer and less discreet moment. In vain. Langham felt a dismal certainty before many weeks were over that Elsmere would miss his first in Greats. He was too curious, too restless, too passionate about many things. Above all he was beginning, in the tutor's opinion, to concern himself disastrously early with that most overwhelming and most brain-confusing of all human interests—the interest of religion. Grey had made him 'earnest' with a vengeance.

Elsmere was now attending Grey's philosophical lectures, following them with enthusiasm, and making use of them, as so often happens, for the defence and fortification of views quite other than his teacher's. The whole basis of Grey's thought was ardently idealist and Hegelian.[76] He had broken with

---

75 Robert is reading Greats, the examination set list for which includes Aristotle's *Nichomachean Ethics* and Tacitus' *Annals*.

76 G. W. F. Hegel (1770–1831), German philosopher whose dialectical theory of human and social development helped shape Green's own Idealist philosophy of progress.

the popular Christianity, but for him, God, consciousness, duty, were the only realities. None of the various forms of materialist thought escaped his challenge; no genuine utterance of the spiritual life of man but was sure of his sympathy. It was known that after having prepared himself for the Christian ministry he had remained a layman because it had become impossible to him to accept miracle; and it was evident that the commoner type of Churchmen regarded him as an antagonist all the more dangerous because he was so sympathetic. But the negative and critical side of him was what in reality told least upon his pupils. He was reserved, he talked with difficulty, and his respect for the immaturity of the young lives near him was complete. So that what he sowed others often reaped, or to quote the expression of a well-known rationalist about him: 'The Tories were always carrying off his honey to their hive.'[77] Elsmere, for instance, took in all that Grey had to give, drank in all the ideal fervour, the spiritual enthusiasm of the great tutor, and then, as Grey himself would have done some twenty years earlier, carried his religious passion so stimulated into the service of the great positive tradition around him.

And at that particular moment in Oxford history, the passage from philosophic idealism to glad acquiescence in the received Christian system, was a peculiarly easy one. It was the most natural thing in the world that a young man of Elsmere's temperament should rally to the Church. The place was passing through one of those periodical crises of reaction against an overdriven rationalism, which show themselves with tolerable regularity in any great centre of intellectual activity.[78] It had begun to be recognised with a great burst of enthusiasm and astonishment, that, after all, Mill and Herbert Spencer had not said the last word on all things in heaven and earth. And now there was exaggerated recoil. A fresh wave of religious romanticism was fast gathering strength; the spirit of Newman had reappeared in the place which Newman had loved and left; religion was becoming once more popular among the most trivial souls, and a deep reality among a large proportion of the nobler ones.[79]

With this movement of opinion Robert had very soon found himself

77 Ward slightly misquotes Mark Pattison on the afterlife of Thomas Hill Green's Idealism in Oxford philosophy and theology in *Memoirs* (London: Macmillan and Co., 1885), 167.

78 Ward borrows heavily from Pattison's analysis of conservative clerical resurgence at Oxford in his *Memoirs*, 165-67.

79 John Stuart Mill (1806-1873), Utilitarian philosopher, political economist, feminist, and Radical politician; Herbert Spencer (1820–1903), philosopher and sociologist, popularizer of Darwin; John Henry Newman (1801–90), a leader of the Oxford Movement before his conversion to Roman Catholicism in 1845.

in close and sympathetic contact. The meagre impression left upon his boy-hood by the somewhat grotesque succession of the Harden curates, and by his mother's shafts of wit at their expense, was soon driven out of him by the stateliness and comely beauty of the Church order as it was revealed to him at Oxford. The religious air, the solemn beauty of the place itself, its innumer-able associations with an organised and venerable faith, the great public func-tions and expressions of that faith, possessed the boy's imagination more and more. As he sat in the undergraduates' gallery at St. Mary's on the Sundays, when the great High Church preacher of the moment occupied the pulpit, and looked down on the crowded building, full of grave black-gowned fig-ures, and framed in one continuous belt of closely packed boyish faces; as he listened to the preacher's vibrating voice, rising and falling with the orator's instinct for musical effect; or as he stood up with the great surrounding body of undergraduates to send the melody of some Latin hymn rolling into the far recesses of the choir, the sight and the experience touched his inmost feeling, and satisfied all the poetical and dramatic instincts of a passionate nature. The system behind the sight took stronger and stronger hold upon him; he began to wish ardently and continuously to become a part of it, to cast in his lot definitely with it.

One May evening he was wandering by himself along the towing-path which skirts the upper river, a prey to many thoughts, to forebodings about the schools which were to begin in three weeks, and to speculations as to how his mother would take the news of the second class, which he himself felt to be inevitable. Suddenly, for no apparent reason, there flashed into his mind the little conversation with his mother, which had taken place nearly four years before, in the garden at Trinity. He remembered the antagonism which the idea of a clerical life for him had raised in both of them, and a smile at his own ignorance and his mother's prejudice passed over his quick young face. He sat down on the grassy bank, a mass of reeds at his feet, the shadows of the poplars behind him lying across the still river; and opposite, the wide green expanse of the great town-meadow, dotted with white patches of geese and herds of grazing horses. There, with a sense of something solemn and critical passing over him, he began to dream out his future life.

And when he rose half an hour afterwards, and turned his steps home-wards, he knew with an inward tremor of heart that the next great step of the way was practically taken. For there by the gliding river, and in view of the distant Oxford spires, which his fancy took to witness the act, he had vowed himself in prayer and self-abasement to the ministry of the Church.

During the three weeks that followed he made some frantic efforts to make up lost ground. He had not been idle for a single day, but he had been unwise, an intellectual spendthrift, living in a continuous succession of enthusiasms, and now at the critical moment his stock of nerve and energy was at a low ebb. He went in depressed and tired, his friends watching anxiously for the result. On the day of the Logic paper, as he emerged into the Schools quadrangle, he felt his arm caught by Mr. Grey.[80]

'Come with me for a walk, Elsmere; you look as if some air would do you good.'

Robert acquiesced, and the two men turned into the passage way leading out on to Radcliffe Square.

'I have done for myself, sir,' said the youth with a sigh, half impatience, half depression. 'It seems to me to-day that I had neither mind nor memory. If I get a second I shall be lucky.'

'Oh, you will get your second whatever happens,' said Mr. Grey quietly, 'and you mustn't be too much cast down about it if you don't get your first.'

This implied acceptance of his partial defeat, coming from another's lips, struck the excitable Robert like a lash. It was only what he had been saying to himself, but in the most pessimist forecasts we make for ourselves, there is always an under protest of hope.

'I have been wasting my time here lately,' he said, hurriedly raising his college cap from his brows as if it oppressed them, and pushing his hair back with a weary restless gesture.

'No,' said Mr. Grey, turning his kind frank eyes upon him. 'As far as general training goes, you have not wasted your time at all. There are many clever men who don't get a first class, and yet it is good for them to be here—so long as they are not loungers and idlers, of course. And you have not been a lounger; you have been headstrong, and a little over-confident, perhaps,' —the speaker's smile took all the sting out of the words—'but you have grown into a man, and you are fit now for man's work. Don't let yourself be depressed, Elsmere. You will do better in life than you have done in examination.'

The young man was deeply touched. This tone of personal comment and admonition was very rare with Mr. Grey. He felt a sudden consciousness of a shared burden which was infinitely soothing, and though he made no answer, his face lost something of its harassed look as the two walked on together down Oriel Street and into Merton Meadows.

'Have you any immediate plans?' said Mr. Grey, as they turned into the Broad Walk, now in the full leafage of June, and rustling under a brisk western wind blowing from the river.

---

80 Logic was one of the required examination topics in Greats.

'No; at least I suppose it will be no good my trying for a fellowship. But I meant to tell you, sir, of one thing—I have made up my mind to take orders.'

'You have? When?'

'Quite lately. So that fixes me, I suppose, to come back for divinity lectures in the autumn.'

Mr. Grey said nothing for a while, and they strolled in and out of the great shadows thrown by the elms across their path.

'You feel no difficulties in the way?' he asked at last, with a certain quick brusqueness of manner.

'No,' said Robert eagerly. 'I never had any. Perhaps,' he added, with a sudden humility, 'it is because I have never gone deep enough. What I believe might have been worth more if I had had more struggle; but it has all seemed so plain.'

The young voice speaking with hesitation and reserve, and yet with a deep inner conviction, was pleasant to hear. Mr. Grey turned towards it, and the great eyes under the furrowed brow had a peculiar gentleness of expression.

'You will probably be very happy in the life,' he said. 'The Church wants men of your sort.'

But through all the sympathy of the tone Robert was conscious of a veil between them. He knew, of course, pretty much what it was, and with a sudden impulse he felt that he would have given worlds to break through it and talk frankly with this man whom he revered beyond all others, wide as was the intellectual difference between them. But the tutor's reticence and the younger man's respect prevented it.

When the unlucky second class was actually proclaimed to the world, Langham took it to heart perhaps more than either Elsmere or his mother. No one knew better than he what Elsmere's gifts were. It was absurd that he should not have made more of them in sight of the public. '*Le cléricalisme, voilà l'ennemi!*' was about the gist of Langham's mood during the days that followed on the class list.[81]

Elsmere, however, did not divulge his intention of taking orders to him till ten days afterwards, when he had carried off Langham to stay at Harden, and he and his old tutor were smoking in his mother's little garden one moonlit night.

When he had finished his statement Langham stood still a moment watching the wreaths of smoke as they curled and vanished. The curious interest in Elsmere's career, which during a certain number of months had made

---

81 Léon Gambetta (1838-82), the French republican politician, in a speech of May 1877. ("Clericalism! That's the enemy!")

him almost practical, almost energetic, had disappeared. He was his own languid, paradoxical self.

'Well, after all,' he said at last, very slowly, 'the difficulty lies in preaching
anything. One may as well preach a respectable mythology as anything else.'

'What do you mean by a mythology?' cried Robert hotly.

'Simply ideas, or experiences, personified,' said Langham, puffing away.
'I take it they are the subject-matter of all theologies.'

'I don't understand you,' said Robert, flushing. 'To the Christian, facts
have been the medium by which ideas the world could not otherwise have
come at have been communicated to man. Christian theology is a system of
ideas indeed, but of ideas realised, made manifest in facts.'

Langham looked at him for a moment, undecided; then that suppressed
irritation we have already spoken of broke through. 'How do you know they
are facts?' he said drily.

The younger man took up the challenge with all his natural eagerness,
and the conversation resolved itself into a discussion of Christian evidences.[82]
Or rather Robert held forth, and Langham kept him going by an occasional
remark which acted like the prick of a spur. The tutor's psychological curiosity
was soon satisfied. He declared to himself that the intellect had precious little
to do with Elsmere's Christianity. He had got hold of all the stock apologetic
arguments, and used them, his companion admitted, with ability and ingenuity. But they were merely the outworks of the citadel. The inmost fortress
was held by something wholly distinct from intellectual conviction—by moral passion, by love, by feeling, by that mysticism, in short, which no healthy
youth should be without.

'He imagines he has satisfied his intellect,' was the inward comment of
one of the most melancholy of sceptics, 'and he has never so much as exerted
it. What a brute I am to protest!'

And suddenly Langham threw up the sponge. He held out his hand to
his companion, a momentary gleam of tenderness in his black eyes, such as
on one or two critical occasions before had disarmed the impetuous Elsmere.

'No use to discuss it further. You have a strong case, of course, and you
have put it well. Only, when you are pegging away at reforming and enlight-
ening the world, don't trample too much on the people who have more than
enough to do to enlighten themselves.'

As to Mrs. Elsmere, in this new turn of her son's fortunes, she realised

---

82 The empirical data used to testify to the truth of Christianity, both outside the
Bible (e.g., historical events, independent testimony to Jesus' existence, scientific or
archaeological discoveries) and inside (quotation, word usage, teachings).

with humorous distinctness that for some years past Robert had been educating her as well as himself. Her old rebellious sense of something inherently absurd in the clerical status had been gradually slain in her by her long contact through him with the finer and more imposing aspects of church life. She was still on light skirmishing terms with the Harden curates, and at times she would flame out into the wildest, wittiest threats and gibes, for the momentary satisfaction of her own essentially lay instincts; but at bottom she knew perfectly well that, when the moment came, no mother could be more loyal, more easily imposed upon, than she would be.

'I suppose, then, Robert, we shall be back at Murewell before very long,' she said to him one morning abruptly, studying him the while out of her small twinkling eyes. What dignity there was already in the young lightly-built frame! what frankness and character in the irregular, attractive face!

'Mother,' cried Elsmere indignantly, 'what do you take me for? Do you imagine I am going to bury myself in the country at five or six-and-twenty, take six hundred a year, and nothing to do for it? That would be a deserter's act indeed.'

Mrs. Elsmere shrugged her shoulders. 'Oh, I supposed you would insist on killing yourself, to begin with. To most people nowadays that seems to be the necessary preliminary of a useful career.'

Robert laughed and kissed her, but her question had stirred him so much that he sat down that very evening to write to his cousin Mowbray Elsmere. He announced to him that he was about to read for orders, and that at the same time he relinquished all claim on the living of Murewell. 'Do what you like with it when it falls vacant,' he wrote, 'without reference to me. My views are strong that before a clergyman in health and strength, and in no immediate want of money, allows himself the luxury of a country parish, he is bound, for some years at any rate, to meet the challenge of evil and poverty where the fight is hardest—among our English town population.'

Sir Mowbray Elsmere replied curtly in a day or two to the effect that Robert's letter seemed to him superfluous. He, Sir Mowbray, had nothing to do with his cousin's views. When the living was vacant—the present holder, however, was uncommon tough and did not mean dying—he should follow out the instructions of his father's will, and if Robert did not want the thing he could say so.

In the autumn Robert and his mother went back to Oxford. The following spring he redeemed his Oxford reputation completely by winning a Fellowship at Merton after a brilliant fight with some of the best men of his year, and in June he was ordained.

In the summer term some teaching work was offered him at Merton, and by Mr. Grey's advice he accepted it, thus postponing for a while that London curacy and that stout grapple with human need at its sorest for which his soul was pining. 'Stay here a year or two,' Grey said bluntly; 'you are at the beginning of your best learning time, and you are not one of the natures who can do without books. You will be all the better worth having afterwards, and there is no lack of work here for a man's moral energies.'

Langham took the same line, and Elsmere submitted. Three happy and fruitful years followed. The young lecturer developed an amazing power of work. That concentration which he had been unable to achieve for himself his will was strong enough to maintain when it was a question of meeting the demands of a college class in which he was deeply interested. He became a stimulating and successful teacher, and one of the most popular of men. His passionate sense of responsibility towards his pupils made him load himself with burdens to which he was constantly physically unequal, and fill the vacations almost as full as the terms. And as he was comparatively a man of means, his generous impetuous temper was able to gratify itself in ways that would have been impossible to others. The story of his summer reading parties, for instance, if one could have unravelled it, would have been found to be one long string of acts of kindness towards men poorer and duller than himself.

At the same time he formed close and eager relations with the heads of the religious party in Oxford. His mother's Evangelical training of him and Mr. Grey's influence, together, perhaps, with certain drifts of temperament, prevented him from becoming a High Churchman. The sacramental, ceremonial view of the Church never took hold upon him. But to the English Church as a great national institution for the promotion of God's work on earth no one could have been more deeply loyal, and none coming close to him could mistake the fervour and passion of his Christian feeling.[83] At the same time he did not know what rancour or bitterness meant, so that men of all shades of Christian belief reckoned a friend in him, and he went through life surrounded by an unusual, perhaps a dangerous amount of liking and affection. He threw himself ardently into the charitable work of Oxford, now helping a High Church vicar, and now toiling with Grey and one or two other Liberal fellows, at the maintenance of a coffee-palace and lecture-room just started by them in one of the suburbs; while in the second year of his lectureship the success of some first attempts at preaching fixed the attention

---

83 Robert's theology is currently tending in a Broad Church direction. This emphasis on the Church of England as a source of national unity draws heavily on Matthew Arnold and Samuel Taylor Coleridge, especially Coleridge's *On the Constitution of Church and State* (1830).

of the religious leaders upon him as upon a man certain to make his mark.[84]

So the three years passed—years not, perhaps, of great intellectual advance, for other forces in him than those of the intellect were mainly to the fore, but years certainly of continuous growth in character and moral experience. And at the end of them Mowbray Elsmere made his offer, and it was accepted.

The secret of it, of course, was overwork. Mrs. Elsmere, from the little house in Merton Street, where she had established herself, had watched her boy's meteoric career through these crowded months with very frequent misgivings. No one knew better than she that Robert was constitutionally not of the toughest fibre, and she realised long before he did that the Oxford life as he was bent on leading it must end for him in premature breakdown. But, as always happens, neither her remonstrances, nor Mr. Grey's common sense, nor Langham's fidgety protests had any effect on the young enthusiast to whom self-slaughter came so easy.[85] During the latter half of his third year of teaching he was continually being sent away by the doctors, and coming back only to break down again. At last, in the January of his fourth year, the collapse became so decided that he consented, bribed by the prospect of the Holy Land, to go away for three months to Egypt and the East, accompanied by his mother and a college friend.

Just before their departure news reached him of the death of the rector of Murewell, followed by a formal offer of the living from Sir Mowbray. At the moment when the letter arrived he was feeling desperately tired and ill, and in after-life he never forgot the half-superstitious thrill and deep sense of depression with which he received it. For within him was a slowly-emerging, despairing conviction that he was indeed physically unequal to the claims of his Oxford work, and if so, still more unequal to grappling with the hardest pastoral labour and the worst forms of English poverty. And the coincidence of the Murewell incumbent's death struck his sensitive mind as a Divine leading.

But it was a painful defeat. He took the letter to Grey, and Grey strongly advised him to accept.

'You overdrive your scruples, Elsmere,' said the Liberal tutor with emphasis. 'No one can say a living with 1200 souls, and no curate, is a sinecure. As for hard town work, it is absurd—you couldn't stand it. And after all, I imagine, there are some souls worth saving out of the towns.'

---

84 In the late nineteenth century, a number of clergy were instrumental in setting up recreational spaces for the urban poor, intended to supply them with food, entertainment, and intellectual stimulation away from the less salubrious environment of pubs and gin sellers.

85 "common sense": hyphen deleted as per both *SE* and *W*.

Elsmere pointed out vindictively that family livings were a corrupt and indefensible institution. Mr. Grey replied calmly that they probably were, but that the fact did not affect, so far as he could see, Elsmere's competence to fulfil all the duties of rector of Murewell.

'After all, my dear fellow,' he said, a smile breaking over his strong expressive face, 'it is well even for reformers to be sane.'

Mrs. Elsmere was passive. It seemed to her that she had foreseen it all along. She was miserable about his health, but she too had a moment of superstition, and would not urge him. Murewell was no name of happy omen to her—she had passed the darkest hours of her life there.

In the end Robert asked for delay, which was grudgingly granted him. Then he and his mother and friend fled over seas: he feverishly determined to get well and cheat the fates. But, after a halcyon time in Palestine and Constantinople, a whiff of poisoned air at Cannes, on their way home, acting on a low constitutional state, settled matters. Robert was laid up for weeks with malarious fever, and when he struggled out again into the hot Riviera sunshine it was clear to himself and everybody else that he must do what he could, and not what he would, in the Christian vineyard.

'Mother,' he said one day, suddenly looking up at her as she sat near him working, 'can *you* be happy at Murewell?'

There was a wistfulness in the long thin face, and a pathetic accent of surrender in the voice, which hurt the mother's heart.

'I can be happy wherever you are,' she said, laying her brown nervous hand on his blanched one.

'Then give me pen and paper and let me write to Mowbray. I wonder whether the place has changed at all. Heigh ho! How is one to preach to people who have stuffed you up with gooseberries, or swung you on gates, or lifted you over puddles to save your petticoats? I wonder what has become of that boy whom I hit in the eye with my bow and arrow, or of that other lout who pummelled me into the middle of next week for disturbing his bird-trap? By the way, is the Squire—is Roger Wendover—living at the Hall now?'

He turned to his mother with a sudden start of interest.

'So I hear,' said Mrs. Elsmere drily. '*He* won't be much good to you.'

He sat on meditating while she went for pen and paper. He had forgotten the Squire of Murewell. But Roger Wendover, the famous and eccentric owner of Murewell Hall, hermit and scholar, possessed of one of the most magnificent libraries in England, and author of books which had carried a revolutionary shock into the heart of English society, was not a figure to be overlooked by any rector of Murewell, least of all by one possessed of Robert's culture and imagination.

The young man ransacked his memory on the subject with a sudden access of interest in his new home that was to be.

Six weeks later they were in England, and Robert, now convalescent, had accepted an invitation to spend a month in Long Whindale with his mother's cousins, the Thornburghs, who offered him quiet, and bracing air. He was to enter on his duties at Murewell in July, the bishop, who had been made aware of his Oxford reputation, welcoming the new recruit to the diocese with marked warmth of manner.

CHAPTER VI

'Agnes, if you want any tea, here it is,' cried Rose, calling from outside through the dining-room window; 'and tell mamma.'

It was the first of June, and the spell of warmth in which Robert Elsmere had arrived was still maintaining itself. An intelligent foreigner dropped into the flower-sprinkled valley might have believed that, after all, England, and even Northern England, had a summer. Early in the season as it was, the sun was already drawing the colour out of the hills; the young green, hardly a week or two old, was darkening. Except the oaks. They were brilliance itself against the luminous gray-blue sky. So were the beeches, their young downy leaves just unpacked, tumbling loosely open to the light. But the larches and the birches and the hawthorns were already sobered by a longer acquaintance with life and Phœbus.

Rose sat fanning herself with a portentous hat, which when in its proper place served her, apparently, both as hat and as parasol. She seemed to have been running races with a fine collie, who lay at her feet panting, but studying her with his bright eyes, and evidently ready to be off again at the first indication that his playmate had recovered her wind. Chattie was coming lazily over the lawn, stretching each leg behind her as she walked, tail arched, green eyes flaming in the sun, a model of treacherous beauty.

'Chattie, you fiend, come here!' cried Rose, holding out a hand to her; 'if Miss Barks were ever pretty she must have looked like you at this moment.'

'I won't have Chattie put upon,' said Agnes, establishing herself at the other side of the little tea-table; 'she has done you no harm. Come to me, beastie. *I* won't compare you to disagreeable old maids.'

The cat looked from one sister to the other, blinking; then with a sudden magnificent spring leaped on to Agnes's lap and curled herself up there.

'Nothing but cupboard love,' said Rose scornfully, in answer to Agnes's laugh; 'she knows you will give her bread and butter and I won't, out of a double regard for my skirts and her morals. Oh, dear me! Miss Barks was quite seraphic last night; she never made a single remark about my clothes, and she didn't even say to me as she generally does, with an air of compassion, that she "*quite* understands how hard it must be to keep in tune."'

'The amusing thing was Mrs. Seaton and Mr. Elsmere,' said Agnes. 'I just love, as Mrs. Thornburgh says, to hear her instructing other people in their own particular trades. She didn't get much change out of him.'

Rose gave Agnes her tea, and then, bending forward, with one hand on her heart, said in a stage whisper, with a dramatic glance round the garden, 'My heart is whole. How is yours?'

'*Intact*,' said Agnes calmly, 'as that French bric-à-brac man in the Brompton Road used to say of his pots. But he is very nice.'

'Oh, charming! But when my destiny arrives'—and Rose, returning to her tea, swept her little hand with a teaspoon in it eloquently round—'he won't have his hair cut close. I must have luxuriant locks, and I will take *no* excuse! *Une chevelure de poète*, the eye of an eagle, the moustache of a hero, the hand of a Rubinstein, and, if it pleases him, the temper of a fiend.[86] He will be odious, insufferable for all the world besides, except for me; and for me he will be heaven.'

She threw herself back, a twinkle in her bright eye, but a little flush of something half real on her cheek.

'No doubt,' said Agnes drily. 'But you can't wonder if under the circumstances I don't pine for a brother-in-law. To return to the subject, however, Catherine liked him. She said so.'

'Oh, that doesn't count,' replied Rose discontentedly; 'Catherine likes everybody—of a certain sort—and everybody likes Catherine.'

'Does that mean, Miss Hasty,' said her sister, 'that you have made up your mind Catherine will never marry?'

'Marry!' cried Rose. 'You might as well talk of marrying Westminster Abbey.'

Agnes looked at her attentively. Rose's fun had a decided lack of sweetness. 'After all,' she said demurely, 'St. Elizabeth married.'

'Yes, but then she was a princess. Reasons of State. If Catherine were "her Royal Highness" it would be her duty to marry, which would just make *all* the difference. Duty! I hate the word.'

---

86 The hair of a poet (with the implication that he will have ample Shelleyan locks); Anton Rubinstein (1829–94), legendary Russian pianist.

And Rose took up a fir-cone lying near and threw it at the nose of the collie, who made a jump at it, and then resumed an attitude of blinking and dignified protest against his mistress's follies.

Agnes again studied her sister. 'What's the matter with you, Rose?'

'The usual thing, my dear,' replied Rose curtly, 'only more so. I had a letter this morning from Carry Ford—the daughter, you know, of those nice people I stayed in Manchester with last year. Well, she wants me to go and stay the winter with them and study under a first-rate man, Franzen, who is to be in Manchester two days a week during the winter. I haven't said a word about it—what's the use? I know all Catherine's arguments by heart. Manchester is not Whindale, and papa wished us to live in Whindale; I am not somebody else and needn't earn my bread; and art is not religion; and——'

'Wheels!' exclaimed Agnes. 'Catherine, I suppose, home from Whinborough.'

Rose got up and peered through the rhododendron bushes at the top of the wall which shut them off from the road.

'Catherine, and an unknown. Catherine driving at a foot's pace, and the unknown walking beside her. Oh, I see, of course—Mr. Elsmere. He will come in to tea, so I'll go for a cup. It is his duty to call on us to-day.'

When Rose came back in the wake of her mother, Catherine and Robert Elsmere were coming up the drive. Something had given Catherine more colour than usual, and as Mrs. Leyburn shook hands with the young clergyman her mother's eyes turned approvingly to her eldest daughter. 'After all, she is as handsome as Rose,' she said to herself—'though it *is* quite a different style.'

Rose, who was always tea-maker, dispensed her wares; Catherine took her favourite low seat beside her mother, clasping Mrs. Leyburn's thin mittened hand awhile tenderly in her own; Robert and Agnes set up a lively gossip on the subject of the Thornburghs' guests, in which Rose joined, while Catherine looked smiling on. She seemed apart from the rest, Robert thought; not, clearly, by her own will, but by virtue of a difference of temperament which could not but make itself felt. Yet once as Rose passed her, Robert saw her stretch out her hand and touch her sister caressingly, with a bright upward look and smile as though she would say, 'Is all well? have you had a good time this afternoon, Röschen?' Clearly the strong contemplative nature was not strong enough to dispense with any of the little wants and cravings of human affection. Compared to the main impression she was making on him, her suppliant attitude at her mother's feet and her caress of her sister were like flowers breaking through the stern March soil and changing the whole spirit of the fields.

Presently he said something of Oxford, and mentioned Merton. Instantly Mrs. Leyburn fell upon him. Had he ever seen Mr. S—— who had been a Fellow there, and Rose's godfather?

'I don't acknowledge him,' said Rose, pouting. 'Other people's god-fathers give them mugs and corals. Mine never gave me anything but a Concordance.'[87]

Robert laughed, and proved to their satisfaction that Mr. S—— had been extinct before his day. But could they ask him any other questions? Mrs. Leyburn became quite animated, and, diving into her memory, produced a number of fragmentary reminiscences of her husband's Queen's friends, asking him for information about each and all of them. The young man disentangled all her questions, racked his brains to answer, and showed all through a quick friendliness, a charming deference as of youth to age, which confirmed the liking of the whole party for him. Then the mention of an associate of Richard Leyburn's youth, who had been one of the Tractarian leaders, led him into talk of Oxford changes and the influences of the present. He drew for them the famous High Church preacher of the moment, described the great spectacle of his Bampton Lectures, by which Oxford had been recently thrilled, and gave a dramatic account of a sermon on evolution preached by the hermit-veteran Pusey, as though by another Elias returning to the world to deliver a last warning message to men.[88] Catherine listened absorbed, her deep eyes fixed upon him. And though all he said was pitched in a vivacious narrative key and addressed as much to the others as to her, inwardly it seemed to him that his one object all through was to touch and keep her attention.

Then, in answer to inquiries about himself, he fell to describing St. Anselm's with enthusiasm,—its growth, its Provost, its effectiveness as a great educational machine, the impression it had made on Oxford and the country. This led him naturally to talk of Mr. Grey, then, next to the Provost, the most

---

87 A Bible concordance.

88 Inaugurated in 1780, the Bampton Lectures are intended to promote Anglican orthodoxy. The High Church preacher is John Wordsworth (1843–1911), whose Bampton Lectures for 1881, *The One Religion: Truth, Holiness, and Peace Desired by the Nations, and Revealed by Jesus Christ*, harshly critiqued the moral implications of an unnamed Matthew Arnold's belief in "culture" as the means of striving towards perfection. Pusey is Edward Bouverie Pusey (1800–82), theologian, one of the most prominent figures in the Oxford and Anglo-Catholic movements. The sermon in question is *Un-science, Not Science, Adverse to Faith* (1878)—but Robert would not have heard Pusey deliver it, as Pusey's advanced age meant that H. P. Liddon (1829-90) took his place in the pulpit. See Henry Parry Liddon, *Life of Edward Bouverie Pusey*, 4 vols. (London: Longmans, Green, and Co., 1897), 4:333-34.

prominent figure in the college; and once embarked on this theme he became more eloquent and interesting than ever. The circle of women listened to him as to a voice from the large world. He made them feel the beat of the great currents of English life and thought; he seemed to bring the stir and rush of our central English society into the deep quiet of their valley. Even the bright-haired Rose, idly swinging her pretty foot, with a head full of dreams and discontent, was beguiled, and for the moment seemed to lose her restless self in listening.

He told an exciting story of a bad election riot in Oxford which had been quelled at considerable personal risk by Mr. Grey, who had gained his influence in the town by a devotion of years to the policy of breaking down as far as possible the old venomous feud between city and university.

When he paused, Mrs. Leyburn said, vaguely, 'Did you say he was a canon of somewhere?'

'Oh no,' said Robert, smiling, 'he is not a clergyman.'

'But you said he preached,' said Agnes.

'Yes—but lay sermons—addresses. He is not one of us even, according to your standard and mine.'

'A Nonconformist?' sighed Mrs. Leyburn. 'Oh, I know they have let in everybody now.'[89]

'Well, if you like,' said Robert. 'What I meant was that his opinions are not orthodox. He could not be a clergyman, but he is one of the noblest of men!'

He spoke with affectionate warmth. Then suddenly Catherine's eyes met his, and he felt an involuntary start. A veil had fallen over them; her sweet moved sympathy was gone; she seemed to have shrunk into herself.

She turned to Mrs. Leyburn. 'Mother, do you know, I have all sorts of messages from Aunt Ellen'—and in an under-voice she began to give Mrs. Leyburn the news of her afternoon expedition.

Rose and Agnes soon plunged young Elsmere into another stream of talk. But he kept his feeling of perplexity. His experience of other women seemed to give him nothing to go upon with regard to Miss Leyburn.

Presently Catherine got up and drew her plain little black cape round her again.

'My dear!' remonstrated Mrs. Leyburn. 'Where are you off to now?'

'To the Backhouses, mother,' she said in a low voice; 'I have not been there for two days. I must go this evening.'

---

89 Nonconformists could matriculate for the BA beginning in 1854, and for the MA in 1871.

Mrs. Leyburn said no more. Catherine's 'musts' were never disputed. She moved towards Elsmere with outstretched hand. But he also sprang up.

'I, too, must be going,' he said; 'I have paid you an unconscionable visit. If you are going past the vicarage, Miss Leyburn, may I escort you so far?'

She stood quietly waiting while he made his farewells. Agnes, whose eye fell on her sister during the pause, was struck with a passing sense of something out of the common. She could hardly have defined her impression, but Catherine seemed more alive to the outer world, more like other people, less nun-like, than usual.

When they had left the garden together, as they had come into it, and Mrs. Leyburn, complaining of chilliness, had retreated to the drawing-room, Rose laid a quick hand on her sister's arm.

'You say Catherine likes him? Owl! what is a great deal more certain is that he likes her.'

'Well,' said Agnes calmly,—'well, I await your remarks.'

'Poor fellow!' said Rose grimly, and removed her hand.

Meanwhile Elsmere and Catherine walked along the valley road towards the Vicarage. He thought, uneasily, she was a little more reserved with him than she had been in those pleasant moments after he had overtaken her in the pony-carriage; but still she was always kind, always courteous. And what a white hand it was, hanging ungloved against her dress! what a beautiful dignity and freedom, as of mountain winds and mountain streams, in every movement!

'You are bound for High Ghyll?' he said to her as they neared the vicarage gate. Is it not a long way for you? You have been at a meeting already, your sister said, and teaching this morning!'

He looked down on her with a charming diffidence as though aware that their acquaintance was very young, and yet with a warm eagerness of feeling piercing through. As she paused under his eye the slightest flush rose to Catherine's cheek. Then she looked up with a smile. It was amusing to be taken care of by this tall stranger!

'It is most unfeminine, I am afraid,' she said, 'but I couldn't be tired if I tried.'

Elsmere grasped her hand.

'You make me feel myself more than ever a shocking example,' he said, letting it go with a little sigh. The smart of his own renunciation was still keen in him. She lingered a moment, could find nothing to say, threw him a look all shy sympathy and lovely pity, and was gone.

In the evening Robert got an explanation of that sudden stiffening in his auditor of the afternoon, which had perplexed him. He and the vicar were sitting smoking in the study after dinner, and the ingenious young man managed to shift the conversation on to the Leyburns, as he had managed to shift it once or twice before that day, flattering himself, of course, on each occasion that his manœuvres were beyond detection. The vicar, good soul, by virtue of his original discovery, detected them all, and with a sense of appropriation in the matter, not at all unmixed with a sense of triumph over Mrs. T., kept the ball rolling merrily.

'Miss Leyburn seems to have very strong religious views,' said Robert, à propos of some remark of the vicar's as to the assistance she was to him in the school.

'Ah, she is her father's daughter,' said the vicar genially. He had his oldest coat on, his favourite pipe between his lips, and a bit of domestic carpentering on his knee at which he was fiddling away; and, being perfectly happy, was also perfectly amiable. 'Richard Leyburn was a fanatic—as mild as you please, but immovable.'

'What line?'

'Evangelical, with a dash of Quakerism. He lent me Madame Guyon's Life once to read.[90] I didn't appreciate it. I told him that for all her religion she seemed to me to have a deal of the vixen in her. He could hardly get over it: it nearly broke our friendship. But I suppose he was very like her, except that, in my opinion, his nature was sweeter. He was a fatalist—saw leadings of Providence in every little thing. And such a dreamer! When he came to live up here just before his death, and all his active life was taken off him, I believe half his time he was seeing visions. He used to wander over the fells and meet you with a start, as though you belonged to another world than the one he was walking in.'

'And his eldest daughter was much with him?'

'The apple of his eye. She understood him. He could talk his soul out to her. The others, of course, were children; and his wife—well, his wife was just what you see her now, poor thing. He must have married her when she was very young and very pretty. She was a squire's daughter somewhere near the school of which he was master—a good family, I believe—she'll tell you so, in a ladylike way. He was always fidgety about her health. He loved her, I suppose, or had loved her. But it was Catherine who had his mind; Catherine who was his friend. She adored him. I believe there was always a sort of pity in

---

90 Jeanne Marie Bouvier de la Motte-Guyon (1648–1717), controversial Catholic figure whose mystical writings brought down charges of heresy. Her Life was first published in 1720.

her heart for him too. But at any rate he made her and trained her. He poured all his ideas and convictions into her.'

'Which were strong?'

'Uncommonly. For all his gentle, ethereal look, you could neither bend nor break him. I don't believe anybody but Richard Leyburn could have gone through Oxford at the height of the Oxford Movement, and, so to speak, have known nothing about it, while living all the time for religion. He had a great deal in common with the Quakers, as I said; a great deal in common with the Wesleyans; but he was very loyal to the Church all the same.[91] He regarded it as the golden mean.[92] George Herbert was his favourite poet.[93] He used to carry his poems about with him on the mountains, and an expurgated *Christian Year*—the only thing he ever took from the High Churchmen—which he had made for himself, and which he and Catherine knew by heart. In some ways he was not a bigot at all. He would have had the Church make peace with the Dissenters; he was all for upsetting tests so far as Nonconformity was concerned.[94] But he drew the most rigid line between belief and unbelief. He would not have dined at the same table with a Unitarian if he could have helped it.[95] I remember a furious article of his in the *Record* against admitting Unitarians to the Universities or allowing them to sit in Parliament.[96] England is a Christian State, he said; they are not Christians; they have no right in her except on sufferance. Well, I suppose he was about right,' said the vicar with a sigh. 'We are all so half-hearted nowadays.'

'Not he,' cried Robert hotly. 'Who are we that because a man differs from us in opinion we are to shut him out from the education of political and civil duty? But never mind, Cousin William. Go on.'

'There's no more that I remember, except that of course Catherine took all these ideas from him. He wouldn't let his children know any unbeliever, however apparently worthy and good. He impressed it upon them as their

---

91 The Wesleyans are the Methodists affiliated with John Wesley (1703–91), called such to distinguish their Arminianism (which emphasizes man's free will in the reception of divine grace) from Calvinistic Methodists (which emphasizes predestination).

92 The *via media*, in which the Church of England strikes a perfect balance between Catholicism and Protestantism.

93 Herbert (1593–1633), Anglican poet and clergyman, best known for *The Temple* (1633).

94 From 1661 to 1828, all those wishing to take office or any government employment were required to receive communion in the Church of England.

95 Leyburn objects to the Unitarian rejection of Christ's divinity.

96 *The Record* was one of the most powerful evangelical papers, founded in 1828.

special sacred duty, in a time of wicked enmity to religion, to cherish the faith and the whole faith. He wished his wife and daughters to live on here after his death that they might be less in danger spiritually than in the big world, and that they might have more opportunity of living the old-fashioned Christian life. There was also some mystical idea, I think, of making up through his children for the godless lives of their forefathers. He used to reproach himself for having in his prosperous days neglected his family, some of whom he might have helped to raise.'

'Well, but,' said Robert, 'all very well for Miss Leyburn, but I don't see the father in the two younger girls.'

'Ah, there is Catherine's difficulty,' said the vicar, shrugging his shoulders. 'Poor thing! How well I remember her after her father's death! She came down to see me in the dining-room about some arrangement for the funeral. She was only sixteen, so pale and thin with nursing. I said something about the comfort she had been to her father. She took my hand and burst into tears. "He was so good!" she said; "I loved him so! Oh, Mr. Thornburgh, help me to look after the others!" And that's been her one thought since then—that, next to following the narrow road.'

The vicar had begun to speak with emotion, as generally happened to him whenever he was beguiled into much speech about Catherine Leyburn. There must have been something great somewhere in the insignificant elderly man. A meaner soul might so easily have been jealous of this girl with her inconveniently high standards, and her influence, surpassing his own, in his own domain.

'I should like to know the secret of the little musician's independence,' said Robert, musing. 'There might be no tie of blood at all between her and the elder, so far as I can see.'

'Oh, I don't know that! There's more than you think, or Catherine wouldn't have kept her hold over her so far as she has. Generally she gets her way, except about the music. There Rose sticks to it.'

'And why shouldn't she?'

'Ah, well, you see, my dear fellow, I am old enough, and you're not, to remember what people in the old days used to think about art. Of course nowadays we all say very fine things about it; but Richard Leyburn would no more have admitted that a girl who hadn't got her own bread or her family's to earn by it was justified in spending her time in fiddling than he would have approved of her spending it in dancing. I have heard him take a text out of the *Imitation* and lecture Rose when she was quite a baby for pestering any stray person she could get hold of to give her music-lessons.[97] "Woe to them"—yes, that was it—"that inquire many curious things of men, and care little about the way of serving me." However, he wasn't consistent. Nobody is. It was actually he that brought Rose her first violin from London in a green baize bag. Mrs. Leyburn took me in one night to see her asleep with it on her pillow, and all her pretty curls lying over the strings. I daresay, poor man, it was one of the acts towards his children that tormented his mind in his last hour.'

'She has certainly had her way about practising it: she plays superbly.'

'Oh yes, she has had her way. She is a queer mixture, is Rose. I see a touch of the old Leyburn recklessness in her; and then there is the beauty and refinement of her mother's side of the family. Lately she has got quite out of hand. She went to stay with some relations they have in Manchester, got drawn into the musical set there, took to these funny gowns, and now she and Catherine are always half at war.[98] Poor Catherine said to me the other day, with tears in her eyes, that she knew Rose thought her as hard as iron. "But what can I do?" she said. "I promised papa." She makes herself miserable, and it's no use. I wish the little wild thing would get herself well married. She's not meant for this humdrum place, and she may kick over the traces.'

'She's pretty enough for anything and anybody,' said Robert.

The vicar looked at him sharply, but the young man's critical and meditative look reassured him.

The next day, just before early dinner, Rose and Agnes, who had been for a walk, were startled, as they were turning into their own gate, by the frantic waving of a white handkerchief from the vicarage garden. It was Mrs. Thornburgh's accepted way of calling the attention of the Burwood inmates, and the girls walked on. They found the good lady waiting for them in the drive in a characteristic glow and flutter.

'My dears, I have been looking out for you all the morning! I should have come over but for the stores coming, and a tiresome man from Randall's. I've had to bargain with him for a whole hour about taking back those sweets. I was swindled, of course, but we should have died if we'd had to eat them up. Well, now, my dears——'

The vicar's wife paused. Her square short figure was between the two girls; she had an arm of each, and she looked significantly from one to another, her

---

97 Thomas à Kempis' *The Imitation of Christ*. The quotation that follows is from the forty-third chapter on the vanity of human learning.

98 Manchester was an important center of Victorian musical culture, especially under the influence of Charles E. Hallé (1819–95), a pianist and conductor who founded the Hallé orchestra in 1858.

gray curls flapping across her face as she did so.

'Go on, Mrs. Thornburgh,' cried Rose. 'You make us quite nervous.'

'How do you like Mr. Elsmere?' she inquired solemnly.

'Very much,' said both in chorus.

Mrs. Thornburgh surveyed Rose's smiling frankness with a little sigh. Things were going grandly, but she could imagine a disposition of affairs which would have given her personally more pleasure.

'*How—would—you—like*—him for a brother-in-law?' she inquired, beginning in a whisper, with slow emphasis, patting Rose's arm, and bringing out the last words with a rush.

Agnes caught the twinkle in Rose's eye, but she answered for them both demurely.

'We have no objection to entertain the idea. But you must explain.'

'Explain!' cried Mrs. Thornburgh. 'I should think it explains itself. At least if you'd been in this house the last twenty-four hours you'd think so. Since the moment when he first met her, it's been "Miss Leyburn," "Miss Leyburn," all the time. One might have seen it with half an eye from the beginning.'

Mrs. Thornburgh had not seen it with two eyes, as we know, till it was pointed out to her; but her imagination worked with equal liveliness backwards or forwards.

'He went to see you yesterday, didn't he—yes, I know he did—and he overtook her in the pony-carriage—the vicar saw them from across the valley—and he brought her back from your house, and then he kept William up till nearly twelve talking of her. And now he wants a picnic. Oh, it's as plain as a pike-staff. And, my dears, *nothing* to be said against him. Fifteen hundred a year if he's a penny. A nice living, only his mother to look after, and as good a young fellow as ever stepped.'

Mrs. Thornburgh stopped, choked almost by her own eloquence. The girls, who had by this time established her between them on a garden-seat, looked at her with smiling composure. They were accustomed to letting her have her budget out.

'And now, of course,' she resumed, taking breath, and chilled a little by their silence, 'now, of course, I want to know about Catherine?' She regarded them with anxious interrogation. Rose, still smiling, slowly shook her head.

'What!' cried Mrs. Thornburgh; then, with charming inconsistency, 'oh, you can't know anything in two days.'

'That's just it,' said Agnes, intervening; 'we can't know anything in two days. No one ever will know anything about Catherine, if she takes to anybody, till the last minute.'

Mrs. Thornburgh's face fell. 'It's very difficult when people will be so reserved,' she said dolefully.

The girls acquiesced, but intimated that they saw no way out of it.

'At any rate we can bring them together,' she broke out, brightening again. 'We can have picnics, you know, and teas, and all that—and watch. Now listen.'

And the vicar's wife sketched out a programme of festivities for the next fortnight she had been revolving in her inventive head, which took the sisters' breath away. Rose bit her lip to keep in her laughter. Agnes with vast self-possession took Mrs. Thornburgh in hand. She pointed out firmly that nothing would be so likely to make Catherine impracticable as fuss. 'In vain is the net spread,' etc.[99] She preached from the text with a worldly wisdom which quickly crushed Mrs. Thornburgh.

'Well, *what* am I to do, my dears?' she said at last helplessly. 'Look at the weather! We must have some picnics, if it's only to amuse Robert.'

Mrs. Thornburgh spent her life between a condition of effervescence and a condition of feeling the world too much for her. Rose and Agnes, having now reduced her to the latter state, proceeded cautiously to give her her head again. They promised her two or three expeditions and one picnic at least; they said they would do their best; they promised they would report what they saw and be very discreet, both feeling the comedy of Mrs. Thornburgh as the advocate of discretion; and then they departed to their early dinner, leaving the vicar's wife decidedly less self-confident than they found her.

'The first matrimonial excitement of the family,' cried Agnes as they walked home. 'So far no one can say the Miss Leyburns have been besieged!'

'It will be all moonshine,' Rose replied decisively. 'Mr. Elsmere may lose his heart; we may aid and abet him; Catherine will live in the clouds for a few weeks, and come down from them at the end with the air of an angel, to give him his *coup de grâce*. As I said before—poor fellow!'

Agnes made no answer. She was never so positive as Rose, and on the whole did not find herself the worse for it in life. Besides, she understood that there was a soreness at the bottom of Rose's heart that was always showing itself in unexpected connections.

There was no necessity, indeed, for elaborate schemes for assisting Providence. Mrs. Thornburgh had her picnics and her expeditions, but without them Robert Elsmere would have been still man enough to see Catherine Leyburn every day. He loitered about the roads along which she must needs

---

99 Proverbs 1.17.

pass to do her many offices of charity; he offered the vicar to take a class in the school, and was naïvely exultant that the vicar curiously happened to fix an hour when he must needs see Miss Leyburn going or coming on the same errand; he dropped into Burwood on any conceivable pretext, till Rose and Agnes lost all inconvenient respect for his cloth and Mrs. Leyburn sent him on errands; and he even insisted that Catherine and the vicar should make use of him and his pastoral services in one or two of the cases of sickness or poverty under their care. Catherine, with a little more reserve than usual, took him one day to the Tysons', and introduced him to the poor crippled son who was likely to live on paralysed for some time, under the weight, moreover, of a black cloud of depression which seldom lifted. Mrs. Tyson kept her talking in the room, and she never forgot the scene. It showed her a new aspect of a man whose intellectual life was becoming plain to her, while his moral life was still something of a mystery. The look in Elsmere's face as he sat bending over the maimed young farmer, the strength and tenderness of the man, the diffidence of the few religious things he said, and yet the reality and force of them, struck her powerfully. He had forgotten her, forgotten everything save the bitter human need, and the comfort it was his privilege to offer. Catherine stood answering Mrs. Tyson at random, the tears rising in her eyes. She slipped out while he was still talking, and went home strangely moved.

As to the festivities, she did her best to join in them. The sensitive soul often reproached itself afterwards for having juggled in the matter. Was it not her duty to manage a little society and gaiety for her sisters sometimes? Her mother could not undertake it, and was always plaintively protesting that Catherine would not be young. So for a short week or two Catherine did her best to be young, and climbed the mountain grass, or forded the mountain streams with the energy and the grace of perfect health, trembling afterwards at night as she knelt by her window to think how much sheer pleasure the day had contained. Her life had always had the tension of a bent bow. It seemed to her once or twice during this fortnight as though something were suddenly relaxed in her, and she felt a swift Bunyan-like terror of backsliding, of falling away.[100] But she never confessed herself fully; she was even blind to what her perspicacity would have seen so readily in another's case—the little arts and manoeuvres of those about her. It did not strike her that Mrs. Thornburgh was more flighty and more ebullient than ever; that the vicar's wife kissed her at odd times, and with a quite unwonted effusion; or that Agnes and Rose,

---

100 This could refer to either John Bunyan's (1628–88) autobiography *Grace Abounding to the Chief of Sinners* (1666), or his allegory *The Pilgrim's Progress* (1678–84), both of which warn of the horrors of turning away from God.

when they were in the wild heart of the mountains, or wandering far and wide in search of sticks for a picnic fire, showed a perfect genius for avoiding Mr. Elsmere, whom both of them liked, and that in consequence his society almost always fell to her. Nor did she ever analyse what would have been the attraction of those walks to her without that tall figure at her side, that bounding step, that picturesque impetuous talk. There are moments when Nature throws a kind of heavenly mist and dazzlement round the soul it would fain make happy. The soul gropes blindly on; if it saw its way it might be timid and draw back, but kind powers lead it genially onward through a golden darkness.

Meanwhile if she did not know herself, she and Elsmere learnt with wonderful quickness and thoroughness to know each other. The two households so near together, and so isolated from the world besides, were necessarily in constant communication. And Elsmere made a most stirring element in their common life. Never had he been more keen, more strenuous. It gave Catherine new lights on modern character altogether to see how he was preparing himself for this Surrey living—reading up the history, geology, and botany of the Weald and its neighbourhood, plunging into reports of agricultural commissions, or spending his quick brain on village sanitation, with the oddest results sometimes, so far as his conversation was concerned.[101] And then in the middle of his disquisitions, which would keep her breathless with a sense of being whirled through space at the tail of an electric kite, the kite would come down with a run, and the preacher and reformer would come hat in hand to the girl beside him, asking her humbly to advise him, to pour out on him some of that practical experience of hers among the poor and suffering, for the sake of which he would in an instant scornfully fling out of sight all his own magnificent plannings. Never had she told so much of her own life to any one; her consciousness of it sometimes filled her with a sort of terror, lest she might have been trading, as it were, for her own advantage on the sacred things of God. But he would have it. His sympathy, his sweetness, his quick spiritual feeling drew the stories out of her. And then how his bright frank eyes would soften! With what a reverence would he touch her hand when she said good-bye!

And on her side she felt that she knew almost as much about Murewell as he did. She could imagine the wild beauty of the Surrey heathland, she could see the white square rectory with its sloping walled garden, the juniper

---

101 Many Victorian social reformers paid close attention to the relationship between sanitation (e.g., waste disposal), physical health, and moral health—among them, the Broad Church clergyman and novelist Charles Kingsley (1819–75), who wrote and lectured extensively on the topic.

common just outside the straggling village; she could even picture the strange squire, solitary in the great Tudor Hall, the author of terrible books against the religion of Christ of which she shrank from hearing, and share the anxieties of the young rector as to his future relations towards a personality so marked, and so important to every soul in the little community he was called to rule. Here all was plain sailing; she understood him perfectly, and her gentle comments, or her occasional sarcasms, were friendliness itself.

But it was when he turned to larger things—to books, movements, leaders of the day—that she was often puzzled, sometimes distressed. Why would he seem to exalt and glorify rebellion against the established order in the person of Mr. Grey? Or why, ardent as his own faith was, would he talk as though opinion was a purely personal matter, hardly in itself to be made the subject of moral judgment at all, and as though right belief were a blessed privilege and boon rather than a law and an obligation? When his comments on men and things took this tinge, she would turn silent, feeling a kind of painful opposition between his venturesome speech and his clergyman's dress.

And yet, as we all know, these ways of speech were not his own. He was merely talking the natural Christian language of this generation; whereas she, the child of a mystic—solitary, intense, and deeply reflective from her earliest youth—was still thinking and speaking in the language of her father's generation.

But although, as often as his unwariness brought him near to these points of jarring, he would hurry away from them, conscious that here was the one profound difference between them, it was clear to him that insensibly she had moved further than she knew from her father's standpoint. Even among these solitudes, far from men and literature, she had unconsciously felt the breath of her time in some degree. As he penetrated deeper into the nature he found it honeycombed, as it were, here and there, with beautiful unexpected softnesses and diffidences. Once, after a long walk, as they were lingering homewards under a cloudy evening sky, he came upon the great problem of her life—Rose and Rose's art. He drew her difficulty from her with the most delicate skill. She had laid it bare, and was blushing to think how she had asked his counsel, almost before she knew where their talk was leading. How was it lawful for the Christian to spend the few short years of the earthly combat in any pursuit, however noble and exquisite, which merely aimed at the gratification of the senses, and implied in the pursuer the emphasising rather than the surrender of self?

He argued it very much as Kingsley would have argued it, tried to lift her to a more intelligent view of a multifarious world, dwelling on the function of pure beauty in life, and on the influence of beauty on character, pointing out the value to the race of all individual development, and pressing home on her the natural religious question: How are the artistic aptitudes to be explained unless the Great Designer meant them to have a use and function in His world?[102] She replied doubtfully that she had always supposed they were lawful for recreation, and like any other trade for bread-winning, but——

Then he told her much that he knew about the humanising effect of music on the poor. He described to her the efforts of a London society, of which he was a subscribing member, to popularise the best music among the lowest class; he dwelt almost with passion on the difference between the joy to be got out of such things and the common brutalising joys of the workman. And you could not have art without artists. In this again he was only talking the commonplaces of his day. But to her they were not commonplaces at all. She looked at him from time to time, her great eyes lightening and deepening as it seemed with every fresh thrust of his.

'I am grateful to you,' she said at last with an involuntary outburst, 'I am *very* grateful to you!'

And she gave a long sigh as if some burden she had long borne in patient silence had been loosened a little, if only by the fact of speech about it. She was not convinced exactly. She was too strong a nature to relinquish a principle without a period of meditative struggle in which conscience should have all its dues. But her tone made his heart leap. He felt in it a momentary self-surrender that, coming from a creature of so rare a dignity, filled him with an exquisite sense of power, and yet at the same time with a strange humility beyond words.

A day or two later he was the spectator of a curious little scene. An aunt of the Leyburns living in Whinborough came to see them. She was their father's youngest sister, and the wife of a man who had made some money as a builder in Whinborough. When Robert came in he found her sitting on the sofa having tea, a large homely-looking woman with gray hair, a high brow, and prominent white teeth. She had unfastened her bonnet strings, and a clean white handkerchief lay spread out on her lap. When Elsmere was introduced to her, she got up, and said with some effusiveness, and a distinct Westmoreland accent—

'Very pleased indeed to make your acquaintance, sir,' while she enclosed his fingers in a capacious hand.

Mrs. Leyburn, looking fidgety and uncomfortable, was sitting near her,

---

102 In both his letters and public speeches, Kingsley insisted that understood properly, beauty could reveal the remaining traces of God in a fallen world.

and Catherine, the only member of the party who showed no sign of embarrassment when Robert entered, was superintending her aunt's tea and talking busily the while.

Robert sat down at a little distance beside Agnes and Rose, who were chattering together a little artificially and of set purpose as it seemed to him. But the aunt was not to be ignored. She talked too loud not to be overheard, and Agnes inwardly noted that as soon as Robert Elsmere appeared she talked louder than before. He gathered presently that she was an ardent Wesleyan, and that she was engaged in describing to Catherine and Mrs. Leyburn the evangelistic exploits of her eldest son, who had recently obtained his first circuit as a Wesleyan minister.[103] He was shrewd enough, too, to guess, after a minute or two, that his presence and probably his obnoxious clerical dress gave additional zest to the recital.

'Oh, his success at Colesbridge has been somethin' marvellous,' he heard her say, with uplifted hands and eyes, 'some-thin' marvellous. The Lord has blessed him indeed! It doesn't matter what it is, whether it's meetin's, or sermons, or parlour work, or just faithful dealin's with souls one by one. Satan has no cliverer foe than Edward. He never shuts his eyes; as Edward says himself, it's like trackin' for game is huntin' for souls. Why, the other day he was walkin' out from Coventry to a service. It was the Sabbath, and he saw a man in a bit of grass by the roadside, mendin' his cart. And he stopped did Edward, and gave him the Word *strong*. The man seemed puzzled like, and said he meant no harm. "No harm!" says Edward, "when you're just doin' the devil's work every nail you put in, and hammerin' away, mon, at your own damnation." But here's his letter.' And while Rose turned away to a far window to hide an almost hysterical inclination to laugh, Mrs. Fleming opened her bag, took out a treasured paper, and read with the emphasis and the unction peculiar to a certain type of revivalism—

"'Poor sinner! He was much put about. I left him, praying the Lord my shaft might rankle in him; ay, might fester and burn in him till he found no peace but in Jesus. He seemed very dark and destitute—no respect for the Word or its ministers. A bit farther I met a boy carrying a load of turnips. To him, too, I was faithful, and he went on, taking, without knowing it, a precious leaflet with him in his bag. Glorious work! If Wesleyans will but go on claiming even the highways for God, sin will skulk yet.'"

A dead silence. Mrs. Fleming folded up the letter and put it back into her bag.

---

103 A circuit is an organization of multiple Methodist churches, or societies; the aunt's son has been appointed as minister to one such circuit.

'There's your true minister,' she said, with a large judicial utterance as she closed the snap. 'Wherever he goes Edward must have souls!'

And she threw a swift searching look at the young clergyman in the window.

'He must have very hard work with so much walking and preaching,' said Catherine gently.

Somehow, as soon as she spoke, Elsmere saw the whole odd little scene with other eyes.

'His work is just wearin' him out,' said the mother fervently; 'but a minister doesn't think of that. Wherever he goes there are sinners saved. He stayed last week at a house near Nuneaton. At family prayer alone there were five saved. And at the prayer-meetin's on the Sabbath such outpourin's of the Spirit! Edward comes home, his wife tells me, just ready to drop. Are you acquainted, sir,' she added, turning suddenly to Elsmere, and speaking in a certain tone of provocation, 'with the labours of our Wesleyan ministers?'

'No,' said Robert, with his pleasant smile, 'not personally. But I have the greatest respect for them as a body of devoted men.'

The look of battle faded from the woman's face. It was not an unpleasant face. He even saw strange reminiscences of Catherine in it at times.

'You're aboot right there, sir. Not that they dare take any credit to themselves—it's grace, sir, all grace.'

'Aunt Ellen,' said Catherine, while a sudden light broke over her face; 'I just want you to take Edward a little story from me. Ministers are good things, but God can do without them.'

And she laid her hand on her aunt's knee with a smile in which there was the slightest touch of affectionate satire.

'I was up among the fells the other day,' she went on; 'I met an elderly man cutting wood in a plantation, and I stopped and asked him how he was. "Ah, miss," he said, "verra weel, verra weel. And yet it was nobbut Friday morning lasst, I cam oop here, awfu' bad in my sperrits like. For my wife she's sick, an' a' dwinnelt away, and I'm gettin' auld, and can't wark as I'd used to, and it did luke to me as thoo there was naethin' afore us nobbut t' Union. And t' mist war low on t' fells, and I sat oonder t' wall, wettish and broodin' like. And theer—all ov a soodent the Lord found me! Yes, puir Reuben Judge, as dawn't matter to naebody, the Lord found un. It war leyke as thoo His feeace cam a-glisterin' an' a-shinin' through t' mist. An' iver sence then, miss, aa've jest felt as thoo aa could a' cut an' stackt all t' wood on t' fell in naw time at a'!" And he waved his hand round the mountain side which was covered with plantation. And all the way along the path for ever so long I could hear him singing, chopping away, and quavering out, "Rock of Ages."[104]

She paused, her delicate face, with just a little quiver in the lip, turned to her aunt, her eyes glowing as though a hidden fire had leapt suddenly outward. And yet the gesture, the attitude, was simplicity and unconsciousness itself. Robert had never heard her say anything so intimate before. Nor had he ever seen her so inspired, so beautiful. She had transmuted the conversation at a touch. It had been barbarous prose; she had turned it into purest poetry. Only the noblest souls have such an alchemy as this at command, thought the watcher on the other side of the room with a passionate reverence.

'I wasn't thinkin' of narrowin' the Lord down to ministers,' said Mrs. Fleming, with a certain loftiness. 'We all know He can do without us puir worms.'

Then, seeing that no one replied, the good woman got up to go. Much of her apparel had slipped away from her in the fervours of revivalist anecdote, and while she hunted for gloves and reticule—officiously helped by the younger girls—Robert crossed over to Catherine.

'You lifted us on to your own high places!' he said, bending down to her; 'I shall carry your story with me through the fells.'

She looked up, and as she met his warm moved look a little glow and tremor crept into the face, destroying its exalted expression. He broke the spell; she sank from the poet into the embarrassed woman.

'You must see my old man,' she said, with an effort; 'he is worth a library of sermons. I must introduce him to you.'

He could think of nothing else to say just then, but could only stand impatiently wishing for Mrs. Fleming's disappearance, that he might somehow appropriate her eldest niece. But alas! when she went, Catherine went out with her, and reappeared no more, though he waited some time.

He walked home in a whirl of feeling; on the way he stopped, and leaning over a gate which led into one of the river-fields gave himself up to the mounting tumult within. Gradually, from the half-articulate chaos of hope and memory, there emerged the deliberate voice of his inmost manhood.

'In her and her only is my heart's desire! She and she only if she will, and God will, shall be my wife!'

He lifted his head and looked out on the dewy field, the evening beauty of the hills, with a sense of immeasurable change—

---

104 The classic hymn by Augustus Toplady (1740–78), first published in 1776.

'Tears
Were in his eyes, and in his ears
The murmur of a thousand years.'[105]

He felt himself knit to his kind, to his race, as he had never felt before. It was as though, after a long apprenticeship, he had sprung suddenly into maturity—entered at last into the full human heritage. But the very intensity and solemnity of his own feeling gave him a rare clear-sightedness. He realised that he had no certainty of success, scarcely even an entirely reasonable hope. But what of that? Were they not together, alone, practically, in these blessed solitudes? Would they not meet to-morrow, and next day, and the day after? Were not time and opportunity all his own? How kind her looks are even now! Courage! And through that maidenly kindness his own passion shall send the last, transmuting glow.

CHAPTER VII

The following morning about noon, Rose, who had been coaxed and persuaded by Catherine, much against her will, into taking a singing class at the school, closed the school door behind her with a sigh of relief, and tripped up the road to Burwood.

'How abominably they sang this morning!' she said to herself with curving lip. 'Talk of the natural north-country gift for music! What ridiculous fictions people set up! Dear me, what clouds! Perhaps we shan't get our walk to Shanmoor after all, and if we don't, and if—if—' her cheek flushed with a sudden excitement—'if Mr. Elsmere doesn't propose, Mrs. Thornburgh will be unmanageable. It is all Agnes and I can do to keep her in bounds as it is, and if *something* doesn't come off to-day, she'll be for reversing the usual proceeding, and asking *Catherine* her intentions, which would ruin everything.'

Then raising her head she swept her eyes round the sky. The wind was freshening, the clouds were coming up fast from the westward; over the summit of High Fell and the crags on either side, a gray straight-edged curtain was already lowering.

'It will hold up yet awhile,' she thought, 'and if it rains later we can get a carriage at Shanmoor and come back by the road.'

And she walked on homewards meditating, her thin fingers clasped before her, the wind blowing her skirts, the blue ribbons on her hat, the little

---

105 A slight misquotation of Matthew Arnold's "Resignation."

gold curls on her temples, in a pretty many-coloured turmoil about her. When she got to Burwood she shut herself into the room which was peculiarly hers, the room which had been a stable. Now it was full of artistic odds and ends—her fiddle, of course, and piles of music, her violin stand, a few deal tables and cane chairs beautified by a number of *chiffons*, bits of Liberty stuffs with the edges still ragged, or cheap morsels of Syrian embroidery.[106] On the tables stood photographs of musicians and friends—the spoils of her visits to Manchester, and of two visits to London which gleamed like golden points in the girl's memory. The plastered walls were covered with an odd medley. Here was a round mirror, of which Rose was enormously proud. She had extracted it from a farmhouse of the neighbourhood, and paid for it with her own money. There a group of unfinished headlong sketches of the most fiercely impressionist description—the work and the gift of a knot of Manchester artists, who had fêted and flattered the beautiful little Westmoreland girl, when she was staying among them, to her heart's content.[107] Manchester, almost alone among our great towns of the present day, has not only a musical, but a pictorial life of its own; its young artists dub themselves 'a school,' study in Paris, and when they come home scout the Academy and its methods, and pine to set up a rival art-centre, skilled in all the methods of the Salon, in the murky north. Rose's uncle, originally a clerk in a warehouse, and a rough diamond enough, had more or less moved with the times, like his brother Richard; at any rate he had grown rich, had married a decent wife, and was glad enough to befriend his dead brother's children, who wanted nothing of him, and did their uncle a credit of which he was sensible, by their good manners and good looks. Music was the only point at which he touched the culture of the times, like so many business men; but it pleased him also to pose as a patron of local art; so that when Rose went to stay with her childless

---

106 Chiffons: delicate decorative fabric; Liberty stuffs: textiles sold by London department store Liberty and Co., a store whose marketing appeal "emphasized the aesthetic over the functional qualities of material goods" (Sonia Ashmore, "Liberty and Lifestyle: Shopping for Art and Luxury in Nineteenth-Century London," *Buying for the Home: Shopping for the Domestic from the Seventeenth Century to the Present*, ed. David Hussey and Margaret Ponsonby [Aldershot: Ashgate, 2008], 78); Syrian embroidery: a popular Middle Eastern decorative import. Ward remembered Liberty stuffs as part of "the fashion of the movement which sprang from Morris and Burne-Jones": *A Writer's Recollections* (London: W. Collins Sons & Co., 1918 [1919]), 119.
107 *Impressionisme*, the art movement underway in France from the 1870s onward, associated with the work of artists such as Georges Seurat, Pierre-Auguste Renoir, and Claude Monet. As the following sentences indicate, Rose's acquaintances are very much the Paris-trained *avant-garde*. The Salon was the most important art exhibit in Europe.

uncle and aunt, she found long-haired artists and fiery musicians about the place, who excited and encouraged her musical gift, who sketched her while she played, and talked to the pretty, clever, unformed creature of London and Paris and Italy, and set her pining for that golden *vie de Bohème* which she alone apparently of all artists was destined never to know.

For she was an artist—she would be an artist—let Catherine say what she would! She came back from Manchester restless for she knew not what, thirsty for the joys and emotions of art, determined to be free, reckless, passionate; with Wagner and Brahms in her young blood; and found Burwood waiting for her—Burwood, the lonely house in the lonely valley, of which Catherine was the presiding genius.[108] *Catherine!* For Rose, what a multitude of associations clustered round the name! To her it meant everything at this moment against which her soul rebelled—the most scrupulous order, the most rigid self-repression, the most determined sacrificing of 'this warm kind world,' with all its indefensible delights, to a cold other-world with its torturing inadmissible claims.[109] Even in the midst of her stolen joys at Manchester or London, this mere name, the mere mental image of Catherine moving through life, wrapped in a religious peace and certainty as austere as they were beautiful, and asking of all about her the same absolute surrender to an awful Master she gave so easily herself, was enough to chill the wayward Rose, and fill her with a kind of restless despair. And at home, as the vicar said, the two sisters were always on the verge of conflict. Rose had enough of her father in her to suffer in resisting, but resist she must by the law of her nature.

Now, as she threw off her walking things, she fell first upon her violin, and rushed through a Brahms's 'Liebeslied,' her eyes dancing, her whole light form thrilling with the joy of it; and then with a sudden revulsion she stopped playing, and threw herself down listlessly by the open window.[110] Close by against the wall was a little looking-glass, by which she often arranged her ruffled locks; she glanced at it now, it showed her a brilliant face enough, but drooping lips, and eyes darkened with the extravagant melancholy of eighteen.

'It is come to a pretty pass,' she said to herself, 'that I should be able to think of nothing but schemes for getting Catherine married and out of my way! Considering what she is and what I am, and how she has slaved for us all her life, I seem to have descended pretty low. Heigh ho!'

---

108 Richard Wagner (1813-83), German composer of such operas as *The Ring* cycle and *Tristan and Isolde*; Johannes Brahms (1833-97), German composer.

109 "[T]his warm kind world," from William Johnson Cory, "Mimnermus in Church" (1858).

110 Brahms' *Neue Liebesliederwalzer*, or "New Love Songs," composed 1869–73.

And with a portentous sigh she dropped her chin on her hand. She was half acting, acting to herself. Life was not really quite unbearable, and she knew it. But it relieved her to overdo it.

'I wonder how much chance there is,' she mused presently. 'Mr. Elsmere will soon be ridiculous. Why, *I* saw him gather up those violets she threw away yesterday on Moor Crag. And as for her, I don't believe she has realised the situation a bit. At least, if she has, she is as unlike other mortals in this as in everything else. But when she does——'

She frowned and meditated, but got no light on the problem. Chattie jumped up on the window-sill, with her usual stealthy *aplomb*, and rubbed herself against the girl's face.

'Oh, Chattie!' cried Rose, throwing her arms round the cat, 'if Catherine 'll *only* marry Mr. Elsmere, my dear, and be happy ever afterwards, and set me free to live my own life a bit, I'll be *so* good, you won't know me, Chattie. And you shall have a new collar, my beauty, and cream till you die of it!'

And springing up she dragged in the cat, and snatching a scarlet anemone from a bunch on the table, stood opposite Chattie, who stood slowly waving her magnificent tail from side to side, and glaring as though it were not at all to her taste to be hustled and bustled in this way.

'Now, Chattie, listen! Will she?'

A leaf of the flower dropped on Chattie's nose.

'Won't she? Will she? Won't she? Will—— Tiresome flower, why did Nature give it such a beggarly few petals? If I'd had a daisy it would have all come right. Come, Chattie, waltz; and let's forget this wicked world!'

And, snatching up her violin, the girl broke into a Strauss waltz, dancing to it the while, her cotton skirts flying, her pretty feet twinkling, till her eyes glowed, and her cheeks blazed with a double intoxication—the intoxication of movement, and the intoxication of sound—the cat meanwhile following her with little mincing perplexed steps, as though not knowing what to make of her.

'Rose, you madcap!' cried Agnes, opening the door.

'Not at all, my dear,' said Rose calmly, stopping to take breath. 'Excellent practice and uncommonly difficult. Try if you can do it, and see!'

The weather held up in a gray grudging sort of way, and Mrs. Thornburgh especially was all for braving the clouds and going on with the expedition. It was galling to her that she herself would have to be driven to Shanmoor behind the fat vicarage pony, while the others would be climbing the fells, and all sorts of exciting things might be happening. Still it was infinitely better to be half in it than not in it at all, and she started by the side of the vicarage 'man' in a most delicious flutter. The skies might fall any day now. Elsmere had not confided in her, though she was unable to count the openings she had given him thereto. For one of the frankest of men he had kept his secret, so far as words went, with a remarkable tenacity. Probably the neighbourhood of Mrs. Thornburgh was enough to make the veriest chatterbox secretive. But notwithstanding, no one possessing the clue could live in the same house with him these June days without seeing that the whole man was absorbed, transformed, and that the crisis might be reached at any moment. Even the vicar was eager and watchful, and playing up to his wife in fine style, and if the situation had so worked on the vicar, Mrs. Thornburgh's state is easier imagined than described.

The walk to Shanmoor need not be chronicled. The party kept together. Robert fancied sometimes that there was a certain note of purpose in the way in which Catherine clung to the vicar. If so it did not disquiet him. Never had she been kinder, more gentle. Nay, as the walk went on a lovely gaiety broke through her tranquil manner, as though she, like the others, had caught exhilaration from the sharpened breeze and the towering mountains, restored to all their grandeur by the storm clouds.

And yet she had started in some little inward trouble. She had promised to join this walk to Shanmoor, she had promised to go with the others on a picnic the following day, but her conscience was pricking her. Twice this last fortnight had she been forced to give up a night-school she held in a little lonely hamlet among the fells, because even *she* had been too tired to walk there and back after a day of physical exertion. Were not the world and the flesh encroaching? She had been conscious of a strange inner restlessness as they all stood waiting in the road for the vicar and Elsmere. Agnes had thought her looking depressed and pale, and even dreamt for a moment of suggesting to her to stay at home. And then ten minutes after they had started it had all gone, her depression, blown away by the winds,—or charmed away by a happy voice, a manly presence, a keen responsive eye?

Elsmere, indeed, was gaiety itself. He kept up an incessant war with Rose; he had a number of little jokes going at the vicar's expense, which kept that good man in a half-protesting chuckle most of the way; he cleared every gate that presented itself in first-rate Oxford form, and climbed every point of rock with a cat-like agility that set the girls scoffing at the pretence of invalid-ism under which he had foisted himself on Whindale.

'How fine all this black purple is!' he cried, as they topped the ridge, and the Shanmoor valley lay before them, bounded on the other side by line after line of mountain, Wetherlam and the Pikes and Fairfield in the far distance, piled sombrely under a sombre sky. 'I had grown quite tired of the sun. He had done his best to make you commonplace.'

'Tired of the sun in Westmoreland?' said Catherine, with a little mocking wonder. 'How wanton, how prodigal!'

'Does it deserve a Nemesis?' he said, laughing. 'Drowning from now till I depart? No matter. I can bear a second deluge with an even mind. On this enchanted soil all things are welcome!'

She looked up, smiling, at his vehemence, taking it all as a tribute to the country, or to his own recovered health. He stood leaning on his stick, gazing, however, not at the view but at her. The others stood a little way off laughing and chattering. As their eyes met, a strange new pulse leapt up in Catherine.

'The wind is very boisterous here,' she said, with a shiver. 'I think we ought to be going on.'

And she hurried up to the others, nor did she leave their shelter till they were in sight of the little Shanmoor inn, where they were to have tea. The pony carriage was already standing in front of the inn, and Mrs. Thornburgh's gray curls shaking at the window.

'William!' she shouted, 'bring them in. Tea is just ready, and Mr. Ruskin was here last week, and there are ever so many new names in the visitors' book!'[111]

While the girls went in Elsmere stood looking a moment at the inn, the bridge, and the village. It was a characteristic Westmoreland scene. The low whitewashed inn, with its newly painted signboard, was to his right, the pony at the door lazily flicking off the flies and dropping its greedy nose in search of the grains of corn among the cobbles; to his left a gray stone bridge over a broad light-filled river; beyond, a little huddled village backed by and apparently built out of the great slate quarry which represented the only industry of the neighbourhood, and a tiny towered church—the scene on the Sabbath of Mr. Mayhew's ministrations. Beyond the village, shoulders of purple fell, and behind the inn masses of broken crag rising at the very head of the valley into a fine pike, along whose jagged edges the rain-clouds were trailing. There was a little lurid storm-light on the river, but, in general, the colour was all dark and rich, the white inn gleaming on a green and purple background. He took it all into his heart, covetously, greedily, trying to fix it there for ever.

Presently he was called in by the vicar, and found a tempting tea spread in a light upper room, where Agnes and Rose were already making fun of

---

111 John Ruskin (1819–1900), art and cultural critic, whose works included *The Stones of Venice* (1851–53) and *Modern Painters* (1843).

the chromo-lithographs and rummaging the visitors' book. The scrambling, chattering meal passed like a flash. At the beginning of it Mrs. Thornburgh's small gray eyes had travelled restlessly from face to face, as though to say, 'What—*no* news yet? Nothing happened?' As for Elsmere, though it seemed to him at the time one of the brightest moments of existence, he remembered little afterwards but the scene: the peculiar clean mustiness of the room only just opened for the summer season, a print of the Princess of Wales on the wall opposite him, a stuffed fox over the mantelpiece, Rose's golden head and heavy amber necklace, and the figure at the vicar's right, in a gown of a little dark blue check, the broad hat shading the white brow and luminous eyes.

When tea was over they lounged out on the bridge. There was to be no long lingering, however. The clouds were deepening, the rain could not be far off. But if they started soon they could probably reach home before it came down. Elsmere and Rose hung over the gray stone parapet, mottled with the green and gold of innumerable mosses, and looked down through a fringe of English maidenhair growing along the coping, into the clear eddies of the stream. Suddenly he raised himself on one elbow, and, shading his eyes, looked to where the vicar and Catherine were standing in front of the inn, touched for an instant by a beam of fitful light slipping between two great rain-clouds.

'How well that hat and dress become your sister!' he said, the words breaking, as it were, from his lips.

'Do you think Catherine pretty?' said Rose with an excellent pretence of innocence, detaching a little pebble and flinging it harmlessly at a water-wagtail balancing on a stone below.

He flushed. 'Pretty! You might as well apply the word to your mountains, to the exquisite river, to that great purple peak!'

'Yes,' thought Rose, 'she is not unlike that high cold peak!' But her girlish sympathy conquered her; it was very exciting, and she liked Elsmere. She turned back to him, her face overspread with a quite irrepressible smile. He reddened still more, then they stared into each other's eyes, and without a word more understood each other perfectly.

Rose held out her hand to him with a little brusque *bon camarade* gesture. He pressed it warmly in his.

'That was nice of you!' he cried. 'Very nice of you! Friends then?'

She nodded, and drew her hand away just as Agnes and the vicar disturbed them.

Meanwhile Catherine was standing by the side of the pony carriage, watching Mrs. Thornburgh's preparations.

'You're sure you don't mind driving home alone?' she said in a troubled voice. 'Mayn't I go with you?'

'My dear, certainly not! As if I wasn't accustomed to going about alone at my time of life! No, no, my dear, you go and have your walk; you'll get home before the rain. Ready, James.'

The old vicarage factotum could not imagine what made his charge so anxious to be off. She actually took the whip out of his hand and gave a flick to the pony, who swerved and started off in a way which would have made his mistress clamorously nervous under any other circumstances. Catherine stood looking after her.

'Now, then, right about face and quick march!' exclaimed the vicar. 'We've got to race that cloud over the Pike. It'll be up with us in no time.'

Off they started, and were soon climbing the slippery green slopes, or crushing through the fern of the fell they had descended earlier in the afternoon. Catherine for some little way walked last of the party, the vicar in front of her. Then Elsmere picked a stonecrop, quarrelled over its precise name with Rose, and waited for Catherine, who had a very close and familiar knowledge of the botany of the district.

'You have crushed me,' he said, laughing, as he put the flower carefully into his pocket-book; 'but it is worth while to be crushed by any one who can give so much ground for their knowledge. How you do know your mountains—from their peasants to their plants!'

'I have had more than ten able-bodied years living and scrambling among them,' she said, smiling.

'Do you keep up all your visits and teaching in the winter?'

'Oh, not so much, of course! But people must be helped and taught in the winter. And our winter is often not as hard as yours down south.'

'Do you go on with that night-school in Poll Ghyll, for instance?' he said, with another note in his voice.

Catherine looked at him and coloured. 'Rose has been telling tales,' she said. 'I wish she would leave my proceedings alone. Poll Ghyll is the family bone of contention at present. Yes, I go on with it. I always take a lantern when the night is dark, and I know every inch of the ground, and Bob is always with me; aren't you, Bob?'

And she stooped down to pat the collie beside her. Bob looked up at her, blinking with a proudly confidential air as though to remind her that there were a good many such secrets between them.

'I like to fancy you with your lantern in the dark,' he cried, the hidden emotion piercing through, 'the night wind blowing about you, the black

mountains to right and left of you, some little stream, perhaps, running beside you for company, your dog guarding you, and all good angels going with
you.'

She flushed still more deeply; the impetuous words affected her strangely.

'Don't fancy it at all,' she said, laughing. 'It is a very small and very natural incident of one's life here. Look back, Mr. Elsmere; the rain has beaten us!'

He looked back and saw the great Pike over Shanmoor village blotted
out in a moving deluge of rain. The quarry opposite on the mountain side
gleamed green and vivid against the ink-black fell; some clothes hanging out
in the field below the church flapped wildly hither and thither in the sudden
gale, the only spot of white in the prevailing blackness; children with their
petticoats over their heads ran homewards along the road the walking party
had just quitted; the stream beneath, spreading broadly through the fields,
shivered and wrinkled under the blast. Up it came, and the rain mists with it.
In another minute the storm was beating in their faces.

'Caught!' cried Elsmere, in a voice almost of jubilation. 'Let me help you
into your cloak, Miss Leyburn.'

He flung it round her, and struggled into his own mackintosh. The vicar
in front of them turned and waved his hand to them in laughing despair, then
hurried after the others, evidently with the view of performing for them the
same office Elsmere had just performed for Catherine.

Robert and his companion struggled on for a while in a breathless silence
against the deluge, which seemed to beat on them from all sides. He walked
behind her, sheltering her by his tall form and his big umbrella as much as
he could. His pulses were all aglow with the joy of the storm. It seemed to
him that he rejoiced with the thirsty grass over which the rain streams were
running, that his heart filled with the shrunken becks as the flood leapt along
them. Let the elements thunder and rave as they pleased. Could he not at a
word bring the light of that face, those eyes, upon him? Was she not his for a
moment in the rain and the solitude, as she had never been in the commonplace sunshine of their valley life?

Suddenly he heard an exclamation, and saw her run on in front of him.
What was the matter? Then he noticed for the first time that Rose, far ahead,
was still walking in her cotton dress. The little scatterbrain had, of course, forgotten her cloak. But, monstrous! There was Catherine stripping off her own,
Rose refusing it. In vain. The sister's determined arms put it round her. Rose
is enwrapped, buttoned up before she knows where she is, and Catherine falls
back, pursued by some shaft from Rose, more sarcastic than grateful, to judge
by the tone of it.

'Miss Leyburn, what have you been doing?'

'Rose had forgotten her cloak,' she said briefly. 'She has a very thin dress on, and she is the only one of us that takes cold easily.'

'You must take my mackintosh,' he said at once.

She laughed in his face.

'As if I should do anything of the sort!'

'You must,' he said, quietly stripping it off. 'Do you think that you are always to be allowed to go through the world taking thought of other people and allowing no one to take thought for you?'

He held it out to her.

'No, no! This is absurd, Mr. Elsmere. You are not strong yet. And I have often told you that nothing hurts me.'

He hung it deliberately over his arm. 'Very well, then, there it stays!'

And they hurried on again, she biting her lip and on the point of laughter.

'Mr. Elsmere, be sensible!' she said presently, her look changing to one of real distress. 'I should never forgive myself if you got a chill after your illness!'

'You will not be called upon,' he said in the most matter-of-fact tone. 'Men's coats are made to keep out weather,' and he pointed to his own, closely buttoned up. 'Your dress—I can't help being disrespectful under the circumstances—will be wet through in ten minutes.'

Another silence. Then he overtook her.

'Please, Miss Leyburn,' he said, stopping her.

There was an instant's mute contest between them. The rain splashed on the umbrellas. She could not help it, she broke down into the merriest, most musical laugh of a child that can hardly stop itself, and he joined.

'Mr. Elsmere, you are ridiculous!'

But she submitted. He put the mackintosh round her, thinking, bold man, as she turned her rosy rain-dewed face to him, of Wordsworth's 'Louisa,' and the poet's cry of longing.[112]

And yet he was not so bold either. Even at this moment of exhilaration he was conscious of a bar that checked and arrested. Something—what was it?— drew invisible lines of defence about her. A sort of divine fear of her mingled with his rising passion. Let him not risk too much too soon.

They walked on briskly, and were soon on the Whindale side of the pass. To the left of them the great hollow of High Fell unfolded, storm-beaten and dark, the river issuing from the heart of it like an angry voice.

---

112 In particular, the poem's last stanza: "Take all that's mine beneath the moon,/ If I with her but half a noon/May sit beneath the walls/Of some old cave, or mossy nook,/When up she winds along the brook,/To hunt the waterfalls."

'What a change!' he said, coming up with her as the path widened. 'How impossible that it should have been only yesterday afternoon I was lounging up here in the heat, by the pool where the stream rises, watching the white butterflies on the turf, and reading "Laodamia"!'[113]

'"Laodamia"!' she said, half sighing as she caught the name. 'Is it one of those you like best?'

'Yes,' he said, bending forward that he might see her in spite of the umbrella. 'How superb it is—the roll, the majesty of it; the severe chastened beauty of the main feeling, the individual lines!'

And he quoted line after line, lingering over the cadences.

'It was my father's favourite of all,' she said, in the low vibrating voice of memory. 'He said the last verse to me the day before he died.'

Robert recalled it—

> 'Yet tears to human suffering are due,
> And mortal hopes defeated and o'erthrown
> Are mourned by man, and not by man alone
> As fondly we believe.'

Poor Richard Leyburn! Yet where had the defeat lain?

'Was he happy in his school life?' he asked gently. 'Was teaching what he liked?'

'Oh yes—only—' Catherine paused and then added hurriedly, as though drawn on in spite of herself by the grave sympathy of his look, 'I never knew anybody so good who thought himself of so little account. He always believed that he had missed everything, wasted everything, and that anybody else would have made infinitely more out of his life. He was always blaming, scourging himself. And all the time he was the noblest, purest, most devoted——'

She stopped. Her voice had passed beyond her control. Elsmere was startled by the feeling she showed. Evidently he had touched one of the few sore places in this pure heart. It was as though her memory of her father had in it elements of almost intolerable pathos, as though the child's brooding love and loyalty were in perpetual protest, even now after this lapse of years, against the verdict which an over-scrupulous, despondent soul had pronounced upon itself. Did she feel that he had gone uncomforted out of life—even by her— even by religion?—was that the sting?

---

113 Another poem by Wordsworth, in which the spirit of Protesilaus rebukes his wife for calling him back from the dead. The lines that follow are a slight misquotation of the opening of the final stanza.

'Oh, I can understand!' he said reverently—'I can understand. I have come across it once or twice, that fierce self-judgment of the good. It is the most stirring and humbling thing in life.' Then his voice dropped. 'And after the last conflict—the last "quailing breath"—the last onslaughts of doubt or fear—think of the Vision waiting—the Eternal Comfort—

> "'Oh, my only Light!
>   It cannot be
>   That I am he
> On whom Thy tempests fell all night!"'[114]

The words fell from the softened voice like noble music.

There was a pause. Then Catherine raised her eyes to his. They swam in tears, and yet the unspoken thanks in them were radiance itself. It seemed to him as though she came closer to him like a child to an elder who has soothed and satisfied an inward smart.

They walked on in silence. They were just nearing the swollen river which roared below them. On the opposite bank two umbrellas were vanishing through the field gate into the road, but the vicar had turned and was waiting for them. They could see his becloaked figure leaning on his stick through the light wreaths of mist that floated above the tumbling stream. The abnormally heavy rain had ceased, but the clouds seemed to be dragging along the very floor of the valley.

The stepping-stones came into sight. He leaped on the first and held out his hand to her. When they started she would have refused his help with scorn. Now, after a moment's hesitation she yielded, and he felt her dear weight on him as he guided her carefully from stone to stone. In reality it is both difficult and risky to be helped over stepping-stones. You had much better manage for yourself; and half way through Catherine had a mind to tell him so. But the words died on her lips which smiled instead. He could have wished that passage from stone to stone could have lasted for ever. She was wrapped up grotesquely in his mackintosh; her hat was all bedraggled; her gloves dripped in his; and in spite of all he could have vowed that anything so lovely as that delicately cut, gravely smiling face, swaying above the rushing brown water, was never seen in Westmoreland wilds before.

'It is clearing,' he cried, with ready optimism, as they reached the bank. 'We shall get our picnic to-morrow after all—we *must* get it! Promise me it shall be fine—and you will be there!'

The vicar was only fifty yards away waiting for them against the field gate.

---

114 George Herbert, "The Flower."

But Robert held her eagerly, imperiously,—and it seemed to her, her head was still dizzy with the water.

'Promise!' he repeated, his voice dropping.

She could not stop to think of the absurdity of promising for Westmoreland weather. She could only say faintly 'Yes!' and so release her hand.

'You *are* pretty wet!' said the vicar, looking from one to the other with a curiosity which Robert's quick sense divined at once was directed to something else than the mere condition of their garments. But Catherine noticed nothing; she walked on wrestling blindly with she knew not what till they reached the vicarage gate. There stood Mrs. Thornburgh, the light drizzle into which the rain had declined beating unheeded on her curls and ample shoulders. She stared at Robert's drenched condition, but he gave her no time to make remarks.

'Don't take it off,' he said with a laughing wave of the hand to Catherine; 'I will come for it to-morrow morning.'

And he ran up the drive, conscious at last that it might be prudent to get himself into something less spongelike than his present attire as quickly as possible.

The vicar followed him.

'Don't keep Catherine, my dear. There's nothing to tell. Nobody's the worse.'

Mrs. Thornburgh took no heed. Opening the iron gate she went through it on to the deserted rain-beaten road, laid both her hands on Catherine's shoulders, and looked her straight in the eyes. The vicar's anxious hint was useless. She could contain herself no longer. She had watched them from the vicarage come down the fell together, had seen them cross the stepping stones, lingeringly, hand in hand.

'My dear Catherine!' she cried, effusively kissing Catherine's glowing cheek under the shelter of the laurustinus that made a bower of the gate. 'My *dear* Catherine!'

Catherine gazed at her in astonishment. Mrs. Thornburgh's eyes were all alive, and swarming with questions. If it had been Rose she would have let them out in one fell flight. But Catherine's personality kept her in awe. And after a second, as the two stood together, a deep flush rose on Catherine's face, and an expression of half-frightened apology dawned in Mrs. Thornburgh's.

Catherine drew herself away. 'Will you please give Mr. Elsmere his mackintosh?' she said, taking it off; 'I shan't want it this little way.'

And putting it on Mrs. Thornburgh's arm she turned away, walking quickly round the bend of the road.

Mrs. Thornburgh watched her open-mouthed, and moved slowly back to the house in a state of complete collapse.

'I always knew'—she said with a groan—'I always knew it would never go right if it was Catherine! *Why* was it Catherine?'

And she went in, still hurling at Providence the same vindictive query.

Meanwhile Catherine, hurrying home, the receding flush leaving a sudden pallor behind it, was twisting her hands before her in a kind of agony.

'What have I been doing?' she said to herself. 'What have I been doing?'

At the gate of Burwood something made her look up. She saw the girls in their own room—Agnes was standing behind, Rose had evidently rushed forward to see Catherine come in, and now retreated as suddenly when she saw her sister look up.

Catherine understood it all in an instant. 'They, too, are on the watch,' she thought to herself bitterly. The strong reticent nature was outraged by the perception that she had been for days the unconscious actor in a drama of which her sisters and Mrs. Thornburgh had been the silent and intelligent spectators.

She came down presently from her room very white and quiet, admitted that she was tired, and said nothing to anybody. Agnes and Rose noticed the change at once, whispered to each other when they found an opportunity, and foreboded ill.

After their tea-supper, Catherine, unperceived, slipped out of the little lane gate, and climbed the stony path above the house leading on to the fell. The rain had ceased, but the clouds hung low and threatening, and the close air was saturated with moisture. As she gained the bare fell, sounds of water met her on all sides. The river cried hoarsely to her from below, the becks in the little ghylls were full and thunderous; and beside her over the smooth grass slid many a new-born rivulet, the child of the storm, and destined to vanish with the night. Catherine's soul went out to welcome the gray damp of the hills. She knew them best in this mood. They were thus most her own.

She climbed on till at last she reached the crest of the ridge. Behind her lay the valley, and on its further side the fells she had crossed in the afternoon. Before her spread a long green vale, compared to which Whindale with its white road, its church, and parsonage, and scattered houses, was the great world itself. Marrisdale had no road and not a single house. As Catherine descended into it she saw not a sign of human life. There were sheep grazing in the silence of the long June twilight; the blackish walls ran down and up again, dividing the green hollow with melancholy uniformity. Here and there was a sheepfold, suggesting the bleakness of winter nights; and here and

there a rough stone barn for storing fodder. And beyond the vale, eastwards
and northwards, Catherine looked out upon a wild sea of moors wrapped in
mists, sullen and storm-beaten, while to the left the clouds hung deepest and
inkiest over the high points of the Ullswater mountains.

When she was once below the pass, man and his world were shut out. The
girl figure in the blue cloak and hood was absolutely alone. She descended till
she reached a point where a little stream had been turned into a stone trough
for cattle. Above it stood a gnarled and solitary thorn. Catherine sank down
on a rock at the foot of the tree. It was a seat she knew well; she had lingered
there with her father; she had thought and prayed there as girl and woman;
she had wrestled there often with despondency or grief, or some of those
subtle spiritual temptations which were all her pure youth had known, till the
inner light had dawned again, and the humble enraptured soul could almost
have traced amid the shadows of that dappled moorland world, between her
and the clouds, the white stoles and 'sleeping wings' of ministering spirits.

But no wrestle had ever been so hard as this. And with what fierce suddenness had it come upon her! She looked back over the day with bewilderment. She could see dimly that the Catherine who had started on that
Shanmoor walk had been full of vague misgivings other than those concerned
with a few neglected duties. There had been an undefined sense of unrest, of
difference, of broken equilibrium. She had shown it in the way in which at
first she had tried to keep herself and Robert Elsmere apart.

And then; beyond the departure from Shanmoor she seemed to lose the
thread of her own history. Memory was drowned in a feeling to which the
resisting soul as yet would give no name. She laid her head on her knees
trembling. She heard again the sweet imperious tones with which he broke
down her opposition about the cloak; she felt again the grasp of his steadying
hand on hers.

But it was only for a very few minutes that she drifted thus. She raised
her head again, scourging herself in shame and self-reproach, recapturing the
empire of the soul with a strong effort. She set herself to a stern analysis of the
whole situation. Clearly Mrs. Thornburgh and her sisters had been aware for
some indefinite time that Mr. Elsmere had been showing a peculiar interest
in her. *Their* eyes had been open. She realised now with hot cheeks how many
meetings and *tête-à-têtes* had been managed for her and Elsmere, and how
complacently she had fallen into Mrs. Thornburgh's snares.

'Have I encouraged him?' she asked herself sternly.

'Yes,' cried the smarting conscience.

'Can I marry him?'

'No,' said conscience again; 'not without deserting your post, not without betraying your trust.'

What post? What trust? Ah, conscience was ready enough with the answer. Was it not just ten years since, as a girl of sixteen, prematurely old and thoughtful, she had sat beside her father's deathbed, while her delicate hysterical mother, in a state of utter collapse, was kept away from him by the doctors? She could see the drawn face, the restless melancholy eyes. 'Catherine, my darling, you are the strong one. They will look to you. Support them.' And she could see in imagination her own young face pressed against the pillows. 'Yes, father, always—always!'—'Catherine, life is harder, the narrow way narrower than ever. I die'—and memory caught still the piteous, long-drawn breath by which the voice was broken—'in much—much perplexity about many things. You have a clear soul, an iron will. Strengthen the others. Bring them safe to the day of account.'—'Yes, father, with God's help. Oh, with God's help!'

That long-past dialogue is clear and sharp to her now, as though it were spoken afresh in her ears. And how has she kept her pledge? She looks back humbly on her life of incessant devotion, on the tie of long dependence which has bound to her her weak and widowed mother, on her relations to her sisters, the efforts she has made to train them in the spirit of her father's life and beliefs.

Have those efforts reached their term? Can it be said in any sense that her work is done, her promise kept?

Oh, no—no! she cries to herself with vehemence. Her mother depends on her every day and hour for protection, comfort, enjoyment. The girls are at the opening of life,—Agnes twenty, Rose eighteen, with all experience to come. And Rose—— Ah! at the thought of Rose, Catherine's heart sinks deeper and deeper—she feels a culprit before her father's memory. What is it has gone so desperately wrong with her training of the child? Surely she has given love enough, anxious thought enough, and here is Rose only fighting to be free from the yoke of her father's wishes, from the galling pressure of the family tradition!

No. Her task has just now reached its most difficult, its most critical, moment. How can she leave it? Impossible.

What claim can she put against these supreme claims—of her promise, her mother's and sisters' need?

His claim? Oh, no—no! She admits with soreness and humiliation unspeakable that she has done him wrong. If he loves her she has opened the way thereto; she confesses in her scrupulous honesty that when the inevitable withdrawal comes she will have given him cause to think of her hardly, slightingly. She flinches painfully under the thought. But it does not alter the matter. This girl, brought up in the austerest school of Christian self-government, knows nothing of the divine rights of passion. Half modern literature is based upon them. Catherine Leyburn knew of no supreme right but the right of God to the obedience of man.

Oh, and besides—besides—it is impossible that he should care so very much. The time is so short—there is so little in her, comparatively, to attract a man of such resource, such attainments, such access to the best things of life.

She cannot—in a kind of terror—she *will* not, believe in her own love-worthiness, in her own power to deal a lasting wound.

Then her *own* claim? Has she any claim, has the poor bounding heart that she cannot silence, do what she will, through all this strenuous debate, no claim to satisfaction, to joy?

She locks her hands round her knees, conscious, poor soul, that the worst struggle is *here*, the quickest agony *here*. But she does not waver for an instant. And her weapons are all ready. The inmost soul of her is a fortress well stored, whence at any moment the mere personal craving of the natural man can be met, repulsed, slain.

'*Man approacheth so much the nearer unto God the farther he departeth from all earthly comfort.*'

'*If thou couldst perfectly annihilate thyself and empty thyself of all created love, then should I be constrained to flow into thee with greater abundance of grace.*'

'*When thou lookest unto the creature the sight of the Creator is withdrawn from thee.*'

'*Learn in all things to overcome thyself for the love of thy Creator....*'[115]

She presses the sentence she has so often meditated in her long solitary walks about the mountains into her heart. And one fragment of George Herbert especially rings in her ears, solemnly, funereally—

'Thy Saviour sentenced joy!'[116]

Ay, sentenced it for ever—the personal craving, the selfish need, that must be filled at any cost. In the silence of the descending night Catherine quietly, with tears, carried out that sentence, and slew her young new-born joy at the feet of the Master.

---

115 From *The Imitation of Christ*, ch. 42.
116 Herbert, "The Size."

She stayed where she was for a while after this crisis in a kind of bewilderment and stupor, but maintaining a perfect outward tranquillity. Then there was a curious little epilogue.

'It is all over,' she said to herself tenderly. 'But he has taught me so much—he has been so good to me—he is so good! Let me take to my heart some counsel—some word of his, and obey it sacredly—silently—for these days' sake.'

Then she fell thinking again, and she remembered their talk about Rose. How often she had pondered it since! In this intense trance of feeling it breaks upon her finally that he is right. May it not be that he with his clearer thought, his wider knowledge of life, has laid his finger on the weak point in her guardianship of her sisters? 'I have tried to stifle her passion,' she thought, 'to push it out of the way as a hindrance. Ought I not rather to have taught her to make of it a step in the ladder—to have moved her to bring her gifts to the altar? Oh, let me take his word for it—be ruled by him in this one thing, once!'

She bowed her face on her knees again. It seemed to her that she had thrown herself at Elsmere's feet, that her cheek was pressed against that young brown hand of his. How long the moment lasted she never knew. When at last she rose stiff and weary, darkness was overtaking even the lingering northern twilight. The angry clouds had dropped lower on the moors; a few sheep beside the glimmering stone trough showed dimly white; the night wind was sighing through the untenanted valley and the scanty branches of the thorn. White mists lay along the hollow of the dale; they moved weirdly under the breeze. She could have fancied them a troop of wraiths to whom she had flung her warm crushed heart, and who were bearing it away to burial.

As she came slowly over the pass and down the Whindale side of the fell a clear purpose was in her mind. Agnes had talked to her only that morning of Rose and Rose's desire, and she had received the news with her habitual silence.

The house was lit up when she returned. Her mother had gone upstairs. Catherine went to her, but even Mrs. Leyburn discovered that she looked worn out, and she was sent off to bed. She went along the passage quickly to Rose's room, listening a moment at the door. Yes, Rose was inside, crooning some German song, and apparently alone. She knocked and went in.

Rose was sitting on the edge of her bed, a white dressing-gown over her shoulders, her hair in a glorious confusion all about her. She was swaying backwards and forwards dreamily singing, and she started up when she saw Catherine.

'Röschen,' said the elder sister, going up to her with a tremor of heart, and putting her motherly arms round the curly golden hair and the half-covered shoulders, 'you never told me of that letter from Manchester, but Agnes did. Did you think, Röschen, I would never let you have your way? Oh, I am not so hard! I may have been wrong—I think I have been wrong; you shall do what you will, Röschen. If you want to go, I will ask mother.'

Rose, pushing herself away with one hand, stood staring. She was struck dumb by this sudden breaking down of Catherine's long resistance. And what a strange white Catherine! What did it mean? Catherine withdrew her arms with a little sigh and moved away.

'I just came to tell you that, Röschen,' she said, 'but I am very tired and must not stay.'

Catherine 'very tired'! Rose thought the skies must be falling.

'Cathie!' she cried, leaping forward just as her sister gained the door. 'Oh, Cathie, you are an angel, and I am a nasty, odious little wretch. But oh, tell me, what is the matter?'

And she flung her strong young arms round Catherine with a passionate strength.

The elder sister struggled to release herself.

'Let me go, Rose,' she said in a low voice. 'Oh, you *must* let me go!'

And wrenching herself free, she drew her hand over her eyes as though trying to drive away the mist from them.

'Good-night! Sleep well.'

And she disappeared, shutting the door noiselessly after her. Rose stood staring a moment, and then swept off her feet by a flood of many feelings—remorse, love, fear, sympathy—threw herself face downwards on her bed and burst into a passion of tears.

CHAPTER VIII

Catherine was much perplexed as to how she was to carry out her resolution; she pondered over it through much of the night. She was painfully anxious to make Elsmere understand without a scene, without a definite proposal and a definite rejection. It was no use letting things drift. Something brusque and marked there must be. She quietly made her dispositions.

It was long after the gray vaporous morning stole on the hills before she fell lightly, restlessly asleep. To her healthful youth a sleepless night was almost unknown. She wondered through the long hours of it, whether now, like other women, she had had her story, passed through her one supreme moment, and she thought of one or two worthy old maids she knew in the neighbourhood with a new and curious pity. Had any of them, too, gone down into Marrisdale and come up widowed indeed?[117]

All through, no doubt, there was a certain melancholy pride in her own spiritual strength. 'It was not mine,' she would have said with perfect sincerity, 'but God's.' Still, whatever its source, it had been there at command, and the reflection carried with it a sad sense of security. It was as though a soldier after his first skirmish should congratulate himself on being bullet-proof.

To be sure, there was an intense trouble and disquiet in the thought that she and Mr. Elsmere must meet again, probably many times. The period of his original invitation had been warmly extended by the Thornburghs. She believed he meant to stay another week or ten days in the valley. But in the spiritual exaltation of the night she felt herself equal to any conflict, any endurance, and she fell asleep, the hands clasped on her breast expressing a kind of resolute patience, like those of some old sepulchral monument.

The following morning Elsmere examined the clouds and the barometer with abnormal interest. The day was sunless and lowering, but not raining, and he represented to Mrs. Thornburgh, with a hypocritical assumption of the practical man, that with rugs and mackintoshes it was possible to picnic on the dampest grass. But he could not make out the vicar's wife. She was all sighs and flightiness. She 'supposed they could go,' and 'didn't see what good it would do them'; she had twenty different views, and all of them more or less mixed up with pettishness, as to the best place for a picnic on a gray day; and at last she grew so difficult that Robert suspected something desperately wrong with the household, and withdrew lest male guests might be in the way. Then she pursued him into the study and thrust a *Spectator* into his hands, begging him to convey it to Burwood.[118] She asked it lugubriously with many sighs, her cap much askew. Robert could have kissed her, curls and all, one moment for suggesting the errand, and the next could almost have signed her committal to the county lunatic asylum with a clear conscience. What an extraordinary person it was!

Off he went, however, with his *Spectator* under his arm, whistling. Mrs. Thornburgh caught the sounds through an open window, and tore the flannel across she was preparing for a mothers' meeting with a noise like the rattle of musketry. Whistling! She would like to know what grounds he had for it, indeed! She always knew—she always said, and she would go on saying—that

---

117 1 Timothy 5.5.
118 One of the three major weekly reviews of the period, founded in 1828.

Catherine Leyburn would die an old maid.

Meanwhile Robert had strolled across to Burwood with the lightest heart. By way of keeping all his anticipations within the bounds of strict reason, he told himself that it was impossible he should see 'her' in the morning. She was always busy in the morning.

He approached the house as a Catholic might approach a shrine. That was her window, that upper casement with the little Banksia rose twining round it. One night, when he and the vicar had been out late on the hills, he had seen a light streaming from it across the valley, and had thought how the mistress of the maiden solitude within shone 'in a naughty world.'[119]

In the drive he met Mrs. Leyburn, who was strolling about the garden. She at once informed him with much languid plaintiveness that Catherine had gone to Whinborough for the day, and would not be able to join the picnic.

Elsmere stood still.

'*Gone!*' he cried. 'But it was all arranged with her yesterday!' Mrs. Leyburn shrugged her shoulders. She too was evidently much put out.

'So I told her. But you know, Mr. Elsmere'—and the gentle widow dropped her voice as though communicating a secret—'when Catherine's once made up her mind, you may as well try to dig away High Fell as move her. She asked me to tell Mrs. Thornburgh—will you, please?—that she found it was her day for the orphan asylum, and one or two other pieces of business, and she must go.'

'*Mrs. Thornburgh!*' And not a word for him—for *him* to whom she had given her promise? She had gone to Whinborough to avoid him, and she had gone in the brusquest way, that it might be unmistakable.

The young man stood with his hands thrust into the pockets of his long coat, hearing with half an ear the remarks that Mrs. Leyburn was making to him about the picnic. Was the wretched thing to come off after all?

He was too proud and sore to suggest an alternative. But Mrs. Thornburgh managed that for him. When he got back, he told the vicar in the hall of Miss Leyburn's flight in the fewest possible words, and then his long legs vanished up the stairs in a twinkling, and the door of his room shut behind him. A few minutes afterwards Mrs. Thornburgh's shrill voice was heard in the hall calling to the servant.

'Sarah, let the hamper alone. Take out the chickens.'

And a minute after the vicar came up to his door.

'Elsmere, Mrs. Thornburgh thinks the day is too uncertain; better put it

---

119 William Shakespeare, *The Merchant of Venice*, 5.1.

off.'

To which Elsmere from inside replied with a vigorous assent. The vicar slowly descended to tackle his spouse, who seemed to have established herself for the morning in his sanctum, though the parish accounts were clamouring to be done, and this morning in the week belonged to them by immemorial usage.

But Mrs. Thornburgh was unmanageable. She sat opposite to him with one hand on each knee, solemnly demanding of him if *he* knew what was to be done with young women nowadays, because *she* didn't.

The tormented vicar declined to be drawn into so illimitable a subject, recommended patience, declared that it might be all a mistake, and tried hard to absorb himself in the consideration of 2s. 8d. *plus* 2s. 11d. *minus* 9d.

'And I suppose, William,' said his wife to him at last, with withering sarcasm, 'that you'd sit by and see Catherine break that young man's heart, and send him back to his mother no better than he came here, in spite of all the beef-tea and jelly Sarah and I have been putting into him, and never lift a finger. You'd see his life *blasted* and you'd do nothing—nothing, I suppose.'

And she fixed him with a fiercely interrogative eye.

'Of course,' cried the vicar, roused; 'I should think so. What good did an outsider ever get by meddling in a love affair? Take care of yourself, Emma. If the girl doesn't care for him, you can't make her.'

The vicar's wife rose, the upturned corners of her mouth saying unutterable things.

'Doesn't care for him!' she echoed in a tone which implied that her husband's headpiece was past praying for.

'Yes, doesn't care for him!' said the vicar, nettled. 'What else should make her give him a snub like this?'

Mrs. Thornburgh looked at him again with exasperation. Then a curious expression stole into her eyes.

'Oh, the Lord only knows!' she said, with a hasty freedom of speech which left the vicar feeling decidedly uncomfortable as she shut the door after her.

However, if the Higher Powers alone *knew*, Mrs. Thornburgh was convinced that she could make a very shrewd guess at the causes of Catherine's behaviour. In her opinion it was all pure 'cussedness.' Catherine Leyburn had always conducted her life on principles entirely different from those of other people. Mrs. Thornburgh wholly denied, as she sat bridling by herself, that it was a Christian necessity to make yourself and other people uncomfortable.[120]

---

120 Possibly an allusion to George Eliot's clergyman Mr. Farebrother in *Middlemarch*

Yet this was what this perverse young woman was always doing. Here was a charming young man who had fallen in love with her at first sight, and had done his best to make the fact plain to her in the most chivalrous devoted ways. Catherine encourages him, walks with him, talks with him, is for a whole three weeks more gay and cheerful and more like other girls than she has ever been known to be, and then, at the end of it, just when everybody is breathlessly awaiting the natural *dénouement*, goes off to spend the day that should have been the day of her betrothal in pottering about orphan asylums, leaving everybody, but especially the poor young man, to look ridiculous! No, Mrs. Thornburgh had no patience with her—none at all. It was all because she would not be happy like anybody else, but must needs set herself up to be peculiar. Why not live on a pillar, and go into hair-shirts at once? Then the rest of the world would know what to be at.

Meanwhile Rose was in no small excitement. While her mother and Elsmere had been talking in the garden she had been discreetly waiting in the back behind the angle of the house, and when she saw Elsmere walk off she followed him with eager sympathetic eyes.

'Poor fellow!' she said to herself, but this time with the little tone of patronage which a girl of eighteen, conscious of graces and good looks, never shrinks from assuming towards an elder male, especially a male in love with some one else. 'I wonder whether he thinks he knows anything about Catherine.'

But her own feeling to-day was very soft and complex. Yesterday it had been all hot rebellion. To-day it was all remorse and wondering curiosity. What had brought Catherine into her room, with that white face, and that bewildering change of policy? What had made her do this brusque, discourteous thing to-day? Rose, having been delayed by the loss of one of her goloshes in a bog, had been once near her and Elsmere during that dripping descent from Shanmoor. They had been so clearly absorbed in one another that she had fled on guiltily to Agnes, golosh in hand, without waiting to put it on; confident, however, that neither Elsmere nor Catherine had been aware of her little adventure. And at the Shanmoor tea Catherine herself had discussed the picnic, offering, in fact, to guide the party to a particular ghyll in High Fell, better known to her than any one else.

'Oh, of course it's our salvation in this world and the next that's in the way,' thought Rose, sitting crouched up in a grassy nook in the garden, her

(1871–72), who doesn't like Mr. Bulstrode's Evangelical party because "they are a narrow, ignorant set, and do more to make their neighbors uncomfortable than to make them better" (ch. 17).

shoulders up to her ears, her chin in her hands. 'I wish to goodness Catherine wouldn't think so much about mine, at any rate. I hate,' added this incorrigible young person—'I hate being the third part of a "moral obstacle" against my will. I declare I don't believe we should any of us go to perdition even if Catherine did marry. And what a wretch I am to think so after last night! Oh dear, I wish she'd let me do something for her; I wish she'd ask me to black her boots for her, or put in her tuckers, or tidy her drawers for her, or anything worse still, and I'd do it and welcome!'

It was getting uncomfortably serious all round, Rose admitted. But there was one element of comedy besides Mrs. Thornburgh, and that was Mrs. Leyburn's unconsciousness.

'Mamma is too good,' thought the girl, with a little ripple of laughter. 'She takes it as a matter of course that all the world should admire us, and she'd scorn to believe that anybody did it from interested motives.'

Which was perfectly true. Mrs. Leyburn was too devoted to her daughters to feel any fidgety interest in their marrying. Of course the most eligible persons would be only too thankful to marry them when the moment came. Meanwhile her devotion was in no need of the confirming testimony of lovers. It was sufficient in itself, and kept her mind gently occupied from morning till night. If it had occurred to her to notice that Robert Elsmere had been paying special attentions to any one in the family, she would have suggested with perfect *naïveté* that it was herself. For he had been to her the very pink of courtesy and consideration, and she was of opinion that 'poor Richard's views' of the degeneracy of Oxford men would have been modified could he have seen this particular specimen.

Later on in the morning Rose had been out giving Bob a run, while Agnes drove with her mother. On the way home she overtook Elsmere returning from an errand for the vicar.

'It is not so bad,' she said to him, laughing, pointing to the sky; 'we really might have gone.'

'Oh, it would have been cheerless,' he said simply. His look of depression amazed her. She felt a quick movement of sympathy, a wild wish to bid him cheer up and fight it out. If she could just have shown him Catherine as she looked last night! Why couldn't she talk it out with him? Absurd conventions! She had half a mind to try.

But the grave look of the man beside her deterred even her young half-childish audacity.

'Catherine will have a good day for all her business,' she said carelessly.

He assented quietly. Oh, after that hand-shake on the bridge yesterday she could not stand it,—she must give him a hint how the land lay.

'I suppose she will spend the afternoon with Aunt Ellen. Mr. Elsmere, what did you think of Aunt Ellen?'

Elsmere started, and could not help smiling into the young girl's beautiful eyes, which were radiant with fun.

'A most estimable person,' he said. 'Are you on good terms with her, Miss Rose?'

'Oh dear, no!' she said, with a little face. 'I'm not a Leyburn; I wear æsthetic dresses, and Aunt Ellen has "special leadings of the spirit" to the effect that the violin is a soul-destroying instrument. Oh dear!'—and the girl's mouth twisted—'it's alarming to think, if Catherine hadn't been Catherine, how like Aunt Ellen she might have been!'

She flashed a mischievous look at him, and thrilled as she caught the sudden change of expression in his face.

'Your sister has the Westmoreland strength in her—one can see that,' he said, evidently speaking with some difficulty.

'Strength! Oh yes. Catherine has plenty of strength,' cried Rose, and then was silent a moment. 'You know, Mr. Elsmere,' she went on at last, obeying some inward impulse—'or perhaps you don't know—that, at home, we are all Catherine's creatures. She does exactly what she likes with us. When my father died she was sixteen, Agnes was ten, I was eight. We came here to live—we were not very rich of course, and mamma wasn't strong. Well, she did everything: she taught us—we have scarcely had any teacher but her since then; she did most of the housekeeping; and you can see for yourself what she does for the neighbours and poor folk. She is never ill, she is never idle, she always knows her own mind. We owe everything we are, almost everything we have, to her. Her nursing has kept mamma alive through one or two illnesses. Our lawyer says he never knew any business affairs better managed than ours, and Catherine manages them. The one thing she never takes any care or thought for is herself. What we should do without her I can't imagine; and yet sometimes I think if it goes on much longer none of us three will have any character of our own left. After all, you know, it may be good for the weak people to struggle on their own feet, if the strong would only believe it, instead of always being carried. The strong people *needn't* be always trampling on themselves,—if they only knew——'

She stopped abruptly, flushing scarlet over her own daring. Her eyes were feverishly bright, and her voice vibrated under a strange mixture of feelings—sympathy, reverence, and a passionate inner admiration struggling with rebellion and protest.

They had reached the gate of the vicarage. Elsmere stopped and looked at his companion with a singular lightening of expression. He saw perfectly that the young impetuous creature understood him, that she felt his cause was not prospering, and that she wanted to help him. He saw that what she meant by this picture of their common life was that no one need expect Catherine Leyburn to be an easy prey; that she wanted to impress on him in her eager way that such lives as her sister's were not to be gathered at a touch, without difficulty, from the branch that bears them. She was exhorting him to courage,—nay, he caught more than exhortation—a sort of secret message from her bright excited looks and incoherent speech that made his heart leap. But pride and delicacy forbade him to put his feeling into words.

'You don't hope to persuade me that your sister reckons *you* among the weak persons of the world?' he said, laughing, his hand on the gate. Rose could have blessed him for thus turning the conversation. What on earth could she have said next?

She stood bantering a little longer, and then ran off with Bob.

Elsmere passed the rest of the morning wandering meditatively over the cloudy fells. After all he was only where he was, before the blessed madness, the upflooding hope, nay, almost certainty, of yesterday. His attack had been for the moment repulsed. He gathered from Rose's manner that Catherine's action with regard to the picnic had not been unmeaning nor accidental, as on second thoughts he had been half-trying to persuade himself. Evidently those about her felt it to be ominous. Well, then, at worst, when they met they would meet on a different footing, with a sense of something critical between them. Oh, if he did but know a little more clearly how he stood! He spent a noonday hour on a gray rock on the side of the fell between Whindale and Marrisdale, studying the path opposite, the stepping-stones, the bit of white road. The minutes passed in a kind of trance of memory. Oh, that soft child-like movement to him, after his speech about her father! that heavenly yielding and self-forgetfulness which shone in her every look and movement as she stood balancing on the stepping-stones! If after all she should prove cruel to him, would he not have a legitimate grievance, a heavy charge to fling against her maiden gentleness? He trampled on the notion. Let her do with him as she would, she would be his saint always, unquestioned, unarraigned.

But with such a memory in his mind it was impossible that any man, least of all a man of Elsmere's temperament, could be very hopeless. Oh yes, he had been rash, foolhardy. Do such divine creatures stoop to mortal men as easily as he had dreamt? He recognises all the difficulties, he enters into the force of all the ties that bind her—or imagines that he does. But he is a man and her lover; and if she loves him, in the end love will conquer—must conquer. For his more modern sense, deeply Christianised as it is, assumes almost without argument the sacredness of passion and its claim—wherein a vast difference between himself and that solitary wrestler in Marrisdale.

Meanwhile he kept all his hopes and fears to himself. Mrs. Thornburgh was dying to talk to him; but though his mobile, boyish temperament made it impossible for him to disguise his change of mood, there was in him a certain natural dignity which life greatly developed, but which made it always possible for him to hold his own against curiosity and indiscretion. Mrs. Thornburgh had to hold her peace. As for the vicar, he developed what were for him a surprising number of new topics of conversation, and in the late afternoon took Elsmere a run up the fells to the nearest fragment of the Roman road which runs, with such magnificent disregard of the humours of Mother Earth, over the very top of High Street towards Penrith and Carlisle.

Next day it looked as though after many waverings the characteristic Westmoreland weather had descended upon them in good earnest. From early morn till late evening the valley was wrapped in damp clouds or moving rain, which swept down from the west through the great basin of the hills, and rolled along the course of the river, wrapping trees and fells and houses in the same misty cheerless drizzle. Under the outward pall of rain, indeed, the valley was renewing its summer youth; the river was swelling with an impetuous music through all its dwindled channels; the crags flung out white waterfalls again, which the heat had almost dried away; and by noon the whole green hollow was vocal with the sounds of water—water flashing and foaming in the river, water leaping downwards from the rocks, water dripping steadily from the larches and sycamores and the slate-eaves of the houses.

Elsmere sat indoors reading up the history of the parish system of Surrey, or pretending to do so. He sat in a corner of the study, where he and the vicar protected each other against Mrs. Thornburgh. That good woman would open the door once and again in the morning, and put her head through in search of prey; but on being confronted with two studious men instead of one, each buried up to the ears in folios, she would give vent to an irritable cough and retire discomfited. In reality Elsmere was thinking of nothing in the world but what Catherine Leyburn might be doing that morning. Judging a North countrywoman by the pusillanimous Southern standard, he found himself glorying in the weather. She could not wander far from him to-day.

After the early dinner he escaped, just as the vicar's wife was devising an excuse on which to convey both him and herself to Burwood, and sallied forth with a mackintosh for a rush down the Whinborough road. It was still raining, but the clouds showed a momentary lightening, and a few gleams of watery sunshine brought out every now and then that sparkle on the trees, that iridescent beauty of distance and atmosphere which goes so far to make a sensitive spectator forget the petulant abundance of mountain rain. Elsmere passed Burwood with a thrill. Should he or should he not present himself? Let him push on a bit and think. So on he swung, measuring his tall frame against the gusts, spirits and masculine energy rising higher with every step. At last the passion of his mood had wrestled itself out with the weather, and he turned back once more determined to seek and find her, to face his fortunes like a man. The warm rain beating from the west struck on his uplifted face. He welcomed it as a friend. Rain and storm had opened to him the gates of a spiritual citadel. What could ever wholly close it against him any more? He felt so strong, so confident! Patience and courage!

Before him the great hollow of High Fell was just coming out from the white mists surging round it. A shaft of sunlight lay across its upper end, and he caught a marvellous apparition of a sunlit valley hung in air, a pale strip of blue above it, a white thread of stream wavering through it, and all around it and below it the rolling rain-clouds.

Suddenly between him and that enchanter's vision he saw a dark slim figure against the mists, walking before him along the road. It was Catherine—Catherine just emerged from a footpath across the fields, battling with wind and rain, and quite unconscious of any spectator. Oh, what a sudden thrill was that! what a leaping together of joy and dread, which sent the blood to his heart! Alone—they two alone again—in the wild Westmoreland mists, and half a mile at least of winding road between them and Burwood. He flew after her, dreading, and yet longing for the moment when he should meet her eyes. Fortune had suddenly given this hour into his hands; he felt it open upon him like that mystic valley in the clouds.

Catherine heard the hurrying steps behind her and turned. There was an evident start when she caught sight of her pursuer—a quick change of expression. She wore a close-fitting waterproof dress and cap. Her hair was lightly loosened, her cheek freshened by the storm. He came up with her; he took her hand, his eyes dancing with the joy he could not hide.

'What are you made of, I wonder!' he said gaily. 'Nothing, certainly, that minds weather.'

'No Westmoreland native thinks of staying at home for this,' she said with her quiet smile, moving on beside him as she spoke.

He looked down upon her with an indescribable mixture of feelings. No stiffness, no coldness in her manner—only the even gentleness which always marked her out from others. He felt as though yesterday were blotted out, and would not for worlds have recalled it to her or reproached her with it. Let it be as though they were but carrying on the scene of the stepping-stones.

'Look,' he said, pointing to the west; 'have you been watching that magical break in the clouds?'

Her eyes followed his to the delicate picture hung high among the moving mists.

'Ah,' she exclaimed, her face kindling, 'that is one of our loveliest effects, and one of the rarest. You are lucky to have seen it.'

'I am conceited enough,' he said joyously, 'to feel as if some enchanter were at work up there drawing pictures on the mists for my special benefit. How welcome the rain is! As I am afraid you have heard me say before, what new charm it gives to your valley!'

There was something in the buoyancy and force of his mood that seemed to make Catherine shrink into herself. She would not pursue the subject of Westmoreland. She asked with a little stiffness whether he had good news from Mrs. Elsmere.

'Oh, yes. As usual, she is doing everything for me,' he said, smiling. 'It is disgraceful that I should be idling here while she is struggling with carpenters and paperers, and puzzling out the decorations of the drawing-room. She writes to me in a fury about the word "artistic." She declares even the little upholsterer at Churton hurls it at her every other minute, and that if it weren't for me she would select everything as frankly, primevally hideous as she could find, just to spite him. As it is, he has so warped her judgment that she has left the sitting-room papers till I arrive. For the drawing-room she avows a passionate preference for one all cabbage-roses and no stalks; but she admits that it may be exasperation. She wants your sister, clearly, to advise her. By the way,' and his voice changed, 'the vicar told me last night that Miss Rose is going to Manchester for the winter to study. He heard it from Miss Agnes, I think. The news interested me greatly after our conversation.'

He looked at her with the most winning interrogative eyes. His whole manner implied that everything which touched and concerned her touched and concerned him; and, moreover, that she had given him in some sort a right to share her thoughts and difficulties. Catherine struggled with herself.

'I trust it may answer,' she said in a low voice.

But she would say no more, and he felt rebuffed. His buoyancy began to desert him.

'It must be a great trial to Mrs. Elsmere,' she said presently with an effort, once more steering away from herself and her concerns, 'this going back to her old home.'

'It is. My father's long struggle for life in that house is a very painful memory. I wished her to put it off till I could go with her, but she declared she would rather get over the first week or two by herself. How I should like you to know my mother, Miss Leyburn!'

At this she could not help meeting his glance and smile, and answering them, though with a kind of constraint most unlike her.

'I hope I may some day see Mrs. Elsmere,' she said.

'It is one of my strongest wishes,' he answered hurriedly, 'to bring you together.'

The words were simple enough; the tone was full of emotion. He was fast losing control of himself. She felt it through every nerve, and a sort of wild dread seized her of what he might say next. Oh, she must, she must prevent it!

'Your mother was with you most of your Oxford life, was she not?' she said, forcing herself to speak in her most everyday tones.

He controlled himself with a mighty effort.

'Since I became a Fellow. We have been alone in the world so long. We have never been able to do without each other.'

'Isn't it wonderful to you?' said Catherine, after a little electric pause— and her voice was steadier and clearer than it had been since the beginning of their conversation—'how little the majority of sons and daughters regard their parents when they come to grow up and want to live their own lives? The one thought seems to be to get rid of them, to throw off their claims, to cut them adrift, to escape them—decently, of course, and under many pretexts, but still to escape them. All the long years of devotion and self-sacrifice go for nothing.'

He looked at her quickly—a troubled, questioning look.

'It is so, often; but not, I think, where the parents have truly understood their problem. The real difficulty for father and mother is not childhood, but youth; how to get over that difficult time when the child passes into the man or woman, and a relation of governor and governed should become the purest and closest of friendships. You and I have been lucky.'

'Yes,' she said, looking straight before her, and still speaking with a distinctness which caught his ear painfully, 'and so are the greater debtors! There is no excuse, I think, for any child, least of all for the child who has had years of understanding love to look back upon, if it puts its own claim first; if it insists on satisfying itself, when there is age and weakness appealing to it on the other side, when it is still urgently needed to help those older, to shield those younger, than itself. Its business first of all is to pay its debt, whatever the cost.'

The voice was low, but it had the clear vibrating ring of steel. Robert's face had darkened visibly.

'But, surely,' he cried, goaded by a new stinging sense of revolt and pain—'surely the child may make a fatal mistake if it imagines that its own happiness counts for nothing in the parents' eyes. What parent but must suffer from the starving of the child's nature? What have mother and father been working for, after all, but the perfecting of the child's life? Their longing is that it should fulfil itself in all directions. New ties, new affections, on the child's part, mean the enriching of the parent. What a cruel fate for the elder generation, to make it the jailer and burden of the younger!'

He spoke with heat and anger, with a sense of dashing himself against an obstacle, and a dumb despairing certainty rising at the heart of him.

'Ah, that is what we are so ready to say,' she answered, her breath coming more quickly, and her eye meeting his with a kind of antagonism in it; 'but it is all sophistry. The only safety lies in following out the plain duty. The parent wants the child's help and care, the child is bound to give it; that is all it needs to know. If it forms new ties, it belongs to them, not to the old ones; the old ones must come to be forgotten and put aside.'

'So you would make all life a sacrifice to the past?' he cried, quivering under the blow she was dealing him.

'No, not all life,' she said, struggling hard to preserve her perfect calm of manner: he could not know that she was trembling from head to foot. 'There are many for whom it is easy and right to choose their own way; their happiness robs no one. There are others on whom a charge has been laid from their childhood, a charge perhaps'—and her voice faltered at last—'impressed on them by dying lips, which must govern, possess their lives; which it would be baseness, treason, to betray. We are not here only to be happy.'

And she turned to him deadly pale, the faintest, sweetest smile on her lip. He was for the moment incapable of speech. He began phrase after phrase, and broke them off. A whirlwind of feeling possessed him. The strangeness, the unworldliness of what she had done struck him singularly. He realised through every nerve that what she had just said to him she had been bracing herself to say to him ever since their last parting. And now he could not tell, or rather, blindly could not see, whether she suffered in the saying it. A passionate protest rose in him, not so much against her words as against her self-control. The man in him rose up against the woman's unlooked-for, unwelcome strength.

But as the hot words she had dared so much in her simplicity to avert from them both were bursting from him, they were checked by a sudden physical difficulty. A bit of road was under water. A little beck, swollen by the rain, had overflowed, and for a few yards' distance the water stood about eight inches deep from hedge to hedge. Robert had splashed through the flood half an hour before, but it had risen rapidly since then. He had to apply his mind to the practical task of finding a way to the other side.

'You must climb the bank,' he said, 'and get through into the field.'

She assented mutely. He went first, drew her up the bank, forced his way through the loosely growing hedge himself, and holding back some young hazel saplings and breaking others, made an opening for her through which she scrambled with bent head; then, stretching out his hand to her, he made her submit to be helped down the steep bank on the other side. Her straight young figure was just above him, her breath almost on his cheek.

'You talk of baseness and treason,' he began passionately, conscious of a hundred wild impulses, as perforce she leant her light weight upon his arm. 'Life is not so simple. It is so easy to sacrifice others with one's self, to slay all claims in honour of one, instead of knitting the new ones to the old. Is life to be allowed no natural expansion? Have you forgotten that, in refusing the new bond for the old bond's sake, the child may be simply wronging the parents, depriving them of another affection, another support, which ought to have been theirs?'

His tone was harsh, almost violent. It seemed to him that she grew suddenly white, and he grasped her more firmly still. She reached the level of the field, quickly withdrew her hand, and for a moment their eyes met, her pale face raised to his. It seemed an age, so much was said in that look. There was appeal on her side, passion on his. Plainly she implored him to say no more, to spare her and himself.

'In some cases,' she said, and her voice sounded strained and hoarse to both of them, 'one cannot risk the old bond. One dare not trust one's self—or circumstance. The responsibility is too great; one can but follow the beaten path, cling to the one thread. But don't let us talk of it any more. We must make for that gate, Mr. Elsmere. It will bring us out on the road again close by home.'

He was quelled. Speech suddenly became impossible to him. He was struck again with that sense of a will firmer and more tenacious than his own, which had visited him in a slight passing way on the first evening they ever met, and now filled him with a kind of despair. As they pushed silently along the edge of the dripping meadow, he noticed with a pang that the stepping-stones lay just below them. The gleam of sun had died away, the aërial valley in the clouds had vanished, and a fresh storm of rain brought back the colour to Catherine's cheek. On their left hand was the roaring of the river, on their right they could already hear the wind moaning and tearing through the trees which sheltered Burwood. The nature which an hour ago had seemed to him so full of stimulus and exhilaration had taken to itself a note of gloom and mourning; for he was at the age when Nature is the mere docile responsive mirror of the spirit, when all her forces and powers are made for us, and are only there to play chorus to our story.[121]

They reached the little lane leading to the gate of Burwood. She paused at the foot of it.

'You will come in and see my mother, Mr. Elsmere?'

Her look expressed a yearning she could not crush. 'Your pardon, your friendship,' it cried, with the usual futility of all good women under the circumstances. But as he met it for one passionate instant, he recognised fully that there was not a trace of yielding in it. At the bottom of the softness there was the iron of resolution.

'No, no; not now,' he said involuntarily: and she never forgot the painful struggle of the face; 'good-bye.' He touched her hand without another word, and was gone.

She toiled up to the gate with difficulty, the gray rain-washed road, the wall, the trees, swimming before her eyes.

In the hall she came across Agnes, who caught hold of her with a start.

'My dear Cathie! you have been walking yourself to death. You look like a ghost. Come and have some tea at once.'

And she dragged her into the drawing-room. Catherine submitted with all her usual outward calm, faintly smiling at her sister's onslaught. But she would not let Agnes put her down on the sofa. She stood with her hand on the back of a chair.

'The weather is very close and exhausting,' she said, gently lifting her hand to her hat. But the hand dropped, and she sank heavily into the chair.

'Cathie, you are faint,' cried Agnes, running to her.

Catherine waved her away, and, with an effort of which none but she would have been capable, mastered the physical weakness.

'I have been a long way, dear,' she said, as though in apology, 'and there is no air. Yes, I will go upstairs and lie down a minute or two. Oh no, don't come, I will be down for tea directly.'

And refusing all help, she guided herself out of the room, her face the

---

121 In *W*, the first "nature" in the sentence is also capitalized, introducing another personification.

colour of the foam on the beck outside. Agnes stood dumfoundered. Never in her life before had she seen Catherine betray any such signs of physical exhaustion.

Suddenly Rose ran in, shut the door carefully behind her, and rushing up to Agnes put her hands on her shoulders.

'He has proposed to her, and she has said no!'

'He? What, Mr. Elsmere? How on earth can you know?'

'I saw them from upstairs come to the bottom of the lane. Then he rushed on, and I have just met her on the stairs. It's as plain as the nose on your face.'

Agnes sat down bewildered.

'It is hard on him,' she said at last.

'Yes, it is *very* hard on him!' cried Rose, pacing the room, her long thin arms clasped behind her, her eyes flashing, 'for she loves him!'

'Rose!'

'She does, my dear, she does,' cried the girl, frowning. 'I know it in a hundred ways.'

Agnes ruminated.

'And it's all because of us?' she said at last reflectively.

'Of course! I put it to you, Agnes'—and Rose stood still with a tragic air—'I put it to you, whether it isn't too bad that three unoffending women should have such a rôle as this assigned them against their will!'

The eloquence of eighteen was irresistible. Agnes buried her head in the sofa cushion, and shook with a kind of helpless laughter. Rose meanwhile stood in the window, her thin form drawn up to its full height, angry with Agnes, and enraged with all the world.

'It's absurd, it's insulting,' she exclaimed. 'I should imagine that you and I, Agnes, were old enough and sane enough to look after mamma, put out the stores, say our prayers, and prevent each other from running away with adventurers! I won't be always in leading-strings. I won't acknowledge that Catherine is bound to be an old maid to keep me in order. I hate it! It is sacrifice run mad.'

And Rose turned to her sister, the defiant head thrown back, a passion of manifold protest in the girlish looks.

'It is very easy, my dear, to be judge in one's own case,' replied Agnes calmly, recovering herself. 'Suppose you tell Catherine some of these home truths?'

Rose collapsed at once. She sat down despondently, and fell, head drooping, into a moody silence. Agnes watched her with a kind of triumph. When it came to the point, she knew perfectly well that there was not a will among them that could measure itself with any chance of success against that lofty but unwavering will of Catherine's. Rose was violent, and there was much reason in her violence. But as for her, she preferred not to dash her head against stone walls.

'Well, then, if you won't say them to Catherine, say them to mamma,' she suggested presently, but half ironically.

'Mamma is no good,' cried Rose angrily; 'why do you bring her in? Catherine would talk her round in ten minutes.'

Long after every one else in Burwood, even the chafing, excited Rose, was asleep, Catherine in her dimly lighted room, where the stormy north-west wind beat noisily against her window, was sitting in a low chair, her head leaning against her bed, her little well-worn Testament open on her knee. But she was not reading. Her eyes were shut; one hand hung down beside her, and tears were raining fast and silently over her cheeks. It was the stillest, most restrained weeping. She hardly knew why she wept, she only knew that there was something within her which must have its way. What did this inner smart and tumult mean, this rebellion of the self against the will which had never yet found its mastery fail it? It was as though from her childhood till now she had lived in a moral world whereof the aims, the dangers, the joys, were all she knew; and now the walls of this world were crumbling round her, and strange lights, strange voices, strange colours were breaking through. All the sayings of Christ which had lain closest to her heart for years, to-night for the first time seem to her no longer sayings of comfort or command, but sayings of fire and flame that burn their coercing way through life and thought. We recite so glibly, 'He that loseth his life shall save it;' and when we come to any of the common crises of experience which are the source and the sanction of the words, flesh and blood recoil.[122] This girl amid her mountains had carried religion as far as religion can be carried before it meets life in the wrestle appointed it. The calm, simple outlines of things are blurring before her eyes; the great placid deeps of the soul are breaking up.

To the purest ascetic temper a struggle of this kind is hardly real. Catherine felt a bitter surprise at her own pain. Yesterday a sort of mystical exaltation upheld her. What had broken it down?

Simply a pair of reproachful eyes, a pale protesting face. What trifles compared to the awful necessities of an infinite obedience! And yet they haunt her, till her heart aches for misery, till she only yearns to be counselled, to be forgiven, to be at least understood.

'Why, why am I so weak?' she cried in utter abasement of soul, and knew

---

122 Matthew 10.39.

not that in that weakness, or rather in the founts of character from which it sprang, lay the innermost safeguard of her life.

CHAPTER IX

Robert was very nearly reduced to despair by the scene with Catherine we have described. He spent a brooding and miserable hour in the vicar's study afterwards, making up his mind as to what he should do. One phrase of hers which had passed almost unnoticed in the shock of the moment was now ringing in his ears, maddening him by a sense of joy just within his reach, and yet barred away from him by an obstacle as strong as it was intangible. '*We are not here only to be happy,*' she had said to him, with a look of ethereal exaltation worthy of her namesake of Alexandria.[123] The words had slipped from her involuntarily in the spiritual tension of her mood. They were now filling Robert Elsmere's mind with a tormenting, torturing bliss. What could they mean? What had her paleness, her evident trouble and weakness meant, but that the inmost self of hers was his, was conquered; and that, but for the shadowy obstacle between them, all would be well?

As for the obstacle in itself, he did not admit its force for a moment. No sane and practical man, least of all when that man happened to be Catherine Leyburn's lover, could regard it as a binding obligation upon her that she should sacrifice her own life and happiness to three persons, who were in no evident moral straits, no physical or pecuniary need, and who, as Rose incoherently put it, might very well be rather braced than injured by the withdrawal of her strong support.

But the obstacle of character—ah, there was a different matter! He realised with despair the brooding scrupulous force of moral passion to which her lonely life, her antecedents, and her father's nature working in her had given so rare and marked a development. No temper in the world is so little open to reason as the ascetic temper. How many a lover and husband, how many a parent and friend, have realised to their pain, since history began, the overwhelming attraction which all the processes of self-annihilation have for a certain order of minds! Robert's heart sank before the memory of that frail indomitable look, that aspect of sad yet immovable conviction with which she had bade him farewell. And yet, surely—surely under the willingness

---

123 St. Catherine of Alexandria (d. 4th century CE), martyred by the Emperor Maxentius after being miraculously saved from being tortured to death on the wheel (with which she is traditionally depicted).

of the spirit there had been a pitiful, a most womanly weakness of the flesh. Surely, now memory reproduced the scene, she had been white—trembling: her hand had rested on the moss-grown wall beside her for support. Oh, why had he been so timid? why had he let that awe of her, which her personality produced so readily, stand between them? why had he not boldly caught her to himself, and, with all the eloquence of a passionate nature, trampled on her scruples, marched through her doubts, convinced—reasoned her into a blessed submission!

'And I will do it yet!' he cried, leaping to his feet with a sudden access of hope and energy. And he stood awhile looking out into the rainy evening, all the keen irregular face and thin pliant form hardening into the intensity of resolve, which had so often carried the young tutor through an Oxford difficulty, breaking down antagonism and compelling consent.

At the high tea which represented the late dinner of the household he was wary and self-possessed. Mrs. Thornburgh got out of him that he had been for a walk, and had seen Catherine, but for all her ingenuities of cross-examination she got nothing more. Afterwards, when he and the vicar were smoking together, he proposed to Mr. Thornburgh that they two should go off for a couple of days on a walking tour to Ullswater.

'I want to go away,' he said, with a hand on the vicar's shoulder, '*and I want to come back.*' The deliberation of the last words was not to be mistaken. The vicar emitted a contented puff, looked the young man straight in the eyes, and without another word began to plan a walk to Patterdale *viâ* High Street, Martindale, and Howtown, and back by Haweswater.

To Mrs. Thornburgh Robert announced that he must leave them on the following Saturday, June 24.

'You *have* given me a good time, Cousin Emma,' he said to her, with a bright friendliness which dumbfounded her. A good time, indeed! with everything begun and nothing finished; with two households thrown into perturbation for a delusion, and a desirable marriage spoilt, all for want of a little common sense and plain speaking, which *one* person at least in the valley could have supplied them with, had she not been ignored and browbeaten on all sides. She contained herself, however, in his presence, but the vicar suffered proportionately in the privacy of the connubial chamber. He had never seen his wife so exasperated. To think what might have been, what she might have done for the race, but for the whims of two stuck-up, superior, impracticable young persons, that would neither manage their own affairs nor allow other people to manage them for them! The vicar behaved gallantly, kept the secret of Elsmere's remark to himself like a man, and allowed himself certain counsels against matrimonial meddling which plunged Mrs. Thornburgh into well-simulated slumber. However, in the morning he was vaguely conscious that some time in the visions of the night his spouse had demanded of him peremptorily, 'When do you get back, William?' To the best of his memory the vicar had sleepily murmured, 'Thursday'; and had then heard, echoed through his dreams, a calculating whisper, 'He goes Saturday—one clear day!'

The following morning was gloomy but fine, and after breakfast the vicar and Elsmere started off. Robert turned back at the top of the High Fell pass and stood leaning on his alpenstock, sending a passionate farewell to the gray distant house, the upper window, the copper beech in the garden, the bit of winding road, while the vicar discreetly stepped on northward, his eyes fixed on the wild regions of Martindale.

Mrs. Thornburgh, left alone, absorbed herself to all appearance in the school treat which was to come off in a fortnight, in a new set of covers for the drawing-room, and in Sarah's love affairs, which were always passing through some tragic phase or other, and into which Mrs. Thornburgh was allowed a more unencumbered view than she was into Catherine Leyburn's. Rose and Agnes dropped in now and then, and found her not at all disposed to talk to them on the great event of the day—Elsmere's absence and approaching departure. They cautiously communicated to her their own suspicions as to the incident of the preceding afternoon; and Rose gave vent to one fiery onslaught on the 'moral obstacle' theory, during which Mrs. Thornburgh sat studying her with small attentive eyes and curls slowly waving from side to side. But for once in her life the vicar's wife was not communicative in return. That the situation should have driven even Mrs. Thornburgh to finesse was a surprising testimony to its gravity. What between her sudden taciturnity and Catherine's pale silence, the girls' sense of expectancy was roused to its highest pitch.

'They come back to-morrow night,' said Rose thoughtfully, 'and he goes Saturday—10.20 from Whinborough—one day for the Fifth Act! By the way, why did Mrs. Thornburgh ask us to say nothing about Saturday at home?'

She *had* asked them, however; and with a pleasing sense of conspiracy they complied.

It was late on Thursday afternoon when Mrs. Thornburgh, finding the Burwood front door open, made her unchallenged way into the hall, and after an unanswered knock at the drawing-room door, opened it and peered in to see who might be there.

'May I come in?'

Mrs. Leyburn, who was a trifle deaf, was sitting by the window absorbed in the intricacies of a heel which seemed to her more than she could manage. Her card was mislaid, the girls were none of them at hand, and she felt as helpless as she commonly did when left alone.

'Oh, do come in, please! So glad to see you. Have you been nearly blown away?'

For, though the rain had stopped, a boisterous north-west wind was still rushing through the valley, and the trees round Burwood were swaying and groaning under the force of its onslaught.

'Well, it is stormy,' said Mrs. Thornburgh, stepping in and undoing all the various safety pins and elastics which had held her dress high above the mud. 'Are the girls out?'

'Yes, Catherine and Agnes are at the school; and Rose, I think, is practising.'

'Ah, well,' said Mrs. Thornburgh, settling herself in a chair close by her friend, 'I wanted to find you alone.'

Her face, framed in bushy curls and an old garden bonnet, was flushed and serious. Her mittened hands were clasped nervously on her lap, and there was about her such an air of forcibly restrained excitement that Mrs. Leyburn's mild eyes gazed at her with some astonishment. The two women were a curious contrast: Mrs. Thornburgh short, inclined, as we know, to be stout, ample and abounding in all things, whether it were curls or cap-strings or conversation; Mrs. Leyburn tall and well proportioned, well dressed, with the same graceful ways and languid pretty manners as had first attracted her husband's attention thirty years before. She was fond of Mrs. Thornburgh, but there was something in the ebullient energies of the vicar's wife which always gave her a sense of bustle and fatigue.

'I am sure you will be sorry to hear,' began her visitor, 'that Mr. Elsmere is going.'

'Going?' said Mrs. Leyburn, laying down her knitting. 'Why, I thought he was going to stay with you another ten days at least.'

'So did I—so did he,' said Mrs. Thornburgh, nodding, and then pausing with a most effective air of sudden gravity and 'recollection.'

'Then why—what's the matter?' asked Mrs. Leyburn, wondering.

Mrs. Thornburgh did not answer for a minute, and Mrs. Leyburn began to feel a little nervous, her visitor's eyes were fixed upon her with so much meaning. Urged by a sudden impulse she bent forward; so did Mrs. Thornburgh, and their two elderly heads nearly touched.

'The young man is in love!' said the vicar's wife in a stage whisper, drawing back after a pause, to see the effect of her announcement.

'Oh! with whom?' asked Mrs. Leyburn, her look brightening. She liked a love affair as much as ever.

Mrs. Thornburgh furtively looked round to see if the door was shut and all safe—she felt herself a criminal, but the sense of guilt had an exhilarating rather than a depressing effect upon her.

'Have you guessed nothing? have the girls told you anything?'

'No!' said Mrs. Leyburn, her eyes opening wider and wider. She never guessed anything; there was no need, with three daughters to think for her, and give her the benefit of their young brains. 'No,' she said again. 'I can't imagine what you mean.'

Mrs. Thornburgh felt a rush of inward contempt for so much obtuseness.

'Well, then, *he is in love with Catherine!*' she said abruptly, laying her hand on Mrs. Leyburn's knee, and watching the effect.

'With Catherine!' stammered Mrs. Leyburn; '*with Catherine!*'

The idea was amazing to her. She took up her knitting with trembling fingers, and went on with it mechanically a second or two. Then laying it down—'Are you quite sure? has he told you?'

'No, but one has eyes,' said Mrs. Thornburgh hastily. 'William and I have seen it from the very first day. And we are both certain that on Tuesday she made him understand in some way or other that she wouldn't marry him, and that is why he went off to Ullswater, and why he made up his mind to go south before his time is up.'

'Tuesday?' cried Mrs. Leyburn. 'In that walk, do you mean, when Catherine looked so tired afterwards? You think he proposed in that walk?'

She was in a maze of bewilderment and excitement.

'Something like it—but if he did, she said "No"; and what I want to know is *why* she said "No."'

'Why, of course, because she didn't care for him!' exclaimed Mrs. Leyburn, opening her blue eyes wider and wider. 'Catherine's not like most girls; she would always know what she felt, and would never keep a man in suspense.'

'Well, I don't somehow believe,' said Mrs. Thornburgh boldly, 'that she doesn't care for him. He is just the young man Catherine might care for. You can see that yourself.'

Mrs. Leyburn once more laid down her knitting and stared at her visitor. Mrs. Thornburgh, after all her meditations, had no very precise idea as to *why* she was at that moment in the Burwood drawing-room bombarding Mrs. Leyburn in this fashion. All she knew was that she had sallied forth determined somehow to upset the situation, just as one gives a shake purposely to a bundle of spillikins on the chance of more favourable openings. Mrs.

Leyburn's mind was just now playing the part of spillikins, and the vicar's wife was shaking it vigorously, though with occasional qualms as to the lawfulness of the process.

'You think Catherine does care for him?' resumed Mrs. Leyburn tremulously.

'Well, isn't he just the kind of man one would suppose Catherine would like?' repeated Mrs. Thornburgh persuasively; 'he is a clergyman, and she likes serious people; and he's sensible and nice and well-mannered. And then he can talk about books, just like her father used—I'm sure William thinks he knows everything! He isn't as nice-looking as he might be just now, but then that's his hair and his fever, poor man. And then he isn't hanging about. He's got a living, and there'd be the poor people all ready, and everything else Catherine likes. And now I'll just ask you—did you ever see Catherine more—more—*lively*—well, I know that's not just the word, but you know what I mean—than she has been the last fortnight?'

But Mrs. Leyburn only shook her head helplessly. She did not know in the least what Mrs. Thornburgh meant. She never thought Catherine doleful, and she agreed that certainly 'lively' was not the word.

'Girls get so frightfully particular nowadays,' continued the vicar's wife, with reflective candour. 'Why, when William fell in love with me, I just fell in love with him—at once—because he did. And if it hadn't been William, but somebody else, it would have been the same. I don't believe girls have got hearts like pebbles—if the man's nice, of course!'

Mrs. Leyburn listened to this summary of matrimonial philosophy with the same yielding flurried attention as she was always disposed to give to the last speaker.

'But,' she said, still in a maze, 'if she did care for him, why should she send him away?'

'*Because she won't have him!*' said Mrs. Thornburgh energetically, leaning over the arm of her chair that she might bring herself nearer to her companion.

The fatuity of the answer left Mrs. Leyburn staring.

'Because she won't have him, my dear Mrs. Leyburn! And—and—I'm sure nothing would make me interfere like this if I weren't so fond of you all, and if William and I didn't know for certain that there never was a better young man born! And then I was just sure you'd be the last person in the world, if you knew, to stand in young people's way!'

'*I!*' cried poor Mrs. Leyburn—'I stand in the way!' She was getting tremulous and tearful, and Mrs. Thornburgh felt herself a brute.

'Well,' she said, plunging on desperately, 'I have been thinking over it night and day. I've been watching him, and I've been talking to the girls, and I've been putting two and two together, and I'm just about sure that there might be a chance for Robert, if only Catherine didn't feel that you and the girls couldn't get on without her!'

Mrs. Leyburn took up her knitting again with agitated fingers. She was so long in answering that Mrs. Thornburgh sat and thought with trepidation of all sorts of unpleasant consequences which might result from this audacious move of hers.

'I don't know how we *should* get on,' cried Mrs. Leyburn at last, with a sort of suppressed sob, while something very like a tear fell on the stocking she held.

Mrs. Thornburgh was still more frightened, and rushed into a flood of apologetic speech. Very likely she was wrong, perhaps it was all a mistake, she was afraid she had done harm, and so on. Mrs. Leyburn took very little heed, but at last she said, looking up and applying a soft handkerchief gently to her eyes—

'Is his mother nice? Where's his living? Would he want to be married soon?'

The voice was weak and tearful, but there was in it unmistakable eagerness to be informed. Mrs. Thornburgh, overjoyed, let loose upon her a flood of particulars, painted the virtues and talents of Mrs. Elsmere, described Robert's Oxford career, with an admirable sense for effect, and a truly feminine capacity for murdering every university detail, drew pictures of the Murewell living and rectory, of which Robert had photographs with him, threw in adroit information about the young man's private means, and in general showed what may be made of a woman's mind under the stimulus of one of the occupations most proper to it. Mrs. Leyburn brightened visibly as the flood proceeded. Alas, poor Catherine! How little room there is for the heroic in this trivial everyday life of ours!

Catherine a bride, Catherine a wife and mother, dim visions of a white soft morsel in which Catherine's eyes and smile should live again—all these thoughts went trembling and flashing through Mrs. Leyburn's mind as she listened to Mrs. Thornburgh. There is so much of the artist in the maternal mind, of the artist who longs to see the work of his hand in fresh combinations and under all points of view. Catherine, in the heat of her own self-surrender, had perhaps forgotten that her mother too had a heart!

'Yes, it all sounds very well,' said Mrs. Leyburn at last, sighing, 'but, you know, Catherine isn't easy to manage.'

'Could you talk to her—find out a little?'

'Well, not to-day; I shall hardly see her. Doesn't it seem to you that when a girl takes up notions like Catherine's, she hasn't time for thinking about the young men? Why, she's as full of business all day long as an egg's full of meat. Well, it was my poor Richard's doing—it was his doing, bless him! I am not going to say anything against it. But it *was* different—once.'

'Yes, I know,' said Mrs. Thornburgh thoughtfully. 'One had plenty of time, when you and I were young, to sit at home and think what one was going to wear, and how one would look, and whether *he* had been paying attention to any one else; and if he had, why; and all that. And now the young women are so superior. But the marrying has got to be done somehow all the same. What is she doing to-day?'

'Oh, she'll be busy all to-day and to-morrow; I hardly expect to see her till Saturday.'

Mrs. Thornburgh gave a start of dismay.

'Why, what *is* the matter now?' she cried in her most aggrieved tones. 'My dear Mrs. Leyburn, one would think we had the cholera in the parish. Catherine just spoils the people.'

'Don't you remember,' said Mrs. Leyburn, staring in her turn, and drawing herself up a little, 'that to-morrow is Midsummer Day, and that Mary Backhouse is as bad as she can be?'

'Mary Backhouse! Why, I had forgotten all about her!' cried the vicar's wife, with sudden remorse. And she sat pensively eyeing the carpet awhile.

Then she got what particulars she could out of Mrs. Leyburn. Catherine, it appeared, was at this moment at High Ghyll, was not to return till late, and would be with the dying girl through the greater part of the following day, returning for an hour or two's rest in the afternoon, and staying in the evening till the twilight, in which the ghost always made her appearances, should have passed into night.

Mrs. Thornburgh listened to it all, her contriving mind working the while at railway speed on the facts presented to her.

'How do you get her home to-morrow night?' she asked, with sudden animation.

'Oh, we send our man Richard at ten. He takes a lantern if it's dark.'

Mrs. Thornburgh said no more. Her eyes and gestures were all alive again with energy and hope. She had given her shake to Mrs. Leyburn's mind. Much good might it do! But, after all, she had the poorest opinion of the widow's capacities as an ally.

She and her companion said a few more excited, affectionate, and apologetic things to one another, and then she departed.

Both mother and knitting were found by Agnes half an hour later in a state of considerable confusion. But Mrs. Leyburn kept her own counsel, having resolved for once, with a timid and yet delicious excitement, to act as the head of the family.

Meanwhile Mrs. Thornburgh was laying plans on her own account.

'Ten o'clock—moonlight,' said that contriving person to herself going home—'at least if the clouds hold up—that'll do—couldn't be better.'

To any person familiar with her character the signs of some unusual pre-occupation were clear enough in Mrs. Leyburn during this Thursday evening. Catherine noticed them at once when she got back from High Ghyll about eight o'clock, and wondered first of all what was the matter; and then, with more emphasis, why the trouble was not immediately communicated to her. It had never entered into her head to take her mother into her confidence with regard to Elsmere. Since she could remember, it had been an axiom in the family to spare the delicate nervous mother all the anxieties and perplexi-ties of life. It was a system in which the subject of it had always acquiesced with perfect contentment, and Catherine had no qualms about it. If there was good news, it was presented in its most sugared form to Mrs. Leyburn; but the moment any element of pain and difficulty cropped up in the common life, it was pounced upon and appropriated by Catherine, aided and abetted by the girls, and Mrs. Leyburn knew no more about it than an unweaned babe.

So that Catherine was thinking at most of some misconduct of a Perth dyer with regard to her mother's best gray poplin, when one of the greatest surprises of her life burst upon her.

She was in Mrs. Leyburn's bedroom that night, helping to put away her mother's things, as her custom was. She had just taken off the widow's cap, caressing as she did so the brown hair underneath, which was still soft and plentiful, when Mrs. Leyburn turned upon her. 'Catherine!' she said in an agitated voice, laying a thin hand on her daughter's arm. 'Oh, Catherine, I want to speak to you!'

Catherine knelt lightly down by her mother's side, and put her arms round her waist.

'Yes, mother darling,' she said, half smiling.

'Oh, Catherine! if—if—you like Mr. Elsmere, don't mind—don't think—about us, dear. We can manage—we can manage, dear!'

The change that took place in Catherine Leyburn's face is indescribable. She rose instantly, her arms falling behind her, her beautiful brows drawn together. Mrs. Leyburn looked up at her with a pathetic mixture of helpless-ness, alarm, entreaty.

'Mother, who has been talking to you about Mr. Elsmere and me?' de-manded Catherine.

'Oh, never mind, dear, never mind,' said the widow hastily; 'I should have seen it myself—oh, I know I should; but I'm a bad mother, Catherine!' And she caught her daughter's dress and drew her towards her. '*Do* you care for him?'

Catherine did not answer. She knelt down again, and laid her head on her mother's hands.

'I want nothing,' she said presently in a low voice of intense emotion—'I want nothing but you and the girls. You are my life, I ask for nothing more. I am abundantly—content.'

Mrs. Leyburn gazed down on her with infinite perplexity. The brown hair, escaped from the cap, had fallen about her still pretty neck, a pink spot of excitement was on each gently-hollowed cheek; she looked almost younger than her pale daughter.

'But—he is very nice,' she said timidly. 'And he has a good living. Catherine, you ought to be a clergyman's wife.'

'I ought to be, and I am your daughter,' said Catherine, smiling a little with an unsteady lip, and kissing her hand.

Mrs. Leyburn sighed and looked straight before her. Perhaps in imagi-nation she saw the vicar's wife. 'I think—I think,' she said very seriously, 'I should like it!'

Catherine straightened herself brusquely at that. It was as though she had felt a blow.

'Mother!' she cried, with a stifled accent of pain, and yet still trying to smile, 'do you want to send me away?'

'No, no!' cried Mrs. Leyburn hastily. 'But if a nice man wants you to marry him, Catherine? Your father would have liked him—oh, I know your father would have liked him! And his manners to me are so pretty, I shouldn't mind being *his* mother-in-law. And the girls have no brother, you know, dear. Your father was always so sorry about that.'

She spoke with pleading agitation, her own tempting imaginations—the pallor, the latent storm of Catherine's look—exciting her more and more.

Catherine was silent a moment, then she caught her mother's hand again.

'Dear little mother—dear, kind little mother! You are an angel, you al-ways are. But I think, if you'll keep me, I'll stay.'

And she once more rested her head clingingly on Mrs. Leyburn's knee.

'But *do* you—*do* you love him, Catherine?'

'I love you, mother, and the girls, and my life here.'

'Oh dear,' sighed Mrs. Leyburn, as though addressing a third person, the tears in her mild eyes, 'she won't, and she *would* like it, and so should I!'

Catherine rose, stung beyond bearing.

'And I count for nothing to you, mother!' her deep voice quivering. 'You could put me aside, you and the girls, and live as though I had never been!'

'But you would be a great deal to us if you did marry, Catherine!' cried Mrs. Leyburn, almost with an accent of pettishness. 'People have to do without their daughters. There's Agnes—I often think, as it is, you might let her do more. And if Rose were troublesome, why, you know it might be a good thing—a very good thing—if there were a man to take her in hand!'

'And you, mother, without me?' cried poor Catherine, choked.

'Oh, I should come and see you,' said Mrs. Leyburn, brightening. 'They say it *is* such a nice house, Catherine, and such pretty country; and I'm sure I should like his mother, though she *is* Irish!'

It was the bitterest moment of Catherine Leyburn's life. In it the heroic dream of years broke down. Nay, the shrivelling ironic touch of circumstance laid upon it made it look even in her own eyes almost ridiculous. What had she been living for, praying for, all these years? She threw herself down by the widow's side, her face working with a passion that terrified Mrs. Leyburn.

'Oh, mother, say you would miss me—say you would miss me if I went!'

Then Mrs. Leyburn herself broke down, and the two women clung to each other, weeping. Catherine's sore heart was soothed a little by her mother's tears, and by the broken words of endearment that were lavished on her. But through it all she felt that the excited imaginative desire in Mrs. Leyburn still persisted. It was the cheapening—the vulgarising, so to speak, of her whole existence.

In the course of their long embrace Mrs. Leyburn let fall various items of news that showed Catherine very plainly who had been at work upon her mother, and one of which startled her.

'He comes back to-night, my dear—and he goes on Saturday. Oh, and, Catherine, Mrs. Thornburgh says he *does* care so much. Poor young man!'

And Mrs. Leyburn looked up at her now standing daughter with eyes as woe-begone for Elsmere as for herself.

'Don't talk about it any more, mother,' Catherine implored. 'You won't sleep, and I shall be more wroth with Mrs. Thornburgh than I am already.'

Mrs. Leyburn let herself be gradually soothed and coerced, and Catherine, with a last kiss to the delicate emaciated fingers on which the

worn wedding-ring lay slipping forward—in itself a history—left her at last
to sleep.

'And I don't know much more than when I began!' sighed the perplexed
widow to herself. 'Oh, I wish Richard was here—I do!'

Catherine's night was a night of intense mental struggle. Her struggle
was one with which the modern world has perhaps but scant sympathy.
Instinctively we feel such things out of place in our easy indifferent generation. We think them more than half unreal. We are so apt to take it for
granted that the world has outgrown the religious thirst for sanctification, for
a perfect moral consistency, as it has outgrown so many of the older complications of the sentiment of honour. And meanwhile half the tragedy of our time
lies in this perpetual clashing of two estimates of life—the estimate which is
the offspring of the scientific spirit, and which is for ever making the visible
world fairer and more desirable in mortal eyes; and the estimate of Saint
Augustine.[124]

As a matter of fact, owing to some travelling difficulties, the vicar and
Elsmere did not get home till noon on Friday. Catherine knew nothing of
either delay or arrival. Mrs. Leyburn watched her with anxious timidity, but
she never mentioned Elsmere's name to any one on the Friday morning, and
no one dared speak of him to her. She came home in the afternoon from the
Backhouses' absorbed apparently in the state of the dying girl, took a couple
of hours' rest, and hurried off again. She passed the vicarage with bent head,
and never looked up.

'She is gone!' said Rose to Agnes as she stood at the window looking after
her sister's retreating figure. 'It is all over! They can't meet now. He will be off
by nine to-morrow.'

The girl spoke with a lump in her throat, and flung herself down by the
window, moodily watching the dark form against the fells. Catherine's coldness seemed to make all life colder and more chilling—to fling a hard denial
in the face of the dearest claims of earth.

The stormy light of the afternoon was fading towards sunset. Catherine
walked on fast towards the group of houses at the head of the valley, in one
of which lived the two old carriers who had worked such havoc with Mrs.
Thornburgh's housekeeping arrangements. She was tired physically, but she
was still more tired mentally. She had the bruised feeling of one who has been

---

124 Augustine's distinction between the fallen and godly cities in *The City of God*, the
former occupied by those incapable of seeing beyond worldly needs and desires and
the latter by those oriented toward the divine.

humiliated before the world and before herself. Her self-respect was for the moment crushed, and the breach made in the wholeness of personal dignity had produced a strange slackness of nerve, extending both to body and mind. She had been convicted, it seemed to her, in her own eyes, and in those of her world, of an egregious over-estimate of her own value. She walked with hung head like one ashamed, the overstrung religious sense deepening her discomfiture at every step. How rich her life had always been in the conviction of usefulness—nay, indispensableness! Her mother's persuasions had dashed it from her. And religious scruple, for her torment, showed her her past, transformed, alloyed with all sorts of personal prides and cravings, which stood unmasked now in a white light.

And he? Still near her for a few short hours! Every pulse in her had thrilled as she had passed the house which sheltered him. But she will see him no more. And she is glad. If he had stayed on, he too would have discovered how cheaply they held her—those dear ones of hers for whom she had lived till now! And she might have weakly yielded to his pity what she had refused to his homage. The strong nature is half tortured, half soothed by the prospect of his going. Perhaps when he is gone she will recover something of that moral equilibrium which has been so shaken. At present she is a riddle to herself, invaded by a force she has no power to cope with, feeling the moral ground of years crumbling beneath her, and struggling feverishly for self-control.

As she neared the head of the valley the wind became less tempestuous. The great wall of High Fell, towards which she was walking, seemed to shelter her from its worst violence. But the hurrying clouds, the gleams of lurid light which every now and then penetrated into the valley from the west, across the dip leading to Shanmoor, the voice of the river answering the voice of the wind, and the deep unbroken shadow that covered the group of houses and trees towards which she was walking, all served to heighten the nervous depression which had taken hold of her. As she neared the bridge, however, leading to the little hamlet, beyond which northwards all was stony loneliness and desolation, and saw in front of her the gray stone house, backed by the sombre red of a great copper beech, and overhung by crags, she had perforce to take herself by both hands, try and realise her mission afresh, and the scene which lay before her.

CHAPTER X

Mary Backhouse, the girl whom Catherine had been visiting with regularity for many weeks, and whose frail life was this evening nearing a terrible and long-expected crisis, was the victim of a fate sordid and common enough, yet not without its elements of dark poetry. Some fifteen months before this Midsummer Day she had been the mistress of the lonely old house in which her father and uncle had passed their whole lives, in which she had been born, and in which, amid snowdrifts so deep that no doctor could reach them, her mother had passed away. She had been then strong and well favoured, possessed of a certain masculine black-browed beauty, and of a temper which sometimes gave to it an edge and glow such as an artist of ambition might have been glad to catch. At the bottom of all the outward *sauvagerie*, however, there was a heart, and strong wants, which only affection and companionship could satisfy and tame.[125] Neither was to be found in sufficient measure within her home. Her father and she were on fairly good terms, and had for each other up to a certain point the natural instincts of kinship. On her uncle, whom she regarded as half-witted, she bestowed alternate tolerance and jeers. She was, indeed, the only person whose remonstrances ever got under the wool with old Jim, and her sharp tongue had sometimes a cowing effect on his curious nonchalance which nothing else had. For the rest, they had no neighbours with whom the girl could fraternise, and Whinborough was too far off to provide any adequate food for her vague hunger after emotion and excitement.

In this dangerous morbid state she fell a victim to the very coarse attractions of a young farmer in the neighbouring valley of Shanmoor. He was a brute with a handsome face, and a nature in which whatever grains of heart and conscience might have been interfused with the original composition had been long since swamped. Mary, who had recklessly flung herself into his power on one or two occasions, from a mixture of motives, partly passion, partly jealousy, partly *ennui*, awoke one day to find herself ruined, and a grim future hung before her. She had realised her doom for the first time in its entirety on the Midsummer Day preceding that we are now describing. On that day she had walked over to Shanmoor in a fever of dumb rage and

---

125 Literally, savagery, but with the looser sense of unfriendliness as well.

despair, to claim from her betrayer the fulfilment of his promise of marriage. He had laughed at her, and she had fled home in the warm rainy dusk, a prey to all those torturing terrors which only a woman *in extremis* can know. And on her way back she had seen the ghost or 'bogle' of Deep Crag; the ghost had spoken to her, and she had reached home more dead than alive, having received what she at once recognised as her death sentence.

What had she seen? An effect of moonlit mist—a shepherd boy bent on a practical joke—a gleam of white waterfall among the darkening rocks? What had she heard? The evening greeting of a passer-by, wafted down to her from some higher path along the fell? distant voices in the farm enclosures beneath her feet? or simply the eerie sounds of the mountain, those weird earth-whispers which haunt the lonely places of nature? Who can tell? Nerves and brain were strained to their uttermost. The legend of the ghost—of the girl who had thrown her baby and herself into the tarn under the frowning precipitous cliffs which marked the western end of High Fell, and who had since then walked the lonely road to Shanmoor every Midsummer Night, with her moaning child upon her arm—had flashed into Mary's mind as she left the white-walled village of Shanmoor behind her, and climbed upward with her shame and her secret into the mists. To see the bogle was merely distressing and untoward; to be spoken to by the phantom voice was death. No one so addressed could hope to survive the following Midsummer Day. Revolving these things in her mind, along with the terrible details of her own story, the exhausted girl had seen her vision, and, as she firmly believed, incurred her doom.

A week later she had disappeared from home and from the neighbourhood. The darkest stories were afloat. She had taken some money with her, and all trace of her was lost. The father had a period of gloomy taciturnity, during which his principal relief was got out of jeering and girding at his elder brother; the noodle's eyes wandered and glittered more; his shrunken frame seemed more shrunken as he sat dangling his spindle legs from the shaft of the carrier's cart; his absence of mind was for a time more marked, and excused with less buoyancy and inventiveness than usual.[126] But otherwise all went on as before. John Backhouse took no step, and for nine months nothing was heard of his daughter.

At last one cheerless March afternoon, Jim, coming back first from the Wednesday round with the cart, entered the farm kitchen, while John Backhouse was still wrangling at one of the other farmhouses of the hamlet about some disputed payment. The old man came in cold and weary, and the

126 "at his elder brother; the noodle's eyes": semi-colon as per *SE* and *W*.

sight of the half-tended kitchen and neglected fire—they paid a neighbour to do the housework, as far as the care of her own seven children would let her—suddenly revived in his slippery mind the memory of his niece, who, with all her faults, had had the makings of a housewife, and for whom, in spite of her flouts and jeers, he had always cherished a secret admiration. As he came in he noticed that the door to the left hand, leading into what Westmoreland folk call the 'house' or sitting-room of the farm, was open. The room had hardly been used since Mary's flight, and the few pieces of black oak and shining mahogany which adorned it had long ago fallen from their pristine polish. The geraniums and fuchsias with which she had filled the window all the summer before had died into dry blackened stalks; and the dust lay heavy on the room, in spite of the well-meant but wholly ineffective efforts of the char-woman next door. The two old men had avoided the place for months past by common consent, and the door into it was hardly ever opened.

Now, however, it stood ajar, and old Jim going up to shut it, and looking in, was struck dumb with astonishment. For there on a wooden rocking-chair, which had been her mother's favourite seat, sat Mary Backhouse, her feet on the curved brass fender, her eyes staring into the parlour grate. Her clothes, her face, her attitude of cowering chill and mortal fatigue, produced an impression which struck through the old man's dull senses, and made him tremble so that his hand dropped from the handle of the door. The slight sound roused Mary, and she turned towards him. She said nothing for a few seconds, her hollow black eyes fixed upon him; then with a ghastly smile, and a voice so hoarse as to be scarcely audible—

'Weel, aa've coom back. Ye'd maybe not expect me?'

There was a sound behind on the cobbles outside the kitchen door.

'Yur feyther!' cried Jim between his teeth. 'Gang upstairs wi' ye.' And he pointed to a door in the wall concealing a staircase to the upper storey.

She sprang up, looked at the door and at him irresolutely, and then stayed where she was, gaunt, pale, fever-eyed, the wreck and ghost of her old self.

The steps neared. There was a rough voice in the kitchen, a surprised ex-clamation, and her father had pushed past his brother into the room.

John Backhouse no sooner saw his daughter than his dull weather-beaten face flamed into violence. With an oath he raised the heavy whip he held in his hand, and flung himself towards her.

'Naw, ye'll not du'at!' cried Jim, throwing himself with all his feeble strength on to his brother's arm. John swore and struggled, but the old man stuck like a limpet.

'You let 'un aleann,' said Mary, drawing her tattered shawl over her breast.

'If he aims to kill me, *aa*'ll not say naa. But he needn't moider hisself! There's them abuve as ha' taken care o' that!'

She sank again into her chair, as though her limbs could not support her, and her eyes closed in the utter indifference of a fatigue which had made even fear impossible.

The father's arm dropped; he stood there sullenly looking at her. Jim, thinking she had fainted, went up to her, took a glass of water out of which she had already been drinking from the mahogany table, and held it to her lips. She drank a little, and then with a desperate effort raised herself, and clutching the arm of the chair, faced her father.

'Ye'll not hev to wait lang. Doan't ye fash yersel. Maybe it ull comfort ye to knaw summat! Lasst Midsummer Day aa was on t' Shanmoor road, i' t' gloaming. An' aa saw theer t' bogle—thee knaws, t' bogle o' Bleacliff Tarn; an' she turned hersel, an' she spoak to me!'

She uttered the last words with a grim emphasis, dwelling on each, the whole life of the wasted face concentrated in the terrible black eyes, which gazed past the two figures within their immediate range into a vacancy peopled with horror. Then a film came over them, the grip relaxed, and she fell back with a lurch of the rocking-chair in a dead swoon.

With the help of the neighbour from next door, Jim got her upstairs into the room that had been hers. She awoke from her swoon only to fall into the torpid sleep of exhaustion, which lasted for twelve hours.

'Keep her oot o' ma way,' said the father with an oath to Jim, 'or aa'll not answer nayther for her nor me!'

She needed no telling. She soon crept downstairs again, and went to the task of house-cleaning. The two men lived in the kitchen as before; when they were at home she ate and sat in the parlour alone. Jim watched her as far as his dull brain was capable of watching, and he dimly understood that she was dying. Both men, indeed, felt a sort of superstitious awe of her, she was so changed, so unearthly. As for the story of the ghost, the old popular superstitions are almost dead in the Cumbrian mountains, and the shrewd north-country peasant is in many places quite as scornfully ready to sacrifice his ghosts to the Time Spirit as any 'bold bad' haunter of scientific associations could wish him to be. But in a few of the remoter valleys they still linger, though beneath the surface. Either of the Backhouses, or Mary in her days of health, would have suffered many things rather than allow a stranger to suppose they placed the smallest credence in the story of Bleacliff Tarn. But, all the same, the story which each had heard in childhood, on stormy nights perhaps, when the mountain side was awful with the sounds of tempest, had grown up with them, had entered deep into the tissue of consciousness. In Mary's imagination the ideas and images connected with it had now, under the stimulus of circumstance, become instinct with a living pursuing terror. But they were present, though in a duller, blunter state, in the minds of her father and uncle; and as the weeks passed on, and the days lengthened towards midsummer, a sort of brooding horror seemed to settle on the house.

Mary grew weaker and weaker; her cough kept Jim awake at nights; once or twice when he went to help her with a piece of work which not even her extraordinary will could carry her through, her hand burnt him like a hot cinder. But she kept all other women out of the house by her mad, strange ways; and if her uncle showed any consciousness of her state, she turned upon him with her old temper, which had lost all its former stormy grace, and had become ghastly by the contrast it brought out between the tempestuous vindictive soul and the shaken weakness of frame.

A doctor would have discovered at once that what was wrong with her was phthisis, complicated with insanity; and the insanity, instead of taking the hopeful optimistic tinge which is characteristic of the insanity of consumption, had rather assumed the colour of the events from which the disease itself had started.[127] Cold, exposure, long-continued agony of mind and body—the madness intertwined with an illness which had such roots as these was naturally a madness of despair. One of its principal signs was the fixed idea as to Midsummer Day. It never occurred to her as possible that her life should be prolonged beyond that limit. Every night, as she dragged herself up the steep little staircase to her room, she checked off the day which had just passed from the days she had still to live. She had made all her arrangements; she had even sewed with her own hands, and that without any sense of special horror, but rather in the provident peasant way, the dress in which she was to be carried to her grave.

At last one day, her father, coming unexpectedly into the yard, saw her carrying a heavy pail of water from the pump. Something stirred within him, and he went up to her and forcibly took it from her. Their looks met, and her poor mad eyes gazed intensely into his. As he moved forward towards the house she crept after him, passing him into the parlour, where she sank down breathless on the settle where she had been sleeping for the last few nights, rather than face climbing the stairs. For the first time he followed her, watching her gasping struggle for breath, in spite of her impatient motion to him to go. After a few seconds he left her, took his hat, went out, saddled his horse, and rode off to Whinborough. He got Dr. Baker to promise to come over on

---

127 Phthisis: tuberculosis.

the morrow, and on his way back he called and requested to see Catherine Leyburn. He stammeringly asked her to come and visit his daughter who was ill and lonesome, and when she consented gladly he went on his way feeling a load off his mind. What he had just done had been due to an undefined, but still vehement prompting of conscience. It did not make it any the less probable that the girl would die on or before Midsummer Day; but, supposing her story were true, it absolved him from any charge of assistance to the designs of those grisly powers in whose clutch she was.

When the doctor came next morning a change for the worse had taken place, and she was too feeble actively to resent his appearance. She lay there on the settle, every now and then making superhuman efforts to get up, which generally ended in a swoon. She refused to take any medicine, she would hardly take any food, and to the doctor's questions she returned no answer whatever. In the same way, when Catherine came, she would be absolutely silent, looking at her with glittering, feverish eyes, but taking no notice at all, whether she read or talked, or simply sat quietly beside her.

After the silent period, as the days went on, and Midsummer Day drew nearer, there supervened a period of intermittent delirium. In the evenings, especially when her temperature rose, she became talkative and incoherent, and Catherine would sometimes tremble as she caught the sentences which, little by little, built up the girl's hidden tragedy before her eyes. London streets, London lights, London darkness, the agony of an endless wandering, the little clinging puny life, which could never be stilled or satisfied, biting cold, intolerable pain, the cheerless workhouse order, and, finally, the arms without a burden, the breast without a child—these were the sharp fragments of experience, so common, so terrible to the end of time, which rose on the troubled surface of Mary Backhouse's delirium, and smote the tender heart of the listener.

Then in the mornings she would lie suspicious and silent, watching Catherine's face with the long gaze of exhaustion, as though trying to find out from it whether her secret had escaped her. The doctor, who had gathered the story of the 'bogle' from Catherine, to whom Jim had told it, briefly and reluctantly, and with an absolute reservation of his own views on the matter, recommended that if possible they should try and deceive her as to the date of the day and month. Mere nervous excitement might, he thought, be enough to kill her when the actual day and hour came round. But all their attempts were useless. Nothing distracted the intense sleepless attention with which the darkened mind kept always in view that one absorbing expectation. Words fell from her at night which seemed to show that she expected a

summons—a voice along the fell, calling her spirit into the dark. And then
would come the shriek, the struggle to get loose, the choked waking, the wandering, horror-stricken eyes, subsiding by degrees into the old silent watch.

On the morning of the 23d, when Robert, sitting at his work, was looking at Burwood through the window in the flattering belief that Catherine
was the captive of the weather, she had spent an hour or more with Mary
Backhouse, and the austere influences of the visit had perhaps had more share
than she knew in determining her own mood that day. The world seemed
such dross, the pretences of personal happiness so hollow and delusive, after
such a sight! The girl lay dying fast, with a look of extraordinary attentiveness
in her face, hearing every noise, every footfall, and, as it seemed to Catherine,
in a mood of inward joy. She took, moreover, some notice of her visitor. As
a rough tomboy of fourteen, she had shown Catherine, who had taught her
in the school sometimes, and had especially won her regard on one occasion
by a present of some article of dress, a good many uncouth signs of affection.
On the morning in question Catherine fancied she saw something of the old
childish expression once or twice. At any rate, there was no doubt her presence was soothing, as she read in her low vibrating voice, or sat silently stroking the emaciated hand, raising it every now and then to her lips with a rush
of that intense pitifulness which was to her the most natural of all moods.

The doctor, whom she met there, said that this state of calm was very possibly only transitory. The night had been passed in a succession of paroxysms,
and they were almost sure to return upon her, especially as he could get her to
swallow none of the sedatives which might have carried her in unconsciousness past the fatal moment. She would have none of them; he thought that
she was determined to allow of no encroachments on the troubled remnants
of intelligence still left to her; so the only thing to be done was to wait and
see the result. 'I will come to-morrow,' said Catherine briefly; 'for the day
certainly, longer if necessary.' She had long ago established her claim to be
treated seriously as a nurse, and Dr. Baker made no objection. '*If* she lives
so long,' he said dubiously. 'The Backhouses and Mrs. Irwin [the neighbour]
shall be close at hand. I will come in the afternoon and try to get her to take
an opiate; but I can't give it her by force, and there is not the smallest chance
of her consenting to it.'

All through Catherine's own struggle and pain during these two days the
image of the dying girl had lain at her heart. It served her as the crucifix serves
the Romanist; as she pressed it into her thought, it recovered from time to
time the failing forces of the will. Need life be empty because self was left un-
satisfied? Now, as she neared the hamlet, the quality of her nature reasserted

itself. The personal want tugging at her senses, the personal soreness, the cry of resentful love, were silenced. What place had they in the presence of this lonely agony of death, this mystery, this opening beyond? The old heroic mood revived in her. Her step grew swifter, her carriage more erect, and as she entered the farm kitchen she felt herself once more ready in spirit for what lay before her.

From the next room there came a succession of husky sibilant sounds, as though some one were whispering hurriedly and continuously.

After her subdued greeting she looked inquiringly at Jim.

'She's in a taaking way,' said Jim, who looked more attenuated and his face more like a pink and white parchment than ever. 'She's been knacking an' taaking a long while. She woan't know ye. Luke ye,' he continued, dropping his voice as he opened the 'house' door for her; 'ef you want ayder ov oos, you jest call oot—sharp! Mrs. Irwin, she'll stay in wi' ye—she's not afeeard!'

The superstitious excitement which the looks and gestures of the old man expressed touched Catherine's imagination, and she entered the room with an inward shiver.

Mary Backhouse lay raised high on her pillows, talking to herself or to imaginary other persons, with eyes wide open but vacant, and senses conscious of nothing but the dream world in which the mind was wandering. Catherine sat softly down beside her, unnoticed, thankful for the chances of disease. If this delirium lasted till the ghost-hour—the time of twilight, that is to say, which would begin about half-past eight, and the duration of which would depend on the cloudiness of the evening—was over, or, better still, till midnight were past, the strain on the girl's agonised senses might be relieved, and death come at last in softer, kinder guise.

'Has she been long like this?' she asked softly of the neighbour who sat quietly knitting by the evening light.

The woman looked up and thought.

'Ay!' she said. 'Aa came in at tea-time, an' she's been maistly taakin' ivver sence!'

The incoherent whisperings and restless movements, which obliged Catherine constantly to replace the coverings over the poor wasted and fevered body, went on for some time. Catherine noticed presently, with a little thrill, that the light was beginning to change. The weather was growing darker and stormier; the wind shook the house in gusts; and the farther shoulder of High Fell, seen in distorted outline through the casemented window, was almost hidden by the trailing rain clouds. The mournful western light coming from behind the house struck the river here and there; almost everything else was gray and dark. A mountain ash, just outside the window, brushed the panes every now and then; and in the silence every surrounding sound—the rare movements in the next room, the voices of quarrelling children round the door of a neighbouring house, the far-off barking of dogs—made itself distinctly audible.

Suddenly Catherine, sunk in painful reverie, noticed that the mutterings from the bed had ceased for some little time. She turned her chair, and was startled to find those weird eyes fixed with recognition on herself. There was a curious malign intensity, a curious triumph in them.

'It must be—eight o'clock,' said the gasping voice—'*eight o'clock*,' and the tone became a whisper, as though the idea thus half involuntarily revealed had been drawn jealously back into the strongholds of consciousness.

'Mary,' said Catherine, falling on her knees beside the bed, and taking one of the restless hands forcibly into her own, 'can't you put this thought away from you? We are not the playthings of evil spirits—we are the children of God! We are in His hands. No evil thing can harm us against His will.'

It was the first time for many days she had spoken openly of the thought which was in the mind of all, and her whole pleading soul was in her pale, beautiful face. There was no response in the sick girl's countenance, and again that look of triumph, of sinister exultation. They had tried to cheat her into sleeping, and living, and in spite of them, at the supreme moment, every sense was awake and expectant. To what was the materialised peasant imagination looking forward? To an actual call, an actual following to the free mountain-side, the rush of the wind, the phantom figure floating on before her, bearing her into the heart of the storm? Dread was gone, pain was gone; there was only rapt excitement and fierce anticipation.

'Mary,' said Catherine again, mistaking her mood for one of tense defiance and despair, 'Mary, if I were to go out now and leave Mrs. Irwin with you, and if I were to go up all the way to the top of Shanmoss and back again, and if I could tell you there was nothing there, nothing!—if I were to stay out till the dark has come—it will be here in half an hour—and you could be quite sure when you saw me again, that there was nothing near you but the dear old hills, and the power of God, could you believe me and try and rest and sleep?'

Mary looked at her intently. If Catherine could have seen clearly in the dim light she would have caught something of the cunning of madness slipping into the dying woman's expression. While she waited for the answer there was a noise in the kitchen outside, an opening of the outer door, and a voice. Catherine's heart stood still. She had to make a superhuman effort to keep her attention fixed on Mary.

'Go!' said the hoarse whisper close beside her, and the girl lifted her wasted hand, and pushed her visitor from her. 'Go!' it repeated insistently, with a sort of wild beseeching; then, brokenly, the gasping breath interrupting, 'There's naw fear—naw fear—fur the likes o' you!'

Catherine rose.

'I'm not afraid,' she said gently, but her hand shook as she pushed her chair back; 'God is everywhere, Mary.'

She put on her hat and cloak, said something in Mrs. Irwin's ear, and stooped to kiss the brow which to the shuddering sense under her will seemed already cold and moist with the sweats of death. Mary watched her go; Mrs. Irwin, with the air of one bewildered, drew her chair nearer to the settle; and the light of the fire, shooting and dancing through the June twilight, threw such fantastic shadows over the face on the pillow that all expression was lost. What was moving in the crazed mind? Satisfaction, perhaps, at having got rid of one witness, one jailer, one of the various antagonistic forces surrounding her? She had a dim frenzied notion she should have to fight for her liberty when the call came, and she lay tense and rigid, waiting—the images of insanity whirling through her brain, while the light slowly, slowly waned.

Catherine opened the door into the kitchen. The two carriers were standing there, and Robert Elsmere also stood with his back to her, talking to them in an undertone.

He turned at the sound behind him, and his start brought a sudden flush to Catherine's cheek. Her face, as the candle-light struck it amid the shadows of the doorway, was like an angelic vision to him—the heavenly calm of it just exquisitely broken by the wonder, the shock, of his presence.

'You here?' he cried, coming up to her, and taking her hand—what secret instinct guided him?—close in both of his. 'I never dreamt of it—so late. My cousin sent me over—she wished for news.'

She smiled involuntarily. It seemed to her she had expected this in some sort all along. But her self-possession was complete.

'The excited state may be over in a short time now,' she answered him in a quiet whisper; 'but at present it is at its height. It seemed to please her'—and withdrawing her hand, she turned to John Backhouse—'when I suggested that I should walk up to Shanmoss and back. I said I would come back to her in half an hour or so, when the daylight was quite gone, and prove to her there was nothing on the path.'

A hand caught her arm. It was Mrs. Irwin, holding the door close with the other hand.

'Miss Leyburn—Miss Catherine! Yur not gawin' oot—not gawin' oop *that* path?' The woman was fond of Catherine, and looked deadly frightened.

'Yes, I am, Mrs. Irwin—but I shall be back very soon. Don't leave her; go back.' And Catherine motioned her back with a little peremptory gesture.

'Doan't ye let 'ur, sir,' said the woman excitedly to Robert. 'One's eneuf aa'm thinking.' And she pointed with a meaning gesture to the room behind her.

Robert looked at Catherine, who was moving towards the outer door.

'I'll go with her,' he said hastily, his face lighting up. 'There is nothing whatever to be afraid of, only don't leave your patient.'

Catherine trembled as she heard the words, but she made no sign, and the two men and the woman watched their departure with blank uneasy wonderment. A second later they were on the fell-side climbing a rough stony path, which in places was almost a watercourse, and which wound up the fell towards a tract of level swampy moss or heath, beyond which lay the descent to Shanmoor. Daylight was almost gone; the stormy yellow west was being fast swallowed up in cloud; below them as they climbed lay the dark group of houses, with a light twinkling here and there. All about them were black mountain forms; a desolate tempestuous wind drove a gusty rain into their faces; a little beck roared beside them, and in the distance from the black gulf of the valley the swollen river thundered.

Elsmere looked down on his companion with an indescribable exultation, a passionate sense of possession which could hardly restrain itself. He had come back that morning with a mind clearly made up. Catherine had been blind indeed when she supposed that any plan of his or hers would have been allowed to stand in the way of that last wrestle with her, of which he had planned all the methods, rehearsed all the arguments. But when he reached the vicarage he was greeted with the news of her absence. She was inaccessible it appeared for the day. No matter! The vicar and he settled in the fewest possible words that he should stay till Monday, Mrs. Thornburgh meanwhile looking on, saying what civility demanded, and surprisingly little else. Then in the evening Mrs. Thornburgh had asked of him with a manner of admirable indifference whether he felt inclined for an evening walk to High Ghyll to inquire after Mary Backhouse. The request fell in excellently with a lover's restlessness, and Robert assented at once. The vicar saw him go with puzzled brows and a quick look at his wife, whose head was bent close over her worsted work.

It never occurred to Elsmere—or if it did occur, he pooh-poohed the notion—that he should find Catherine still at her post far from home on this dark stormy evening. But in the glow of joy which her presence had brought him he was still capable of all sorts of delicate perceptions and reasonings. His quick imagination carried him through the scene from which she had just momentarily escaped. He had understood the exaltation of her look and tone. If love spoke at all, ringed with such surroundings, it must be with its most inward and spiritual voice, as those speak who feel 'the Eternities' about them.

But the darkness hid her from him so well that he had to feel out the situation for himself. He could not trace it in her face.

'We must go right up to the top of the pass,' she said to him as he held a gate open for her which led them into a piece of larch plantation on the mountain-side. 'The ghost is supposed to walk along this bit of road above the houses, till it reaches the heath on the top, and then it turns towards Bleacliff Tarn, which lies higher up to the right, under High Fell.'

'Do you imagine your report will have any effect?'

'At any rate,' she said sighing, 'it seemed to me that it might divert her thoughts a little from the actual horror of her own summons. Anything is better than the torture of that one fixed idea as she lies there.'

'What is that?' said Robert, startled a little by some ghostly sounds in front of them. The little wood was almost dark, and he could see nothing.

'Only a horse trotting on in front of us,' said Catherine; 'our voices frightened him, I suppose. We shall be out on the fell again directly.'

And as they quitted the trees, a dark bulky form to the left suddenly lifted a shadowy head from the grass, and clattered down the slope.

A cluster of white-stemmed birches just ahead of them caught whatever light was still left in the atmosphere, their feathery tops bending and swaying against the sky.

'How easily, with mind attuned, one could people this whole path with ghosts!' said Robert. 'Look at those stems, and that line of stream coming down to the right, and listen to the wind among the fern.'

For they were passing a little gully deep in bracken, up which the blast was tearing its tempestuous way.

Catherine shivered a little, and the sense of physical exhaustion, which had been banished like everything else—doubt, humiliation, bitterness—by the one fact of his presence, came back on her.

'There *is* something rather awful in this dark and storm,' she said, and paused.

'Would you have faced it alone?' he asked, his voice thrilling her with a hundred different meanings. 'I am glad I prevented it.'

'I have no fear of the mountains,' she said, trembling. 'I know them, and they me.'

'But you are tired—your voice is tired—and the walk might have been more of an effort than you thought it. Do you never think of yourself?'

'Oh dear, yes,' said Catherine, trying to smile, and could find nothing else to say. They walked on a few moments in silence, splashes of rain breaking in their faces. Robert's inward excitement was growing fast. Suddenly Catherine's pulse stood still. She felt her hand lifted, drawn within his arm, covered close with his warm trembling clasp.

'Catherine, let it stay there. Listen one moment. You gave me a hard lesson yesterday, too hard—I cannot learn it—I am bold—I claim you. Be my wife. Help me through this difficult world. I have loved you from the first moment. Come to me. Be kind to me.'

She could hardly see his face, but she could feel the passion in his voice and touch. Her cheek seemed to droop against his arm. He felt her tottering.

'Let me sit down,' she said; and after one moment of dizzy silence he guided her to a rock, sinking down himself beside her, longing, but not daring, to shelter her under his broad Inverness cloak against the storm.

'I told you,' she said, almost whispering, 'that I was bound, tied to others.'

'I do not admit your plea,' he said passionately; 'no, not for a moment. For two days have I been tramping over the mountains thinking it out for yourself and me. Catherine, your mother has no son—she should find one in me. I have no sisters—give me yours. I will cherish them as any brother could. Come and enrich my life; you shall still fill and shelter theirs. I dare not think what my future might be with you to guide, to inspire, to bless—dare not, lest with a word you should plunge me into an outer darkness I cannot face.'

He caught her unresisting hand, and raised it to his lips.

'Is there no sacredness,' he said brokenly, 'in the fate that has brought us together—out of all the world—here in this lonely valley? Come to me, Catherine. You shall never fail the old ties, I promise you; and new hands shall cling to you—new voices shall call you blessed.'

Catherine could hardly breathe. Every word had been like balm upon a wound—like a ray of intense light in the gloom about them. Oh, where was this softness bearing her—this emptiness of all will, of all individual power? She hid her eyes with her other hand, struggling to recall that far-away moment in Marrisdale. But the mind refused to work. Consciousness seemed to retain nothing but the warm grasp of his hand—the tones of his voice. [128]

He saw her struggle, and pressed on remorselessly.

---

128 "far-away": hyphenated as per *W.*

'Speak to me—say one little kind word. Oh, you cannot send me away miserable and empty!'

She turned to him, and laid her trembling free hand on his arm. He clasped them both with rapture.

'Give me a little time.'

'No, no,' he said, and it almost seemed to her that he was smiling: 'time for you to escape me again, my wild mountain bird; time for you to think yourself and me into all sorts of moral mists! No, you shall not have it. Here, alone with God and the dark—bless me or undo me. Send me out to the work of life maimed and sorrowful, or send me out your knight, your possession, pledged——'

But his voice failed him. What a note of youth, of imagination, of impulsive eagerness there was through it all! The more slowly-moving inarticulate nature was swept away by it. There was but one object clear to her in the whole world of thought or sense, everything else had sunk out of sight—drowned in a luminous mist.

He rose and stood before her as he delivered his ultimatum, his tall form drawn up to its full height. In the east, across the valley, above the farther buttress of High Fell, there was a clearer strip of sky, visible for a moment among the moving storm clouds, and a dim haloed moon shone out in it. Far away a white-walled cottage glimmered against the fell; the pools at their feet shone in the weird passing light.

She lifted her head, and looked at him, still irresolute. Then she too rose, and helplessly, like some one impelled by a will not her own, she silently held out to him two white trembling hands.

'Catherine—my angel—my wife!'

There was something in the pale virginal grace of look and form which kept his young passion in awe. But he bent his head again over those yielded hands, kissing them with dizzy unspeakable joy.

About twenty minutes later Catherine and Robert, having hurried back with all speed from the top of Shanmoss, reached the farmhouse door. She knocked. No one answered. She tried the lock; it yielded, and they entered. No one in the kitchen. She looked disturbed and conscience-stricken.

'Oh!' she cried to him, under her breath; 'have we been too long?' And hurrying into the inner room she left him waiting.

Inside was a mournful sight. The two men and Mrs. Irwin stood close round the settle, but as she came nearer, Catherine saw Mary Backhouse lying panting on her pillows, her breath coming in loud gasps, her dress and all the coverings of the bed showing signs of disorder and confusion, her black hair tossed about her.

'It's bin awfu' work sence you left, miss,' whispered Mrs. Irwin to Catherine excitedly, as she joined them. 'She thowt she heerd soombody fley-tin' and callin'—it was t' wind came skirlin' round t' place, an' she aw' but thrown hirsel' oot o' t' bed, an' aa shooted for Jim, and they came, and they and I—it's bin as much as we could a' du to hod 'er.'

'Luke! Steady!' exclaimed Jim. 'She'll try it again.'

For the hands were moving restlessly from side to side, and the face was working again. There was one more desperate effort to rise, which the two men checked—gently enough, but effectually—and then the exhaustion seemed complete. The lids fell, and the struggle for breath was pitiful.

Catherine flew for some drugs which the doctor had left, and shown her how to use. After some twenty minutes they seemed to give relief, and the great haunted eyes opened once more.

Catherine held barley-water to the parched lips, and Mary drank me-chanically, her gaze still intently fixed on her nurse. When Catherine put down the glass the eyes followed her with a question which the lips had no power to frame.

'Leave her now a little,' said Catherine to the others. 'The fewer people and the more air the better. And please let the door be open; the room is too hot.'

They went out silently, and Catherine sank down beside the bed. Her heart went out in unspeakable longing towards the poor human wreck before her. For her there was no morrow possible, no dawn of other and softer skies. All was over: life was lived, and all its heavenly capabilities missed for ever. Catherine felt her own joy hurt her, and her tears fell fast.

'Mary,' she said, laying her face close beside the chill face on the pillow, 'Mary, I went out; I climbed all the path as far as Shanmoss. There was noth-ing evil there. Oh, I must tell you! *Can* I make you understand? I want you to feel that it is only God and love that are real. Oh, think of them! He would not let you be hurt and terrified in your pain, poor Mary. He loves you. He is waiting to comfort you—to set you free from pain for ever; and He has sent you a sign by me.' ... She lifted her head from the pillow, trembling and hesi-tating. Still that feverish questioning gaze on the face beneath her, as it lay in deep shadow cast by a light on the window-sill some paces away.

'You sent me out, Mary, to search for something, the thought of which has been tormenting and torturing you. You thought God would let a dark lost spirit trouble you and take you away from Him—you, His child, whom

He made and whom He loves! And listen! While you thought you were sending me out to face the evil thing, you were really my kind angel—God's mes-
senger—sending me to meet the joy of my whole life!

'There was some one waiting here just now,' she went on hurriedly,
breathing her sobbing words into Mary's ear. 'Some one who has loved me,
and whom I love. But I had made him sad, and myself; then when you sent
me out he came too; we walked up that path, you remember, beyond the
larchwood, up to the top, where the stream goes under the road. And there
he spoke to me, and I couldn't help it any more. And I promised to love him
and be his wife. And if it hadn't been for you, Mary, it would never have happened. God had put it into your hand, this joy, and I bless you for it! Oh,
and Mary—Mary—it is only for a little little while this life of ours! Nothing
matters—not our worst sin and sorrow—but God, and our love to Him. I
shall meet you some day—I pray I may—in His sight and all will be well, the
pain all forgotten—all!'

She raised herself again and looked down with yearning passionate pity
on the shadowed form. Oh, blessed answer of heart to heart! There were tears
forming under the heavy lids, the corners of the lips were relaxed and soft.
Slowly the feeble hand sought her own. She waited in an intense expectant
silence.

There was a faint breathing from the lips; she stooped and caught it.

'Kiss me!' said the whisper; and she laid her soft fresh lips to the parched
mouth of the dying. When she lifted her head again Mary still held her hand;
Catherine softly stretched out hers for the opiate Dr. Baker had left; it was
swallowed without resistance, and a quiet to which the invalid had been a
stranger for days stole little by little over the wasted frame. The grasp of the
fingers relaxed, the laboured breath came more gently, and in a few more
minutes she slept. Twilight was long over. The ghost-hour was past, and the
moon outside was slowly gaining a wider empire in the clearing heavens.

It was a little after ten o'clock when Rose drew aside the curtain at
Burwood and looked out.

'There is the lantern,' she said to Agnes, 'just by the vicarage. How the
night has cleared!'

She turned back to her book. Agnes was writing letters. Mrs. Leyburn was
sitting by the bit of fire that was generally lit for her benefit in the evenings,
her white shawl dropping gracefully about her, a copy of the *Cornhill* on her
lap.[129] But she was not reading, she was meditating, and the girls thought her

---

129 The *Cornhill Magazine*, a leading literary journal of the Victorian period founded

out of spirits. The hall door opened.

'There is some one with Catherine!' cried Rose, starting up. Agnes suspended her letter.

'Perhaps the vicar,' said Mrs. Leyburn, with a little sigh.

A hand turned the drawing-room door, and in the doorway stood Elsmere. Rose caught a gray dress disappearing up the little stairs behind him.

Elsmere's look was enough for the two girls. They understood in an instant. Rose flushed all over. The first contact with love is intoxicating to any girl of eighteen, even though the romance be not hers. But Mrs. Leyburn sat bewildered.

Elsmere went up to her, stooped and took her hand.

'Will you give her to me, Mrs. Leyburn?' he said, his boyish looks aglow, his voice unsteady. 'Will you let me be a son to you?'

Mrs. Leyburn rose. He still held her hand. She looked up at him helplessly.

'Oh, Mr. Elsmere, where is Catherine?'

'I brought her home,' he said gently. 'She is mine, if you will it. Give her to me again!'

Mrs. Leyburn's face worked pitifully. The rectory and the wedding dress, which had lingered so regretfully in her thoughts since her last sight of Catherine, sank out of them altogether.

'She has been everything in the world to us, Mr. Elsmere.'

'I know she has,' he said simply. 'She shall be everything in the world to you still. I have had hard work to persuade her. There will be no chance for me if you don't help me.'

Another breathless pause. Then Mrs. Leyburn timidly drew him to her, and he stooped his tall head and kissed her like a son.

'Oh, I must go to Catherine!' she said, hurrying away, her pretty withered cheeks wet with tears.

Then the girls threw themselves on Elsmere. The talk was all animation and excitement for the moment, not a tragic touch in it. It was as well perhaps that Catherine was not there to hear!

'I give you fair warning,' said Rose, as she bade him good-night, 'that I don't know how to behave to a brother. And I am equally sure that Mrs. Thornburgh doesn't know how to behave to a *fiancé*.'

Robert threw up his arms in mock terror at the name, and departed.

'We are abandoned,' cried Rose, flinging herself into the chair again—then with a little flash of half irresolute wickedness—'and we are free! Oh, I hope she will be happy!'

---

in 1860. Its first editor was novelist and satirist W. M. Thackeray.

And she caught Agnes wildly round the neck as though she would drown her first words in her last.

'Madcap!' cried Agnes, struggling. 'Leave me at least a little breath to wish Catherine joy!'

And they both fled upstairs.

There was indeed no prouder woman in the three kingdoms than Mrs. Thornburgh that night. After all the agitation downstairs she could not persuade herself to go to bed. She first knocked up Sarah and communicated the news; then she sat down before a pier-glass in her own room studying the person who had found Catherine Leyburn a husband.

'My doing from beginning to end,' she cried with a triumph beyond words. 'William has had *nothing* to do with it. Robert has had scarcely as much. And to think how little I dreamt of it when I began! Well, to be sure, no one could have *planned* marrying those two. There's no one but Providence could have foreseen it—they're so different. And after all it's *done*. Now then, whom shall I have next year?'

BOOK II - SURREY

CHAPTER XI

Farewell to the mountains!

The scene in which the next act of this unpretending history is to run its course is of a very different kind. In place of the rugged northern nature—a nature wild and solitary indeed, but still rich, luxuriant, and friendly to the senses of the traveller, even in its loneliest places. The heaths and woods of some districts of Surrey are scarcely more thickly peopled than the fells of Westmoreland; the walker may wander for miles, and still enjoy an untamed primitive earth, guiltless of boundary or furrow, the undisturbed home of all that grows and flies, where the rabbits, the lizards, and the birds live their life as they please, either ignorant of intruding man or strangely little incommoded by his neighbourhood. And yet there is nothing forbidding or austere in these wide solitudes. The patches of graceful birch-wood; the miniature lakes nestling among them; the brakes of ling—pink, faintly scented, a feast for every sense; the stretches of purple heather, glowing into scarlet under the touch of the sun; the scattered farm-houses, so mellow in colour, so pleasant in outline; the general softness and lavishness of the earth and all it bears, make these Surrey commons not a wilderness but a paradise. Nature, indeed, here is like some spoilt petulant child. She will bring forth nothing, or almost nothing, for man's grosser needs. Ask her to bear corn or pasture flocks, and she will be miserly and grudging. But ask her only to be beautiful, enticing, capriciously lovely, and she will throw herself into the task with all the abandonment, all the energy, that heart could wish.

It is on the borders of one of the wilder districts of a county, which is throughout a strange mixture of suburbanism and the desert, that we next meet with Robert and Catherine Elsmere. The rectory of Murewell occupied the highest point of a gentle swell of ground which sloped through cornfields and woods to a plain of boundless heather on the south, and climbed away on the north towards the long chalk ridge of the Hog's Back. It was a square white house pretending neither to beauty nor state, a little awkwardly and barely placed, with only a small stretch of grass and a low hedge between it and the road. A few tall firs climbing above the roof gave a little grace and clothing to its southern side, and behind it there was a garden sloping softly down towards the village at its foot—a garden chiefly noticeable for its grass walks, the luxuriance of the fruit trees clinging to its old red walls, and the masses of pink and white phloxes which now in August gave it the floweriness and the gaiety of an Elizabethan song. Below in the hollow and to the right lay the picturesque medley of the village—roofs and gables and chimneys, yellow-gray thatch, shining whitewash, and mellowed brick, making a bright patchwork among the softening trees, thin wreaths of blue smoke, like airy ribbons, tangled through it all. Rising over the rest was a house of some dignity. It had been an old manor-house, now it was half ruinous and the village inn. Some generations back the squire of the day had dismantled it, jealous that so big a house should exist in the same parish as the Hall, and the spoils of it had furnished the rectory; so that the homely house was fitted inside with mahogany doors and carved cupboard fronts, in which Robert delighted, and in which even Catherine felt a proprietary pleasure.

Altogether a quiet, rural, English spot. If the house had no beauty, it commanded a world of loveliness. All around it—north, south, and west—there spread, as it were, a vast playground of heather and wood and grassy common, in which the few workaday patches of hedge and ploughed land seemed ingulfed and lost. Close under the rectory windows, however, was a vast sloping cornfield, belonging to the glebe, the largest and fruitfulest of the neighbourhood. At the present moment it was just ready for the reaper—the golden ears had clearly but a few more days or hours to ripple in the sun. It was bounded by a dark summer-scorched belt of wood, and beyond, over the distance, rose a blue pointed hill, which seemed to be there only to attract and make a centre for the sunsets.

As compared with her Westmoreland life, the first twelve months of wifehood had been to Catherine Elsmere a time of rapid and changing experience. A few days out of their honeymoon had been spent at Oxford. It was a week before the opening of the October term, but many of the senior members of the University were already in residence, and the stagnation of the Long Vacation was over.[1] Langham was up; so was Mr. Grey, and many another old friend of Robert's. The bride and bridegroom were much fêted in a quiet way. They dined in many common rooms and bursaries; they were invited to many luncheons, whereat the superabundance of food and the length of

---

1   The summer break, which lasts from July through September. Serious-minded students would use the summer to organize "reading parties" with a tutor.

time spent upon it made the Puritan Catherine uncomfortable; and Langham devoted himself to taking the wife through colleges and gardens, Schools and Bodleian, in most orthodox fashion, indemnifying himself afterwards for the sense of constraint her presence imposed upon him by a talk and a smoke with Robert.

He could not understand the Elsmere marriage. That a creature so mobile, so sensitive, so susceptible as Elsmere should have fallen in love with this stately silent woman, with her very evident rigidities of thought and training, was only another illustration of the mysteries of matrimony. He could not get on with her, and after a while did not try to do so.

There could be no doubt as to Elsmere's devotion. He was absorbed, wrapped up in her.

'She has affected him,' thought the tutor, 'at a period of life when he is more struck by the difficulty of being morally strong than by the difficulty of being intellectually clear. The touch of religious genius in her braces him like the breath of an Alpine wind. One can see him expanding, glowing under it. *Bien!* sooner he than I. To be fair, however, let me remember that she decidedly does not like me—which may cut me off from Elsmere. However'—and Langham sighed over his fire—'what have he and I to do with one another in the future? By all the laws of character something untoward might come out of this marriage. But she will mould him, rather than he her. Besides, she will have children—and that solves most things.'

Meanwhile, if Langham dissected the bride as he dissected most people, Robert, with that keen observation which lay hidden somewhere under his careless boyish ways, noticed many points of change about his old friend. Langham seemed to him less human, more strange, than ever; the points of contact between him and active life were lessening in number term by term. He lectured only so far as was absolutely necessary for the retention of his post, and he spoke with wholesale distaste of his pupils. He had set up a book on 'The Schools of Athens,' but when Robert saw the piles of disconnected notes already accumulated, he perfectly understood that the book was a mere blind, a screen, behind which a difficult fastidious nature trifled and procrastinated as it pleased.[2]

Again, when Elsmere was an undergraduate Langham and Grey had been intimate. Now, Langham's tone *à propos* of Grey's politics and Grey's dreams of Church Reform was as languidly sarcastic as it was with regard to most of the strenuous things of life. 'Nothing particular is true,' his manner said, 'and

---

2   The ancient philosophical schools.

all action is a degrading *pis-aller*.[3] Get through the day somehow, with as little harm to yourself and other people as may be; do your duty if you like it, but, for heaven's sake, don't cant about it to other people!'

If the affinities of character count for much, Catherine and Henry Grey should certainly have understood each other. The tutor liked the look of Elsmere's wife. His kindly brown eyes rested on her with pleasure; he tried in his shy but friendly way to get at her, and there was in both of them a touch of homeliness, a sheer power of unworldliness that should have drawn them together. And indeed Catherine felt the charm, the spell of this born leader of men. But she watched him with a sort of troubled admiration, puzzled, evidently, by the halo of moral dignity surrounding him, which contended with something else in her mind respecting him. Some words of Robert's, uttered very early in their acquaintance, had set her on her guard. Speaking of religion, Robert had said, 'Grey is not one of us'; and Catherine, restrained by a hundred ties of training and temperament, would not surrender herself, and could not if she would.

Then had followed their home-coming to the rectory, and that first institution of their common life, never to be forgotten for the tenderness and the sacredness of it. Mrs. Elsmere had received them, and had then retired to a little cottage of her own close by. She had of course already made the acquaintance of her daughter-in-law, for she had been the Thornburghs' guest for ten days before the marriage in September, and Catherine, moreover, had paid her a short visit earlier in the summer. But it was now that for the first time she realised to the full the character of the woman Robert had married. Catherine's manner to her was sweetness itself. Parted from her own mother as she was, the younger woman's strong filial instincts spent themselves in tending the mother who had been the guardian and life of Robert's youth. And Mrs. Elsmere in return was awed by Catherine's moral force and purity of nature, and proud of her personal beauty, which was so real, in spite of the severity of the type, and to which marriage had given, at any rate for the moment, a certain added softness and brilliancy.

But there were difficulties in the way. Catherine was a little too apt to treat Mrs. Elsmere as she would have treated her own mother. But to be nursed and protected, to be screened from draughts, and run after with shawls and stools was something wholly new and intolerable to Mrs. Elsmere. She could not away with it, and as soon as she had sufficiently lost her first awe of her daughter-in-law she would revenge herself in all sorts of droll ways, and with occasional flashes of petulant Irish wit which would make Catherine colour

---

3   Bottom of the barrel, worst option.

and draw back. Then Mrs. Elsmere, touched with remorse, would catch her by the neck and give her a resounding kiss, which perhaps puzzled Catherine no less than her sarcasm of a minute before.

Moreover Mrs. Elsmere felt ruefully from the first that her new daughter was decidedly deficient in the sense of humour.

'I believe it's that father of hers,' she would say to herself crossly. 'By what Robert tells me of him he must have been one of the people who get ill in their minds for want of a good mouth-filling laugh now and then. The man who can't amuse himself a bit out of the world is sure to get his head addled somehow, poor creature.'

Certainly it needed a faculty of laughter to be always able to take Mrs. Elsmere on the right side. For instance, Catherine was more often scandalised than impressed by her mother-in-law's charitable performances.

Mrs. Elsmere's little cottage was filled with workhouse orphans sent to her from different London districts. The training of these girls was the chief business of her life, and a very odd training it was, conducted in the noisiest way and on the most familiar terms. It was undeniable that the girls generally did well, and they invariably adored Mrs. Elsmere, but Catherine did not much like to think about them. Their household teaching under Mrs. Elsmere and her old servant Martha—as great an original as herself—was so irregular, their religious training so extraordinary, the clothes in which they were allowed to disport themselves so scandalous to the sober taste of the rector's wife, that Catherine involuntarily regarded the little cottage on the hill as a spot of misrule in the general order of the parish. She would go in, say, at eleven o'clock in the morning, find her mother-in-law in bed, half-dressed, with all her handmaidens about her, giving her orders, reading her letters and the newspaper, cutting out her girls' frocks, instructing them in the fashions, or delivering little homilies on questions suggested by the news of the day to the more intelligent of them. The room, the whole house, would seem to Catherine in a detestable litter. If so, Mrs. Elsmere never apologised for it. On the contrary, as she saw Catherine sweep a mass of miscellaneous *débris* off a chair in search of a seat, the small bright eyes would twinkle with something that was certainly nearer amusement than shame.

And in a hundred other ways Mrs. Elsmere's relations with the poor of the parish often made Catherine miserable. She herself had the most angelic pity and tenderness for sorrows and sinners; but sin was sin to her, and when she saw Mrs. Elsmere more than half attracted by the stronger vices, and in many cases more inclined to laugh with what was human in them than to weep over what was vile, Robert's wife would go away and wrestle with herself, that she might be betrayed into nothing harsh towards Robert's mother.

But fate allowed their differences, whether they were deep or shallow, no time to develop. A week of bitter cold at the beginning of January struck down Mrs. Elsmere, whose strange ways of living were more the result of certain long-standing delicacies of health than she had ever allowed any one to imagine. A few days of acute inflammation of the lungs,[4] borne with a patience and heroism which showed the Irish character at its finest—a moment of agonised wrestling with that terror of death which had haunted the keen vivacious soul from its earliest consciousness, ending in a glow of spiritual victory—and Robert found himself motherless. He and Catherine had never left her since the beginning of the illness. In one of the intervals towards the end, when there was a faint power of speech, she drew Catherine's cheek down to her and kissed her.

'God bless you!' the old woman's voice said, with a solemnity in it which Robert knew well, but which Catherine had never heard before. 'Be good to him, Catherine—be always good to him!'

And she lay looking from the husband to the wife with a certain wistfulness which pained Catherine, she knew not why. But she answered with tears and tender words, and at last the mother's face settled into a peace which death did but confirm.

This great and unexpected loss, which had shaken to their depths all the feelings and affections of his youth, had thrown Elsmere more than ever on his wife. To him, made as it seemed for love and for enjoyment, grief was a novel and difficult burden. He felt with passionate gratitude that his wife helped him to bear it so that he came out from it not lessened but ennobled, that she preserved him from many a lapse of nervous weariness and irritation into which his temperament might easily have been betrayed.

And how his very dependence had endeared him to Catherine! That vibrating responsive quality in him, so easily mistaken for mere weakness, which made her so necessary to him—there is nothing perhaps which wins more deeply upon a woman. For all the while it was balanced in a hundred ways by the illimitable respect which his character and his doings compelled from those about him. To be the strength, the inmost joy of a man who within the conditions of his life seems to you a hero at every turn—there is no happiness more penetrating for a wife than this.

On this August afternoon the Elsmeres were expecting visitors. Catherine had

---

4   A catch-all that could cover anything from pneumonia to tuberculosis; in this case, probably pneumonia or bronchitis.

sent the pony-carriage to the station to meet Rose and Langham, who was to escort her from Waterloo. For various reasons, all characteristic, it was Rose's first visit to Catherine's new home.

Now she had been for six weeks in London, and had been persuaded to come on to her sister, at the end of her stay. Catherine was looking forward to her coming with many tremors. The wild ambitious creature had been not one atom appeased by Manchester and its opportunities. She had gone back to Whindale in April only to fall into more hopeless discontent than ever. 'She can hardly be civil to anybody,' Agnes wrote to Catherine. 'The cry now is all "London" or at least "Berlin," and she cannot imagine why papa should ever have wished to condemn us to such a prison.'

Catherine grew pale with indignation as she read the words, and thought of her father's short-lived joy in the old house and its few green fields, or of the confidence which had soothed his last moments, that it would be well there with his wife and children, far from the hubbub of the world.

But Rose and her whims were not facts which could be put aside. They would have to be grappled with, probably humoured. As Catherine strolled out into the garden, listening alternately for Robert and for the carriage, she told herself that it would be a difficult visit. And the presence of Mr. Langham would certainly not diminish its difficulty. The mere thought of him set the wife's young form stiffening. A cold breath seemed to blow from Edward Langham, which chilled Catherine's whole being. Why was Robert so fond of him?

But the more Langham cut himself off from the world, the more Robert clung to him in his wistful affectionate way. The more difficult their intercourse became, the more determined the younger man seemed to be to maintain it. Catherine imagined that he often scourged himself in secret for the fact that the gratitude which had once flowed so readily had now become a matter of reflection and resolution.

'Why should we always expect to get pleasure from our friends?' he had said to her once with vehemence. 'It should be pleasure enough to love them.' And she knew very well of whom he was thinking.

How late he was this afternoon. He must have been a long round. She had news for him of great interest. The lodge-keeper from the Hall had just looked in to tell the rector that the squire and his widowed sister were expected home in four days.

But, interesting as the news was, Catherine's looks as she pondered it were certainly not looks of pleased expectation. Neither of them, indeed, had much cause to rejoice in the squire's advent. Since their arrival in the parish the splendid Jacobean Hall had been untenanted. The squire, who was abroad with his sister at the time of their coming, had sent a civil note to the new rector on his settlement in the parish, naming some common Oxford acquaintances, and desiring him to make what use of the famous Murewell Library he pleased. 'I hear of you as a friend to letters,' he wrote; 'do my books a service by using them.' The words were graceful enough. Robert had answered them warmly. He had also availed himself largely of the permission they had conveyed. We shall see presently that the squire, though absent, had already made a deep impression on the young man's imagination.

But unfortunately he came across the squire in two capacities. Mr. Wendover was not only the owner of Murewell, he was also the owner of the whole land of the parish, where, however, by a curious accident of inheritance, dating some generations back, and implying some very remote connection between the Wendover and Elsmere families, he was not the patron of the living. Now the more Elsmere studied him under this aspect, the deeper became his dismay. The estate was entirely in the hands of an agent who had managed it for some fifteen years, and of whose character the rector, before he had been two months in the parish, had formed the very poorest opinion. Robert, entering upon his duties with the ardour of the modern reformer, armed not only with charity but with science, found himself confronted by the opposition of a man who combined the shrewdness of an attorney with the callousness of a drunkard. It seemed incredible that a great landowner should commit his interests and the interests of hundreds of human beings to the hands of such a person.

By and by, however, as the rector penetrated more deeply into the situation, he found his indignation transferring itself more and more from the man to the master. It became clear to him that in some respects Henslowe suited the squire admirably. It became also clear to him that the squire had taken pains for years to let it be known that he cared not one rap for any human being on his estate in any other capacity than as a rent-payer or wage-receiver. What! Live for thirty years in that great house, and never care whether your tenants and labourers lived like pigs or like men, whether the old people died of damp, or the children of diphtheria, which you might have prevented! Robert's brow grew dark over it.

The click of an opening gate. Catherine shook off her dreaminess at once, and hurried along the path to meet her husband. In another moment Elsmere came in sight, swinging along, a holly stick in his hand, his face aglow with health and exercise and kindling at the sight of his wife. She hung on his arm, and, with his hand laid tenderly on hers, he asked her how she fared. She answered briefly, but with a little flush, her eyes raised to his. She was within a few weeks of motherhood.

Then they strolled along talking. He gave her an account of his afternoon, which, to judge from the worried expression which presently effaced the joy of their meeting, had been spent in some unsuccessful effort or other. They paused after a while, and stood looking over the plain before them to a spot beyond the nearer belt of woodland, where from a little hollow about three miles off there rose a cloud of bluish smoke.

'He will do nothing!' cried Catherine, incredulous.

'Nothing! It is the policy of the estate, apparently, to let the old and bad cottages fall to pieces. He sneers at one for supposing any landowner has money for "philanthropy" just now. If the people don't like the houses they can go. I told him I should appeal to the squire as soon as he came home.'

'What did he say?'

'He smiled, as much as to say, "Do as you like, and be a fool for your pains." How the squire can let that man tyrannise over the estate as he does, I cannot conceive. Oh, Catherine, I am full of qualms about the squire!'

'So am I,' she said, with a little darkening of her clear look. 'Old Benham has just been in to say they are expected on Thursday.'

Robert started. 'Are these our last days of peace?' he said wistfully—'the last days of our honeymoon, Catherine?'

She smiled at him with a little quiver of passionate feeling under the smile.

'Can anything touch that?' she said under her breath.

'Do you know,' he said presently, his voice dropping, 'that it is only a month to our wedding day? Oh, my wife, have I kept my promise—is the new life as rich as the old?'

She made no answer, except the dumb sweet answer that love writes on eyes and lips. Then a tremor passed over her.

'Are we too happy? Can it be well—be right?'

'Oh, let us take it like children!' he cried, with a shiver, almost petulantly. 'There will be dark hours enough. It is so good to be happy.'

She leant her cheek fondly against his shoulder. To her life always meant self-restraint, self-repression, self-deadening, if need be. The Puritan distrust of personal joy as something dangerous and ensnaring was deep ingrained in her. It had no natural hold on him.

They stood a moment hand in hand fronting the cornfield and the sun-filled west, while the afternoon breeze blew back the man's curly reddish hair, long since restored to all its natural abundance.

Presently Robert broke into a broad smile.

'What do you suppose Langham has been entertaining Rose with on the way, Catherine? I wouldn't miss her remarks to-night on the escort we provided her for a good deal.'

Catherine said nothing, but her delicate eyebrows went up a little. Robert stooped and lightly kissed her.

'You never performed a greater act of virtue even in *your* life, Mrs. Elsmere, than when you wrote Langham that nice letter of invitation.'

And then the young rector sighed, as many a boyish memory came crowding upon him.

A sound of wheels! Robert's long legs took him to the gate in a twinkling, and he flung it open just as Rose drove up in fine style, a thin dark man beside her.

Rose lent her bright cheek to Catherine's kiss, and the two sisters walked up to the door together, while Robert and Langham loitered after them talking.

'Oh, Catherine!' said Rose under her breath, as they got into the drawing-room, with a little theatrical gesture, 'why on earth did you inflict that man and me on each other for two mortal hours?'

'Sh-sh!' said Catherine's lips, while her face gleamed with laughter.

Rose sank flushed upon a chair, her eyes glancing up with a little furtive anger in them as the two gentlemen entered the room.

'You found each other easily at Waterloo?' asked Robert.

'Mr. Langham would never have found *me*,' said Rose drily; 'but I pounced on him at last—just, I believe, as he was beginning to cherish the hope of an empty carriage and the solitary enjoyment of his *Saturday Review*.'[5]

Langham smiled nervously. 'Miss Leyburn is too hard on a blind man,' he said, holding up his eyeglass apologetically; 'it was my eyes, not my will, that were at fault.'

Rose's lip curled a little. 'And Robert,' she cried, bending 'forward as though something had just occurred to her, 'do tell me—I vowed I would ask—*is* Mr. Langham a Liberal or a Conservative? *He* doesn't know!'

Robert laughed, so did Langham.

'Your sister,' he said, flushing, 'will have one so very precise in all one says.'

He turned his handsome olive face towards her, an unwonted spark of animation lighting up his black eyes. It was evident that he felt himself

---

5   Another important weekly, founded in 1855. Its frequently slashing reviews earned its writers the nickname of the "Saturday Revilers."

persecuted, but it was not so evident whether he enjoyed the process or disliked it.

'Oh dear, no!' said Rose nonchalantly. 'Only I have just come from a
house where everybody either loathes Mr. Gladstone or would die for him
to-morrow. There was a girl of seven and a boy of nine who were always discussing "Coercion" in the corners of the schoolroom.[6] So, of course, I have
grown political too, and began to catechise Mr. Langham at once, and when
he said "he didn't know," I felt I should like to set those children at him! They
would soon put some principles into him!'

'It is not generally lack of principle, Miss Rose,' said her brother-in-law,
'that turns a man a doubter in politics, but too much!'

And while he spoke, his eyes resting on Langham, his smile broadened
as he recalled all those instances in their Oxford past, when he had taken a
humble share in one of the herculean efforts on the part of Langham's friends,
which were always necessary whenever it was a question of screwing a vote
out of him on any debated University question.

'How dull it must be to have too much principle!' cried Rose. 'Like a mill
choked with corn. No bread because the machine can't work!'

'Defend me from my friends!' cried Langham, roused. 'Elsmere, when
did I give you a right to caricature me in this way? If I were interested,' he
added, subsiding into his usual hesitating ineffectiveness, 'I suppose I should
know my own mind.'

And then seizing the muffins, he stood presenting them to Rose as though
in deprecation of any further personalities. Inside him there was a hot protest
against an unreasonable young beauty whom he had done his miserable best
to entertain for two long hours, and who in return had made him feel himself
more of a fool than he had done for years. Since when had young women put
on all these airs? In his young days they knew their place.

Catherine meanwhile sat watching her sister. The child was more beautiful than ever, but in other outer respects the Rose of Long Whindale had
undergone much transformation. The puffed sleeves, the æsthetic skirts, the
naïve adornments of bead and shell, the formless hat, which it pleased her to
imagine 'after Gainsborough,' had all disappeared. She was clad in some soft
fawn-coloured garment, cut very much in the fashion; her hair was closely
rolled and twisted about her lightly-balanced head; everything about her was
neat and fresh and tight-fitting. A year ago she had been a damsel from the

---

6   William Gladstone (1809–98), Liberal politician and Prime Minister; "Coercion"
refers to the Irish Coercion Act (1881), which allowed dissidents to be jailed without
trial.

'Earthly Paradise'; now, so far as an English girl can achieve it, she might have been a model for Tissot.[7] In this phase, as in the other, there was a touch of extravagance. The girl was developing fast, but had clearly not yet developed. The restlessness, the self-consciousness of Long Whindale were still there; but they spoke to the spectator in different ways.

But in her anxious study of her sister Catherine did not forget her place of hostess. 'Did our man bring you through the park, Mr. Langham?' she asked him timidly.

'Yes. What an exquisite old house!' he said, turning to her, and feeling through all his critical sense the difference between the gentle matronly dignity of the one sister and the young self-assertion of the other.

'Ah,' said Robert, 'I kept that as a surprise! Did you ever see a more perfect place?'

'What date?'

'Early Tudor—as to the oldest part. It was built by a relation of Bishop Fisher's; then largely rebuilt under James I. Elizabeth stayed there twice. There is a trace of a visit of Sidney's. Waller was there, and left a copy of verses in the library. Evelyn laid out a great deal of the garden. Lord Clarendon wrote part of his History in the garden, et cetera, et cetera. The place is steeped in associations, and as beautiful as a dream to begin with.'[8]

'And the owner of all this is the author of *The Idols of the Market-place*?'

Robert nodded.

'Did you ever meet him at Oxford? I believe he was there once or twice during my time, but I never saw him.'

'Yes,' said Langham, thinking. 'I met him at dinner at the Vice-Chancellor's, now I remember. A bizarre and formidable person—very difficult to talk to,' he added reflectively.

Then as he looked up he caught a sarcastic twitch of Rose Leyburn's lip and understood it in a moment. Incontinently he forgot the squire and fell to asking himself what had possessed him on that luckless journey down. He

7   William Morris' poetic cycle (1868–70), another link between Rose and the Pre-Raphaelites; James Tissot (1836–1902), French Catholic artist associated with both religious and society painting.

8   St. John Fisher (d. 1535), beheaded for rejecting Henry VIII as head of the Church of England; James VI and I (1566–1625), Elizabeth I's successor, King of England, Scotland, and Ireland; Elizabeth I (1533–1603), Queen of England; Sir Philip Sidney (1554-86), poet, literary theorist, military officer; Edmund Waller (1606–1687), poet and politician; John Evelyn (1620-1706), leading figure in the Royal Society, diarist, author; Edward Hyde, 1st Earl of Clarendon (1609–74), politician, author of *History of the Rebellion and Civil Wars in England* (1717).

had never seemed to himself more perverse, more unmanageable; and for once his philosophy did not enable him to swallow the certainty that this slim flashing creature must have thought him a morbid idiot with as much *sang-froid* as usual.

Robert interrupted his reflections by some Oxford question, and presently Catherine carried off Rose to her room. On their way they passed a door, beside which Catherine paused hesitating, and then with a bright flush on the face, which had such maternal calm in it already, she threw her arm round Rose and drew her in. It was a white empty room, smelling of the roses outside, and waiting in the evening stillness for the life that was to be. Rose looked at it all—at the piles of tiny garments, the cradle, the pictures from Retsch's 'Song of the Bell,'[9] which had been the companion of their own childhood, on the walls—and something stirred in the girl's breast.

'Catherine, I believe you have everything you want, or you soon will have!' she cried, almost with a kind of bitterness, laying her hands on her sister's shoulders.

'Everything but worthiness!' said Catherine softly, a mist rising in her calm gray eyes. 'And you, Röschen,' she added wistfully, 'have you been getting a little more what you want?'

'What's the good of asking?' said the girl, with a little shrug of impatience. 'As if creatures like me ever got what they want! London has been good fun certainly—if one could get enough of it. Catherine, how long is that marvellous person going to stay?' and she pointed in the direction of Langham's room.

'A week,' said Catherine, smiling at the girl's disdainful tone. 'I was afraid you didn't take to him.'

'I never saw such a being before,' declared Rose—'never! I thought I should never get a plain answer from him about anything. He wasn't even quite certain it was a fine day! I wonder if you set fire to him whether he would be sure it hurt! A week, you say? Heigh ho! what an age!'

'Be kind to him,' said Catherine, discreetly veiling her own feelings, and caressing the curly golden head as they moved towards the door. 'He's a poor lone don, and he was so good to Robert!'

'Excellent reason for you, Mrs. Elsmere,' said Rose, pouting; 'but——'

Her further remarks were cut short by the sound of the front-door bell.

'Oh, I had forgotten Mr. Newcome!' cried Catherine, starting. 'Come down soon, Rose, and help us through.'

---

9   Moritz Retzsch (1779–1857), German artist; his illustrations to Friedrich Schiller's *Lied von der Glocke* appeared in 1833.

'Who is he?' inquired Rose sharply.

'A High Church clergyman near here, whom Robert asked to tea this afternoon,' said Catherine, escaping.

Rose took her hat off very leisurely. The prospect downstairs did not seem to justify despatch. She lingered and thought of 'Lohengrin' and Albani,[10] of the crowd of artistic friends that had escorted her to Waterloo, of the way in which she had been applauded the night before, of the joys of playing Brahms with a long-haired pupil of Rubinstein's, who had dropped on one knee and kissed her hand at the end of it, etc. During the last six weeks the colours of 'this threadbare world' had been freshening before her in marvellous fashion. And now, as she stood looking out, the quiet fields opposite, the sight of a cow pushing its head through the hedge, the infinite sunset sky, the quiet of the house, filled her with a sudden depression. How dull it all seemed—how wanting in the glow of life!

CHAPTER XII

Meanwhile downstairs a curious little scene was passing, watched by Langham, who, in his usual anti-social way, had retreated into a corner of his own as soon as another visitor appeared. Beside Catherine sat a Ritualist clergyman in cassock and long cloak—a saint clearly, though perhaps, to judge from the slight restlessness of movement that seemed to quiver through him perpetually, an irritable one. But he had the saint's wasted unearthly look, the ascetic brow high and narrow, the veins showing through the skin, and a personality as magnetic as it was strong.

Catherine listened to the new-comer, and gave him his tea, with an aloofness of manner which was not lost on Langham. 'She is the Thirty-nine Articles in the flesh!' he said to himself.[11] 'For her there must neither be too much nor too little. How can Elsmere stand it?'

Elsmere apparently was not perfectly happy. He sat balancing his long person over the arm of a chair listening to the recital of some of the High Churchman's parish troubles with a slight half-embarrassed smile. The vicar of Mottringham was always in trouble. The narrative he was pouring out took shape in Langham's sarcastic sense as a sort of classical epic, with the High Churchman as a new champion of Christendom, harassed on all

---

10   Richard Wagner's opera, first performed in 1850; Emma Albani (1847–1930), stage name of French-Canadian soprano Marie-Louise-Emma-Cécile Lajeunesse.

11   The core doctrines of the Church of England, as officially enumerated in 1563.

sides by pagan parishioners, crass church-wardens, and treacherous bishops. Catherine's fine face grew more and more set, nay disdainful. Mr. Newcome was quite blind to it. Women never entered into his calculations except as sisters or as penitents. At a certain diocesan conference he had discovered a sympathetic fibre in the young rector of Murewell, which had been to the imperious persecuted zealot like water to the thirsty. He had come to-day, drawn by the same quality in Elsmere as had originally attracted Langham to the St. Anselm's undergraduate, and he sat pouring himself out with as much freedom as if all his companions had been as ready as he was to die for an alb, or to spend half their days in piously circumventing a bishop.

But presently the conversation had slid, no one knew how, from Mottringham and its intrigues to London and its teeming East. Robert was leading, his eye now on the apostolic-looking priest, now on his wife. Mr. Newcome resisted, but Robert had his way. Then it came out that behind these battles of kites and crows at Mottringham, there lay an heroic period, when the pale ascetic had wrestled ten years with London poverty, leaving health and youth and nerves behind him in the *mêlée*. Robert dragged it out at last, that struggle, into open view, but with difficulty. The Ritualist may glory in the discomfiture of an Erastian bishop[12]—what Christian dare parade ten years of love to God and man? And presently round Elsmere's lip there dawned a little smile of triumph. Catherine had shaken off her cold silence, her Puritan aloofness, was bending forward eagerly—listening. Stroke by stroke, as the words and facts were beguiled from him, all that was futile and quarrelsome in the sharp-featured priest sank out of sight; the face glowed with inward light; the stature of the man seemed to rise; the angel in him unsheathed its wings. Suddenly a story of the slums that Mr. Newcome was telling—a story of the purest Christian heroism told in the simplest way—came to an end, and Catherine leaned towards him with a long quivering breath.

'Oh, thank you, thank you! That must have been a joy, a privilege!'

Mr. Newcome turned and looked at her with surprise.

'Yes, it was a privilege,' he said slowly—the story had been an account of the rescue of a young country lad from a London den of thieves and profligates—'you are right; it was just that.'

And then some sensitive inner fibre of the man was set vibrating, and he would talk no more of himself or his past, do what they would.

So Robert had hastily to provide another subject, and he fell upon that of the squire.

---

12 One who condones the State's governing role in the Church.

Mr. Newcome's eyes flashed.

'He is coming back? I am sorry for you, Elsmere. "Woe is me that I am constrained to dwell with Mesech, and to have my habitation among the tents of Kedar!"'[13]

And he fell back in his chair, his lips tightening, his thin long hand lying along the arm of it, answering to that general impression of combat, of the spiritual athlete, that hung about him.

'I don't know,' said Robert brightly, as he leant against the mantelpiece looking curiously at his visitor. 'The squire is a man of strong character, of vast learning. His library is one of the finest in England, and it is at my service. I am not concerned with his opinions.'

'Ah, I see,' said Newcome in his driest voice, but sadly. 'You are one of the people who believe in what you call tolerance—I remember.'

'Yes, that is an impeachment to which I plead guilty,' said Robert, perhaps with equal dryness; 'and you—have your worries driven you to throw tolerance overboard?'

Newcome bent forward quickly. Strange glow and intensity of the fanatical eyes—strange beauty of the wasted persecuting lips!

'Tolerance!' he said with irritable vehemence—'tolerance! Simply another name for betrayal, cowardice, desertion—nothing else. God, Heaven, Salvation on the one side, the devil and hell on the other—and one miserable life, one wretched sin-stained will, to win the battle with; and in such a state of things *you*—' he dropped his voice, throwing out every word with a scornful, sibilant emphasis—'*you* would have us behave as though our friends were our enemies and our enemies our friends, as though eternal misery were a bagatelle and our faith a mere alternative. *I stand for Christ*, and His foes are mine.'

'By which I suppose you mean,' said Robert quietly, 'that you would shut your door on the writer of *The Idols of the Market-place*?'

'Certainly.'

And the priest rose, his whole attention concentrated on Robert, as though some deeper-lying motive were suddenly brought into play than any suggested by the conversation itself.

'Certainly. *Judge not*—so long as a man has not judged himself,—only till then. As to an open enemy, the Christian's path is clear. We are but soldiers under orders. What business have we to be truce-making on our own account? The war is not ours, but God's!'

Robert's eyes had kindled. He was about to indulge himself in such a

---

13 Psalm 120.5.

quick passage of arms as all such natures as his delight in, when his look travelled past the gaunt figure of the Ritualist vicar to his wife. A sudden pang
smote, silenced him. She was sitting with her face raised to Newcome; and
her beautiful gray eyes were full of a secret passion of sympathy. It was like the
sudden re-emergence of something repressed, the satisfaction of something
hungry. Robert moved closer to her, and the colour flushed over all his young
boyish face.

'To me,' he said in a low voice, his eyes fixed rather on her than on
Newcome, 'a clergyman has enough to do with those foes of Christ he cannot choose but recognise. There is no making truce with vice or cruelty. Why
should we complicate our task and spend in needless struggle the energies we
might give to love and to our brother?'

His wife turned to him. There was trouble in her look, then a swift lovely
dawn of something indescribable. Newcome moved away with a gesture that
was half bitterness, half weariness.

'Wait, my friend,' he said slowly, 'till you have watched that man's books
eating the very heart out of a poor creature as I have. When you have once
seen Christ robbed of a soul that might have been His, by the infidel of genius, you will loathe all this Laodicean cant of tolerance as I do!'[14]

There was an awkward pause. Langham, with his eyeglass on, was carefully examining the make of a carved paper-knife lying near him. The strained
preoccupied mind of the High Churchman had never taken the smallest account of his presence, of which Robert had been keenly, not to say humor-
ously, conscious throughout.

But after a minute or so the tutor got up, strolled forward, and addressed
Robert on some Oxford topic of common interest. Newcome, in a kind of
dream which seemed to have suddenly descended on him, stood near them,
his priestly cloak falling in long folds about him, his ascetic face grave and
rapt. Gradually, however, the talk of the two men dissipated the mystical
cloud about him. He began to listen, to catch the savour of Langham's modes
of speech, and of his languid indifferent personality.

'I must go,' he said abruptly, after a minute or two, breaking in upon the
friends' conversation. 'I shall hardly get home before dark.'

He took a cold punctilious leave of Catherine, and a still colder and
slighter leave of Langham. Elsmere accompanied him to the gate.

On the way the older man suddenly caught him by the arm.

'Elsmere, let me—I am the elder by so many years—let me speak to you.

---

14 The Laodicean Church became proverbial for its lack of enthusiasm or commit-
ment; see Revelation 3.15-16.

My heart goes out to you!'

And the eagle face softened; the harsh commanding presence became enveloping, magnetic. Robert paused and looked down upon him, a quick light of foresight in his eye. He felt what was coming.

And down it swept upon him, a hurricane of words hot from Newcome's inmost being, a protest winged by the gathered passion of years against certain 'dangerous tendencies' the elder priest discerned in the younger, against the worship of intellect and science as such which appeared in Elsmere's talk, in Elsmere's choice of friends. It was the eternal cry of the mystic of all ages.

'Scholarship! learning!' Eyes and lips flashed into a vehement scorn. 'You allow them a value in themselves, apart from the Christian's test. It is the modern canker, the modern curse! Thank God, my years in London burnt it out of me! Oh, my friend, what have you and I to do with all these curious triflings, which lead men oftener to rebellion than to worship? Is this a time for wholesale trust, for a maudlin universal sympathy? Nay, rather a day of suspicion, a day of repression!—a time for trampling on the lusts of the mind no less than the lusts of the body, a time when it is better to believe than to know, to pray than to understand!'

Robert was silent a moment, and they stood together, Newcome's gaze of fiery appeal fixed upon him.

'We are differently made, you and I,' said the young rector at last with difficulty. 'Where you see temptation I see opportunity. I cannot conceive of God as the Arch-plotter against His own creation!'

Newcome dropped his hold abruptly.

'A groundless optimism,' he said with harshness. 'On the track of the soul from birth to death there are two sleuth-hounds—Sin and Satan. Mankind for ever flies them, is for ever vanquished and devoured. I see life always as a thread-like path between abysses along which man *creeps*'—and his gesture illustrated the words—'with bleeding hands and feet towards one—narrow—solitary outlet. Woe to him if he turn to the right hand or the left—"I will repay, saith the Lord!"'[15]

Elsmere drew himself up suddenly; the words seemed to him a blasphemy. Then something stayed the vehement answer on his lips. It was a sense of profound intolerable pity. What a maimed life! what an indomitable soul! Husbandhood, fatherhood, and all the sacred education that flows from human joy for ever self-forbidden, and this grim creed for recompense!

He caught Newcome's hand with a kind of filial eagerness.

'You are a perpetual lesson to me,' he said, most gently. 'When the world

---

15 Romans 12.19.

is too much with me, I think of you and am rebuked. God bless you! But
I know myself. If I could see life and God as you see them for one hour, I
should cease to be a Christian in the next!'

A flush of something like sombre resentment passed over Newcome's
face. There is a tyrannical element in all fanaticism, an element which makes
opposition a torment. He turned abruptly away, and Robert was left alone.

It was a still clear evening, rich in the languid softness and balm which
mark the first approaches of autumn. Elsmere walked back to the house,
his head uplifted to the sky which lay beyond the cornfield, his whole being wrought into a passionate protest—a passionate invocation of all things
beautiful and strong and free, a clinging to life and nature as to something
wronged and outraged.

Suddenly his wife stood beside him. She had come down to warn him
that it was late and that Langham had gone to dress; but she stood lingering
by his side after her message was given, and he made no movement to go in.
He turned to her, the exaltation gradually dying out of his face, and at last
he stooped and kissed her with a kind of timidity unlike him. She clasped
both hands on his arm and stood pressing towards him as though to make
amends—for she knew not what. Something—some sharp momentary sense
of difference, of antagonism, had hurt that inmost fibre which is the conscience of true passion. She did the most generous, the most ample penance
for it as she stood there talking to him of half-indifferent things, but with a
magic, a significance of eye and voice which seemed to take all the severity
from her beauty and make her womanhood itself.

At the evening meal Rose appeared in pale blue, and it seemed to
Langham, fresh from the absolute seclusion of college rooms in vacation, that
everything looked flat and stale beside her, beside the flash of her white arms,
the gleam of her hair, the confident grace of every movement. He thought
her much too self-conscious and self-satisfied; and she certainly did not make
herself agreeable to him; but for all that he could hardly take his eyes off her;
and it occurred to him once or twice to envy Robert the easy childish friendliness she showed to him, and to him alone of the party. The lack of real sympathy between her and Catherine was evident to the stranger at once—what, indeed, could the two have in common? He saw that Catherine was constantly
on the point of blaming, and Rose constantly on the point of rebelling. He
caught the wrinkling of Catherine's brow as Rose presently, in emulation apparently of some acquaintances she had been making in London, let slip the
names of some of her male friends without the 'Mr.,' or launched into some

bolder affectation than usual of a comprehensive knowledge of London society. The girl, in spite of all her beauty, and her fashion, and the little studied details of her dress, was in reality so crude, so much of a child under it all, that it made her audacities and assumptions the more absurd, and he could see that Robert was vastly amused by them.

But Langham was not merely amused by her. She was too beautiful and too full of character.

It astonished him to find himself afterwards edging over to the corner where she sat with the rectory cat on her knee—an inferior animal, but the best substitute for Chattie available. So it was, however; and once in her neighbourhood he made another serious effort to get her to talk to him. The Elsmeres had never seen him so conversational. He dropped his paradoxical melancholy; he roared as gently as any sucking dove; and Robert, catching from the pessimist of St. Anselm's, as the evening went on, some hesitating commonplaces worthy of a bashful undergraduate on the subject of the boats and Commemoration, had to beat a hasty retreat, so greatly did the situation tickle his sense of humour.

But the tutor made his various ventures under a discouraging sense of failure. What a capricious ambiguous creature it was, how fearless, how disagreeably alive to all his own damaging peculiarities! Never had he been so piqued for years, and as he floundered about trying to find some common ground where he and she might be at ease, he was conscious throughout of her mocking indifferent eyes, which seemed to be saying to him all the time, 'You are not interesting—no, not a bit! You are tiresome, and I see through you, but I must talk to you, I suppose, *faute de mieux*.'[16]

Long before the little party separated for the night Langham had given it up, and had betaken himself to Catherine, reminding himself with some sharpness that he had come down to study his friend's life, rather than the humours of a provoking girl. How still the summer night was round the isolated rectory; how fresh and spotless were all the appointments of the house; what a Quaker neatness and refinement everywhere! He drank in the scent of air and flowers with which the rooms were filled; for the first time his fastidious sense was pleasantly conscious of Catherine's grave beauty; and even the mystic ceremonies of family prayer had a certain charm for him, pagan as he was. How much dignity and persuasiveness it has still, he thought to himself, this commonplace country life of ours, on its best sides!

Half-past ten arrived. Rose just let him touch her hand; Catherine gave him a quiet good-night, with various hospitable wishes for his nocturnal

16 *Faute de mieux*: no better option.

comfort, and the ladies withdrew. He saw Robert open the door for his wife, and catch her thin white fingers as she passed him with all the secrecy and passion of a lover.

Then they plunged into the study, he and Robert, and smoked their fill. The study was an astonishing medley. Books, natural history specimens, a half-written sermon, fishing-rods, cricket-bats, a huge medicine cupboard—all the main elements of Elsmere's new existence were represented there. In the drawing-room with his wife and his sister-in-law he had been as much of a boy as ever; here clearly he was a man, very much in earnest. What about? What did it all come to? Can the English country clergyman do much with his life and his energies? Langham approached the subject with his usual scepticism.

Robert for a while, however, did not help him to solve it. He fell at once to talking about the squire, as though it cleared his mind to talk out his difficulties even to so ineffective a counsellor as Langham. Langham, indeed, was but faintly interested in the squire's crimes as a landlord, but there was a certain interest to be got out of the struggle in Elsmere's mind between the attractiveness of the squire, as one of the most difficult and original personalities of English letters, and that moral condemnation of him as a man of possessions and ordinary human responsibilities with which the young reforming rector was clearly penetrated. So that, as long as he could smoke under it, he was content to let his companion describe to him Mr. Wendover's connection with the property, his accession to it in middle life after a long residence in Germany, his ineffectual attempts to play the English country gentleman, and his subsequent complete withdrawal from the life about him.

'You have no idea what a queer sort of existence he lives in that huge place,' said Robert with energy. 'He is not unpopular exactly with the poor down here. When they want to belabour anybody they lay on at the agent, Henslowe. On the whole, I have come to the conclusion the poor like a mystery. They never see him; when he is here the park is shut up; the common report is that he walks at night; and he lives alone in that enormous house with his books. The county folk have all quarrelled with him, or nearly. It pleases him to get a few of the humbler people about, clergy, professional men, and so on, to dine with him sometimes. And he often fills the Hall, I am told, with London people for a day or two. But otherwise he knows no one, and nobody knows him.'

'But you say he has a widowed sister? How does she relish the kind of life?'

'Oh; by all accounts,' said the rector with a shrug, 'she is as little like other people as himself. A queer elfish little creature, they say, as fond of solitude down here as the squire, and full of hobbies. In her youth she was about the court. Then she married a canon of Warham, one of the popular preachers, I believe, of the day. There is a bright little cousin of hers, a certain Lady Helen Varley, who lives near here, and tells me stories of her. She must be the most whimsical little aristocrat imaginable. She liked her husband apparently, but she never got over leaving London and the fashionable world, and is as hungry now, after her long fast, for titles and big-wigs, as though she were the purest parvenu. The squire of course makes mock of her, and she has no influence with him. However, there is something naïve in the stories they tell of her. I feel as if I might get on with *her*. But the squire!'

And the rector, having laid down his pipe, took to studying his boots with a certain dolefulness.

Langham, however, who always treated the subjects of conversation presented to him as an epicure treats foods, felt at this point that he had had enough of the Wendovers, and started something else.

'So you physic bodies as well as minds?' he said, pointing to the medicine cupboard.

'I should think so!' cried Robert, brightening at once. 'Last winter I causticked all the diphtheritic throats in the place with my own hand.[17] Our parish doctor is an infirm old noodle, and I just had to do it. And if the state of part of the parish remains what it is, it's a pleasure I may promise myself most years. But it shan't remain what it is.'

And the rector reached out his hand again for his pipe, and gave one or two energetic puffs to it as he surveyed his friend stretched before him in the depths of an armchair.

'I will make myself a public nuisance, but the people shall have their drains!'

'It seems to me,' said Langham, musing, 'that in my youth people talked about Ruskin; now they talk about drains.'

'And quite right too. Dirt and drains, Catherine says I have gone mad upon them. It's all very well, but they are the foundations of a sound religion.'

'Dirt, drains, and Darwin,' said Langham meditatively, taking up Darwin's *Earthworms*, which lay on the study table beside him, side by side with a volume of Grant Allen's *Sketches*.[18] 'I didn't know you cared for this

---

17 Doctors burnt away the pseudomembranes that impeded breathing by applying some sort of caustic solution (silver nitrate was increasingly popular by mid-century) directly to the affected areas.

18 Charles Darwin (1809–82), famed for his theories of evolution and natural selection; Langham is looking at his final book, *The Formation of Vegetable Mould through*

sort of thing!'

Robert did not answer for a moment, and a faint flush stole into his face.

'Imagine, Langham!' he said presently, 'I had never read even *The Origin of Species* before I came here. We used to take the thing half for granted, I remember, at Oxford, in a more or less modified sense. But to drive the mind through all the details of the evidence, to force one's self to understand the whole hypothesis and the grounds for it, is a very different matter. It is a revelation.'

'Yes,' said Langham; and could not forbear adding, 'but it is a revelation, my friend, that has not always been held to square with other revelations.'

In general these two kept carefully off the religious ground. The man who is religious by nature tends to keep his treasure hid from the man who is critical by nature, and Langham was much more interested in other things. But still it had always been understood that each was free to say what he would.

'There was a natural panic,' said Robert, throwing back his head at the challenge. 'Men shrank and will always shrink, say what you will, from what seems to touch things dearer to them than life. But the panic is passing. The smoke is clearing away, and we see that the battle-field is falling into new lines. But the old truth remains the same. Where and when and how you will, but somewhen and somehow, God created the heavens and the earth!'

Langham said nothing. It had seemed to him for long that the clergy were becoming dangerously ready to throw the Old Testament overboard, and all that it appeared to him to imply was that men's logical sense is easily benumbed where their hearts are concerned.[19]

'Not that every one need be troubled with the new facts,' resumed Robert after a while, going back to his pipe. 'Why should they? We are not saved by Darwinism. I should never press them on my wife, for instance, with all her clearness and courage of mind.'

His voice altered as he mentioned his wife—grew extraordinarily soft, even reverential.

'It would distress her?' said Langham interrogatively, and inwardly conscious of pursuing investigations begun a year before.

---

the *Actions of Worms* (1881). Grant Allen (1848–99): novelist and popular science writer; *Sketches* does not exist, but Clyde de L. Ryals (606n171.1) suggests that Ward probably has *Vignettes from Nature* (1881) or *Nature Studies* (1885) in mind.
19 Refers to current trends in both English and German Biblical scholarship, which argued that the Old Testament was, in effect, a document relevant only to a pre-civilized, savage race—and which, therefore, had nothing of any importance to say to Christian cultures. In this line of argument, Christianity stood on its own, without needing Old Testament prophecy to authorize itself.

'Yes, it would distress her. She holds the old ideas as she was taught them. It is all beautiful to her, what may seem doubtful or grotesque to others. And why should I or any one else trouble her? I above all, who am not fit to tie her shoe-strings.'

The young husband's face seemed to gleam in the dim light which fell upon it. Langham involuntarily put up his hand in silence and touched his sleeve. Robert gave him a quiet friendly look, and the two men instantly plunged into some quite trivial and commonplace subject.

Langham entered his room that night with a renewed sense of pleasure in the country quiet, the peaceful flower-scented house. Catherine, who was an admirable housewife, had put out her best guest-sheets for his benefit, and the tutor, accustomed for long years to the second-best of college service, looked at their shining surfaces and frilled edges, at the freshly matted floor, at the flowers on the dressing-table, at the spotlessness of everything in the room, with a distinct sense that matrimony had its advantages. He had come down to visit the Elsmeres, sustained by a considerable sense of virtue. He still loved Elsmere and cared to see him. It was a much colder love, no doubt, than that which he had given to the undergraduate. But the man altogether was a colder creature, who for years had been drawing in tentacle after tentacle, and becoming more and more content to live without his kind. Robert's parsonage, however, and Robert's wife had no attractions for him; and it was with an effort that he had made up his mind to accept the invitation which Catherine had made an effort to write.

And, after all, the experience promised to be pleasant. His fastidious love for the quieter, subtler sorts of beauty was touched by the Elsmere surroundings. And whatever Miss Leyburn might be, she was not commonplace. The demon of convention had no large part in *her!* Langham lay awake for a time analysing his impressions of her with some gusto, and meditating, with a whimsical candour which seldom failed him, on the manner in which she had trampled on him, and the reasons why.

He woke up, however, in a totally different frame of mind. He was pre-eminently a person of moods, dependent, probably, as all moods are, on certain obscure physical variations. And his mental temperature had run down in the night. The house, the people who had been fresh and interesting to him twelve hours before, were now the burden he had more than half expected them to be. He lay and thought of the unbroken solitude of his college rooms, of Senancour's flight from human kind, of the uselessness of all friendship, the absurdity of all effort, and could hardly persuade himself to get up and face a futile world, which had, moreover, the enormous disadvantage for the moment of being a new one.

Convention, however, is master even of an Obermann.[20] That prototype of all the disillusioned had to cut himself adrift from the society of the eagles on the Dent du Midi, to go and hang like any other ridiculous mortal on the Paris law-courts. Langham, whether he liked it or no, had to face the parsonic breakfast and the parsonic day.

He had just finished dressing when the sound of a girl's voice drew him to the window, which was open. In the garden stood Rose, on the edge of the sunk fence dividing the rectory domain from the cornfield. She was stooping forward playing with Robert's Dandie Dinmont.[21] In one hand she held a mass of poppies, which showed a vivid scarlet against her blue dress; the other was stretched out seductively to the dog leaping round her. A crystal buckle flashed at her waist; the sunshine caught the curls of auburn hair, the pink cheek, the white moving hand, the lace ruffles at her throat and wrist. The lithe glittering figure stood thrown out against the heavy woods behind, the gold of the cornfield, the blues of the distance. All the gaiety and colour which is as truly representative of autumn as the gray languor of a September mist had passed into it.

Langham stood and watched, hidden, as he thought, by the curtain, till a gust of wind shook the casement window beside him, and threatened to blow it in upon him. He put out his hand perforce to save it, and the slight noise caught Rose's ear. She looked up; her smile vanished. 'Go down, Dandie,' she said severely, and walked quickly into the house with as much dignity as nineteen is capable of.

At breakfast the Elsmeres found their guest a difficulty. But they also, as we know, had expected it. He was languor itself; none of their conversational efforts succeeded; and Rose, studying him out of the corners of her eyes, felt that it would be of no use even to torment so strange and impenetrable a being. Why on earth should people come and visit their friends if they could not keep up even the ordinary decent pretences of society?

Robert had to go off to some clerical business afterwards, and Langham wandered out into the garden by himself. As he thought of his Greek texts and his untenanted Oxford rooms, he had the same sort of craving that an opium-eater has cut off from his drugs. How was he to get through?

Presently he walked back into the study, secured an armful of volumes, and carried them out. True to himself in the smallest things, he could never

---

20 In Senancour's epistolary novel *Obermann* (1804), the unhappy and self-isolated protagonist frequently reflects on his general discomfort with the world around him.
21 The breed of terrier named after one of Sir Walter Scott's popular characters from *Guy Mannering* (1815).

in his life be content with the companionship of one book. To cut off the possibility of choice and change in anything whatever was repugnant to him.

He sat himself down under the shade of a great chestnut near the house, and an hour glided pleasantly away. As it happened, however, he did not open one of the books he had brought with him. A thought had struck him as he sat down, and he went groping in his pockets in search of a yellow-covered *brochure*, which, when found, proved to be a new play by Dumas, just about to be produced by a French company in London. Langham, whose passion for the French theatre supplied him, as we know, with a great deal of life without the trouble of living, was going to see it, and always made a point of reading the piece beforehand.

The play turned upon a typical French situation, treated in a manner rather more French than usual. The reader shrugged his shoulders a good deal as he read on. 'Strange nation!' he muttered to himself after an act or two. 'How they do revel in mud!'

Presently, just as the fifth act was beginning to get hold of him with that force which, after all, only a French playwright is master of, he looked up and saw the two sisters coming round the corner of the house from the great kitchen garden, which stretched its grass paths and tangled flower-masses down the further slope of the hill. The transition was sharp from Dumas's heated atmosphere of passion and crime to the quiet English rectory, its rural surroundings, and the figures of the two Englishwomen advancing towards him.

Catherine was in a loose white dress with a black lace scarf draped about her head and form. Her look hardly suggested youth, and there was certainly no touch of age in it. Ripeness, maturity, serenity—these were the chief ideas which seemed to rise in the mind at sight of her.

'Are you amusing yourself, Mr. Langham?' she said, stopping beside him and retaining with slight imperceptible force Rose's hand, which threatened to slip away.

'Very much. I have been skimming through a play, which I hope to see next week, by way of preparation.'

Rose turned involuntarily. Not wishing to discuss *Marianne* with either Catherine or her sister, Langham had just closed the book and was returning it to his pocket.[22] But she had caught sight of it.

'You are reading *Marianne*,' she exclaimed, the slightest possible touch of wonder in her tone.

---

22 Alexandre Dumas *fils* (1824–95). Ward appears to have invented this play, but the vague description suggests that she has Dumas' smash hit *Denise* (1885) in mind.

'Yes, it is *Marianne*,' said Langham, surprised in his turn. He had very old-fashioned notions about the limits of a girl's acquaintance with the world, knowing nothing, therefore, as may be supposed, about the modern young woman, and he was a trifle scandalised by Rose's accent of knowledge.

'I read it last week,' she said carelessly; 'and the Piersons'—turning to her sister—'have promised to take me to see it next winter if Desforêts comes again, as every one expects.'

'Who wrote it?' asked Catherine innocently. The theatre not only gave her little pleasure, but wounded in her a hundred deep unconquerable instincts. But she had long ago given up in despair the hope of protesting against Rose's dramatic instincts with success.

'Dumas *fils*,' said Langham drily. He was distinctly a good deal astonished.

Rose looked at him, and something brought a sudden flame into her cheek.

'It is one of the best of his,' she said defiantly. 'I have read a good many others. Mrs. Pierson lent me a volume. And when I was introduced to Madame Desforêts last week, she agreed with me that *Marianne* is nearly the best of all.'

All this, of course, with the delicate nose well in air.

'You were introduced to Madame Desforêts?' cried Langham, surprised this time quite out of discretion. Catherine looked at him with anxiety. The reputation of the black-eyed little French actress, who had been for a year or two the idol of the theatrical public of Paris and London, had reached even to her, and the tone of Langham's exclamation struck her painfully.

'I was,' said Rose proudly. 'Other people may think it a disgrace. *I* thought it an honour!'

Langham could not help smiling, the girl's *naïveté* was so evident. It was clear that, if she had read *Marianne*, she had never understood it.

'Rose, you don't know!' exclaimed Catherine, turning to her sister with a sudden trouble in her eyes. 'I don't think Mrs. Pierson ought to have done that, without consulting mamma especially.'

'Why not?' cried Rose vehemently. Her face was burning, and her heart was full of something like hatred of Langham, but she tried hard to be calm.

'I think,' she said, with a desperate attempt at crushing dignity, 'that the way in which all sorts of stories are believed against a woman, just because she is an actress, is *disgraceful!* Just because a woman is on the stage, everybody thinks they may throw stones at her. I *know*, because—because she told me,' cried the speaker, growing, however, half embarrassed as she spoke, 'that she feels the things that are said of her deeply! She has been ill, very ill, and one of her friends said to me, "You know it isn't her work, or a cold, or anything else that's made her ill—it's calumny!" And so it is.'

The speaker flashed an angry glance at Langham. She was sitting on the arm of the cane chair into which Catherine had fallen, one hand grasping the back of the chair for support, one pointed foot beating the ground restlessly in front of her, her small full mouth pursed indignantly, the greenish-gray eyes flashing and brilliant.

As for Langham, the cynic within him was on the point of uncontrollable laughter. Madame Desforêts complaining of calumny to this little Westmoreland maiden! But his eyes involuntarily met Catherine's, and the expression of both fused into a common wonderment—amused on his side, anxious on hers. 'What a child, what an infant it is!' they seemed to confide to one another. Catherine laid her hand softly on Rose's, and was about to say something soothing, which might secure her an opening for some sisterly advice later on, when there was a sound of calling from the gate. She looked up and saw Robert waving to her. Evidently he had just run up from the school to deliver a message. She hurried across the drive to him and afterwards into the house, while he disappeared.

Rose got up from her perch on the armchair and would have followed, but a movement of obstinacy or Quixotic wrath, or both, detained her.

'At any rate, Mr. Langham,' she said, drawing herself up, and speaking with the most lofty accent, 'if you don't know anything personally about Madame Desforêts, I think it would be much fairer to say nothing—and not to assume at once that all you hear is true!'

Langham had rarely felt more awkward than he did then, as he sat leaning forward under the tree, this slim indignant creature standing over him, and his consciousness about equally divided between a sense of her absurdity and a sense of her prettiness.

'You are an advocate worth having, Miss Leyburn,' he said at last, an enigmatical smile he could not restrain playing about his mouth. 'I could not argue with you; I had better not try.'

Rose looked at him, at his dark regular face, at the black eyes which were much vivider than usual, perhaps because they could not help reflecting some of the irrepressible memories of Madame Desforêts and her *causes célèbres* which were coursing through the brain behind them, and with a momentary impression of rawness, defeat, and yet involuntary attraction, which galled her intolerably, she turned away and left him.

In the afternoon Robert was still unavailable, to his own great chagrin, and

Langham summoned up all his resignation and walked with the ladies. The general impression left upon his mind by the performance was, first, that the dust of an English August is intolerable, and, secondly, that women's society ought only to be ventured on by the men who are made for it. The views of Catherine and Rose may be deduced from his with tolerable certainty.

But in the late afternoon, when they thought they had done their duty by him, and he was again alone in the garden reading, he suddenly heard the sounds of music.

Who was playing, and in that way? He got up and strolled past the drawing-room window to find out.

Rose had got hold of an accompanist, the timid dowdy daughter of a local solicitor, with some capacity for reading, and was now, in her lavish impetuous fashion, rushing through a quantity of new music, the accumulations of her visit to London. She stood up beside the piano, her hair gleaming in the shadow of the drawing-room, her white brow hanging forward over her violin as she peered her way through the music, her whole soul absorbed in what she was doing. Langham passed unnoticed.

What astonishing playing! Why had no one warned him of the presence of such a gift in this dazzling, prickly, unripe creature? He sat down against the wall of the house, as close as possible, but out of sight, and listened. All the romance of his spoilt and solitary life had come to him so far through music, and through such music as this! For she was playing Wagner, Brahms, and Rubinstein, interpreting all those passionate voices of the subtlest moderns, through which the heart of our own day has expressed itself even more freely and exactly than through the voice of literature. Hans Sachs' immortal song, echoes from the love duets in 'Tristan und Isolde,' fragments from a wild and alien dance-music, they rippled over him in a warm intoxicating stream of sound, stirring association after association, and rousing from sleep a hundred bygone moods of feeling.[23]

What magic and mastery in the girl's touch! What power of divination, and of rendering! Ah! she too was floating in passion and romance, but of a different sort altogether from the conscious reflected product of the man's nature. She was not thinking of the past, but of the future; she was weaving her story that was to be into the flying notes, playing to the unknown of her Whindale dreams, the strong ardent unknown,—'insufferable, if he pleases, to all the world besides, but to *me* heaven!' She had caught no breath yet of his coming, but her heart was ready for him.

---

23 Two of Richard Wagner's operas, *Die Meistersinger von Nürnberg* (1868) and *Tristan und Isolde* (1865).

Suddenly, as she put down her violin, the French window opened, and Langham stood before her. She looked at him with a quick stiffening of the face which a minute before had been all quivering and relaxed, and his instant perception of it chilled the impulse which had brought him there.

He said something *banal* about his enjoyment, something totally different from what he had meant to say. The moment presented itself, but he could not seize it or her.

'I had no notion you cared for music,' she said carelessly, as she shut the piano, and then she went away.

Langham felt a strange fierce pang of disappointment. What had he meant to do or say? Idiot! What common ground was there between him and any such exquisite youth? What girl would ever see in him anything but the dull remains of what once had been a man!

CHAPTER XIII

The next day was Sunday. Langham, who was as depressed and home-sick as ever, with a certain new spice of restlessness, not altogether intelligible to himself, thrown in, could only brace himself to the prospect by the determination to take the English rural Sunday as the subject of severe scientific investigation. He would 'do it' thoroughly.

So he donned a black coat and went to church with the rest. There, in spite of his boredom with the whole proceeding, Robert's old tutor was a good deal more interested by Robert's sermon than he had expected to be. It was on the character of David, and there was a note in it, a note of historical imagination, a power of sketching in a background of circumstance, and of biting into the mind of the listener, as it were, by a detail or an epithet, which struck Langham as something new in his experience of Elsmere. He followed it at first as one might watch a game of skill, enjoying the intellectual form of it, and counting the good points, but by the end he was not a little carried away. The peroration was undoubtedly very moving, very intimate, very modern, and Langham up to a certain point was extremely susceptible to oratory, as he was to music and acting. The critical judgment, however, at the root of him kept coolly repeating as he stood watching the people defile out of the church: 'This sort of thing will go down, will make a mark; Elsmere is at the beginning of a career!'

In the afternoon Robert, who was feeling deeply guilty towards his wife, in that he had been forced to leave so much of the entertainment of Langham to her, asked his old friend to come for him to the school at four o'clock and take him for a walk between two engagements. Langham was punctual, and Robert carried him off first to see the Sunday cricket, which was in full swing. During the past year the young rector had been developing a number of outdoor capacities which were probably always dormant in his Elsmere blood, the blood of generations of country gentlemen, but which had never had full opportunity before. He talked of fishing as Kingsley might have talked of it, and, indeed, with constant quotations from Kingsley; and his cricket, which had been good enough at Oxford to get him into his College eleven, had stood him in specially good stead with the Murewell villagers.[24] That his play was not elegant they were not likely to find out; his bowling they set small store by; but his batting was of a fine, slashing, superior sort which soon carried the Murewell Club to a much higher position among the clubs of the neighbourhood than it had ever yet aspired to occupy.

The rector had no time to play on Sundays, however, and, after they had hung about the green a little while, he took his friend over to the Workmen's Institute, which stood at the edge of it. He explained that the Institute had been the last achievement of the agent before Henslowe, a man who had done his duty to the estate according to his lights, and to whom it was owing that those parts of it, at any rate, which were most in the public eye, were still in fair condition.

The Institute was now in bad repair and too small for the place. 'But catch that man doing anything for us!' exclaimed Robert hotly. 'He will hardly mend the roof now, merely, I believe, to spite me. But come and see my new Naturalists' Club.'

And he opened the Institute door. Langham followed in the temper of one getting up a subject for examination.

Poor Robert! His labour and his enthusiasm deserved a more appreciative eye. He was wrapped up in his Club, which had been the great success of his first year, and he dragged Langham through it all, not indeed, sympathetic creature that he was, without occasional qualms. 'But after all,' he would say to himself indignantly, 'I must do *something* with him.'

Langham, indeed, behaved with resignation. He looked at the collections for the year, and was quite ready to take it for granted that they were extremely creditable. Into the old-fashioned window-sills glazed compartments had been fitted, and these were now fairly filled with specimens, with eggs, butterflies, moths, beetles, fossils, and what not. A case of stuffed tropical birds

---

24 Kingsley's best-known essay on fishing was "Chalk-Stream Studies" (1858). Cricket teams have eleven players.

presented by Robert stood in the centre of the room; another containing the birds of the district was close by. On a table farther on stood two large open books, which served as records of observations on the part of members of the Club. In one, which was scrawled over with mysterious hieroglyphs, any one might write what he would. In the other, only such facts and remarks as had passed the gauntlet of a Club meeting were recorded in Robert's neatest hand. On the same table stood jars full of strange creatures—tadpoles and water larvæ of all kinds, over which Robert hung now absorbed, poking among them with a straw, while Langham, to whom only the generalisations of science were congenial, stood by and mildly scoffed.

As they came out a great loutish boy, who had evidently been hanging about waiting for the rector, came up to him, boorishly touched his cap, and then, taking a cardboard box out of his pocket, opened it with infinite caution, something like a tremor of emotion passing over his gnarled countenance.

The rector's eyes glistened.

'Hullo! I say, Irwin, where in the name of fortune did you get that? You lucky fellow! Come in, and let's look it out!'

And the two plunged back into the Club together, leaving Langham to the philosophic and patient contemplation of the village green, its geese, its donkeys, and its surrounding fringe of houses. He felt that quite indisputably life would have been better worth living if, like Robert, he could have taken a passionate interest in rare moths or common ploughboys; but Nature having denied him the possibility, there was small use in grumbling.

Presently the two naturalists came out again, and the boy went off, bearing his treasure with him.

'Lucky dog!' said Robert, turning his friend into a country road leading out of the village, 'he's found one of the rarest moths of the district. Such a hero he'll be in the Club to-morrow night. It's extraordinary what a rational interest has done for that fellow! I nearly fought him in public last winter.'

And he turned to his friend with a laugh, and yet with a little quick look of feeling in the gray eyes.

'Magnificent, but not war,' said Langham drily. 'I wouldn't have given much for your chances against those shoulders.'

'Oh, I don't know. I should have had a little science on my side, which counts for a great deal. We turned him out of the Club for brutality towards the old grandmother he lives with—turned him out in public. Such a scene! I shall never forget the boy's face. It was like a corpse, and the eyes burning out of it. He made for me, but the others closed up round, and we got him put out.'

'Hard lines on the grandmother,' remarked Langham.

'She thought so—poor old thing! She left her cottage that night, think-ing he would murder her, and went to a friend. At the end of a week he came into the friend's house, where she was alone in bed. She cowered under the bedclothes, she told me, expecting him to strike her. Instead of which he threw his wages down beside her and gruffly invited her to come home. "He wouldn't do her no mischief." Everybody dissuaded her, but the plucky old thing went. A week or two afterwards she sent for me and I found her crying. She was sure the lad was ill, he spoke to nobody at his work. "Lord, sir!" she said, "it do remind me, when he sits glowering at nights, of those folks in the Bible, when the devils inside 'em kep' a-tearing 'em. But he's like a new-born babe to me, sir—never does me no 'arm. And it do go to my heart, sir, to see how poorly he do take his vittles!" So I made tracks for that lad,' said Robert, his eyes kindling, his whole frame dilating. 'I found him in the fields one morning. I have seldom lived through so much in half an hour. In the even-ing I walked him up to the Club, and we re-admitted him, and since then the boy has been like one clothed and in his right mind. If there is any trouble in the Club I set him on, and he generally puts it right. And when I was laid up with a chill in the spring, and the poor fellow came trudging up every night after his work to ask for me—well, never mind! but it gives one a good glow at one's heart to think about it.'

The speaker threw back his head impulsively, as though defying his own feeling. Langham looked at him curiously. The pastoral temper was a novelty to him, and the strong development of it in the undergraduate of his Oxford recollections had its interest.

'A quarter to six,' said Robert, as on their return from their walk they were descending a low-wooded hill above the village, and the church clock rang out. 'I must hurry, or I shall be late for my story-telling.'

'Story-telling!' said Langham, with a half-exasperated shrug. 'What next? You clergy are too inventive by half!'

Robert laughed a trifle bitterly.

'I can't congratulate you on your epithets,' he said, thrusting his hands far into his pockets. 'Good heavens, if we *were*—if we were inventive as a body, the Church wouldn't be where she is in the rural districts! My story-telling is the simplest thing in the world. I began it in the winter with the object of somehow or other getting at the *imagination* of these rustics. Force them for only half an hour to live some one else's life—it is the one thing worth doing with them. That's what I have been aiming at. I *told* my stories all the winter—Shakespeare, Don Quixote, Dumas—Heaven knows what! And on the whole it answers best. But now we are reading *The Talisman*.[25] Come and inspect us, unless you're a purist about your Scott! None other of the immortals have such *longueurs* as he, and we cut him freely.'

'By all means,' said Langham; 'lead on.' And he followed his companion without repugnance. After all, there was something contagious in so much youth and hopefulness.

The story-telling was held in the Institute.

A group of men and boys were hanging round the door when they reached it. The two friends made their way through, greeted in the dumb friendly English fashion on all sides, and Langham found himself in a room half-filled with boys and youths, a few grown men, who had just put their pipes out, lounging at the back.

Langham not only endured, but enjoyed the first part of the hour that followed. Robert was an admirable reader, as most enthusiastic imaginative people are. He was a master of all those arts of look and gesture which make a spoken story telling and dramatic, and Langham marvelled with what energy, after his hard day's work and with another service before him, he was able to throw himself into such a *hors d'œuvre* as this. He was reading to-night one of the most perfect scenes that even the Wizard of the North has ever conjured: the scene in the tent of Richard Lion-Heart, when the disguised slave saves the life of the king, and Richard first suspects his identity. As he read on, his arms resting on the high desk in front of him, and his eyes, full of infectious enjoyment, travelling from the book to his audience, surrounded by human beings whose confidence he had won, and whose lives he was brightening from day to day, he seemed to Langham the very type and model of a man who had found his *métier*, found his niche in the world, and the best means of filling it. If to attain to an 'adequate and masterly expression of one's self' be the aim of life, Robert was fast achieving it. This parish of twelve hundred souls gave him now all the scope he asked. It was evident that he felt his work to be rather above than below his deserts. He was content—more than content—to spend ability which would have distinguished him in public life, or carried him far to the front in literature, on the civilising of a few hundred of England's rural poor. The future might bring him worldly success—Langham thought it must and would. Clergymen of Robert's stamp are rare among us. But if so, it would be in response to no conscious effort of his. Here, in the country living he had so long dreaded and put from him, lest it should tax his

---

25 Historical novel (1825) by Walter Scott, set during the Crusades. The "disguised slave" mentioned a few paragraphs down is the novel's protagonist, Sir Kenneth.

young energies too lightly, he was happy—deeply, abundantly happy, at peace with God, at one with man.

Happy! Langham, sitting at the outer corner of one of the benches, by the open door, gradually ceased to listen, started on other lines of thought by this realisation, warm, stimulating, provocative, of another man's happiness.

Outside, the shadows lengthened across the green; groups of distant children or animals passed in and out of the golden light-spaces; the patches of heather left here and there glowed as the sunset touched them. Every now and then his eye travelled vaguely past a cottage garden, gay with the pinks and carmines of the phloxes, into the cool browns and bluish-grays of the raftered room beyond; babies toddled across the road, with stooping mothers in their train; the whole air and scene seemed to be suffused with suggestions of the pathetic expansiveness and helplessness of human existence, which, generation after generation, is still so vulnerable, so confiding, so eager. Life after life flowers out from the darkness and sinks back into it again. And in the interval what agony, what disillusion! All the apparatus of a universe that men may know what it is to hope and fail, to win and lose! *Happy!*—in this world, 'where men sit and hear each other groan.'[26] His friend's confidence only made Langham as melancholy as Job.

What was it based on? In the first place, on Christianity—'on the passionate acceptance of an exquisite fairy tale,' said the dreaming spectator to himself, 'which at the first honest challenge of the critical sense withers in our grasp! That challenge Elsmere has never given it, and in all probability never will. No! A man sees none the straighter for having a wife he adores, and a profession that suits him, between him and unpleasant facts!'

In the evening Langham, with the usual reaction of his afternoon self against his morning self, felt that wild horses should not take him to Church again, and, with a longing for something purely mundane, he stayed at home with a volume of Montaigne, while apparently all the rest of the household went to evening service.[27]

After a warm day the evening had turned cold and stormy; the west was streaked with jagged strips of angry cloud, the wind was rising in the trees, and the temperature had suddenly fallen so much that when Langham shut himself up in Robert's study he did what he had been admonished to do in case of need, set a light to the fire, which blazed out merrily into the darkening room. Then he drew the curtains and threw himself down into Robert's

---

26 John Keats, "Ode to a Nightingale" (1819), l. 24.
27 The essayist Michel de Montaigne (1533–92).

chair with a sigh of Sybaritic satisfaction. 'Good! Now for something that takes the world less naïvely,' he said to himself; 'this house is too virtuous for anything.'

He opened his Montaigne and read on very happily for half an hour. The house seemed entirely deserted.

'All the servants gone too!' he said presently, looking up and listening. 'Anybody who wants the spoons needn't trouble about me. I don't leave this fire.'

And he plunged back again into his book. At last there was a sound of the swing door which separated Robert's passage from the front hall opening and shutting. Steps came quickly towards the study, the handle was turned, and there on the threshold stood Rose.

He turned quickly round in his chair with a look of astonishment. She also started as she saw him.

'I did not know any one was in,' she said awkwardly, the colour spreading over her face. 'I came to look for a book.'

She made a delicious picture as she stood framed in the darkness of the doorway, her long dress caught up round her in one hand, the other resting on the handle. A gust of some delicate perfume seemed to enter the room with her, and a thrill of pleasure passed through Langham's senses.

'Can I find anything for you?' he said, springing up.

She hesitated a moment, then apparently made up her mind that it would be foolish to retreat, and, coming forward, she said, with an accent as coldly polite as she could make it,—

'Pray don't disturb yourself. I know exactly where to find it.'

She went up to the shelves where Robert kept his novels, and began running her fingers over the books, with slightly knitted brows and a mouth severely shut. Langham, still standing, watched her and presently stepped forward.

'You can't reach those upper shelves,' he said; 'please let me.'

He was already beside her, and she gave way.

'I want *Charles Auchester*,' she said, still forbiddingly. 'It ought to be there.'[28]

'Oh, that queer musical novel—I know it quite well. No sign of it here,' and he ran over the shelves with the practised eye of one accustomed to deal with books.

'Robert must have lent it,' said Rose, with a little sigh. 'Never mind,

---

28 Novel (1853) by Elizabeth Sara Sheppard, about a fictionalized version of the composer Felix Mendelssohn (1809–47).

please. It doesn't matter,' and she was already moving away.

'Try some other instead,' he said, smiling, his arm still upstretched. 'Robert has no lack of choice.' His manner had an animation and ease usually quite foreign to it. Rose stopped, and her lips relaxed a little.

'He is very nearly as bad as the novel-reading bishop, who was reduced at last to stealing the servant's *Family Herald* out of the kitchen cupboard,' she said, a smile dawning.

Langham laughed.

'Has he such an episcopal appetite for them? That accounts for the fact that when he and I begin to talk novels I am always nowhere.'

'I shouldn't have supposed you ever read them,' said Rose, obeying an irresistible impulse, and biting her lip the moment afterwards.

'Do you think that we poor people at Oxford are always condemned to works on the "enclitic δέ"?' he asked, his fine eyes lit up with gaiety, and his head, of which the Greek outlines were ordinarily so much disguised by his stoop and hesitating look, thrown back against the books behind him.[29]

Natures like Langham's, in which the nerves are never normal, have their moments of felicity, balancing their weeks of timidity and depression. After his melancholy of the last two days the tide of reaction had been mounting within him, and the sight of Rose had carried it to its height.

She gave a little involuntary stare of astonishment. What had happened to Robert's silent and finicking friend?

'I know nothing of Oxford,' she said a little primly, in answer to his question. 'I never was there—but I never was anywhere, I have seen nothing,' she added hastily, and, as Langham thought, bitterly.

'Except London, and the great world, and Madame Desforêts!' he answered, laughing. 'Is that so little?'

She flashed a quick defiant look at him, as he mentioned Madame Desforêts, but his look was imperturbably kind and gay. She could not help softening towards him. What magic had passed over him?

'Do you know,' said Langham, moving, 'that you are standing in a draught, and that it has turned extremely cold?'

For she had left the passage-door wide open behind her, and as the window was partially open the curtains were swaying hither and thither, and her

---

29　From Robert Browning's "A Grammarian's Funeral" (1855), l. 31. This may also be a roundabout link back to Mark Pattison, as Rhoda Broughton's Professor Forth from *Belinda* (1883), who was based on Pattison, quotes "A Grammarian's Funeral" during courtship. Enclitics "are words attaching themselves closely to the preceding word, after which they are pronounced rapidly" (Herbert Weir Smyth, *A Greek Grammar for Colleges*, pt. 1, ch. 7, sec. 12 [www.perseus.tufts.edu]).

muslin dress was being blown in coils round her feet.

'So it has,' said Rose, shivering. 'I don't envy the Church people. You haven't found me a book, Mr. Langham?'

'I will find you one in a minute, if you will come and read it by the fire,' he said, with his hand on the door.

She glanced at the fire and at him, irresolute. His breath quickened. She too had passed into another phase. Was it the natural effect of night, of solitude, of sex? At any rate, she sank softly into the armchair opposite to that in which he had been sitting.

'Find me an exciting one, please.'

Langham shut the door securely, and went back to the bookcase, his hand trembling a little as it passed along the books. He found *Villette* and offered it to her.[30] She took it, opened it, and appeared deep in it at once. He took the hint and went back to his Montaigne.

The fire crackled cheerfully, the wind outside made every now and then a sudden gusty onslaught on their silence, dying away again as abruptly as it had risen. Rose turned the pages of her book, sitting a little stiffly in her long chair, and Langham gradually began to find Montaigne impossible to read. He became instead more and more alive to every detail of the situation into which he had fallen. At last seeing, or imagining, that the fire wanted attending to, he bent forward and thrust the poker into it. A burning coal fell on the hearth, and Rose hastily withdrew her foot from the fender and looked up.

'I am so sorry!' he interjected. 'Coals never do what you want them to do. Are you very much interested in *Villette*?'

'Deeply,' said Rose, letting the book, however, drop on her lap. She laid back her head with a little sigh, which she did her best to check, half way through. What ailed her to-night? She seemed wearied; for the moment there was no fight in her with anybody. Her music, her beauty, her mutinous mocking gaiety—these things had all worked on the man beside her; but this new softness, this touch of childish fatigue, was adorable.

'Charlotte Brontë wrote it out of her Brussels experience, didn't she?' she resumed languidly. 'How sorry she must have been to come back to that dull home and that awful brother after such a break!'[31]

'There were reasons more than one that must have made her sorry to come back,' said Langham reflectively. 'But how she pined for her wilds all through! I am afraid you don't find your wilds as interesting as she found

---

30 Charlotte Brontë's novel (1853), which was inspired by her studies in Belgium at the Pensionnat Heger in 1842–43.

31 The alcoholic and unsuccessful Branwell Brontë (1817–48).

hers?'

His question and his smile startled her.

Her first impulse was to take up her book again, as a hint to him that her likings were no concern of his. But something checked it, probably the new brilliancy of that look of his, which had suddenly grown so personal, so manly. Instead, *Villette* slid a little farther from her hand, and her pretty head still lay lightly back against the cushion.

'No, I don't find my wilds interesting at all,' she said forlornly.

'You are not fond of the people as your sister is?'

'Fond of them?' cried Rose hastily. 'I should think not; and what is more, they don't like me. It is quite intolerable since Catherine left. I have so much more to do with them. My other sister and I have to do all her work. It is dreadful to have to work after somebody who has a genius for doing just what you do worst.'

The young girl's hands fell across one another with a little impatient ges-ture. Langham had a movement of the most delightful compassion towards the petulant, childish creature. It was as though their relative positions had been in some mysterious way reversed. During their two days together she had been the superior, and he had felt himself at the mercy of her scornful sharp-eyed youth. Now, he knew not how or why, Fate seemed to have re-stored to him something of the man's natural advantage, combined, for once, with the impulse to use it.

'Your sister, I suppose, has been always happy in charity?' he said.

'Oh dear, yes,' said Rose irritably; 'anything that has two legs and is ill, that is all Catherine wants to make her happy.'

'And *you* want something quite different, something more exciting?' he asked, his diplomatic tone showing that he felt he dared something in thus pressing her, but dared it at least with his wits about him. Rose met his look irresolutely, a little tremor of self-consciousness creeping over her.

'Yes, I want something different,' she said in a low voice and paused; then, raising herself energetically, she clasped her hands round her knees. 'But it is not idleness I want. I want to work, but at things I was born for; I *can't* have patience with old women, but I could slave all day and all night to play the violin.'

'You want to give yourself up to study then, and live with musicians?' he said quietly.

She shrugged her shoulders by way of answer, and began nervously to play with her rings.

That under-self which was the work and the heritage of her father in her, and which, beneath all the wilfulnesses and defiances of the other self, held its own moral debates in its own way, well out of Catherine's sight generally, began to emerge, wooed into the light by his friendly gentleness.

'But it is all so difficult, you see,' she said despairingly. 'Papa thought it wicked to care about anything except religion. If he had lived, of course I should never have been allowed to study music. It has been all mutiny so far, every bit of it, whatever I have been able to do.'

'He would have changed with the times,' said Langham.

'I know he would,' cried Rose. 'I have told Catherine so a hundred times. People—good people—think quite differently about art now, don't they, Mr. Langham?'

She spoke with perfect *naïveté*. He saw more and more of the child in her, in spite of that one striking development of her art.

'They call it the handmaid of religion,' he answered, smiling.

Rose made a little face.

'I shouldn't,' she said, with frank brevity. 'But then there's something else. You know where we live—at the very ends of the earth, seven miles from a station, in the very loneliest valley of all Westmoreland. What's to be done with a fiddle in such a place? Of course, ever since papa died I've just been plotting and planning to get away. But there's the difficulty,' and she crossed one white finger over another as she laid out her case. 'That house where we live has been lived in by Leyburns ever since—the Flood! Horrid set they were, I know, because I can't ever make mamma or even Catherine talk about them. But still, when papa retired, he came back and bought the old place from his brother. Such a dreadful, dreadful mistake!' cried the child, letting her hands fall over her knee.

'Had he been so happy there?'

'Happy!'—and Rose's lip curled. 'His brothers used to kick and cuff him, his father was awfully unkind to him, he never had a day's peace till he went to school, and after he went to school he never came back for years and years and years, till Catherine was fifteen. What *could* have made him so fond of it?'

And again looking despondently into the fire she pondered that far-off perversity of her father's.

'Blood has strange magnetisms,' said Langham, seized as he spoke by the pensive prettiness of the bent head and neck, 'and they show themselves in the oddest ways.'

'Then I wish they wouldn't,' she said irritably. 'But that isn't all. He went there, not only because he loved that place, but because he hated other places. I think he must have thought'—and her voice dropped—'he wasn't going to live long—he wasn't well when he gave up the school—and then we could grow up there safe, without any chance of getting into mischief. Catherine says he thought the world was getting very wicked and dangerous and irreligious, and that it comforted him to know that we should be out of it.'

Then she broke off suddenly.

'Do you know,' she went on wistfully, raising her beautiful eyes to her companion, 'after all, he gave me my first violin?'

Langham smiled.

'I like that little inconsequence,' he said.

'Then of course I took to it, like a duck to water, and it began to scare him that I loved it so much. He and Catherine only loved religion, and us, and the poor. So he always took it away on Sundays. Then I hated Sundays, and would never be good on them. One Sunday I cried myself nearly into a fit on the dining-room floor because I mightn't have it. Then he came in, and he took me up, and he tied a Scotch plaid round his neck, and he put me into it, and carried me away right up on to the hills, and he talked to me like an angel. He asked me not to make him sad before God that he had given me that violin; so I never screamed again—on Sundays!'

Her companion's eyes were not quite as clear as before.

'Poor little naughty child,' he said, bending over to her. 'I think your father must have been a man to be loved.'

She looked at him, very near to weeping, her face all working with a soft remorse.

'Oh, so he was—so he was! If he had been hard and ugly to us, why, it would have been much easier for *me*; but he was so good! And there was Catherine just like him, always preaching to us what he wished. You see what a chain it's been—what a weight! And as I must struggle—*must*, because I was I—to get back into the world on the other side of the mountains, and do what all the dear wicked people there were doing, why, I have been a criminal all my life! And *that* isn't exhilarating always.'

And she raised her arm and let it fall beside her with the quick over-tragic emotion of nineteen.

'I wish your father could have heard you play as I heard you play yesterday,' he said gently.

She started.

'*Did* you hear me—that Wagner?'

He nodded, smiling. She still looked at him, her lips slightly open.

'Do you want to know what I thought? I have heard much music, you know.'

He laughed into her eyes, as much as to say, 'I am not quite the mummy you thought me, after all!' And she coloured slightly.

'I have heard every violinist of any fame in Europe play, and play often; and it seemed to me that with time—and work—you might play as well as any of them.'

The slight flush became a glow that spread from brow to chin. Then she gave a long breath and turned away, her face resting on her hand.

'And I can't help thinking,' he went on, marvelling inwardly at his own rôle of mentor, and his strange enjoyment of it, 'that if your father had lived till now, and had gone with the times a little, as he must have gone, he would have learnt to take pleasure in your pleasure, and to fit your gift somehow into his scheme of things.'

'Catherine hasn't moved with the times,' said Rose dolefully.

Langham was silent. *Gaucherie* seized him again when it became a question of discussing Mrs. Elsmere, his own view was so inconveniently emphatic.[32]

'And you think,' she went on, 'you *really* think, without being too ungrateful to papa, and too unkind to the old Leyburn ghosts'—and a little laugh danced through the vibrating voice—'I might try and get them to give up Burwood—I might struggle to have my way? I shall, of course I shall! I never was a meek martyr, and never shall be. But one can't help having qualms, though one doesn't tell them to one's sisters and cousins and aunts. And sometimes'—she turned her chin round on her hand and looked at him with a delicious shy impulsiveness—'sometimes a stranger sees clearer. Do *you* think me a monster, as Catherine does?'

Even as she spoke her own words startled her—the confidence, the abandonment of them. But she held to them bravely; only her eyelids quivered. She had absurdly misjudged this man, and there was a warm penitence in her heart. How kind he had been, how sympathetic!

He rose with her last words, and stood leaning against the mantelpiece, looking down upon her gravely, with the air, as it seemed to her, of her friend, her confessor. Her white childish brow, the little curls of bright hair upon her temples, her parted lips, the pretty folds of the muslin dress, the little foot on the fender—every detail of the picture impressed itself once for all. Langham will carry it with him to his grave.

'Tell me,' she said again, smiling divinely, as though to encourage him—'tell me quite frankly, down to the bottom, what you think?'

The harsh noise of an opening door in the distance, and a gust of wind

---

32 *Gaucherie*: awkwardness.

sweeping through the house, voices and steps approaching. Rose sprang up, and, for the first time during all the latter part of their conversation, felt a sharp sense of embarrassment.

'How early you are, Robert!' she exclaimed, as the study door opened, and Robert's wind-blown head and tall form, wrapped in an Inverness cape, appeared on the threshold. 'Is Catherine tired?'

'Rather,' said Robert, the slightest gleam of surprise betraying itself on his face. 'She has gone to bed, and told me to ask you to come and say good-night to her.'

'You got my message about not coming from old Martha?' asked Rose. 'I met her on the common.'

'Yes, she gave it us at the church door.' He went out again into the passage to hang up his greatcoat. She followed, longing to tell him that it was pure accident that took her to the study, but she could not find words in which to do it, and could only say good-night a little abruptly.

'How tempting that fire looks!' said Robert, re-entering the study. 'Were you very cold, Langham, before you lit it?'

'Very,' said Langham, smiling, his arm behind his head, his eyes fixed on the blaze; 'but I have been delightfully warm and happy since.'

CHAPTER XIV

Catherine stopped beside the drawing-room window with a start, caught by something she saw outside.

It was nothing, however, but the figures of Rose and Langham strolling round the garden. A bystander would have been puzzled by the sudden knitting of Catherine's brows over it.

Rose held a red parasol, which gleamed against the trees; Dandie leapt about her, but she was too busy talking to take much notice of him. Talking, chattering, to that cold cynic of a man, for whom only yesterday she had scarcely had a civil word! Catherine felt herself a prey to all sorts of vague unreasonable alarms.

Robert had said to her the night before, with an odd look: 'Wifie, when I came in I found Langham and Rose had been spending the evening together in the study. And I don't know when I have seen Langham so brilliant or so alive as in our smoking talk just now!'

Catherine had laughed him to scorn; but, all the same, she had been a little longer going to sleep than usual. She felt herself almost as much as ever the guardian of her sisters, and the old sensitive nerve was set quivering. And now there could be no question about it—Rose had changed her ground towards Mr. Langham altogether. Her manner at breakfast was evidence enough of it.

Catherine's self-torturing mind leapt on for an instant to all sorts of horrors. *That* man!—and she and Robert responsible to her mother and her dead father! Never! Then she scolded herself back to common sense. Rose and he had discovered a common subject in music and musicians. That would be quite enough to account for the new-born friendship on Rose's part. And in five more days, the limit of Langham's stay, nothing very dreadful *could* happen, argued the reserved Catherine.

But she was uneasy, and after a bit, as that *tête-à-tête* in the garden still went on, she could not, for the life of her, help interfering. She strolled out to meet them with some woollen stuff hanging over her arm, and made a plaintive and smiling appeal to Rose to come and help her with some preparations for a mothers' meeting to be held that afternoon. Rose, who was supposed by the family to be 'taking care' of her sister at a critical time, had a moment's prick of conscience, and went off with a good grace. Langham felt vaguely that he owed Mrs. Elsmere another grudge, but he resigned himself and took out a cigarette, wherewith to console himself for the loss of his companion.

Presently, as he stood for a moment turning over some new books on the drawing-room table, Rose came in. She held an armful of blue serge, and, going up to a table in the window, she took from it a little work-case, and was about to vanish again when Langham went up to her.

'You look intolerably busy,' he said to her, discontentedly.

'Six dresses, ten cloaks, eight petticoats to cut out by luncheon time,' she answered demurely, with a countenance of most Dorcas-like seriousness, 'and if I spoil them I shall have to pay for the stuff!'[33]

He shrugged his shoulders and looked at her, smiling, still master of himself and of his words.

'And no music—none at all? Perhaps you don't know that I too can accompany?'

'You play!' she exclaimed, incredulous.

'Try me.'

The light of his fine black eyes seemed to encompass her. She moved backward a little, shaking her head. 'Not this morning,' she said. 'Oh dear, no, not this morning! I am afraid you don't know anything about tacking or fixing, or the abominable time they take. Well, it could hardly be expected. There is nothing in the world'—and she shook her serge vindictively—'that

---

33 Dorcas, a "woman full of good works and almsdeeds," Acts 9.36.

I hate so much!'

'And not this afternoon, for Robert and I go fishing. But this evening?' he said, detaining her.

She nodded lightly, dropped her lovely eyes with a sudden embarrassment, and went away with lightning quickness.

A minute or two later Elsmere laid a hand on his friend's shoulder. 'Come and see the Hall, old fellow. It will be our last chance, for the squire and his sister come back this afternoon. I must parochialise a bit afterwards, but you shan't be much victimised.'

Langham submitted, and they sallied forth. It was a soft rainy morning, one of the first heralds of autumn. Gray mists were drifting silently across the woods and the wide stubbles of the now shaven cornfield, where white lines of reapers were at work, as the morning cleared, making and stacking the sheaves. After a stormy night the garden was strewn with *débris*, and here and there noiseless prophetic showers of leaves were dropping on the lawn.

Elsmere took his guest along a bit of common, where great black junipers stood up like magnates in council above the motley undergrowth of fern and heather, and then they turned into the park. A great stretch of dimpled land it was, falling softly towards the south and west, bounded by a shining twisted river, and commanding from all its highest points a heathery world of distance, now turned a stormy purple under the drooping fringes of the rain clouds. They walked downwards from the moment of entering it, till at last, when they reached a wooded plateau about a hundred feet above the river, the house itself came suddenly into view.

That was a house of houses! The large main building, as distinguished from the lower stone portions to the north which represented a fragment of the older Elizabethan house, had been in its day the crown and boast of Jacobean house-architecture. It was fretted and jewelled with Renaissance terra-cotta work from end to end; each gable had its lace work, each window its carved setting. And yet the lines of the whole were so noble, genius had hit the general proportions so finely, that no effect of stateliness or grandeur had been missed through all the accumulation of ornament. Majestic relic of a vanished England, the house rose amid the August woods rich in every beauty that site, and wealth, and centuries could give to it. The river ran about it as though it loved it. The cedars which had kept it company for well-nigh two centuries gathered proudly round it; the deer grouped themselves in the park beneath it, as though they were conscious elements in a great whole of loveliness.

The two friends were admitted by a housemaid who happened to be busy in the hall, and whose red cheeks and general breathlessness bore witness to the energy of the storm of preparation now sweeping through the house.

The famous hall to which Elsmere at once drew Langham's attention was, however, in no way remarkable for size or height. It told comparatively little of seignorial dignity, but it was as though generation after generation had employed upon its perfecting the craft of its most delicate fingers, the love of its most fanciful and ingenious spirits. Overhead, the stucco-work ceiling, covered with stags and birds and strange heraldic creatures unknown to science, had the deep creamy tint, the consistency and surface of antique ivory. From the white and gilt frieze beneath, untouched, so Robert explained, since the Jacobean days when it was first executed, hung Renaissance tapestries which would have made the heart's delight of any romantic child, so rich they were in groves of marvellous trees hung with red and golden fruits, in far-reaching palaces and rock-built citadels, in flying shepherdesses and pursuing shepherds. Between the tapestries, again, there were breadths of carved panelling, crowded with all things round and sweet, with fruits and flowers and strange musical instruments, with flying cherubs, and fair faces in laurel-wreathed medallions; while in the middle of the wall a great oriel window broke the dim venerable surfaces of wood and tapestry with stretches of jewelled light. Tables crowded with antiques, with Tanagra figures or Greek vases, with Florentine bronzes or specimens of the wilful vivacious wood-carving of seventeenth-century Spain, stood scattered on the Persian carpets.[34] And, to complete the whole, the gardeners had just been at work on the corners of the hall, and of the great window, so that the hard-won subtleties of man's bygone handiwork, with which the splendid room was encrusted from top to bottom, were masked and relieved here and there by the careless easy splendour of flowers, which had but to bloom in order to eclipse them all.

Robert was at home in the great pile, where for many months he had gone freely in and out on his way to the library, and the housekeeper only met him to make an apology for her working dress, and to hand over to him the keys of the library bookcases, with the fretful comment that seemed to have in it the ghostly voice of generations of housemaids, 'Oh lor', sir, they are a trouble, them books!'

From the drawing-rooms, full of a more modern and less poetical magnificence, where Langham turned restless and refractory, Elsmere with a smile took his guest silently back into the hall, and opened a carved door behind a curtain. Passing through, they found themselves in a long passage lighted by

---

34 Tanagra figures: Greek terracotta statues dating from the late fourth century BCE, popularized in England thanks to the collector Alexander Ionides (1840-1898).

small windows on the left-hand side.

'This passage, please notice,' said Robert, 'leads to nothing but the wing containing the library, or rather libraries, which is the oldest part of the house. I always enter it with a kind of pleasing awe! Consider these carpets, which keep out every sound, and look how everything gets older as we go on.'

For half-way down the passage the ceiling seemed to descend upon their heads, the flooring became uneven and woodwork and walls showed that they had passed from the Jacobean house into the much older Tudor building. Presently Robert led the way up a few shallow steps, pushed open a heavy door, also covered by curtains, and bade his companion enter.

They found themselves in a low immense room, running at right angles to the passage they had just quitted. The long diamond-paned window, filling almost half of the opposite wall, faced the door by which they had come in; the heavy carved mantelpiece was to their right; an open doorway on their left, closed at present by tapestry hangings, seemed to lead into yet other rooms.

The walls of this one were completely covered from floor to ceiling with latticed bookcases, enclosed throughout in a frame of oak carved in light classical relief by what appeared to be a French hand of the sixteenth century. The chequered bindings of the books, in which the creamy tints of vellum predominated, lined the whole surface of the wall with a delicate sobriety of colour; over the mantelpiece, the picture of the founder of the house— a Holbein portrait,[35] glorious in red robes and fur and golden necklace— seemed to gather up and give voice to all the dignity and impressiveness of the room beneath him; while on the window side the book-lined wall was, as it were, replaced by the wooded face of a hill, clothed in dark lines of trimmed yews, which rose abruptly about a hundred yards from the house and overshadowed the whole library wing. Between the window and the hill, however, was a small old English garden, closely hedged round with yew hedges, and blazing now with every flower that an English August knows— with sun-flowers, tiger-lilies, and dahlias white and red. The window was low, so that the flowers seemed to be actually in the room, challenging the pale tints of the books, the tawny browns and blues of the Persian carpet, and the scarlet splendours of the courtier over the mantelpiece. The room was lit up besides by a few gleaming casts from the antique, by the 'Diane Chasseresse' of the Louvre, by the Hermes of Praxiteles smiling with immortal kindness on the child enthroned upon his arm, and by a Donatello figure of a woman

---

35 Hans Holbein the Younger (c. 1497–1543), sixteenth-century portrait painter renowned for his work at the court of Henry VIII.

in marble, its subtle sweet austerity contrasting with the Greek frankness and blitheness of its companions.[36]

Langham was penetrated at once by the spell of this strange and beautiful place. The fastidious instincts which had been half revolted by the costly accumulations, the overblown splendours of the drawing-room, were abundantly satisfied here.

'So it was here,' he said, looking round him, 'that that man wrote *The Idols of the Market-place?*'

'I imagine so,' said Robert; 'if so, he might well have felt a little more charity towards the human race in writing it. The race cannot be said to have treated him badly on the whole. But now look, Langham, look at these books—the most precious things are here.'

And he turned the key of a particular section of the wall, which was not only latticed but glazed.

'Here is *A Mirror for Magistrates*. Look at the title-page; you will find Gabriel Harvey's name on it. Here is a first edition of *Astrophel and Stella*, another of the Arcadia. They may very well be presentation copies, for the Wendover of that day is known to have been a wit and a writer.[37] Imagine finding them *in situ* like this in the same room, perhaps on the same shelves, as at the beginning! The other rooms on this floor have been annexed since, but this room was always a library.'

Langham took the volumes reverently from Robert's hands into his own, the scholar's passion hot within him. That glazed case was indeed a storehouse of treasures. Ben Jonson's *Underwoods* with his own corrections; a presentation copy of Andrew Marvell's *Poems*, with autograph notes; manuscript volumes of letters, containing almost every famous name known to English literature in the seventeenth and eighteenth centuries, the literary cream, in fact, of all the vast collection which filled the muniment room upstairs; books which had belonged to Addison, to Sir William Temple, to Swift, to Horace Walpole; the first four folios of Shakespeare, all perfect, and most of the

---

36 The Diana: a Roman statue (from the Greek original) of the goddess Diana, famed as one of the masterpieces of classical antiquity. The Hermes: the then very recently rediscovered statue by Praxiteles (4th c. BCE), who was and is considered one of the greatest sculptors of ancient Greece. Donatello (1386-1466), an Italian sculptor, primarily based in Florence.

37 *A Mirror for Magistrates* (first published 1559), a multi-author collection of exemplary verse lives; Harvey (1545–1630), contentious scholar and versifier; *Astrophel and Stella* (1591), sonnet sequence by Sir Philip Sidney (1554–86); the *Arcadia* in question, also by Sidney, is the *New Arcadia* (1590). It is unclear who would have done the presenting, as both were published posthumously.

quartos—everything that the heart of the English collector could most desire was there.[38] And the charm of it was that only a small proportion of these precious things represented conscious and deliberate acquisition. The great majority of them had, as it were, drifted thither one by one, carried there by the tide of English letters as to a warm and natural resting-place.

But Robert grew impatient, and hurried on his guest to other things— to the shelves of French rarities, ranging from Du Bellay's *Visions*, with his autograph, down to the copy of *Les Mémoires d'Outre-Tombe* presented by Chateaubriand to Madame Récamier, or to a dainty manuscript volume in the fine writing of Lamartine.[39]

'These,' Robert explained, 'were collected, I believe, by the squire's father. He was not in the least literary, so they say, but it had always been a point of honour to carry on the library, and as he had learnt French well in his youth he bought French things, taking advice, but without knowing much about them, I imagine. It was in the room overhead,' said Robert, laying down the book he held, and speaking in a lower key, 'so the old doctor of the house told me a few weeks ago, that the same poor soul put an end to himself twenty years ago.'

'What in the name of fortune did he do that for?'

'Mania,' said Robert quietly.

'Whew!' said the other, lifting his eyebrows. 'Is that the skeleton in this very magnificent cupboard?'

'It has been the Wendover scourge from the beginning, so I hear. Every one about here of course explains this man's eccentricities by the family history. But I don't know,' said Robert, his lip hardening, 'it may be extremely convenient sometimes to have a tradition of the kind. A man who knew how

---

38   Ben Jonson (1572–1637), dramatist and poet; *The Underwood* (1640), a posthumously published collection of Jonson's poetry (and therefore could not have Jonson's corrections, unless. Ward means us to understand this is a manuscript); Andrew Marvell (1621–1678), Metaphysical poet and satirist; Joseph Addison (1672–1719), co-author of *The Tatler* and *The Spectator*, author of the play *Cato*; Sir William Temple (1628–90), politician and author, now best remembered for *Of Ancient and Modern Learning*; Jonathan Swift (1667–1745), legendary satirist, author of *Gulliver's Travels*; Horace Walpole (1717–97), author and antiquarian, invented the Gothic novel with *The Castle of Otranto*.

39   Joachim Du Bellay (1522–60), French poet especially well-known for his sonnets; *Visions*: the title is not Du Bellay's, but Edmund Spenser's translation, *The Visions of Bellay*; *Les Mémoires* (1848–50): forty-two volume autobiography of François-René de Chateaubriand (1768–1848), Romantic novelist, travel writer, and politician; Madame Juliette Récamier (1777–1849), influential French *salonniére*; Alphonse de Lamartine (1790–1869), French poet, novelist, and politician.

to work it might very well enjoy all the advantages of sanity and the privileges of insanity at the same time. The poor old doctor I was telling you of—old Meyrick—who has known the squire since his boyhood, and has a dog-like attachment to him, is always hinting at mysterious excuses. Whenever I let out to him, as I do sometimes, as to the state of the property, he talks of "inherited melancholy," "rash judgments," and so forth. I like the good old soul, but I don't believe much of it. A man who is sane enough to make a great name for himself in letters is sane enough to provide his estate with a decent agent.'

'It doesn't follow,' said Langham, who was, however, so deep in a collection of Spanish romances and chronicles that the squire's mental history did not seem to make much impression upon him. 'Most men of letters are mad, and I should be inclined,' he added, with a sudden and fretful emphasis, 'to argue much worse things for the sanity of your squire, Elsmere, from the fact that this room is undoubtedly allowed to get damp sometimes, than from any of those absurd parochial tests of yours.'

And he held up a couple of priceless books, of which the Spanish sheep-skin bindings showed traces here and there of moisture.

'It is no use, I know, expecting you to preserve a moral sense when you get among books,' said Robert with a shrug. 'I will reserve my remarks on that subject. But you must really tear yourself away from this room, Langham, if you want to see the rest of the squire's quarters. Here you have what we may call the ornamental sensational part of the library, that part of it which would make a stir at Sotheby's; the working parts are all to come.'

Langham reluctantly allowed himself to be dragged away. Robert held back the hangings over the doorway leading into the rest of the wing, and, passing through, they found themselves in a continuation of the library totally different in character from the magnificent room they had just left. The walls were no longer latticed and carved; they were closely packed, in the most business-like way, with books which represented the squire's own collection, and were in fact a chart of his own intellectual history.

'This is how I interpret this room,' said Robert, looking round it. 'Here are the books he collected at Oxford in the Tractarian Movement and afterwards. Look here,' and he pulled out a volume of St. Basil.[40]

Langham looked, and saw on the title-page a note in faded characters: '*Given to me by Newman at Oxford, in* 1845.'[41]

'Ah, of course, he was one of them in '45; he must have left them very

---

40 St. Basil of Caesarea (c. 329–379 CE), one of the Cappadocian Fathers.

41 Newman converted to Catholicism that year.

soon after,' said Langham reflectively.

Robert nodded. 'But look at them! There are the Tracts, all the Fathers, all the Councils, and masses, as you see, of Anglican theology. Now look at the next case, nothing but eighteenth century!'

'I see,—from the Fathers to the Philosophers, from Hooker to Hume.[42] How history repeats itself in the individual!'

'And there again,' said Robert, pointing to the other side of the room, 'are the results of his life as a German student.'

'Germany—ah, I remember! How long was he there?'

'Ten years, at Berlin and Heidelberg.[43] According to old Meyrick, he buried his last chance of living like other men at Berlin. His years of extravagant labour there have left marks upon him physically that can never be effaced. But that bookcase fascinates me. Half the great names of modern thought are in those books.'

And so they were. The first Langham opened had a Latin dedication in a quavering old man's hand, 'Amico et discipulo meo,' signed 'Fredericus Gulielmus Schelling.'[44] The next bore the autograph of Alexander von Humboldt, the next that of Boeckh, the famous classic, and so on.[45] Close by was Niebuhr's History, in the title-page of which a few lines in the historian's handwriting bore witness to much 'pleasant discourse between the writer and Roger Wendover, at Bonn, in the summer of 1847.'[46] Judging from other shelves farther down, he must also have spent some time, perhaps an academic year, at Tübingen, for here were most of the early editions of the *Leben Jesu*, with some corrections from Strauss's hand, and similar records of Baur, Ewald, and other members or opponents of the Tübingen

---

42 Richard Hooker (1554–1600), one of Anglicanism's foundational theologians; David Hume (1711–76), Scottish Enlightenment philosopher and skeptic.

43 The German universities were at the forefront of intellectual endeavor during the eighteenth and nineteenth centuries, but they were also feared for their apparent "free-thinking" propensities; as the next paragraph makes clear, Wendover encountered the new Biblical scholarship, dubbed the Higher Criticism, during his stay. Berlin was Germany's academic hub; Wendover studied at the University of Heidelberg, one of Germany's premiere research universities.

44 To my friend and student; Schelling (1775–1854), Idealist philosopher.

45 Von Humboldt (1769–1859), pioneering scientist and botanist whose work influenced Romantic theories of nature; Philip August Böckh (1785–1867), influential classicist who would have been at the Humboldt University in Berlin during Wendover's stay.

46 Barthold Georg Niebuhr (1776–1831), Roman historian; his *History of Rome* (1st ed., 1811-12; 2nd ed., 1827-32) strongly influenced Ward's grandfather, Thomas Arnold.

school.[47] And so on, through the whole bookcase. Something of everything was there—Philosophy, Theology, History, Philology. The collection was a medley, and made almost a spot of disorder in the exquisite neatness and system of the vast gathering of which it formed part. Its bond of union was simply that it represented the forces of an epoch, the thoughts, the men, the occupations which had absorbed the energies of ten golden years. Every book seemed to be full of paper marks; almost every title-page was covered with minute writing, which, when examined, proved to contain a record of lectures, or conversations with the author of the volume, sometimes a string of anecdotes or a short biography, rapidly sketched out of the fulness of personal knowledge, and often seasoned with a subtle causticity and wit. A history of modern thinking Germany, of that 'unextinguished hearth' whence the mind of Europe has been kindled for three generations, might almost have been evolved from that bookcase and its contents alone.

Langham, as he stood peering among the ugly, vilely-printed German volumes, felt suddenly a kind of magnetic influence creeping over him. The room seemed instinct with a harsh commanding presence. The history of a mind and soul was written upon the face of it; every shelf, as it were, was an autobiographical fragment, an 'Apologia pro Vita Mea.'[48] He drew away from the books at last with the uneasy feeling of one who surprises a confidence, and looked for Robert. Robert was at the end of the room, a couple of volumes under his arm, another, which he was reading, in his hand.

'This is *my* corner,' he said, smiling and flushing a little, as his friend moved up to him. 'Perhaps you don't know that I too am engaged upon a great work.'

'A great work—you?'

Langham looked at his companion as though to find out whether his remark was meant seriously or whether he might venture to be cynical. Elsmere writing! Why should everybody write books? It was absurd! The scholar who knows what toll scholarship takes of life is always apt to resent the intrusion of the man of action into his domains. It looks to him like a kind of ridiculous assumption that any one *d'un cœur léger* can do what has cost him his heart's

---

47 Ferdinand Christian Baur (1792–1860), theologian at the University of Tübingen and Biblical scholar; under Baur's influence, Tübingen became an important center of the new historicist scholarship. Heinrich Ewald (1803–75), theologian and Hebraist. David Friedrich Strauss' (1808–74) *The Life of Jesus, Critically Examined* (1835–36) set off shockwaves in Europe because it treated Jesus from an entirely historicist point of view, analyzing the gospels as myths instead of divinely inspired scriptures. The standard translation into English remains that of Marian Evans, later George Eliot.
48 An allusion to John Henry Newman's *Apologia pro Vita Sua* (1864).

blood.[49]

Robert understood something of the meaning of his tone, and replied almost apologetically; he was always singularly modest about himself on the intellectual side.

'Well, Grey is responsible. He gave me such a homily before I left Oxford on the absolute necessity of keeping up with books, that I could do nothing less than set up a "subject" at once. "Half the day," he used to say to me, "you will be king of your world; the other half be the slave of something which will take you out of your world into the general world;" and then he would quote to me that saying he was always bringing into lectures—I forget whose it is—"*The decisive events of the world take place in the intellect. It is the mission of books that they help one to remember it.*"[50] Altogether it was striking, coming from one who has always had such a tremendous respect for practical life and work, and I was much impressed by it. So blame him!'

Langham was silent. Elsmere had noticed that any allusion to Grey found Langham less and less responsive.

'Well, what is the "great work"?' he said at last, abruptly.

'Historical. Oh, I should have written something without Grey; I have always had a turn for it since I was a child. But he was clear that history was especially valuable—especially necessary to a clergyman. I felt he was right, entirely right. So I took my Final Schools' history for a basis, and started on the Empire, especially the decay of the Empire. Some day I mean to take up one of the episodes in the great birth of Europe—the makings of France, I think, most likely. It seems to lead farthest and tell most. I have been at work now nine months.'

'And are just getting into it?'

'Just about. I have got down below the surface, and am beginning to feel the joys of digging;' and Robert threw back his head with one of his most brilliant enthusiastic smiles. 'I have been shy about boring you with the thing, but the fact is, I am very keen indeed; and this library has been a godsend!'

'So I should think.' Langham sat down on one of the carved wooden stools placed at intervals along the bookcases and looked at his friend, his psychological curiosity rising a little.

'Tell me,' he said presently—'tell me what interests you specially—what seizes you—in a subject like the making of France, for instance?'

'Do you really want to know?' said Robert, incredulously.

---

49 *d'un cœur léger*: with a light heart.
50 Adapted from *Amiel's Journal: The Journal Intime of Henri Frédéric Amiel,* trans. Mrs. Humphry Ward (London: Macmillan, 1885), 1.453.

The other nodded. Robert left his place, and began to walk up and down, trying to answer Langham's question, and at the same time to fix in speech a number of sentiments and impressions bred in him by the work of the past few months. After a while Langham began to see his way. Evidently the forces at the bottom of this new historical interest were precisely the same forces at work in Elsmere's parish plans, in his sermons, in his dealings with the poor and the young—forces of imagination and sympathy. What was enchaining him to this new study was not, to begin with, that patient love of ingenious accumulation which is the learned temper proper, the temper, in short, of science. It was simply a passionate sense of the human problems which underlie all the dry and dusty detail of history and give it tone and colour, a passionate desire to rescue something more of human life from the drowning, submerging past, to realise for himself and others the solidarity and continuity of mankind's long struggle from the beginning until now.

Langham had had much experience of Elsmere's versatility and pliancy, but he had never realised it so much as now, while he sat listening to the vivid, many-coloured speech getting quicker and quicker, and more and more telling and original as Robert got more absorbed and excited by what he had to say. He was endeavouring to describe to Langham the sort of book he thought might be written on the rise of modern society in Gaul, dwelling first of all on the outward spectacle of the blood-stained Frankish world as it was, say, in the days of Gregory the Great, on its savage kings, its fiendish women, its bishops and its saints; and then, on the conflict of ideas going on behind all the fierce incoherence of the Empire's decay, the struggle of Roman order and of German freedom, of Roman luxury and of German hardness; above all, the war of orthodoxy and heresy, with its strange political complications. And then, discontented still, as though the heart of the matter were still untouched, he went on, restlessly wandering the while, with his long arms linked behind him, 'throwing out' words at an object in his mind, trying to grasp and analyse that strange sense which haunts the student of Rome's decline as it once overshadowed the infancy of Europe, that sense of a slowly departing majesty, of a great presence just withdrawn, and still incalculably potent, traceable throughout in that humbling consciousness of Goth or Frank that they were but 'beggars hutting in a palace—the place had harboured greater men than they!'

'There is one thing,' Langham said presently, in his slow nonchalant voice, when the tide of Robert's ardour ebbed for a moment, 'that doesn't seem to have touched you yet. But you will come to it. To my mind, it makes almost the chief interest of history. It is just this. History depends on *testimony*.[51] What is the nature and the value of testimony at given times? In other words, did the man of the third century understand, or report, or interpret facts in the same way as the man of the sixteenth or the nineteenth? And if not, what are the differences, and what are the deductions to be made from them, if any?' He fixed his keen look on Robert, who was now lounging against the books, as though his harangue had taken it out of him a little.

'Ah, well,' said the rector, smiling, 'I am only just coming to that. As I told you, I am only now beginning to dig for myself. Till now it has all been work at second hand. I have been getting a general survey of the ground as quickly as I could with the help of other men's labours. Now I must go to work inch by inch, and find out what the ground is made of. I won't forget your point. It is enormously important, I grant—enormously,' he repeated reflectively.

'I should think it is,' said Langham to himself as he rose; 'the whole of orthodox Christianity is in it, for instance!'

There was not much more to be seen. A little wooden staircase led from the second library to the upper rooms, curious old rooms, which had been annexed one by one as the squire wanted them, and in which there was noth-ing at all—neither chair, nor table, nor carpet—but books only. All the doors leading from room to room had been taken off; the old worm-eaten boards had been roughly stained; a few old French engravings had been hung here and there where the encroaching books left an opening; but otherwise all was bare. There was a curious charm in the space and air of these empty rooms, with their latticed windows opening on to the hill, and letting in day by day the summer sun-risings or the winter dawns, which had shone upon them for more than three centuries.

'This is my last day of privilege,' said Robert. 'Everybody is shut out when once he appears, from this wing, and this part of the grounds. This was his fa-ther's room,' and the rector led the way into the last of the series; 'and through there,' pointing to a door on the right, 'lies the way to his own sleeping room,

---

51 According to Ward, this conversation arose from her own experience of pon-dering the status of testimony while writing entries for the *Dictionary of Christian Biography* (*A Writer's Recollections* [London: W. Collins Sons & Co., 1918], 165–66). The status of Biblical testimony was a heated topic amongst philosophers and theolo-gians, especially in the wake of David Hume's critique of miracles. Richard Whately (1787–1863) famously pushed this argument to a *reductio ad absurdum* in *Historic Doubts Relative to Napoleon Bonaparte* (1819), in which he used Hume's theories of testimony to "prove" that Napoleon had never existed.

which is of course connected with the more modern side of the house.'

'So this is where that old man ventured "what Cato did and Addison approved,"' murmured Langham, standing in the middle of the room and looking round him.[52] This particular room was now used as a sort of lumber place, a receptacle for the superfluous or useless books gradually thrown off by the great collection all around. There were innumerable volumes in frayed or broken bindings lying on the ground. A musty smell hung over it all; the gray light from outside, which seemed to give only an added subtlety and charm to the other portions of the ancient building through which they had been moving, seemed here *triste* and dreary. Or Langham fancied it.

He passed the threshold again with a little sigh, and saw suddenly before him at the end of the suite of rooms, and framed in the doorways facing him, an engraving of a Greuze picture—a girl's face turned over her shoulder, the hair waving about her temples, the lips parted, the teeth gleaming, mirth and provocation and tender yielding in every line.[53] Langham started, and the blood rushed to his heart. It was as though Rose herself stood there and beckoned to him.

CHAPTER XV

'Now, having seen our sight,' said Robert, as they left the great mass of Murewell behind them, 'come and see our scandal. Both run by the same proprietor, if you please. There is a hamlet down there in the hollow'—and he pointed to a gray speck in the distance—'which deserves a Royal Commission all to itself, which is a *disgrace*'—and his tone warmed—'to any country, any owner, any agent! It is owned by Mr. Wendover, and I see the pleasing prospect straight before me of beginning my acquaintance with him by a fight over it. You will admit that it is a little hard on a man who wants to live on good terms with the possessor of the Murewell library to have to open relations with him by a fierce attack on his drains and his pigsties.'

He turned to his companion with a half-rueful spark of laughter in his gray eyes. Langham hardly caught what he said. He was far away in meditations of his own.

---

52 From the suicide note of Addison's erstwhile collaborator Eustace Budgell (1686–1737): "What Cato did, and Addison approved, cannot be wrong."

53 Jean-Baptiste Greuze (1725–1805), French artist; the description resembles a number of Greuze's paintings of young women, although it is very close to "Young Woman Seen from the Back."

'An attack,' he repeated vaguely; 'why an attack?'

Robert plunged again into the great topic of which his quick mind was evidently full. Langham tried to listen, but was conscious that his friend's social enthusiasms bored him a great deal. And side by side with the consciousness there slid in a little stinging reflection that four years ago no talk of Elsmere's could have bored him.

'What's the matter with this particular place?' he asked languidly, at last, raising his eyes towards the group of houses now beginning to emerge from the distance.

An angry red mounted in Robert's cheek.

'What isn't the matter with it? The houses, which were built on a swamp originally, are falling into ruin; the roofs, the drains, the accommodation per head, are all about equally scandalous. The place is harried with illness; since I came there has been both fever and diphtheria there. They are all crippled with rheumatism, but *that* they think nothing of; the English labourer takes rheumatism as quite in the day's bargain! And as to *vice*—the vice that comes of mere endless persecuting opportunity—I can tell you one's ideas of personal responsibility get a good deal shaken up by a place like this! And I can do nothing. I brought over Henslowe to see the place, and he behaved like a brute. He scoffed at all my complaints, said that no landlord would be such a fool as to build fresh cottages on such a site, that the old ones must just be allowed to go to ruin; that the people might live in them if they chose, or turn out of them if they chose. Nobody forced them to do either; it was their own look-out.'

'That was true,' said Langham, 'wasn't it?'

Robert turned upon him fiercely.

'Ah! you think it so easy for those poor creatures to leave their homes, their working places! Some of them have been there thirty years. They are close to the two or three farms that employ them, close to the osier beds which give them extra earnings in the spring. If they were turned out there is nothing nearer than Murewell, and not a single cottage to be found there. I don't say it is a landlord's duty to provide more cottages than are wanted; but if the labour is wanted, the labourer should be decently housed. He is worthy of his hire, and woe to the man who neglects or ill-treats him!'[54]

Langham could not help smiling, partly at the vehemence of the speech, partly at the lack of adjustment between his friend's mood and his own. He braced himself to take the matter more seriously, but meanwhile Robert had caught the smile, and his angry eyes melted at once into laughter.

---

54 An allusion to Luke 10.7.

'There I am, ranting as usual,' he said penitently. 'Took you for Henslowe, I suppose! Ah, well, never mind. I hear the Provost has another book on the stocks.'

So they diverged into other things, talking politics and new books, public men and what not, till, at the end of a long and gradual descent through wooded ground, some two miles to the north-west of the park, they emerged from the trees beneath which they had been walking, and found themselves on a bridge, a gray sluggish stream flowing beneath them, and the hamlet they sought rising among the river flats on the farther side.

'There,' said Robert, stopping, 'we are at our journey's end. Now then, what sort of a place of human habitation do you call *that*?'

The bridge whereon they stood crossed the main channel of the river, which just at that point, however, parted into several branches, and came meandering slowly down through a little bottom or valley, filled with osier beds, long since robbed of their year's growth of shoots. On the other side of the river, on ground all but level with the osier beds which interposed between them and the stream, rose a miserable group of houses, huddled together as though their bulging walls and rotten roofs could only maintain themselves at all by the help and support which each wretched hovel gave to its neighbour. The mud walls were stained with yellow patches of lichen, the palings round the little gardens were broken and ruinous. Close beside them all was a sort of open drain or water-course, stagnant and noisome, which dribbled into the river a little above the bridge. Behind them rose a high gravel bank edged by firs, and a line of oak trees against the sky. The houses stood in the shadow of the bank looking north, and on this gray, lowering day, the dreariness, the gloom, the squalor of the place were indescribable.

'Well, that *is* a God-forsaken hole!' said Langham, studying it, his interest roused at last, rather, perhaps, by the Ruysdael-like melancholy and picturesqueness of the scene than by its human suggestiveness.[55] 'I could hardly have imagined such a place existed in southern England. It is more like a bit of Ireland.'

'If it were Ireland it might be to somebody's interest to ferret it out,' said Robert bitterly. 'But these poor folks are out of the world. They may be brutalised with impunity. Oh, such a case as I had here last autumn! A young girl of sixteen or seventeen, who would have been healthy and happy anywhere else, stricken by the damp and the poison of the place, dying in six weeks, of complications due to nothing in the world but preventable cruelty and

---

55   There were multiple landscape painters in this Dutch family; the most likely candidate is Jacob Izaacksoon van Ruisdale (1628–82).

neglect! It was a sight that burnt into my mind, once for all, what is meant by a landlord's responsibility. I tried, of course, to move her, but neither she nor her parents—elderly folk—had energy enough for a change. They only prayed to be let alone. I came over the last evening of her life to give her the communion. "Ah, sir!" said the mother to me—not bitterly—that is the strange thing, they have so little bitterness—"if Mister 'Enslowe would jest 'a mended that bit 'o roof of ours last winter, Bessie needn't have laid in the wet so many nights as she did, and she coughin' fit to break your heart, for all the things yer could put over 'er.'"

Robert paused, his strong young face, so vehemently angry a few minutes before, tremulous with feeling. 'Ah, well,' he said at last with a long breath, moving away from the parapet of the bridge on which he had been leaning, 'better be oppressed than oppressor, any day! Now, then, I must deliver my stores. There's a child here Catherine and I have been doing our best to pull through typhoid.'

They crossed the bridge and turned down the track leading to the hamlet. Some planks carried them across the ditch, the main sewer of the community, as Robert pointed out, and they made their way through the filth surrounding one of the nearest cottages.

A feeble elderly man, whose shaking limbs and sallow bloodless skin make him look much older than he actually was, opened the door and invited them to come in. Robert passed on into an inner room, conducted thither by a woman who had been sitting working over the fire. Langham stood irresolute; but the old man's quavering 'kindly take a chair, sir; you've come a long way,' decided him, and he stepped in.

Inside the hovel was miserable indeed. It belonged to that old and evil type which the efforts of the last twenty years have done so much all over England to sweep away: four mud walls, enclosing an oblong space about eight yards long, divided into two unequal portions by a lath and plaster partition, with no upper storey, a thatched roof, now entirely out of repair, and letting in the rain in several places, and a paved floor little better than the earth itself, so large and cavernous were the gaps between the stones. The dismal place had no small adornings—none of those little superfluities which, however ugly and trivial, are still so precious in the dwellings of the poor, as showing the existence of some instinct or passion which is not the creation of the sheerest physical need; and Langham, as he sat down, caught the sickening marsh smell which the Oxford man, accustomed to the odours of damp meadows in times of ebbing flood and festering sun, knows so well. As old Milsom began to talk to him in his weak tremulous voice, the visitor's attention was irresistibly held by the details about him. Fresh as he was from all the delicate sights, the harmonious colours and delightful forms of the squire's house, they made an unusually sharp impression on his fastidious senses. What does human life become lived on reeking floors and under stifling roofs like these? What strange abnormal deteriorations, physical and spiritual, must it not inevitably undergo? Langham felt a sudden inward movement of disgust and repulsion. 'For heaven's sake, keep your superstitions!' he could have cried to the whole human race, 'or any other narcotic that a grinding fate has left you. What does *anything* matter to the mass of mankind but a little ease, a little lightening of pressure on this side or on that?'

Meanwhile the old man went maundering on, talking of the weather, and of his sick child, and 'Mr. Elsmere,' with a kind of listless incoherence which hardly demanded an answer, though Langham threw in a word or two here and there.

Among other things, he began to ask a question or two about Robert's predecessor, a certain Mr. Preston, who had left behind him a memory of amiable evangelical indolence.

'Did you see much of him?' he asked.

'Oh law, no, sir!' replied the man, surprised into something like energy. 'Never seed 'im more 'n once a year, and sometimes not that!'

'Was he liked here?'

'Well, sir, it was like this, you see. My wife, she's north-country, she is, comes from Yorkshire; sometimes she'd used to say to me, "Passon 'ee ain't much good, and passon 'ee ain't much harm. 'Ee's no more good nor more 'arm, so fer as *I* can see, nor a chip in a basin o' parritch." And that was just about it, sir,' said the old man, pleased for the hundredth time with his wife's bygone flight of metaphor and his own exact memory of it.

As to the rector's tendance of his child, his tone was very cool and guarded.

'It do seem strange, sir, as nor he nor Doctor Grimes 'ull let her have anything to put a bit of flesh on her, nothin' but them messy things as he brings—milk an' that. An' the beef jelly—lor, such a trouble! Missis Elsmere, he tells my wife, strains all the stuff through a cloth, she do; never seed anythin' like it, nor my wife neither. People is clever nowadays,' said the speaker dubiously. Langham realised that, in this quarter of his parish at any rate, his friend's pastoral vanity, if he had any, would not find much to feed on. Nothing, to judge from this specimen at least, greatly affected an inhabitant of Mile End. Gratitude, responsiveness, imply health and energy, past or present. The only constant defence which the poor have against such physical conditions as those which prevailed at Mile End is apathy.

As they came down the dilapidated steps at the cottage door, Robert drew in with avidity a long draught of the outer air.

'Ugh!' he said with a sort of groan, 'that bedroom! Nothing gives one such a sense of the toughness of human life as to see a child recovering, actually recovering, in such a pestilential den! Father, mother, grown-up son, girl of thirteen, and grandchild, all huddled in a space just fourteen feet square. Langham!' and he turned passionately on his companion, 'what defence can be found for a man who lives in a place like Murewell Hall, and can take money from human beings for the use of a sty like that?'

'Gently, my friend. Probably the squire, being the sort of recluse he is, has never seen the place, or, at any rate, not for years, and knows nothing about it!'

'More shame for him!'

'True in a sense,' said Langham, a little drily; 'but as you *may* want hereafter to make excuses for your man, and he *may* give you occasion, I wouldn't begin by painting him to yourself any blacker than need be.'

Robert laughed, sighed and acquiesced. 'I am a hot-headed, impatient kind of creature at the best of times,' he confessed. 'They tell me that great things have been done for the poor round here in the last twenty years. Something has been done, certainly. But why are the old ways, the old evil neglect and apathy, so long, so terribly long in dying? This social progress of ours we are so proud of is a clumsy limping jade at best!'

They prowled a little more about the hamlet, every step almost revealing some new source of poison and disease. Of their various visits, however, Langham remembered nothing afterwards but a little scene in a miserable cottage, where they found a whole family party gathered round the mid-day meal. A band of puny, black, black-eyed children were standing or sitting at the table. The wife, confined of twins three weeks before, sat by the fire, deathly pale, a 'bad leg' stretched out before her on some improvised support, one baby on her lap and another dark-haired bundle asleep in a cradle beside her. There was a pathetic pinched beauty about the whole family. Even the tiny twins were comparatively shapely; all the other children had delicate transparent skins, large eyes, and small colourless mouths. The father, a picturesque handsome fellow, looking as though he had gipsy blood in his veins, had opened the door to their knock. Robert, seeing the meal, would have retreated at once, in spite of the children's shy inviting looks, but a glance past them at the mother's face checked the word of refusal and apology on his lips, and he stepped in.

In after years Langham was always apt to see him in imagination as he saw him then, standing beside the bent figure of the mother, his quick pitiful eyes taking in the pallor and exhaustion of face and frame, his hand resting instinctively on the head of a small creature that had crept up beside him, his look all attention and softness as the woman feebly told him some of the main facts of her state. The young rector at the moment might have stood for the modern 'Man of Feeling,' as sensitive, as impressionable, and as free from the burden of self, as his eighteenth-century prototype.[56]

On the way home Robert suddenly remarked to his companion, 'Have you heard my sister-in-law play yet, Langham? What did you think of it?'

'Extraordinary!' said Langham briefly. 'The most considerable gift I ever came across in an amateur.'

His olive cheek flushed a little involuntarily. Robert threw a quick observant look at him.

'The difficulty,' he exclaimed, 'is to know what to do with it!'

'Why do you make the difficulty? I gather she wants to study abroad. What is there to prevent it?'

Langham turned to his companion with a touch of asperity. He could not stand it that Elsmere should be so much narrowed and warped by that wife of his, and her prejudices. Why should that gifted creature be cribbed, cabined, and confined in this way?

'I grant you,' said Robert, with a look of perplexity, 'there is not much to prevent it.'

And he was silent a moment, thinking, on his side, very tenderly of all the antecedents and explanations of that old-world distrust of art and the artistic life so deeply rooted in his wife, even though in practice and under his influence she had made concession after concession.

'The great solution of all,' he said presently, brightening, 'would be to get her married. I don't wonder her belongings dislike the notion of anything so pretty and so flighty going off to live by itself. And to break up the home in Whindale would be to undo everything their father did for them, to defy his most solemn last wishes.'

'To talk of a father's wishes, in a case of this kind, ten years after his death, is surely excessive?' said Langham with dry interrogation; then, suddenly recollecting himself, 'I beg your pardon, Elsmere. I am interfering.'

'Nonsense,' said Robert brightly, 'I don't wonder, it seems like a difficulty of our own making. Like so many difficulties, it depends on character, present character, bygone character——' And again he fell musing on his

---

56 A novel (1771) by Henry Mackenzie (1745–1831), which along with *The Vicar of Wakefield* shaped the field of sentimental fiction.

Westmoreland experiences, and on the intensity of that Puritan type it had revealed to him. 'However, as I said, marriage would be the natural way out of it.'

'An easy way, I should think,' said Langham, after a pause.

'It won't be so easy to find the right man. She is a young person with a future, is Miss Rose. She wants somebody in the stream; somebody with a strong hand who will keep her in order and yet give her a wide range; a rich man, I think—she hasn't the ways of a poor man's wife; but, at any rate, some one who will be proud of her, and yet have a full life of his own in which she may share.'

'Your views are extremely clear,' said Langham, and his smile had a touch of bitterness in it. 'If hers agree, I prophesy you won't have long to wait. She has beauty, talent, charm—everything that rich and important men like.'

There was the slightest sarcastic note in the voice. Robert winced. It was borne in upon one of the least worldly of mortals that he had been talking like the veriest schemer. What vague quick impulse had driven him on?

By the time they emerged again upon the Murewell Green the rain had cleared altogether away, and the autumnal morning had broken into sunshine, which played mistily on the sleeping woods, on the white fronts of the cottages, and the wide green where the rain-pools glistened. On the hill leading to the rectory there was the flutter of a woman's dress. As they hurried on, afraid of being late for luncheon, they saw that it was Rose in front of them.

Langham started as the slender figure suddenly defined itself against the road. A tumult within, half rage, half feeling, showed itself only in an added rigidity of the finely-cut features.

Rose turned directly she heard the steps and voices, and over the dreaminess of her face there flashed a sudden brightness.

'You *have* been a long time!' she exclaimed, saying the first thing that came into her head, joyously, rashly, like the child she in reality was. 'How many halt and maimed has Robert taken you to see, Mr. Langham?'

'We went to Murewell first. The library was well worth seeing. Since then we have been a parish round, distributing stores.'

Rose's look changed in an instant. The words were spoken by the Langham of her earliest acquaintance. The man who that morning had asked her to play to him had gone—vanished away.

'How exhilarating!' she said scornfully. 'Don't you wonder how any one can ever tear themselves away from the country?'

'Rose, don't be abusive,' said Robert, opening his eyes at her tone. Then, passing his arm through hers, he looked banteringly down upon her. 'For the first time since you left the metropolis you have walked yourself into a colour. It's becoming—and it's Murewell—so be civil!'

'Oh, nobody denies you a high place in milkmaids!' she said, with her head in air—and they went off into a minute's sparring.

Meanwhile Langham, on the other side of the road, walked up slowly, his eyes on the ground. Once, when Rose's eye caught him, a shock ran through her. There was already a look of slovenly age about his stooping bookworm's gait. Her companion of the night before—handsome, animated, human— where was he? The girl's heart felt a singular contraction. Then she turned and rent herself, and Robert found her more mocking and sprightly than ever.

At the rectory gate Robert ran on to overtake a farmer on the road. Rose stooped to open the latch; Langham mechanically made a quick movement forward to anticipate her. Their fingers touched; she drew hers hastily away and passed in, an erect and dignified figure, in her curving garden hat.

Langham went straight up to his room, shut the door, and stood before the open window, deaf and blind to everything save an inward storm of sensation.

'Fool! Idiot!' he said to himself at last, with fierce stifled emphasis, while a kind of dumb fury with himself and circumstance swept through him.

That he, the poor and solitary student whose only sources of self-respect lay in the deliberate limitations, the reasoned and reasonable renunciations he had imposed upon his life, should have needed the reminder of his old pupil not to fall in love with his brilliant ambitious sister! His irritable self-consciousness enormously magnified Elsmere's motive and Elsmere's words. That golden vagueness and softness of temper which had possessed him since his last sight of her gave place to one of bitter tension.

With sardonic scorn he pointed out to himself that his imagination was still held by, his nerves were still thrilling under, the mental image of a girl looking up to him as no woman had ever looked—a girl, white-armed, white-necked—with softened eyes of appeal and confidence. He bade himself mark that during the whole of his morning walk with Robert down to its last stage, his mind had been really absorbed in some preposterous dream he was now too self-contemptuous to analyse. Pretty well for a philosopher, in four days! What a ridiculous business is life—what a contemptible creature is man, how incapable of dignity, of consistency!

At luncheon he talked rather more than usual, especially on literary matters with Robert. Rose, too, was fully occupied in giving Catherine a sarcastic account of a singing lesson she had been administering in the school that morning. Catherine winced sometimes at the tone of it.

That afternoon Robert, in high spirits, his rod over his shoulder, his basket at his back, carried off his guest for a lounging afternoon along the river. Elsmere enjoyed these fishing expeditions like a boy. They were his holidays, relished all the more because he kept a jealous account of them with his conscience. He sauntered along, now throwing a cunning and effectual fly, now resting, smoking, and chattering, as the fancy took him. He found a great deal of the old stimulus and piquancy in Langham's society, but there was an occasional irritability in his companion, especially towards himself personally, which puzzled him. After a while, indeed, he began to feel himself the unreasonably cheerful person which he evidently appeared to his companion. A mere ignorant enthusiast, banished for ever from the realm of pure knowledge by certain original and incorrigible defects—after a few hours' talk with Langham Robert's quick insight always showed him some image of himself resembling this in his friend's mind.

At last he turned restive. He had been describing to Langham his acquaintance with the Dissenting minister of the place—a strong coarse-grained fellow of sensuous excitable temperament, famous for his noisy 'conversion meetings,' and for a gymnastic dexterity in the quoting and combining of texts, unrivalled in Robert's experience. Some remark on the Dissenter's logic, made, perhaps, a little too much in the tone of the Churchman conscious of University advantages, seemed to irritate Langham.

'You think your Anglican logic in dealing with the Bible so superior! On the contrary, I am all for your Ranter.[57] He is your logical Protestant. Historically, you Anglican parsons are where you are and what you are, because Englishmen, as a whole, like attempting the contradictory—like, above all, to eat their cake and have it. The nation has made you and maintains you for its own purposes. But that is another matter.'

Robert smoked on a moment in silence. Then he flushed and laid down his pipe.

'We are all fools in your eyes, I know! *À la bonne heure!* I have been to the University, and talk what he is pleased to call "philosophy"—therefore Mr. Colson denies me faith. You have always, in your heart of hearts, denied me knowledge. But I cling to both in spite of you.'

There was a ray of defiance, of emotion, in his look. Langham met it in silence.

'I deny you nothing,' he said at last, slowly. 'On the contrary, I believe you to be the possessor of all that is best worth having in life and mind.'

---

57 Langham alludes to the Ranters, a breakaway radical Protestant sect of the seventeenth century.

His irritation had all died away. His tone was one of indescribable depression, and his great black eyes were fixed on Robert with a melancholy which startled his companion. By a subtle transition Elsmere felt himself touched with a pang of profound pity for the man who an instant before had seemed to pose as his scornful superior. He stretched out his hand, and laid it on his friend's shoulder.

Rose spent the afternoon in helping Catherine with various parochial occupations. In the course of them Catherine asked many questions about Long Whindale. Her thoughts clung to the hills, to the gray farmhouses, the rough men and women inside them. But Rose gave her small satisfaction.

'Poor old Jim Backhouse!' said Catherine, sighing. 'Agnes tells me he is quite bedridden now.'

'Well, and a good thing for John, don't you think,' said Rose briskly, covering a parish library book the while in a way which made Catherine's fingers itch to take it from her, 'and for us? It's some use having a carrier now.'

Catherine made no reply. She thought of the 'noodle' fading out of life in the room where Mary Backhouse died; she actually saw the white hair, the blurred eyes, the palsied hands, the poor emaciated limbs stretched along the settle. Her heart rose, but she said nothing.

'And has Mrs. Thornburgh been enjoying her summer?'

'Oh! I suppose so,' said Rose, her tone indicating a quite measureless indifference. 'She had another young Oxford man staying with her in June—a missionary—and it annoyed her very much that neither Agnes nor I would intervene to prevent his resuming his profession. She seemed to think it was a question of saving him from being eaten, and apparently he would have proposed to either of us.'

Catherine could not help laughing. 'I suppose she still thinks she married Robert and me.'

'Of course. So she did.'

Catherine coloured a little, but Rose's hard lightness of tone was unconquerable.

'Or if she didn't,' Rose resumed, 'nobody could have the heart to rob her of the illusion. Oh, by the way, Sarah has been under warning since June! Mrs. Thornburgh told her desperately that she must either throw over her young man, who was picked up drunk at the vicarage gate one night, or vacate the vicarage kitchen. Sarah cheerfully accepted her month's notice, and is still making the vicarage jams and walking out with the young man every Sunday. Mrs. Thornburgh sees that it will require a convulsion of nature to get rid either of Sarah or the young man, and has succumbed.'

'And the Tysons? And that poor Walker girl?'

'Oh, dear me, Catherine!' said Rose, a strange disproportionate flash of impatience breaking through. 'Every one in Long Whindale is always just where and what they were last year. I admit they are born and die, but they do nothing else of a decisive kind.'

Catherine's hands worked away for a while, then she laid down her book and said, lifting her clear large eyes on her sister,—

'Was there *never* a time when you loved the valley, Rose?'

'Never!' cried Rose.

Then she pushed away her work, and leaning her elbows on the table turned her brilliant face to Catherine. There was frank mutiny in it.

'By the way, Catherine, are you going to prevent mamma from letting me go to Berlin for the winter?'

'And after Berlin, Rose?' said Catherine, presently, her gaze bent upon her work.

'After Berlin? What next?' said Rose recklessly. 'Well, after Berlin I shall try to persuade mamma and Agnes, I suppose, to come and back me up in London. We could still be some months of the year at Burwood.'

Now she had said it out. But there was something else surely goading the girl than mere intolerance of the family tradition. The hesitancy, the moral doubt of her conversation with Langham, seemed to have vanished wholly in a kind of acrid self-assertion.

Catherine felt a shock sweep through her. It was as though all the pieties of life, all the sacred assumptions and self-surrenders at the root of it, were shaken, outraged by the girl's tone.

'Do you ever remember,' she said, looking up, while her voice trembled, 'what papa wished when he was dying?'

It was her last argument. To Rose she had very seldom used it in so many words. Probably, it seemed to her too strong, too sacred, to be often handled.

But Rose sprang up, and pacing the little workroom with her white wrists locked behind her, she met that argument with all the concentrated passion which her youth had for years been storing up against it. Catherine sat presently overwhelmed, bewildered. This language of a proud and tameless individuality, this modern gospel of the divine right of self-development—her soul loathed it! And yet, since that night in Marrisdale, there had been a new yearning in her to understand.

Suddenly, however, Rose stopped, lost her thread. Two figures were crossing the lawn, and their shadows were thrown far beyond them by the fast disappearing sun.

She threw herself down on her chair again with an abrupt—

'Do you see they have come back? We must go and dress.'

And as she spoke she was conscious of a new sensation altogether—the sensation of the wild creature lassoed on the prairie, of the bird exchanging in an instant its glorious freedom of flight for the pitiless meshes of the net. It was stifling—her whole nature seemed to fight with it.

Catherine rose and began to put away the books they had been covering. She had said almost nothing in answer to Rose's tirade. When she was ready she came and stood beside her sister a moment, her lips trembling. At last she stooped and kissed the girl—the kiss of deep suppressed feeling—and went away. Rose made no response.

Unmusical as she was, Catherine pined for her sister's music that evening. Robert was busy in his study, and the hours seemed interminable. After a little difficult talk Langham subsided into a book and a corner. But the only words of which he was conscious for long were the words of an inner dialogue. 'I promised to play for her.—Go and offer then!—Madness! let me keep away from her. If she asks me, of course I will go. She is much too proud, and already she thinks me guilty of a rudeness.'

Then, with a shrug, he would fall to his book again, abominably conscious, however, all the while of the white figure between the lamp and the open window, and of the delicate head and cheek lit up against the trees and the soft August dark.

When the time came to go to bed he got their candles for the two ladies. Rose just touched his hand with cool fingers.

'Good-night, Mr. Langham. You are going in to smoke with Robert, I suppose?'

Her bright eyes seemed to look him through. Their mocking hostility seemed to say to him as plainly as possible: 'Your purgatory is over—go, smoke and be happy!'

'I will go and help him wind up his sermon,' he said, with an attempt at a laugh, and moved away.

Rose went upstairs, and it seemed to her that a Greek brow, and a pair of wavering melancholy eyes, went before her in the darkness chased along the passages by the light she held. She gained her room, and stood by the window, seized again by that stifling sense of catastrophe, so strange, so undefined. Then she shook it off with an angry laugh, and went to work to see how far her stock of light dresses had suffered by her London dissipations.

CHAPTER XVI

The next morning after breakfast the rectory party were in the garden—the gentlemen smoking, Catherine and her sister strolling arm-in-arm among the flowers. Catherine's vague terrors of the morning before had all taken to themselves wings. It seemed to her that Rose and Mr. Langham had hardly spoken to each other since she had seen them walking about together. Robert had already made merry over his own alarms, and hers, and she admitted he was in the right. As to her talk with Rose her deep meditative nature was slowly working upon and digesting it. Meanwhile, she was all tenderness to her sister, and there was even a reaction of pity in her heart towards the lonely sceptic who had once been so good to Robert.

Robert was just bethinking himself that it was time to go off to the school, when they were all startled by an unexpected visitor—a short old lady, in a rusty black dress and bonnet, who entered the drive and stood staring at the rectory party, a tiny hand in a black thread glove shading the sun from a pair of wrinkled eyes.

'Mrs. Darcy!' exclaimed Robert to his wife after a moment's perplexity, and they walked quickly to meet her.

Rose and Langham exchanged a few commonplaces till the others joined them, and then for a while the attention of everybody in the group was held by the squire's sister. She was very small, as thin and light as thistle-down, ill-dressed, and as communicative as a babbling child. The face and all the features were extraordinarily minute, and moreover, blanched and etherealised by age. She had the elfish look of a little withered fairy godmother. And yet through it all it was clear that she was a great lady. There were certain poses and gestures about her, which made her thread gloves and rusty skirts seem a mere whim and masquerade, adopted, perhaps deliberately, from a high-bred love of congruity, to suit the country lanes.

She had come to ask them all to dinner at the Hall on the following evening, and she either brought or devised on the spot the politest messages from the squire to the new rector, which pleased the sensitive Robert and silenced for the moment his various misgivings as to Mr. Wendover's advent. Then she stayed chattering, studying Rose every now and then out of her strange little eyes, restless and glancing as a bird's, which took stock also of the garden, of the flower-beds, of Elsmere's lanky frame, and of Elsmere's handsome friend in the background. She was most odd when she was grateful, and she was grateful for the most unexpected things. She thanked Elsmere effusively for coming to live there, 'sacrificing yourself so nobly to us country folk,' and she thanked him with an appreciative glance at Langham, for having his clever friends to stay with him. 'The squire will be so pleased. My brother, you know, is very clever; oh yes, frightfully clever!'

And then there was a long sigh, at which Elsmere could hardly keep his countenance.

She thought it particularly considerate of them to have been to see the squire's books. It would make conversation so easy when they came to dinner.

'Though I don't know anything about his books. He doesn't like women to talk about books. He says they only pretend—even the clever ones. Except, of course, Madame de Staël.[58] He can only say she was ugly, and I don't deny it. But I have about used up Madame de Staël,' she added, dropping into another sigh as soft and light as a child's.

Robert was charmed with her, and even Langham smiled. And as Mrs. Darcy adored 'clever men,' ranking them, as the London of her youth had ranked them, only second to 'persons of birth,' she stood among them beaming, becoming more and more whimsical and inconsequent, more and more deliciously incalculable, as she expanded. At last she fluttered off, only, however, to come hurrying back, with little, short, scudding steps, to implore them all to come to tea with her as soon as possible in the garden that was her special hobby, and in her last new summer-house.

'I build two or three every summer,' she said. 'Now, there are twenty-one! Roger laughs at me,' and there was a momentary bitterness in the little eerie face, 'but how can one live without hobbies? That's one—then I've two more. My album—oh, you *will* all write in my album, won't you? When I was young—when I was Maid of Honour'—and she drew herself up slightly—'everybody had albums.[59] Even the dear Queen herself! I remember how she made M. Guizot write in it; something quite stupid, after all.[60] *Those* hobbies—the garden and the album—are *quite* harmless, aren't they? They hurt nobody, do they?' Her voice dropped a little, with a pathetic expostulating

---

58 Anne Louise Germaine de Staël-Holstein (1766–1817), novelist, *salonnière*, and intellectual, best remembered for the novel *Corinne* (1807) and *De l'Allemagne* (*On Germany*) (1810).

59 Autograph albums.

60 François Pierre Guillaume Guizot (1787–1874), French politician and historian, author of the historical autobiography *Mémoires pour servir à l'histoire de mon temps* (1858–61).

intonation in it, as of one accustomed to be rebuked.

'Let me remind you of a saying of Bacon's,' said Langham, studying her, and softened perforce into benevolence.

'Yes, yes,' said Mrs. Darcy in a flutter of curiosity.

'God Almighty first planted a garden,' he quoted; 'and indeed, it is the purest of all human pleasures.'[61]

'Oh, but how *delightful*!' cried Mrs. Darcy, clasping her diminutive hands in their thread gloves. 'You must write that in my album, Mr. Langham, that very sentence; oh, how *clever* of you to remember it! What it is to be clever and have a brain! But, then—I've another hobby——'

Here, however, she stopped, hung her head and looked depressed. Robert, with a little ripple of laughter, begged her to explain.

'No,' she said plaintively, giving a quick uneasy look at him, as though it occurred to her that it might some day be his pastoral duty to admonish her. 'No, it's wrong. I know it is—only I can't help it. Never mind. You'll know soon.'

And again she turned away, when, suddenly, Rose attracted her attention, and she stretched out a thin white bird-claw of a hand and caught the girl's arm.

'There won't be much to amuse you to-morrow, my dear, and there ought to be—you're so pretty!' Rose blushed furiously and tried to draw her hand away. 'No, no! don't mind, don't mind. I didn't at your age. Well, we'll do our best. But your own party is so *charming*!' and she looked round the little circle, her gaze stopping specially at Langham before it returned to Rose. 'After all, you will amuse each other.'

Was there any malice in the tiny withered creature? Rose, unsympathetic and indifferent as youth commonly is when its own affairs absorb it, had stood coldly outside the group which was making much of the squire's sister. Was it so the strange little visitor revenged herself?

At any rate Rose was left feeling as if some one had pricked her. While Catherine and Elsmere escorted Mrs. Darcy to the gate she turned to go in, her head thrown back stag-like, her cheek still burning. Why should it be always open to the old to annoy the young with impunity?

Langham watched her mount the first step or two; his eye travelled up the slim figure so instinct with pride and will—and something in him suddenly gave way. It was like a man who feels his grip relaxing on some attacking thing he has been holding by the throat.

---

61 In Essay XVI, "Of Gardens." Francis Bacon (1561–1626), politician and polymath, regarded as the inventor of the modern scientific method.

He followed her hastily.

'Must you go in? And none of us have paid our respects yet to those phloxes in the back garden?'

Oh woman—flighty woman! An instant before, the girl, sore and bruised in every fibre, she only half knew why, was thirsting that this man might somehow offer her his neck that she might trample on it. He offers it, and the angry instinct wavers, as a man wavers in a wrestling match when his opponent unexpectedly gives ground. She paused, she turned her white throat. His eyes upturned met hers.

'The phloxes did you say?' she asked, coolly redescending the steps. 'Then round here, please.'

She led the way, he followed, conscious of an utter relaxation of nerve and will which for the moment had something intoxicating in it.

'There are your phloxes,' she said, stopping before a splendid line of plants in full blossom. Her self-respect was whole again; her spirits rose at a bound. 'I don't know why you admire them so much. They have no scent, and they are only pretty in the lump,' and she broke off a spike of blossom, studied it a little disdainfully, and threw it away.

He stood beside her, the southern glow and life of which it was intermittently capable once more lighting up the strange face.

'Give me leave to enjoy everything countrified more than usual,' he said. 'After this morning it will be so long before I see the true country again.'

He looked, smiling, round on the blue and white brilliance of the sky, clear again after a night of rain; on the sloping garden, on the village beyond, on the hedge of sweet peas close beside them, with its blooms

'On tiptoe for a flight,
With wings of gentle flush o'er delicate white.'[62]

'Oh! Oxford is countrified enough,' she said indifferently, moving down the broad grass-path which divided the garden into two equal portions.

'But I am leaving Oxford, at any rate for a year,' he said quietly. 'I am going to London.'

Her delicate eyebrows went up. 'To London?' Then, in a tone of mock meekness and sympathy, 'How you will dislike it!'

'Dislike it—why?'

'Oh! because—' she hesitated, and then laughed her daring girlish laugh—'because there are so many stupid people in London; the clever people are not all picked out like prize apples, as I suppose they are in Oxford.'

---

62 From John Keats' "I stood tip-toe upon a little hill."

'At Oxford?' repeated Langham, with a kind of groan. 'At Oxford? You imagine that Oxford is inhabited only by clever people?'

'I can only judge by what I see,' she said demurely. 'Every Oxford man always behaves as if he were the cream of the universe. Oh! I don't mean to be rude,' she cried, losing for a moment her defiant control over herself, as though afraid of having gone too far. 'I am not the least disrespectful, really. When you and Robert talk, Catherine and I feel quite as humble as we ought.'

The words were hardly out before she could have bitten the tongue that spoke them. He had made her feel her indiscretions of Sunday night as she deserved to feel them, and now after three minutes' conversation she was on the verge of fresh ones. Would she never grow up, never behave like other girls? That word *humble*! It seemed to burn her memory.

Before he could possibly answer she barred the way by a question as short and dry as possible—

'What are you going to London for?'

'For many reasons,' he said, shrugging his shoulders. 'I have told no one yet—not even Elsmere. And indeed I go back to my rooms for a while from here. But as soon as Term begins I become a Londoner.'

They had reached the gate at the bottom of the garden, and were leaning against it. She was disturbed, conscious, lightly flushed. It struck her as another *gaucherie* on her part that she should have questioned him as to his plans. What did his life matter to her?

He was looking away from her, studying the half-ruined, degraded man-or house spread out below them. Then suddenly he turned—

'If I could imagine for a moment it would interest you to hear my reasons for leaving Oxford, I could not flatter myself you would see any sense in them. I *know* that Robert will think them moonshine; nay, more, that they will give him pain.'

He smiled sadly. The tone of gentleness, the sudden breach in the man's melancholy reserve affected the girl beside him for the second time, precisely as they had affected her the first time. The result of twenty-four hours' resentful meditation turned out to be precisely *nil*. Her breath came fast, her proud look melted, and his quick sense caught the change in an instant.

'Are you tired of Oxford?' the poor child asked him, almost shyly.

'Mortally!' he said, still smiling. 'And what is more important still, Oxford is tired of me. I have been lecturing there for ten years. They have had more than enough of me.'

'Oh! but Robert said——' began Rose impetuously, then stopped, crimson, remembering many things Robert had said.

'That I helped him over a few stiles?' returned Langham calmly. 'Yes, there was a time when I was capable of that—there was a time when I could teach, and teach with pleasure.' He paused. Rose could have scourged herself for the tremor she felt creeping over her. Why should it be to her so new and strange a thing that *a man*, especially a man of these years and this calibre, should confide in her, should speak to her intimately of himself? After all, she said to herself angrily, with a terrified sense of importance, she was a child no longer, though her mother and sisters would treat her as one. 'When we were chatting the other night,' he went on, turning to her again as he stood leaning on the gate, 'do you know what it was struck me most?'

His tone had in it the most delicate, the most friendly deference. But Rose flushed furiously.

'That girls are very ready to talk about themselves, I imagine,' she said scornfully.

'Not at all! Not for a moment! No, but it seemed to me so pathetic, so strange that anybody should wish for anything so much as you wished for the musician's life.'

'And you never wish for anything?' she cried.

'When Elsmere was at college,' he said, smiling, 'I believe I wished he should get a first class. This year I have certainly wished to say good-bye to St. Anselm's, and to turn my back for good and all on my men. I can't remember that I have wished for anything else for six years.'

She looked at him perplexed. Was his manner merely languid, or was it from him that the emotion she felt invading herself first started? She tried to shake it off.

'And *I* am just a bundle of wants,' she said, half-mockingly. 'Generally speaking I am in the condition of being ready to barter all I have for some folly or other—one in the morning, another in the afternoon. What have you to say to such people, Mr. Langham?'

Her eyes challenged him magnificently, mostly out of sheer nervousness. But the face they rested on seemed suddenly to turn to stone before her. The life died out of it. It grew still and rigid.

'Nothing,' he said quietly. 'Between them and me there is a great gulf fixed. I watch them pass, and I say to myself: "There are *the living*—that is how they look, how they speak! Realise once for all that you have nothing to do with them. Life is theirs—belongs to *them*. You are already outside it. Go your way, and be a spectre among the active and the happy no longer."'

He leant his back against the gate. Did he see her? Was he conscious of her at all in this rare impulse of speech which had suddenly overtaken one of the most withdrawn and silent of human beings? All her airs dropped off her; a kind of fright seized her; and involuntarily she laid her hand on his arm.

'Don't—don't—Mr. Langham! Oh, don't say such things! Why should you be so unhappy? Why should you talk so? Can no one do anything? Why do you live so much alone? Is there no one you care about?'

He turned. What a vision! His artistic sense absorbed it in an instant—the beautiful tremulous lip, the drawn white brow. For a moment he drank in the pity, the emotion, of those eyes. Then a movement of such self-scorn as even he had never felt swept through him. He gently moved away; her hand dropped.

'Miss Leyburn,' he said, gazing at her, his olive face singularly pale, 'don't waste your pity on me, for Heaven's sake. Some madness made me behave as I did just now. Years ago the same sort of idiocy betrayed me to your brother; never before or since. I ask your pardon, humbly,' and his tone seemed to scorch her, 'that this second fit of ranting should have seized me in your presence.'

But he could not keep it up. The inner upheaval had gone too far. He stopped and looked at her—piteously, the features quivering. It was as though the man's whole nature had for the moment broken up, become disorganised. She could not bear it. Some ghastly infirmity seemed to have been laid bare to her. She held out both her hands. Swiftly he caught them, stooped, kissed them, let them go. It was an extraordinary scene—to both a kind of lifetime.

Then he gathered himself together by a mighty effort.

'That was *adorable* of you,' he said with a long breath. 'But I stole it—I despise myself. Why should you pity me? What is there to pity me for? My troubles, such as I have, are my own making—every one.'

And he laid a sort of vindictive emphasis on the words. The tears of excitement were in her eyes.

'Won't you let me be your friend?' she said, trembling, with a kind of reproach. 'I thought—the other night—we were to be friends. Won't you tell me——'

'More of yourself?' her eyes said, but her voice failed her. And as for him, as he gazed at her, all the accidents of circumstance, of individual character, seemed to drop from her. He forgot the difference of years; he saw her no longer as she was—a girl hardly out of the schoolroom, vain, ambitious, dangerously responsive, on whose crude romantic sense he was wantonly playing; she was to him pure beauty, pure woman. For one tumultuous moment the cold critical instinct which had been for years draining his life of all its natural energies was powerless. It was sweet to yield, to speak, as it had never been sweet before.

So, leaning over the gate, he told her the story of his life, of his cramped childhood and youth, of his brief moment of happiness and success at college, of his first attempts to make himself a power among younger men, of the gradual dismal failure of all his efforts, the dying down of desire and ambition. From the general narrative there stood out little pictures of individual persons or scenes, clear cut and masterly—of his father, the Gainsborough churchwarden; of his Methodistical mother, who had all her life lamented her own beauty as a special snare of Satan, and who since her husband's death had refused to see her son on the ground that his opinions 'had vexed his father'; of his first ardent worship of knowledge, and passion to communicate it; and of the first intuitions in lecture, face to face with an undergraduate, alone in college rooms, sometimes alone on Alpine heights, of something cold, impotent and baffling in himself, which was to stand for ever between him and action, between him and human affection; the growth of the critical pessimist sense which laid the axe to the root of enthusiasm after enthusiasm, friendship after friendship—which made other men feel him inhuman, intangible, a skeleton at the feast; and the persistence through it all of a kind of hunger for life and its satisfactions, which the will was more and more powerless to satisfy: all these Langham put into words with an extraordinary magic and delicacy of phrase. There was something in him which found a kind of pleasure in the long analysis, which took pains that it should be infinitely well done.

Rose followed him breathlessly. If she had known more of literature she would have realised that she was witnessing a masterly dissection of one of those many morbid growths of which our nineteenth century psychology is full. But she was anything but literary, and she could not analyse her excitement. The man's physical charm, his melancholy, the intensity of what he said, affected, unsteadied her as music was apt to affect her. And through it all there was the strange girlish pride that this should have befallen *her*; a first crude intoxicating sense of the power over human lives which was to be hers, mingled with a desperate anxiety to be equal to the occasion, to play her part well.

'So you see,' said Langham at last, with a great effort (to do him justice) to climb back on to some ordinary level of conversation; 'all these transcendentalisms apart, I am about the most unfit man in the world for a college tutor. The undergraduates regard me as a shilly-shallying pedant. On my part,' he added drily, 'I am not slow to retaliate. Every term I live I find the young man a less interesting animal. I regard the whole university system as a wretched sham. Knowledge! It has no more to do with knowledge than my boots.'

And for one curious instant he looked out over the village, his fastidious scholar's soul absorbed by some intellectual irritation, of which Rose understood absolutely nothing. She stood bewildered, silent, longing childishly to speak, to influence him, but not knowing what cue to take.

'And then—' he went on presently (but was the strange being speaking to her?)—'so long as I stay there, worrying those about me, and eating my own heart out, I am cut off from the only life that might be mine, that I might find the strength to live.'

The words were low and deliberate. After his moment of passionate speech, and hers of passionate sympathy, she began to feel strangely remote from him.

'Do you mean the life of the student?' she asked him after a pause, timidly.

Her voice recalled him. He turned and smiled at her.

'Of the dreamer, rather.'

And as her eyes still questioned, as he was still moved by the spell of her responsiveness, he let the new wave of feeling break in words. Vaguely at first, and then with a growing flame and force, he fell to describing to her what the life of thought may be to the thinker, and those marvellous moments which belong to that life when the mind which has divorced itself from desire and sense sees spread out before it the vast realms of knowledge, and feels itself close to the secret springs and sources of being. And as he spoke, his language took an ampler turn, the element of smallness which attaches to all mere personal complaint vanished, his words flowed, became eloquent, inspired, till the bewildered child beside him, warm through and through as she was with youth and passion, felt for an instant by sheer fascinated sympathy the cold spell, the ineffable prestige, of the thinker's voluntary death in life.

But only for an instant. Then the natural sense of chill smote her to the heart.

'You make me shiver,' she cried, interrupting him. 'Have those strange things—I don't understand them—made you happy? Can they make any one happy? Oh no, no! Happiness is to be got from living, seeing, experiencing, making friends, enjoying nature! Look at the world, Mr. Langham!' she said, with bright cheeks, half smiling at her own magniloquence, her hand waving over the view before them. 'What has it done that you should hate it so? If you can't put up with people you might love nature. I—I can't be content with nature, because I want some life first. Up in Whindale there is too much nature, not enough life. But if I had got through life—if it had disappointed me—then I should love nature. I keep saying to the mountains at home: "Not *now*, not *now*; I want something else, but afterwards if I can't get it, or if I get too much of it, why then I will love you, live with you. You are my second string, my reserve. You—and art—and poetry."'

'But everything depends on feeling,' he said softly, but lightly, as though to keep the conversation from slipping back into those vague depths it had emerged from; 'and if one has forgotten how to feel—if when one sees or hears something beautiful that used to stir one, one can only say "I remember it moved me once!"—if feeling dies, like life, like physical force, but prematurely, long before the rest of the man!'

She gave a long quivering sigh of passionate antagonism.

'Oh, I cannot imagine it!' she cried. 'I shall feel to my last hour.' Then, after a pause, in another tone, 'But, Mr. Langham, you say music excites you, Wagner excites you?'

'Yes, a sort of strange second life I can still get out of music,' he admitted, smiling.

'Well then,' and she looked at him persuasively, 'why not give yourself up to music? It is so easy—so little trouble to one's self—it just takes you and carries you away.'

Then, for the first time, Langham became conscious—probably through these admonitions of hers—that the situation had absurdity in it.

'It is not my *métier*,' he said hastily. 'The self that enjoys music is an outer self, and can only bear with it for a short time. No, Miss Leyburn, I shall leave Oxford, the college will sing a *Te Deum*, I shall settle down in London, I shall keep a big book going, and cheat the years after all, I suppose, as well as most people.'

'And you will know, you will remember,' she said faltering, reddening, her womanliness forcing the words out of her, 'that you have friends: Robert— my sister—all of us?'

He faced her with a little quick movement. And as their eyes met each was struck once more with the personal beauty of the other. His eyes shone— their black depths seemed all tenderness.

'I will never forget this visit, this garden, this hour,' he said slowly, and they stood looking at each other. Rose felt herself swept off her feet into a world of tragic mysterious emotion. She all but put her hand into his again, asking him childishly to hope, to be consoled. But the maidenly impulse restrained her, and once more he leant on the gate, burying his face in his hands.

Suddenly he felt himself utterly tired, relaxed. Strong nervous reaction set in. What had all this scene, this tragedy, been about? And then in another instant was that sense of the ridiculous again clamouring to be heard.

He—the man of thirty-five—confessing himself, making a tragic scene, playing Manfred or Cain to this adorable half-fledged creature, whom he had
known five days![63] Supposing Elsmere had been there to hear—Elsmere with
his sane eye, his laugh! As he leant over the gate he found himself quivering
with impatience to be away—by himself—out of reach—the critic in him
making the most bitter remorseless mock of all these heroics and despairs the
other self had been indulging in. But for the life of him he could not find a
word to say—a move to make. He stood hesitating, *gauche*, as usual.

'Do you know, Mr. Langham,' said Rose lightly, by his side, 'that there is
no time at all left for *you* to give *me* good advice in? That is an obligation still
hanging over you. I don't mean to release you from it, but if I don't go in now
and finish the covering of those library books, the youth of Murewell will be
left without any literature till Heaven knows when!'

He could have blessed her for the tone, for the escape into common
mundanity.

'Hang literature—hang the parish library!' he said with a laugh as he
moved after her. Yet his real inner feeling towards that parish library was one
of infinite friendliness.

'Hear these men of letters!' she said scornfully. But she was happy; there
was a glow on her cheek.

A bramble caught her dress; she stopped and laid her white hand to it,
but in vain. He knelt in an instant, and between them they wrenched it away,
but not till those soft slim fingers had several times felt the neighbourhood
of his brown ones, and till there had flown through and through him once
more, as she stooped over him, the consciousness that she was young, that she
was beautiful, that she had pitied him so sweetly, that they were alone.

'Rose!'

It was Catherine calling—Catherine, who stood at the end of the grass-
path, with eyes all indignation and alarm.

Langham rose quickly from the ground.

He felt as though the gods had saved him—or damned him—which?

CHAPTER XVII

Murewell Rectory during the next forty-eight hours was the scene of much
that might have been of interest to a psychologist gifted with the power of

---

63 Two of Lord Byron's most famous anti-heroes (in verse dramas of the same name,
1817 and 1821). Both figures are dark, conflicted, and on the road to damnation.

divining his neighbours.

In the first place Catherine's terrors were all alive again.[64] Robert had never seen her so moved since those days of storm and stress before their engagement.

'I cannot bear it!' she said to Robert at night in their room. 'I cannot bear it! I hear it always in my ears: "What hast thou done with thy sister?" Oh, Robert, don't mind, dear, though he is your friend. My father would have shrunk from him with horror—*An alien from the household of faith! An enemy to the Cross of Christ!*'[65]

She flung out the words with low intense emphasis and frowning brow, standing rigid by the window, her hands locked behind her. Robert stood by her much perplexed, feeling himself a good deal of a culprit, but inwardly conscious that he knew a great deal more about Langham than she did.

'My dear wifie,' he said to her, 'I am certain Langham has no intention of marrying.'

'Then more shame for him,' cried Catherine, flushing. 'They could not have looked more conscious, Robert, when I found them together, if he had just proposed.'

'What, in five days?' said Robert, more than half inclined to banter his wife. Then he fell into meditation as Catherine made no answer. 'I believe with men of that sort,' he said at last, 'relations to women are never more than half-real—always more or less literature—acting. Langham is tasting an experience, to be bottled up for future use.'

It need hardly be said, however, that Catherine got small consolation out of this point of view. It seemed to her Robert did not take the matter quite rightly.

'After all, darling,' he said at last, kissing her, 'you can act dragon splendidly; you have already—so can I. And you really cannot make me believe in anything very tragic in a week.'

But Catherine was conscious that she had already played the dragon hard, to very little purpose. In the forty hours that intervened between the scene in the garden and the squire's dinner-party, Robert was always wanting to carry off Langham, Catherine was always asking Rose's help in some household business or other. In vain. Langham said to himself calmly, this time, that Elsmere and his wife were making a foolish mistake in supposing that his friendship with Miss Leyburn was anything to be alarmed about, that they

---

64 The one-volume Macmillan edition accidentally omits the punctuation here; all other editions have a period.

65 "Household of faith" alludes to Galatians 6.10; "an enemy…" to Philippians 3.18.

would soon be amply convinced of it themselves, and meanwhile he should take his own way. And as for Rose, they had no sooner turned back all three from the house to the garden than she had divined everything in Catherine's mind, and set herself against her sister with a wilful force in which many a past irritation found expression.

How Catherine hated the music of that week! It seemed to her she never opened the drawing-room door but she saw Langham at the piano, his head with its crown of glossy, curling black hair, and his eyes lit with unwonted gleams of laughter and sympathy, turned towards Rose, who was either chatting wildly to him, mimicking the airs of some professional, or taking off the ways of some famous teacher; or else, which was worse, playing with all her soul, flooding the house with sound—now as soft and delicate as first love, now as full and grand as storm waves on an angry coast. And the sister going with compressed lip to her work-table would recognise sorely that never had the girl looked so handsome, and never had the lightnings of a wayward genius played so finely about her.

As to Langham, it may well be believed that after the scene in the garden he had rated, satirised, examined himself in the most approved introspective style. One half of him declared that scene to have been the heights of melodramatic absurdity; the other thought of it with a thrill of tender gratitude towards the young pitiful creature who had evoked it. After all, why, because he was alone in the world and must remain so, should he feel bound to refuse this one gift of the gods, the delicate passing gift of a girl's—a child's friendship? As for her, the man's very real, though wholly morbid, modesty scouted the notion of love on her side. *He* was a likely person for a beauty on the threshold of life and success to fall in love with; but she meant to be kind to him, and he smiled a little inward indulgent smile over her very evident compassion, her very evident intention of reforming him, reconciling him to life. And, finally, he was incapable of any further resistance. He had gone too far with her. Let her do what she would with him, dear child, with the sharp tongue and the soft heart, and the touch of genius and brilliancy which made her future so interesting! He called his age and his disillusions to the rescue; he posed to himself as stooping to her in some sort of elder-brotherly fashion; and if every now and then some disturbing memory of that strange scene between them would come to make his present rôle less plausible, or some whim of hers made it difficult to play, why then at bottom there was always the consciousness that sixty hours, or thereabouts, would see him safely settled in that morning train to London. Throughout it is probable that that morning train occupied the saving background of his thoughts.

The two days passed by, and the squire's dinner-party arrived. About seven on the Thursday evening a party of four might have been seen hurrying across the park—Langham and Catherine in front, Elsmere and Rose behind. Catherine had arranged it so, and Langham, who understood perfectly that his friendship with her young sister was not at all to Mrs. Elsmere's taste, and who had by now taken as much of a dislike to her as his nature was capable of, was certainly doing nothing to make his walk with her otherwise than difficult. And every now and then some languid epigram would bring Catherine's eyes on him with a fiery gleam in their gray depths. Oh, fourteen more hours and she would have shut the rectory gate on this most unwelcome of intruders! She had never felt so vindictively anxious to see the last of any one in her life. There was in her a vehemence of antagonism to the man's manner, his pessimism, his infidelity, his very ways of speaking and looking, which astonished even herself.

Robert's eager soul meanwhile, for once irresponsive to Catherine's, was full of nothing but the squire. At last the moment was come, and that dumb spiritual friendship he had formed through these long months with the philosopher and the *savant* was to be tested by sight and speech of the man. He bade himself a hundred times pitch his expectations low. But curiosity and hope were keen, in spite of everything.

Ah, those parish worries! Robert caught the smoke of Mile End in the distance, curling above the twilight woods, and laid about him vigorously with his stick on the squire's shrubs, as he thought of those poisonous hovels, those ruined lives! But, after all, it might be mere ignorance, and that wretch Henslowe might have been merely trading on his master's morbid love of solitude.

And then—all men have their natural conceits. Robert Elsmere would not have been the very human creature he was if, half-consciously, he had not counted a good deal on his own powers of influence. Life had been to him so far one long social success of the best kind. Very likely as he walked on to the great house over whose threshold lay the answer to the enigma of months, his mind gradually filled with some naïve young dream of winning the squire, playing him with all sorts of honest arts, beguiling him back to life—to his kind.

Those friendly messages of his through Mrs. Darcy had been very pleasant.

'I wonder whether my Oxford friends have been doing me a good turn with the squire,' he said to Rose, laughing. 'He knows the Provost, of course.[66] If they talked me over it is to be hoped my scholarship didn't come

---

66 "Provost": capitalization restored as per *SE* and *W*.

up. Precious little the Provost used to think of my abilities for Greek prose!'

Rose yawned a little behind her gloved hand. Robert had already talked a good deal about the squire, and he was certainly the only person in the group who was thinking of him. Even Catherine, absorbed in other anxieties, had forgotten to feel any thrill at their approaching introduction to the man who must of necessity mean so much to herself and Robert.

'Mr. and Mrs. Robert Elsmere,' said the butler, throwing open the carved and gilded doors.

Catherine—following her husband, her fine grave head and beautiful neck held a little more erect than usual—was at first conscious of nothing but the dazzle of western light which flooded the room, striking the stands of Japanese lilies, and the white figure of a clown in the famous Watteau opposite the window.[67]

Then she found herself greeted by Mrs. Darcy, whose odd habit of holding her lace handkerchief in her right hand on festive occasions only left her two fingers for her guests. The mistress of the Hall—as diminutive and elflike as ever in spite of the added dignity of her sweeping silk and the draperies of black lace with which her tiny head was adorned—kept tight hold of Catherine, and called a gentleman standing in a group just behind her.

'Roger, here are Mr. and Mrs. Robert Elsmere. Mr. Elsmere, the squire remembers you in petticoats, and I'm not sure that I don't too.'

Robert, smiling, looked beyond her to the advancing figure of the squire, but if Mr. Wendover heard his sister's remark he took no notice of it. He held out his hand stiffly to Robert, bowed to Catherine and Rose before extending to them the same formal greeting, and just recognised Langham as having met him at Oxford.

Having done so he turned back to the knot of people with whom he had been engaged on their entrance. His manner had been reserve itself. The *hauteur* of the grandee on his own ground was clearly marked in it, and Robert could not help fancying that towards himself there had even been something more. And not one of those phrases which, under the circumstances, would have been so easy and so gracious, as to Robert's childish connection with the place, or as to the squire's remembrance of his father, even though Mrs. Darcy had given him a special opening of the kind.

The young rector instinctively drew himself together, like one who has received a blow, as he moved across to the other side of the fireplace to shake hands with the worthy family doctor, old Meyrick, who was already well

---

67 Jean-Antoine Watteau (1684–1721)'s "Pierrot" (1718–19).

known to him. Catherine, in some discomfort, for she too had felt their reception at the squire's hands to be a chilling one, sat down to talk to Mrs. Darcy, disagreeably conscious the while that Rose and Langham left to themselves were practically *tête-à-tête*, and that, moreover, a large stand of flowers formed a partial screen between her and them. She could see, however, the gleam of Rose's upstretched neck, as Langham, who was leaning on the piano beside her, bent down to talk to her; and when she looked next she caught a smiling motion of Langham's head and eyes towards the Romney portrait of Mr. Wendover's grandmother, and was certain when he stooped afterwards to say something to his companion, that he was commenting on a certain surface likeness there was between her and the young auburn-haired beauty of the picture. Hateful! And they would be sent down to dinner together to a certainty.

The other guests were Lady Charlotte Wynnstay, a cousin of the squire— a tall, imperious, loud-voiced woman, famous in London society for her relationships, her audacity, and the *salon* which in one way or another she managed to collect round her; her dark, thin, irritable-looking husband; two neighbouring clerics—the first, by name Longstaffe, a somewhat inferior specimen of the cloth, whom Robert cordially disliked; and the other, Mr. Bickerton, a gentle Evangelical, one of those men who help to ease the harshness of a cross-grained world, and to reconcile the cleverer or more impatient folk in it to the worries of living.

Lady Charlotte was already known by name to the Elsmeres as the aunt of one of their chief friends of the neighbourhood—the wife of a neighbouring squire whose property joined that of Murewell Hall, one Lady Helen Varley, of whom more presently. Lady Charlotte was the sister of the Duke of Sedbergh, one of the greatest of dukes, and the sister also of Lady Helen's mother, Lady Wanless. Lady Wanless had died prematurely, and her two younger children, Helen and Hugh Flaxman, creatures both of them of unusually fine and fiery quality, had owed a good deal to their aunt. There were family alliances between the Sedberghs and the Wendovers, and Lady Charlotte made a point of keeping up with the squire. She adored cynics and people who said piquant things, and it amused her to make her large tyrannous hand felt by the squire's timid, crack-brained, ridiculous little sister.

As to Dr. Meyrick, he was tall and gaunt as Don Quixote. His gray hair made a ragged fringe round his straight-backed head; he wore an old-fashioned neck-cloth; his long body had a perpetual stoop, as though of deference, and his spectacled look of mild attentiveness had nothing in common with that medical self-assurance with which we are all nowadays so familiar.

Robert noticed presently that when he addressed Mrs. Darcy he said 'Ma'am,' making no bones at all about it; and his manner generally was the manner of one to whom class distinctions were the profoundest reality, and no burden at all on a naturally humble temper. Dr. Baker, of Whindale, accustomed to trouncing Mrs. Seaton, would have thought him a poor creature.

When dinner was announced, Robert found himself assigned to Mrs. Darcy; the squire took Lady Charlotte. Catherine fell to Mr. Bickerton, Rose to Mr. Wynnstay, and the rest found their way in as best they could. Catherine seeing the distribution was happy for a moment, till she found that if Rose was covered on her right she was exposed to the full fire of the enemy on her left, in other words that Langham was placed between her and Dr. Meyrick.

'Are your spirits damped at all by this magnificence?' Langham said to his neighbour as they sat down. The table was entirely covered with Japanese lilies, save for the splendid silver candelabra from which the light flashed, first on to the faces of the guests, and then on to those of the family portraits, hung thickly round the room. A roof embossed with gilded Tudor roses on a ground of black oak hung above them; a rose-water dish in which the Merry Monarch had once dipped his hands, and which bore a record of the fact in the inscription on its sides, stood before them; and the servants were distributing to each guest silver soup-plates which had been the gift of Sarah, Duchess of Marlborough, in some moment of generosity or calculation, to the Wendover of her day.[68]

'Oh dear, no!' said Rose carelessly. 'I don't know how it is, I think I must have been born for a palace.'

Langham looked at her, at the daring harmony of colour made by the reddish gold of her hair, the warm whiteness of her skin, and the brown-pink tints of her dress, at the crystals playing the part of diamonds on her beautiful neck, and remembered Robert's remarks to him. The same irony mingled with the same bitterness returned to him, and the elder brother's attitude became once more temporarily difficult. 'Who is your neighbour?' he inquired of her presently.

'Lady Charlotte's husband,' she answered mischievously, under her breath. 'One needn't know much more about him I imagine!'

'And that man opposite?'

'Robert's pet aversion,' she said calmly, without a change of countenance, so that Mr. Longstaffe opposite, who was studying her as he always studied pretty young women, stared at her through her remark in sublime ignorance

---

68 King Charles II (1630–85); Sarah Churchill (1660–1744), court favorite of Queen Anne (1665–1714).

of its bearing.

'And your sister's neighbour?'

'I can't hit him off in a sentence, he's too good!' said Rose laughing; 'all I can say is that Mrs. Bickerton has too many children, and the children have too many ailments for her ever to dine out.'

'That will do; I see the existence,' said Langham with a shrug. 'But he has the look of an apostle, though a rather hunted one. Probably nobody here, except Robert, is fit to tie his shoes.'

'The squire could hardly be called *empressé*,' said Rose, after a second, with a curl of her red lips. Mr. Wynnstay was still safely engaged with Mrs. Darcy, and there was a buzz of talk largely sustained by Lady Charlotte.

'No,' Langham admitted; 'the manners I thought were not quite equal to the house.'

'What possible reason could he have for treating Robert with those airs?' said Rose indignantly, ready enough in girl fashion to defend her belongings against the outer world. 'He ought to be only too glad to have the opportunity of knowing him and making friends with him.'

'You are a sister worth having;' and Langham smiled at her as she leant back in her chair, her white arms and wrists lying on her lap, and her slightly flushed face turned towards him. They had been on these pleasant terms of *camaraderie* all day, and the intimacy between them had been still making strides.

'Do you imagine I don't appreciate Robert because I make bad jokes about the choir and the clothing club?' she asked him, with a little quick repentance passing like a shadow through her eyes. 'I always feel I play an odious part here. I can't like it—I can't—their life. I should hate it! And yet——'

She sighed remorsefully, and Langham, who five minutes before could have wished her to be always smiling, could now have almost asked to fix her as she was: the eyes veiled, the soft lips relaxed in this passing instant of gravity.

'Ah! I forgot—' and she looked up again with light bewitching appeal— 'there is still that question, my poor little question of Sunday night, when I was in that fine moral frame of mind and you were near giving me, I believe, the only good advice you ever gave in your life,—how shamefully you have treated it!'

One brilliant look, which Catherine for her torment caught from the other side of the table, and then in an instant the quick face changed and stiffened. Mr. Wynnstay was speaking to her, and Langham was left to the intermittent mercies of Dr. Meyrick, who though glad to talk, was also quite content, apparently, to judge from the radiant placidity of his look, to examine his wine, study his *menu*, and enjoy his *entrées* in silence, undisturbed by the uncertain pleasures of conversation.

Robert, meanwhile, during the first few minutes, in which Mr. Wynnstay had been engaged in some family talk with Mrs. Darcy, had been allowing himself a little deliberate study of Mr. Wendover across what seemed the safe distance of a long table. The squire was talking shortly and abruptly, yet with occasional flashes of shrill ungainly laughter, to Lady Charlotte, who seemed to have no sort of fear of him and to find him good company, and every now and then Robert saw him turn to Catherine on the other side of him, and with an obvious change of manner address some formal and constrained remark to her.

Mr. Wendover was a man of middle height and loose bony frame, of which, as Robert had noticed in the drawing-room, all the lower half had a thin and shrunken look. But the shoulders, which had the scholar's stoop, and the head were massive and squarely outlined. The head was specially remarkable for its great breadth and comparative flatness above the eyes, and for the way in which the head itself dwarfed the face, which, as contrasted with the large angularity of the skull, had a pinched and drawn look. The hair was reddish-gray, the eyes small, but deep-set under fine brows, and the thin-lipped wrinkled mouth and long chin had a look of hard sarcastic strength.

Generally the countenance was that of an old man, the furrows were deep, the skin brown and shrivelled. But the alertness and force of the man's whole expression showed that, if the body was beginning to fail, the mind was as fresh and masterful as ever. His hair, worn rather longer than usual, his loosely-fitting dress and slouching carriage gave him an un-English look. In general he impressed Robert as a sort of curious combination of the foreign *savant* with the English grandee, for while his manner showed a considerable consciousness of birth and social importance, the gulf between him and the ordinary English country gentleman could hardly have been greater, whether in points of appearance or, as Robert very well knew, in points of social conduct. And as Robert watched him, his thoughts flew back again to the library, to this man's past, to all that those eyes had seen and those hands had touched. He felt already a mysterious, almost a yearning, sense of acquaintance with the being who had just received him with such chilling, such unexpected, indifference.

The squire's manners, no doubt, were notorious, but even so, his reception of the new rector of the parish, the son of a man intimately connected for years with the place, and with his father, and to whom he had himself shown what was for him considerable civility by letter and message, was sufficiently startling.

Robert, however, had no time to speculate on the causes of it, for Mrs. Darcy, released from Mr. Wynnstay, threw herself with glee on to her longed-for prey, the young and interesting-looking rector. First of all she cross-examined him as to his literary employments, and when by dint of much questioning she had forced particulars from him, Robert's mouth twitched as he watched her scuttling away from the subject, seized evidently with internal terrors lest she should have precipitated herself beyond hope of rescue into the jaws of the sixth century. Then with a view to regaining the lead and opening another and more promising vein, she asked him his opinion of Lady Selden's last novel, *Love in a Marsh*; and when he confessed ignorance she paused a moment, fork in hand, her small wrinkled face looking almost as bewildered as when, three minutes before, her rashness had well-nigh brought her face to face with Gregory of Tours as a topic of conversation.

But she was not daunted long. With little airs and bridlings infinitely diverting, she exchanged inquiry for the most beguiling confidence. She could appreciate 'clever men,' she said, for she—she too—was literary. Did Mr. Elsmere know—this in a hurried whisper, with sidelong glances to see that Mr. Wynnstay was safely occupied with Rose, and the squire with Lady Charlotte—that she had once *written a novel?*

Robert, who had been posted up in many things concerning the neighbourhood by Lady Helen Varley, could answer most truly that he had. Whereupon Mrs. Darcy beamed all over.

'Ah! but you haven't read it,' she said regretfully. 'It was when I was Maid of Honour, you know. No Maid of Honour had ever written a novel before. It was quite an event. Dear Prince Albert borrowed a copy of me one night to read in bed—I have it still, with the page turned down where he left off.' She hesitated. 'It was only in the second chapter,' she said at last with a fine truthfulness, 'but you know he was so busy, all the Queen's work to do, of course, besides his own—poor man!'

Robert implored her to lend him the work, and Mrs. Darcy, with blushes which made her more weird than ever, consented.

Then there was a pause, filled by an acid altercation between Lady Charlotte and her husband, who had not found Rose as grateful for his attentions as, in his opinion, a pink and white nobody at a country dinner-party ought to be, and was glad of the diversion afforded him by some aggressive remark of his wife. He and she differed on three main points—politics; the decoration of their London house, Mr. Wynnstay being a lover of Louis

Quinze, and Lady Charlotte a preacher of Morris; and the composition of their dinner-parties.[69] Lady Charlotte, in the pursuit of amusement and notoriety, was fond of flooding the domestic hearth with all the people possessed of any sort of a name for any sort of a reason in London. Mr. Wynnstay loathed such promiscuity; and the company in which his wife compelled him to drink his wine had seriously soured a small irritable Conservative with more family pride than either nerves or digestion.

During the whole passage of arms, Mrs. Darcy watched Elsmere, cat-and-mouse fashion, with a further confidence burning within her, and as soon as there was once more a general burst of talk, she pounced upon him afresh. Would he like to know that after thirty years she had just finished her *second* novel, unbeknown to her brother—as she mentioned him the little face darkened, took a strange bitterness—and it was just about to be entrusted to the post and a publisher?

Robert was all interest, of course, and inquired the subject. Mrs. Darcy expanded still more—could, in fact, have hugged him. But, just as she was launching into the plot a thought, apparently a scruple of conscience, struck her.

'Do you remember,' she began, looking at him a little darkly, askance, 'what I said about my hobbies the other day? Now, Mr. Elsmere, will you tell me—don't mind me—don't be polite—have you ever heard people tell stories of me? Have you ever, for instance, heard them call me a—a—tuft-hunter?'[70]

'Never!' said Robert heartily.

'They might,' she said, sighing. 'I *am* a tuft-hunter. I can't help it. And yet we *are* a good family, you know. I suppose it was that year at Court, and that horrid Warham afterwards. Twenty years in a cathedral town—and a very *little* cathedral town, after Windsor, and Buckingham Palace, and dear Lord Melbourne![71] Every year I came up to town to stay with my father for a month in the season, and if it hadn't been for that I should have died—my husband knew I should. It was the world, the flesh, and the devil, of course,

---

69 Louis Quinze refers to the French Rococo style originating in the eighteenth century and later imitated extensively during the mid-Victorian period; by the time of *Robert Elsmere*'s composition, it was out of fashion. Morris is the Arts and Crafts Movement associated with William Morris, an originally socialist enterprise that was opposed, in both aesthetics and politics, to Louis Quinze.

70 Someone who ostentatiously seeks out the company of (and, if possible, lives off of) the wealthy and aristocratic.

71 Windsor Castle and Buckingham Palace are two of the primary royal residences, the latter the palace in London; Lord Melbourne is William Lamb, 2nd Viscount Melbourne (1779–1848), Whig prime minister very close to the young Queen Victoria.

but it couldn't be helped. But now,' and she looked plaintively at her companion, as though challenging him to a candid reply: 'You *would* be more interesting, wouldn't you, to tell the truth, if you had a handle to your name?'

'Immeasurably,' cried Robert, stifling his laughter with immense difficulty, as he saw she had no inclination to laugh.

'Well, yes, you know. But it isn't right;' and again she sighed. 'And so I have been writing this novel just for that. It is called—what do you think?— "Mr. Jones." Mr. Jones is my hero—it's so good for me, you know, to think about a Mr. Jones.'

She looked beamingly at him. 'It must be indeed! Have you endowed him with every virtue?'

'Oh yes, and in the end, you know—' and she bent forward eagerly—'it all comes right. His father didn't die in Brazil without children after all, and the title——'

'What!' cried Robert, 'so he *wasn't* Mr. Jones?'

Mrs. Darcy looked a little conscious.

'Well, no,' she said guiltily, 'not just at the end. But it *really* doesn't matter—not to the story.'

Robert shook his head, with a look of protest as admonitory as he could make it, which evoked in her an answering expression of anxiety. But just at that moment a loud wave of conversation and of laughter seemed to sweep down upon them from the other end of the table, and their little private eddy was effaced. The squire had been telling an anecdote, and his clerical neighbours had been laughing at it.

'Ah!' cried Mr. Longstaffe, throwing himself back in his chair with a chuckle, 'that was an Archbishop worth having!'

'A curious story,' said Mr. Bickerton, benevolently, the point of it, however, to tell the truth, not being altogether clear to him. It seemed to Robert that the squire's keen eye, as he sat looking down the table, with his large nervous hands clasped before him, was specially fixed upon himself.

'May we hear the story?' he said, bending forward. Catherine, faintly smiling in her corner beside the host, was looking a little flushed and moved out of her ordinary quiet.

'It is a story of Archbishop Manners Sutton,' said Mr. Wendover, in his dry nasal voice. 'You probably know it, Mr. Elsmere. After Bishop Heber's consecration to the See of Calcutta, it fell to the Archbishop to make a valedictory speech, in the course of the luncheon at Lambeth which followed the ceremony. "I have very little advice to give you as to your future career," he said to the young bishop, "but all that experience has given me I hand on to you. Place before your eyes two precepts, and two only. One is, Preach the Gospel; and the other is—*Put down enthusiasm!*"[72]

There was a sudden gleam of steely animation in the squire's look as he told his story, his eye all the while fixed on Robert. Robert divined in a moment that the story had been re-told for his special benefit, and that in some unexplained way the relations between him and the squire were already biassed. He smiled a little with faint politeness, and falling back into his place made no comment on the squire's anecdote. Lady Charlotte's eyeglass, having adjusted itself for a moment to the distant figure of the rector, with regard to whom she had been asking Dr. Meyrick for particulars, quite unmindful of Catherine's neighbourhood, turned back again towards the squire.

'An unblushing old worldling, I should call your Archbishop,' she said briskly. 'And a very good thing for him that he lived when he did. Our modern good people would have dusted his apron for him.'

Lady Charlotte prided herself on these vigorous forms of speech, and the squire's neighbourhood generally called out an unusual crop of them. The squire was still sitting with his hands on the table, his great brows bent, surveying his guests.

'Oh, of course all the sensible men are dead!' he said indifferently. 'But that is a pet saying of mine—the Church of England in a nutshell.'

Robert flushed, and after a moment's hesitation bent forward.

'What do you suppose,' he asked quietly, 'your Archbishop meant, Mr. Wendover, by enthusiasm? Nonconformity, I imagine.'

'Oh, very possibly!' and again Robert found the hawk-like glance concentrated on himself. 'But I like to give his remark a much wider extension. One may make it a maxim of general experience, and take it as fitting all the fools with a mission who have teased our generation—all your Kingsleys, and Maurices,[73] and Ruskins—every one bent upon making any sort of aimless commotion, which may serve him both as an investment for the next world, and an advertisement for this.'

'Upon my word, squire,' said Lady Charlotte, 'I hope you don't expect Mr. Elsmere to agree with you?'

---

72 Charles Manners Sutton (1755–1828), Archbishop of Canterbury; Reginald Heber (1783–1826), Bishop of Calcutta and religious poet. The story, however, is actually about the *previous* Bishop of Calcutta, Thomas Middleton, although by the 1880s the anecdote had migrated to Heber; see, among others, E. A. Varley, *The Last of the Prince Bishops: William Van Mildert and the High Church Movement of the Nineteenth Century* (Cambridge: Cambridge University Press, 1992), 77.
73 Frederick Denison Maurice (1805–72), theologian associated with the Broad Church Movement and Christian Socialism.

Mr. Wendover made her a little bow.

'I have very little sanguineness of any sort in my composition,' he said drily.

'I should like to know,' said Robert, taking no notice of this by-play; 'I should like to know, Mr. Wendover, leaving the Archbishop out of count, what *you* understand by this word enthusiasm in this maxim of yours?'

'An excellent manner,' thought Lady Charlotte, who, for all her noisiness, was an extremely shrewd woman, 'an excellent manner and an unprovoked attack.'

Catherine's trained eye, however, had detected signs in Robert's look and bearing which were lost on Lady Charlotte, and which made her look nervously on. As to the rest of the table, they had all fallen to watching the 'break' between the new rector and their host with a good deal of curiosity.

The squire paused a moment before replying,—

'It is not easy to put it tersely,' he said at last; 'but I may define it, perhaps, as the mania for mending the roof of your right-hand neighbour with straw torn off the roof of your left-hand neighbour; the custom, in short, of robbing Peter to propitiate Paul.'

'Precisely,' said Mr. Wynnstay warmly; 'all the ridiculous Radical nostrums of the last fifty years—you have hit them off exactly. Sometimes you rob more and propitiate less; sometimes you rob less and propitiate more. But the principle is always the same.' And mindful of all those intolerable evenings, when these same Radical nostrums had been forced down his throat at his own table, he threw a pugnacious look at his wife, who smiled back serenely in reply. There is small redress indeed for these things, when out of the common household stock the wife possesses most of the money, and a vast proportion of the brains.

'And the cynic takes pleasure in observing,' interrupted the squire, 'that the man who effects the change of balance does it in the loftiest manner, and profits in the vulgarest way. Other trades may fail. The agitator is always sure of *his* market.'

He spoke with a harsh contemptuous insistence which was gradually setting every nerve in Robert's body tingling. He bent forward again, his long thin frame and boyish bright-complexioned face making an effective contrast to the squire's bronzed and wrinkled squareness.

'Oh, if you and Mr. Wynnstay are prepared to draw an indictment against your generation and all its works, I have no more to say,' he said, smiling still, though his voice had risen a little in spite of himself. 'I should be content to withdraw with my Burke into the majority.[74] I imagined your attack on enthusiasm had a narrower scope, but if it is to be made synonymous with social progress I give up. The subject is too big. Only——'

He hesitated. Mr. Wynnstay was studying him with somewhat insolent coolness; Lady Charlotte's eyeglass never wavered from his face, and he felt through every fibre the tender timid admonitions of his wife's eyes.

'However,' he went on after an instant, 'I imagine that we should find it difficult anyhow to discover common ground. I regard your Archbishop's maxim, Mr. Wendover,' and his tone quickened and grew louder, 'as first of all a contradiction in terms; and in the next place, to me, almost all enthusiasms are respectable!'

'You are one of those people, I see,' returned Mr. Wendover, after a pause, with the same nasal emphasis and the same *hauteur*, 'who imagine we owe civilisation to the heart; that mankind has *felt* its way—literally. The school of the majority, of course—I admit it amply. I, on the other hand, am with the benighted minority who believe that the world, so far as it has lived to any purpose, has lived by the *head*,' and he flung the noun at Robert scornfully. 'But I am quite aware that in a world of claptrap the philosopher gets all the kicks, and the philanthropists, to give them their own label, all the halfpence.'

The impassive tone had gradually warmed to a heat which was unmistakable. Lady Charlotte looked on with increasing relish. To her all society was a comedy played for her entertainment, and she detected something more dramatic than usual in the juxtaposition of these two men. That young rector might be worth looking after. The dinners in Martin Street were alarmingly in want of fresh blood. As for poor Mr. Bickerton, he had begun to talk hastily to Catherine, with a sense of something tumbling about his ears; while Mr. Longstaffe, eyeglass in hand, surveyed the table with a distinct sense of pleasurable entertainment. He had not seen much of Elsmere yet, but it was as clear as daylight that the man was a firebrand, and should be kept in order.

Meanwhile there was a pause between the two main disputants; the storm-clouds were deepening outside, and rain had begun to patter on the windows. Mrs. Darcy was just calling attention to the weather when the squire unexpectedly returned to the charge.

'The one necessary thing in life,' he said, turning to Lady Charlotte, a slight irritating smile playing round his strong mouth, 'is—not to be duped. Put too much faith in these fine things the altruists talk of, and you arrive one day at the condition of Louis XIV. after the battle of Ramillies: "Dieu a donc

---

74 *Burke's Peerage.*

oublié tout ce que j'ai fait pour lui?"[75] Read your Renan; remind yourself at every turn that it is quite possible after all the egotist *may* turn out to be in the right of it, and you will find at any rate that the world gets on excellently well without your blundering efforts to set it straight.[76] And so we get back to the Archbishop's maxim—adapted, no doubt, to English requirements,' and he shrugged his great shoulders expressively: '*Pace* Mr. Elsmere, of course, and the rest of our clerical friends!'

Again he looked down the table, and the strident voice sounded harsher than ever as it rose above the sudden noise of the storm outside. Robert's bright eyes were fixed on the squire, and before Mr. Wendover stopped Catherine could see the words of reply trembling on his lips.

'I am well content,' he said, with a curious dry intensity of tone. 'I give you your Renan. Only leave us poor dupes our illusions. We will not quarrel with the division. With you all the cynics of history; with us all the "scorners of the ground" from the world's beginning until now!'[77]

The squire make a quick impatient movement. Mr. Wynnstay looked significantly at his wife, who dropped her eyeglass with a little irrepressible smile.

As for Robert, leaning forward with hastened breath, it seemed to him that his eyes and the squire's crossed like swords. In Robert's mind there had arisen a sudden passion of antagonism. Before his eyes there was a vision of a child in a stifling room, struggling with mortal disease, imposed upon her, as he hotly reminded himself, by this man's culpable neglect. The dinner-party, the splendour of the room, the conversation, excited a kind of disgust in him. If it were not for Catherine's pale face opposite, he could hardly have maintained his self-control.

Mrs. Darcy, a little bewildered, and feeling that things were not going particularly well, thought it best to interfere.

'Roger,' she said plaintively, 'you must not be so philosophical. It's too hot! He used to talk like that,' she went on, bending over to Mr. Wynnstay, 'to the French priests who came to see us last winter in Paris. They never minded a bit—they used to laugh. "Monsieur votre frère, madame, c'est un homme

---

75 Louis XIV of France (1638–1715) fought and lost the Battle of Ramillies (1706) as part of the War of the Spanish Succession (1701–14). "Has God then forgotten everything I have done for him?"

76 Ernest Renan (1823-92), French scholar infamous for *The Life of Jesus* (1863), which studied Jesus purely as a human being. Cf. Strauss' *Life of Jesus*, referenced above.

77 A slight misquotation from Percy Bysshe Shelley, "To a Skylark" (1820), l. 100.

qui a trop lu," they would say to me when I gave them their coffee.[78] Oh, they were such dears, those old priests! Roger said they had great hopes of me.'

The chatter was welcome, the conversation broke up. The squire turned to Lady Charlotte, and Rose to Langham.

'Why didn't you support Robert?' she said to him, impulsively, with a dissatisfied face. 'He was alone, against the table!'

'What good should I have done him?' he asked, with a shrug. 'And pray, my lady confessor, what enthusiasms do you suspect me of?'

He looked at her intently. It seemed to her they were by the gate again—the touch of his lips on her hand. She turned from him hastily to stoop for her fan which had slipped away. It was only Catherine who, for her annoyance, saw the scarlet flush leap into the fair face. An instant later Mrs. Darcy had given the signal.

CHAPTER XVIII

After dinner Lady Charlotte fixed herself at first on Catherine, whose quiet dignity during the somewhat trying ordeal of the dinner had impressed her, but a few minutes' talk produced in her the conviction that without a good deal of pains—and why should a Londoner, accustomed to the cream of things, take pains with a country clergyman's wife?—she was not likely to get much out of her. Her appearance promised more, Lady Charlotte thought, than her conversation justified, and she looked about for easier game.

'Are you Mr. Elsmere's sister?' said a loud voice over Rose's head; and Rose, who had been turning over an illustrated book, with a mind wholly detached from it, looked up to see Lady Charlotte's massive form standing over her.

'No, his sister-in-law,' said Rose, flushing in spite of herself, for Lady Charlotte was distinctly formidable.

'Hum,' said her questioner, depositing herself beside her. 'I never saw two sisters more unlike. You have got a very argumentative brother-in-law.'

Rose said nothing, partly from awkwardness, partly from rising antagonism.

'Did you agree with him?' asked Lady Charlotte, putting up her glass and remorselessly studying every detail of the pink dress, its ornaments, and the slippered feet peeping out beneath it.

'Entirely,' said Rose fearlessly, looking her full in the face.

---

78 Monsieur your brother is a man who has read too much, Madame.

'And what can you know about it, I wonder? However, you are on the right side. It is the fashion nowadays to have enthusiasms. I suppose you muddle about among the poor like other people?'

'I know nothing about the poor,' said Rose.

'Oh, then, I suppose you feel yourself effective enough in some other line?' said the other coolly. 'What is it—lawn tennis, or private theatricals, or—hem—prettiness?' And again the eyeglass went up.

'Whichever you like,' said Rose calmly, the scarlet on her cheek deepening, while she resolutely reopened her book. The manner of the other had quite effaced in her all that sense of obligation, as from the young to the old, which she had been very carefully brought up in. Never had she beheld such an extraordinary woman.

'Don't read,' said Lady Charlotte complacently. 'Look at me. It's your duty to talk to me, you know; and I won't make myself any more disagreeable than I can help. I generally make myself disagreeable, and yet, after all, there are a great many people who like me.'

Rose turned a countenance rippling with suppressed laughter on her companion. Lady Charlotte had a large fair face, with a great deal of nose and chin, and an erection of lace and feathers on her head that seemed in excellent keeping with the masterful emphasis of those features. Her eyes stared frankly and unblushingly at the world, only softened at intervals by the glasses which were so used as to make them a most effective adjunct of her conversation. Socially, she was absolutely devoid of weakness or of shame. She found society extremely interesting, and she always struck straight for the desirable things in it, making short work of all those delicate tentative processes of acquaintanceship by which men and women ordinarily sort themselves. Rose's brilliant vivacious beauty had caught her eye at dinner; she adored beauty as she adored anything effective, and she always took a queer pleasure in bullying her way into a girl's liking. It is a great thing to be persuaded that at bottom you have a good heart. Lady Charlotte was so persuaded, and allowed herself many things in consequence.

'What shall we talk about?' said Rose demurely. 'What a magnificent old house this is!'

'Stuff and nonsense! I don't want to talk about the house. I am sick to death of it. And if your people live in the parish, you are too. I return to my question. Come, tell me, what is your particular line in life? I am sure you have one, by your face. You had better tell me; it will do you no harm.'

Lady Charlotte settled herself comfortably on the sofa, and Rose, seeing that there was no chance of escaping her tormentor, felt her spirits rise to an encounter.

'Really—Lady Charlotte—' and she looked down, and then up, with a feigned bashfulness—'I—I—play a little.'

'Humph!' said her questioner again, rather disconcerted by the obvious missishness of the answer. 'You do, do you? More's the pity. No woman who respects herself ought to play the piano nowadays. A professional told me the other day that until nineteen-twentieths of the profession were strung up, there would be no chance for the rest; and as for amateurs, there is simply *no* room for them whatever. I can't conceive anything more *passé* than amateur pianoforte playing!'

'I don't play the piano,' said Rose meekly.

'What—the fashionable instrument, the banjo?' laughed Lady Charlotte. 'That would be really striking.'

Rose was silent again, the corners of her mouth twitching.

'Mrs. Darcy,' said her neighbour, raising her voice, 'this young lady tells me she plays something; what is it?'

Mrs. Darcy looked in a rather helpless way at Catherine. She was dreadfully afraid of Lady Charlotte.

Catherine, with a curious reluctance, gave the required information; and then Lady Charlotte insisted that the violin should be sent for, as it had not been brought.

'Who accompanies you?' she inquired of Rose.

'Mr. Langham plays very well,' said Rose indifferently.

Lady Charlotte raised her eyebrows. 'That dark, Byronic-looking creature who came with you? I should not have imagined him capable of anything sociable. Letitia, shall I send my maid to the rectory, or can you spare a man?'

Mrs. Darcy hurriedly gave orders, and Rose, inwardly furious, was obliged to submit. Then Lady Charlotte, having gained her point, and secured a certain amount of diversion for the evening, lay back on the sofa, used her fan, and yawned till the gentlemen appeared.

When they came in, the precious violin which Rose never trusted to any other hands but her own without trepidation had just arrived, and its owner, more erect than usual, because more nervous, was trying to prop up a dilapidated music-stand which Mrs. Darcy had unearthed for her. As Langham came in, she looked up and beckoned to him.

'Do you see?' she said to him impatiently, 'they have made me play. Will you accompany me? I am very sorry, but there is no one else.'

If there was one thing Langham loathed on his own account, it was any sort of performance in public. But the half-plaintive look which accompanied her last words showed that she knew it, and he did his best to be amiable.

'I am altogether at your service,' he said, sitting down with resignation.

'It is all that tiresome woman, Lady Charlotte Wynnstay,' she whispered to him behind the music-stand. 'I never saw such a person in my life.'

'Macaulay's Lady Holland without the brains,' suggested Langham with languid vindictiveness as he gave her the note.[79]

Meanwhile Mr. Wynnstay and the squire sauntered in together.

'A village Norman-Néruda?' whispered the guest to the host.[80] The squire shrugged his shoulders.

'Hush!' said Lady Charlotte, looking severely at her husband. Mr. Wynnstay's smile instantly disappeared; he leant against the doorway and stared sulkily at the ceiling. Then the musicians began, on some Hungarian melodies put together by a younger rival of Brahms. They had not played twenty bars before the attention of every one in the room was more or less seized—unless we except Mr. Bickerton, whose children, good soul, were all down with some infantile ailment or other, and who was employed in furtively watching the clock all the time to see when it would be decent to order round the pony-carriage which would take him back to his pale overweighted spouse.

First came wild snatches of march music, primitive, savage, non-European; then a waltz of the lightest, maddest rhythm, broken here and there by strange barbaric clashes; then a song, plaintive and clinging, rich in the subtlest shades and melancholies of modern feeling.

'Ah, but *excellent*!' said Lady Charlotte once, under her breath, at a pause; 'and what *entrain*—what beauty!'

For Rose's figure was standing thrown out against the dusky blue of the tapestried walls, and from that delicate relief every curve, every grace, each tint—hair and cheek and gleaming arm gained an enchanting picture-like distinctness. There was jessamine at her waist and among the gold of her hair; the crystals on her neck, and on the little shoe thrown forward beyond her dress, caught the lamplight.

'How can that man play with her and not fall in love with her?' thought Lady Charlotte to herself, with a sigh, perhaps, for her own youth. 'He looks cool enough, however; the typical don with his nose in the air!'

Then the slow passionate sweetness of the music swept her away with it, she being in her way a connoisseur, and she ceased to speculate. When the

---

79 Thomas Babington Macaulay (1800–59), historian, politician, and reformer, author of the bestselling *History of England* (1848); Elizabeth, Lady Holland (1770–1845), prominent Whig society hostess.

80 Wilma Neruda, later Lady Hallé (1838–1911), famed violinist.

sounds ceased there was silence for a moment. Mrs. Darcy, who had a piano in her sitting-room whereon she strummed every morning with her tiny
rheumatic fingers, and who had, as we know, strange little veins of sentiment
running all about her, stared at Rose with open mouth. So did Catherine.
Perhaps it was then for the first time that, touched by this publicity, this contagion of other people's feeling, Catherine realised fully against what a depth
of stream she had been building her useless barriers.

'More! more!' cried Lady Charlotte.

The whole room seconded the demand save the squire and Mr. Bickerton.
They withdrew together into a distant oriel. Robert, who was delighted with
his little sister-in-law's success, went smiling to talk of it to Mrs. Darcy, while
Catherine with a gentle coldness answered Mr. Longstaffe's questions on the
same theme.

'Shall we?' said Rose, panting a little, but radiant, looking down on her
companion.

'Command me!' he said, his grave lips slightly smiling, his eyes taking
in the same vision that had charmed Lady Charlotte's. What a 'child of grace
and genius!'[81]

'But do you like it?' she persisted.

'Like it—like accompanying your playing?'

'Oh no!'—impatiently; 'showing off, I mean. I am quite ready to stop.'

'Go on; go on!' he said, laying his finger on the A. 'You have driven all
my *mauvaise honte* away.[82] I have not heard you play so splendidly yet.'

She flushed all over. 'Then we will go on,' she said briefly.

So they plunged again into an Andante and Scherzo of Beethoven.
How the girl threw herself into it, bringing out the wailing love-song of the
Andante, the dainty tripping mirth of the Scherzo, in a way which set every
nerve in Langham vibrating! Yet the art of it was wholly unconscious. The
music was the mere natural voice of her inmost self. A comparison full of
excitement was going on in that self between her first impressions of the man
beside her, and her consciousness of him, as he seemed to-night, human,
sympathetic, kind. A blissful sense of a mission filled the young silly soul.
Like David, she was pitting herself and her gift against those dark powers
which may invade and paralyse a life.[83]

After the shouts of applause at the end had yielded to a burst of talk, in
the midst of which Lady Charlotte, with exquisite infelicity, might have been

---

81 Percy Bysshe Shelley, "Alastor, or the Spirit of Solitude" (1816), l. 690.

82 *Mauvaise honte*: shyness.

83 e.g., David and Goliath from 1 Samuel 17.

heard laying down the law to Catherine as to how her sister's remarkable musical powers might be best perfected, Langham turned to his companion,—

'Do you know that for years I have enjoyed nothing so much as the music of the last two days?'

His black eyes shone upon her, transfused with something infinitely soft and friendly. She smiled. 'How little I imagined that first evening that you cared for music!'

'Or about anything else worth caring for?' he asked her, laughing, but with always that little melancholy note in the laugh.

'Oh, if you like,' she said, with a shrug of her white shoulders. 'I believe you talked to Catherine the whole of the first evening, when you weren't reading *Hamlet* in the corner, about the arrangements for women's education at Oxford.'[84]

'Could I have found a more respectable subject?' he inquired of her.

'The adjective is excellent,' she said with a little face, as she put her violin into its case. 'If I remember right, Catherine and I felt it personal. None of us were ever educated, except in arithmetic, sewing, English history, the Catechism, and *Paradise Lost*. I taught myself French at seventeen, because one Molière wrote plays in it, and German because of Wagner. But they are *my* French and *my* German. I wouldn't advise anybody else to steal them!'

Langham was silent, watching the movements of the girl's agile fingers.

'I wonder,' he said at last, slowly, 'when I shall play that Beethoven again?'

'To-morrow morning if you have a conscience,' she said drily; 'we murdered one or two passages in fine style.'

He looked at her, startled. 'But I go by the morning train!' There was an instant's silence. Then the violin case shut with a snap.

'I thought it was to be Saturday,' she said abruptly.

'No,' he answered with a sigh, 'it was always Friday. There is a meeting in London I must get to to-morrow afternoon.'

'Then we shan't finish these Hungarian duets,' she said slowly, turning away from him to collect some music on the piano.

Suddenly a sense of the difference between the week behind him, with all its ups and downs, its quarrels, its *ennuis*, its moments of delightful intimity, of artistic freedom and pleasure, and those threadbare monotonous weeks into which he was to slip back on the morrow, awoke in him a mad inconsequent sting of disgust, of self-pity.

---

84 By the time *Robert Elsmere* was published, Oxford had four colleges for women, with the first two, Lady Margaret Hall and Somerville Hall, opening to students in 1879. Although women could study at Oxford, they could not actually receive a BA.

'No, we shall finish nothing,' he said in a voice which only she could hear, his hands lying on the keys; 'there are some whose destiny it is never to finish—never to have enough—to leave the feast on the table, and all the edges of life ragged!'

Her lips trembled. They were far away, in the vast room, from the group Lady Charlotte was lecturing. Her nerves were all unsteady with music and feeling, and the face looking down on him had grown pale.

'We make our own destiny,' she said impatiently. '*We* choose. It is all our own doing. Perhaps destiny begins things—friendship, for instance; but afterwards it is absurd to talk of anything but ourselves. We keep our friends, our chances, our—our joys,' she went on hurriedly, trying desperately to generalise, 'or we throw them away wilfully, because we choose.'

Their eyes were riveted on each other.

'Not wilfully,' he said under his breath. 'But—no matter. May I take you at your word, Miss Leyburn? Wretched shirker that I am, whom even Robert's charity despairs of: have I made a friend? Can I keep her?'

Extraordinary spell of the dark effeminate face—of its rare smile! The girl forgot all pride, all discretion. 'Try,' she whispered, and as his hand, stretching along the keyboard, instinctively felt for hers, for one instant—and another, and another—she gave it to him.

'Albert, come here!' exclaimed Lady Charlotte, beckoning to her husband; and Albert, though with a bad grace, obeyed. 'Just go and ask that girl to come and talk to me, will you? Why on earth didn't you make friends with her at dinner?'

The husband made some irritable answer, and the wife laughed.

'Just like you!' she said, with a good humour which seemed to him solely caused by the fact of his non-success with the beauty at table. 'You always expect to kill at the first stroke. I mean to take her in tow. Go and bring her here.'

Mr. Wynnstay sauntered off with as much dignity as his stature was capable of. He found Rose tying up her music at one end of the piano, while Langham was preparing to shut up the keyboard.

There was something appeasing in the girl's handsomeness. Mr. Wynnstay laid down his airs, paid her various compliments, and led her off to Lady Charlotte.

Langham stood by the piano, lost in a kind of miserable dream. Mrs. Darcy fluttered up to him.

'Oh, Mr. Langham, you play so *beautifully*! Do play a solo!'

He subsided on to the music-bench obediently. On any ordinary occasion tortures could not have induced him to perform in a room full of strangers. He had far too lively and fastidious a sense of the futility of the amateur.

But he played—what, he knew not. Nobody listened but Mrs. Darcy, who sat lost in an armchair a little way off, her tiny foot beating time. Rose stopped talking, started, tried to listen. But Lady Charlotte had had enough music, and so had Mr. Longstaffe, who was endeavouring to joke himself into the good graces of the Duke of Sedbergh's sister. The din of conversation rose at the challenge of the piano, and Langham was soon overcrowded.

Musically, it was perhaps as well, for the player's inward tumult was so great, that what his hands did he hardly knew or cared. He felt himself the greatest criminal unhung. Suddenly, through all that wilful mist of epicurean feeling which had been enwrapping him, there had pierced a sharp illumining beam from a girl's eyes aglow with joy, with hope, with tenderness. In the name of Heaven, what had this growing degeneracy of every moral muscle led him to now? What! smile and talk, and smile—and be a villain all the time?[85] What! encroach on a young life, like some creeping parasitic growth, taking all, able to give nothing in return—not even one genuine spark of genuine passion? Go philandering on till a child of nineteen shows you her warm impulsive heart, play on her imagination, on her pity, safe all the while in the reflection that by the next day you will be far away, and her task and yours will be alike to forget! He shrinks from himself as one shrinks from a man capable of injuring anything weak and helpless. To despise the world's social code, and then to fall conspicuously below its simplest articles; to aim at being pure intelligence, pure open-eyed rationality, and not even to succeed in being a gentleman, as the poor commonplace world understands it! Oh, to fall at her feet, and ask her pardon before parting for ever! But no—no more posing; no more dramatising. How can he get away most quietly—make least sign? The thought of that walk home in the darkness fills him with a passion of irritable impatience.

'Look at that Romney, Mr. Elsmere; just look at it!' cried Dr. Meyrick excitedly; 'did you ever see anything finer? There was one of those London dealer fellows down here last summer offered the squire four thousand pounds down on the nail for it.'

In this way Meyrick had been taking Robert round the drawing-room, doing the honours of every stick and stone in it, his eyeglass in his eye, his thin old face shining with pride over the Wendover possessions. And so the two

---

85 Adapted from *Hamlet*, 1.5: "That one may smile, and smile, and be a villain."

gradually neared the oriel where the squire and Mr. Bickerton were standing.

Robert was in twenty minds as to any further conversation with the squire. After the ladies had gone, while every nerve in him was still tingling with anger, he had done his best to keep up indifferent talk on local matters with Mr. Bickerton. Inwardly he was asking himself whether he should ever sit at the squire's table and eat his bread again. It seemed to him that they had had a brush which would be difficult to forget. And as he sat there before the squire's wine, hot with righteous heat, all his grievances against the man and the landlord crowded upon him. A fig for intellectual eminence if it make a man oppress his inferiors and bully his equals!

But as the minutes passed on, the rector had cooled down. The sweet, placable, scrupulous nature began to blame itself. 'What, play your cards so badly, give up the game so rashly, the very first round? Nonsense! Patience and try again. There must be some cause in the background. No need to be white-livered, but every need, in the case of such a man as the squire, to take no hasty needless offence.'

So he had cooled and cooled, and now here were Meyrick and he close to the squire and his companion. The two men, as the rector approached, were discussing some cases of common enclosure that had just taken place in the neighbourhood. Robert listened a moment, then struck in. Presently, when the chat dropped, he began to express to the squire his pleasure in the use of the library. His manner was excellent, courtesy itself, but without any trace of effusion.

'I believe,' he said at last, smiling, 'my father used to be allowed the same privileges. If so, it quite accounts for the way in which he clung to Murewell.'

'I had never the honour of Mr. Edward Elsmere's acquaintance,' said the squire frigidly. 'During the time of his occupation of the rectory I was not in England.'

'I know. Do you still go much to Germany? Do you keep up your relations with Berlin?'

'I have not seen Berlin for fifteen years,' said the squire briefly, his eyes in their wrinkled sockets fixed sharply on the man who ventured to question him about himself, uninvited. There was an awkward pause. Then the squire turned again to Mr. Bickerton.

'Bickerton, have you noticed how many trees that storm of last February has brought down at the north-east corner of the park?'

Robert was inexpressibly galled by the movement, by the words themselves. The squire had not yet addressed a single remark of any kind about Murewell to *him*. There was a deliberate intention to exclude implied in this appeal to the man who was not the man of the place, on such a local point, which struck Robert very forcibly.

He walked away to where his wife was sitting.

'What time is it?' whispered Catherine, looking up at him.

'Time to go,' he returned, smiling, but she caught the discomposure in his tone and look at once, and her wifely heart rose against the squire. She got up, drawing herself together with a gesture that became her.

'Then let us go at once,' she said. 'Where is Rose?'

A minute later there was a general leave-taking. Oddly enough it found the squire in the midst of a conversation with Langham. As though to show more clearly that it was the rector personally who was in his black books, Mr. Wendover had already devoted some cold attention to Catherine both at and after dinner, and he had no sooner routed Robert than he moved in his slouching away across from Mr. Bickerton to Langham. And now, another man altogether, he was talking and laughing—describing apparently a reception at the French Academy—the epigrams flying, the harsh face all lit up, the thin bony fingers gesticulating freely.

The husband and wife exchanged glances as they stood waiting, while Lady Charlotte, in her loudest voice, was commanding Rose to come and see her in London any Thursday after the first of November. Robert was very sore. Catherine passionately felt it, and forgetting everything but him, longed to be out with him in the park comforting him.

'What an absurd fuss you have been making about that girl,' Wynnstay exclaimed to his wife as the Elsmere party left the room, the squire conducting Catherine with a chill politeness. 'And now, I suppose, you will be having her up in town, and making some young fellow who ought to know better fall in love with her. I am told the father was a grammar-school headmaster. Why can't you leave people where they belong?'

'I have already pointed out to you,' Lady Charlotte observed calmly, 'that the world has moved on since you were launched into it. I can't keep up class-distinctions to please you; otherwise, no doubt, being the devoted wife I am, I might try. However, my dear, we both have our fancies. You collect Sèvres china with or without a pedigree,' and she coughed drily; 'I collect promising young women.[86] On the whole, I think my hobby is more beneficial to you than yours is profitable to me.'

Mr. Wynnstay was furious. Only a week before he had been childishly,

---

86 The highly-desirable Sèvres make of china originated in France in the mid-eighteenth century under the protection of Louis XV. Given its value, it was (and is) frequently faked (hence the quip about "with or without a pedigree").

shamefully taken in by a Jew curiosity-dealer from Vienna, to his wife's huge amusement. If looks could have crushed her, Lady Charlotte would have been crushed. But she was far too substantial as she lay back in her chair, one large foot crossed over the other, and, as her husband very well knew, the better man of the two. He walked away, murmuring under his moustache words that would hardly have borne publicity, while Lady Charlotte, through her glasses, made a minute study of a little French portrait hanging some two yards from her.

Meanwhile the Elsmere party were stepping out into the warm damp of the night. The storm had died away, but a soft Scotch mist of rain filled the air. Everything was dark, save for a few ghostly glimmerings through the trees of the avenue; and there was a strong sweet smell of wet earth and grass. Rose had drawn the hood of her waterproof over her head, and her face gleamed an indistinct whiteness from its shelter. Oh this leaping pulse—this bright glow of expectation! How had she made this stupid blunder about his going? Oh, it was Catherine's mistake, of course, at the beginning. But what matter? Here they were in the dark, side by side, friends now, friends always. Catherine should not spoil their last walk together. She felt a passionate trust that *he* would not allow it.

'Wifie!' exclaimed Robert, drawing her a little apart, 'do you know it has just occurred to me that, as I was going through the park this afternoon by the lower footpath, I crossed Henslowe coming away from the house. Of course this is what has happened! *He* has told his story first. No doubt just before I met him he had been giving the squire a full and particular account—*à la* Henslowe—of my proceedings since I came. Henslowe lays it on thick—paints with a will. The squire receives me afterwards as the meddlesome pragmatical priest he understands me to be; puts his foot down to begin with; and, *hinc illæ lacrymæ*.[87] It's as clear as daylight! I thought that man had an odd twist of the lip as he passed me.'

'Then a disagreeable evening will be the worst of it,' said Catherine proudly. 'I imagine, Robert, you can defend yourself against that bad man?'

'He has got the start; he has no scruples; and it remains to be seen whether the squire has a heart to appeal to,' replied the young rector with sore reflectiveness. 'Oh, Catherine, have you ever thought, wifie, what a business it will be for us if I *can't* make friends with that man? Here we are at his gates—all our people in his power; the *comfort*, at any rate, of our social life depending on him. And what a strange, unmanageable, inexplicable being!'

---

87 "Hence these tears." From the Roman playwright Terence, *Andria*.

Elsmere sighed aloud. Like all quick imaginative natures he was easily depressed, and the squire's sombre figure had for the moment darkened his whole horizon. Catherine laid her cheek against his arm in the darkness, consoling, remonstrating, every other thought lost in her sympathy with Robert's worries. Langham and Rose slipped out of her head; Elsmere's step had quickened, as it always did when he was excited, and she kept up without thinking.

When Langham found the others had shot ahead in the darkness, and he and his neighbour were *tête-à-tête*, despair seized him. But for once he showed a sort of dreary presence of mind. Suddenly, while the girl beside him was floating in a golden dream of feeling, he plunged with a stiff deliberation born of his inner conflict into a discussion of the German system of musical training. Rose, startled, made some vague and flippant reply. Langham pursued the matter. He had some information about it, it appeared, garnered up in his mind, which might perhaps some day prove useful to her. A St. Anselm's undergraduate, one Dashwood, an old pupil of his, had been lately at Berlin for six months, studying at the Conservatorium. Not long ago, being anxious to become a schoolmaster, he had written to Langham for a testimonial. His letter had contained a full account of his musical life. Langham proceeded to recapitulate it.

His careful and precise report of hours, fees, masters, and methods lasted till they reached the park gate. He had the smallest powers of social acting, and his rôle was dismally overdone. The girl beside him could not know that he was really defending her from himself. His cold altered manner merely seemed to her a sudden and marked withdrawal of his petition for her friendship. No doubt she had received that petition too effusively—and he wished there should be no mistake.

What a young smarting soul went through in that half-mile of listening is better guessed than analysed. There are certain moments of shame, which only women know, and which seem to sting and burn out of youth all its natural sweet self-love. A woman may outlive them, but never forget them. If she pass through one at nineteen her cheek will grow hot over it at seventy. Her companion's measured tone, the flow of deliberate speech which came from him, the nervous aloofness of his attitude—every detail in that walk seemed to Rose's excited sense an insult.

As the park gate swung behind them she felt a sick longing for Catherine's shelter. Then all the pride in her rushed to the rescue and held that swooning dismay at the heart of her in check. And forthwith she capped Langham's minute account of the scale-method of a famous Berlin pianist by some witty stories of the latest London prodigy, a child-violinist, incredibly gifted, dirty,

and greedy, whom she had made friends with in town. The girl's voice rang
out sharp and hard under the trees. Where, in fortune's name, were the lights
of the rectory? Would this nightmare never come to an end?

At the rectory gate was Catherine waiting for them, her whole soul one
repentant alarm.

'Mr. Langham, Robert has gone to the study; will you go and smoke with
him?'

'By all means. Good-night, then, Mrs. Elsmere.'

Catherine gave him her hand. Rose was trying hard to fit the lock of the
gate into the hasp, and had no hand free. Besides, he did not approach her.

'Good-night!' she said to him over her shoulder.

'Oh, and Mr. Langham!' Catherine called after him as he strode away,
'will you settle with Robert about the carriage?'

He turned, made a sound of assent, and went on.

'When?' asked Rose lightly.

'For the nine o'clock train.'

'There should be a law against interfering with people's breakfast hour,'
said Rose; 'though, to be sure, a guest may as well get himself gone early and
be done with it. How you and Robert raced, Cathie! We did our best to catch
you up, but the pace was too good.'

Was there a wild taunt, a spice of malice in the girl's reckless voice?
Catherine could not see her in the darkness, but the sister felt a sudden trouble invade her.

'Rose, darling, you are not tired?'

'Oh dear, no! Good-night, sleep well. What a goose Mrs. Darcy is!'

And, barely submitting to be kissed, Rose ran up the steps and upstairs.

Langham and Robert smoked till midnight. Langham for the first time
gave Elsmere an outline of his plans for the future, and Robert, filled with
dismay at this final breach with Oxford and human society, and the only
form of practical life possible to such a man, threw himself into protests more
and more vigorous and affectionate. Langham listened to them at first with
sombre silence, then with an impatience which gradually reduced Robert to
a sore puffing at his pipe. There was a long space during which they sat together, the ashes of the little fire Robert had made dropping on the hearth,
and not a word on either side.

At last Elsmere could not bear it, and when midnight struck he sprang up
with an impatient shake of his long body, and Langham took the hint, gave
him a cold good-night, and went.

As the door shut upon him Robert dropped back into his chair, and sat on, his face in his hands, staring dolefully at the fire. It seemed to him the world was going crookedly. A day on which a man of singularly open and responsive temper makes a new enemy, and comes nearer than ever before to losing an old friend, shows very blackly to him in the calendar, and, by way of aggravation, Robert Elsmere says to himself at once that somehow or other there must be fault of his own in the matter.

Rose!—pshaw! Catherine little knows what stuff that cold intangible soul is made of.

Meanwhile, Langham was standing heavily, looking out into the night. The different elements in the mountain of discomfort that weighed upon him were so many that the weary mind made no attempt to analyse them. He had a sense of disgrace, of having stabbed something gentle that had leant upon him, mingled with a strong intermittent feeling of unutterable relief. Perhaps his keenest regret was that, after all, it had not been love! He had offered himself up to a girl's just contempt, but he had no recompense in the shape of a great addition to knowledge, to experience. Save for a few doubtful moments at the beginning, when he had all but surprised himself in something more poignant, what he had been conscious of had been nothing more than a suave and delicate charm of sentiment, a subtle surrender to one exquisite æsthetic impression after another. And these things in other relations the world had yielded him before.

'Am I sane?' he muttered to himself. 'Have I ever been sane? Probably not. The disproportion between my motives and other men's is too great to be normal. Well, at least I am sane enough to shut myself up. Long after that beautiful child has forgotten she ever saw me I shall still be doing penance in the desert.'

He threw himself down beside the open window with a groan. An hour later he lifted a face blanched and lined, and stretched out his hand with avidity towards a book on the table. It was an obscure and difficult Greek text, and he spent the greater part of the night over it, rekindling in himself with feverish haste the embers of his one lasting passion.

Meanwhile, in a room overhead, another last scene in this most futile of dramas was passing. Rose, when she came in, had locked the door, torn off her dress and her ornaments, and flung herself on the edge of the bed, her hands on her knees, her shoulders drooping, a fierce red spot on either cheek. There for an indefinite time she went through a torture of self-scorn. The incidents of the week passed before her one by one—her sallies, her defiances, her impulsive friendliness, the *élan*, the happiness of the last two days, the self-abandonment of this evening. Oh, intolerable—intolerable!

And all to end with the intimation that she had been behaving like a forward child—had gone too far and must be admonished—made to feel accordingly! The poisoned arrow pierced deeper and deeper into the girl's shrinking pride. The very foundations of self-respect seemed overthrown.

Suddenly her eye caught a dim and ghostly reflection of her own figure, as she sat with locked hands on the edge of the bed, in a long glass near, the only one of the kind which the rectory household possessed. Rose sprang up, snatched at the candle, which was flickering in the air of the open window, and stood erect before the glass, holding the candle above her head.

What the light showed her was a slim form in a white dressing-gown, that fell loosely about it; a rounded arm upstretched; a head, still crowned with its jessamine wreath, from which the bright hair fell heavily over shoulders and bosom; eyes, under frowning brows, flashing a proud challenge at what they saw; two lips, 'indifferent red,'[88] just open to let the quick breath come through—all thrown into the wildest chiaroscuro by the wavering candle flame.

Her challenge was answered. The fault was not there. Her arm dropped. She put down the light.

'I *am* handsome,' she said to herself, her mouth quivering childishly. 'I am. I may say it to myself.'

Then, standing by the window, she stared into the night. Her room, on the opposite side of the house from Langham's, looked over the cornfields and the distance. The stubbles gleamed faintly; the dark woods, the clouds teased by the rising wind, sent a moaning voice to greet her.

'I hate him! I hate him!' she cried to the darkness, clenching her cold little hand.

Then presently she slipped on to her knees, and buried her head in the bed-clothes. She was crying—angry stifled tears which had the hot impatience of youth in them. It all seemed to her so untoward. This was not the man she had dreamed of—the unknown of her inmost heart. *He* had been young, ardent, impetuous like herself. Hand in hand, eye flashing into eye, pulse answering to pulse, they would have flung aside the veil hanging over life and plundered the golden mysteries behind it.

She rebels; she tries to see the cold alien nature which has laid this paralysing spell upon her as it is, to reason herself back to peace—to indifference. The poor child flies from her own half-understood trouble; will none of it; murmurs again wildly—

'I hate him! I hate him! Cold-blooded—ungrateful—unkind!'

---

88 Shakespeare, *Twelfth Night*, 1.5.

In vain. A pair of melancholy eyes haunt, enthral her inmost soul. The charm of the denied, the inaccessible is on her, womanlike.

That old sense of capture, of helplessness, as of some lassoed struggling creature, descended upon her. She lay sobbing there, trying to recall what she had been a week before; the whirl of her London visit, the ambitions with which it had filled her; the bewildering many-coloured lights it had thrown upon life, the intoxicating sense of artistic power. In vain.

> 'The stream will not flow, and the hills will not rise;
> And the colours have all passed away from her eyes.'[89]

She felt herself bereft, despoiled. And yet through it all, as she lay weeping, there came flooding a strange contradictory sense of growth, of enrichment. In such moments of pain does a woman first begin to live? Ah! why should it hurt so—this long-awaited birth of the soul?

---

89 A slight misquotation of the last two lines from William Wordsworth, "The Reverie of Poor Susan."

BOOK III - THE SQUIRE

CHAPTER XIX

The evening of the Murewell Hall dinner-party proved to be a date of some importance in the lives of two or three persons. Rose was not likely to forget it; Langham carried about with him the picture of the great drawing-room, its stately light and shade, and its scattered figures, through many a dismal subsequent hour; and to Robert it was the beginning of a period of practical difficulties such as his fortunate youth had never yet encountered.

His conjecture had hit the mark. The squire's sentiments towards him, which had been on the whole friendly enough, with the exception of a slight *nuance* of contempt provoked in Mr. Wendover's mind by all forms of the clerical calling, had been completely transformed in the course of the afternoon before the dinner-party, and transformed by the report of his agent. Henslowe, who knew certain sides of the squire's character by heart, had taken Time by the forelock. For fourteen years before Robert entered the parish he had been king of it. Mr. Preston, Robert's predecessor, had never given him a moment's trouble. The agent had developed a habit of drinking, had favoured his friends and spited his enemies, and had allowed certain distant portions of the estate to go finely to ruin, quite undisturbed by any sentimental meddling of the priestly sort. Then the old rector had been gathered to the majority, and this long-legged busybody had taken his place, a man, according to the agent, as full of communistical notions as an egg is full of meat, and always ready to poke his nose into other people's business. And as all men like mastery, but especially Scotchmen, and as during even the first few months of the new rector's tenure of office it became tolerably evident to Henslowe that young Elsmere would soon become the ruling force of the neighbourhood unless measures were taken to prevent it, the agent, over his nocturnal drams, had taken sharp and cunning counsel with himself concerning the young man.

The state of Mile End had been originally the result of indolence and caprice on his part rather than of any set purpose of neglect. As soon, however, as it was brought to his notice by Elsmere, who did it, to begin with, in the friendliest way, it became a point of honour with the agent to let the place go to the devil, nay, to hurry it there. For some time notwithstanding, he avoided an open breach with the rector. He met Elsmere's remonstrances by a more or less civil show of argument, belied every now and then by the sarcasm of his coarse blue eye, and so far the two men had kept outwardly on terms. Elsmere had reason to know that on one or two occasions of difficulty in the parish Henslowe had tried to do him a mischief. The attempts, however, had not greatly succeeded, and their ill-success had probably excited in Elsmere a confidence of ultimate victory which had tended to keep him cool in the presence of Henslowe's hostility. But Henslowe had been all along merely waiting for the squire. He had served the owner of the Murewell estate for fourteen years, and if he did not know that owner's peculiarities by this time, might he obtain certain warm corners in the next life to which he was fond of consigning other people! It was not easy to cheat the squire out of money, but it was quite easy to play upon his ignorance of the details of English land management—ignorance guaranteed by the learned habits of a lifetime—on his complete lack of popular sympathy, and on the contempt felt by the disciple of Bismarck and Mommsen for all forms of altruistic sentiment.[1] The squire despised priests. He hated philanthropic cants. Above all things he respected his own leisure, and was abnormally, irritably sensitive as to any possible inroads upon it.

All these things Henslowe knew, and all these things he utilised. He saw the squire within forty-eight hours of his arrival at Murewell. His fancy picture of Robert and his doings was introduced with adroitness, and coloured with great skill, and he left the squire walking up and down his library, chafing alternately at the monstrous fate which had planted this sentimental agitator at his gates, and at the memory of his own misplaced civilities towards the intruder. In the evening those civilities were abundantly avenged, as we have seen.

Robert was much perplexed as to his next step. His heart was very sore. The condition of Mile End—those gaunt-eyed women and wasted children, all the sordid details of their unjust avoidable suffering weighed upon his nerves perpetually. But he was conscious that this state of feeling was one of tension, perhaps of exaggeration, and though it was impossible he should let the matter alone, he was anxious to do nothing rashly.

However, two days after the dinner-party he met Henslowe on the hill

---

1   Otto von Bismarck (1815–98), politician, architect of German unification; Theodor Mommsen (1817–1903), the most important classicist of the nineteenth century.

leading up to the rectory. Robert would have passed the man with a stiffening of his tall figure and the slightest possible salutation. But the agent, just returned from a round wherein the bars of various local inns had played a conspicuous part, was in a truculent mood and stopped to speak. He took up the line of insolent condolence with the rector on the impossibility of carrying his wishes with regard to Mile End into effect. They had been laid before the squire, of course, but the squire had his own ideas and wasn't just easy to manage.

'Seen him yet, sir?' Henslowe wound up jauntily, every line of his flushed countenance, the full lips under the fair beard, and the light prominent eyes, expressing a triumph he hardly cared to conceal.

'I have seen him, but I have not talked to him on this particular matter,' said the rector quietly, though the red mounted in his cheek. 'You may, however, be very sure, Mr. Henslowe, that everything I know about Mile End the squire shall know before long.'

'Oh, lor' bless me, sir!' cried Henslowe with a guffaw, 'it's all one to me. And if the squire ain't satisfied with the way his work's done now, why he can take you on as a second string, you know. You'd show us all, I'll be bound, how to make the money fly.'

Then Robert's temper gave way, and he turned upon the half-drunken brute before him with a few home-truths delivered with a rapier-like force which for the moment staggered Henslowe, who turned from red to purple. The rector, with some of those pitiful memories of the hamlet, of which we had glimpses in his talk with Langham, burning at his heart, felt the man no better than a murderer, and as good as told him so. Then, without giving him time to reply, Robert strode on, leaving Henslowe planted in the pathway. But he was hardly up the hill before the agent, having recovered himself by dint of copious expletives, was looking after him with a grim chuckle. He knew his master, and he knew himself, and he thought between them they would about manage to keep that young spark in order.

Robert meanwhile went straight home into his study, and there fell upon ink and paper. What was the good of protracting the matter any longer? Something must and should be done for these people, if not one way, then another.

So he wrote to the squire, showing the letter to Catherine when it was done, lest there should be anything over-fierce in it. It was the simple record of twelve months' experience told with dignity and strong feeling. Henslowe was barely mentioned in it, and the chief burden of the letter was to implore the squire to come and inspect certain portions of his property with his own eyes. The rector would be at his service any day or hour.

Husband and wife went anxiously through the document, softening here, improving there, and then it was sent to the Hall. Robert waited nervously through the day for an answer. In the evening, while he and Catherine were in the footpath after dinner, watching a chilly autumnal moonrise over the stubbles of the cornfield, the answer came.

'H'm,' said Robert dubiously as he opened it, holding it up to the moonlight; 'can't be said to be lengthy.'

He and Catherine hurried into the house. Robert read the letter, and handed it to her without a word.

After some curt references to one or two miscellaneous points raised in the latter part of the rector's letter, the squire wound up as follows:—

'As for the bulk of your communication, I am at a loss to understand the vehemence of your remarks on the subject of my Mile End property. My agent informed me shortly after my return home that you had been concerning yourself greatly, and, as he conceived, unnecessarily about the matter. Allow me to assure you that I have full confidence in Mr. Henslowe, who has been in the district for as many years as you have spent months in it, and whose authority on points connected with the business management of my estate naturally carries more weight with me, if you will permit me to say so, than your own.—I am, sir, your obedient servant,

'ROGER WENDOVER.'

Catherine returned the letter to her husband with a look of dismay. He was standing with his back to the chimney-piece, his hands thrust far into his pockets, his upper lip quivering. In his happy expansive life this was the sharpest personal rebuff that had ever happened to him. He could not but smart under it.

'Not a word,' he said, tossing his hair back impetuously, as Catherine stood opposite watching him—'not one single word about the miserable people themselves! What kind of stuff can the man be made of?'

'Does he believe you?' asked Catherine, bewildered.

'If not, one must try and make him,' he said energetically, after a moment's pause. 'To-morrow, Catherine, I go down to the Hall and see him.'

She quietly acquiesced, and the following afternoon, first thing after luncheon, she watched him go, her tender inspiring look dwelling with him as he crossed the park, which was lying delicately wrapped in one of the whitest of autumnal mists, the sun just playing through it with pale invading shafts.

The butler looked at him with some doubtfulness. It was never safe to admit visitors for the squire without orders. But he and Robert had special relations. As the possessor of a bass voice worthy of his girth, Vincent, under Robert's rule, had become the pillar of the choir, and it was not easy for him to refuse the rector.

So Robert was led in, through the hall, and down the long passage to the curtained door, which he knew so well.

'Mr. Elsmere, sir!'

There was a sudden hasty movement. Robert passed a magnificent lacquered screen newly placed round the door, and found himself in the squire's presence.

The squire had half risen from his seat in a capacious chair, with a litter of books round it, and confronted his visitor with a look of surprised annoyance. The figure of the rector, tall, thin, and youthful, stood out against the delicate browns and whites of the book-lined walls. The great room, so impressively bare when Robert and Langham had last seen it, was now full of the signs of a busy man's constant habitation. An odour of smoke pervaded it; the table in the window was piled with books just unpacked, and the half-emptied case from which they had been taken lay on the ground beside the squire's chair.

'I persuaded Vincent to admit me, Mr. Wendover,' said Robert, advancing hat in hand, while the squire hastily put down the German professor's pipe he had just been enjoying, and coldly accepted his proffered greeting. 'I should have preferred not to disturb you without an appointment, but after your letter it seemed to me some prompt personal explanation was necessary.'

The squire stiffly motioned towards a chair, which Robert took, and then slipped back into his own, his wrinkled eyes fixed on the intruder.

Robert, conscious of almost intolerable embarrassment, but maintaining in spite of it an excellent degree of self-control, plunged at once into business. He took the letter he had just received from the squire as a text, made a good-humoured defence of his own proceedings, described his attempt to move Henslowe, and the reluctance of his appeal from the man to the master. The few things he allowed himself to say about Henslowe were in perfect temper, though by no means without an edge.

Then, having disposed of the more personal aspects of the matter, he paused, and looked hesitatingly at the face opposite him, more like a bronzed mask at this moment than a human countenance. The squire, however, gave him no help. He had received his remarks so far in perfect silence, and seeing that there were more to come, he waited for them with the same rigidity of look and attitude.

So, after a moment or two, Robert went on to describe in detail some of those individual cases of hardship and disease at Mile End, during the preceding year, which could be most clearly laid to the sanitary condition of the place. Filth, damp, leaking roofs, foul floors, poisoned water—he traced to each some ghastly human ill, telling his stories with a nervous brevity, a suppressed fire, which would have burnt them into the sense of almost any other listener. Not one of these woes but he and Catherine had tended with sickening pity and labour of body and mind. That side of it he kept rigidly out of sight. But all that he could hurl against the squire's feeling, as it were, he gathered up, strangely conscious through it all of his own young persistent yearning to right himself with this man, whose mental history, as it lay chronicled in these rooms, had been to him, at a time of intellectual hunger, so stimulating, so enriching.

But passion and reticence and hidden sympathy were alike lost upon the squire. Before he paused Mr. Wendover had already risen restlessly from his chair, and from the rug was glowering down on his unwelcome visitor.

Good heavens! had he come home to be lectured in his own library by this fanatical slip of a parson? As for his stories, the squire barely took the trouble to listen to them.

Every popularity-hunting fool, with a passion for putting his hand into other people's pockets, can tell pathetic stories; but it was intolerable that his scholar's privacy should be at the mercy of one of the tribe.

'Mr. Elsmere,' he broke out at last with contemptuous emphasis, 'I imagine it would have been better—infinitely better—to have spared both yourself and me the disagreeables of this interview. However, I am not sorry we should understand each other. I have lived a life which is at least double the length of yours in very tolerable peace and comfort. The world has been good enough for me, and I for it, so far. I have been master in my own estate, and intend to remain so. As for the new-fangled ideas of a landowner's duty, with which your mind seems to be full'—the scornful irritation of the tone was unmistakable—'I have never dabbled in them, nor do I intend to begin now. I am like the rest of my kind; I have no money to chuck away in building schemes, in order that the rector of the parish may pose as the apostle of the agricultural labourer. That, however, is neither here nor there. What is to the purpose is, that my business affairs are in the hands of a business man, deliberately chosen and approved by me, and that I have nothing to do with them. Nothing at all!' he repeated with emphasis. 'It may seem to you very shocking. You may regard it as the object in life of the English landowner to inspect the pigstyes and amend the habits of the English labourer. I don't quarrel with the conception, I only ask you not to expect me to live up to it. I am a student first and foremost, and desire to be left to my books. Mr. Henslowe is there on purpose to protect my literary freedom. What he thinks desirable is good enough for me, as I have already informed you. I am sorry for it if his methods do not commend themselves to you. But I have yet to learn that the rector of the parish has an ex-officio right to interfere between a landlord and his tenants.'

Robert kept his temper with some difficulty. After a pause he said, feeling desperately, however, that the suggestion was not likely to improve matters,—

'If I were to take all the trouble and all the expense off your hands, Mr. Wendover, would it be impossible for you to authorise me to make one or two alterations most urgently necessary for the improvement of the Mile End cottages?'

The squire burst into an angry laugh.

'I have never yet been in the habit, Mr. Elsmere, of doing my repairs by public subscription. You ask a little too much from an old man's powers of adaptation.'

Robert rose from his seat, his hand trembling as it rested on his walking-stick.

'Mr. Wendover,' he said, speaking at last with a flash of answering scorn in his young vibrating voice, 'what I think you cannot understand is that at any moment a human creature may sicken and die, poisoned by the state of your property, for which you—and nobody else—are ultimately responsible.'

The squire shrugged his shoulders.

'So you say, Mr. Elsmere. If true, every person in such a condition has a remedy in his own hands. I force no one to remain on my property.'

'The people who live there,' exclaimed Robert, 'have neither home nor subsistence if they are driven out. Murewell is full—times bad—most of the people old.'

'And eviction "a sentence of death," I suppose,' interrupted the squire, studying him with sarcastic eyes. 'Well, I have no belief in a Gladstonian Ireland, still less in a Radical England.[2] Supply and demand, cause and effect, are enough for me. The Mile End cottages are out of repair, Mr. Elsmere, so Mr. Henslowe tells me, because the site is unsuitable, the type of cottage out of date. People live in them at their peril; I don't pull them down, or rather'—correcting himself with exasperating consistency—'Mr. Henslowe doesn't pull them down, because, like other men, I suppose, he dislikes an

---

2   Gladstone advocated Irish Home Rule.

outcry. But if the population stays, it stays at its own risk. Now have I made myself plain?'

The two men eyed one another.

'Perfectly plain,' said Robert quietly. 'Allow me to remind you, Mr. Wendover, that there are other matters than eviction capable of provoking an outcry.'

'As you please,' said the other indifferently. 'I have no doubt I shall find myself in the newspapers before long. If so, I daresay I shall manage to put up with it. Society is made up of fanatics and the creatures they hunt. If I am to be hunted, I shall be in good company.'

Robert stood hat in hand, tormented with a dozen cross-currents of feeling. He was forcibly struck with the blind and comparatively motiveless pugnacity of the squire's conduct. There was an extravagance in it which for the first time recalled to him old Meyrick's lucubrations.

'I have done no good, I see, Mr. Wendover,' he said at last, slowly. 'I wish I could have induced you to do an act of justice and mercy. I wish I could have made you think more kindly of myself. I have failed in both. It is useless to keep you any longer. Good-morning.'

He bowed. The squire also bent forward. At that moment Robert caught sight beside his shoulder of an antique, standing on the mantelpiece, which was a new addition to the room. It was a head of Medusa, and the frightful stony calm of it struck on Elsmere's ruffled nerves with extraordinary force. It flashed across him that here was an apt symbol of that absorbing and overgrown life of the intellect which blights the heart and chills the senses. And to that spiritual Medusa, the man before him was not the first victim he had known.

Possessed with the fancy the young man made his way into the hall. Arrived there, he looked round with a kind of passionate regret: 'Shall I ever see this again?' he asked himself. During the past twelve months his pleasure in the great house had been much more than sensuous. Within those walls his mind had grown, had reached to a fuller stature than before, and a man loves, or should love, all that is associated with the maturing of his best self.

He closed the ponderous doors behind him sadly. The magnificent pile, grander than ever in the sunny autumnal mist which enwrapped it, seemed to look after him as he walked away, mutely wondering that he should have allowed anything so trivial as a peasant's grievance to come between him and its perfections.

In the wooded lane outside the rectory gate he overtook Catherine. He gave her his report, and they walked on together arm-in-arm, a very depressed pair.

'What shall you do next?' she asked him.

'Make out the law of the matter,' he said briefly.

'If you get over the inspector,' said Catherine anxiously, 'I am tolerably certain Henslowe will turn out the people.'

He would not dare, Robert thought. At any rate, the law existed for such cases, and it was his bounden duty to call the inspector's attention.

Catherine did not see what good could be done thereby, and feared harm. But her wifely chivalry felt that he must get through his first serious practical trouble his own way. She saw that he felt himself distressingly young and inexperienced, and would not for the world have harassed him by over advice.

So she let him alone, and presently Robert threw the matter from him with a sigh.

'Let it be a while,' he said, with a shake of his long frame. 'I shall get morbid over it if I don't mind. I am a selfish wretch too. I know you have worries of your own, wifie.'

And he took her hand under the trees and kissed it with a boyish tenderness.

'Yes,' said Catherine, sighing, and then paused. 'Robert,' she burst out again, 'I am certain that man made love of a kind to Rose. *He* will never think of it again, but since the night before last she, to my mind, is simply a changed creature.'

'*I* don't see it,' said Robert doubtfully.

Catherine looked at him with a little angel scorn in her gray eyes. That men should make their seeing in such matters the measure of the visible!

'You have been studying the squire, sir—I have been studying Rose.'

Then she poured out her heart to him, describing the little signs of change and suffering her anxious sense had noted, in spite of Rose's proud effort to keep all the world, but especially Catherine, at arm's length. And at the end her feeling swept her into a denunciation of Langham, which was to Robert like a breath from the past, from those stern hills wherein he met her first. The happiness of their married life had so softened or masked all her ruggedness of character, that there was a certain joy in seeing those strong forces in her which had struck him first reappear.

'Of course I feel myself to blame,' he said when she stopped. 'But how could one foresee, with such an inveterate hermit and recluse? And I owed him—I owe him—so much.'

'I know,' said Catherine, but frowning still. It probably seemed to her that that old debt had been more than effaced.

'You will have to send her to Berlin,' said Elsmere after a pause. 'You must play off her music against this unlucky feeling. If it exists it is your only chance.'

'Yes, she must go to Berlin,' said Catherine slowly.

Then presently she looked up, a flash of exquisite feeling breaking up the delicate resolution of the face.

'I am not sad about that, Robert. Oh, how you have widened my world for me!'

Suddenly that hour in Marrisdale came back to her. They were in the woodpath. She crept inside her husband's arm and put up her face to him, swept away by an overmastering impulse of self-humiliating love.

The next day Robert walked over to the little market town of Churton, saw the discreet and long-established solicitor of the place, and got from him a complete account of the present state of the rural sanitary law. The first step clearly was to move the sanitary inspector; if that failed for any reason, then any *bonâ fide* inhabitant had an appeal to the local sanitary authority, viz. the board of guardians. Robert walked home pondering his information, and totally ignorant that Henslowe, who was always at Churton on market-days, had been in the market-place at the moment when the rector's tall figure had disappeared within Mr. Dunstan's office-door. That door was unpleasantly known to the agent in connection with some energetic measures for raising money he had been lately under the necessity of employing, and it had a way of attracting his eyes by means of the fascination that often attaches to disagreeable objects.

In the evening Rose was sitting listlessly in the drawing-room. Catherine was not there, so her novel was on her lap and her eyes were staring intently into a world whereof they only had the key. Suddenly there was a ring at the bell. The servant came, and there were several voices and a sound of much shoe-scraping. Then the swing-door leading to the study opened and Elsmere and Catherine came out. Elsmere stopped with an exclamation.

His visitors were two men from Mile End. One was old Milsom, more sallow and palsied than ever. As he stood bent almost double, his old knotted hand resting for support on the table beside him, everything in the little hall seemed to shake with him. The other was Sharland, the handsome father of the twins, whose wife had been fed by Catherine with every imaginable delicacy since Robert's last visit to the hamlet. Even his strong youth had begun to show signs of premature decay. The rolling gipsy eyes were growing sunken, the limbs dragged a little.

They had come to implore the rector to let Mile End alone. Henslowe had been over there in the afternoon, and had given them all very plainly to understand that if Mr. Elsmere meddled any more they would be all turned out at a week's notice to shift as they could. 'And if you don't find Thurston Common nice lying this weather, with the winter coming on, you'll know who to thank for it,' the agent had flung behind him as he rode off.

Robert turned white. Rose, watching the little scene with listless eyes, saw him towering over the group like an embodiment of wrath and pity.

'If they turn us out, sir,' said old Milsom, wistfully looking up at Elsmere with blear eyes, 'there'll be nothing left but the House for us old 'uns. Why, lor' bless you, sir, it's not so bad but we can make shift.'

'You, Milsom!' cried Robert; 'and you've just all but lost your grandchild! And you know your wife 'll never be the same woman since that bout of fever in the spring. And——'

His quick eyes ran over the old man's broken frame with a world of indignant meaning in them.

'Ay, ay, sir,' said Milsom, unmoved. 'But if it isn't fevers, it's summat else. I can make a shilling or two where I be, speshally in the first part of the year, in the basket work, and my wife she goes charring up at Mr. Carter's farm, and Mr. Dodson, him at the farther farm, he do give us a bit sometimes. Ef you git us turned away it will be a bad day's work for all on us, sir, you may take my word on it.'

'And my wife so ill, Mr. Elsmere,' said Sharland, 'and all those childer! I can't walk three miles farther to my work, Mr. Elsmere, I can't nohow. I haven't got the legs for it. Let un be, sir. We'll rub along.'

Robert tried to argue the matter.

If they would but stand by him he would fight the matter through, and they should not suffer, if he had to get up a public subscription, or support them out of his own pocket all the winter. A bold front, and Mr. Henslowe must give way. The law was on their side, and every labourer in Surrey would be the better off for their refusal to be housed like pigs and poisoned like vermin.

In vain. There is an inexhaustible store of cautious endurance in the poor against which the keenest reformer constantly throws himself in vain. Elsmere was beaten. The two men got his word, and shuffled off back to their pestilential hovels, a pathetic content beaming on each face.

Catherine and Robert went back into the study. Rose heard her brother-in-law's passionate sigh as the door swung behind them.

'Defeated!' she said to herself with a curious accent. 'Well, everybody must have his turn. Robert has been too successful in his life, I think.—You wretch!' she added, after a minute, laying her bright head down on the book before her.

Next morning his wife found Elsmere after breakfast busily packing a case of books in the study. They were books from the Hall library, which so far had been for months the inseparable companions of his historical work.

Catherine stood and watched him sadly.

'Must you, Robert?'

'I won't be beholden to that man for anything an hour longer than I can help,' he answered her.

When the packing was nearly finished he came up to where she stood in the open window.

'Things won't be as easy for us in the future, darling,' he said to her. 'A rector with both squire and agent against him is rather heavily handicapped. We must make up our minds to that.'

'I have no great fear,' she said, looking at him proudly.

'Oh, well—nor I—perhaps,' he admitted, after a moment. 'We can hold our own. But I wish—oh, I wish'—and he laid his hand on his wife's shoulder—'I could have made friends with the squire.'

Catherine looked less responsive.

'As squire, Robert, or as Mr. Wendover?'

'As both, of course, but specially as Mr. Wendover.'

'We can do without his friendship,' she said with energy.

Robert gave a great stretch, as though to work off his regrets.

'Ah, but,' he said, half to himself, as his arms dropped, 'if you are just filled with the hunger to *know*, the people who know as much as the squire become very interesting to you!'

Catherine did not answer. But probably her heart went out once more in protest against a knowledge that was to her but a form of revolt against the awful powers of man's destiny.

'However, here go his books,' said Robert.

Two days later Mrs. Leyburn and Agnes made their appearance, Mrs. Leyburn all in a flutter concerning the event over which, in her own opinion, she had come to preside.[3] In her gentle fluid mind all impressions were short-lived. She had forgotten how she had brought up her own babies, but Mrs. Thornburgh, who had never had any, had filled her full of nursery lore. She

---

3   "appearance, Mrs. Leyburn": Punctuation missing in the one-volume Macmillan edition, but is always a comma elsewhere.

sat retailing a host of second-hand hints and instructions to Catherine, who would every now and then lay her hand smiling on her mother's knee, well pleased to see the flush of pleasure on the pretty old face, and ready, in her patient filial way, to let herself be experimented on to the utmost, if it did but make the poor foolish thing happy.

Then came a night when every soul in the quiet rectory, even hot, smarting Rose, was possessed by one thought through many terrible hours, and one only—the thought of Catherine's safety. It was strange and unexpected, but Catherine, the most normal and healthy of women, had a hard struggle for her own life and her child's, and it was not till the gray autumn morning, after a day and night which left a permanent mark on Robert, that he was summoned at last, and with the sense of one emerging from black gulfs of terror, received from his wife's languid hand the tiny fingers of his firstborn.

The days that followed were full of emotion for these two people, who were perhaps always over-serious, over-sensitive. They had no idea of minimising the great common experiences of life. Both of them were really simple, brought up in old-fashioned simple ways, easily touched, responsive to all that high spiritual education which flows from the familiar incidents of the human story, approached poetically and passionately. As the young husband sat in the quiet of his wife's room, the occasional restless movements of the small brown head against her breast causing the only sound perceptible in the country silence, he felt all the deep familiar currents of human feeling sweeping through him—love, reverence, thanksgiving—and all the walls of the soul, as it were, expanding and enlarging as they passed.

Responsive creature that he was, the experience of these days was hardly happiness. It went too deep; it brought him too poignantly near to all that is most real and therefore most tragic in life.

Catherine's recovery also was slower than might have been expected, considering her constitutional soundness, and for the first week, after that faint moment of joy when her child was laid upon her arm, and she saw her husband's quivering face above her, there was a kind of depression hovering over her. Robert felt it, and felt too that all his devotion could not soothe it away. At last she said to him one evening, in the encroaching September twilight, speaking with a sudden hurrying vehemence, wholly unlike herself, as though a barrier of reserve had given way,—

'Robert, I cannot put it out of my head. I cannot forget it, *the pain of the world!*'

He shut the book he was reading, her hand in his, and bent over her with questioning eyes.

'It seems,' she went on, with that difficulty which a strong nature always feels in self-revelation, 'to take the joy even out of our love—and the child. I feel ashamed almost that mere physical pain should have laid such hold on me—and yet I can't get away from it. It's not for myself,' and she smiled faintly at him. 'Comparatively I had so little to bear! But I know now for the first time what physical pain may mean—and I never knew before! I lie thinking, Robert, about all creatures in pain—workmen crushed by machinery, or soldiers—or poor things in hospitals—above all of women! Oh, when I get well, how I will take care of the women here! What women must suffer even here in out-of-the-way cottages—no doctor, no kind nursing, all blind agony and struggle! And women in London in dens like those Mr. Newcome got into, degraded, forsaken, ill-treated, the thought of the child only an extra horror and burden! And the pain all the time so merciless, so cruel—no escape! Oh, to give all one is, or ever can be, to comforting! And yet the great sea of it one can never touch! It is a nightmare—I am weak still, I suppose; I don't know myself; but I can see nothing but jarred, tortured creatures everywhere. All my own joys and comforts seem to lift me selfishly above the common lot.'

She stopped, her large gray-blue eyes dim with tears, trying once more for that habitual self-restraint which physical weakness had shaken.

'You *are* weak,' he said, caressing her, 'and that destroys for a time the normal balance of things. It is true, darling, but we are not meant to see it always so clearly. God knows we could not bear it if we did.'

'And to think,' she said, shuddering a little, 'that there are men and women who in the face of it can still refuse Christ and the Cross, can still say this life is all! How can they live—how dare they live?'

Then he saw that not only man's pain, but man's defiance, had been haunting her, and he guessed what persons and memories had been flitting through her mind. But he dared not talk lest she should exhaust herself. Presently, seeing a volume of Augustine's *Confessions*, her favourite book, lying beside her, he took it up, turning over the pages, and weaving passages together as they caught his eye.

'*Speak to me, for Thy compassion's sake, O Lord my God, and tell me what art Thou to me! Say unto my soul, "I am thy salvation!" Speak it that I may hear. Behold the ears of my heart, O Lord; open them and say unto my soul, "I am thy salvation!" I will follow after this voice of Thine, I will lay hold on Thee. The temple of my soul, wherein Thou shouldest enter, is narrow, do Thou enlarge it. It falleth into ruins—do Thou rebuild it!... Woe to that bold soul which hopeth, if it do but let Thee go, to find something better than Thee! It turneth hither and thither, on this side and on that, and all things are hard and bitter unto it. For*

Thou only art rest!... Whithersoever the soul of man turneth it findeth sorrow, except only in Thee. Fix there, then, thy resting-place, my soul! Lay up in Him whatever thou hast received from Him. Commend to the keeping of the Truth whatever the Truth hath given thee, and thou shalt lose nothing. And thy dead things shall revive and thy weak things shall be made whole!'

She listened, appropriating and clinging to every word, till the nervous clasp of the long delicate fingers relaxed, her head dropped a little, gently, against the head of the child, and tired with much feeling she slept.

Robert slipped away and strolled out into the garden in the fast-gathering darkness. His mind was full of that intense spiritual life of Catherine's which in its wonderful self-containedness and strength was always a marvel, sometimes a reproach, to him. Beside her, he seemed to himself a light creature, drawn hither and thither by this interest and by that, tangled in the fleeting shows of things—the toy and plaything of circumstance. He thought ruefully and humbly, as he wandered on through the dusk, of his own lack of inwardness: 'Everything divides me from Thee!' he could have cried in St. Augustine's manner. 'Books, and friends, and work—all seem to hide Thee from me. Why am I so passionate for this and that, for all these sections and fragments of Thee? Oh, for the One, the All! Fix there thy resting-place, my soul!'

And presently, after this cry of self-reproach, he turned to muse on that intuition of the world's pain which had been troubling Catherine, shrinking from it even more than she had shrunk from it, in proportion as his nature was more imaginative than hers. And Christ the only clue, the only remedy—no other anywhere in this vast universe, where all men are under sentence of death, where the whole creation groaneth and travaileth in pain together until now!

And yet what countless generations of men had borne their pain, knowing nothing of the one Healer. He thought of Buddhist patience and Buddhist charity; of the long centuries during which Chaldean or Persian or Egyptian lived, suffered, and died, trusting the gods they knew. And how many other generations, nominally children of the Great Hope, had used it as the mere instrument of passion or of hate, cursing in the name of love, destroying in the name of pity! For how much of the world's pain was not Christianity itself responsible? His thoughts recurred with a kind of anguished perplexity to some of the problems stirred in him of late by his historical reading. The strifes and feuds and violences of the early Church returned to weigh upon him—the hair-splitting superstition, the selfish passion for power. He recalled Gibbon's lamentation over the age of the Antonines, and Mommsen's grave doubt whether, taken as a whole, the area once covered by the Roman Empire can be said to be substantially happier now than in the days of Severus.[4]

O corruptio optimi![5] That men should have been so little affected by that shining ideal of the New Jerusalem, 'descended out of Heaven from God,'[6] into their very midst—that the print of the 'blessed feet' along the world's highway should have been so often buried in the sands of cruelty and fraud!

The September wind blew about him as he strolled through the darkening column, set thick with great bushes of sombre juniper among the yellowing fern, which stretched away on the left-hand side of the road leading to the Hall. He stood and watched the masses of restless discordant cloud which the sunset had left behind it, thinking the while of Mr. Grey, of his assertions and his denials. Certain phrases of his which Robert had heard drop from him on one or two rare occasions during the later stages of his Oxford life ran through his head.

'*The fairy-tale of Christianity*'—'*The origins of Christian Mythology.*' He could recall, as the words rose in his memory, the simplicity of the rugged face, and the melancholy mingled with fire which had always marked the great tutor's sayings about religion.

'*Fairy Tale!*' Could any reasonable man watch a life like Catherine's and believe that nothing but a delusion lay at the heart of it? And as he asked the question, he seemed to hear Mr. Grey's answer: 'All religions are true, and all are false. In them all, more or less visibly, man grasps at the one thing needful—self forsaken, God laid hold of. The spirit in them all is the same, answers eternally to reality; it is but the letter, the fashion, the imagery, that are relative and changing.'

He turned and walked homeward, struggling, with a host of tempestuous ideas as swift and varying as the autumn clouds hurrying overhead. And then, through a break in a line of trees, he caught sight of the tower and chancel window of the little church. In an instant he had a vision of early summer mornings—dewy, perfumed, silent, save for the birds, and all the soft stir of rural birth and growth, of a chancel fragrant with many flowers, of a distant church with scattered figures, of the kneeling form of his wife close beside him, himself bending over her, the sacrament of the Lord's death in his hand. The emotion, the intensity, the absolute self-surrender of innumerable such moments in the past—moments of a common faith, a common

---

4   In *The Decline and Fall of the Roman Empire*, 1.3 and the introduction to *The Provinces of the Roman Empire*, respectively.

5   Variant on *corruptio optimi pessima*, lit. "corruption of the best is the worst [kind]."

6   Revelation 21.2.

self-abasement—came flooding back upon him. With a movement of joy and penitence he threw himself at the feet of Catherine's Master and his own: *'Fix there thy resting-place, my soul!'*

CHAPTER XX

Catherine's later convalescence dwelt in her mind in after years as a time of peculiar softness and peace. Her baby-girl throve; Robert had driven the squire and Henslowe out of his mind, and was all eagerness as to certain negotiations with a famous naturalist for a lecture at the village club. At Mile End, as though to put the rector in the wrong, serious illness had for the time disappeared; and Mrs. Leyburn's mild chatter, as she gently poked about the house and garden, went out in Catherine's pony-carriage, inspected Catherine's stores, and hovered over Catherine's babe, had a constantly cheering effect on the still languid mother. Like all theorists, especially those at second-hand, Mrs. Leyburn's maxims had been very much routed by the event. The babe had ailments she did not understand, or it developed likes and dislikes she had forgotten existed in babies, and Mrs. Leyburn was nonplussed. She would sit with it on her lap, anxiously studying its peculiarities. She was sure it squinted, that its back was weaker than other babies, that it cried more than hers had ever done. She loved to be plaintive; it would have seemed to her unladylike to be too cheerful, even over a first grandchild.

Agnes meanwhile made herself practically useful, as was her way, and she did almost more than anybody to beguile Catherine's recovery by her hours of Long Whindale chat. She had no passionate feeling about the place and the people as Catherine had, but she was easily content, and she had a good wholesome feminine curiosity as to the courtings and weddings and buryings of the human beings about her. So she would sit and chat, working the while with the quickest, neatest of fingers, till Catherine knew as much about Jenny Tyson's Whinborough lover, and Farmer Tredall's troubles with his son, and the way in which that odious woman Molly Redgold bullied her little consumptive husband, as Agnes knew, which was saying a good deal.

About themselves Agnes was frankness itself.

'Since you went,' she would say with a shrug, 'I keep the coach steady, perhaps, but Rose drives, and we shall have to go where she takes us. By the way, Cathie, what have you been doing to her here? She is not a bit like herself. I don't generally mind being snubbed. It amuses her and doesn't hurt me; and, of course, I know I am meant to be her foil. But, really, sometimes she is too bad even for me.'

Catherine sighed, but held her peace. Like all strong persons, she kept things very much to herself. It only made vexations more real to talk about them. But she and Agnes discussed the winter and Berlin.

'You had better let her go,' said Agnes significantly; 'she will go anyhow.'

A few days afterwards Catherine, opening the drawing-room door unexpectedly, came upon Rose sitting idly at the piano, her hands resting on the keys, and her great gray eyes straining out of her white face with an expression which sent the sister's heart into her shoes.

'How you steal about, Catherine!' cried the player, getting up and shutting the piano. 'I declare you are just like Millais's Gray Lady in that ghostly gown.'[7]

Catherine came swiftly across the floor. She had just left her child, and the sweet dignity of motherhood was in her step, her look. She came and threw her arms round the girl.

'Rose, dear, I have settled it all with mamma. The money can be managed, and you shall go to Berlin for the winter when you like.'

She drew herself back a little, still with her arms round Rose's waist, and looked at her smiling, to see how she took it.

Rose had a strange movement of irritation. She drew herself out of Catherine's grasp.

'I don't know that I had settled on Berlin,' she said coldly. 'Very possibly Leipsic would be better.'

Catherine's face fell.

'Whichever you like, dear. I have been thinking about it ever since that day you spoke of it—you remember—and now I have talked it over with mamma. If she can't manage all the expense we will help. Oh, Rose,' and she came nearer again, timidly, her eyes melting, 'I know we haven't understood each other. I have been ignorant, I think, and narrow. But I meant it for the best, dear—I did——'

Her voice failed her, but in her look there seemed to be written the history of all the prayers and yearnings of her youth over the pretty wayward child who had been her joy and torment. Rose could not but meet that look—its nobleness, its humble surrender.

Suddenly two large tears rolled down her cheeks. She dashed them away impatiently.

'I am not a bit well,' she said, as though in irritable excuse both to herself

---

7   Possibly *A Somnambulist* (1871), which fits Ward's description here better than any of the portraits of his wife, Effie Gray (as suggested by Clyde de L. Ryals [626]).

and Catherine. 'I believe I have had a headache for a fortnight.'

And then she put her arms down on a table near and hid her face upon them. She was one bundle of jarring nerves—sore, poor passionate child, that she was betraying herself; sorer still that, as she told herself, Catherine was sending her to Berlin as a consolation. When girls have love-troubles the first thing their elders do is to look for a diversion. She felt sick and humiliated. Catherine had been talking her over with the family, she supposed.

Meanwhile Catherine stood by her tenderly, stroking her hair and saying soothing things.

'I am sure you will be happy at Berlin, Rose. And you mustn't leave me out of your life, dear, though I am so stupid and unmusical. You must write to me about all you do. We must begin a new time. Oh, I feel so guilty sometimes,' she went on, falling into a low intensity of voice that startled Rose, and made her look hurriedly up. 'I fought against your music, I suppose, because I thought it was devouring you—leaving no room for—for religion—for God. I was jealous of it for Christ's sake. And all the time I was blundering! Oh, Rose,' and she sank on her knees beside the chair, resting her head against the girl's shoulder, 'papa charged me to make you love God, and I torture myself with thinking that, instead, it has been my doing, my foolish clumsy doing, that you have come to think religion dull and hard. Oh, my darling, if I could make amends—if I could get you not to love your art less but to love it in God! Christ is the first reality; all things else are real and lovely in Him. Oh, I have been frightening you away from Him! I ought to have drawn you near. I have been so—so silent, so shut up, I have never tried to make you feel what it was kept *me* at His feet! Oh, Rose, darling, you think the world real, and pleasure and enjoyment real. But if I could have made you see and know the things I have seen up in the mountains—among the poor, the dying—you would have *felt* Him saving, redeeming, interceding, as I did. Oh, then you *must*, you *would* have known that Christ only is real, that our joys can only truly exist in Him. I should have been more open—more faithful—more humble.'

She paused with a long quivering sigh. Rose suddenly lifted herself, and they fell into each other's arms.

Rose, shaken and excited, thought, of course, of that night at Burwood, when she had won leave to go to Manchester. This scene was the sequel to that—the next stage in one and the same process. Her feeling was much the same as that of the naturalist who comes close to any of the hidden operations of life. She had come near to Catherine's spirit in the growing. Beside that sweet expansion, how poor and feverish and earth-stained the poor child felt herself!

But there were many currents in Rose—many things striving for the mastery. She kissed Catherine once or twice, then she drew herself back suddenly, looking into the other's face. A great wave of feeling rushed up and broke.

'Catherine, could you ever have married a man that did not believe in Christ?'

She flung the question out—a kind of morbid curiosity, a wild wish to find an outlet of some sort for things pent up in her, driving her on.

Catherine started. But she met Rose's half-frowning eyes steadily.

'Never, Rose! To me it would not be marriage.'

The child's face lost its softness. She drew one hand away.

'What have we to do with it?' she cried. 'Each one for himself.'

'But marriage makes two one,' said Catherine, pale, but with a firm clearness. 'And if husband and wife are only one in body and estate, not one in soul, why, who that believes in the soul would accept such a bond, endure such a miserable second best?'

She rose. But though her voice had recovered all its energy, her attitude, her look was still tenderness, still yearning itself.

'Religion does not fill up the soul,' said Rose slowly. Then she added carelessly, a passionate red flying into her cheek against her will, 'However, I cannot imagine any question that interests me personally less. I was curious what you would say.'

And she too got up, drawing her hand lightly along the keyboard of the piano. Her pose had a kind of defiance in it; her knit brows forbade Catherine to ask questions. Catherine stood irresolute. Should she throw herself on her sister, imploring her to speak, opening her own heart on the subject of this wild unhappy fancy for a man who would never think again of the child he had played with?

But the North-country dread of words, of speech that only defines and magnifies, prevailed. Let there be no words, but let her love and watch.

So, after a moment's pause, she began in a different tone upon the inquiries she had been making, the arrangements that would be wanted for this musical winter. Rose was almost listless at first. A stranger would have thought she was being persuaded into something against her will. But she could not keep it up. The natural instinct reasserted itself, and she was soon planning and deciding as sharply, and with as much young omniscience, as usual.

By the evening it was settled. Mrs. Leyburn, much bewildered, asked Catherine doubtfully, the last thing at night, whether she wanted Rose to be a professional. Catherine exclaimed.

'But, my dear,' said the widow, staring pensively into her bedroom fire, 'what's she to do with all this music?' Then after a second she added half severely: 'I don't believe her father would have liked it; I don't, indeed, Catherine!'

Poor Catherine smiled and sighed in the background, but made no reply.

'However, she never looks so pretty as when she's playing the violin— never!' said Mrs. Leyburn presently in the distance, with a long breath of satisfaction. 'She's got such a lovely hand and arm, Catherine! They're prettier than mine, and even your father used to notice mine.'

'*Even.*' The word had a little sound of bitterness. In spite of all his love, had the gentle puzzle-headed woman found her unearthly husband often very hard to live with?

Rose meanwhile was sitting up in bed, with her hands round her knees, dreaming. So she had got her heart's desire! There did not seem to be much joy in the getting, but that was the way of things, one was told. She knew she should hate the Germans—great, bouncing, over-fed, sentimental creatures!

Then her thoughts ran into the future. After six months—yes, by April— she would be home, and Agnes and her mother could meet her in London.

London. Ah, it was London she was thinking of all the time, not Berlin! She could not stay in the present; or rather the Rose of the present went straining to the Rose of the future, asking to be righted, to be avenged.

'I will learn—I will learn fast—many things besides music!' she said to herself feverishly. 'By April I shall be *much* cleverer. Oh, *then* I won't be a fool so easily. We shall be sure to meet, of course. But he shall find out that it was only a *child*, only a silly soft-hearted baby he played with down here. I shan't care for him in the least, of course not, not after six months. I don't *mean* to. And I will make him know it—oh, I will, though he is so wise, and so much older, and mounts on such stilts when he pleases!'

So once more Rose flung her defiance at fate. But when Catherine came along the passage an hour later she heard low sounds from Rose's room, which ceased abruptly as her step drew near. The elder sister paused; her eyes filled with tears; her hand closed indignantly. Then she came closer, all but went in, thought better of it, and moved away. If there is any truth in brain-waves, Langham should have slept restlessly that night.

Ten days later an escort had been found, all preparations had been made, and Rose was gone.

Mrs. Leyburn and Agnes lingered a while, and then they too departed under an engagement to come back after Christmas for a long stay, that Mrs. Leyburn might cheat the northern spring a little.

So husband and wife were alone again. How they relished their solitude! Catherine took up many threads of work which her months of comparative weakness had forced her to let drop. She taught vigorously in the school; in the afternoons, so far as her child would let her, she carried her tender presence and her practical knowledge of nursing to the sick and feeble; and on two evenings in the week she and Robert threw open a little room there was on the ground-floor between the study and the dining-room to the women and girls of the village, as a sort of drawing-room. Hard-worked mothers would come, who had put their fretful babes to sleep, and given their lords to eat, and had just energy left, while the eldest daughter watched, and the men were at the club or the 'Blue Boar,' to put on a clean apron and climb the short hill to the rectory. Once there, there was nothing to think of for an hour but the bright room, Catherine's kind face, the rector's jokes, and the illustrated papers or the photographs that were spread out for them to look at if they would. The girls learned to come, because Catherine could teach them a simple dressmaking, and was clever in catching stray persons to set them singing; and because Mr. Elsmere read exciting stories, and because nothing any one of them ever told Mrs. Elsmere was forgotten by her, or failed to interest her. Any of her social equals of the neighbourhood would have hardly recognised the reserved and stately Catherine on these occasions. Here she felt herself at home, at ease. She would never, indeed, have Robert's pliancy, his quick divination, and for some time after her transplanting the North-country woman had found it very difficult to suit herself to a new shade of local character. But she was learning from Robert every day; she watched him among the poor, recognising all his gifts with a humble intensity of admiring love, which said little but treasured everything, and for herself her inward happiness and peace shone through her quiet ways, making her the mother and the friend of all about her.

As for Robert, he, of course, was living at high pressure all round. Outside his sermons and his school, his Natural History Club had perhaps most of his heart, and the passion for science, little continuous work as he was able to give it, grew on him more and more. He kept up as best he could, working with one hand, so to speak, when he could not spare two, and in his long rambles over moor and hill, gathering in with his quick eye a harvest of local fact wherewith to feed their knowledge and his own.

The mornings he always spent at work among his books, the afternoons in endless tramps over the parish, sometimes alone, sometimes with Catherine; and in the evenings, if Catherine was 'at home,' twice a week to womankind, he had his nights when his study became the haunt and prey of half the boys in the place, who were free of everything, as soon as he had taught them to respect his books, and not to taste his medicines; other nights when he was lecturing or story-telling in the club or in some outlying hamlet; or others again, when with Catherine beside him he would sit trying to think some of that religious passion which burned in both their hearts, into clear words or striking illustrations for his sermons.

Then his choir was much upon his mind. He knew nothing about music, nor did Catherine; their efforts made Rose laugh irreverently when she got their letters at Berlin. But Robert believed in a choir chiefly as an excellent social and centralising instrument. There had been none in Mr. Preston's day. He was determined to have one, and a good one, and by sheer energy he succeeded, delighting in his boyish way over the opposition some of his novelties excited among the older and more stiff-backed inhabitants.

'Let them talk,' he would say brightly to Catherine. 'They will come round; and talk is good. Anything to make them think, to stir the pool!'

Of course that old problem of the agricultural labourer weighed upon him—his grievances, his wants. He went about pondering the English land system, more than half inclined one day to sink part of his capital in a peasant-proprietor experiment,[8] and ingulfed the next in all the moral and economical objections to the French system.[9] Land for allotments, at any rate, he had set his heart on. But in this direction, as in many others, the way was barred. All the land in the parish was the squire's, and not one inch of the squire's land would Henslowe let young Elsmere have anything to do with if he knew it. He would neither repair nor enlarge the Workmen's Institute; and he had a way of forgetting the squire's customary subscriptions to parochial objects, always paid through him, which gave him much food for chuckling whenever he passed Elsmere in the country lanes. The man's coarse insolence and mean hatred made themselves felt at every turn, besmirching and embittering.

Still it was very true that neither Henslowe nor the squire could do Robert much harm. His hold on the parish was visibly strengthening; his sermons were not only filling the church with his own parishioners, but attracting hearers from the districts round Murewell, so that even on these winter Sundays there was almost always a sprinkling of strange faces among the congregation; and his position in the county and diocese was becoming every month more honourable and important. The gentry about showed

---

8   In peasant-proprietorship, farmers own their own land instead of paying rent to a landlord. France's example in this respect was regularly cited in the contemporary economic literature.

9   "moral and economical objections": incorrect use of singular and a comma corrected as per *SE(1)* and *W.*

them much kindness, and would have shown them much hospitality if they had been allowed. But though Robert had nothing of the ascetic about him, and liked the society of his equals as much as most good-tempered and vivacious people do, he and Catherine decided that for the present they had no time to spare for visits and county society. Still, of course, there were many occasions on which the routine of their life brought them across their neighbours, and it began to be pretty widely recognised that Elsmere was a young fellow of unusual promise and intelligence, that his wife too was remarkable, and that between them they were likely to raise the standard of clerical effort considerably in their part of Surrey.

All the factors of this life—his work, his influence, his recovered health, the lavish beauty of the country, Elsmere enjoyed with all his heart. But at the root of all there lay what gave value and savour to everything else—that exquisite home-life of theirs, that tender, triple bond of husband, wife, and child.

Catherine, coming home tired from teaching or visiting, would find her step quickening as she reached the gate of the rectory, and the sense of delicious possession waking up in her, which is one of the first fruits of motherhood. There, at the window, between the lamplight behind and the winter dusk outside, would be the child in its nurse's arms, little wondering, motiveless smiles passing over the tiny puckered face that was so oddly like Robert already. And afterwards, in the fire-lit nursery, with the bath in front of the high fender, and all the necessaries of baby life beside it, she would go through those functions which mothers love and linger over, let the kicking dimpled creature principally concerned protest as it may against the over-refinements of civilisation. Then, when the little restless voice was stilled, and the cradle left silent in the darkened room, there would come the short watching for Robert, his voice, his kiss, their simple meal together, a moment of rest, of laughter and chat, before some fresh effort claimed them. Every now and then—white-letter days—there would drop on them a long evening together. Then out would come one or the few books—Dante or Virgil or Milton—which had entered into the fibre of Catherine's strong nature. The two heads would draw close over them, or Robert would take some thought of hers as a text, and spout away from the hearthrug, watching all the while for her smile, her look of assent. Sometimes, late at night, when there was a sermon on his mind, he would dive into his pocket for his Greek Testament and make her read, partly for the sake of teaching her—for she knew some Greek and longed to know more—but mostly that he might get from her some of that garnered wealth of spiritual experience which he adored in her. They would go from verse to verse, from thought to thought, till suddenly perhaps the tide of feeling would rise, and while the wind swept round the house, and the owls hooted in the elms, they would sit hand in hand, lost in love and faith,— Christ near them—Eternity, warm with God, enwrapping them.

So much for the man of action, the husband, the philanthropist. In reality, great as was the moral energy of this period of Elsmere's life, the dominant distinguishing note of it was not moral but intellectual.

In matters of conduct he was but developing habits and tendencies already strongly present in him; in matters of thinking, with every month of this winter he was becoming conscious of fresh forces, fresh hunger, fresh horizons.

'*One half of your day be the king of your world,*' Mr. Grey had said to him; '*the other half be the slave of something which will take you out of your world,* into the general life, the life of thought, of man as a whole, of the universe.'

The counsel, as we have seen, had struck root and flowered into action. So many men of Elsmere's type give themselves up once and for all as they become mature to the life of doing and feeling, practically excluding the life of thought. It was Henry Grey's influence in all probability, perhaps, too, the training of an earlier Langham, that saved for Elsmere the life of thought.

The form taken by this training of his own mind he had been thus encouraged not to abandon, was, as we know, the study of history. He had well mapped out before him that book on the origins of France which he had described to Langham. It was to take him years, of course, and meanwhile, in his first enthusiasm, he was like a child, revelling in the treasure of work that lay before him. As he had told Langham, he had just got below the surface of a great subject and was beginning to dig into the roots of it. Hitherto he had been under the guidance of men of his own day, of the nineteenth century historian, who refashions the past on the lines of his own mind, who gives it rationality, coherence, and, as it were, modernness, so that the main impression he produces on us, so long as we look at that past through him only, is on the whole an impression of *continuity*, of *resemblance*.

Whereas, on the contrary, the first impression left on a man by the attempt to plunge into the materials of history for himself is almost always an extraordinarily sharp impression of *difference*, of *contrast*. Ultimately, of course, he sees that these men and women whose letters and biographies, whose creeds and general conceptions he is investigating, are in truth his ancestors, bone of his bone, flesh of his flesh. But at first the student who goes back, say, in the history of Europe, behind the Renaissance or behind the Crusades into the actual deposits of the past, is often struck with a kind of *vertige*.[10] The men and women whom he has dragged forth into the light of his own mind are to him like some strange puppet-show. They are called by names he knows—kings, bishops, judges, poets, priests, men of letters— but what a gulf between him and them! What motives, what beliefs, what embryonic processes of thought and morals, what bizarre combinations of ignorance and knowledge, of the highest sanctity with the lowest credulity or falsehood; what extraordinary prepossessions, born with a man and tainting his whole ways of seeing and thinking from childhood to the grave! Amid all the intellectual dislocation of the spectacle, indeed, he perceives certain Greeks and certain Latins who represent a forward strain, who belong as it seems to a world of their own, a world ahead of them. To them he stretches out his hand: '*You*,' he says to them, 'though your priests spoke to you not of Christ, but of Zeus and Artemis, *you* are really my kindred!' But intellectually they stand alone. Around them, after them, for long ages the world 'spake as a child, felt as a child, understood as a child.'[11]

Then he sees what it is makes the difference, digs the gulf. '*Science*,' the mind cries, '*ordered knowledge*.' And so for the first time the modern recognises what the accumulations of his forefathers have done for him. He takes the torch which man has been so long and patiently fashioning to his hand, and turns it on the past, and at every step the sight grows stranger, and yet more moving, more pathetic. The darkness into which he penetrates does but make him grasp his own guiding light the more closely. And yet, bit by bit, it has been prepared for him by these groping half conscious generations, and the scrutiny which began in repulsion and laughter ends in a marvelling gratitude.

But the repulsion and the laughter come first, and during this winter of work Elsmere felt them both very strongly. He would sit in the morning buried among the records of decaying Rome and emerging France, surrounded by Chronicles, by Church Councils, by lives of the Saints, by primitive systems of law, pushing his imaginative impetuous way through them. Sometimes Catherine would be there, and he would pour out on her something of what was in his own mind.

One day he was deep in the life of a certain saint.[12] The saint had been bishop of a diocese in Southern France. His biographer was his successor

---

10 *Vertige*: vertigo.

11 1 Corinthians 13.11.

12 The anecdote that follows is Ward's own invention; see R. J. Schork, "Victorian Hagiography: A Pattern of Allusions in *Robert Elsmere* and *Helbeck of Bannisdale*," *Studies in the Novel* 21.3 (1989): 301.

in the see, a man of high political importance in the Burgundian state, renowned besides for sanctity and learning. Only some twenty years separated
the biography, at the latest, from the death of its subject. It contained some
curious material for social history, and Robert was reading it with avidity. But
it was, of course, a tissue of marvels. The young bishop had practised every
virtue known to the time, and wrought every conceivable miracle, and the
miracles were better told than usual, with more ingenuity, more imagination.
Perhaps on that account they struck the reader's sense more sharply.

'And the saint said to the sorcerers and to the practisers of unholy arts,
that they should do those evil things no more, for he had bound the spirits of
whom they were wont to inquire, and they would get no further answers to
their incantations. Then those stiff-necked sons of the devil fell upon the man
of God, scourged him sore, and threatened him with death, if he would not
instantly loose those spirits he had bound. And seeing he could prevail nothing, and being, moreover, admonished by God so to do, he permitted them to
work their own damnation. For he called for a parchment and wrote upon it,
"*Ambrose unto Satan—Enter!*" Then was the spell loosed, the spirits returned,
the sorcerers inquired as they were accustomed, and received answers. But in
a short space of time every one of them perished miserably and was delivered
unto his natural lord Satanas, whereunto he belonged.'

Robert made a hasty exclamation, and turning to Catherine, who was
working beside him, read the passage to her, with a few words as to the book
and its author.

Catherine's work dropped a moment on to her knee.

'What extraordinary superstition!' she said, startled. 'A bishop, Robert,
and an educated man?'

Robert nodded.

'But it is the whole habit of mind,' he said half to himself, staring into
the fire, 'that is so astounding. No one escapes it. The whole age really is
non-sane.'

'I suppose the devout Catholic would believe that?'

'I am not sure,' said Robert dreamily, and remained sunk in thought for
long after, while Catherine worked, and pondered a Christmas entertainment
for her girls.

Perhaps it was his scientific work, fragmentary as it was, that was really
quickening and sharpening these historical impressions of his. Evolution—
once a mere germ in the mind—was beginning to press, to encroach, to intermeddle with the mind's other furniture.

And the comparative instinct—that tool, *par excellence*, of modern science—was at last fully awake, was growing fast, taking hold, now here, now there.

'It is tolerably clear to me,' he said to himself suddenly one winter afternoon, as he was trudging home alone from Mile End, 'that some day or other I must set to work to bring a little order into one's notions of the Old Testament. At present they are just a chaos!'

He walked on a while, struggling with the rainstorm which had overtaken him, till again the mind's quick life took voice.

'But what matter? God in the beginning—God in the prophets—in Israel's best life—God in Christ! How are any theories about the Pentateuch to touch that?'

And into the clear eyes, the young face aglow with wind and rain, there leapt a light, a softness indescribable.

But the vivider and the keener grew this new mental life of Elsmere's, the more constant became his sense of soreness as to that foolish and motiveless quarrel which divided him from the squire. Naturally he was for ever being harassed and pulled up in his work by the mere loss of the Murewell library. To have such a collection so close, and to be cut off from it, was a state of things no student could help feeling severely. But it was much more than that: it was the man he hankered after; the man who was a master where he was a beginner; the man who had given his life to learning, and was carrying all his vast accumulations sombrely to the grave, unused, untransmitted.

'He might have given me his knowledge,' thought Elsmere sadly, 'and I—I—would have been a son to him. Why is life so perverse?'

Meanwhile he was as much cut off from the great house and its master as though both had been surrounded by the thorn hedge of fairy tale. The Hall had its visitors during these winter months, but the Elsmeres saw nothing of them. Robert gulped down a natural sigh when one Saturday evening, as he passed the Hall gates, he saw driving through them the chief of English science side by side with the most accomplished of English critics.

'"There are good times in the world and I ain't in 'em!"' he said to himself with a laugh and a shrug as he turned up the lane to the rectory, and then, boy-like, was ashamed of himself, and greeted Catherine with all the tenderer greeting.[13]

Only on two occasions during three months could he be sure of having

---

13 This quotation may be a loose recollection of '"Sech lots of good times in the world, and I ain't in 'em!,"' from Adeline Dutton T. Whitney, *Faith Gartney's Girlhood*, in *Faith Gartney's Girlhood and A Summer in Leslie Goldthwaite's Life* (London: Ward, Lock, and Co., 1872), 22.

seen the squire. Both were in the twilight, when, as the neighbourhood declared, Mr. Wendover always walked, and both made a sharp impression on
the rector's nerves. In the heart of one of the loneliest commons of the parish
Robert, swinging along one November evening through the scattered furze
bushes, growing ghostly in the darkness, was suddenly conscious of a cloaked
figure with slouching shoulders and head bent forward coming towards him.
It passed without recognition of any kind, and for an instant Robert caught
the long sharpened features and haughty eyes of the squire.

At another time Robert was walking, far from home, along a bit of level
road. The pools in the ruts were just filmed with frost, and gleamed under
the sunset; the winter dusk was clear and chill. A horseman turned into the
road from a side lane. It was the squire again, alone. The sharp sound of the
approaching hoofs stirred Robert's pulse, and as they passed each other the
rector raised his hat. He thought his greeting was acknowledged, but could
not be quite sure. From the shelter of a group of trees he stood a moment and
looked after the retreating figure. It and the horse showed dark against a wide
sky barred by stormy reds and purples. The wind whistled through the withered oaks; the long road with its lines of glimmering pools seemed to stretch
endlessly into the sunset; and with every minute the night strode on. Age and
loneliness could have found no fitter setting. A shiver ran through Elsmere as
he stepped forward.

Undoubtedly the quarrel, helped by his work, and the perpetual presence
of that beautiful house commanding the whole country round it from its plateau above the river, kept Elsmere specially in mind of the squire. As before
their first meeting, and in spite of it, he became more and more imaginatively
preoccupied with him. One of the signs of it was a strong desire to read
the squire's two famous books: one, *The Idols of the Market-place*, an attack
on English beliefs; the other, *Essays on English Culture*, an attack on English
ideals of education. He had never come across them as it happened, and
perhaps Newcome's denunciation had some effect in inducing him for a time
to refrain from reading them. But in December he ordered them and waited
their coming with impatience. He said nothing of the order to Catherine;
somehow there were by now two or three portions of his work, two or three
branches of his thought, which had fallen out of their common discussion.
After all she was not literary, and with all their oneness of soul there could not
be an *identity* of interests or pursuits.

The books arrived in the morning. (Oh, how dismally well, with what a
tightening of the heart, did Robert always remember that day in after years!)
He was much too busy to look at them, and went off to a meeting. In the

evening, coming home late from his night-school, he found Catherine tired, sent her to bed, and went himself into his study to put together some notes for a cottage lecture he was to give the following day. The packet of books, unopened, lay on his writing-table. He took off the wrapper, and in his eager way fell to reading the first he touched.

It was the first volume of *The Idols of the Market-place*.

Ten or twelve years before, Mr. Wendover had launched this book into a startled and protesting England. It had been the fruit of his first renewal of contact with English life and English ideas after his return from Berlin. Fresh from the speculative ferment of Germany and the far profaner scepticism of France, he had returned to a society where the first chapter of Genesis and the theory of verbal inspiration were still regarded as valid and important counters on the board of thought. The result had been this book. In it each stronghold of English popular religion had been assailed in turn, at a time when English orthodoxy was a far more formidable thing than it is now.

The Pentateuch, the Prophets, the Gospels, St. Paul, Tradition, the Fathers, Protestantism and Justification by Faith, the Eighteenth Century, the Broad Church Movement, Anglican Theology—the squire had his say about them all. And while the coolness and frankness of the method sent a shock of indignation and horror through the religious public, the subtle and caustic style, and the epigrams with which the book was strewn, forced both the religious and irreligious public to read, whether they would or no. A storm of controversy rose round the volumes, and some of the keenest observers of English life had said at the time, and maintained since, that the publication of the book had made or marked an epoch.

Robert had lit on those pages in the Essay on the Gospels where the squire fell to analysing the evidence for the Resurrection, following up his analysis by an attempt at reconstructing the conditions out of which the belief in 'the legend' arose. Robert began to read vaguely at first, then to hurry on through page after page, still standing, seized at once by the bizarre power of the style, the audacity and range of the treatment.

Not a sound in the house. Outside, the tossing moaning December night; inside, the faintly crackling fire, the standing figure. Suddenly it was to Robert as though a cruel torturing hand were laid upon his inmost being. His breath failed him; the book slipped out of his grasp; he sank down upon his chair, his head in his hands. Oh, what a desolate intolerable moment! Over the young idealist soul there swept a dry destroying whirlwind of thought. Elements gathered from all sources—from his own historical work, from the squire's book, from the secret half-conscious recesses of the mind—entered into it, and as it passed it seemed to scorch the heart.

He stayed bowed there a while, then he roused himself with a half-groan, and hastily extinguishing his lamp he groped his way upstairs to his wife's room. Catherine lay asleep. The child, lost among its white coverings, slept too; there was a dim light over the bed, the books, the pictures. Beside his wife's pillow was a table on which there lay open her little Testament and the *Imitation* her father had given her. Elsmere sank down beside her, appalled by the contrast between this soft religious peace and that black agony of doubt which still overshadowed him. He knelt there, restraining his breath lest it should wake her, wrestling piteously with himself, crying for pardon, for faith, feeling himself utterly unworthy to touch even the dear hand that lay so near him. But gradually the traditional forces of his life reasserted themselves. The horror lifted. Prayer brought comfort and a passionate healing self-abasement. 'Master, forgive—defend—purify,' cried the aching heart. '*There is none other that fighteth for us, but only Thou, O God!*'[14]

He did not open the book again. Next morning he put it back into his shelves. If there were any Christian who could affront such an antagonist with a light heart, he felt with a shudder of memory it was not he.

'I have neither learning nor experience enough—yet,' he said to himself slowly as he moved away, 'of course it can be met, but *I* must grow; must think—first.'

And of that night's wrestle he said not a word to any living soul. He did penance for it in the tenderest, most secret ways, but he shrank in misery from the thought of revealing it even to Catherine.

CHAPTER XXI

Meanwhile the poor poisoned folk at Mile End lived and apparently throve, in defiance of all the laws of the universe. Robert, as soon as he found that radical measures were for the time hopeless, had applied himself with redoubled energy to making the people use such palliatives as were within their reach, and had preached boiled water and the removal of filth till, as he declared to Catherine, his dreams were one long sanitary nightmare. But he was not confiding enough to believe that the people paid much heed, and he hoped more from a dry hard winter than from any exertion either of his or theirs.

But, alas! with the end of November a season of furious rain set in.

---

14 One of the responses in the Book of Common Prayer.

Then Robert began to watch Mile End with anxiety, for so far every outbreak of illness there had followed upon unusual damp. But the rains passed, leaving behind them no worse results than the usual winter crop of lung ailments and rheumatism, and he breathed again.

Christmas came and went, and with the end of December the wet weather returned. Day after day rolling masses of south-west cloud came up from the Atlantic and wrapped the whole country in rain, which reminded Catherine of her Westmoreland rain more than any she had yet seen in the South. Robert accused her of liking it for that reason, but she shook her head with a sigh, declaring that it was 'nothing without the becks.'

One afternoon she was shutting the door of the school behind her, and stepping out on the road skirting the green—the bedabbled wintry green—when she saw Robert emerging from the Mile End lane. She crossed over to him, wondering as she neared him that he seemed to take no notice of her. He was striding along, his wideawake over his eyes, and so absorbed that she had almost touched him before he saw her.

'Darling, is that you? Don't stop me, I am going to take the pony-carriage in for Meyrick. I have just come back from that accursed place; three cases of diphtheria in one house, Sharland's wife—and two others down with fever.'

She made a horrified exclamation.

'It will spread,' he said gloomily, 'I know it will. I never saw the children look such a ghastly crew before. Well, I must go for Meyrick and a nurse, and we must isolate and make a fight for it.'

In a few days the diphtheria epidemic in the hamlet had reached terrible proportions. There had been one death, others were expected, and soon Robert in his brief hours at home could find no relief in anything, so heavy was the oppression of the day's memories. At first Catherine for the child's sake kept away; but the little Mary was weaned, had a good Scotch nurse, was in every way thriving, and after a day or two Catherine's craving to help, to be with Robert in his trouble, was too strong to be withstood. But she dared not go backwards and forwards between her baby and the diphtheritic children. So she bethought herself of Mrs. Elsmere's servant, old Martha, who was still inhabiting Mrs. Elsmere's cottage till a tenant could be found for it, and doing good service meanwhile as an occasional parish nurse. The baby and its nurse went over to the cottage. Catherine carried the child there, wrapped close in maternal arms, and leaving her on old Martha's lap, went back to Robert.

Then she and he devoted themselves to a hand-to-hand fight with the epidemic. At the climax of it there were about twenty children down with it in different stages, and seven cases of fever. They had two hospital nurses; one of the better cottages, turned into a sanatorium, accommodated the worst cases under the nurses, and Robert and Catherine, directed by them and the doctors, took the responsibility of the rest, he helping to nurse the boys and she the girls. Of the fever cases Sharland's wife was the worst. A feeble creature at all times, it seemed almost impossible she could weather through. But day after day passed, and by dint of incessant nursing she still lived. A youth of twenty, the main support of a mother and five or six younger children, was also desperately ill. Robert hardly ever had him out of his thoughts, and the boy's dog-like affection for the rector, struggling with his deathly weakness, was like a perpetual exemplification of Ahriman and Ormuzd—the power of life struggling with the power of death.[15]

It was a fierce fight. Presently it seemed to the husband and wife as though the few daily hours spent at the rectory were mere halts between successive acts of battle with the plague-fiend—a more real and grim Grendel of the Marshes—for the lives of children.[16] Catherine could always sleep in these intervals, quietly and dreamlessly; Robert very soon could only sleep by the help of some prescription of old Meyrick's. On all occasions of strain since his boyhood there had been signs in him of a certain lack of constitutional hardness which his mother knew very well, but which his wife was only just beginning to recognise. However, he laughed to scorn any attempt to restrain his constant goings and comings, or those hours of night-nursing, in which, as the hospital nurses were the first to admit, no one was so successful as the rector. And when he stood up on Sundays to preach in Murewell Church, the worn and spiritual look of the man, and the knowledge warm at each heart of those before him of how the rector not only talked but lived, carried every word home.

This strain upon all the moral and physical forces, however, strangely enough, came to Robert as a kind of relief. It broke through a tension of brain which of late had become an oppression. And for both him and Catherine these dark times had moments of intensest joy, points of white light illuminating heaven and earth. There were cloudy nights—wet, stormy January nights—when sometimes it happened to them to come back both together from the hamlet, Robert carrying a lantern, Catherine clothed in waterproof from head to foot, walking beside him, the rays flashing now on her face, now on the wooded sides of the lane, while the wind howled through the dark vault of branches overhead. And then, as they talked or were silent, suddenly

---

15 The opposing principles of Good and Evil in Zoroastrianism.
16 A monster from the poem *Beowulf*, slain by the eponymous hero.

a sense of the intense blessedness of this comradeship of theirs would rise like a flood in the man's heart, and he would fling his free arm round her, forcing her to stand a moment in the January night and storm while he said to her words of passionate gratitude, of faith in an immortal union reaching beyond change or death, lost in a kiss which was a sacrament. Then there were the moments when they saw their child, held high in Martha's arms at the window, and leaping towards her mother; the moments when one pallid sickly being after another was pronounced out of danger; and by the help of them the weeks passed away.

Nor were they left without help from outside. Lady Helen Varley no sooner heard the news than she hurried over. Robert, on his way one morning from one cottage to another, saw her pony-carriage in the lane. He hastened up to her before she could dismount.

'No, Lady Helen, you mustn't come here,' he said to her peremptorily, as she held out her hand.

'Oh, Mr. Elsmere, let me. My boy is in town with his grandmother. Let me just go through, at any rate, and see what I can send you.'

Robert shook his head, smiling. A common friend of theirs and hers had once described this little lady to Elsmere by a French sentence which originally applied to the Duchesse de Choiseul. 'Une charmante petite fée sortie d'un œuf enchanté!'—so it ran.[17] Certainly, as Elsmere looked down upon her now, fresh from those squalid death-stricken hovels behind him, he was brought more abruptly than ever upon the contrasts of life. Lady Helen wore a green velvet and fur mantle, in the production of which even Worth had felt some pride; a little green velvet bonnet perched on her fair hair; one tiny hand, ungloved, seemed ablaze with diamonds; there were opals and diamonds somewhere at her throat, gleaming among her sables. But she wore her jewels as carelessly as she wore her high birth, her quaint irregular prettiness, or the one or two brilliant gifts which made her sought after wherever she went. She loved her opals as she loved all bright things; if it pleased her to wear them in the morning, she wore them; and in five minutes she was capable of making the sourest puritan forget to frown on her and them. To Robert she always seemed the quintessence of breeding, of aristocracy at their best. All her freaks, her sallies, her absurdities even, were graceful. At her freest and gayest there were things in her—restraints, reticences, perceptions—which implied behind her generations of rich, happy, important people, with ample leisure to cultivate all the more delicate niceties of social feeling and relation.

17 Louise Honorine Crozat du Châtel (1737–1801), who was arrested during the Terror; "a charming little fairy born out of an enchanted egg."

Robert was often struck by the curious differences between her and Rose. Rose was far the handsomer; she was at least as clever; and she had a strong imperious will where Lady Helen had only impulses and sympathies and *engouements*.[18] But Rose belonged to the class which struggles, where each individual depends on himself and knows it. Lady Helen had never struggled for anything—all the best things of the world were hers so easily that she hardly gave them a thought; or rather, what she had gathered without pain she held so lightly, she dispensed so lavishly, that men's eyes followed her, fluttering through life, with much the same feeling as was struck from Clough's radical hero by the peerless Lady Maria—

> 'Live, be lovely, forget us, be beautiful, even to proudness,
> Even for their poor sakes whose happiness is to behold you;
> Live, be uncaring, be joyous, be sumptuous; only be lovely!'[19]

'Uncaring,' however, little Lady Helen never was. If she was a fairy, she was a fairy all heart, all frank foolish smiles and tears.

'No, Lady Helen—no,' Robert said again. 'This is no place for you, and we are getting on capitally.'

She pouted a little.

'I believe you and Mrs. Elsmere are just killing yourselves all in a corner, with no one to see,' she said indignantly. 'If you won't let me see, I shall send Sir Harry. But who'—and her brown fawn's eyes ran startled over the cottages before her—'who, Mr. Elsmere, does this *dreadful* place belong to?'

'Mr. Wendover,' said Robert shortly.

'Impossible!' she cried incredulously. 'Why, I wouldn't ask one of my dogs to sleep there,' and she pointed to the nearest hovel, whereof the walls were tottering outwards, the thatch was falling to pieces, and the windows were mended with anything that came handy—rags, paper, or the crown of an old hat.

'No, you would be ill advised,' said Robert, looking with a bitter little smile at the sleek dachshund that sat blinking beside its mistress.

'But what is the agent about?'

Then Robert told her the story, not mincing his words. Since the epidemic had begun, all that sense of imaginative attraction which had been reviving in him towards the squire had been simply blotted out by a fierce heat

---

18 *Engouements*: here in the sense of "craze" (Collins) or enthusiasm.
19 Arthur Hugh Clough (1819–61), poet, follower of Florence Nightingale, the subject of Matthew Arnold's *Thyrsis*; the lines are slightly misquoted from his *The Bothie of Toper-Na-Fuosich: A Long Vacation Pastoral* (1848), canto 5.

of indignation. When he thought of Mr. Wendover now, he thought of him as the man to whom in strict truth it was owing that helpless children died in choking torture. All that agony of wrath and pity he had gone through in the last ten days sprang to his lips now as he talked to Lady Helen, and poured itself into his words.

'Old Meyrick and I have taken things into our own hands now,' he said at last briefly. 'We have already made two cottages fairly habitable. To-morrow the inspector comes. I told the people yesterday I wouldn't be bound by my promise a day longer. He must put the screw on Henslowe, and if Henslowe dawdles, why we shall just drain and repair and sink for a well ourselves. I can find the money somehow. At present we get all our water from one of the farms on the brow.'

'Money!' said Lady Helen impulsively, her looks warm with sympathy for the pale harassed young rector. 'Sir Harry shall send you as much as you want. And anything else—blankets—coals?'

Out came her note-book, and Robert was drawn into a list. Then, full of joyfulness at being allowed to help, she gathered up her reins, she nodded her pretty little head at him, and was just starting off her ponies at full speed, equally eager 'to tell Harry' and to ransack Churton for the stores required, when it occurred to her to pull up again.

'Oh, Mr. Elsmere, my aunt, Lady Charlotte, does nothing but talk about your sister-in-law. *Why* did you keep her all to yourself? Is it kind, is it neighbourly, to have such a wonder to stay with you and let nobody share?'

'A wonder?' said Robert, amused. 'Rose plays the violin very well, but——'

'As if relations ever saw one in proper perspective!' exclaimed Lady Helen. 'My aunt wants to be allowed to have her in town next season if you will all let her. I think she would find it fun. Aunt Charlotte knows all the world and his wife. And if I'm there, and Miss Leyburn will let me make friends with her, why, you know, *I* can just protect her a little from Aunt Charlotte!'

The little laughing face bent forward again; Robert, smiling, raised his hat, and the ponies whirled her off. In anybody else Elsmere would have thought all this effusion insincere or patronising. But Lady Helen was the most spontaneous of mortals, and the only high-born woman he had ever met who was really, and not only apparently, free from the 'nonsense of rank.' Robert shrewdly suspected Lady Charlotte's social tolerance to be a mere varnish. But this little person, and her favourite brother Hugh, to judge from the accounts of him, must always have found life too romantic, too wildly and delightfully interesting from top to bottom, to be measured by any but romantic standards.

Next day Sir Harry Varley, a great burly country squire, who adored his wife, kept the hounds, owned a model estate, and thanked God every morning that he was an Englishman, rode over to Mile End. Robert, who had just been round the place with the inspector and was dead tired, had only energy to show him a few of the worst enormities. Sir Harry, leaving a cheque behind him, rode off with a discharge of strong language, at which Robert, clergyman as he was, only grimly smiled.

A few days later Mr. Wendover's crimes as a landowner, his agent's brutality, young Elsmere's devotion, and the horrors of the Mile End outbreak, were in everybody's mouths. The county was roused. The Radical newspaper came out on the Saturday with a flaming article; Robert, much to his annoyance, found himself the local hero; and money began to come in to him freely.

On the Monday morning Henslowe appeared on the scene with an army of workmen. A racy communication from the inspector had reached him two days before, so had a copy of the *Churton Advertiser*. He had spent Sunday in a drinking bout, turning over all possible plans of vengeance and evasion. Towards the evening, however, his wife, a gaunt clever Scotchwoman, who saw ruin before them, and had on occasion an even sharper tongue than her husband, managed to capture the supplies of brandy in the house and effectually conceal them. Then she waited for the moment of collapse which came on towards morning, and with her hands on her hips she poured into him a volley of home-truths which not even Sir Harry Varley could have bettered. Henslowe's nerve gave way. He went out at daybreak, white and sullen, to look for workmen.

Robert, standing on the step of a cottage, watched him give his orders, and took vigilant note of their substance. They embodied the inspector's directions, and the rector was satisfied. Henslowe was obliged to pass him on his way to another group of houses. At first he affected not to see the rector, then suddenly Elsmere was conscious that the man's bloodshot eyes were on him. Such a look! If hate could have killed, Elsmere would have fallen where he stood. Yet the man's hand mechanically moved to his hat, as though the spell of his wife's harangue were still potent over his shaking muscles.

Robert took no notice whatever of the salutation. He stood calmly watching till Henslowe disappeared into the last house. Then he called one of the agent's train, heard what was to be done, gave a sharp nod of assent, and turned on his heel. So far so good: the servant had been made to feel, but he wished it had been the master. Oh, those three little emaciated creatures whose eyes he had closed, whose clammy hands he had held to the last!—what reckoning should be asked for their undeserved torments when the Great Account came to be made up?

Meanwhile not a sound apparently of all this reached the squire in the sublime solitude of Murewell. A fortnight had passed. Henslowe had been conquered, the county had rushed to Elsmere's help, and neither he nor Mrs. Darcy had made a sign. Their life was so abnormal that it was perfectly possible they had heard nothing. Elsmere wondered when they *would* hear.

The rector's chief help and support all through had been old Meyrick. The parish doctor had been in bed with rheumatism when the epidemic broke out, and Robert, feeling it a comfort to be rid of him, had thrown the whole business into the hands of Meyrick and his son. This son was nominally his father's junior partner, but as he was, besides, a young and brilliant M.D. fresh from a great hospital, and his father was just a poor old general practitioner, with the barest qualification, and only forty years' experience to recommend him, it will easily be imagined that the subordination was purely nominal. Indeed young Meyrick was fast ousting his father in all directions, and the neighbourhood, which had so far found itself unable either to enter or to quit this mortal scene without old Meyrick's assistance, was beginning to send notes to the house in Churton High Street, whereon the superscription 'Dr. *Edward* Meyrick' was underlined with ungrateful emphasis. The father took his deposition very quietly. Only on Murewell Hall would he allow no trespassing, and so long as his son left him undisturbed there, he took his effacement in other quarters with perfect meekness.

Young Elsmere's behaviour to him, however, at a time when all the rest of the Churton world was beginning to hold him cheap and let him see it, had touched the old man's heart, and he was the rector's slave in this Mile End business. Edward Meyrick would come whirling in and out of the hamlet once a day. Robert was seldom sorry to see the back of him. His attainments, of course, were useful, but his cocksureness was irritating, and his manner to his father abominable. The father, on the other hand, came over in the shabby pony-cart he had driven for the last forty years, and having himself no press of business, would spend hours with the rector over the cases, giving them an infinity of patient watching, and amusing Robert by the cautious hostility he would allow himself every now and then towards his son's new-fangled devices.

At first Meyrick showed himself fidgety as to the squire. Had he been seen, been heard from? He received Robert's sharp negatives with long sighs, but Robert clearly saw that, like the rest of the world, he was too much afraid of Mr. Wendover to go and beard him. Some months before, as it happened,

Elsmere had told him the story of his encounter with the squire, and had been a good deal moved and surprised by the old man's concern.

One day, about three weeks from the beginning of the outbreak, when the state of things in the hamlet was beginning decidedly to mend, Meyrick arrived for his morning round, much preoccupied. He hurried his work a little, and after it was done asked Robert to walk up the road with him.

'I have seen the squire, sir,' he said, turning on his companion with a certain excitement.

Robert flushed.

'Have you?' he replied with his hands behind him, and a world of expression in his sarcastic voice.

'You misjudge him! You misjudge him, Mr. Elsmere!' the old man said tremulously. 'I told you he could know nothing of this business—and he didn't! He has been in town part of the time, and down here—how is he to know anything? He sees nobody. That man Henslowe, sir, must be a real *bad* fellow.'

'Don't abuse the man,' said Robert, looking up. 'It's not worth while, when you can say your mind of the master.'

Old Meyrick sighed.

'Well,' said Robert, after a moment, his lip drawn and quivering, 'you told him the story, I suppose? Seven deaths, is it, by now? Well, what sort of impression did these unfortunate accidents'—and he smiled—'produce?'

'He talked of sending money,' said Meyrick doubtfully; 'he said he would have Henslowe up and inquire. He seemed put about and annoyed. Oh, Mr. Elsmere, you think too hardly of the squire, that you do!'

They strolled on together in silence. Robert was not inclined to discuss the matter. But old Meyrick seemed to be labouring under some suppressed emotion, and presently he began upon his own experiences as a doctor of the Wendover family. He had already broached the subject more or less vaguely with Robert. Now, however, he threw his medical reserve, generally his strongest characteristic, to the winds. He insisted on telling his companion, who listened reluctantly, the whole miserable and ghastly story of the old squire's suicide. He described the heir's summons, his arrival just in time for the last scene with all its horrors, and that mysterious condition of the squire for some months afterwards, when no one, not even Mrs. Darcy, had been admitted to the Hall, and old Meyrick, directed at intervals by a great London doctor, had been the only spectator of Roger Wendover's physical and mental breakdown, the only witness of that dark consciousness of inherited fatality which at that period of his life not even the squire's iron will had been able wholly to conceal.

Robert, whose attention was inevitably roused after a while, found himself with some curiosity realising the squire from another man's totally different point of view. Evidently Meyrick had seen him at such moments as wring from the harshest nature whatever grains of tenderness, of pity, or of natural human weakness may be in it. And it was clear, too, that the squire, conscious perhaps of a shared secret, and feeling a certain soothing influence in the *naïveté* and simplicity of the old man's sympathy, had allowed himself at times, in the years succeeding that illness of his, an amount of unbending in Meyrick's presence, such as probably no other mortal had ever witnessed in him since his earliest youth.

And yet how childish the old man's whole mental image of the squire was after all! What small account it made of the subtleties, the gnarled intricacies and contradictions of such a character! Horror at his father's end, and dread of a like fate for himself! Robert did not know very much of the squire, but he knew enough to feel sure that this confiding indulgent theory of Meyrick's was ludicrously far from the mark as an adequate explanation of Mr. Wendover's later life.

Presently Meyrick became aware of the sort of tacit resistance which his companion's mind was opposing to his own. He dropped the wandering narrative he was busy upon with a sigh.

'Ah well, I daresay it's hard, it's hard,' he said with patient acquiescence in his voice, 'to believe a man can't help himself. I daresay we doctors get to muddle up right and wrong. But if ever there was a man sick in mind—for all his book-learning they talk about—and sick in soul, that man is the squire.'

Robert looked at him with a softer expression. There was a new dignity about the simple old man. The old-fashioned deference, which had never let him forget in speaking to Robert that he was speaking to a man of family, and which showed itself in all sorts of antiquated locutions which were a torment to his son, had given way to something still more deeply ingrained. His gaunt figure, with the stoop, and the spectacles and the long straight hair—like the figure of a superannuated schoolmaster—assumed, as he turned again to his younger companion, something of authority, something almost of stateliness.

'Ah, Mr. Elsmere,' he said, laying his shrunk hand on the younger man's sleeve and speaking with emotion, 'you're very good to the poor. We're all proud of you—you and your good lady. But when you were coming, and I heard tell all about you, I thought of my poor squire, and I said to myself, "That young man 'll be good to *him*. The squire will make friends with him, and Mr. Elsmere will have a good wife—and there'll be children born to him—and the squire will take an interest—and—and—maybe——'"

The old man paused. Robert grasped his hand silently.

'And there was something in the way between you,' the speaker went on, sighing. 'I daresay you were quite right—quite right. I can't judge. Only there are ways of doing a thing. And it was a last chance; and now its missed—it's missed. Ah! it's no good talking; he has a heart—he has! Many's the kind thing he's done in old days for me and mine—I'll never forget them! But all these last few years—oh, I know, I know. You can't go and shut your heart up, and fly in the face of all the duties the Lord laid on you, without losing yourself and setting the Lord against you. But it is pitiful, Mr. Elsmere, it's pitiful!'

It seemed to Robert suddenly as though there was a Divine breath passing through the wintry lane and through the shaking voice of the old man. Beside the spirit looking out of those wrinkled eyes, his own hot youth, its justest resentments, its most righteous angers, seemed crude, harsh, inexcusable.

'Thank you, Meyrick, thank you, and God bless you! Don't imagine I will forget a word you have said to me.'

The rector shook the hand he held warmly twice over, a gentle smile passed over Meyrick's ageing face, and they parted.

That night it fell to Robert to sit up after midnight with John Allwood, the youth of twenty whose case had been a severer tax on the powers of the little nursing staff than perhaps any other. Mother and neighbours were worn out, and it was difficult to spare a hospital nurse for long together from the diphtheria cases. Robert, therefore, had insisted during the preceding week on taking alternate nights with one of the nurses. During the first hours before midnight he slept soundly on a bed made up in the ground-floor room of the little sanatorium. Then at twelve the nurse called him, and he went out, his eyes still heavy with sleep, into a still frosty winter's night.

After so much rain, so much restlessness of wind and cloud, the silence and the starry calm of it were infinitely welcome. The sharp cold air cleared his brain and braced his nerves, and by the time he reached the cottage whither he was bound, he was broad awake. He opened the door softly, passed through the lower room, crowded with sleeping children, climbed the narrow stairs as noiselessly as possible, and found himself in a garret, faintly lit, a bed in one corner and a woman sitting beside it. The woman glided away, the rector looked carefully at the table of instructions hanging over the bed, assured himself that wine and milk and beef essence and medicines were ready to his hand, put out his watch on the wooden table near the bed, and sat him down to his task. The boy was sleeping the sleep of weakness. Food was to be given every half-hour, and in this perpetual impulse to the system lay his only chance.

The rector had his Greek Testament with him, and could just read it by the help of the dim light. But after a while, as the still hours passed on, it dropped on to his knee, and he sat thinking—endlessly thinking. The young labourer lay motionless beside him, the lines of the long emaciated frame showing through the bed-clothes. The night-light flickered on the broken discoloured ceiling; every now and then a mouse scratched in the plaster; the mother's heavy breathing came from the next room; sometimes a dog barked or an owl cried outside. Otherwise deep silence, such silence as drives the soul back upon itself.

Elsmere was conscious of a strange sense of moral expansion. The stern judgments, the passionate condemnations which his nature housed so painfully, seemed lifted from it. The soul breathed an 'ampler æther, a diviner air.' Oh! the mysteries of life and character, the subtle inexhaustible claims of pity! The problems which hang upon our being here; its mixture of elements; the pressure of its inexorable physical environment; the relations of mind to body, of man's poor will to this tangled tyrannous life—it was along these old, old lines his thought went painfully groping; and always at intervals it came back to the squire, pondering, seeking to understand, a new soberness, a new humility and patience entering in.

And yet it was not Meyrick's facts exactly that had brought this about. Robert thought them imperfect, only half true. Rather was it the spirit of love, of infinite forbearance in which the simpler, duller nature had declared itself that had appealed to him, nay, reproached him.

Then these thoughts led him on farther and farther from man to God, from human defect to the Eternal Perfectness. Never once during those hours did Elsmere's hand fail to perform its needed service to the faint sleeper beside him, and yet that night was one long dream and strangeness to him, nothing real anywhere but consciousness, and God its source; the soul attacked every now and then by phantom stabs of doubt, of bitter brief misgiving, as the barriers of sense between it and the eternal enigma grew more and more transparent, wrestling awhile, and then prevailing. And each golden moment of certainty, of conquering faith, seemed to Robert in some sort a gift from Catherine's hand. It was she who led him through the shades; it was her voice murmuring in his ear.

When the first gray dawn began to creep in slowly perceptible waves into the room, Elsmere felt as though not hours but years of experience lay between him and the beginnings of his watch.

'It is by these moments we should date our lives,' he murmured to himself as he rose; 'they are the only real landmarks.'

It was eight o'clock, and the nurse who was to relieve him had come. The results of the night for his charge were good: the strength had been maintained, the pulse was firmer, the temperature lower. The boy, throwing off his drowsiness, lay watching the rector's face as he talked in an undertone to the nurse, his haggard eyes full of a dumb friendly wistfulness. When Robert bent over him to say good-bye, this expression brightened into something more positive, and Robert left him, feeling at last that there was a promise of life in his look and touch.

In another moment he had stepped out into the January morning. It was clear and still as the night had been. In the east there was a pale promise of sun; the reddish-brown trunks of the fir woods had just caught it, and rose faintly glowing in endless vistas and colonnades one behind the other. The flooded river itself rushed through the bridge as full and turbid as before, but all the other water surfaces had gleaming films of ice. The whole ruinous place had a clean, almost a festal air under the touch of the frost, while on the side of the hill leading to Murewell, tree rose above tree, the delicate network of their wintry twigs and branches set against stretches of frost-whitened grass, till finally they climbed into the pale all-completing blue. In a copse close at hand there were woodcutters at work, and piles of gleaming laths shining through the underwood. Robins hopped along the frosty road, and as he walked on through the houses towards the bridge, Robert's quick ear distinguished that most wintry of all sounds—the cry of a flock of fieldfares passing overhead.

As he neared the bridge he suddenly caught sight of a figure upon it, the figure of a man wrapped in a large Inverness cloak, leaning against the stone parapet. With a start he recognised the squire.

He went up to him without an instant's slackening of his steady step. The squire heard the sound of some one coming, turned, and saw the rector.

'I am glad to see you here, Mr. Wendover,' said Robert, stopping and holding out his hand. 'I meant to have come to talk to you about this place this morning. I ought to have come before.'

He spoke gently, and quite simply, almost as if they had parted the day before. The squire touched his hand for an instant.

'You may not, perhaps, be aware, Mr. Elsmere,' he said, endeavouring to speak with all his old hauteur, while his heavy lips twitched nervously, 'that, for one reason and another, I knew nothing of the epidemic here till yesterday, when Meyrick told me.'

'I heard from Mr. Meyrick that it was so. As you are here now, Mr.

Wendover, and I am in no great hurry to get home, may I take you through and show you the people?'

The squire at last looked at him straight—at the face worn and pale, yet still so extraordinarily youthful, in which something of the solemnity and high emotion of the night seemed to be still lingering.

'Are you just come?' he said abruptly, 'or are you going back?'

'I have been here through the night, sitting up with one of the fever cases. It's hard work for the nurses, and the relations sometimes, without help.'

The squire moved on mechanically towards the village, and Robert moved beside him.

'And Mrs. Elsmere?'

'Mrs. Elsmere was here most of yesterday. She used to stay the night when the diphtheria was at its worst; but there are only four anxious cases left—the rest all convalescent.'

The squire said no more, and they turned into the lane, where the ice lay thick in the deep ruts, and on either hand curls of smoke rose into the clear cold sky. The squire looked about him with eyes which no detail escaped. Robert, without a word of comment, pointed out this feature and that, showed where Henslowe had begun repairs, where the new well was to be, what the water supply had been till now, drew the squire's attention to the roofs, the pigstyes, the drainage, or rather complete absence of drainage, and all in the dry voice of some one going through a catalogue. Word had already fled like wildfire through the hamlet that the squire was there. Children and adults, a pale emaciated crew, poured out into the wintry air to look. The squire knit his brows with annoyance as the little crowd in the lane grew. Robert took no notice.

Presently he pushed open the door of the house where he had spent the night. In the kitchen a girl of sixteen was clearing away the various nondescript heaps on which the family had slept, and was preparing breakfast. The squire looked at the floor.

'I thought I understood from Henslowe,' he muttered, as though to himself, 'that there were no mud floors left on the estate——'

'There are only three houses in Mile End without them,' said Robert, catching what he said.

They went upstairs, and the mother stood open-eyed while the squire's restless look gathered in the details of the room, the youth's face, as he lay back on his pillows, whiter than they, exhausted and yet refreshed by the sponging with vinegar and water which the mother had just been administering to him; the bed, the gaps in the worm-eaten boards, the spots in the roof where the plaster bulged inward, as though a shake would bring it down; the coarse china shepherdesses on the mantel-shelf, and the flowers which Catherine had put there the day before. He asked a few questions, said an abrupt word or two to the mother, and they tramped downstairs again and into the street. Then Robert took him across to the little improvised hospital, saying to him on the threshold, with a moment's hesitation,—

'As you know, for adults there is not much risk, but there is always some risk——'

A peremptory movement of the squire's hand stopped him, and they went in. In the downstairs room were half-a-dozen convalescents, pale, shadowy creatures, four of them under ten, sitting up in their little cots, each of them with a red flannel jacket drawn from Lady Helen's stores, and enjoying the breakfast which a nurse in white cap and apron had just brought them. Upstairs, in a room from which a lath-and-plaster partition had been removed, and which had been adapted, warmed and ventilated by various contrivances to which Robert and Meyrick had devoted their practical minds, were the 'four anxious cases.' One of them, a little creature of six, one of Sharland's black-eyed children, was sitting up, supported by the nurse, and coughing its little life away. As soon as he saw it, Robert's step quickened. He forgot the squire altogether. He came and stood by the bedside, rigidly still, for he could do nothing, but his whole soul absorbed in that horrible struggle for air. How often he had seen it now, and never without the same wild sense of revolt and protest! At last the hideous membrane was loosened, the child got relief, and lay back white and corpse-like, but with a pitiful momentary relaxation of the drawn lines on its little brow. Robert stooped and kissed the damp tiny hand. The child's eyes remained shut, but the fingers made a feeble effort to close on his.

'Mr. Elsmere,' said the nurse, a motherly body, looking at him with friendly admonition, 'if you don't go home and rest you'll be ill too, and I'd like to know who'll be the better for that?'

'How many deaths?' asked the squire abruptly, touching Elsmere's arm, and so reminding Robert of his existence. 'Meyrick spoke of deaths.'

He stood near the door, but his eyes were fixed on the little bed, on the half-swooning child.

'Seven,' said Robert, turning upon him. 'Five of diphtheria, two of fever. That little one will go too.'

'Horrible!' said the squire under his breath, and then moved to the door.

The two men went downstairs in perfect silence. Below, in the convalescent room, the children were capable of smiles, and of quick coquettish beckonings to the rector to come and make game with them as usual. But he could only kiss his hand to them and escape, for there was more to do.

He took the squire through all the remaining fever cases, and into several of the worst cottages—Milsom's among them—and when it was all over they emerged into the lane again, near the bridge. There was still a crowd of children and women hanging about, watching eagerly for the squire, whom many of them had never seen at all, and about whom various myths had gradually formed themselves in the countryside. The squire walked away from them hurriedly, followed by Robert, and again they halted on the centre of the bridge. A horse led by a groom was being walked up and down on a flat piece of road just beyond.

It was an awkward moment. Robert never forgot the thrill of it, or the association of wintry sunshine streaming down upon a sparkling world of ice and delicate woodland and foam-flecked river.

The squire turned towards him irresolutely; his sharply-cut wrinkled lips opening and closing again. Then he held out his hand: 'Mr. Elsmere, I did you a wrong—I did this place and its people a wrong. In my view, regret for the past is useless. Much of what has occurred here is plainly irreparable; I will think what can be done for the future. As for my relation to you, it rests with you to say whether it can be amended. I recognise that you have just cause of complaint.'

What invincible pride there was in the man's very surrender! But Elsmere was not repelled by it. He knew that in their hour together the squire had *felt*. His soul had lost its bitterness. The dead and their wrong were with God.

He took the squire's outstretched hand, grasping it cordially, a pure unworldly dignity in his whole look and bearing.

'Let us be friends, Mr. Wendover. It will be a great comfort to us—my wife and me. Will you remember us both very kindly to Mrs. Darcy?'

Commonplace words, but words that made an epoch in the life of both. In another minute the squire, on horseback, was trotting along the side road leading to the Hall, and Robert was speeding home to Catherine as fast as his long legs could carry him.

She was waiting for him on the steps, shading her eyes against the unwonted sun. He kissed her with the spirits of a boy and told her all his news.

Catherine listened bewildered, not knowing what to say or how all at once to forgive, to join Robert in forgetting. But that strange spiritual glow about him was not to be withstood. She threw her arms about him at last with a half sob,—

'Oh, Robert—yes! Dear Robert—thank God!'

'Never think any more,' he said at last, leading her in from the little hall, 'of what has been, only of what shall be! Oh, Catherine, give me some tea; and never did I see anything so tempting as that armchair.'

He sank down into it, and when she put his breakfast beside him she saw with a start that he was fast asleep. The wife stood and watched him, the signs of fatigue round eyes and mouth, the placid expression, and her face was soft with tenderness and joy. 'Of course—of course, even that hard man must love him. Who could help it? My Robert!'

And so now in this disguise, now in that, the supreme hour of Catherine's life stole on and on towards her.

CHAPTER XXII

As may be imagined, the *Churton Advertiser* did not find its way to Murewell. It was certainly no pressure of social disapproval that made the squire go down to Mile End in that winter's dawn. The county might talk, or the local press might harangue, till Doomsday, and Mr. Wendover would either know nothing or care less.

Still his interview with Meyrick in the park after his return from a week in town, whither he had gone to see some old Berlin friends, had been a shock to him. A man may play the intelligent recluse, may refuse to fit his life to his neighbours' notions as much as you please, and still find death, especially death for which he has some responsibility, as disturbing a fact as the rest of us.

He went home in much irritable discomfort. It seemed to him probably that fortune need not have been so eager to put him in the wrong. To relieve his mind he sent for Henslowe, and in an interview, the memory of which sent a shiver through the agent to the end of his days, he let it be seen that though it did not for the moment suit him to dismiss the man who had brought this upon him, that man's reign in any true sense was over.

But afterwards the squire was still restless. What was astir in him was not so much pity or remorse as certain instincts of race which still survived under the strange superstructure of manners he had built upon them. It may be the part of a gentleman and a scholar to let the agent whom you have interposed between yourself and a boorish peasantry have a free hand; but, after all, the estate is yours, and to expose the rector of the parish to all sorts of avoidable risks in the pursuit of his official duty by reason of the gratuitous filth of your property, is an act of doubtful breeding. The squire in his most rough-and-tumble days at Berlin had always felt himself the grandee as well as the student. He abhorred sentimentalism, but neither did he choose to cut an unseemly figure in his own eyes.

After a night, therefore, less tranquil or less meditative than usual, he rose early and sallied forth at one of those unusual hours he generally chose for walking. The thing must be put right somehow, and at once, with as little waste of time and energy as possible, and Henslowe had shown himself not to be trusted; so telling a servant to follow him, the squire had made his way with difficulty to a place he had not seen for years.

Then had followed the unexpected and unwelcome apparition of the rector. The squire did not want to be impressed by the young man, did not want to make friends with him. No doubt his devotion had served his own purposes. Still Mr. Wendover was one of the subtlest living judges of character when he pleased, and his enforced progress through these hovels with Elsmere had not exactly softened him, but had filled him with a curious contempt for his own hastiness of judgment.

'History would be inexplicable after all without the honest fanatic,' he said to himself on the way home. 'I suppose I had forgotten it. There is nothing like a dread of being bored for blunting your psychological instinct.'

In the course of the day he sent off a letter to the rector intimating in the very briefest, driest way that the cottages should be rebuilt on a different site as soon as possible, and enclosing a liberal contribution towards the expenses incurred in fighting the epidemic. When the letter was gone he drew his books towards him with a sound which was partly disgust, partly relief. This annoying business had wretchedly interrupted him, and his concessions left him mainly conscious of a strong nervous distaste for the idea of any fresh interview with young Elsmere. He had got his money and his apology; let him be content.

However, next morning after breakfast Mr. Wendover once more saw his study door open to admit the tall figure of the rector. The note and cheque had reached Robert late the night before, and, true to his new-born determination to make the best of the squire, he had caught up his wideawake at the first opportunity and walked off to the Hall to acknowledge the gift in person. The interview opened as awkwardly as it was possible, and with their former conversation on the same spot fresh in their minds both men spent a sufficiently difficult ten minutes. The squire was asking himself, indeed, impatiently, all the time, whether he could possibly be forced in the future to put up with such an experience again, and Robert found his host, if less sarcastic than before, certainly as impenetrable as ever.

At last, however, the Mile End matter was exhausted, and then Robert, as good luck would have it, turned his longing eyes on the squire's books, especially on the latest volumes of a magnificent German *Weltgeschichte* lying near his elbow, which he had coveted for months without being able to conquer his conscience sufficiently to become the possessor of it. He took it up with an exclamation of delight, and a quiet critical remark that exactly hit the value and scope of the book. The squire's eyebrows went up, and the corners of his mouth slackened visibly. Half an hour later the two men, to the amazement of Mrs. Darcy, who was watching them from the drawing-room window, walked back to the park gates together, and what Robert's nobility and beauty of character would never have won him, though he had worn himself to death in the service of the poor and the tormented under the squire's eyes, a chance coincidence of intellectual interest had won him almost in a moment.

The squire walked back to the house under a threatening sky, his mackintosh cloak wrapped about him, his arms folded, his mind full of an unwonted excitement.

The sentiment of long-past days—days in Berlin, in Paris, where conversations such as that he had just passed through were the daily relief and reward of labour, was stirring in him. Occasionally he had endeavoured to import the materials for them from the Continent, from London. But as a matter of fact it was years since he had had any such talk as this with an Englishman on English ground, and he suddenly realised that he had been unwholesomely solitary, and that for the scholar there is no nerve stimulus like that of an occasional interchange of ideas with some one acquainted with his *Fach*.

'Who would ever have thought of discovering instincts and aptitudes of such a kind in this long-legged optimist?' The squire shrugged his shoulders as he thought of the attempt involved in such a personality to combine both worlds, the world of action and the world of thought. Absurd! Of course, ultimately one or other must go to the wall.

Meanwhile, what a ludicrous waste of time and opportunity that he and this man should have been at cross-purposes like this! 'Why the deuce couldn't he have given some rational account of himself to begin with!' thought the squire irritably, forgetting, of course, who it was that had wholly denied him the opportunity. 'And then the sending back of those books: what a piece of idiocy!'

Granted an historical taste in this young parson, it was a curious chance, Mr. Wendover reflected, that in his choice of a subject he should just have fallen on the period of the later empire—of the passage from the old world to the new, where the squire was a master. The squire fell to thinking of the kind of knowledge implied in his remarks, of the stage he seemed to have reached, and then to cogitating as to the books he must be now in want of. He went back to his library, ran over the shelves, picking out volumes here and there with an unwonted glow and interest all the while. He sent for a case, and made a youth who sometimes acted as his secretary pack them. And still as he went back to his own work new names would occur to him, and full of the scholar's avaricious sense of the shortness of time, he would shake his head and frown over the three months which young Elsmere had already passed, grappling with problems like Teutonic Arianism, the spread of Monasticism in Gaul, and Heaven knows what besides, half a mile from the man and the library which could have supplied him with the best help to be got in England, unbenefited by either! Mile End was obliterated, and the annoyance of the morning forgotten.

The next day was Sunday, a wet January Sunday, raw and sleety, the frost breaking up on all sides and flooding the roads with mire.

Robert, rising in his place to begin morning service, and wondering to see the congregation so good on such a day, was suddenly startled, as his eye travelled mechanically over to the Hall pew, usually tenanted by Mrs. Darcy in solitary state, to see the characteristic figure of the squire. His amazement was so great that he almost stumbled in the exhortation, and his feeling was evidently shared by the congregation, which throughout the service showed a restlessness, an excited tendency to peer round corners and pillars, that was not favourable to devotion.

'Has he come to spy out the land?' the rector thought to himself, and could not help a momentary tremor at the idea of preaching before so formidable an auditor. Then he pulled himself together by a great effort, and fixing his eyes on a shock-headed urchin half way down the church, read the service to him. Catherine meanwhile in her seat on the northern side of the nave, her soul lulled in Sunday peace, knew nothing of Mr. Wendover's appearance.

Robert preached on the first sermon of Jesus, on the first appearance of the young Master in the synagogue at Nazareth:—

'*This day is this scripture fulfilled in your ears!*'[20]

The sermon dwelt on the Messianic aspect of Christ's mission, on the mystery and poetry of that long national expectation, on the pathos of Jewish disillusion, on the sureness and beauty of Christian insight as faith gradually transferred trait after trait of the Messiah of prophecy to the Christ of Nazareth. At first there was a certain amount of hesitation, a slight wavering

20 Luke 4.21.

hither and thither—a difficult choice of words—and then the soul freed itself from man, and the preacher forgot all but his Master and his people.

At the door as he came out stood Mr. Wendover, and Catherine, slightly flushed and much puzzled for conversation, beside him. The Hall carriage was drawn close up to the door, and Mrs. Darcy, evidently much excited, had her small head out of the window, and was showering a number of flighty inquiries and suggestions on her brother, to which he paid no more heed than to the patter of the rain.

When Robert appeared the squire addressed him ceremoniously—

'With your leave. Mr. Elsmere, I will walk with you to the rectory.' Then, in another voice, 'Go home, Lætitia, and don't send anything or anybody.'

He made a signal to the coachman, and the carriage started, Mrs. Darcy's protesting head remaining out of window as long as anything could be seen of the group at the church door. The odd little creature had paid one or two hurried and recent visits to Catherine during the quarrel, visits so filled, however, with vague railing against her brother and by a queer incoherent melancholy, that Catherine felt them extremely uncomfortable, and took care not to invite them. Clearly she was mortally afraid of 'Roger,' and yet ashamed of being afraid. Catherine could see that all the poor thing's foolish whims and affectations were trampled on; that she suffered, rebelled, found herself no more able to affect Mr. Wendover than if she had been a fly buzzing round him, and became all the more foolish and whimsical in consequence.

The squire and the Elsmeres crossed the common to the rectory, followed at a discreet interval by groups of villagers curious to get a look at the squire. Robert was conscious of a good deal of embarrassment, but did his best to hide it. Catherine felt all through as if the skies had fallen. The squire alone was at his ease, or as much at his ease as he ever was. He commented on the congregation, even condescended to say something of the singing, and passed over the staring of the choristers with a magnanimity of silence which did him credit.

They reached the rectory door, and it was evidently the squire's purpose to come in, so Robert invited him in. Catherine threw open her little drawing-room door, and then was seized with shyness as the squire passed in, and she saw over his shoulder her baby, lying kicking and crowing on the hearth-rug, in anticipation of her arrival, the nurse watching it. The squire in his great cloak stopped, and looked down at the baby as if it had been some curious kind of reptile. The nurse blushed, curtsied, and caught up the gurgling creature in a twinkling.

Robert made a laughing remark on the tyranny and ubiquity of babies.

The squire smiled grimly. He supposed it was necessary that the human race should be carried on. Catherine meanwhile slipped out and ordered another place to be laid at the dinner-table, devoutly hoping that it might not be used.

It was used. The squire stayed till it was necessary to invite him, then accepted the invitation, and Catherine found herself dispensing boiled mutton to him, while Robert supplied him with some very modest claret, the sort of wine which a man who drinks none thinks it necessary to have in the house, and watched the nervousness of their little parlour-maid with a fellow-feeling which made it difficult for him during the early part of the meal to keep a perfectly straight countenance. After a while, however, both he and Catherine were ready to admit that the squire was making himself agreeable. He talked of Paris, of a conversation he had had with M. Renan, whose name luckily was quite unknown to Catherine, as to the state of things in the French Chamber.

'A set of chemists and quill-drivers,' he said contemptuously; 'but as Renan remarked to me, there is one thing to be said for a government of that sort, "Ils ne font pas la guerre."[21] And so long as they don't run France into adventures, and a man can keep a roof over his head and a sou in his pocket, the men of letters at any rate can rub along. The really interesting thing in France just now is not French politics—Heaven save the mark!—but French scholarship. There never was so little original genius going in Paris, and there never was so much good work being done.'

Robert thought the point of view eminently characteristic.

'Catholicism, I suppose,' he said, 'as a force to be reckoned with, is dwindling more and more?'

'Absolutely dead,' said the squire emphatically, 'as an *intellectual* force. They haven't got a writer, scarcely a preacher. Not one decent book has been produced on that side for years.'

'And the Protestants, too,' said Robert, 'have lost all their best men of late,' and he mentioned one or two well-known French Protestant names.

'Oh, as to French Protestantism'—and the squire's shrug was superb—'Teutonic Protestantism is in the order of things, so to speak, but *Latin* Protestantism! There is no more sterile hybrid in the world!'

Then, becoming suddenly aware that he might have said something inconsistent with his company, the squire stopped abruptly. Robert, catching Catherine's quick compression of the lips, was grateful to him, and the conversation moved on in another direction.

Yes, certainly, all things considered, Mr. Wendover made himself

---

21 They don't make war.

agreeable. He ate his boiled mutton and drank his *ordinaire* like a man, and when the meal was over, and he and Robert had withdrawn into the study, he gave an emphatic word of praise to the coffee which Catherine's housewifely care sent after them, and accepting a cigar, he sank into the armchair by the fire and spread a bony hand to the blaze, as if he had been at home in that particular corner for months. Robert, sitting opposite to him, and watching his guest's eyes travel round the room, with its medicine shelves, its rods and nets, and preparations of uncanny beasts, its parish litter, and its teeming bookcases, felt that the Mile End matter was turning out oddly indeed.

'I have packed you a case of books, Mr. Elsmere,' said the squire, after a puff or two at his cigar. 'How have you got on without that collection of Councils?'

He smiled a little awkwardly. It was one of the books Robert had sent back. Robert flushed. He did not want the squire to regard him as wholly dependent on Murewell.

'I bought it,' he said, rather shortly. 'I have ruined myself in books lately, and the London Library too supplies me really wonderfully well.'

'Are these your books?' The squire got up to look at them. 'Hum, not at all bad for a beginning. I have sent you so and so,' and he named one or two costly folios that Robert had long pined for in vain.

The rector's eyes glistened.

'That was very good of you,' he said simply. 'They will be most welcome.'

'And now, how much *time*,' said the other, settling himself again to his cigar, his thin legs crossed over each other, and his great head sunk into his shoulders, 'how much time do you give to this work?'

'Generally the mornings—not always. A man with twelve hundred souls to look after, you know, Mr. Wendover,' said Elsmere, with a bright half-defiant accent, 'can't make grubbing among the Franks his main business.'

The squire said nothing, and smoked on. Robert gathered that his companion thought his chances of doing anything worth mentioning very small.

'Oh no,' he said, following out his own thought with a shake of his curly hair; 'of course I shall never do very much. But if I don't, it won't be for want of knowing what the scholar's ideal is.' And he lifted his hand with a smile towards the squire's book on *English Culture*, which stood in the bookcase just above him. The squire, following the gesture, smiled too. It was a faint, slight illumining, but it changed the face agreeably.

Robert began to ask questions about the book, about the pictures contained in it of foreign life and foreign universities. The squire consented to be drawn out, and presently was talking at his very best.

Racy stories of Mommsen or Von Ranke were followed by a description of an evening of mad carouse with Heine—a talk at Nohant with George Sand—scenes in the Duchesse de Broglie's salon—a contemptuous sketch of Guizot—a caustic sketch of Renan.[22] Robert presently even laid aside his pipe, and stood in his favourite attitude, lounging against the mantelpiece, looking down, absorbed, on his visitor. All that intellectual passion which his struggle at Mile End had for the moment checked in him revived. Nay, after his weeks of exclusive contact with the most hideous forms of bodily ill, this interruption, these great names, this talk of great movements and great causes, had a special savour and relish. All the horizons of the mind expanded, the currents of the blood ran quicker.

Suddenly, however, he sprang up.

'I beg your pardon? Mr. Wendover, it is too bad to interrupt you—I have enjoyed it immensely—but the fact is I have only two minutes to get to Sunday School in!'

Mr. Wendover rose also, and resumed his ordinary manner.

'It is I who should apologise,' he said with stiff politeness, 'for having encroached in this way on your busy day, Mr. Elsmere.'

Robert helped him on with his coat, and then suddenly the squire turned to him.

'You were preaching this morning on one of the Isaiah quotations in St. Matthew. It would interest you, I imagine, to see a recent Jewish book on the subject of the prophecies quoted in the Gospels which reached me yesterday. There is nothing particularly new in it, but it looked to me well done.'

'Thank you,' said Robert, not, however, with any great heartiness, and the squire moved away. They parted at the gate, Robert running down the hill to the village as fast as his long legs could carry him.

'Sunday School—pshaw!' cried the squire, as he tramped homeward in the opposite direction.

Next morning a huge packing-case arrived from the Hall, and Robert could not forbear a little gloating over the treasures in it before he tore himself away to pay his morning visit to Mile End. There everything was improving; the poor Sharland child indeed had slipped away on the night after the squire's visit, but the other bad cases in the diphtheria ward were mending fast. John Allwood was gaining strength daily, and poor Mary Sharland was feebly struggling back to a life which seemed hardly worth so much effort to

22 Leopold von Ranke (1795–1886), German historian credited with inventing modern "scientific" history; Heinrich Heine (1797–1856), German poet; [Albertine] Hedvig Gustava Albertina, Baroness de Staël-Holstein (1797–1838), *salonnière*, daughter of Germaine de Staël.

keep. Robert felt, with a welcome sense of slackening strain, that the daily and hourly superintendence which he and Catherine had been giving to the place might lawfully be relaxed, that the nurses on the spot were now more than equal to their task, and after having made his round he raced home again in order to secure an hour with his books before luncheon.

The following day a note arrived, while they were at luncheon, in the squire's angular precise handwriting. It contained a request that, unless otherwise engaged, the rector would walk with Mr. Wendover that afternoon.

Robert flung it across to Catherine.

'Let me see,' he said, deliberating, 'have I any engagement I must keep?'

There was a sort of jealousy for his work within him contending with this new fascination of the squire's company. But, honestly, there was nothing in the way, and he went.

That walk was the first of many. The squire had no sooner convinced himself that young Elsmere's society did in reality provide him with a stimulus and recreation he had been too long without, than in his imperious wilful way he began to possess himself of it as much as possible. He never alluded to the trivial matters which had first separated and then united them. He worked the better, he thought the more clearly, for these talks and walks with Elsmere, and therefore these talks and walks became an object with him. They supplied a long-stifled want, the scholar's want of disciples, of some form of investment for all that heaped-up capital of thought he had been accumulating during a lifetime.

As for Robert, he soon felt himself so much under the spell of the squire's strange and powerful personality that he was forced to make a fight for it, lest this new claim should encroach upon the old ones. He would walk when the squire liked, but three times out of four these walks must be parish rounds, interrupted by descents into cottages and chats in farmhouse parlours. The squire submitted. The neighbourhood began to wonder over the strange spectacle of Mr. Wendover waiting grimly in the winter dusk outside one of his own farmhouses while Elsmere was inside, or patrolling a bit of lane till Elsmere should have inquired after an invalid or beaten up a recruit for his confirmation class, dogged the while by stealthy children, with fingers in their mouths, who ran away in terror directly he turned.

Rumours of this new friendship spread. One day, on the bit of road between the Hall and the rectory, Lady Helen behind her ponies whirled past the two men, and her arch look at Elsmere said as plain as words, 'Oh, you young wonder! what hook has served you with this leviathan?'

On another occasion, close to Churton, a man in a cassock and cloak came towards them. The squire put up his eyeglass.

'Humph!' he remarked; 'do you know this merryandrew, Elsmere?'

It was Newcome. As they passed, Robert with slightly heightened colour gave him an affectionate nod and smile. Newcome's quick eye ran over the companions, he responded stiffly, and his step grew more rapid. A week or two later Robert noticed with a little prick of remorse that he had seen nothing of Newcome for an age. If Newcome would not come to him, he must go to Mottringham. He planned an expedition, but something happened to prevent it.

And Catherine? Naturally this new and most unexpected relation of Robert's to the man who had begun by insulting him was of considerable importance to the wife. In the first place it broke up to some extent the exquisite *tête-à-tête* of their home life; it encroached often upon time that had always been hers; it filled Robert's mind more and more with matters in which she had no concern. All these things many wives might have resented. Catherine Elsmere resented none of them. It is probable, of course, that she had her natural moments of regret and comparison, when love said to itself a little sorely and hungrily, 'It is hard to be even a fraction less to him than I once was!' But if so, these moments never betrayed themselves in word or act. Her tender common sense, her sweet humility, made her recognise at once Robert's need of intellectual comradeship, isolated as he was in this remote rural district. She knew perfectly that a clergyman's life of perpetual giving forth becomes morbid and unhealthy if there is not some corresponding taking in.

If only it had not been Mr. Wendover! She marvelled over the fascination Robert found in his dry cynical talk. She wondered that a Christian pastor could ever forget Mr. Wendover's antecedents; that the man who had nursed those sick children could forgive Mile End. All in all as they were to each other, she felt for the first time that she often understood her husband imperfectly. His mobility, his eagerness, were sometimes now a perplexity, even a pain to her.

It must not be imagined, however, that Robert let himself drift into this intellectual intimacy with one of the most distinguished of anti-Christian thinkers without reflecting on its possible consequences. The memory of that night of misery which *The Idols of the Market-place* had inflicted on him was enough. He was no match in controversy for Mr. Wendover, and he did not mean to attempt it.

One morning the squire unexpectedly plunged into an account of a German monograph he had just received on the subject of the Johannine

authorship of the Fourth Gospel.[23] It was almost the first occasion on which
he had touched what may strictly be called the *matériel* of orthodoxy in their
discussions—at any rate directly. But the book was a striking one, and in the
interest of it he had clearly forgotten his ground a little. Suddenly the man
who was walking beside him interrupted him.

'I think we ought to understand one another perhaps, Mr. Wendover,'
Robert said, speaking under a quick sense of oppression, but with his usual
dignity and bright courtesy. 'I know your opinions, of course, from your
books; you know what mine, as an honest man, must be, from the position
I hold. My conscience does not forbid me to discuss anything, only—I am
no match for you on points of scholarship, and I should just like to say once
for all, that to me, whatever else is true, the religion of Christ is true. I am a
Christian and a Christian minister. Therefore, whenever we come to discuss
what may be called Christian evidence, I do it with reserves, which you would
not have. I believe in an Incarnation, a Resurrection, a Revelation. If there
are literary difficulties, I must want to smooth them away—you may want to
make much of them. We come to the matter from different points of view.
You will not quarrel with me for wanting to make it clear. It isn't as if we differed slightly. We differ fundamentally—is it not so?'

The squire was walking beside him with bent shoulders, the lower lip
pushed forward, as was usual with him when he was considering a matter
with close attention, but did not mean to communicate his thoughts.

After a pause he said, with a faint inscrutable smile,—

'Your reminder is perfectly just. Naturally we all have our reserves.
Neither of us can be expected to stultify his own.'

And the talk went forward again, Robert joining in more buoyantly than
ever, perhaps because he had achieved a necessary but disagreeable thing and
got done with it.

In reality he had but been doing as the child does when it sets up its sand-
barrier against the tide.

CHAPTER XXIII

It was the beginning of April. The gorse was fast extending its golden empire over the commons. On the sunny slopes of the copses primroses were

---

23 Debates over John were key to nineteenth-century controversies over Biblical
history and inspiration; see Michael Wheeler, *St. John and the Victorians* (Cambridge:
Cambridge University Press, 2012), 29-41.

breaking through the hazel roots and beginning to gleam along the edges of the river. On the grass commons between Murewell and Mile End the birches rose like green clouds against the browns and purples of the still leafless oaks and beeches. The birds were twittering and building. Every day Robert was on the look-out for the swallows, or listening for the first notes of the nightingale amid the bare spring coverts.

But the spring was less perfectly delightful to him than it might have been, for Catherine was away. Mrs. Leyburn, who was to have come south to them in February, was attacked by bronchitis instead at Burwood and forbidden to move, even to a warmer climate. In March, Catherine, feeling restless and anxious about her mother, and thinking it hard that Agnes should have all the nursing and responsibility, tore herself from her man and her baby, and went north to Whindale for a fortnight, leaving Robert forlorn.

Now, however, she was in London, whither she had gone for a few days on her way home, to meet Rose and to shop. Robert's opinion was that all women, even St. Elizabeths, have somewhere rooted in them an inordinate partiality for shopping; otherwise why should that operation take four or five mortal days? Surely with a little energy, one might buy up the whole of London in twelve hours! However, Catherine lingered, and as her purchases were made, Robert crossly supposed it must be all Rose's fault. He believed that Rose spent a great deal too much on dress.

Catherine's letters, of course, were full of her sister. Rose, she said, had come back from Berlin handsomer than ever, and playing, she supposed, magnificently. At any rate, the letters which followed her in shoals from Berlin flattered her to the skies, and during the three months preceding her return Joachim himself had taken her as a pupil and given her unusual attention.[24]

'And now, of course,' wrote Catherine, 'she is desperately disappointed that mamma and Agnes cannot join her in town, as she had hoped. She does her best, I know, poor child, to conceal it and to feel as she ought about mamma, but I can see that the idea of an indefinite time at Burwood is intolerable to her. As to Berlin, I think she has enjoyed it, but she talks very scornfully of German *Schwärmerei*[25] and German women, and she tells the oddest stories of her professors. With one or two of them she seems to have been in a state of war from the beginning; but some of them, my dear Robert, I am persuaded were just simply in love with her!

'I don't—no, I never *shall* believe, that independent exciting student's life is good for a girl. But I never say so to Rose. When she forgets to be irritable

---

24 Joseph Joachim (1831–1907), a violinist of the first rank.

25 *Schwärmerei:* over-enthusiasm.

and to feel that the world is going against her, she is often very sweet to me, and I can't bear there should be any conflict.'

His next day's letter contained the following:—

'Are you properly amused, sir, at your wife's performances in town? Our three concerts you have heard all about. I still can't get over them. I go about haunted by the *seriousness*, the life-and-death interest people throw into music. It is astonishing! And outside, as we got into our hansom, such sights and sounds!—such starved fierce-looking men, such ghastly women!

'But since then Rose has been taking me into society. Yesterday afternoon, after I wrote to you, we went to see Rose's artistic friends—the Piersons— with whom she was staying last summer, and to-day we have even called on Lady Charlotte Wynnstay.

'As to Mrs. Pierson, I never saw such an odd bundle of ribbons and rags and queer embroideries as she looked when we called. However, Rose says that, for "an æsthete"—she despises them now herself—Mrs. Pierson has wonderful taste, and that her wall-papers and her gowns, if I only understood them, are not the least like those of other æsthetic persons, but very *recherché*—which may be. She talked to Rose of nothing but acting, especially of Madame Desforêts. No one, according to her, has anything to do with an actress's private life, or ought to take it into account. But, Robert, dear,—an actress is a woman, and has a soul!

'Then Lady Charlotte,—you would have laughed at our *entrée*.

'We found she was in town, and went on her "day," as she had asked Rose to do. The room was rather dark—none of these London rooms seem to me to have any light and air in them. The butler got our names wrong, and I marched in first, more shy than I ever have been before in my life. Lady Charlotte had two gentlemen with her. She evidently did not know me in the least; she stood staring at me with her eyeglass on, and her cap so crooked I could think of nothing but a wish to put it straight. Then Rose followed, and in a few minutes it seemed to me as though it were Rose who were hostess, talking to the two gentlemen and being kind to Lady Charlotte. I am sure everybody in the room was amused by her self-possession, Lady Charlotte included. The gentlemen stared at her a great deal, and Lady Charlotte paid her one or two compliments on her looks, which *I* thought she would not have ventured to pay to any one in her own circle.

'We stayed about half an hour. One of the gentlemen was, I believe, a member of the Government, an under-secretary for something, but he and Rose and Lady Charlotte talked again of nothing but musicians and actors. It is strange that politicians should have time to know so much of these things.

The other gentleman reminded me of Hotspur's popinjay.[26] I think now I made out that he wrote for the newspapers, but at the moment I should have felt it insulting to accuse him of anything so humdrum as an occupation in life. He discovered somehow that I had an interest in the Church, and he asked me, leaning back in his chair and lisping, whether I really thought "the Church could still totter on a while in the rural dithtricts." He was informed her condition was so "vewy dethperate."

'Then I laughed outright, and found my tongue. Perhaps his next article on the Church will have a few facts in it. I did my best to put some into him. Rose at last looked round at me, astonished. But he did not dislike me, I think. I was not impertinent to him, husband mine. If I might have described just *one* of your days to his high-and-mightiness! There is no need to tell you, I think, whether I did or not.

'Then when we got up to go, Lady Charlotte asked Rose to stay with her. Rose explained why she couldn't, and Lady Charlotte pitied her dreadfully for having a family, and the under-secretary said that it was one's first duty in life to trample on one's relations, and that he hoped nothing would prevent his hearing her play some time later in the year. Rose said very decidedly she should be in town for the winter. Lady Charlotte said she would have an evening specially for her, and as I said nothing, we got away at last.'

The letter of the following day recorded a little adventure:—

'I was much startled this morning. I had got Rose to come with me to the National Gallery on our way to her dressmaker. We were standing before Raphael's "Vigil of the Knight,"[27] when suddenly I saw Rose, who was looking away towards the door into the long gallery, turn perfectly white. I followed her eyes, and there, in the doorway, disappearing,—I am almost certain,—was Mr. Langham! One cannot mistake his walk or his profile. Before I could say a word Rose had walked away to another wall of pictures, and when we joined again we did not speak of it. Did he see us, I wonder, and purposely avoid us? Something made me think so.

'Oh, I wish I could believe she had forgotten him! I am certain she would laugh me to angry scorn if I mentioned him; but there she sits by the fire now, while I am writing, quite drooping and pale, because she thinks I am not noticing. If she did but love me a little more! It must be my fault, I know.

'Yes, as you say, Burwood may as well be shut up or let. My dear, dear father!'

---

26 Shakespeare's *Henry IV, Part One*, 1.3. A "certain lord" who infuriates Hotspur by his foppery and idle chatter, entirely out of place on a battlefield filled with corpses.
27 *Vision of the Knight* (1504), one of several titles for this painting. Raphael (1483–1520), Italian Renaissance painter.

Robert could imagine the sigh with which Catherine had laid down her
pen. Dear tender soul, with all its old-world fidelities and pieties pure and
unimpaired! He raised the signature to his lips.

Next day Catherine came back to him. Robert had no words too oppro-
brious for the widowed condition from which her return had rescued him. It
seemed to Catherine, however, that life had been very full and keen with him
since her departure! He lingered with her after supper, vowing that his club
boys might make what hay in the study they pleased; he was going to tell her
the news, whatever happened.

'I told you of my two dinners at the Hall? The first was just *tête-à-tête* with
the squire—oh, and Mrs. Darcy, of course. I am always forgetting her, poor
little thing, which is most ungrateful of me. A pathetic life that, Catherine.
She seems to me, in her odd way, perpetually hungering for affection, for
praise. No doubt, if she got them, she wouldn't know what to do with them.
She would just touch and leave them as she does everything. Her talk and
she are both as light and wandering as thistledown. But still, meanwhile, she
hungers, and is never satisfied. There seems to be something peculiarly antipathetic in her to the squire. I can't make it out. He is sometimes quite brutal
to her when she is more inconsequent than usual. I often wonder she goes on
living with him.'

Catherine made some indignant comment.

'Yes,' said Robert, musing. 'Yes, it is bad.'

But Catherine thought his tone might have been more unqualified, and
marvelled again at the curious lenity of judgment he had always shown of
late towards Mr. Wendover. And all his judgments of himself and others were
generally so quick, so uncompromising!

'On the second occasion we had Freake and Dashwood,' naming two
well-known English antiquarians. 'Very learned, very jealous, and very snuffy;
altogether "too genuine," as poor mother used to say of those old chairs we
got for the dining-room. But afterwards when we were all smoking in the
library, the squire came out of his shell and talked. I never heard him more
brilliant!'

He paused a moment, his bright eyes looking far away from her, as
though fixed on the scene he was describing.

'Such a mind!' he said at last with a long breath, 'such a memory!
Catherine, my book has been making great strides since you left. With Mr.
Wendover to go to, all the problems are simplified. One is saved all false
starts, all beating about the bush. What a piece of luck it was that put one
down beside such a guide, such a living storehouse of knowledge!'

He spoke in a glow of energy and enthusiasm. Catherine sat looking at him wistfully, her gray eyes crossed by many varying shades of memory and feeling.

At last his look met hers, and the animation of it softened at once, grew gentle.

'Do you think I am making knowledge too much of a god just now, Madonna mine?' he said, throwing himself down beside her. 'I have been full of qualms myself. The squire excites one so, makes one feel as though intellect—accumulation—were the whole of life. But I struggle against it—I do. I go on, for instance, trying to make the squire do his social duties—behave like "a human."'

Catherine could not help smiling at his tone.

'Well?' she inquired.

He shook his head ruefully.

'The squire is a tough customer—most men of sixty-seven with strong wills are, I suppose. At any rate, he is like one of the Thurston trout—sees through all my manœuvres. But one piece of news will astonish you, Catherine!' And he sprang up to deliver it with effect. 'Henslowe is dismissed.'

'Henslowe dismissed!' Catherine sat properly amazed while Robert told the story.

The dismissal of Henslowe indeed represented the price which Mr. Wendover had been so far willing to pay for Elsmere's society. Some *quid pro quo* there must be—that he was prepared to admit—considering their relative positions as squire and parson. But, as Robert shrewdly suspected, not one of his wiles so far had imposed on the master of Murewell. He had his own sarcastic smiles over them, and over Elsmere's pastoral *naïveté* in general. The evidences of the young rector's power and popularity were, however, on the whole, pleasant to Mr. Wendover. If Elsmere had his will with all the rest of the world, Mr. Wendover knew perfectly well who it was that at the present moment had his will with Elsmere. He had found a great piquancy in this shaping of a mind more intellectually eager and pliant than any he had yet come across among younger men; perpetual food too, for his sense of irony, in the intellectual contradictions, wherein Elsmere's developing ideas and information were now, according to the squire, involving him at every turn.

'His religious foundations are gone already, if he did but know it,' Mr. Wendover grimly remarked to himself one day about this time, 'but he will take so long finding it out that the results are not worth speculating on.'

Cynically assured, therefore, at bottom of his own power with this ebullient nature, the squire was quite prepared to make external concessions, or, as we have said, to pay his price. It annoyed him that when Elsmere would press for allotment land, or a new institute, or a better supply of water for the village, it was not open to him merely to give *carte blanche*, and refer his petitioner to Henslowe. Robert's opinion of Henslowe, and Henslowe's now more cautious but still incessant hostility to the rector, were patent at last even to the squire. The situation was worrying and wasted time. It must be changed.

So one morning he met Elsmere with a bundle of letters in his hand, calmly informed him that Henslowe had been sent about his business, and that it would be a kindness if Mr. Elsmere would do him the favour of looking through some applications for the vacant post just received.

Elsmere, much taken by surprise, felt at first as it was natural for an over-sensitive, over-scrupulous man to feel. His enemy had been given into his hand, and instead of victory he could only realise that he had brought a man to ruin.

'He has a wife and children,' he said quickly, looking at the squire.

'Of course I have pensioned him,' replied the squire impatiently; 'otherwise I imagine he would be hanging round our necks to the end of the chapter.'

There was something in the careless indifference of the tone which sent a shiver through Elsmere. After all, this man had served the squire for fifteen years, and it was not Mr. Wendover who had much to complain of.

No one with a conscience could have held out a finger to keep Henslowe in his post. But though Elsmere took the letters and promised to give them his best attention, as soon as he got home he made himself irrationally miserable over the matter. It was not his fault that, from the moment of his arrival in the parish, Henslowe had made him the target of a vulgar and embittered hostility, and so far as he had struck out in return it had been for the protection of persecuted and defenceless creatures. But all the same, he could not get the thought of the man's collapse and humiliation out of his mind. How at his age was he to find other work, and how was he to endure life at Murewell without his comfortable house, his smart gig, his easy command of spirits, and the cringing of the farmers?

Tormented by the sordid misery of the situation almost as though it had been his own, Elsmere ran down impulsively in the evening to the agent's house. Could nothing be done to assure the man that he was not really his enemy, and that anything the parson's influence and the parson's money could do to help him to a more decent life, and work which offered fewer temptations and less power over human beings, should be done?

It need hardly be said that the visit was a complete failure. Henslowe, who was drinking hard, no sooner heard Elsmere's voice in the little hall than he dashed open the door which separated them, and, in a paroxysm of drunken rage, hurled at Elsmere all the venomous stuff he had been garnering up for months against some such occasion. The vilest abuse, the foulest charges—there was nothing that the maddened sot, now fairly unmasked, denied himself. Elsmere, pale and erect, tried to make himself heard. In vain. Henslowe was physically incapable of taking in a word.

At last the agent, beside himself, made a rush, his three untidy children, who had been hanging open-mouthed in the background, set up a howl of terror, and his Scotch wife, more pinched and sour than ever, who had been so far a gloomy spectator of the scene, interposed.

'Have doon wi' ye,' she said sullenly, putting out a long bony arm in front of her husband, 'or I'll just lock oop that brandy where ye'll naw find it if ye pull the house doon. Now, sir,' turning to Elsmere, 'would ye jest be going? Ye mean it weel, I daur say, but ye've doon yer wark, and ye maun leave it.'

And she motioned him out, not without a sombre dignity. Elsmere went home crestfallen. The enthusiast is a good deal too apt to under-estimate the stubbornness of moral fact, and these rebuffs have their stern uses for character.

'They intend to go on living here, I am told,' Elsmere said, as he wound up the story, 'and as Henslowe is still churchwarden, he may do us a world of mischief yet. However, I think that wife will keep him in order. No doubt vengeance would be sweet to her as to him, but she has a shrewd eye, poor soul, to the squire's remittances. It is a wretched business, and I don't take a man's hate easily, Catherine!—though it may be a folly to say so.'

Catherine was irresponsive. The Old Testament element in her found a lawful satisfaction in Henslowe's fall, and a wicked man's hatred, according to her, mattered only to himself. The squire's conduct, on the other hand, made her uneasily proud. To her, naturally, it simply meant that he was falling under Robert's spell. So much the better for him, but——

CHAPTER XXIV

That same afternoon Robert started on a walk to a distant farm, where one of his Sunday-school boys lay recovering from rheumatic fever. The rector had his pocket full of articles—a story-book in one, a puzzle map in the other—destined for Master Carter's amusement. On the way he was to pick up Mr.

Wendover at the park gates.

It was a delicious April morning. A soft west wind blew through leaf and grass—

'Driving sweet buds, like flocks, to feed in air.'[28]

The spring was stirring everywhere, and Robert raced along, feeling in every vein a life, an ebullience akin to that of nature. As he neared the place of meeting it occurred to him that the squire had been unusually busy lately, unusually silent and absent too on their walks. What *was* he always at work on? Robert had often inquired of him as to the nature of those piles of proof and manuscript with which his table was littered. The squire had never given any but the most general answer, and had always changed the subject. There was an invincible *personal* reserve about him which, through all his walks and talks with Elsmere, had never as yet broken down. He would talk of other men and other men's labours by the hour, but not of his own. Elsmere reflected on the fact, mingling with the reflection a certain humorous scorn of his own constant openness and readiness to take counsel with the world.

'However, *his* book isn't a mere excuse, as Langham's is,' Elsmere inwardly remarked. 'Langham, in a certain sense, plays even with learning; Mr. Wendover plays at nothing.'

By the way, he had a letter from Langham in his pocket much more cheerful and human than usual. Let him look through it again.

Not a word, of course, of that National Gallery experience!—a circumstance, however, which threw no light on it either way.

'I find myself a good deal reconciled to life by this migration of mine,' wrote Langham. 'Now that my enforced duties to them are all done with, my fellow-creatures seem to me much more decent fellows than before. The great stir of London, in which, unless I please, I have no part whatever, attracts me more than I could have thought possible. No one in these noisy streets has any rightful claim upon me. I have cut away at one stroke lectures, and Boards of Studies, and tutors' meetings, and all the rest of the wearisome Oxford make-believe, and the creature left behind feels lighter and nimbler than he has felt for years. I go to concerts and theatres; I look at the people in the streets; I even begin to take an outsider's interest in social questions, in the puny dykes which well-meaning people are trying to raise all round us against the encroaching, devastating labour-troubles of the future. By dint of running away from life, I may end by cutting a much more passable figure in it than before. Be consoled, my dear Elsmere; reconsider your remonstrances.'

---

28 Percy Bysshe Shelley, "Ode to the West Wind," l. 11.

There, under the great cedar by the gate, stood Mr. Wendover. Illumined as he was by the spring sunshine, he struck Elsmere as looking unusually shrunken and old. And yet under the look of physical exhaustion there was a new serenity, almost a peacefulness of expression, which gave the whole man a different aspect.

'Don't take me far,' he said abruptly, as they started. 'I have not got the energy for it. I have been over-working, and must go away.'

'I have been sure of it for some time,' said Elsmere warmly. 'You ought to have a long rest. But mayn't I know, Mr. Wendover, before you take it, what this great task is you have been toiling at? Remember, you have never told me a word of it.'

And Elsmere's smile had in it a touch of most friendly reproach. Fatigue had left the scholar relaxed, comparatively defenceless. His sunk and wrinkled eyes lit up with a smile, faint indeed, but of unwonted softness.

'A task indeed,' he said with a sigh, 'the task of a lifetime. To-day I finished the second third of it. Probably before the last section is begun some interloping German will have stepped down before me; it is the way of the race! But for the moment there is the satisfaction of having come to an end of some sort—a natural halt, at any rate.'

Elsmere's eyes were still interrogative. 'Oh, well,' said the squire hastily, 'it is a book I planned just after I took my doctor's degree at Berlin. It struck me then as the great want of modern scholarship. It is a History of Evidence, or rather, more strictly, "A History of *Testimony*."'

Robert started. The library flashed into his mind, and Langham's figure in the long gray coat sitting on the stool.

'A great subject,' he said slowly, 'a magnificent subject. How have you conceived it, I wonder?'

'Simply from the standpoint of evolution, of development. The philosophical value of the subject is enormous. You must have considered it, of course; every historian must. But few people have any idea in detail of the amount of light which the history of human witness in the world, systematically carried through, throws on the history of the human mind; that is to say, on the history of ideas.'

The squire paused, his keen scrutinising look dwelling on the face beside him, as though to judge whether he were understood.

'Oh, true!' cried Elsmere; 'most true. Now I know what vague want it is that has been haunting me for months——'

He stopped short, his look, aglow with all the young thinker's ardour, fixed on the squire.

The squire received the outburst in silence—a somewhat ambiguous silence.

'But go on,' said Elsmere; 'please go on.'

'Well, you remember,' said the squire slowly, 'that when Tractarianism began I was for a time one of Newman's victims. Then, when Newman departed, I went over body and bones to the Liberal reaction which followed his going. In the first ardour of what seemed to me a release from slavery I migrated to Berlin, in search of knowledge which there was no getting in England, and there, with the taste of a dozen aimless theological controversies still in my mouth, this idea first took hold of me. It was simply this:—Could one through an exhaustive examination of human records, helped by modern physiological and mental science, get at the conditions, physical and mental, which govern the greater or lesser correspondence between human witness and the fact it reports?'

'A giant's task!' cried Robert: 'hardly conceivable!'

The squire smiled slightly—the smile of a man who looks back with indulgent half-melancholy satire on the rash ambitions of his youth.

'Naturally,' he resumed, 'I soon saw I must restrict myself to European testimony, and that only up to the Renaissance. To do that, of course, I had to dig into the East, to learn several Oriental languages—Sanskrit among them. Hebrew I already knew. Then, when I had got my languages, I began to work steadily through the whole mass of existing records, sifting and comparing. It is thirty years since I started. Fifteen years ago I finished the section dealing with classical antiquity—with India, Persia, Egypt, and Judæa. To-day I have put the last strokes to a History of Testimony from the Christian era down to the sixth century—from Livy to Gregory of Tours, from Augustus to Justinian.'

Elsmere turned to him with wonder, with a movement of irrepressible homage. Thirty years of unbroken solitary labour for one end, one cause! In our hurried fragmentary life, a purpose of this tenacity, this power of realising itself, strikes the imagination.

'And your two books?'

'Were a mere interlude,' replied the squire briefly. 'After the completion of the first part of my work, there were certain deposits left in me which it was a relief to get rid of, especially in connection with my renewed impressions of England,' he added drily.

Elsmere was silent, thinking this then was the explanation of the squire's minute and exhaustive knowledge of the early Christian centuries, a knowledge into which—apart from certain forbidden topics—he had himself dipped so freely. Suddenly, as he mused, there awoke in the young man a new hunger, a new unmanageable impulse towards frankness of speech. All his nascent intellectual powers were alive and clamorous. For the moment his past reticences and timidities looked to him absurd. The mind rebelled against the barriers it had been rearing against itself. It rushed on to sweep them away, crying out that all this shrinking from free discussion had been at bottom 'a mere treason to faith.'

'Naturally, Mr. Wendover,' he said at last, and his tone had a half-defiant, half-nervous energy, 'you have given your best attention all these years to the Christian problems.'

'Naturally,' said the squire drily. Then, as his companion still seemed to wait, keenly expectant, he resumed, with something cynical in the smile which accompanied the words,—

'But I have no wish to infringe our convention.'

'A convention was it?' replied Elsmere, flushing. 'I think I only wanted to make my own position clear and prevent misunderstanding. But it is impossible that I should be indifferent to the results of thirty years' such work as you can give to so great a subject.'

The squire drew himself up a little under his cloak and seemed to consider. His tired eyes, fixed on the spring lane before them, saw in reality only the long retrospects of the past. Then a light broke in them, transformed them—a light of battle. He turned to the man beside him, and his sharp look swept over him from head to foot. Well, if he would have it, let him have it. He had been contemptuously content so far to let the subject be. But Mr. Wendover, in spite of his philosophy, had never been proof all his life against an anti-clerical instinct worthy almost of a Paris municipal councillor. In spite of his fatigue there woke in him a kind of cruel whimsical pleasure at the notion of speaking, once for all, what he conceived to be the whole bare truth to this clever attractive dreamer, to the young fellow who thought he could condescend to science from the standpoint of the Christian miracles!

'Results?' he said interrogatively. 'Well, as you will understand, it is tolerably difficult to summarise such a mass at a moment's notice. But I can give you the lines of my last volumes, if it would interest you to hear them.'

That walk prolonged itself far beyond Mr. Wendover's original intention. There was something in the situation, in Elsmere's comments, or arguments, or silences, which after a while banished the scholar's sense of exhaustion and made him oblivious of the country distances. No man feels another's soul quivering and struggling in his grasp without excitement, let his nerve and his self-restraint be what they may.

As for Elsmere, that hour and a half, little as he realised it at the time, represented the turning-point of life. He listened, he suggested, he put in an acute remark here, an argument there, such as the squire had often difficulty in meeting. Every now and then the inner protest of an attacked faith would break through in words so full of poignancy, in imagery so dramatic, that the squire's closely-knit sentences would be for the moment wholly disarranged. On the whole, he proved himself no mean guardian of all that was most sacred to himself and to Catherine, and the squire's intellectual respect for him rose considerably.

All the same, by the end of their conversation that first period of happy unclouded youth we have been considering was over for poor Elsmere. In obedience to certain inevitable laws and instincts of the mind, he had been for months tempting his fate, inviting catastrophe. None the less did the first sure approaches of that catastrophe fill him with a restless resistance which was in itself anguish.

As to the squire's talk, it was simply the outpouring of one of the richest, most sceptical, and most highly-trained of minds on the subject of Christian origins. At no previous period of his life would it have greatly affected Elsmere. But now at every step the ideas, impressions, arguments bred in him by his months of historical work and ordinary converse with the squire rushed in, as they had done once before, to cripple resistance, to check an emerging answer, to justify Mr. Wendover.

We may quote a few fragmentary utterances taken almost at random from the long wrestle of the two men, for the sake of indicating the main lines of a bitter after-struggle.

'Testimony like every other human product has *developed*. Man's power of apprehending and recording what he sees and hears has grown from less to more, from weaker to stronger, like any other of his faculties, just as the reasoning powers of the cave-dweller have developed into the reasoning powers of a Kant. What one wants is the ordered proof of this, and it can be got from history and experience.'

'To plunge into the Christian period without having first cleared the mind as to what is meant in history and literature by "the critical method," which in history may be defined as the "science of what is credible," and in literature as "the science of what is rational," is to invite fiasco. The theologian in such a state sees no obstacle to accepting an arbitrary list of documents with all the strange stuff they may contain, and declaring them to be sound historical material, while he applies to all the strange stuff of a similar kind surrounding them the most rigorous principles of modern science. Or he has to make believe that the reasoning processes exhibited in the speeches of the Acts, in certain passages of St. Paul's Epistles, or in the Old Testament quotations in the Gospels, have a validity for the mind of the nineteenth century, when in truth they are the imperfect, half-childish products of the mind of the first century, of quite insignificant or indirect value to the historian of fact, of enormous value to the historian of *testimony* and its varieties.'

'Suppose, for instance, before I begin to deal with the Christian story, and the earliest Christian development, I try to make out beforehand what are the moulds, the channels into which the testimony of the time must run. I look for these moulds, of course, in the dominant ideas, the intellectual preconceptions and preoccupations existing when the period begins.

'In the first place, I shall find present in the age which saw the birth of Christianity, as in so many other ages, a universal preconception in favour of miracle—that is to say, of deviations from the common norm of experience, governing the work of *all* men of *all* schools. Very well, allow for it then. Read the testimony of the period in the light of it. Be prepared for the inevitable differences between it and the testimony of your own day. The witness of the time is not true, nor, in the strict sense, false. It is merely incompetent, half-trained, pre-scientific, but all through perfectly natural. The wonder would have been to have had a life of Christ without miracles. The air teems with them. The East is full of Messiahs. Even a Tacitus is superstitious. Even a Vespasian works miracles. Even a Nero cannot die, but fifty years after his death is still looked for as the inaugurator of a millennium of horror.[29] The Resurrection is partly invented, partly imagined, partly ideally true—in any case wholly intelligible and natural, as a product of the age, when once you have the key of that age.

'In the next place, look for the preconceptions that have a definite historical origin; those, for instance, flowing from the pre-Christian, apocalyptic literature of the Jews, taking the Maccabean legend of Daniel as the centre of inquiry—those flowing from Alexandrian Judaism and the school of Philo—those flowing from the Palestinian schools of exegesis. Examine your synoptic gospels, your Gospel of St. John, your Apocalypse, in the light of these. You

---

29   Publius Cornelius Tacitus (56–117 CE), Roman historian and politician; Vespasian (d. 79 CE), Roman Emperor; Nero (37–68 CE), Roman Emperor who became a byword for depravity.

have no other chance of understanding them. But so examined, they fall into place, become explicable and rational; such material as science can make full use of. The doctrine of the Divinity of Christ, Christian eschatology, and Christian views of prophecy will also have found *their* place in a sound historical scheme!'

'It is discreditable now for the man of intelligence to refuse to read his Livy in the light of his Mommsen. My object has been to help in making it discreditable to him to refuse to read his Christian documents in the light of a trained scientific criticism. We shall have made some positive advance in rationality when the man who is perfectly capable of dealing sanely with legend in one connection, and, in another, will insist on confounding it with history proper, cannot do so any longer without losing caste, without falling *ipso facto* out of court with men of education. It is enough for a man of letters if he has helped ever so little in the final staking out of the boundaries between reason and unreason!'

And so on. These are mere ragged gleanings from an ample store. The discussion in reality ranged over the whole field of history, plunged into philosophy, and into the subtlest problems of mind. At the end of it, after he had been conscious for many bitter moments of that same constriction of heart which had overtaken him once before at Mr. Wendover's hands, the religious passion in Elsmere once more rose with sudden stubborn energy against the iron negations pressed upon it.

'I will not fight you any more, Mr. Wendover,' he said, with his moved flashing look. 'I am perfectly conscious that my own mental experience of the last two years has made it necessary to re-examine some of these intellectual foundations of faith. But as to the faith itself, that is its own witness. It does not depend, after all, upon anything external, but upon the living voice of the Eternal in the soul of man!'

Involuntarily his pace quickened. The whole man was gathered into one great, useless, pitiful defiance, and the outer world was forgotten. The squire kept up with difficulty a while, a faint glimmer of sarcasm playing now and then round the straight thin-lipped mouth. Then suddenly he stopped.

'No, let it be. Forget me and my book, Elsmere. Everything can be got out of in this world. By the way, we seem to have reached the ends of the earth. Those are the new Mile End cottages, I believe. With your leave, I'll sit down in one of them, and send to the Hall for the carriage.'

Elsmere's repentant attention was drawn at once to his companion.

'I am a selfish idiot,' he said hotly, 'to have led you into over-walking and over-talking like this.'

The squire made some short reply and instantly turned the matter off. The momentary softness which had marked his meeting with Elsmere had entirely vanished, leaving only the Mr. Wendover of every day, who was merely made awkward and unapproachable by the slightest touch of personal sympathy. No living being, certainly not his foolish little sister, had any *right* to take care of the squire. And as the signs of age became more apparent, this one fact had often worked powerfully on the sympathies of Elsmere's chivalrous youth, though as yet he had been no more capable than any one else of breaking through the squire's haughty reserve.

As they turned down the newly-worn track to the cottages, whereof the weekly progress had been for some time the delight of Elsmere's heart, they met old Meyrick in his pony-carriage. He stopped his shambling steed at sight of the pair. The bleared spectacled eyes lit up, the prim mouth broke into a smile which matched the April sun.

'Well, Squire; well, Mr. Elsmere, are you going to have a look at those places? Never saw such palaces. I only hope I may end my days in anything so good. Will you give me a lease, Squire?'

Mr. Wendover's deep eyes took a momentary survey, half indulgent, half contemptuous, of the naïve, awkward-looking old creature in the pony-carriage. Then, without troubling to find an answer, he went his way.

Robert stayed chatting a moment or two, knowing perfectly well what Meyrick's gay garrulity meant. A sharp and bitter sense of the ironies of life swept across him. The squire humanised, influenced by him—he knew that was the image in Meyrick's mind; he remembered with a quiet scorn its presence in his own. And never, never had he felt his own weakness and the strength of that grim personality so much as at that instant.

That evening Catherine noticed an unusual silence and depression in Robert. She did her best to cheer it away, to get at the cause of it. In vain. At last, with her usual wise tenderness, she left him alone, conscious herself, as she closed the study door behind her, of a momentary dreariness of soul, coming she knew not whence, and only dispersed by the instinctive upward leap of prayer.

Robert was no sooner alone than he put down his pipe and sat brooding over the fire. All the long debate of the afternoon began to fight itself out again in the shrinking mind. Suddenly, in his restless pain, a thought occurred to him. He had been much struck in the squire's conversation by certain allusions to arguments drawn from the Book of Daniel. It was not a subject with which Robert had any great familiarity. He remembered his Pusey dimly, certain Divinity lectures, an article of Westcott's.[30]

He raised his hand quickly and took down the monograph on *The Use of the Old Testament in the New*, which the squire had sent him in the earliest days of their acquaintance. A secret dread and repugnance had held him from it till now. Curiously enough it was not he but Catherine, as we shall see, who had opened it first. Now, however, he got it down and turned to the section on Daniel.

It was a change of conviction on the subject of the date and authorship of this strange product of Jewish patriotism in the second century before Christ that drove M. Renan out of the Church of Rome. 'For the Catholic Church to confess,' he says in his *Souvenirs*, 'that Daniel is an apocryphal book of the time of the Maccabees, would be to confess that she had made a mistake; if she had made this mistake, she may have made others; she is no longer divinely inspired.'

The Protestant, who is in truth more bound to the Book of Daniel than M. Renan, has various ways of getting over the difficulties raised against the supposed authorship of the book by modern criticism. Robert found all these ways enumerated in the brilliant and vigorous pages of the book before him.

In the first place, like the orthodox Saint-Sulpicien, the Protestant meets the critic with a flat *non possumus*.[31] 'Your arguments are useless and irrelevant,' he says in effect. 'However plausible may be your objections, the Book of Daniel is what it professes to be, *because* our Lord quoted it in such a manner as to distinctly recognise its authority. The All-True and All-Knowing cannot have made a mistake, nor can He have expressly led His disciples to regard as genuine and Divine, prophecies which were in truth the inventions of an ingenious romancer.'

But the liberal Anglican—the man, that is to say, whose logical sense is inferior to his sense of literary probabilities—proceeds quite differently.

'Your arguments are perfectly just,' he says to the critic; 'the book is a patriotic fraud, of no value except to the historian of literature. But how do you know that our Lord quoted it as *true* in the strict sense? In fact He quoted it as *literature*, as a Greek might have quoted Homer, as an Englishman might quote Shakespeare.'

And many a harassed Churchman takes refuge forthwith in the new explanation. It is very difficult, no doubt, to make the passages in the Gospels

---

30 Brooke Foss Westcott (1825–1901), one of the leading British specialists in the history and translation of the Bible, and Bishop of Durham from 1890 onward.
31 The Society of Saint-Sulpice, the seminary organization founded in the seventeenth century, known for its more "conservative" theological bent; "we cannot."

agree with it, but at the bottom of his mind there is a saving silent scorn for the old theories of inspiration. He admits to himself that probably Christ was not correctly reported in the matter.

Then appears the critic, having no interests to serve, no *parti pris* to defend, and states the matter calmly, dispassionately, as it appears to him. 'No reasonable man,' says the ablest German exponent of the Book of Daniel, 'can doubt'—that this most interesting piece of writing belongs to the year 169 or 170 B.C. It was written to stir up the courage and patriotism of the Jews, weighed down by the persecutions of Antiochus Epiphanes.[32] It had enormous vogue. It inaugurated a new Apocalyptic literature. And clearly the youth of Jesus of Nazareth was vitally influenced by it. It entered into his thought, it helped to shape his career.[33]

But Elsmere did not trouble himself much with the critic, as at any rate he was reported by the author of the book before him. Long before the critical case was reached, he had flung the book heavily from him. The mind accomplished its further task without help from outside. In the stillness of the night there rose up weirdly before him a whole new mental picture—effacing, pushing out, innumerable older images of thought. It was the image of a purely human Christ—a purely human, explicable, yet always wonderful Christianity. It broke his heart, but the spell of it was like some dream-country wherein we see all the familiar objects of life in new relations and perspectives. He gazed upon it fascinated, the wailing underneath checked a while by the strange beauty and order of the emerging spectacle. Only a little while! Then with a groan Elsmere looked up, his eyes worn, his lips white and set.

'I must face it—I must face it through! God help me!'

A slight sound overhead in Catherine's room sent a sudden spasm of feeling through the young face. He threw himself down, hiding from his own foresight of what was to be.

'My darling, my darling! But she shall know nothing of it—yet.'

CHAPTER XXV

And he did face it through.

The next three months were the bitterest months of Elsmere's life. They

---

32 As recorded in 2 Maccabees.

33 Loosely adapted from Heinrich Ewald, *Die Jüngsten Propheten des Alten Bundes mit den Büchern Barukh und Daniel* (Göttingen: Vandenhoeck & Ruprecht's Verlag, 1868), 301-2.

were marked by anguished mental struggle, by a consciousness of painful separation from the soul nearest to his own, and by a constantly increasing sense of oppression, of closing avenues and narrowing alternatives, which for weeks together seemed to hold the mind in a grip whence there was no escape.

That struggle was not hurried and embittered by the bodily presence of the squire. Mr. Wendover went off to Italy a few days after the conversation we have described. But though he was not present in the flesh the great book of his life was in Elsmere's hands, he had formally invited Elsmere's remarks upon it; and the air of Murewell seemed still echoing with his sentences, still astir with his thoughts. That curious instinct of pursuit, that avid imperious wish to crush an irritating resistance, which his last walk with Elsmere had first awakened in him with any strength, persisted. He wrote to Robert from abroad, and the proud fastidious scholar had never taken more pains with anything than with those letters.

Robert might have stopped them, might have cast the whole matter from him with one resolute effort. In other relations he had will enough and to spare.

Was it an unexpected weakness of fibre that made it impossible?—that had placed him in this way at the squire's disposal? Half the world would answer yes. Might not the other half plead that in every generation there is a minority of these mobile, impressionable, defenceless natures, who are ultimately at the mercy of experience, at the mercy of thought, at the mercy (shall we say?) of truth; and that, in fact, it is from this minority that all human advance comes?

During these three miserable months it cannot be said—poor Elsmere!— that he attempted any systematic study of Christian evidence. His mind was too much torn, his heart too sore. He pounced feverishly on one test point after another, on the Pentateuch, the Prophets, the relation of the New Testament to the thoughts and beliefs of its time, the Gospel of St. John, the evidence as to the Resurrection, the intellectual and moral conditions surrounding the formation of the Canon. His mind swayed hither and thither, driven from each resting-place in turn by the pressure of some new difficulty. And—let it be said again—all through, the only constant element in the whole dismal process was his trained historical sense. If he had gone through this conflict at Oxford, for instance, he would have come out of it unscathed: for he would simply have remained throughout it ignorant of the true problems at issue. As it was, the keen instrument he had sharpened so laboriously on indifferent material now ploughed its agonising way, bit by bit, into the most intimate recesses of thought and faith.

Much of the actual struggle he was able to keep from Catherine's view, as he had vowed to himself to keep it. For after the squire's departure Mrs. Darcy too went joyously up to London to flutter a while through the golden alleys of Mayfair; and Elsmere was left once more in undisturbed possession of the Murewell library. There for a while on every day—oh, pitiful relief!— he could hide himself from the eyes he loved.

But, after all, married love allows of nothing but the shallowest concealments. Catherine had already had one or two alarms. Once, in Robert's study, among a tumbled mass of books he had pulled out in search of something missing, and which she was putting in order, she had come across that very book on the Prophecies which at a critical moment had so deeply affected Elsmere. It lay open, and Catherine was caught by the heading of a section: 'The Messianic Idea.'

She began to read, mechanically at first, and read about a page. That page so shocked a mind accustomed to a purely traditional and mystical interpretation of the Bible that the book dropped abruptly from her hand, and she stood a moment by her husband's table, her fine face pale and frowning.

She noticed, with bitterness, Mr. Wendover's name on the title-page. Was it right for Robert to have such books? Was it wise, was it prudent, for the Christian to measure himself against such antagonism as this? She wrestled painfully with the question. 'Oh, but I can't understand,' she said to herself with an almost agonised energy. 'It is I who am timid, faithless! He *must*— he *must*—know what they say; he must have gone through the dark places if he is to carry others through them.'

So she stilled and trampled on the inward protest. She yearned to speak of it to Robert, but something withheld her. In her passionate wifely trust she could not bear to seem to question the use he made of his time and thought; and a delicate moral scruple warned her she might easily allow her dislike of the Wendover friendship to lead her into exaggeration and injustice.

But the stab of that moment recurred—dealt now by one slight incident, now by another. And after the squire's departure Catherine suddenly realised that the whole atmosphere of their home-life was changed.

Robert was giving himself to his people with a more scrupulous energy than ever. Never had she seen him so pitiful, so full of heart for every human creature. His sermons, with their constant imaginative dwelling on the earthly life of Jesus, affected her now with a poignancy, a pathos, which were almost unbearable. And his tenderness to *her* was beyond words. But with that tenderness there was constantly mixed a note of remorse, a painful self-depreciation which she could hardly notice in speech, but which every now and then wrung her heart. And in his parish work he often showed a depression, an irritability, entirely new to her. He who had always the happiest power of forgetting to-morrow all the rubs of to-day, seemed now quite incapable of saving himself and his cheerfulness in the old ways, nay, had developed a capacity for sheer worry she had never seen in him before. And meanwhile all the old gossips of the place spoke their mind freely to Catherine on the subject of the rector's looks, coupling their remarks with a variety of prescriptions, out of which Robert did sometimes manage to get one of his old laughs. His sleeplessness, too, which had always been a constitutional tendency, had become now so constant and wearing that Catherine began to feel a nervous hatred of his book-work, and of those long mornings at the Hall; a passionate wish to put an end to it, and carry him away for a holiday.

But he would not hear of the holiday, and he could hardly bear any talk of himself. And Catherine had been brought up in a school of feeling which bade love be very scrupulous, very delicate, and which recognised in the strongest way the right of every human soul to its own privacy, its own reserves. That something definite troubled him she was certain. What it was he clearly avoided telling her, and she could not hurt him by impatience.

He would tell her soon—when it was right—she cried pitifully to herself. Meantime both suffered, she not knowing why, clinging to each other the while more passionately than ever.

One night, however, coming down in her dressing-gown into the study in search of a *Christian Year* she had left behind her, she found Robert with papers strewn before him, his arms on the table and his head laid down upon them. He looked up as she came in, and the expression of his eyes drew her to him irresistibly.

'Were you asleep, Robert? Do come to bed!'

He sat up, and with a pathetic gesture held out his arms to her. She came on to his knee, putting her white arms round his neck, while he leant his head against her breast.

'Are you tired with all your walking to-day?' she said presently, a pang at her heart.

'I am tired,' he said, 'but not with walking.'

'Does your book worry you? You shouldn't work so hard, Robert—you shouldn't!'

He started.

'Don't talk of it. Don't let us talk or think at all, only feel!'

And he tightened his arms round her, happy once more for a moment in this environment of a perfect love. There was silence for a few moments,

Catherine feeling more and more disturbed and anxious.

'Think of your mountains,' he said presently, his eyes still pressed against her, 'of High Fell, and the moonlight, and the house where Mary Backhouse died. Oh! Catherine, I see you still, and shall always see you, as I saw you then, my angel of healing and of grace!'

'I too have been thinking of her to-night,' said Catherine softly, 'and of the walk to Shanmoor. This evening in the garden it seemed to me as though there were Westmoreland scents in the air! I was haunted by a vision of bracken, and rocks, and sheep browsing up the fell slopes.'

'Oh for a breath of the wind on High Fell!' cried Robert,—it was so new to her, the dear voice with this accent in it of yearning depression! 'I want more of the spirit of the mountains, their serenity, their strength. Say me that Duddon sonnet you used to say to me there, as you said it to me that last Sunday before our wedding, when we walked up the Shanmoor road to say good-bye to that blessed spot. Oh! how I sit and think of it sometimes, when life seems to be going crookedly, that rock on the fell-side where I found you, and caught you, and snared you, my dove, for ever.'

And Catherine, whose mere voice was as balm to this man of many impulses, repeated to him, softly in the midnight silence, those noble lines in which Wordsworth has expressed, with the reserve and yet the strength of the great poet, the loftiest yearning of the purest hearts—

> 'Enough, if something from our hand have power
> To live and move, and serve the future hour,
> And if, as towards the silent tomb we go,
> Through love, through hope, and faith's transcendent dower,
> We feel that we are greater than we know.'[34]

'He has divined it all,' said Robert, drawing a long breath when she stopped, which seem to relax the fibres of the inner man, 'the fever and the fret of human thought, the sense of littleness, of impotence, of evanescence—and he has soothed it all!'[35]

'Oh, not all, not all!' cried Catherine, her look kindling, and her rare passion breaking through; 'how little in comparison!'

For her thoughts were with him of whom it was said, *'He needed not that any one should bear witness concerning man, for he knew what was in man.'*[36] But Robert's only response was silence and a kind of quivering sigh.

---

34 William Wordsworth, "After-Thought," ll. 10-14.
35 This is loosely inspired by John Keats' "Ode to a Nightingale," ll. 21-30.
36 John 2.25.

'Robert!' she cried, pressing her cheek against his temple, 'tell me, my dear, dear husband, what it is troubles you. Something does—I am certain—certain!'

'Catherine—wife—beloved!' he said to her, after another pause, in a tone of strange tension she never forgot; 'generations of men and women have known what it is to be led spiritually into the desert, into that outer wilderness where even the Lord was "tempted." What am I that I should claim to escape it? And you cannot come through it with me, my darling—no, not even you! It is loneliness—it is solitariness itself——' and he shuddered. 'But pray for me—pray that *He* may be with me, and that at the end there may be light!'

He pressed her to him convulsively, then gently released her. His solemn eyes, fixed upon her as she stood there beside him, seemed to forbid her to say a word more. She stooped; she laid her lips to his; it was a meeting of soul with soul; then she went softly out, breaking the quiet of the house by a stifled sob as she passed upstairs.

Oh! but at last she thought she understood him. She had not passed her girlhood, side by side with a man of delicate fibre, of melancholy and scrupulous temperament, and within hearing of all the natural interests of a deeply religious mind, religious biography, religious psychology, and—within certain sharply defined limits—religious speculation, without being brought face to face with the black possibilities of 'doubts' and 'difficulties' as barriers in the Christian path. Has not almost every Christian of illustrious excellence been tried and humbled by them? Catherine, looking back upon her own youth, could remember certain crises of religious melancholy, during which she had often dropped off to sleep at night on a pillow wet with tears. They had passed away quickly, and for ever. But she went back to them now, straining her eyes through the darkness of her own past, recalling her father's days of spiritual depression, and the few difficult words she had sometimes heard from him as to those bitter times of religious dryness and hopelessness, by which God chastens from time to time His most faithful and heroic souls. A half-contempt awoke in her for the unclouded serenity and confidence of her own inner life. If her own spiritual experience had gone deeper, she told herself with the strangest self-blame, she would have been able now to understand Robert better—to help him more.

She thought as she lay awake after those painful moments in the study, the tears welling up slowly in the darkness, of many things that had puzzled her in the past. She remembered the book she had seen on his table; her thoughts travelled over his months of intercourse with the squire; and the memory of Mr. Newcome's attitude towards the man whom he conceived to be his Lord's adversary, as contrasted with Robert's, filled her with a shrinking pain she dared not analyse.

Still all through, her feeling towards her husband was in the main akin to that of the English civilian at home towards English soldiers abroad, suffering and dying that England may be great. *She* had sheltered herself all her life from those deadly forces of unbelief which exist in English society, by a steady refusal to know what, however, any educated university man must perforce know. But such a course of action was impossible for Robert. He had been forced into the open, into the full tide of the Lord's battle. The chances of that battle are many; and the more courage the more risk of wounds and pain. But the great Captain knows—the great Captain does not forget His own!

For never, never had she the smallest doubt as to the issue of this sudden crisis in her husband's consciousness, even when she came nearest to apprehending its nature. As well might she doubt the return of daylight, as dream of any permanent eclipse descending upon the faith which had shone through every detail of Robert's ardent impulsive life, with all its struggles, all its failings, all its beauty, since she had known him first. The dread did not even occur to her. In her agony of pity and reverence she thought of him as passing through a trial, which is specially the believer's trial—the chastening by which God proves the soul He loves. Let her only love and trust in patience.

So that day by day as Robert's depression still continued, Catherine surrounded him with the tenderest and wisest affection. Her quiet common sense made itself heard, forbidding her to make too much of the change in him, which might after all, she thought, be partly explained by the mere physical results of his long strain of body and mind during the Mile End epidemic. And for the rest she would not argue; she would not inquire. She only prayed that she might so lead the Christian life beside him, that the Lord's tenderness, the Lord's consolation, might shine upon him through her. It had never been her wont to speak to him much about his own influence, his own effect, in the parish. To the austerer Christian considerations of this kind are forbidden: 'It is not I, but Christ that worketh in me.' But now, whenever she came across any striking trace of his power over the weak or the impure, the sick or the sad, she would in some way make it known to him, offering it to him in her delicate tenderness, as though it were a gift that the Father had laid in her hand for him—a token that the Master was still indeed with His servant, and that all was fundamentally well!

And so much, perhaps, the contact with his wife's faith, the power of her love, wrought in Robert, that during these weeks and months he also never lost his own certainty of emergence from the shadow which had overtaken him. And, indeed, driven on from day to day as he was by an imperious intellectual thirst which would be satisfied, the religion of the heart, the imaginative emotional habit of years, that incessant drama which the soul enacts with the Divine Powers to which it feels itself committed, lived and persisted through it all. Feeling was untouched. The heart was still passionately on the side of all its old loves and adorations, still blindly trustful that in the end, by some compromise as yet unseen, they would be restored to it intact.

Some time towards the end of July Robert was coming home from the Hall before lunch, tired and worn, as the morning always left him, and meditating some fresh sheets of the squire's proofs which had been in his hands that morning. On the road crossing that to the rectory he suddenly saw Reginald Newcome, thinner and whiter than ever, striding along as fast as cassock and cloak would let him, his eyes on the ground, and his wideawake drawn over them. He and Elsmere had scarcely met for months, and Robert had lately made up his mind that Newcome was distinctly less friendly, and wished to show it.

Elsmere had touched his arm before Newcome had perceived any one near him. Then he drew back with a start.

'Elsmere, you here! I had an idea you were away for a holiday!'

'Oh dear, no!' said Robert, smiling. 'I may get away in September, perhaps—not till then.'

'Mr. Wendover at home?' said the other, his eyes turning to the Hall, of which the chimneys were just visible from where they stood.

'No, he is abroad.'

'You and he have made friends, I understand,' said the other abruptly, his eagle look returning to Elsmere; 'I hear of you as always together.'

'We have made friends, and we walk a great deal when the squire is here,' said Robert, meeting Newcome's harshness of tone with a bright dignity. 'Mr. Wendover has even been doing something for us in the village. You should come and see the new Institute. The roof is on, and we shall open it in August or September. The best building of the kind in the country by far, and Mr. Wendover's gift.'

'I suppose you use the library a great deal?' said Newcome, paying no attention to these remarks, and still eyeing his companion closely.

'A great deal.'

Robert had at that moment under his arm a German treatise on the history of the Logos doctrine,[37] which afterwards, looking back on the little scene, he thought it probable Newcome recognised. They turned towards the rectory together, Newcome still asking abrupt questions as to the squire, the length of time he was to be away, Elsmere's work, parochial and literary, during the past six months, the numbers of his Sunday congregation, of his communicants, etc. Elsmere bore his catechism with perfect temper, though Newcome's manner had in it a strange and almost judicial imperativeness.

'Elsmere,' said his questioner presently, after a pause, 'I am going to have a retreat for priests at the Clergy House next month. Father H——,' mentioning a famous High Churchman, 'will conduct it. You would do me a special favour'—and suddenly the face softened, and shone with all its old magnetism on Elsmere—'if you would come. I believe you would find nothing to dislike in it, or in our rule, which is a most simple one.'

Robert smiled, and laid his hand on the other's arm.

'No, Newcome, no; I am in no mood for H——.'

The High Churchman looked at him with a quick and painful anxiety visible in the stern eyes.

'Will you tell me what that means?'

'It means,' said Robert, clasping his hands tightly behind him, his pace slackening a little to meet that of Newcome—'it means that if you will give me your prayers, Newcome, your companionship sometimes, your pity always, I will thank you from the bottom of my heart. But I am in a state just now when I must fight my battles for myself, and in God's sight only!'

It was the first burst of confidence which had passed his lips to any one but Catherine.

Newcome stood still, a tremor of strong emotion running through the emaciated face.

'You are in trouble, Elsmere; I felt it, I knew it, when I first saw you!'

'Yes, I am in trouble,' said Robert quietly.

'Opinions?'

'Opinions, I suppose—or facts,' said Robert, his arms dropping wearily beside him. 'Have you ever known what it is to be troubled in mind, I wonder, Newcome?'

And he looked at his companion with a sudden pitiful curiosity.

A kind of flash passed over Mr. Newcome's face.

'*Have I ever known?*' he repeated vaguely, and then he drew his thin hand, the hand of the ascetic and the mystic, hastily across his eyes, and was silent—his lips moving, his gaze on the ground, his whole aspect that of a man

---

37 That is, that Christ is the Word of God.

wrought out of himself by a sudden passion of memory.

Robert watched him with surprise, and was just speaking, when Mr. Newcome looked up, every drawn attenuated feature working painfully.

'Did you never ask yourself, Elsmere,' he said slowly, 'what it was drove me from the bar and journalism to the East End? Do you think I don't know,' and his voice rose, his eyes flamed, 'what black devil it is that is gnawing at your heart now? Why, man, I have been through darker gulfs of hell than you have ever sounded! Many a night I have felt myself *mad—mad of doubt*—a castaway on a shoreless sea; doubting not only God or Christ, but myself, the soul, the very existence of good. I found only one way out of it, and *you* will find only one way.'

The lithe hand caught Robert's arm impetuously—the voice with its accent of fierce conviction was at his ear.

'Trample on yourself! Pray down the demon, fast, scourge, kill the body, that the soul may live! What are we, miserable worms, that we should defy the Most High, that we should set our wretched faculties against His Omnipotence? Submit—submit—humble yourself, my brother! Fling away the freedom which is your ruin. There is no freedom for man. Either a slave to Christ, or a slave to his own lusts—there is no other choice. Go away; exchange your work here for a time for work in London. You have too much leisure here: Satan has too much opportunity. I foresaw it—I foresaw it when you and I first met. I felt I had a message for you, and here I deliver it. In the Lord's name, I bid you fly; I bid you yield in time. Better to be the Lord's captive than *the Lord's betrayer!*'

The wasted form was drawn up to its full height, the arm was outstretched, the long cloak fell back from it in long folds—voice and eye were majesty itself. Robert had a tremor of responsive passion. How easy it sounded, how tempting, to cut the knot, to mutilate and starve the rebellious intellect which would assert itself against the soul's purest instincts! Newcome had done it—why not he?

And then, suddenly, as he stood gazing at his companion, the spring sun, and murmur all about them, another face, another life, another message, flashed on his inmost sense—the face and life of Henry Grey. Words torn from their context, but full for him of intensest meaning, passed rapidly through his mind: '*God is not wisely trusted when declared unintelligible.*' '*Such honour rooted in dishonour stands; such faith unfaithful makes us falsely true.*' '*God is for ever reason: and His communication, His revelation, is reason.*'[38]

He turned away with a slight sad shake of the head. The spell was broken.

---

38 Quoted from T. H. Green's essay "The Witness of God."

Mr. Newcome's arm dropped, and he moved sombrely on beside Robert—the hand, which held a little book of Hours against his cloak, trembling slightly.

At the rectory gate he stopped.

'Good-bye—I must go home.'

'You won't come in?—No, no, Newcome; believe me, I am no rash careless egotist, risking wantonly the most precious things in life! But the call is on me, and I must follow it. All life is God's, and all thought—not only a fraction of it. He cannot let me wander very far!'

But the cold fingers he held so warmly dropped from his, and Newcome turned away.

A week afterwards, or thereabouts, Robert had in some sense followed Newcome's counsel. Admonished perhaps by sheer physical weakness, as much as by anything else, he had for the moment laid down his arms; he had yielded to an invading feebleness of the will, which refused, as it were, to carry on the struggle any longer, at such a life-destroying pitch of intensity. The intellectual oppression of itself brought about wild reaction and recoil, and a passionate appeal to that inward witness of the soul which holds its own long after the reason has practically ceased to struggle.

It came about in this way. One morning he stood reading in the window of the library the last of the squire's letters. It contained a short but masterly analysis of the mental habits and idiosyncrasies of St. Paul, *à propos* of St. Paul's witness to the Resurrection. Every now and then, as Elsmere turned the pages, the orthodox protest would assert itself, the orthodox arguments make themselves felt as though in mechanical involuntary protest. But their force and vitality was gone. Between the Paul of Anglican theology and the fiery fallible man of genius—so weak logically, so strong in poetry, in rhetoric, in moral passion, whose portrait has been drawn for us by a free and temperate criticism—the rector knew, in a sort of dull way, that his choice was made.[39] The one picture carried reason and imagination with it; the other contented neither.

But as he put down the letter something seemed to snap within him. Some chord of physical endurance gave way. For five months he had been living intellectually at a speed no man maintains with impunity, and this letter of the squire's, with its imperious demands upon the tired irritable brain, was the last straw.

He sank down on the oriel seat, the letter dropping from his hands. Outside, the little garden, now a mass of red and pink roses, the hill and the

---

39 The "free and temperate criticism" is that of Matthew Arnold, *St. Paul and Protestantism* (1870).

distant stretches of park were wrapped in a thick sultry mist, through which a dim far-off sunlight struggled on to the library floor, and lay in ghostly patches on the polished boards and lower ranges of books.

The simplest religious thoughts began to flow over him—the simplest childish words of prayer were on his lips. He felt himself delivered, he knew not how or why.

He rose deliberately, laid the squire's letter among his other papers, and tied them up carefully; then he took up the books which lay piled on the squire's writing-table: all those volumes of German, French, and English criticism, liberal or apologetic, which he had been accumulating round him day by day with a feverish toilsome impartiality, and began rapidly and methodically to put them back in their places on the shelves.

'I have done too much thinking, too much reading,' he was saying to himself as he went through his task. 'Now let it be the turn of something else!'

And still as he handled the books, it was as though Catherine's figure glided backwards and forwards beside him, across the smooth floor, as though her hand were on his arm, her eyes shining into his. Ah—he knew well what it was had made the sharpest sting of this wrestle through which he had been passing! It was not merely religious dread, religious shame; that terror of disloyalty to the Divine Images which have filled the soul's inmost shrine since its first entry into consciousness, such as every good man feels in a like strait. This had been strong indeed; but men are men, and love is love! Ay, it was to the dark certainty of Catherine's misery that every advance in knowledge and intellectual power had brought him nearer. It was from that certainty that he now, and for the last time, recoiled. It was too much. It could not be borne.

He walked home, counting up the engagements of the next few weeks—the school-treat, two club field-days, a sermon in the county town, the probable opening of the new Workmen's Institute, and so on. Oh! to be through them all and away, away amid Alpine scents and silences. He stood a moment beside the gray slowly-moving river, half hidden beneath the rank flower-growth, the tansy and willow-herb, the luxuriant elder and trailing brambles of its August banks, and thought with hungry passion of the clean-swept Alpine pasture, the fir-woods, and the tameless mountain streams. In three weeks or less he and Catherine should be climbing the Jaman or the Dent du Midi. And till then he would want all his time for men and women. Books should hold him no more.

Catherine only put her arms round his neck in silence when he told her. The relief was too great for words. He, too, held her close, saying nothing. But that night, for the first time for weeks, Elsmere's wife slept in peace and woke without dread of the day before her.

BOOK IV - CRISIS

CHAPTER XXVI

The next fortnight was a time of truce. Elsmere neither read nor reasoned. He spent his days in the school, in the village, pottering about the Mile End cottages, or the new Institute—sometimes fishing, sometimes passing long summer hours on the commons with his club boys, hunting the ponds for caddises, newts, and water-beetles, peering into the furze-bushes for second broods, or watching the sand-martins in the gravel-pits, and trudging home at night in the midst of an escort of enthusiasts, all of them with pockets as full and miry as his own, to deposit the treasures of the day in the club-room. Once more the rector, though physically perhaps less ardent than of yore, was the life of the party, and a certain awe and strangeness which had developed in his boys' minds towards him, during the last few weeks, passed away.

It was curious that in these days he would neither sit nor walk alone if he could help it. Catherine or a stray parishioner was almost always with him. All the while, vaguely, in the depths of consciousness, there was the knowledge that behind this piece of quiet water on which his life was now sailing, there lay storm and darkness, and that in front loomed fresh possibilities of tempest. He knew, in a way, that it was a treacherous peace which had overtaken him. And yet it was peace. The pressure exerted by the will had temporarily given way, and the deepest forces of the man's being had reasserted themselves. He could feel and love and pray again; and Catherine, seeing the old glow in the eyes, the old spring in the step, made the whole of life one thank-offering.

On the evening following that moment of reaction in the Murewell library, Robert had written to the squire. His letter had been practically a withdrawal from the correspondence.

'I find,' he wrote, 'that I have been spending too much time and energy lately on these critical matters. It seems to me that my work as a clergyman has suffered. Nor can I deny that your book and your letters have been to me a source of great trouble of mind.

'My heart is where it was, but my head is often confused. Let controversy rest a while. My wife says I want a holiday; I think so myself, and we are off in three weeks; not, however, I hope, before we have welcomed you home again, and got you to open the new Institute, which is already dazzling the eyes of the village by its size and splendour, and the white paint that Harris the builder has been lavishing upon it.'

Ten days later, rather earlier than was expected, the squire and Mrs. Darcy were at home again. Robert re-entered the great house the morning after their arrival with a strange reluctance. Its glow and magnificence, the warm perfumed air of the hall, brought back a sense of old oppressions, and he walked down the passage to the library with a sinking heart. There he found the squire busy as usual with one of those fresh cargoes of books which always accompanied him on any homeward journey. He was more brown, more wrinkled, more shrunken; more full of force, of harsh epigram, of grim anecdote than ever. Robert sat on the edge of the table laughing over his stories of French Orientalists, or Roman cardinals, or modern Greek professors, enjoying the impartial sarcasm which one of the greatest of *savants* was always ready to pour out upon his brethren of the craft.

The squire, however, was never genial for a moment during the interview. He did not mention his book nor Elsmere's letter. But Elsmere suspected in him a good deal of suppressed irritability; and, as after a while he abruptly ceased to talk, the visit grew difficult.

The rector walked home feeling restless and depressed. The mind had begun to work again. It was only by a great effort that he could turn his thoughts from the squire, and all that the squire had meant to him during the past year, and so woo back to himself 'the shy bird Peace.'

Mr. Wendover watched the door close behind him, and then went back to his work with a gesture of impatience.

'Once a priest, always a priest. What a fool I was to forget it! You think you make an impression on the mystic, and at the bottom there is always something which defies you and common sense. "Two and two do not, and shall not, make four," he said to himself, in a mincing voice of angry sarcasm. "'It would give me too much pain that they should." Well, and so I suppose what might have been a rational friendship will go by the board like everything else. What can make the man shilly-shally in this way? He is convinced already, as he knows—those later letters were conclusive! His living, perhaps, and his work! Not for the money's sake—there never was a more incredibly disinterested person born. But his work? Well, who is to hinder his work? Will he be the first parson in the Church of England who looks after the poor and holds his tongue? If you can't speak your mind, it is something at any rate to possess one—nine-tenths of the clergy being without the appendage. But Elsmere—pshaw! he will go muddling on to the end of the chapter!'

The squire, indeed, was like a hunter whose prey escapes him at the very moment of capture, and there grew on him a mocking aggressive mood which Elsmere often found hard to bear.

One natural symptom of it was his renewed churlishness as to all local matters. Elsmere one afternoon spent an hour in trying to persuade him to open the new Institute.

'What on earth do you want me for?' inquired Mr. Wendover, standing before the fire in the library, the Medusa head peering over his shoulder. 'You know perfectly well that all the gentry about here—I suppose you will have some of them—regard me as an old reprobate, and the poor people, I imagine, as a kind of ogre. To me it doesn't matter a twopenny damn—I apologise; it was the Duke of Wellington's favourite standard of value—but I can't see what good it can do either you or the village, under the circumstances, that I should stand on my head for the popular edification.'

Elsmere, however, merely stood his ground, arguing and bantering, till the squire grudgingly gave way. This time, after he departed, Mr. Wendover, instead of going to his work, still stood gloomily ruminating in front of the fire. His frowning eyes wandered round the great room before him. For the first time he was conscious that now, as soon as the charm of Elsmere's presence was withdrawn, his working hours were doubly solitary; that his loneliness weighed upon him more; and that it mattered to him appreciably whether that young man went or stayed. The stirring of a new sensation, however,—unparalleled since the brief days when even Roger Wendover had his friends and his attractions like other men,—was soon lost in renewed chafing at Elsmere's absurdities. The squire had been at first perfectly content—so he told himself—to limit the field of their intercourse, and would have been content to go on doing so. But Elsmere himself had invited freedom of speech between them.

'I would have given him my best,' Mr. Wendover reflected impatiently. 'I could have handed on to him all I shall never use, and he might use, admirably. And now we might as well be on the terms we were to begin with for all the good I get out of him, or he out of me. Clearly nothing but cowardice! He cannot face the intellectual change, and he must, I suppose, dread lest it should affect his work. Good God, what nonsense! As if any one inquired what an English parson believed nowadays, so long as he performs all the usual antics decently!'

And, meanwhile, it never occurred to the squire that Elsmere had a wife, and a pious one. Catherine had been dropped out of his calculation as to Elsmere's future, at a very early stage.

The following afternoon Robert, coming home from a round, found Catherine out, and a note awaiting him from the Hall.

'Can you and Mrs. Elsmere come in to tea?' wrote the squire. 'Madame de Netteville is here, and one or two others.'

Robert grumbled a good deal, looked for Catherine to devise an excuse for him, could not find her, and at last reluctantly set out again alone.

He was tired and his mood was heavy. As he trudged through the park he never once noticed the soft sun-flooded distance, the shining loops of the river, the feeding deer, or any of those natural witcheries to which eye and sense were generally so responsive. The labourers going home, the children—with aprons full of crab-apples, and lips dyed by the first blackberries—who passed him, got but an absent smile or salute from the rector. The interval of exaltation and recoil was over. The ship of the mind was once more labouring in alien and dreary seas.

He roused himself to remember that he had been curious to see Madame de Netteville. She was an old friend of the squire's, the holder of a London salon, much more exquisite and select than anything Lady Charlotte could show.

'She had the same thing in Paris before the war,' the squire explained. 'Renan gave me a card to her. An extraordinary woman. No particular originality; but one of the best persons "to consult about ideas," like Joubert's Madame de Beaumont, I ever saw.[1] Receptiveness itself. A beauty, too, or was one, and a bit of a sphinx, which adds to the attraction. Mystery becomes a woman vastly. One suspects her of adventures just enough to find her society doubly piquant.'

Vincent directed him to the upper terrace, whither tea had been taken. This terrace, which was one of the features of Murewell, occupied the top of the yew-clothed hill on which the library looked out. Evelyn himself had planned it. Along its upper side ran one of the most beautiful of old walls, broken by niches and statues, tapestried with roses and honeysuckle, and opening in the centre to reveal Evelyn's darling conceit of all—a semicircular space, holding a fountain, and leading to a grotto. The grotto had been scooped out of the hill; it was peopled with dim figures of fauns and nymphs

---

1   Joseph Joubert (1754–1824), French man of letters; Pauline de Beaumont (1768–1803), *salonnière*.

who showed white amid its moist greenery; and in front a marble Silence
drooped over the fountain, which held gold and silver fish in a singularly clear
water. Outside ran the long stretch of level turf, edged with a jewelled rim
of flowers; and as the hill fell steeply underneath, the terrace was like a high
green platform raised into air, in order that a Wendover might see his domain,
which from thence lay for miles spread out before him.

Here, beside the fountain, were gathered the squire, Mrs. Darcy, Madame
de Netteville, and two unknown men. One of them was introduced to Elsmere
as Mr. Spooner, and recognised by him as a Fellow of the Royal Society, a famous mathematician, sceptic, *bon vivant*, and sayer of good things. The other
was a young Liberal Catholic, the author of a remarkable collection of essays on mediæval subjects in which the squire, treating the man's opinions of
course as of no account, had instantly recognised the note of the true scholar.
A pale, small, hectic creature, possessed of that restless energy of mind which
often goes with the heightened temperature of consumption.

Robert took a seat by Madame de Netteville, whose appearance was picturesqueness itself. Her dress, a skilful mixture of black and creamy yellow, lay
about her in folds, as soft, as carelessly effective as her manner. Her plumed
hat shadowed a face which was no longer young in such a way as to hide all
the lines possible; while the half-light brought admirably out the rich dark
smoothness of the tints, the black lustre of the eyes. A delicate blue-veined
hand lay upon her knee, and Robert was conscious after ten minutes or so
that all her movements, which seemed at first merely slow and languid, were
in reality singularly full of decision and purpose.

She was not easy to talk to on a first acquaintance. Robert felt that she
was studying him, and was not so much at his ease as usual, partly owing to
fatigue and mental worry.

She asked him little abrupt questions about the neighbourhood, his
parish, his work, in a soft tone which had, however, a distinct aloofness,
even *hauteur*. His answers, on the other hand, were often a trifle reckless and
offhand. He was in a mood to be impatient with a *mondaine's* languid inquiries into clerical work, and it seemed to him the squire's description had been
overdone.

'So you try to civilise your peasants,' she said at last. 'Does it succeed—is
it worth while?'

'That depends upon your general ideas of what is worth while,' he answered smiling.

'Oh, everything is worth while that passes the time,' she said hurriedly.
'The clergy of the old *régime* went through life half asleep. That was their way

of passing it. Your way, being a modern, is to bustle and try experiments.'

Her eyes, half closed but none the less provocative, ran over Elsmere's keen face and pliant frame. An atmosphere of intellectual and social assumption enwrapped her, which annoyed Robert in much the same way as Langham's philosophical airs were wont to do. He was drawn without knowing it into a match of wits wherein his strokes, if they lacked the finish and subtlety of hers, showed certainly no lack of sharpness or mental resource. Madame de Netteville's tone insensibly changed, her manner quickened, her great eyes gradually unclosed.

Suddenly, as they were in the middle of a skirmish as to the reality of influence, Madame de Netteville paradoxically maintaining that no human being had ever really converted, transformed, or convinced another, the voice of young Wishart, shrill and tremulous, rose above the general level of talk.

'I am quite ready; I am not the least afraid of a definition. Theology is organised knowledge in the field of religion, a science like any other science!'

'Certainly, my dear sir, certainly,' said Mr. Spooner, leaning forward with his hands round his knees, and speaking with the most elegant and good-humoured *sangfroid* imaginable, 'the science of the world's ghosts! I cannot imagine any more fascinating.'

'Well,' said Madame de Netteville to Robert, with a deep breath, '*that* was a remark to have hurled at you all at once out of doors on a summer's afternoon! Oh, Mr. Spooner!' she said, raising her voice, 'don't play the heretic here! There is no fun in it; there are too many with you.'

'I did not begin it, my dear madam, and your reproach is unjust. On one side of me Archbishop Manning's *fidus Achates*,'[2] and the speaker took off his large straw hat and gracefully waved it—first to the right, then to the left. 'On the other, the rector of the parish. "Cannon to right of me, cannon to left of me."[3] I submit my courage is unimpeachable!'

He spoke with a smiling courtesy as excessive as his silky moustache, his long straw-coloured beard, and his Panama hat. Madame de Netteville surveyed him with cool critical eyes. Robert smiled slightly, acknowledged the bow, but did not speak.

Mr. Wishart evidently took no heed of anything but his own thoughts. He sat bolt upright with shining excited eyes.

'Ah, I remember that article of yours in the *Fortnightly*! How you sceptics miss the point!'

---

2   Henry Edward Manning (1808–92), Cardinal and Archbishop of Westminster; "faithful Achilles" (from the *Aeneid*).

3   Adapted from Tennyson, "The Charge of the Light Brigade" (1854), ll. 18-19.

And out came a stream of argument and denunciation which had probably lain lava-hot at the heart of the young convert for years, waiting for such a moment as this, when he had before him at close quarters two of the most famous antagonists of his faith. The outburst was striking, but certainly unpardonably ill-timed. Madame de Netteville retreated into herself with a shrug. Robert, in whom a sore nerve had been set jarring, did his utmost to begin his talk with her again.

In vain!—for the squire struck in. He had been sitting huddled together—his cynical eyes wandering from Wishart to Elsmere—when suddenly some extravagant remark of the young Catholic, and Robert's effort to edge away from the conversation, caught his attention at the same moment. His face hardened, and in his nasal voice he dealt a swift epigram at Mr. Wishart, which for the moment left the young disputant floundering.

But only for the moment. In another minute or two the argument, begun so casually, had developed into a serious trial of strength, in which the squire and young Wishart took the chief parts, while Mr. Spooner threw in a laugh and a sarcasm here and there.

And as long as Mr. Wendover talked, Madame de Netteville listened. Robert's restless repulsion to the whole incident, his passionate wish to escape from these phrases and illustrations and turns of argument which were all so wearisomely stale and familiar to him, found no support in her. Mrs. Darcy dared not second his attempts at chat, for Mr. Wendover, on the rare occasions when he held forth, was accustomed to be listened to; and Elsmere was of too sensitive a social fibre to break up the party by an abrupt exit, which could only have been interpreted in one way.

So he stayed, and perforce listened, but in complete silence. None of Mr. Wendover's side-hits touched him. Only as the talk went on, the rector in the background got paler and paler; his eyes, as they passed from the mobile face of the Catholic convert, already, for those who knew, marked with the signs of death, to the bronzed visage of the squire, grew duller—more instinct with a slowly-dawning despair.

Half an hour later he was once more on the road leading to the park gate. He had a vague memory that at parting the squire had shown him the cordiality of one suddenly anxious to apologise by manner, if not by word. Otherwise everything was forgotten. He was only anxious, half dazed as he was, to make out wherein lay the vital difference between his present self and the Elsmere who had passed along that road an hour before.

He had heard a conversation on religious topics, wherein nothing was new to him, nothing affected him intellectually at all. What was there in that to break the spring of life like this? He stood still, heavily trying to understand himself.

Then gradually it became clear to him. A month ago, every word of that hectic young pleader for Christ and the Christian certainties would have roused in him a leaping passionate sympathy—the heart's yearning assent, even when the intellect was most perplexed. Now that inmost strand had given way. Suddenly the disintegrating force he had been so pitifully, so blindly, holding at bay had penetrated once for all into the sanctuary! What had happened to him had been the first real failure of *feeling*, the first treachery of the *heart*. Wishart's hopes and hatreds, and sublime defiances of man's petty faculties, had aroused in him no echo, no response. His soul had been dead within him.

As he gained the shelter of the wooded lane beyond the gate it seemed to Robert that he was going through, once more, that old fierce temptation of Bunyan's,—

'For after the Lord had in this manner thus graciously delivered me, and had set me down so sweetly in the faith of His Holy Gospel, and had given me such strong consolation and blessed evidence from heaven, touching my interest in His love through Christ, the tempter came upon me again, and that with a more grievous and dreadful temptation than before. And that was, "To sell and part with this most blessed Christ; to exchange Him for the things of life, for anything!" The temptation lay upon me for the space of a year, and did follow me so continually that I was not rid of it one day in a month: no, not sometimes one hour in many days together, for it did always, in almost whatever I thought, intermix itself therewith, in such sort that I could neither eat my food, stoop for a pin, chop a stick, or cast mine eyes to look on this or that, but still the temptation would come: "Sell Christ for this, or sell Christ for that, sell Him, sell Him!"'[4]

Was this what lay before the minister of God now in this *selva oscura* of life?[5] The selling of the Master, of 'the love so sweet, the unction spiritual,' for an intellectual satisfaction, the ravaging of all the fair places of the heart by an intellectual need![6]

And still through all the despair, all the revolt, all the pain, which made the summer air a darkness, and closed every sense in him to the evening beauty, he felt the irresistible march and pressure of the new instincts, the

---

4   From Bunyan's *Grace Abounding to the Chief of Sinners*.

5   Dark forest. A reference to Dante's *Inferno*, 1.2.

6   The hymn "Come, Holy Ghost," sung at the ordination of Anglican priests.

new forces, which life and thought had been calling into being. The words of St. Augustine which he had read to Catherine, taken in a strange new sense, came back to him—'Commend to the keeping of the Truth whatever the Truth hath given thee, and thou shalt lose nothing!'

Was it the summons of Truth which was rending the whole nature in this way?

Robert stood still, and with his hands locked behind him, and his face turned like the face of a blind man towards a world of which it saw nothing, went through a desperate catechism of himself.

'*Do I believe in God?* Surely, surely! "Though He slay me yet will I trust in Him!" *Do I believe in Christ?* Yes,—in the teacher, the martyr, the symbol to us Westerns of all things heavenly and abiding, the image and pledge of the invisible life of the spirit—with all my soul and all my mind!

'*But in the Man-God*, the Word from Eternity,—in a wonder-working Christ, in a risen and ascended Jesus, in the living Intercessor and Mediator for the lives of His doomed brethren?'

He waited, conscious that it was the crisis of his history, and there rose in him, as though articulated one by one by an audible voice, words of irrevocable meaning.

'Every human soul in which the voice of God makes itself felt, enjoys, equally with Jesus of Nazareth, the divine sonship, and "*miracles do not happen!*"'[7]

It was done. He felt for the moment as Bunyan did after his lesser defeat.

'Now was the battle won, and down fell I as a bird that is shot from the top of a tree into great guilt and fearful despair. Thus getting out of my bed I went moping in the field; but God knows with as heavy an heart as mortal man I think could bear, where for the space of two hours I was like a man bereft of life.'

All these years of happy spiritual certainty, of rejoicing oneness with Christ, to end in this wreck and loss! Was not this indeed '*il gran rifiuto*'—the greatest of which human daring is capable?[8] The lane darkened round him. Not a soul was in sight. The only sounds were the sounds of a gently-breathing nature, sounds of birds and swaying branches and intermittent gusts of air rustling through the gorse and the drifts of last year's leaves in the wood beside him. He moved mechanically onward, and presently, after the first

---

7   Probably a reference to Matthew Arnold, "A Comment on Christmas" (1884): "So angry are some good people at being told that miracles do not happen, that if we say this, they cannot bear to have us using the Bible at all, or recommending the Bible."

8   The great refusal. The quotation is from Dante, *The Inferno*, 3.60.

flutter of desolate terror had passed away, with a new inrushing sense which seemed to him a sense of liberty—of infinite expansion.

Suddenly the trees before him thinned, the ground sloped away, and there to the left on the westernmost edge of the hill lay the square stone rectory, its windows open to the evening coolness, a white flutter of pigeons round the dovecote on the side lawn, the gold of the August wheat in the great cornfield showing against the heavy girdle of oak-wood.

Robert stood gazing at it—the home consecrated by love, by effort, by faith. The high alternations of intellectual and spiritual debate, the strange emerging sense of deliverance, gave way to a most bitter human pang of misery.

'O God! My wife—my work!'

...There was a sound of a voice calling—Catherine's voice calling for him. He leant against the gate of the wood-path, struggling sternly with himself. This was no simple matter of his own intellectual consistency or happiness. Another's whole life was concerned. Any precipitate speech, or hasty action, would be a crime. A man is bound above all things to protect those who depend on him from his own immature or revocable impulses. Not a word yet, till this sense of convulsion and upheaval had passed away, and the mind was once more its own master.

He opened the gate and went towards her. She was strolling along the path looking out for him, one delicate hand gathering up her long evening dress—that very same black brocade she had worn in the old days at Burwood—the other playing with their Dandie Dinmont puppy who was leaping beside her. As she caught sight of him, there was the flashing smile, the hurrying step. And he felt he could but just drag himself to meet her.

'Robert, how long you have been! I thought you must have stayed to dinner after all! And how tired you seem!'

'I had a long walk,' he said, catching her hand, as it slipped itself under his arm, and clinging to it as though to a support. 'And I am tired. There is no use whatever in denying it.'

His voice was light, but if it had not been so dark she must have been startled by his face. As they went on towards the house, however, she scolding him for over-walking, he won his battle with himself. He went through the evening so that even Catherine's jealous eyes saw nothing but extra fatigue. In the most desperate straits of life love is still the fountain of all endurance, and if ever a man loved it was Robert Elsmere.

But that night, as he lay sleepless in their quiet room, with the window open to the stars and to the rising gusts of wind, which blew the petals of the cluster-rose outside in drifts of 'fair weather snow' on to the window-sill, he went through an agony which no words can adequately describe.

He must, of course, give up his living and his orders. His standards and judgments had always been simple and plain in these respects. In other men it might be right and possible that they should live on in the ministry of the Church, doing the humane and charitable work of the Church, while refusing assent to the intellectual and dogmatic framework on which the Church system rests; but for himself it would be neither right nor wrong, but simply impossible. He did not argue or reason about it. There was a favourite axiom of Mr. Grey's which had become part of his pupil's spiritual endowment, and which was perpetually present to him at this crisis of his life, in the spirit, if not in the letter—'*Conviction is the Conscience of the Mind.*' And with this intellectual conscience he was no more capable of trifling than with the moral conscience.

The night passed away. How the rare intermittent sounds impressed themselves upon him!—the stir of the child's waking soon after midnight in the room overhead; the cry of the owls on the oak-wood; the purring of the night-jars on the common; the morning chatter of the swallows round the eaves.

With the first invasion of the dawn Robert raised himself and looked at Catherine. She was sleeping with that light sound sleep which belongs to health of body and mind, one hand under her face, the other stretched out in soft relaxation beside her. Her husband hung over her in a bewilderment of feeling. Before him passed all sorts of incoherent pictures of the future; the mind was caught by all manner of incongruous details in that saddest uprooting which lay before him. How her sleep, her ignorance, reproached him! He thought of the wreck of all her pure ambitions—for him, for their common work, for the people she had come to love; the ruin of her life of charity and tender usefulness, the darkening of all her hopes, the shaking of all her trust. Two years of devotion, of exquisite self-surrender, had brought her to this! It was for this he had lured her from the shelter of her hills, for this she had opened to him all her sweet stores of faith, all the deepest springs of her womanhood. Oh, how she must suffer! The thought of it and his own helplessness wrung his heart.

Oh, could he keep her love through it all? There was an unspeakable dread mingled with his grief—his remorse. It had been there for months. In her eyes would not only pain but *sin* divide them? Could he possibly prevent her whole relation to him from altering and dwindling?

It was to be the problem of his remaining life. With a great cry of the soul to that God it yearned and felt for through all the darkness and ruin which encompassed it, he laid his hand on hers with the timidest passing touch.

'Catherine, I will make amends! My wife, I will make amends!'

CHAPTER XXVII

The next morning Catherine, finding that Robert still slept on after their usual waking time, and remembering his exhaustion of the night before, left him softly, and kept the house quiet that he might not be disturbed. She was in charge of the now toddling Mary in the dining-room when the door opened and Robert appeared.

At sight of him she sprang up with a half-cry; the face seemed to have lost all its fresh colour, its look of sun and air; the eyes were sunk; the lips and chin lined and drawn. It was like a face from which the youth had suddenly been struck out.

'Robert!—' but her question died on her lips.

'A bad night, darling, and a bad headache,' he said, groping his way, as it seemed to her, to the table, his hand leaning on her arm. 'Give me some breakfast.'

She restrained herself at once, put him into an armchair by the window, and cared for him in her tender noiseless way. But she had grown almost as pale as he, and her heart was like lead.

'Will you send me off for the day to Thurston ponds?' he said presently, trying to smile with lips so stiff and nerveless that the will had small control over them.

'Can you walk so far? You did overdo it yesterday, you know. You have never got over Mile End, Robert.'

But her voice had a note in it which in his weakness he could hardly bear. He thirsted to be alone again, to be able to think over quietly what was best for her—for them both. There must be a next step, and in her neighbourhood he was too feeble, too tortured, to decide upon it.

'No more, dear—no more,' he said impatiently, as she tried to feed him; then he added as he rose: 'Don't make arrangements for our going next week, Catherine; it can't be so soon.'

Catherine looked at him with eyes of utter dismay. The sustaining hope of all these difficult weeks, which had slipped with such terrible unexpectedness into their happy life, was swept away from her.

'Robert, you *ought* to go.'

'I have too many things to arrange,' he said sharply, almost irritably. Then his tone changed: 'Don't urge it, Catherine.'

His eyes in their weariness seemed to entreat her not to argue. She stooped and kissed him, her lips trembling.

'When do you want to go to Thurston?'

'As soon as possible. Can you find me my fishing-basket and get me some sandwiches? I shall only lounge there and take it easy.'

She did everything for him that wifely hands could do. Then when his fishing-basket was strapped on, and his lunch was slipped into the capacious pocket of the well-worn shooting coat, she threw her arms round him.

'Robert, you will come away *soon*.'

He roused himself and kissed her.

'I will,' he said simply, withdrawing, however, from her grasp as though he could not bear those close pleading eyes. 'Good-bye! I shall be back some time in the afternoon.'

From her post beside the study window she watched him take the short cut across the cornfield. She was miserable, and all at sea. A week ago he had been so like himself again, and now——! Never had she seen him in anything like this state of physical and mental collapse.

'Oh, Robert,' she cried under her breath, with an abandonment like a child's, strong soul that she was, 'why *won't* you tell me, dear? Why won't you let me share? I might help you through—I might.'

She supposed he must be again in trouble of mind. A weaker woman would have implored, tormented, till she knew all. Catherine's very strength and delicacy of nature, and that respect which was inbred in her for the *sacra* of the inner life, stood in her way. She could not catechise him, and force his confidence on this subject of all others. It must be given freely. And oh! it was so long in coming!

Surely, surely, it must be mainly physical, the result of over-strain—expressing itself in characteristic mental worry, just as daily life reproduces itself in dreams. The worldly man suffers at such times through worldly things, the religious man through his religion. Comforting herself a little with thoughts of this kind, and with certain more or less vague preparations for departure, Catherine got through the morning as best she might.

Meanwhile, Robert was trudging along to Thurston under a sky which, after a few threatening showers, promised once more to be a sky of intense heat. He had with him all the tackle necessary for spooning pike, a sport the novelty and success of which had hugely commended it the year before to those Esau-like instincts Murewell had so much developed in him.

And now—oh the weariness of the August warmth, and the long stretch-es of sandy road! By the time he reached the ponds he was tired out; but instead of stopping at the largest of the three, where a picturesque group of old brick cottages brought a reminder of man and his works into the prairie solitude of the common, he pushed on to a smaller pool just beyond, now hidden in a green cloud of birch-wood. Here, after pushing his way through the closely-set trees, he made some futile attempts at fishing, only to put up his rod long before the morning was over and lay it beside him on the bank. And there he sat for hours, vaguely watching the reflection of the clouds, the gambols and quarrels of the waterfowl, the ways of the birds, the alternations of sun and shadow on the softly-moving trees,—the real self of him passing all the while through an interminable inward drama, starting from the past, stretching to the future, steeped in passion, in pity, in regret.

He thought of the feelings with which he had taken orders, of Oxford scenes and Oxford persons, of the efforts, the pains, the successes of his first year at Murewell. What a ghastly mistake it had all been! He felt a kind of sore contempt for himself, for his own lack of prescience, of self-knowledge. His life looked to him so shallow and worthless. How does a man ever retrieve such a false step? He groaned aloud as he thought of Catherine linked to one born to defeat her hopes, and all that natural pride that a woman feels in the strength and consistency of the man she loves. As he sat there by the water he touched the depths of self-humiliation.

As to religious belief, everything was a chaos. What might be to him the ultimate forms and condition of thought, the tired mind was quite incapable of divining. To every stage in the process of destruction it was feverishly alive. But its formative energy was for the moment gone. The foundations were swept away, and everything must be built up afresh. Only the *habit* of faith held, the close instinctive clinging to a Power beyond sense—a Goodness, a Will, not man's. The soul had been stripped of its old defences, but at his worst there was never a moment when Elsmere felt himself *utterly* forsaken.

But his people—his work! Every now and then into the fragmentary de-bate still going on within him there would flash little pictures of Murewell. The green, with the sun on the house-fronts, the awning over the village shop, the vane on the old 'Manor-house,' the familiar figures at the doors; his church, with every figure in the Sunday congregation as clear to him as though he were that moment in the pulpit; the children he had taught, the sick he had nursed, this or that weather-beaten or brutalised peasant whose history he knew, whose tragic secrets he had learnt,—all these memories and images clung about him as though with ghostly hands, asking, 'Why will you desert us? You are ours—stay with us!'

Then his thoughts would run over the future, dwelling, with a tense realistic sharpness, on every detail which lay before him—the arrangements with his *locum tenens*, the interview with the bishop, the parting with the rectory. It even occurred to him to wonder what must be done with Martha and his mother's cottage.

His mother? As he thought of her a wave of unutterable longing rose and broke. The difficult tears stood in his eyes. He had a strange conviction that at this crisis of his life she of *all* human beings would have understood him best.

When would the squire know? He pictured the interview with him, divining, with the same abnormal clearness of inward vision, Mr. Wendover's start of mingled triumph and impatience—triumph in the new recruit, impatience with the Quixotic folly which could lead a man to look upon orthodox dogma as a thing real enough to be publicly renounced, or clerical pledges as more than a form of words. So henceforth he was on the same side with the squire, held by an indiscriminating world as bound to the same negations, the same hostilities! The thought roused in him a sudden fierceness of moral repugnance. The squire and Edward Langham—they were the only sceptics of whom he had ever had close and personal experience. And with all his old affection for Langham, all his frank sense of pliancy in the squire's hands, yet in this strait of life how he shrinks from them both!—souls at war with life and man, without holiness, without perfume!

Is it the law of things? 'Once loosen a man's *religio*, once fling away the old binding elements, the old traditional restraints which have made him what he is, and moral deterioration is certain.' How often he has heard it said! How often he has endorsed it! Is it true? His heart grows cold within him. What good man can ever contemplate with patience the loss, not of friends or happiness, but of his best self? What shall it profit a man, indeed, if he gain the whole world—the whole world of knowledge and speculation—and *lose his own soul?*[9]

And then, for his endless comfort, there rose on the inward eye the vision of an Oxford lecture room, of a short sturdy figure, of a great brow over honest eyes, of words alive with moral passion, of thought instinct with the beauty of holiness. Thank God for the saint in Henry Grey! Thinking of it, Robert felt his own self-respect re-born.

Oh! to see Grey in the flesh, to get his advice, his approval! Even though it was the depth of vacation, Grey was so closely connected with the town, as distinguished from the university, life of Oxford, it might be quite possible

---

9   Mark 8.36.

to find him at home. Elsmere suddenly determined to find out at once if he could be seen.

And if so, he would go over to Oxford at once. *This* should be the next step, and he would say nothing to Catherine till afterwards. He felt himself so dull, so weary, so resourceless. Grey should help and counsel him, should send him back with a clearer brain—a quicker ingenuity of love, better furnished against her pain and his own.

Then everything else was forgotten; and he thought of nothing but that grisly moment of waking in the empty room, when still believing it night, he had put out his hand for his wife, and with a superstitious pang had felt himself alone. His heart torn with a hundred inarticulate cries of memory and grief, he sat on beside the water, unconscious of the passing of time, his gray eyes staring sightlessly at the wood-pigeons as they flew past him, at the occasional flash of a kingfisher, at the moving panorama of summer clouds above the trees opposite.

At last he was startled back to consciousness by the fall of a few heavy drops of warm rain. He looked at his watch. It was nearly four o'clock. He rose, stiff and cramped with sitting, and at the same instant he saw beyond the birchwood on the open stretch of common a boy's figure, which, after a step or two, he recognised as Ned Irwin.

'You here, Ned?' he said, stopping, the pastoral temper in him reasserting itself at once. 'Why aren't you harvesting?'

'Please, sir, I finished with the Hall medders yesterday, and Mr. Carter's job don't begin till to-morrow. He's got a machine coming from Witley, he hev, and they won't let him have it till Thursday, so I've been out after things for the club.'

And opening the tin box strapped on his back, he showed the day's capture of butterflies, and some belated birds' eggs, the plunder of a bit of common where the turf for the winter's burning was just being cut.

'Goatsucker, linnet, stonechat,' said the rector, fingering them. 'Well done for August, Ned. If you haven't got anything better to do with them, give them to that small boy of Mr. Carter's that's been ill so long. He'd thank you for them, I know.'

The lad nodded with a guttural sound of assent. Then his new-born scientific ardour seemed to struggle with his rustic costiveness of speech.

'I've been just watching a queer creetur,' he said at last hurriedly; 'I b'leeve he's that un.'

And he pulled out a well-thumbed handbook, and pointed to a cut of the grasshopper warbler.

'Whereabouts?' asked Robert, wondering the while at his own start of interest.

'In that bit of common t'other side the big pond,' said Ned, pointing, his brick-red countenance kindling into suppressed excitement.

'Come and show me!' said the rector, and the two went off together. And sure enough, after a little beating about, they heard the note which had roused the lad's curiosity, the loud whirr of a creature that should have been a grasshopper, and was not.

They stalked the bird a few yards, stooping and crouching, Robert's eager hand on the boy's arm, whenever the clumsy rustic movements made too much noise among the underwood. They watched it uttering its jarring imitative note on bush after bush, just dropping to the ground as they came near, and flitting a yard or two farther, but otherwise showing no sign of alarm at their presence. Then suddenly the impulse which had been leading him on died in the rector. He stood upright, with a long sigh.

'I must go home, Ned,' he said abruptly. 'Where are you off to?'

'Please, sir, there's my sister at the cottage, her as married Jim, the underkeeper. I be going there for my tea.'

'Come along, then, we can go together.'

They trudged along in silence; presently Robert turned on his companion.

'Ned, this natural history has been a fine thing for you, my lad; mind you stick to it. That and good work will make a man of you. When I go away——'

The boy started and stopped dead, his dumb animal eyes fixed on his companion.

'You know I shall soon be going off on my holiday,' said Robert, smiling faintly; adding hurriedly as the boy's face resumed its ordinary expression: 'But some day, Ned, I shall go for good. I don't know whether you've been depending on me—you and some of the others. I think perhaps you have. If so, don't depend on me, Ned, any more! It must all come to an end—everything must—*everything!*—except the struggle to be a man in the world, and not a beast—to make one's heart clean and soft, and not hard and vile. That is the *one* thing that matters, and lasts. Ah, never forget that, Ned! Never forget it!'

He stood still, towering over the slouching thick-set form beside him, his pale intensity of look giving a rare dignity and beauty to the face which owed so little of its attractiveness to comeliness of feature. He had the makings of a true shepherd of men, and his mind as he spoke was crossed by a hundred different currents of feeling—bitterness, pain, and yearning unspeakable. No man could feel the wrench that lay before him more than he.

Ned Irwin said not a word. His heavy lids were dropped over his deep-set eye; he stood motionless, nervously fiddling with his butterfly net—awkwardness, and, as it seemed, irresponsiveness, in his whole attitude.

Robert gathered himself together.

'Well, good-night, my lad,' he said with a change of tone. 'Good luck to you; be off to your tea!'

And he turned away, striding swiftly over the short burnt August grass in the direction of the Murewell woods, which rose in a blue haze of heat against the slumberous afternoon sky. He had not gone a hundred yards before he heard a clattering after him. He stopped, and Ned came up with him.

'They're heavy, them things,' said the boy, desperately blurting it out, and pointing, with heaving chest and panting breath, to the rod and basket. 'I am going that way, I can leave un at the rectory.'

Robert's eyes gleamed.

'They are no weight, Ned—'cause why? I've been lazy and caught no fish! But there,'—after a moment's hesitation he slipped off the basket and rod, and put them into the begrimed hands held out for them. 'Bring them when you like; I don't know when I shall want them again. Thank you, and God bless you!'

The boy was off with his booty in a second.

'Perhaps he'll like to think he did it for me, by and by,' said Robert sadly to himself, moving on, a little moisture in the clear gray eye.

About three o'clock next day Robert was in Oxford. The night before he had telegraphed to ask if Grey was at home. The reply had been—'Here for a week on way north; come by all means.' Oh! that look of Catherine's when he had told her of his plan, trying in vain to make it look merely casual and ordinary.

'It is more than a year since I have set eyes on Grey, Catherine. And the day's change would be a boon. I could stay the night at Merton, and get home early next day.'

But as he turned a pleading look to her, he had been startled by the sudden rigidity of face and form. Her silence had in it an intense, almost a haughty, reproach, which she was too keenly hurt to put into words.

He caught her by the arm, and drew her forcibly to him. There he made her look into the eyes which were full of nothing but the most passionate imploring affection.

'Have patience a little more, Catherine!' he just murmured. 'Oh, how I have blessed you for silence! Only till I come back!'

'Till you come back,' she repeated slowly. 'I cannot bear it any longer, Robert, that you should give others your confidence, and not me.'

He groaned and let her go. No—there should be but one day more of silence, and that day was interposed for her sake. If Grey from his calmer standpoint bade him wait and test himself, before taking any irrevocable step, he would obey him. And if so, the worst pang of all need not yet be inflicted on Catherine, though as to his state of mind he would be perfectly open with her.

A few hours later his cab deposited him at the well-known door. It seemed to him that he and the scorched plane-trees lining the sides of the road were the only living things in the wide sun-beaten street.

Every house was shut up. Only the Greys' open windows, amid their shuttered neighbours, had a friendly human air.

Yes; Mr. Grey was in, and expecting Mr. Elsmere. Robert climbed the dim familiar staircase, his heart beating fast.

'Elsmere, this is a piece of good fortune!'

And the two men, after a grasp of the hand, stood fronting each other: Mr. Grey, a light of pleasure on the rugged dark-complexioned face, looking up at his taller and paler visitor.

But Robert could find nothing to say in return; and in an instant Mr. Grey's quick eye detected the strained nervous emotion of the man before him.

'Come and sit down, Elsmere—there, in the window, where we can talk. One has to live on this east side of the house this weather.'

'In the first place,' said Mr. Grey, scrutinising him, as he returned to his own book-littered corner of the window-seat. 'In the first place, my dear fellow, I can't congratulate you on your appearance. I never saw a man look in worse condition—to be up and about.'

'That's nothing!' said Robert almost impatiently. 'I want a holiday, I believe. Grey!' and he looked nervously out over garden and apple-trees, 'I have come—very selfishly—to ask your advice; to throw a trouble upon you, to claim all your friendship can give me.'

He stopped. Mr. Grey was silent—his expression changing instantly, the bright eyes profoundly, anxiously attentive.

'I have just come to the conclusion,' said Robert, after a moment, with quick abruptness, 'that I ought now—at this moment—to leave the Church, and give up my living, for reasons which I will describe to you. But before I act on the conclusion, I wanted the light of your mind upon it, seeing that—that—other persons than myself are concerned.'

'Give up your living!' echoed Mr. Grey in a low voice of astonishment. He sat looking at the face and figure of the man before him with a half-frowning expression. How often Robert had seen some rash exuberant youth quelled by that momentary frown! Essentially conservative as was the inmost nature of the man, for all his radicalism there were few things for which Henry Grey felt more instinctive distaste than for unsteadiness of will and purpose, however glorified by fine names. Robert knew it, and, strangely enough, felt for a moment in the presence of the heretical tutor as a culprit before a judge.

'It is, of course, a matter of opinions,' he said, with an effort. 'Do you remember, before I took orders, asking whether I had ever had difficulties, and I told you that I had probably never gone deep enough. It was profoundly true, though I didn't really mean it. But this year—— No, no, I have not been merely vain and hasty! I may be a shallow creature, but it has been natural growth, not wantonness.'

And at last his eyes met Mr. Grey's firmly, almost with solemnity. It was as if in the last few moments he had been instinctively testing the quality of his own conduct and motives by the touchstone of the rare personality beside him; and they had stood the trial. There was such pain, such sincerity, above all such freedom from littleness of soul implied in words and look, that Mr. Grey quickly held out his hand. Robert grasped it, and felt that the way was clear before him.

'Will you give me an account of it?' said Mr. Grey, and his tone was grave sympathy itself. 'Or would you rather confine yourself to generalities and accomplished facts?'

'I will try and give you an account of it,' said Robert; and sitting there with his elbows on his knees, his gaze fixed on the yellowing afternoon sky, and the intricacies of the garden-walls between them and the new Museum, he went through the history of the last two years.[10] He described the beginnings of his historical work, the gradual enlargement of the mind's horizons, and the intrusion within them of question after question, and subject after subject. Then he mentioned the squire's name.

'Ah!' exclaimed Mr. Grey, 'I had forgotten you were that man's neighbour. I wonder he didn't set you against the whole business, inhuman old cynic!'

He spoke with the strong dislike of the idealist, devoted in practice to an everyday ministry to human need, for the intellectual egotist. Robert caught and relished the old pugnacious flash in the eye, the Midland strength of

---

10 The newest museum would have been the anthropological Pitt Rivers Museum, which opened in 1884.

accent.

'Cynic he is, not altogether inhuman, I think. I fought him about his drains and his cottages, however,'—and he smiled sadly—'before I began to read his books. But the man's genius is incontestable, his learning enormous. He found me in a susceptible state, and I recognise that his influence immensely accelerated a process already begun.'

Mr. Grey was struck with the simplicity and fulness of the avowal. A lesser man would hardly have made it in the same way. Rising to pace up and down the room—the familiar action recalling vividly to Robert the Sunday afternoons of bygone years—he began to put questions with a clearness and decision that made them so many guides to the man answering, through the tangle of his own recollections.

'I see,' said the tutor at last, his hands in the pockets of his short gray coat, his brow bent and thoughtful. 'Well, the process in you has been the typical process of the present day. Abstract thought has had little or nothing to say to it. It has been all a question of literary and historical evidence. *I* am old-fashioned enough'—and he smiled—'to stick to the *à priori* impossibility of miracles, but then I am a philosopher! *You* have come to see how miracle is manufactured, to recognise in it merely a natural inevitable outgrowth of human testimony, in its pre-scientific stages. It has been all experimental, inductive. I imagine'—he looked up—'you didn't get much help out of the orthodox apologists?'

Robert shrugged his shoulders.

'It often seemed to me,' he said drearily, 'I might have got through, but for the men whose books I used to read and respect most in old days. The point of view is generally so extraordinarily limited. Westcott, for instance, who means so much nowadays to the English religious world, first isolates Christianity from all the other religious phenomena of the world, and then argues upon its details. You might as well isolate English jurisprudence, and discuss its details without any reference to Teutonic custom or Roman law! You may be as logical or as learned as you like within the limits chosen, but the whole result is false! You treat Christian witness and Biblical literature as you would treat no other witness, and no other literature in the world. And you cannot show cause enough. For your reasons depend on the very witness under dispute. And so you go on arguing in a circle, *ad infinitum.*'

But his voice dropped. The momentary eagerness died away as quickly as it had risen, leaving nothing but depression behind it.

Mr. Grey meditated. At last he said, with a delicate change of tone,—

'And now—if I may ask it, Elsmere—how far has this destructive process gone?'

'I can't tell you,' said Robert, turning away almost with a groan; 'I only know that the things I loved once I love still, and that—that—if I had the heart to think at all, I should see more of God in the world than I ever saw before!'

The tutor's eye flashed. Robert had gone back to the window, and was miserably looking out. After all, he had told only half his story.

'And so you feel you must give up your living?'

'What else is there for me to do?' cried Robert, turning upon him, startled by the slow deliberate tone.

'Well, of course, you know that there are many men, men with whom both you and I are acquainted, who hold very much what I imagine your opinions now are, or will settle into, who are still in the Church of England, doing admirable work there!'

'I know,' said Elsmere quickly—'I know; I cannot conceive it, nor could you. Imagine standing up Sunday after Sunday to say the things you do *not* believe,—using words as a convention which those who hear you receive as literal truth,—and trusting the maintenance of your position either to your neighbour's forbearance or to your own powers of evasion! With the ideas at present in my head, nothing would induce me to preach another Easter Day sermon to a congregation that have both a moral and a legal right to demand from me an implicit belief in the material miracle!'

'Yes,' said the other gravely—'yes, I believe you are right. It can't be said the Broad Church movement has helped us much! How greatly it promised!—how little it has performed! For the private person, the worshipper, it is different—or I think so. No man pries into our prayers; and to cut ourselves off from common worship is to lose that fellowship which is in itself a witness and vehicle of God.'

But his tone had grown hesitating, and touched with melancholy.

There was a moment's silence. Then Robert walked up to him again.

'At the same time,' he said falteringly, standing before the elder man, as he might have stood as an undergraduate, 'let me not be rash! If you think this change has been too rapid to last—if you, knowing me better than at this moment I can know myself—if you bid me wait a while, before I take any overt step, I will wait—oh, God knows I will wait!—my wife——' and his husky voice failed him utterly.

'Your wife!' cried Mr. Grey, startled. 'Mrs. Elsmere does not know?'

'My wife knows nothing, or almost nothing—and it will break her heart!'

He moved hastily away again, and stood with his back to his friend, his tall narrow form outlined against the window. Mr. Grey was left in dismay, rapidly turning over the impressions of Catherine left on him by his last year's sight of her. That pale distinguished woman with her look of strength and character,—he remembered Langham's analysis of her, and of the silent religious intensity she had brought with her from her training among the northern hills.

Was there a bitterly human tragedy preparing under all this thought-drama he had been listening to?

Deeply moved, he went up to Robert, and laid his rugged hand almost timidly upon him.

'Elsmere, it won't break her heart! You are a good man. She is a good woman.' What an infinity of meaning there was in the simple words! 'Take courage. Tell her at once—tell her everything—and let *her* decide whether there shall be any waiting. I cannot help you there; she can; she will probably understand you better than you understand yourself.'

He tightened his grasp, and gently pushed his guest into a chair beside him. Robert was deadly pale, his face quivering painfully. The long physical strain of the past months had weakened for the moment all the controlling forces of the will. Mr. Grey stood over him—the whole man dilating, expanding, under a tyrannous stress of feeling.

'It is hard, it is bitter,' he said slowly, with a wonderful manly tenderness. 'I know it, I have gone through it. So has many and many a poor soul that you and I have known! But there need be no sting in the wound unless we ourselves envenom it. I know—oh! I know very well—the man of the world scoffs, but to him who has once been a Christian of the old sort, the parting with the Christian mythology is the rending asunder of bones and marrow. It means parting with half the confidence, half the joy, of life! But take heart,' and the tone grew still more solemn, still more penetrating. 'It is the education of God! Do not imagine it will put you farther from Him! He is in criticism, in science, in doubt, so long as the doubt is a pure and honest doubt, as yours is. He is in all life, in all thought. The thought of man, as it has shaped itself in institutions, in philosophies, in science, in patient critical work, or in the life of charity, is the one continuous revelation of God! Look for Him in it all; see how, little by little, the Divine indwelling force, using as its tools—but *merely* as its tools!—man's physical appetites and conditions, has built up conscience and the moral life; think how every faculty of the mind has been trained in turn to take its part in the great work of faith upon the visible world! Love and imagination built up religion,—shall reason destroy it? No!—reason is God's like the rest! Trust it,—trust him. The leading strings of the past are dropping from you; they are dropping from the world, not wantonly, or by chance, but in the providence of God. Learn the lesson of your own pain,—learn to seek God, not in any single event of past history, *but in your own soul,*—in the constant verifications of experience, in the life of Christian love. Spiritually you have gone through the last wrench; I promise it you! You being what you are, nothing can cut this ground from under your feet. Whatever may have been the forms of human belief, *faith,* the faith which saves, has always been rooted here! All things change,—creeds and philosophies and outward systems,—but God remains!

> "'Life, that in me has rest,
> As I, undying Life, have power in Thee!'"[11]

The lines dropped with low vibrating force from lips unaccustomed indeed to such an outburst. The speaker stood a moment longer in silence beside the figure in the chair, and it seemed to Robert, gazing at him with fixed eyes, that the man's whole presence, at once so homely and so majestic, was charged with benediction. It was as though invisible hands of healing and consecration had been laid upon him. The fiery soul beside him had kindled anew the drooping life of his own. So the torch of God passes on its way, hand reaching out to hand.

He bent forward, stammering incoherent words of assent and gratitude, he knew not what. Mr. Grey, who had sunk into his chair, gave him time to recover himself. The intensity of the tutor's own mood relaxed; and presently he began to talk to his guest, in a wholly different tone, of the practical detail of the step before him, supposing it to be taken immediately, discussing the probable attitude of Robert's bishop, the least conspicuous mode of withdrawing from the living, and so on—all with gentleness and sympathy indeed, but with an indefinable change of manner, which showed that he felt it well both for himself and Elsmere to repress any further expression of emotion. There was something, a vein of stoicism perhaps, in Mr. Grey's temper of mind, which, while it gave a special force and sacredness to his rare moments of fervent speech, was wont in general to make men more self-controlled than usual in his presence. Robert felt now the bracing force of it.

'Will you stay with us to dinner?' Mr. Grey asked when at last Elsmere got up to go. 'There are one or two lone Fellows coming—asked before your telegram came, of course. Do exactly as you like.'

'I think not,' said Robert, after a pause. 'I longed to see you, but I am not fit for general society.'

Mr. Grey did not press him. He rose and went with his visitor to the

---

11 Emily Brontë, "No Coward Soul is Mine" (1848), ll. 7-8.

door.

'Good-bye, good-bye! Let me always know what I can do for you. And your wife—poor thing, poor thing! Go and tell her, Elsmere; don't lose a moment you can help. God help her and you!'

They grasped each other's hands. Mr. Grey followed him down the stairs and along the narrow hall. He opened the hall door, and smiled a last smile of encouragement and sympathy into the eyes that expressed such a young moved gratitude. The door closed. Little did Elsmere realise that never, in this life, would he see that smile or hear that voice again!

CHAPTER XXVIII

In half an hour from the time Mr. Grey's door closed upon him, Elsmere had caught a convenient cross-country train, and had left the Oxford towers and spires, the shrunken summer Isis, and the flat hot river meadows far behind him. He had meant to stay at Merton, as we know, for the night. Now, his one thought was to get back to Catherine. The urgency of Mr. Grey's words was upon him, and love had a miserable pang that it should have needed to be urged.

By eight o'clock he was again at Churton. There were no carriages waiting at the little station, but the thought of the walk across the darkening common through the August moonrise had been a refreshment to him in the heat and crowd of the train. He hurried through the small town, where the streets were full of summer idlers, and the lamps were twinkling in the still balmy air, along a dusty stretch of road, leaving man and his dwellings farther and farther to the rear of him, till at last he emerged on a boundless tract of common, and struck to the right into a cart-track leading to Murewell.

He was on the top of a high sandy ridge, looking west and north, over a wide evening world of heather and wood and hill. To the right, far ahead, across the misty lower grounds into which he was soon to plunge, rose the woods of Murewell, black and massive in the twilight distance. To the left, but on a nearer plane, the undulating common stretching downwards from where he stood rose suddenly towards a height crowned with a group of gaunt and jagged firs—landmarks for all the plain—of which every ghostly bough and crest was now sharply outlined against a luminous sky. For the wide heaven in front of him was still delicately glowing in all its under parts with soft harmonies of dusky red or blue, while in its higher zone the same tract of sky was closely covered with the finest network of pearl-white cloud, suffused

at the moment with a silver radiance so intense that a spectator might almost
have dreamed the moon had forgotten its familiar place of rising, and was
about to mount into a startled expectant west. Not a light in all the wide
expanse, and for a while not a sound of human life, save the beat of Robert's
step, or the occasional tap of his stick against the pebbles of the road.

Presently he reached the edge of the ridge whence the rough track he
was following sank sharply to the lower levels. Here was a marvellous point
of view, and the rector stood a moment, beside a bare weather-blasted fir, a
ghostly shadow thrown behind him. All around the gorse and heather seemed
still radiating light, as though the air had been so drenched in sunshine that
even long after the sun had vanished the invading darkness found itself still
unable to win firm possession of earth and sky. Every little stone in the sandy
road was still weirdly visible; the colour of the heather, now in lavish bloom,
could be felt though hardly seen.

Before him melted line after line of woodland, broken by hollow after
hollow, filled with vaporous wreaths of mist. About him were the sounds of a
wild nature. The air was resonant with the purring of the night-jars, and every
now and then he caught the loud clap of their wings as they swayed unstead-
ily through the furze and bracken. Overhead a trio of wild ducks flew across,
from pond to pond, their hoarse cry descending through the darkness. The
partridges on the hill called to each other, and certain sharp sounds betrayed
to the solitary listener the presence of a flock of swans on a neighbouring
pool.

The rector felt himself alone on a wide earth. It was almost with a start
of pleasure that he caught at last the barking of dogs on a few distant farms,
or the dim thunderous rush of a train through the wide wooded landscape
beyond the heath. Behind that frowning mass of wood lay the rectory. The
lights must be lit in the little drawing-room; Catherine must be sitting by the
lamp, her fine head bent over book or work, grieving for him perhaps, her
anxious expectant heart going out to him through the dark. He thinks of the
village lying wrapped in the peace of the August night, the lamp rays from
shop-front or casement streaming out on to the green; he thinks of his child,
of his dead mother, feeling heavy and bitter within him all the time the message of separation and exile.

But his mood was no longer one of mere dread, of helpless pain, of miserable self-scorn. Contact with Henry Grey had brought him that rekindling of
the flame of conscience, that medicinal stirring of the soul's waters, which is
the most precious boon that man can give to man. In that sense which attaches to every successive resurrection of our best life from the shades of despair

or selfishness, he had that day, almost that hour, been born again. He was no longer filled mainly with the sense of personal failure, with scorn for his own blundering impetuous temper, so lacking in prescience and in balance; or, in respect to his wife, with such an anguished impotent remorse. He was nerved and braced; whatever oscillations the mind might go through in its search for another equilibrium, to-night there was a moment of calm. The earth to him was once more full of God, existence full of value.

'The things I have always loved, I love still!' he had said to Mr. Grey. And in this healing darkness it was as if the old loves, the old familiar images of thought, returned to him new-clad, re-entering the desolate heart in a white-winged procession of consolation. On the heath beside him the Christ stood once more, and as the disciple felt the sacred presence he could bear for the first time to let the chafing pent-up current of love flow into the new channels, so painfully prepared for it by the toil of thought. '*Either God or an impostor.*' What scorn the heart, the intellect, threw on the alternative! Not in the dress of speculations which represent the product of long past, long superseded looms of human thought, but in the guise of common manhood, laden like his fellows with the pathetic weight of human weakness and human ignorance, the Master moves towards him—

'*Like you, my son, I struggled and I prayed. Like you, I had my days of doubt and nights of wrestling. I had my dreams, my delusions, with my fellows. I was weak; I suffered; I died. But God was in me, and the courage, the patience, the love He gave to me, the scenes of the poor human life He inspired, have become by His will the world's eternal lesson—man's primer of Divine things, hung high in the eyes of all, simple and wise, that all may see and all may learn. Take it to your heart again—that life, that pain, of mine! Use it to new ends; apprehend it in new ways; but knowledge shall not take it from you; and love, instead of weakening or forgetting, if it be but faithful, shall find ever fresh power of realising and renewing itself.*'

So said the vision; and carrying the passion of it deep in his heart the rector went his way, down the long stony hill, past the solitary farm amid the trees at the foot of it, across the grassy common beyond, with its sentinel clumps of beeches, past an ethereal string of tiny lakes just touched by the moonrise, beside some of the first cottages of Murewell, up the hill, with pulse beating and step quickening, and round into the stretch of road leading to his own gate.

As soon as he had passed the screen made by the shrubs on the lawn, he saw it all as he had seen it in his waking dream on the common—the lamp-light, the open windows, the white muslin curtains swaying a little in the soft evening air, and Catherine's figure seen dimly through them.

The noise of the gate, however—of the steps on the drive—had startled her. He saw her rise quickly from her low chair, put some work down beside her, and move in haste to the window.

'Robert!' she cried in amazement.

'Yes,' he answered, still some yards from her, his voice coming strangely to her out of the moonlit darkness. 'I did my errand early; I found I could get back; and here I am.'

She flew to the door, opened it, and felt herself caught in his arms.

'Robert, you are quite damp!' she said, fluttering and shrinking, for all her sweet habitual gravity of manner—was it the passion of that yearning embrace? 'Have you walked?'

'Yes. It is the dew on the common, I suppose. The grass was drenched.'

'Will you have some food? They can bring back the supper directly.'

'I don't want any food now,' he said, hanging up his hat. 'I got some lunch in town, and a cup of soup at Reading coming back. Perhaps you will give me some tea soon—not yet.'

He came up to her, pushing back the thick disordered locks of hair from his eyes with one hand, the other held out to her. As he came under the light of the hall lamp she was so startled by the gray pallor of the face that she caught hold of his outstretched hand with both hers. What she said he never knew—her look was enough. He put his arm round her, and as he opened the drawing-room door holding her pressed against him, she felt the desperate agitation in him penetrating, beating against an almost iron self-control of manner. He shut the door behind them.

'Robert, dear Robert!' she said, clinging to him, 'there is bad news,—tell me—there is something to tell me! Oh! what is it—what is it?'

It was almost like a child's wail. His brow contracted still more painfully.

'My darling,' he said; 'my darling—my dear dear wife!' and he bent his head down to her as she lay against his breast, kissing her hair with a passion of pity, of remorse, of tenderness, which seemed to rend his whole nature.

'Tell me—tell me—Robert!'

He guided her gently across the room, past the sofa over which her work lay scattered, past the flower-table, now a many-coloured mass of roses, which was her especial pride, past the remains of a brick castle which had delighted Mary's wondering eyes and mischievous fingers an hour or two before, to a low chair by the open window looking on the wide moonlit expanse of cornfield. He put her into it, walked to the window on the other side of the room, shut it, and drew down the blind. Then he went back to her, and sank down beside her, kneeling, her hands in his.

'My dear wife—you have loved me—you do love me?'

She could not answer, she could only press his hands with her cold fingers, with a look and gesture that implored him to speak.

'Catherine,' he said, still kneeling before her, 'you remember that night you came down to me in the study, the night I told you I was in trouble and you could not help me. Did you guess from what I said what the trouble was?'

'Yes,' she answered, trembling, 'yes, I did, Robert; I thought you were depressed—troubled—about religion.'

'And I know,' he said with an outburst of feeling, kissing her hands as they lay in his—'I know very well that you went upstairs and prayed for me, my white-souled angel! But Catherine, the trouble grew—it got blacker and blacker. You were there beside me, and you could not help me. I dared not tell you about it; I could only struggle on alone, so terribly alone, sometimes; and now I am beaten, beaten. And I come to you to ask you to help me in the only thing that remains to me. Help me, Catherine, to be an honest man—to follow conscience—to say and do the truth!'

'Robert,' she said piteously, deadly pale, 'I don't understand.'

'Oh, my poor darling!' he cried, with a kind of moan of pity and misery. Then still holding her, he said, with strong deliberate emphasis, looking into the gray-blue eyes—the quivering face so full of austerity and delicacy,—

'For six or seven months, Catherine—really for much longer, though I never knew it—I have been fighting with *doubt*—doubt of orthodox Christianity—doubt of what the Church teaches—of what I have to say and preach every Sunday. First it crept on me I knew not how. Then the weight grew heavier, and I began to struggle with it. I felt I must struggle with it. Many men, I suppose, in my position would have trampled on their doubts—would have regarded them as sin in themselves, would have felt it their duty to ignore them as much as possible, trusting to time and God's help. I *could* not ignore them. The thought of questioning the most sacred beliefs that you and I'—and his voice faltered a moment—'held in common was misery to me. On the other hand, I knew myself. I knew that I could no more go on living to any purpose, with a whole region of the mind shut up, as it were, barred away from the rest of me, than I could go on living with a secret between myself and you. I could not hold my faith by a mere tenure of tyranny and fear. Faith that is not free—that is not the faith of the whole creature, body, soul, and intellect—seemed to me a faith worthless both to God and man!'

Catherine looked at him stupefied. The world seemed to be turning round her. Infinitely more terrible than his actual words was the accent running through words and tone and gesture—the accent of irreparableness, as of something dismally *done* and *finished*. What did it all mean? For what had he brought her there? She sat stunned, realising with awful force the feebleness, the inadequacy, of her own fears.

He, meanwhile, had paused a moment, meeting her gaze with those yearning sunken eyes. Then he went on, his voice changing a little,—

'But if I had wished it ever so much, I could not have helped myself. The process, so to speak, had gone too far by the time I knew where I was. I think the change must have begun before the Mile End time. Looking back, I see the foundations were laid in—in—the work of last winter.'

She shivered. He stooped and kissed her hands again passionately. 'Am I poisoning even the memory of our past for you?' he cried. Then, restraining himself at once, he hurried on again: 'After Mile End you remember I began to see much of the squire. Oh, my wife, don't look at me so! It was not his doing in any true sense. I am not such a weak shuttlecock as that! But being where I was before our intimacy began, his influence hastened everything. I don't wish to minimise it. I was not made to stand alone!'

And again that bitter, perplexed, half-scornful sense of his own pliancy at the hands of circumstance as compared with the rigidity of other men descended upon him. Catherine made a faint movement as though to draw her hands away.

'Was it well,' she said, in a voice which sounded like a harsh echo of her own, 'was it right for a clergyman to discuss sacred things—with such a man?'

He let her hands go, guided for the moment by a delicate imperious instinct which bade him appeal to something else than love. Rising, he sat down opposite to her on the low window seat, while she sank back into her chair, her fingers clinging to the arm of it, the lamplight far behind deepening all the shadows of the face, the hollows in the cheeks, the line of experience and will about the mouth. The stupor in which she had just listened to him was beginning to break up. Wild forces of condemnation and resistance were rising in her; and he knew it. He knew, too, that as yet she only half realised the situation, and that blow after blow still remained to him to deal.

'Was it right that I should discuss religious matters with the squire?' he repeated, his face resting on his hands. 'What are religious matters, Catherine, and what are not?'

Then, still controlling himself rigidly, his eyes fixed on the shadowy face of his wife, his ear catching her quick uneven breath, he went once more through the dismal history of the last few months, dwelling on his state of thought before the intimacy with Mr. Wendover began, on his first attempts to escape the squire's influence, on his gradual pitiful surrender. Then he told the story of the last memorable walk before the squire's journey, of the moment in the study afterwards, and of the months of feverish reading and wrestling which had followed. Half-way through it a new despair seized him. What was the good of all he was saying? He was speaking a language she did not really understand. What were all these critical and literary considerations to her?

The rigidity of her silence showed him that her sympathy was not with him, that in comparison with the vibrating protest of her own passionate faith which must be now ringing through her, whatever he could urge must seem to her the merest culpable trifling with the soul's awful destinies. In an instant of tumultuous speech he could not convey to her the temper and results of his own complex training, and on that training, as he very well knew, depended the piercing, convincing force of all that he was saying. There were gulfs between them—gulfs which, as it seemed to him, in a miserable insight, could never be bridged again. Oh, the frightful separateness of experience!

Still he struggled on. He brought the story down to the conversation at the Hall, described—in broken words of fire and pain—the moment of spiritual wreck which had come upon him in the August lane, his night of struggle, his resolve to go to Mr. Grey. And all through he was not so much narrating as pleading a cause, and that not his own, but Love's. Love was at the bar, and it was for love that the eloquent voice, the pale varying face, were really pleading, through all the long story of intellectual change.

At the mention of Mr. Grey Catherine grew restless; she sat up suddenly, with a cry of bitterness.

'Robert, why did you go away from me? It was cruel. I should have known first. He had no right—no right!'

She clasped her hands round her knees, her beautiful mouth set and stern. The moon had been sailing westward all this time, and as Catherine bent forward the yellow light caught her face, and brought out the haggard change in it. He held out his hands to her with a low groan, helpless against her reproach, her jealousy. He dared not speak of what Mr. Grey had done for him, of the tenderness of his counsel towards her specially. He felt that everything he could say would but torture the wounded heart still more.

But she did not notice the outstretched hands. She covered her face in silence a moment, as though trying to see her way more clearly through the mazes of disaster; and he waited. At last she looked up.

'I cannot follow all you have been saying,' she said, almost harshly. 'I know so little of books, I cannot give them the place you do. You say you have convinced yourself the Gospels are like other books, full of mistakes, and credulous, like the people of the time; and therefore you can't take what they say as you used to take it. But what does it all quite mean? Oh, I am not clever—I cannot see my way clear from thing to thing as you do. If there are mistakes, does it matter so—so—terribly to you?' and she faltered. 'Do you think *nothing* is true because something may be false? Did not—did not—Jesus still live, and die, and rise again?—*can* you doubt—*do* you doubt—that He rose—that He is God—that He is in heaven—that we shall see Him?'

She threw an intensity into every word, which made the short breathless questions thrill through him, through the nature saturated and steeped as hers was in Christian association, with a bitter accusing force. But he did not flinch from them.

'I can believe no longer in an Incarnation and Resurrection,' he said slowly, but with a resolute plainness. 'Christ is risen in our hearts, in the Christian life of charity. Miracle is a natural product of human feeling and imagination; and God was in Jesus—pre-eminently, as He is in all great souls, but not otherwise—not otherwise in kind than He is in me or you.'

His voice dropped to a whisper. She grew paler and paler.

'So to you,' she said presently in the same strange altered voice. 'My father—when I saw that light on his face before he died, when I heard him cry, "Master, *I come!*" was dying—deceived—deluded. Perhaps even,' and she trembled, 'you think it ends here—our life—our love?'

It was agony to him to see her driving herself through this piteous catechism. The lantern of memory flashed a moment on to the immortal picture of Faust and Margaret. Was it not only that winter they had read the scene together?

Forcibly he possessed himself once more of those closely locked hands, pressing their coldness on his own burning eyes and forehead in hopeless silence.

'*Do* you, Robert?' she repeated insistently.

'I know nothing,' he said, his eyes still hidden. 'I know nothing! But I trust God with all that is dearest to me, with our love, with the soul that is His breath, His work in us!'

The pressure of her despair seemed to be wringing his own faith out of him, forcing into definiteness things and thoughts that had been lying in an accepted, even a welcomed, obscurity.

She tried again to draw her hands away, but he would not let them go. 'And the end of it all, Robert?' she said—'the end of it?'

Never did he forget the note of that question, the desolation of it, the indefinable change of accent. It drove him into a harsh abruptness of reply.

'The end of it—so far—must be, if I remain an honest man, that I must give up my living, that I must cease to be a minister of the Church of England. What the course of our life after that shall be is in your hands—absolutely.'

She caught her breath painfully. His heart was breaking for her, and yet there was something in her manner now which kept down caresses and repressed all words.

Suddenly, however, as he sat there mutely watching her, he found her at his knees, her dear arms around him, her face against his breast.

'Robert, my husband, my darling, it *cannot* be! It is a madness—a delusion. God is trying you, and me! You cannot be planning so to desert Him, so to deny Christ—you cannot, my husband. Come away with me, away from books and work, into some quiet place where He can make Himself heard. You are overdone, overdriven. Do nothing now—say nothing—except to me. Be patient a little, and He will give you back Himself! What can books and arguments matter to you or me? Have we not *known* and *felt* Him as He is— have we not, Robert? Come!'

She pushed herself backwards, smiling at him with an exquisite tenderness. The tears were streaming down her cheeks. They were wet on his own. Another moment and Robert would have lost the only clue which remained to him through the mists of this bewildering world. He would have yielded again as he had many times yielded before, for infinitely less reason, to the urgent pressure of another's individuality, and having jeopardised love for truth, he would now have murdered—or tried to murder—in himself the sense of truth for love.

But he did neither.

Holding her close pressed against him, he said in breaks of intense speech: 'If you wish, Catherine, I will wait—I will wait till you bid me speak—but I warn you—there is something dead in me—something gone and broken. It can never live again—except in forms which now it would only pain you more to think of. It is not that I think differently of this point or that point— but of life and religion altogether. I see God's purposes in quite other proportions as it were. Christianity seems to me something small and local. Behind it, around it—including it—I see the great drama of the world, sweeping on—led by God—from change to change, from act to act. It is not that Christianity is false, but that it is only an imperfect human reflection of a part of truth. Truth has never been, can never be, contained in any one creed or system!'

She heard, but through her exhaustion, through the bitter sinking of hope, she only half understood. Only she realised that she and he were alike helpless—both struggling in the grip of some force outside themselves, inexorable, ineluctable.

Robert felt her arms relaxing, felt the dead weight of her form against him. He raised her to her feet, he half carried her to the door, and on to the stairs. She was nearly fainting, but her will held it at bay. He threw open the door of their room, led her in, lifted her—unresisting—on to the bed. Then her head fell to one side, and her lips grew ashen. In an instant or two he had done for her all that his medical knowledge could suggest with rapid decided hands. She was not quite unconscious; she drew up round her, as though with a strong vague sense of chill, the shawl he laid over her, and gradually the slightest shade of colour came back to her lips. But as soon as she opened her eyes and met those of Robert fixed upon her, the heavy lids dropped again.

'Would you rather be alone?' he said to her, kneeling beside her.

She made a faint affirmative movement of the head, and the cold hand he had been chafing tried feebly to withdraw itself. He rose at once, and stood a moment beside her, looking down at her. Then he went.

CHAPTER XXIX

He shut the door softly, and went downstairs again. It was between ten and eleven. The lights in the lower passage were just extinguished; every one else in the house had gone to bed. Mechanically he stooped and put away the child's bricks, he pushed the chairs back into their places, and then he paused a while before the open window. But there was not a tremor on the set face. He felt himself capable of no more emotion. The fount of feeling, of pain, was for the moment dried up. What he was mainly noticing was the effect of some occasional gusts of night-wind on the moonlit cornfield; the silver ripples they sent through it; the shadows thrown by some great trees in the western corners of the field; the glory of the moon itself in the pale immensity of the sky.

Presently he turned away, leaving one lamp still burning in the room, softly unlocked the hall door, took his hat, and went out. He walked up and down the woodpath or sat on the bench there for some time, thinking indeed, but thinking with a certain stern practical dryness. Whenever he felt the thrill of feeling stealing over him again, he would make a sharp effort at repression. Physically he could not bear much more, and he knew it. A part remained for him to play, which must be played with tact, with prudence, and with firmness. Strength and nerves had been sufficiently weakened already. For his wife's sake, his people's sake, his honourable reputation's sake, he must guard himself from a collapse which might mean far more than physical failure.

So in the most patient methodical way he began to plan out the immediate future. As to waiting, the matter was still in Catherine's hands; but he knew that finely tempered soul; he knew that when she had mastered her poor woman's self, as she had always mastered it from her childhood, she would not bid him wait. He hardly took the possibility into consideration. The proposal had had some reality in his eyes when he went to see Mr. Grey; now it had none, though he could hardly have explained why.

He had already made arrangements with an old Oxford friend to take his duty during his absence on the Continent. It had been originally suggested that this Mr. Armitstead should come to Murewell on the Monday following the Sunday they were now approaching, spend a few days with them before their departure, and be left to his own devices in the house and parish, about the Thursday or Friday. An intense desire now seized Robert to get hold of the man at once, before the next Sunday. It was strange how the interview with his wife seemed to have crystallised, precipitated, everything. How infinitely more real the whole matter looked to him since the afternoon! It had passed—at any rate for the time—out of the region of thought, into the hurrying evolution of action, and as soon as action began it was characteristic of Robert's rapid energetic nature to feel this thirst, to make it as prompt, as complete, as possible. The fiery soul yearned for a fresh consistency, though it were a consistency of loss and renunciation.

To-morrow he must write to the bishop. The bishop's residence was only eight or ten miles from Murewell; he supposed his interview with him would take place about Monday or Tuesday. He could see the tall stooping figure of the kindly old man rising to meet him; he knew exactly the sort of arguments that would be brought to bear upon him. Oh, that it were done with—this wearisome dialectical necessity! His life for months had been one long argument. If he were but left free to feel, and live again!

The practical matter which weighed most heavily upon him was the function connected with the opening of the new Institute, which had been fixed for the Saturday—the next day but one. How was he—but much more how was Catherine—to get through it? His lips would be sealed as to any possible withdrawal from the living, for he could not by then have seen the bishop. He looked forward to the gathering, the crowds, the local enthusiasm, the signs of his own popularity, with a sickening distaste. The one thing real to him through it all would be Catherine's white face, and their bitter joint consciousness.

And then he said to himself, sharply, that his own feelings counted for nothing. Catherine should be tenderly shielded from all avoidable pain, but for himself there must be no flinching, no self-indulgent weakness. Did he not owe every last hour he had to give to the people amongst whom he had planned to spend the best energies of life, and from whom his own act was about to part him in this lame impotent fashion?[12]

Midnight! The sounds rolled silverly out, effacing the soft murmurs of the night. So the long interminable day was over, and a new morning had begun. He rose, listening to the echoes of the bell, and—as the tide of feeling surged back upon him—passionately commending the new-born day to God.

Then he turned towards the house, put the light out in the drawing-room, and went upstairs, stepping cautiously. He opened the door of Catherine's room. The moonlight was streaming in through the white blinds. Catherine, who had undressed, was lying now with her face hidden in the pillow, and one white-sleeved arm flung across little Mary's cot. The night was hot, and the child would evidently have thrown off all its coverings had it not been for the mother's hand, which lay lightly on the tiny shoulder, keeping one thin blanket in its place.

'Catherine,' he whispered, standing beside her.

She turned, and by the light of the candle he held shaded from her he saw the austere remoteness of her look, as of one who had been going through deep waters of misery, alone with God. His heart sank. For the first time that look seemed to exclude him from her inmost life.

He sank down beside her, took the hand lying on the child, and laid down his head upon it, mutely kissing it. But he said nothing. Of what further avail could words be just then to either of them? Only he felt through every fibre the coldness, the irresponsiveness of those fingers lying in his.

'Would it prevent your sleeping,' he asked her presently, 'if I came to read here, as I used to when you were ill? I could shade the light from you, of course.'

She raised her head suddenly.

'But you—you ought to sleep.'

Her tone was anxious, but strangely quiet and aloof.

'Impossible!' he said, pressing his hand over his eyes as he rose. 'At any

12 "and from whom his own act": "for" in 1888 corrected to "from" as per *SE(1)* and *W*.

rate I will read first.'

His sleeplessness at any time of excitement or strain was so inveterate, and so familiar to them both by now, that she could say nothing. She turned away with a long sobbing breath, which seemed to go through her from head to foot. He stood a moment beside her, fighting strong impulses of remorse and passion, and ultimately maintaining silence and self-control.

In another minute or two he was sitting beside her feet, in a low chair drawn to the edge of the bed, the light arranged so as to reach his book without touching either mother or child. He had run over the book-shelf in his own room, shrinking painfully from any of his common religious favourites as one shrinks from touching a still sore and throbbing nerve, and had at last carried off a volume of Spenser.

And so the night began to wear away. For the first hour or two, every now and then, a stifled sob would make itself just faintly heard. It was a sound to wring the heart, for what it meant was that not even Catherine Elsmere's extraordinary powers of self-suppression could avail to check the outward expression of an inward torture. Each time it came and went, it seemed to Elsmere that a fraction of his youth went with it.

At last exhaustion brought her a restless sleep. As soon as Elsmere caught the light breathing which told him she was not conscious of her grief, or of him, his book slipped on to his knee.

> 'Open the temple gates unto my love,
>   Open them wide that she may enter in,
> And all the posts adorn as doth behove,
>   And all the pillars deck with garlands trim,
> For to receive this saint with honour due
>   That cometh in to you.
>   With trembling steps and humble reverence,
> She cometh in before the Almighty's view.'[13]

The leaves fell over as the book dropped, and these lines, which had been to him, as to other lovers, the utterance of his own bridal joy, emerged. They brought about him a host of images—a little gray church penetrated everywhere by the roar of a swollen river; outside, a road filled with empty farmers' carts, and shouting children carrying branches of mountain-ash—winding on and up into the heart of wild hills dyed with reddening fern, the sun-gleams stealing from crag to crag, and shoulder to shoulder; inside, row after row of

13 Edmund Spenser, "Epithalamion," ll. 204-11. The quotation that follows is from the same poem, l. 151.

intent faces, all turned towards the central passage, and, moving towards him, a figure 'clad all in white, that seems a virgin best,' whose every step brings nearer to him the heaven of his heart's desire. Everything is plain to him—Mrs. Thornburgh's round cheeks and marvellous curls and jubilant airs, Mrs. Leyburn's mild and tearful pleasure, the vicar's solid satisfaction. With what confiding joy had those who loved her given her to him! And he knows well that out of all griefs, the grief he has brought upon her in two short years is the one which will seem to her hardest to bear. Very few women of the present day could feel this particular calamity as Catherine Elsmere must feel it.

'Was it a crime to love and win you, my darling?' he cried to her in his heart. 'Ought I to have had more self-knowledge? could I have guessed where I was taking you? Oh, how could I know—how could I know.'

But it was impossible to him to sink himself wholly in the past. Inevitably such a nature as Elsmere's turns very quickly from despair to hope; from the sense of failure to the passionate planning of new effort. In time will he not be able to comfort her, and, after a miserable moment of transition, to repair her trust in him and make their common life once more rich towards God and man? There must be painful readjustment and friction, no doubt. He tries to see the facts as they truly are, fighting against his own optimist tendencies, and realising as best he can all the changes which his great change must introduce into their most intimate relations. But after all can love and honesty and a clear conscience do nothing to bridge over, nay, to efface, such differences as theirs will be?

Oh to bring her to understand him! At this moment he shrinks painfully from the thought of touching her faith—his own sense of loss is too heavy, too terrible. But if she will only be still open with him!—still give him her deepest heart, any lasting difference between them will surely be impossible. Each will complete the other, and love knit up the ravelled strands again into a stronger unity.

Gradually he lost himself in half-articulate prayer, in the solemn girding of the will to this future task of a recreating love. And by the time the morning light had well established itself sleep had fallen on him. When he became sensible of the longed-for drowsiness, he merely stretched out a tired hand and drew over him a shawl hanging at the foot of the bed. He was too utterly worn out to think of moving.

When he woke the sun was streaming into the room, and behind him sat the tiny Mary on the edge of the bed, the rounded apple cheeks and wild-bird eyes aglow with mischief and delight. She had climbed out of her cot, and, finding no check to her progress, had crept on, till now she sat triumphantly, with one diminutive leg and rosy foot doubled under her, and her father's thick hair at the mercy of her invading fingers, which, however, were as yet touching him half timidly, as though something in his sleep had awed the baby sense.

But Catherine was gone.

He sprang up with a start. Mary was frightened by the abrupt movement, perhaps disappointed by the escape of her prey, and raised a sudden wail.

He carried her to her nurse, even forgetting to kiss the little wet cheek, ascertained that Catherine was not in the house, and then came back, miserable, with the bewilderment of sleep still upon him. A sense of wrong rose high within him. How *could* she have left him thus without a word?

It had been her way, sometimes, during the summer, to go out early to one or other of the sick folk who were under her especial charge. Possibly she had gone to a woman, just confined, on the farther side of the village, who yesterday had been in danger.

But, whatever explanation he could make for himself, he was none the less irrationally wretched. He bathed, dressed, and sat down to his solitary meal in a state of tension and agitation indescribable. All the exaltation, the courage of the night, was gone.

Nine o'clock, ten o'clock, and no sign of Catherine.

'Your mistress must have been detained somewhere,' he said as quietly and carelessly as he could to Susan, the parlour-maid, who had been with them since their marriage. 'Leave breakfast things for one.'

'Mistress took a cup of milk when she went out, cook says,' observed the little maid with a consoling intention, wondering the while at the rector's haggard mien and restless movements.

'Nursing other people indeed!' she observed severely downstairs, glad as we all are at times to pick holes in excellence which is inconveniently high. 'Missis had a deal better stay at home and nurse *him*!'

The day was excessively hot. Not a leaf moved in the garden; over the cornfield the air danced in long vibrations of heat; the woods and hills beyond were indistinct and colourless. Their dog Dandy lay sleeping in the sun, waking up every now and then to avenge himself on the flies. On the far edge of the cornfield reaping was beginning. Robert stood on the edge of the sunk fence, his blind eyes resting on the line of men, his ear catching the shouts of the farmer directing operations from his gray horse. He could do nothing. The night before, in the wood-path, he had clearly mapped out the day's work. A mass of business was waiting, clamouring to be done. He tried to begin on this or that, and gave up everything with a groan, wandering out again to the gate on to the wood-path to sweep the distances of road or field with hungry straining eyes.

The wildest fears had taken possession of him. Running in his head was a passage from *The Confessions*, describing Monica's horror of her son's heretical opinions. 'Shrinking from and detesting the blasphemies of his error, she began to doubt whether it was right in her to allow her son to live in her house and to eat at the same table with her;' and the mother's heart, he remembered, could only be convinced of the lawfulness of its own yearning by a prophetic vision of the youth's conversion.[14] He recalled, with a shiver, how in the life of Madame Guyon, after describing the painful and agonising death of a kind but comparatively irreligious husband, she quietly adds, 'As soon as I heard that my husband had just expired, I said to Thee, O my God, Thou hast broken my bonds, and I will offer to Thee a sacrifice of praise!'[15] He thought of John Henry Newman, disowning all the ties of kinship with his younger brother because of divergent views on the question of baptismal regeneration; of the long tragedy of Blanco White's life, caused by the slow dropping-off of friend after friend, on the ground of heretical belief.[16] What right had he, or any one in such a strait as his, to assume that the faith of the present is no longer capable of the same stern self-destructive consistency as the faith of the past? He knew that to such Christian purity, such Christian inwardness as Catherine's, the ultimate sanction and legitimacy of marriage rest, both in theory and practice, on a common acceptance of the definite commands and promises of a miraculous revelation. He had had a proof of it in Catherine's passionate repugnance to the idea of Rose's marriage with Edward Langham.

Eleven o'clock striking from the distant tower. He walked desperately along the wood-path, meaning to go through the copse at the end of it towards the park, and look there. He had just passed into the copse, a thick interwoven mass of young trees, when he heard the sound of the gate which on the farther side of it led on to the road. He hurried on; the trees closed behind him; the grassy path broadened; and there, under an arch of young oak and hazel, stood Catherine, arrested by the sound of his step. He, too, stopped at the sight of her; he could not go on. Husband and wife looked at

---

14 Augustine, *The Confessions*, bk. 3.

15 *Autobiography of Madame Guyon*, pt. 1, ch. 22.

16 Francis William Newman (1805–1897), religious skeptic. In *Phases of Faith; Or, Passages from the History of My Creed* (1850), F. W. Newman notes that he and his brother had parted ways over baptismal regeneration in the early 1820s (7). Joseph Blanco White (1775–1841), Spanish Catholic priest who joined the Church of England and wrote anti-Catholic controversial works before finally becoming a Unitarian.

each other one long quivering moment. Then Catherine sprang forward with a sob and threw herself on his breast.

They clung to each other, she in a passion of tears—tears of such self-abandonment as neither Robert nor any other living soul had ever seen Catherine Elsmere shed before. As for him he was trembling from head to foot, his arms scarcely strong enough to hold her, his young worn face bent down over her.

'Oh, Robert!' she sobbed at last, putting up her hand and touching his hair, 'you look so pale, so sad.'

'I have you again!' he said simply.

A thrill of remorse ran through her.

'I went away,' she murmured, her face still hidden—'I went away, because when I woke up it all seemed to me, suddenly, too ghastly to be believed; I could not stay still and bear it. But, Robert, Robert, I kissed you as I passed! I was so thankful you could sleep a little and forget. I hardly know where I have been most of the time—I think I have been sitting in a corner of the park, where no one ever comes. I began to think of all you said to me last night—to put it together—to try and understand it, and it seemed to me more and more horrible! I thought of what it would be like to have to hide my prayers from you—my faith in Christ—my hope of heaven. I thought of bringing up the child—how all that was vital to me would be a superstition to you, which you would bear with for my sake. I thought of death,' and she shuddered—'your death, or my death, and how this change in you would cleave a gulf of misery between us. And then I thought of losing my own faith, of denying Christ. It was a nightmare—I saw myself on a long road, escaping with Mary in my arms, escaping from you! Oh, Robert! it wasn't only for myself,'—and she clung to him as though she were a child, confessing, explaining away, some grievous fault hardly to be forgiven. 'I was agonised by the thought that I was not my own—I and my child were *Christ's*. Could I risk what was His? Other men and women had died, had given up all for His sake. Is there no one now strong enough to suffer torment, to kill even love itself rather than deny Him—rather than crucify Him afresh?'

She paused, struggling for breath. The terrible excitement of that bygone moment had seized upon her again and communicated itself to him.

'And then—and then,' she said sobbing, 'I don't know how it was. One moment I was sitting up looking straight before me, without a tear, thinking of what was the least I must do, even—even—if you and I stayed together—of all the hard compacts and conditions I must make—judging you all the while from a long, long distance, and feeling as though I had buried the old self—sacrificed the old heart—for ever! And the next I was lying on the ground crying for you, Robert, crying for you! Your face had come back to me as you lay there in the early morning light. I thought how I had kissed you—how pale and gray and thin you looked. Oh, how I loathed myself! That I should think it could be God's will that I should leave you, or torture you, my poor husband! I had not only been wicked towards you—I had offended Christ. I could think of nothing as I lay there—again and again—but *"Little children, love one another; little children, love one another."*[17] Oh, my beloved,'—and she looked up with the solemnest, tenderest smile breaking on the marred tear-stained face,—'I will never give up hope, I will pray for you night and day. God will bring you back. You cannot lose yourself so. No, no! His grace is stronger than our wills. But I will not preach to you—I will not persecute you—I will only live beside you—in your heart—and love you always. Oh, how could I—how could I have such thoughts!'

And again she broke off, weeping, as if to the tender torn heart the only crime that could not be forgiven was its own offence against love. As for him he was beyond speech. If he had ever lost his vision of God, his wife's love would that moment have given it back to him.

'Robert,' she said presently, urged on by the sacred yearning to heal, to atone, 'I will not complain—I will not ask you to wait. I take your word for it that it is best not, that it would do no good. The only hope is in time—and prayer. I must suffer, dear, I must be weak sometimes; but oh, I am so sorry for you! Kiss me, forgive me, Robert; I will be your faithful wife unto our lives' end.'

He kissed her, and in that kiss, so sad, so pitiful, so clinging, their new life was born.

CHAPTER XXX

But the problem of these two lives was not solved by a burst of feeling. Without that determining impulse of love and pity in Catherine's heart the salvation of an exquisite bond might indeed have been impossible. But in spite of it the laws of character had still to work themselves inexorably out on either side.

The whole gist of the matter for Elsmere lay really in this question: Hidden in Catherine's nature, was there, or was there not, the true stuff of fanaticism? Madame Guyon left her infant children to the mercies of chance,

---

17 Ascribed by St. Jerome to St. John the Apostle.

while she followed the voice of God to the holy war with heresy.[18] Under similar conditions Catherine Elsmere might have planned the same. Could she ever have carried it out?

And yet the question is still ill stated. For the influences of our modern time on religious action are so blunting and dulling, because in truth the religious motive itself is being constantly modified, whether the religious person knows it or not. Is it possible now for a good woman with a heart, in Catherine Elsmere's position, to maintain herself against love, and all those subtle forces to which such a change as Elsmere's opens the house doors, without either hardening, or greatly yielding? Let Catherine's further story give some sort of an answer.

Poor soul! As they sat together in the study, after he had brought her home, Robert, with averted eyes, went through the plans he had already thought into shape. Catherine listened, saying almost nothing. But never, never had she loved this life of theirs so well as now that she was called on, at barely a week's notice, to give it up for ever! For Robert's scheme, in which her reason fully acquiesced, was to keep to their plan of going to Switzerland, he having first, of course, settled all things with the bishop, and having placed his living in the hands of Mowbray Elsmere. When they left the rectory, in a week or ten days' time, he proposed, in fact, his voice almost inaudible as he did so, that Catherine should leave it for good.

'Everybody had better suppose,' he said choking, 'that we are coming back. Of course we need say nothing. Armitstead will be here for next week certainly. Then afterwards I can come down and manage everything. I shall get it over in a day if I can, and see nobody. I cannot say good-bye, nor can you.'

'And next Sunday, Robert?' she asked him, after a pause.

'I shall write to Armitstead this afternoon and ask him, if he possibly can, to come to-morrow afternoon, instead of Monday, and take the service.'

Catherine's hands clasped each other still more closely. So then she had heard her husband's voice for the last time in the public ministry of the Church, in prayer, in exhortation, in benediction! One of the most sacred traditions of her life was struck from her at a blow.

It was long before either of them spoke again. Then she ventured another question.

'And have you any idea of what we shall do next, Robert—of—of our future?'

---

18 After her husband and two of her children died, Mme. Guyon temporarily relinquished two of her remaining three children in order to pursue her spiritual goals.

'Shall we try London for a little?' he answered in a queer strained voice, leaning against the window, and looking out, that he might not see her. 'I should find work among the poor—so would you—and I could go on with my book. And your mother and sister will probably be there part of the winter.'

She acquiesced silently. How mean and shrunken a future it seemed to them both, beside the wide and honourable range of his clergyman's life as he and she had developed it. But she did not dwell long on that. Her thoughts were suddenly invaded by the memory of a cottage tragedy in which she had recently taken a prominent part. A girl, a child of fifteen, from one of the crowded Mile End hovels, had gone at Christmas to a distant farm as servant, and come back a month ago, ruined, the victim of an outrage over which Elsmere had ground his teeth in fierce and helpless anger. Catherine had found her a shelter, and was to see her through her 'trouble'; the girl, a frail half-witted creature, who could find no words even to bewail herself, clinging to her the while with the dumbest, pitifulest tenacity.

How *could* she leave that girl? It was as if all the fibres of life were being violently wrenched from all their natural connections.

'Robert!' she cried at last with a start. 'Had you forgotten the Institute to-morrow?'

'No—no,' he said with the saddest smile. 'No, I had not forgotten it. Don't go, Catherine—don't go. I must. But why should you go through it?'

'But there are all those flags and wreaths,' she said, getting up in pained bewilderment. 'I must go and look after them.'

He caught her in his arms.

'Oh, my wife, my wife, forgive me!' It was a groan of misery. She put up her hands and pressed his hair back from his temples.

'I love you, Robert,' she said simply, her face colourless, but perfectly calm.

Half an hour later, after he had worked through some letters, he went into the workroom and found her surrounded with flags, and a vast litter of paper roses and evergreens, which she and the new agent's daughters who had come up to help her were putting together for the decorations of the morrow. Mary was tottering from chair to chair in high glee, a big pink rose stuck in the belt of her pinafore. His pale wife, trying to smile and talk as usual, her lap full of evergreens, and her politeness exercised by the chatter of the two Miss Batesons, seemed to Robert one of the most pitiful spectacles he had ever seen. He fled from it out into the village driven by a restless longing for change and movement.

Here he found a large gathering round the new Institute. There were carpenters at work on a triumphal arch in front, and close by, an admiring circle of children and old men, huddling in the shade of a great chestnut.

Elsmere spent an hour in the building, helping and superintending, stabbed every now and then by the unsuspecting friendliness of those about him, or worried by their blunt comments on his looks. He could not bear more than a glance into the new rooms apportioned to the Naturalists' Club. There against the wall stood the new glass cases he had wrung out of the squire, with various new collections lying near, ready to be arranged and unpacked when time allowed. The old collections stood out bravely in the added space and light; the walls were hung here and there with a wonderful set of geographical pictures he had carried off from a London exhibition, and fed his boys on for weeks; the floors were freshly matted; the new pine fittings gave out their pleasant cleanly scent; the white paint of doors and windows shone in the August sun. The building had been given by the squire. The fittings and furniture had been mainly of his providing. What uses he had planned for it all!—only to see the fruits of two years' effort out of doors, and personal frugality at home, handed over to some possibly unsympathetic stranger. The heart beat painfully against the iron bars of fate, rebelling against the power of a mental process so to affect a man's whole practical and social life!

He went out at last by the back of the Institute, where a little bit of garden, spoilt with building materials, led down to a lane.

At the end of the garden, beside the untidy gap in the hedge made by the builders' carts, he saw a man standing, who turned away down the lane, however, as soon as the rector's figure emerged into view.

Robert had recognised the slouching gait and unwieldy form of Henslowe. There were at this moment all kinds of gruesome stories afloat in the village about the ex-agent. It was said that he was breaking up fast; it was known that he was extensively in debt; and the village shopkeepers had already held an agitated meeting or two, to decide upon the best mode of getting their money out of him, and upon a joint plan of cautious action towards his custom in future. The man, indeed, was sinking deeper and deeper into a pit of sordid misery, maintaining all the while a snarling exasperating front to the world, which was rapidly converting the careless half-malicious pity wherewith the village had till now surveyed his fall into that more active species of baiting which the human animal is never very loth to try upon the limping specimens of his race.

Henslowe stopped and turned as he heard the steps behind him. Six months' self-murdering had left ghastly traces. He was many degrees nearer the brute than he had been even when Robert made his ineffectual visit. But at this actual moment Robert's practised eye—for every English parish clergyman becomes dismally expert in the pathology of drunkenness—saw that there was no fight in him. He was in one of the drunkard's periods of collapse—shivering, flabby, starting at every sound, a misery to himself and a spectacle to others.

'Mr. Henslowe!' cried Robert, still pursuing him, 'may I speak to you a moment?'

The ex-agent turned, his prominent bloodshot eyes glowering at the speaker. But he had to catch at his stick for support, or at the nervous shock of Robert's summons his legs would have given way under him.

Robert came up with him and stood a second, fronting the evil silence of the other, his boyish face deeply flushed. Perhaps the grotesqueness of that former scene was in his mind. Moreover, the vestry meetings had furnished Henslowe with periodical opportunities for venting his gall on the rector, and they had never been neglected. But he plunged on boldly.

'I am going away next week, Mr. Henslowe; I shall be away some considerable time. Before I go I should like to ask you whether you do not think the feud between us had better cease. Why will you persist in making an enemy of me? If I did you an injury it was neither wittingly nor willingly. I know you have been ill, and I gather that—that—you are in trouble. If I could stand between you and further mischief I would—most gladly. If help—or—or money——' He paused. He shrewdly suspected, indeed, from the reports that reached him, that Henslowe was on the brink of bankruptcy.

The rector had spoken with the utmost diffidence and delicacy, but Henslowe found energy in return for an outburst of quavering animosity, from which, however, physical weakness had extracted all its sting.

'I'll thank you to make your canting offers to some one else, Mr. Elsmere. When I want your advice I'll ask it. Good day to you.' And he turned away with as much of an attempt at dignity as his shaking limbs would allow of.

'Listen, Mr. Henslowe,' said Robert firmly, walking beside him; 'you know—I know—that if this goes on, in a year's time you will be in your grave, and your poor wife and children struggling to keep themselves from the workhouse. You may think that I have no right to preach to you—that you are the older man—that it is an intrusion. But what is the good of blinking facts that you must know all the world knows? Come, now, Mr. Henslowe, let us behave for a moment as though this were our last meeting. Who knows? the chances of life are many. Lay down your grudge against me, and let me speak to you as one struggling human being to another. The fact that you have, as you say, become less prosperous, in some sort through me, seems to give me a right—to make it a duty for me, if you will—to help you if I can. Let me send a good doctor to see you. Let me implore you as a last chance to put yourself into his hands, and to obey him, and your wife; and let me,'—the rector hesitated,—'let me make things pecuniarily easier for Mrs. Henslowe till you have pulled yourself out of the hole in which, by common report at least, you are now.'

Henslowe stared at him, divided between anger caused by the sore stirring of his old self-importance, and a tumultuous flood of self-pity, roused irresistibly in him by Robert's piercing frankness, and aided by his own more or less maudlin condition. The latter sensation quickly undermined the former; he turned his back on the rector and leant over the railings of the lane, shaken by something it is hardly worth while to dignify by the name of emotion. Robert stood by, a pale embodiment of mingled judgment and compassion. He gave the man a few moments to recover himself, and then, as Henslowe turned round again, he silently and appealingly held out his hand—the hand of the good man, which it was an honour for such as Henslowe to touch. Constrained by the moral force radiating from his look, the other took it with a kind of helpless sullenness.

Then, seizing at once on the slight concession, with that complete lack of inconvenient self-consciousness, or hindering indecision, which was one of the chief causes of his effect on men and women, Robert began to sound the broken repulsive creature as to his affairs. Bit by bit, compelled by a will and nervous strength far superior to his own, Henslowe was led into abrupt and blurted confidences which surprised no one so much as himself. Robert's quick sense possessed itself of point after point, seeing presently ways of escape and relief which the besotted brain beside him had been quite incapable of devising for itself. They walked on into the open country, and what with the discipline of the rector's presence, the sobering effect wrought by the shock to pride and habit, and the unwonted brain exercise of the conversation, the demon in Henslowe had been for the moment most strangely tamed after half an hour's talk. Actually some reminiscences of his old ways of speech and thought, the ways of the once prosperous and self-reliant man of business, had reappeared in him before the end of it, called out by the subtle influence of a manner which always attracted to the surface whatever decent element there might be left in a man, and then instantly gave it a recognition which was more redeeming than either counsel or denunciation.

By the time they parted Robert had arranged with his old enemy that he should become his surety with a rich cousin in Churton, who, always supposing there were no risk in the matter, and that benevolence ran on all-fours with security of investment, was prepared to shield the credit of the family by the advance of a sufficient sum of money to rescue the ex-agent from his most pressing difficulties. He had also wrung from him the promise to see a specialist in London—Robert writing that evening to make the appointment.

How had it been done? Neither Robert nor Henslowe ever quite knew. Henslowe walked home in a bewilderment which for once had nothing to do with brandy, but was simply the result of a moral shock acting on what was still human in the man's debased consciousness, just as electricity acts on the bodily frame.

Robert, on the other hand, saw him depart with a singular lightening of mood. What he seemed to have achieved might turn out to be the merest moonshine. At any rate, the incident had appeased in him a kind of spiritual hunger—the hunger to escape a while from that incessant process of destructive analysis with which the mind was still beset, into some use of energy, more positive, human, and beneficent.

The following day was one long trial of endurance for Elsmere and for Catherine. She pleaded to go, promising quietly to keep out of his sight, and they started together—a miserable pair.

Crowds, heat, decorations, the grandees on the platform, and conspicuous among them the squire's slouching frame and striking head, side by side with a white and radiant Lady Helen—the outer success, the inner revolt and pain—and the constant seeking of his truant eyes for a face that hid itself as much as possible in dark corners, but was in truth the one thing sharply present to him—these were the sort of impressions that remained with Elsmere afterwards of this last meeting with his people.

He had made a speech, of which he never could remember a word. As he sat down, there had been a slight flutter of surprise in the sympathetic looks of those about him, as though the tone of it had been somewhat unexpected and disproportionate to the occasion. Had he betrayed himself in any way? He looked for Catherine, but she was nowhere to be seen. Only in his search he caught the squire's ironical glance, and wondered with quick shame what sort of nonsense he had been talking.

Then a neighbouring clergyman, who had been his warm supporter and admirer from the beginning, sprang up and made a rambling panegyric on him and on his work, which Elsmere writhed under. His work! absurdity! What could be done in two years? He saw it all as the merest nothing, a ragged beginning which might do more harm than good.

But the cheering was incessant, the popular feeling intense. There was old Milsom waving a feeble arm; John Allwood gaunt, but radiant; Mary Sharland, white still as the ribbons on her bonnet, egging on her flushed and cheering husband; and the club boys grinning and shouting, partly for love of Elsmere, mostly because to the young human animal mere noise is heaven. In front was an old hedger and ditcher, who came round the parish periodically, and never failed to take Elsmere's opinion as to 'a bit of prap-perty' he and two other brothers as ancient as himself had been quarrelling over for twenty years, and were likely to go on quarrelling over, till all three litigants had closed their eyes on a mortal scene which had afforded them on the whole vast entertainment, though little pelf. Next him was a bowed and twisted old tramp who had been shepherd in the district in his youth, had then gone through the Crimea and the Mutiny,[19] and was now living about the commons, welcome to feed here and sleep there for the sake of his stories and his queer innocuous wit. Robert had had many a gay argumentative walk with him, and he and his companion had tramped miles to see the function, to rattle their sticks on the floor in Elsmere's honour, and satiate their curious gaze on the squire.

When all was over, Elsmere, with his wife on his arm, mounted the hill to the rectory, leaving the green behind them still crowded with folk. Once inside the shelter of their own trees, husband and wife turned instinctively and caught each other's hands. A low groan broke from Elsmere's lips; Catherine looked at him one moment, then fell weeping on his breast. The first chapter of their common life was closed.

One thing more, however, of a private nature, remained for Elsmere to do. Late in the afternoon he walked over to the Hall.

He found the squire in the inner library, among his German books, his pipe in his mouth, his old smoking coat and slippers bearing witness to the rapidity and joy with which he had shut the world out again after the futilities of the morning. His mood was more accessible than Elsmere had yet found it since his return.

'Well, have you done with all those tomfooleries, Elsmere? Precious elo-quent speech you made! When I see you and people like you throwing your-selves at the heads of the people, I always think of Scaliger's remark about the

---

19 The Crimean War (1853–56), waged against Russia in an attempt to seize con-trol of parts of the Ottoman Empire, in which British military preparedness came under frequent and hostile scrutiny; the Mutiny, or Indian Rebellion (1857), nation-alist resistance movement sparked by a sepoy uprising against their officers, which eventually led to the emergence of the Raj.

Basques: "They say they understand one another—*I don't believe a word of it!*"[20] All that the lower class *wants* to understand, at any rate, is the shortest way to the pockets of you and me; all that you and I need understand, according to me, is how to keep 'em off! There you have the sum and substance of *my* political philosophy.'

'You remind me,' said Robert drily, sitting down on one of the library stools, 'of some of those sentiments you expressed so forcibly on the first evening of our acquaintance.'

The squire received the shaft with equanimity.

'I was not amiable, I remember, on that occasion,' he said coolly, his thin, old man's fingers moving the while among the shelves of books, 'nor on several subsequent ones. I had been made a fool of, and you were not particularly adroit. But of course you won't acknowledge it. Who ever yet got a parson to confess himself!'

'Strangely enough, Mr. Wendover,' said Robert, fixing him with a pair of deliberate feverish eyes, 'I am here at this moment for that very purpose.'

'Go on,' said the squire, turning, however, to meet the rector's look, his gold spectacles falling forward over his long hooked nose, his attitude one of sudden attention. 'Go on.'

All his grievances against Elsmere returned to him. He stood aggressively waiting.

Robert paused a moment, and then said abruptly—

'Perhaps even you will agree, Mr. Wendover, that I had some reason for sentiment this morning. Unless I read the lessons to-morrow, which is possible, to-day has been my last public appearance as rector of this parish!'

The squire looked at him dumfoundered.

'And your reasons?' he said, with quick imperativeness.

Robert gave them. He admitted, as plainly and bluntly as he had done to Grey, the squire's own part in the matter; but here a note of antagonism, almost of defiance, crept even into his confession of wide and illimitable defeat. He was there, so to speak, to hand over his sword. But to the squire, his surrender had all the pride of victory.

'Why should you give up your living?' asked the squire after several minutes' complete silence.

He too had sat down, and was now bending forward, his sharp small eyes peering at his companion.

---

20 Joseph Scaliger (1540–1609), French Huguenot theologian and historian. The quotation is ascribed to him by Chamfort ("On dit qu'ils s'entendent, mais je n'en crois rien") in his *Maximes*.

'Simply because I prefer to feel myself an honest man. However, I have not acted without advice. Grey of St. Anselm's—you know him of course—was a very close personal friend of mine at Oxford. I have been to see him, and we agreed it was the only thing to do.'

'Oh, Grey,' exclaimed the squire, with a movement of impatience. 'Grey of course wanted you to set up a church of your own, or to join his! He is like all idealists, he has the usual foolish contempt for the compromise of institutions.'

'Not at all,' said Robert calmly, 'you are mistaken; he has the most sacred respect for institutions. He only thinks it well, and I agree with him, that with regard to a man's public profession and practice he should recognise that two and two make four.'

It was clear to him from the squire's tone and manner that Mr. Wendover's instincts on the point were very much what he had expected, the instincts of the philosophical man of the world, who scorns the notion of taking popular beliefs seriously, whether for protest or for sympathy. But he was too weary to argue. The squire, however, rose hastily and began to walk up and down in a gathering storm of irritation. The triumph gained for his own side, the tribute to his life's work, were at the moment absolutely indifferent to him. They were effaced by something else much harder to analyse. Whatever it was, it drove him to throw himself upon Robert's position with a perverse bewildering bitterness.

'Why should you break up your life in this wanton way? Who, in God's name, is injured if you keep your living? It is the business of the thinker and the scholar to clear his mind of cobwebs. Granted. You have done it. But it is also the business of the practical man to live! If I had your altruist emotional temperament, I should not hesitate for a moment. I should regard the historical expressions of an eternal tendency in men as wholly indifferent to me. If I understand you aright, you have flung away the sanctions of orthodoxy. There is no other in the way. Treat words as they deserve. *You*'—and the speaker laid an emphasis on the pronoun which for the life of him he could not help making sarcastic—'*you* will always have Gospel enough to preach.'

'I cannot,' Robert repeated quietly, unmoved by the taunt, if it was one. 'I am in a different stage, I imagine, from you. Words—that is to say, the specific Christian formulæ—may be indifferent to you, though a month or two ago I should hardly have guessed it; they are just now anything but indifferent to me.'

The squire's brow grew darker. He took up the argument again, more pugnaciously than ever. It was the strangest attempt ever made to gibe and flout a wandering sheep back into the fold. Robert's resentment was roused at last. The squire's temper seemed to him totally inexplicable, his arguments contradictory, the conversation useless and irritating. He got up to take his leave.

'What you are about to do, Elsmere,' the squire wound up with saturnine emphasis, 'is a piece of *cowardice!* You will live bitterly to regret the haste and the unreason of it.'

'There has been no haste,' exclaimed Robert in the low tone of passionate emotion; 'I have not rooted up the most sacred growths of life as a careless child devastates its garden. There are some things which a man only does because he *must.*'

There was a pause. Robert held out his hand. The squire would hardly touch it. Outwardly his mood was one of the strangest eccentricity and anger; and as to what was beneath it, Elsmere's quick divination was dulled by worry and fatigue. It only served him so far that at the door he turned back, hat in hand, and said, looking lingeringly the while at the solitary sombre figure, at the great library, with all its suggestive and exquisite detail: 'If Monday is fine, Squire, will you walk?'

The squire made no reply except by another question.

'Do you still keep to your Swiss plans for next week?' he asked sharply.

'Certainly. The plan, as it happens, is a Godsend. But there,' said Robert, with a sigh, 'let me explain the details of this dismal business to you on Monday. I have hardly the courage for it now.'

The curtain dropped behind him. Mr. Wendover stood a minute looking after him; then, with some vehement expletive or other, walked up to his writing-table, drew some folios that were lying on it towards him, with hasty maladroit movements which sent his papers flying over the floor, and plunged doggedly into work.

He and Mrs. Darcy dined alone. After dinner the squire leant against the mantelpiece sipping his coffee, more gloomily silent than even his sister had seen him for weeks. And, as always happened when he became more difficult and morose, she became more childish. She was now wholly absorbed with a little electric toy she had just bought for Mary Elsmere, a number of infinitesimal little figures dancing fantastically under the stimulus of an electric current, generated by the simplest means. She hung over it absorbed, calling to her brother every now and then, as though by sheer perversity, to come and look whenever the pink or the blue *danseuse* executed a more surprising somersault than usual.

He took not the smallest spoken notice of her, though his eyes followed her contemptuously as she moved from window to window with her toy in pursuit of the fading light.

'Oh, Roger,' she called presently, still throwing herself to this side and that, to catch new views of her pith puppets, 'I have got something to show you. You must admire them—you shall! I have been drawing them all day, and they are nearly done. You remember what I told you once about my "imps"? I have seen them all my life, since I was a child in France with papa, and I have never been able to draw them till the last few weeks. They are such dears—such darlings; every one will know them when he sees them! There is the Chinese imp, the low smirking creature, you know, that sits on the edge of your cup of tea; there is the flipperty-flopperty creature that flies out at you when you open a drawer; there is the twisty-twirly person that sits jeering on the edge of your hat when it blows away from you; and'—her voice dropped—'that *ugly, ugly* thing I always see waiting for me on the top of a gate. They have teased me all my life, and now at *last* I have drawn them. If they were to take offence to-morrow I should have them—the beauties—all safe.'

She came towards him, her *bizarre* little figure swaying from side to side, her eyes glittering, her restless hands pulling at the lace round her blanched head and face. The squire, his hands behind him, looked at her frowning, an involuntary horror dawning on his dark countenance, turned abruptly, and left the room.

Mr. Wendover worked till midnight; then, tired out, he turned to the bit of fire to which, in spite of the oppressiveness of the weather, the chilliness of age and nervous strain had led him to set a light. He sat there for long, sunk in the blackest reverie. He was the only living creature in the great library wing which spread around and above him—the only waking creature in the whole vast pile of Murewell. The silver lamps shone with a steady melancholy light on the chequered walls of books. The silence was a silence that could be felt; and the gleaming Artemis, the tortured frowning Medusa, were hardly stiller in their frozen calm than the crouching figure of the squire.

So Elsmere was going! In a few weeks the rectory would be once more tenanted by one of those nonentities the squire had either patronised or scorned all his life. The park, the lanes, the room in which he sits, will know that spare young figure, that animated voice, no more. The outlet which had brought so much relief and stimulus to his own mental powers is closed; the friendship on which he had unconsciously come to depend so much is broken before it had well begun.

All sorts of strange thwarted instincts make themselves felt in the squire. The wife he had once thought to marry, the children he might have had, come to sit like ghosts with him beside the fire. He had never, like Augustine, 'loved to love'; he had only loved to know. But none of us escapes to the last the yearnings which make us men. The squire becomes conscious that certain fibres he had thought long since dead in him had been all the while twining themselves silently round the disciple who had shown him in many respects such a filial consideration and confidence. That young man might have become to him the son of his old age, the one human being from whom, as weakness of mind and body break him down, even his indomitable spirit might have accepted the sweetness of human pity, the comfort of human help.

And it is his own hand which has done most to break the nascent slowly-forming tie. He has bereft himself.

With what incredible recklessness had he been acting all these months!

It was the *levity* of his own proceeding which stared him in the face. His rough hand had closed on the delicate wings of a soul as a boy crushes the butterfly he pursues. As Elsmere had stood looking back at him from the library door, the suffering which spoke in every line of that changed face had stirred a sudden troubled remorse in Roger Wendover. It was mere justice that one result of that suffering should be to leave himself forlorn.

He had been thinking and writing of religion, of the history of ideas, all his life. Had he ever yet grasped the meaning of religion *to the religious man*? *God* and *faith*—what have these venerable ideas ever mattered to him personally, except as the subjects of the most ingenious analysis, the most delicate historical inductions? Not only sceptical to the core, but constitutionally indifferent, the squire had always found enough to make life amply worth living in the mere dissection of other men's beliefs.

But to-night! The unexpected shock of feeling, mingled with the terrible sense, periodically alive in him, of physical doom, seems to have stripped from the thorny soul its outer defences of mental habit. He sees once more the hideous spectacle of his father's death, his own black half-remembered moments of warning, the teasing horror of his sister's increasing weakness of brain. Life has been on the whole a burden, though there has been a certain joy no doubt in the fierce intellectual struggle of it. And to-night it seems so nearly over! A cold prescience of death creeps over the squire as he sits in the lamplit silence. His eye seems to be actually penetrating the eternal vastness which lies about our life. He feels himself old, feeble, alone. The awe, the terror which are at the root of all religions have fallen even upon him at last.

The fire burns lower, the night wears on; outside, an airless, misty moonlight lies over park and field. Hark! was that a sound upstairs, in one of those silent empty rooms?

The squire half rises, one hand on his chair, his blanched face strained, listening. Again! Is it a footstep or simply a delusion of the ear? He rises, pushes aside the curtains into the inner library, where the lamps have almost burnt away, creeps up the wooden stair, and into the deserted upper story.

Why was that door into the end room—his father's room—open? He had seen it closed that afternoon. No one had been there since. He stepped nearer. Was that simply a gleam of moonlight on the polished floor—confused lines of shadow thrown by the vine outside? And was that sound nothing but the stirring of the rising wind of dawn against the open casement window? Or——

'*My God!*'

The squire fled downstairs. He gained his chair again. He sat upright an instant, impressing on himself, with sardonic vindictive force, some of those truisms as to the action of mind on body, of brain-process on sensation, which it had been part of his life's work to illustrate. The philosopher had time to realise a shuddering fellowship of weakness with his kind, to see himself as a helpless instance of an inexorable law, before he fell back in his chair; a swoon, born of pitiful human terror—terror of things unseen—creeping over heart and brain.

BOOK V - ROSE

CHAPTER XXXI

It was a November afternoon. London lay wrapped in rainy fog. The atmosphere was such as only a Londoner can breathe with equanimity, and the gloom was indescribable.

Meanwhile, in defiance of the Inferno outside, festal preparations were being made in a little house on Campden Hill. Lamps were lit; in the drawing-room chairs were pushed back; the piano was open, and a violin stand towered beside it; chrysanthemums were everywhere; an invalid lady in a 'best cap' occupied the sofa; and two girls were flitting about, clearly making the last arrangements necessary for a 'musical afternoon.'

The invalid was Mrs. Leyburn, the girls, of course, Rose and Agnes. Rose at last was safely settled in her longed-for London, and an artistic company, of the sort her soul loved, was coming to tea with her.

Of Rose's summer at Burwood very little need be said. She was conscious that she had not borne it very well. She had been off-hand with Mrs. Thornburgh, and had enjoyed one or two open skirmishes with Mrs. Seaton. Her whole temper had been irritating and irritable—she was perfectly aware of it. Towards her sick mother, indeed, she had controlled herself; nor, for such a restless creature, had she made a bad nurse. But Agnes had endured much, and found it all the harder because she was so totally in the dark as to the whys and wherefores of her sister's moods.

Rose herself would have scornfully denied that any whys and wherefores—beyond her rooted dislike of Whindale—existed. Since her return from Berlin, and especially since that moment when, as she was certain, Mr. Langham had avoided her and Catherine at the National Gallery, she had been calmly certain of her own heart-wholeness. Berlin had developed her precisely as she had desired that it might. The necessities of the Bohemian student's life had trained her to a new independence and shrewdness, and in her own opinion she was now a woman of the world judging all things by pure reasons.

Oh, of course, she understood him perfectly. In the first place, at the time of their first meeting she had been a mere bread-and-butter miss, the easiest of preys for any one who might wish to get a few hours' amusement and distraction out of her temper and caprices. In the next place, even supposing he had been ever inclined to fall in love with her, which her new sardonic fairness of mind obliged her to regard as entirely doubtful, he was a man to whom marriage was impossible. How could any one expect such a superfine dreamer to turn bread-winner for a wife and household? Imagine Mr. Langham interviewed by a rate-collector or troubled about coals! As to her—simply—she had misunderstood the laws of the game. It was a little bitter to have to confess it; a little bitter that he should have seen it, and have felt reluctantly compelled to recall the facts to her. But, after all, most girls have some young follies to blush over.

So far the little cynic would get, becoming rather more scarlet, however, over the process of reflection than was quite compatible with the ostentatious worldly wisdom of it. Then a sudden inward restlessness would break through, and she would spend a passionate hour pacing up and down, and hungering for the moment when she might avenge upon herself and him the week of silly friendship he had found it necessary as her elder and monitor to cut short!

In September came the news of Robert's resignation of his living. Mother and daughters sat looking at each other over the letter, stupefied. That this calamity, of all others, should have fallen on Catherine, of all women! Rose said very little, and presently jumped up with shining excited eyes, and ran out for a walk with Bob, leaving Agnes to console their tearful and agitated mother. When she came in she went singing about the house as usual. Agnes, who was moved by the news out of all her ordinary *sangfroid*, was outraged by what seemed to her Rose's callousness. *She* wrote a letter to Catherine, which Catherine put among her treasures, so strangely unlike it was to the quiet indifferent Agnes of every day. Rose spent a morning over an attempt at a letter, which when it reached its destination only wounded Catherine by its constraint and convention.

And yet that same night when the child was alone, suddenly some phrase of Catherine's letter recurred to her. She *saw*, as only imaginative people see, with every detail visualised, her sister's suffering, her sister's struggle that was to be. She jumped into bed, and, stifling all sounds under the clothes, cried herself to sleep, which did not prevent her next morning from harbouring somewhere at the bottom of her, a wicked and furtive satisfaction that Catherine might now learn there were more opinions in the world than one.

As for the rest of the valley, Mrs. Leyburn soon passed from bewailing to a plaintive indignation with Robert, which was a relief to her daughters. It seemed to her a reflection on 'Richard' that Robert should have behaved so. Church opinions had been good enough for 'Richard.' 'The young men seem to think, my dears, their fathers were all fools!'

The vicar, good man, was sincerely distressed, but sincerely confident, also, that in time Elsmere would find his way back into the fold. In Mrs. Thornburgh's dismay there was a secret superstitious pang. Perhaps she had better not have meddled. Perhaps it was never well to meddle. One event bears many readings, and the tragedy of Catherine Elsmere's life took shape in the uneasy consciousness of the vicar's spouse as a more or less sharp admonition against wilfulness in match-making.

Of course Rose had her way as to wintering in London. They came up in the middle of October while the Elsmeres were still abroad, and settled into a small house in Lerwick Gardens, Campden Hill, which Catherine had secured for them on her way through town to the Continent.

As soon as Mrs. Leyburn had been made comfortable, Rose set to work to look up her friends. She owed her acquaintance in London hitherto mainly to Mr. and Mrs. Pierson, the young barrister and his æsthetic wife whom she had originally met and made friends with in a railway-carriage. Mr. Pierson was bustling and shrewd; not made of the finest clay, yet not at all a bad fellow. His wife, the daughter of a famous Mrs. Leo Hunter of a bygone generation, was small, untidy, and in all matters of religious or political opinion 'emancipated' to an extreme. She had also a strong vein of inherited social ambition, and she and her husband welcomed Rose with greater effusion than ever, in proportion as she was more beautiful and more indisputably gifted than ever. They placed themselves and their house at the girl's service, partly out of genuine admiration and good-nature, partly also because they divined in her a profitable social appendage.

For the Piersons, socially, were still climbing, and had by no means attained. Their world, so far, consisted too much of the odds and ends of most other worlds. They were not satisfied with it, and the friendship of the girl-violinist, whose vivacious beauty and artistic gift made a stir wherever she went, was a very welcome addition to their resources. They fêted her in their own house; they took her to the houses of other people; society smiled on Miss Leyburn's protectors more than it had ever smiled on Mr. and Mrs. Pierson taken alone; and meanwhile Rose, flushed, excited, and totally unsuspicious, thought the world a fairy tale, and lived from morning till night in a perpetual din of music, compliments, and bravos, which seemed to her life indeed—life at last!

With the beginning of November the Elsmeres returned, and about the same time Rose began to project tea-parties of her own, to which Mrs. Leyburn gave a flurried assent. When the invitations were written, Rose sat staring at them a little, pen in hand.

'I wonder what Catherine will say to some of these people!' she remarked in a dubious voice to Agnes. 'Some of them are queer, I admit; but, after all, those two superior persons will have to get used to my friends some time, and they may as well begin.'

'You cannot expect poor Cathie to come,' said Agnes with sudden energy.

Rose's eyebrows went up. Agnes resented her ironical expression, and with a word or two of quite unusual sharpness got up and went.

Rose, left alone, sprang up suddenly, and clasped her white fingers above her head, with a long breath.

'Where my heart used to be there is now just—a black—cold—cinder,' she remarked with sarcastic emphasis. 'I am sure I used to be a nice girl once, but it is so long ago I can't remember it!'

She stayed so a minute or more; then two tears suddenly broke and fell. She dashed them angrily away, and sat down again to her note-writing.

Amongst the cards she had still to fill up was one of which the envelope was addressed to the Hon. Hugh Flaxman, 90 St. James's Place. Lady Charlotte, though she had afterwards again left town, had been in Martin Street at the end of October. The Leyburns had lunched there, and had been introduced by her to her nephew, and Lady Helen's brother, Mr. Flaxman. The girls had found him agreeable; he had called the week afterwards when they were not at home; and Rose now carelessly sent him a card, with the inward reflection that he was much too great a man to come, and was probably enjoying himself at country houses, as every aristocrat should, in November.

The following day the two girls made their way over to Bedford Square, where the Elsmeres had taken a house in order to be near the British Museum. They pushed their way upstairs through a medley of packing-cases, and a sickening smell of paint. There was a sound of an opening door, and a gentleman stepped out of the back room, which was to be Elsmere's study, on to the landing.

It was Edward Langham. He and Rose stood and stared at each other a moment. Then Rose in the coolest, lightest voice introduced him to Agnes. Agnes, with one curious glance, took in her sister's defiant smiling ease and the stranger's embarrassment; then she went on to find Catherine. The two left behind exchanged a few *banal* questions and answers. Langham had only allowed himself one look at the dazzling face and eyes framed in fur cap and boa. Afterwards he stood making a study of the ground, and answering her remarks in his usual stumbling fashion. What was it had gone out of her voice—simply the soft callow sounds of first youth? And what a personage she had grown in these twelve months—how formidably, consciously brilliant in look and dress and manner!

Yes, he was still in town—settled there, indeed, for some time. And she—was there any special day on which Mrs. Leyburn received visitors? He asked the question, of course, with various hesitations and circumlocutions.

'Oh dear, yes! Will you come next Wednesday, for instance, and inspect a musical menagerie? The animals will go through their performances from four till seven. And I can answer for it that some of the specimens will be entirely new to you.'

The prospect offered could hardly have been more repellent to him, but he got out an acceptance somehow. She nodded lightly to him and passed on, and he went downstairs, his head in a whirl. Where had the crude pretty child of yester-year departed to—impulsive, conceited, readily offended, easily touched, sensitive as to what all the world might think of her and her performances? The girl he had just left had counted all her resources, tried the edge of all her weapons, and knew her own place too well to ask for anybody else's appraisement. What beauty—good heavens!—what *aplomb!* The rich husband Elsmere talked of would hardly take much waiting for.

So cogitating, Langham took his way westward to his Beaumont Street rooms. They were on the second floor, small, dingy, choked with books. Ordinarily he shut the door behind him with a sigh of content. This evening they seemed to him intolerably confined and stuffy. He thought of going out to his club and a concert, but did nothing, after all, but sit brooding over the fire till midnight, alternately hugging and hating his solitude.

And so we return to the Wednesday following this unexpected meeting.

The drawing-room at No. 27 was beginning to fill. Rose stood at the door receiving the guests as they flowed in, while Agnes in the background dispensed tea. She was discussing with herself the probability of Langham's appearance. 'Whom shall I introduce him to first?' she pondered, while she shook hands. 'The poet? I see mamma is now struggling with him. The 'cellist with the hair—or the lady in Greek dress—or the esoteric Buddhist? What a fascinating selection! I had really no notion we should be quite so curious!'

'Mees Rose, they vait for you,' said a charming golden-bearded young German, viola in hand, bowing before her. He and his kind were most of them in love with her already, and all the more so because she knew so well how to keep them at a distance.

She went off, beckoning to Agnes to take her place, and the quartette began. The young German aforesaid played the viola, while the 'cello was divinely played by a Hungarian, of whose outer man it need only be said that in wild profusion of much-tortured hair, in Hebraism of feature, and swarthy smoothness of cheek, he belonged to that type which Nature would seem to have already used to excess in the production of the continental musician. Rose herself was violinist, and the instruments dashed into the opening allegro with a precision and an *entrain* that took the room by storm.

In the middle of it, Langham pushed his way into the crowd round the drawing-room door. Through the heads about him, he could see her standing a little in advance of the others, her head turned to one side, really in the natural attitude of violin-playing, but, as it seemed to him, in a kind of ravishment of listening—cheeks flushed, eyes shining, and the right arm and high-curved wrist managing the bow with a grace born of knowledge and fine training.

'Very much improved, eh?' said an English professional to a German neighbour, lifting his eyebrows interrogatively.

The other nodded with the business-like air of one who knows. 'Joachim, they say, *war darüber entzückt*,[1] and did his best vid her, and now D—— has got her'—naming a famous violinist—'she vill make fast brogress. He vill schtamp upon her treecks!'

'But will she ever be more than a very clever amateur? Too pretty, eh?' And the questioner nudged his companion, dropping his voice.

Langham would have given worlds to get on into the room, over the prostrate body of the speaker by preference, but the laws of mass and weight had him at their mercy, and he was rooted to the spot.

The other shrugged his shoulders. 'Vell, vid a bretty woman—*überhaupt*— it *doesn't* mean business![2] It's zoziety—the dukes and the duchesses—that ruins all the yong talents.'

This whispered conversation went on during the andante. With the scherzo the two hirsute faces broke into broad smiles. The artist behind each woke up, and Langham heard no more, except guttural sounds of delight and quick notes of technical criticism.

How that Scherzo danced and coquetted, and how the Presto flew as though all the winds were behind it, chasing its mad eddies of notes through

---

1 Was also delighted.

2 *überhaupt*: in the sense of "in general."

listening space! At the end, amid a wild storm of applause, she laid down her violin, and, proudly smiling, her breast still heaving with excitement and exertion, received the praises of those crowding round her. The group round the door was precipitated forward, and Langham with it. She saw him in a moment. Her white brow contracted, and she gave him a quick but hardly smiling glance of recognition through the crowd. He thought there was no chance of getting at her, and moved aside amid the general hubbub to look at a picture.

'Mr. Langham, how do you do?'

He turned sharply and found her beside him. She had come to him with malice in her heart—malice born of smart and long smouldering pain; but as she caught his look, the look of the nervous short-sighted scholar and recluse, as her glance swept over the delicate refinement of the face, a sudden softness quivered in her own. The game was so defenceless!

'You will find nobody here you know,' she said abruptly, a little under her breath. 'I am morally certain you never saw a single person in the room before! Shall I introduce you?'

'Delighted, of course. But don't disturb yourself about me, Miss Leyburn. I come out of my hole so seldom, everything amuses me—but especially looking and listening.'

'Which means,' she said, with frank audacity, 'that you dislike new people!'

His eye kindled at once. 'Say rather that it means a preference for the people that are not new! There is such a thing as concentrating one's attention. I came to hear you play, Miss Leyburn!'

'Well?'

She glanced at him from under her long lashes, one hand playing with the rings on the other. He thought, suddenly, with a sting of regret, of the confiding child who had flushed under his praise that Sunday evening at Murewell.

'Superb!' he said, but half-mechanically. 'I had no notion a winter's work would have done so much for you. Was Berlin as stimulating as you expected? When I heard you had gone, I said to myself—"Well, at least, now, there is one completely happy person in Europe!"'

'Did you? How easily we all dogmatise about each other!'[3] she said scornfully. Her manner was by no means simple. He did not feel himself at all at ease with her. His very embarrassment, however, drove him into rashness, as often happens.

---

3   Question mark changed to exclamation point as per *W*.

'I thought I had enough to go upon!' he said in another tone; and his black eyes, sparkling as though a film had dropped from them, supplied the reference his words forbore.

She turned away from him with a perceptible drawing up of the whole figure.

'Will you come and be introduced?' she asked him coldly. He bowed as coldly and followed her. Wholesome resentment of her manner was denied him. He *had* asked for her friendship, and had then gone away and forgotten her. Clearly what she meant him to see now was that they were strangers again. Well, she was amply in her right. He suspected that his allusion to their first talk over the fire had not been unwelcome to her, as an opportunity.

And he had actually debated whether he should come, lest in spite of himself she might beguile him once more into those old lapses of will and common sense! Coxcomb!

He made a few spasmodic efforts at conversation with the lady to whom she had introduced him, then awkwardly disengaged himself and went to stand in a corner and study his neighbours.

Close to him, he found, was the poet of the party, got up in the most correct professional costume—long hair, velvet coat, eyeglass and all.[4] His extravagance, however, was of the most conventional type. Only his vanity had a touch of the sublime. Langham, who possessed a sort of fine-ear gift for catching conversation, heard him saying to an open-eyed *ingénue* beside him,—

'Oh, my literary baggage is small as yet. I have only done, perhaps, three things that will live.'

'Oh, Mr. Wood!' said the maiden, mildly protesting against so much modesty.

He smiled, thrusting his hand into the breast of the velvet coat. 'But then,' he said, in a tone of the purest candour, 'at my age I don't think Shelley had done more!'

Langham, who, like all shy men, was liable to occasional explosions, was seized with a convulsive fit of coughing, and had to retire from the neighbourhood of the bard, who looked round him, disturbed and slightly frowning.

At last he discovered a point of view in the back room whence he could watch the humours of the crowd without coming too closely in contact with them. What a miscellaneous collection it was! He began to be irritably jealous for Rose's place in the world. She ought to be more adequately surrounded than this. What was Mrs. Leyburn—what were the Elsmeres about? He

---

4   The marks of an aesthete in Oscar Wilde's mode.

rebelled against the thought of her living perpetually among her inferiors, the centre of a vulgar publicity, queen of the second-rate.

It provoked him that she should be amusing herself so well. Her laughter, every now and then, came ringing into the back room. And presently there was a general hubbub. Langham craned his neck forward, and saw a struggle going on over a roll of music, between Rose and the long-haired, long-nosed violoncellist. Evidently she did not want to play some particular piece, and wished to put it out of sight. Whereupon the Hungarian, who had been clamouring for it, rushed to its rescue, and there was a mock fight over it. At last, amid the applause of the room, Rose was beaten, and her conqueror, flourishing the music on high, executed a kind of *pas seul* of triumph.

'*Victoria!*' he cried. 'Now denn for de conditions of peace. Mees Rose, vill you kindly tune up? You are as moch beaten as the French at Sedan.'[5]

'Not a stone of my fortresses, not an inch of my territory!' said Rose, with fine emphasis, crossing her white wrists before her.

The Hungarian looked at her, the wild poetic strain in him which was the strain of race asserting itself.

'But if de victor bows,' he said, dropping on one knee before her. 'If force lay down his spoils at de feet of beauty?'

The circle round them applauded hotly, the touch of theatricality finding immediate response. Langham was remorselessly conscious of the man's absurd *chevelure* and ill-fitting clothes. But Rose herself had evidently nothing but relish for the scene. Proudly smiling, she held out her hand for her property, and as soon as she had it safe, she whisked it into the open drawer of a cabinet standing near, and drawing out the key, held it up a moment in her taper fingers, and then, depositing it in a little velvet bag hanging at her girdle, she closed the snap upon it with a little vindictive wave of triumph. Every movement was graceful, rapid, effective.

Half a dozen German throats broke into guttural protest. Amid the storm of laughter and remonstrance, the door suddenly opened. The fluttered parlour-maid mumbled a long name, and, with a port of soldierly uprightness, there advanced behind her a large fair-haired woman, followed by a gentleman, and in the distance by another figure.

Rose drew back a moment astounded, one hand on the piano, her dress sweeping round her. An awkward silence fell on the chattering circle of musicians.

'Good heavens!' said Langham to himself, 'Lady Charlotte Wynnstay!'

'How do you do, Miss Leyburn?' said one of the most piercing of voices.

5　　The French suffered a devastating loss to Prussia in the Battle of Sedan (1870).

'Are you surprised to see me? You didn't ask me—perhaps you don't want me. But I have come, you see, partly because my nephew was coming,' and she pointed to the gentleman behind her, 'partly because I meant to punish you for not having come to see me last Thursday. Why didn't you?'

'Because we thought you were still away,' said Rose, who had by this time recovered her self-possession. 'But if you meant to punish me, Lady Charlotte, you have done it badly. I am delighted to see you. May I introduce my sister? Agnes, will you find Lady Charlotte Wynnstay a chair by mamma?'

'Oh, you wish, I see, to dispose of me at once,' said the other imperturbably. 'What is happening? Is it music?'

'Aunt Charlotte, that is most disingenuous on your part. I gave you ample warning.'

Rose turned a smiling face towards the speaker. It was Mr. Flaxman, Lady Charlotte's companion.

'You need not have drawn the picture too black, Mr. Flaxman. There is an escape. If Lady Charlotte will only let my sister take her into the next room, she will find herself well out of the clutches of the music. Oh, Robert! Here you are at last! Lady Charlotte, you remember my brother-in-law? Robert, will you get Lady Charlotte some tea?'

'*I* am not going to be banished,' said Mr. Flaxman, looking down upon her, his well-bred, slightly worn face aglow with animation and pleasure.

'Then you will be deafened,' said Rose, laughing, as she escaped from him a moment, to arrange for a song from a tall formidable maiden, built after the fashion of Mr. Gilbert's contralto heroines, with a voice which bore out the ample promise of her frame.[6]

'Your sister is a terribly self-possessed young person, Mr. Elsmere,' said Lady Charlotte, as Robert piloted her across the room.

'Does that imply praise or blame on your part, Lady Charlotte?' asked Robert, smiling.

'Neither at present. I don't know Miss Leyburn well enough. I merely state a fact. No tea, Mr. Elsmere. I have had three teas already, and I am not like the American woman who could always worry down another cup.'

She was introduced to Mrs. Leyburn; but the plaintive invalid was immediately seized with terror of her voice and appearance, and was infinitely grateful to Robert for removing her as promptly as possible to a chair on the border of the two rooms where she could talk or listen as she pleased. For a few moments she listened to Fraülein Adelmann's veiled unmanageable

---

6   W. S. Gilbert (1836–1911), famed for his comic operettas written with composer Arthur Sullivan (1842–1900).

contralto; then she turned magisterially to Robert standing behind her.

'The art of singing has gone out.' she declared, 'since the Germans have been allowed to meddle in it. By the way, Mr. Elsmere, how do you manage to be here? Are you taking a holiday?'

Robert looked at her with a start.

'I have left Murewell, Lady Charlotte.'

'Left Murewell!' she said in astonishment, turning round to look at him, her eyeglass in her eye. 'Why has Helen told me nothing about it? Have you got another living?'

'No. My wife and I are settling in London. We only told Lady Helen of our intentions a few weeks ago.'

To which it may be added that Lady Helen, touched and dismayed by Elsmere's letter to her, had not been very eager to hand over the woes of her friends to her aunt's cool and irresponsible comments.

Lady Charlotte deliberately looked at him a minute longer through her glass. Then she let it fall.

'You don't mean to tell me any more, I can see, Mr. Elsmere. But you will allow me to be astonished?'

'Certainly,' he said, smiling sadly, and immediately afterwards relapsing into silence.

'Have you heard of the squire lately?' he asked her after a pause.

'Not from him. We are excellent friends when we meet, but he doesn't consider me worth writing to. His sister—little idiot—writes to me every now and then. But she has not vouchsafed me a letter since the summer. I should say from the last accounts that he was breaking.'

'He had a mysterious attack of illness just before I left,' said Robert gravely. 'It made one anxious.'

'Oh, it is the old story. All the Wendovers have died of weak hearts or queer brains—generally of both together. I imagine you had some experience of the squire's queerness at one time, Mr. Elsmere. I can't say you and he seemed to be on particularly good terms on the only occasion I ever had the pleasure of meeting you at Murewell.'

She looked up at him, smiling grimly. She had a curiously exact memory for the unpleasant scenes of life.

'Oh, you remember that unlucky evening!' said Robert, reddening a little. 'We soon got over that. We became great friends.'

Again, however, Lady Charlotte was struck by the quiet melancholy of his tone. How strangely the look of youth—which had been so attractive in him the year before—had ebbed from the man's face—from complexion, eyes, expression! She stared at him, full of a brusque tormenting curiosity as to the how and why.

'I hope there is some one among you strong enough to manage Miss Rose,' she said presently, with an abrupt change of subject. 'That little sister-in-law of yours is going to be the rage.'

'Heaven forbid!' cried Robert fervently.

'Heaven will do nothing of the kind. She is twice as pretty as she was last year; I am told she plays twice as well. She had always the sort of manner that provoked people one moment and charmed them the next. And, to judge by my few words with her just now, I should say she had developed it finely. Well, now, Mr. Elsmere, who is going to take care of her?'

'I suppose we shall all have a try at it, Lady Charlotte.'

'Her mother doesn't look to me a person of nerve enough,' said Lady Charlotte coolly. 'She is a girl certain—absolutely certain—to have adventures, and you may as well be prepared for them.'

'I can only trust she will disappoint your expectations, Lady Charlotte,' said Robert, with a slightly sarcastic emphasis.

'Elsmere, who is that man talking to Miss Leyburn?' asked Langham as the two friends stood side by side, a little later, watching the spectacle.

'A certain Mr. Flaxman, brother to a pretty little neighbour of ours in Surrey—Lady Helen Varley—and nephew to Lady Charlotte. I have not seen him here before; but I think the girls like him.'

'Is he the Flaxman who got the mathematical prize at Berlin last year?'

'Yes, I believe so. A striking person altogether. He is enormously rich, Lady Helen tells me, in spite of an elder brother. All the money in his mother's family has come to him, and he is the heir to Lord Daniel's great Derbyshire property. Twelve years ago I used to hear him talked about incessantly by the Cambridge men one met. "Citizen Flaxman" they called him, for his opinions' sake. He would ask his scout to dinner, and insist on dining with his own servants, and shaking hands with his friends' butlers. The scouts and the butlers put an end to that, and altogether, I imagine, the world disappointed him. He has a story, poor fellow, too—a young wife, who died with her first baby ten years ago. The world supposes him never to have got over it, which makes him all the more interesting. A distinguished face, don't you think?— the good type of English aristocrat.'

Langham assented. But his attention was fixed on the group in which Rose's bright hair was conspicuous; and when Robert left him and went to amuse Mrs. Leyburn, he still stood rooted to the same spot watching. Rose was leaning against the piano, one hand behind her, her whole attitude full of a young, easy, self-confident grace. Mr. Flaxman was standing beside her, and they were deep in talk—serious talk apparently, to judge by her quiet manner and the charmed attentive interest of his look. Occasionally, however, there was a sally on her part, and an answering flash of laughter on his; but the stream of conversation closed immediately over the interruption, and flowed on as evenly as before.

Unconsciously Langham retreated farther and farther into the comparative darkness of the inner room. He felt himself singularly insignificant and out of place, and he made no more efforts to talk. Rose played a violin solo, and played it with astonishing delicacy and fire. When it was over Langham saw her turn from the applauding circle crowding in upon her and throw a smiling interrogative look over her shoulder at Mr. Flaxman. Mr. Flaxman bent over her, and as he spoke Langham caught her flush, and the excited sparkle of her eyes. Was this the 'some one in the stream'? No doubt!—no doubt!

When the party broke up Langham found himself borne towards the outer room, and before he knew where he was going he was standing beside her.

'Are *you* here still?' she said to him, startled, as he held out his hand. He replied by some comments on the music, a little lumbering and infelicitous, as all his small-talk was. She hardly listened, but presently she looked up nervously, compelled as it were by the great melancholy eyes above her.

'We are not always in this turmoil, Mr. Langham. Perhaps some other day you will come and make friends with my mother?'

CHAPTER XXXII

Naturally, it was during their two months of autumn travel that Elsmere and Catherine first realised in detail what Elsmere's act was to mean to them, as husband and wife, in the future. Each left England with the most tender and heroic resolves. And no one who knows anything of life will need to be told that even for these two finely-natured people such resolves were infinitely easier to make than to carry out.

'I will not preach to you—I will not persecute you!' Catherine had said to her husband at the moment of her first shock and anguish. And she did her utmost, poor thing, to keep her word! All through the innumerable bitter-nesses which accompanied Elsmere's withdrawal from Murewell—the letters which followed them, the remonstrances of public and private friends, the paragraphs which found their way, do what they would, into the newspapers—the pain of deserting, as it seemed to her, certain poor and helpless folk who had been taught to look to her and Robert, and whose bewildered lamentations came to them through young Armitstead—through all this she held her peace; she did her best to soften Robert's grief; she never once reproached him with her own.

But at the same time the inevitable separation of their inmost hopes and beliefs had thrown her back on herself, had immensely strengthened that puritan independent fibre in her which her youth had developed, and which her happy marriage had only temporarily masked, not weakened. Never had Catherine believed so strongly and intensely as now, when the husband, who had been the guide and inspirer of her religious life, had given up the old faith and practices. By virtue of a kind of nervous instinctive dread, his relaxations bred increased rigidity in her. Often when she was alone—or at night—she was seized with a lonely, an awful sense of responsibility. Oh! let her guard her faith, not only for her own sake, her child's, her Lord's, but for *his*—that it might be given to her patience at last to lead him back.

And the only way in which it seemed to her possible to guard it was to set up certain barriers of silence. She feared that fiery persuasive quality in Robert she had so often seen at work on other people. With him conviction was life—it was the man himself, to an extraordinary degree. How was she to resist the pressure of those new ardours with which his mind was filling—she who loved him!—except by building, at any rate for the time, an enclosure of silence round her Christian beliefs? It was in some ways a pathetic repetition of the situation between Robert and the squire in the early days of their friendship, but in Catherine's mind there was no troubling presence of new knowledge conspiring from within with the forces without. At this moment of her life she was more passionately convinced than ever that the only knowledge truly worth having in this world was the knowledge of God's mercies in Christ.

So gradually with a gentle persistency she withdrew certain parts of herself from Robert's ken; she avoided certain subjects, or anything that might lead to them; she ignored the religious and philosophical books he was constantly reading; she prayed and thought alone—always for him, of him—but still resolutely alone. It was impossible, however, that so great a change in their life could be effected without a perpetual sense of breaking links, a perpetual series of dumb wounds and griefs on both sides. There came a moment when, as he sat alone one evening in a pine wood above the Lake of Geneva,

Elsmere suddenly awoke to the conviction that in spite of all his efforts and illusions, their relation to each other *was* altering, dwindling, impoverishing; the terror of that summer night at Murewell was being dismally justified.

His own mind during this time was in a state of perpetual discovery, 'sailing the seas where there was never sand'—the vast shadowy seas of speculative thought. All his life, reserve to those nearest to him had been pain and grief to him. He was one of those people, as we know, who throw off readily; to whom sympathy, expansion, are indispensable; who suffer physically and mentally from anything cold and rigid beside them. And now, at every turn, in their talk, their reading, in many of the smallest details of their common existence, Elsmere began to feel the presence of this cold and rigid something. He was ever conscious of self-defence on her side, of pained drawing back on his. And with every succeeding effort of his at self-repression, it seemed to him as though fresh nails were driven into the coffin of that old free habit of perfect confidence which had made the heaven of their life since they had been man and wife.

He sat on for long, through the September evening, pondering, wrestling. Was it simply inevitable, the natural result of his own act, and of her antecedents, to which he must submit himself, as to any mutilation or loss of power in the body? The young lover and husband rebelled—the believer rebelled—against the admission. Probably if his change had left him anchorless and forsaken, as it leaves many men, he would have been ready enough to submit, in terror lest his own forlornness should bring about hers. But in spite of the intellectual confusion, which inevitably attends any wholesale reconstruction of a man's platform of action, he had never been more sure of God, or the Divine aims of the world, than now; never more open than now, amid this exquisite Alpine world, to those passionate moments of religious trust which are man's eternal defiance to the iron silences about him. Originally, as we know, he had shrunk from the thought of change in her corresponding to his own; now that his own foothold was strengthening, his longing for a new union was overpowering that old dread. The proselytising instinct may be never quite morally defensible, even as between husband and wife. Nevertheless, in all strong, convinced, and ardent souls it exists, and must be reckoned with.

At last one evening he was overcome by a sudden impulse which neutralised for the moment his nervous dread of hurting her. Some little incident of their day together was rankling, and it was borne in upon him that almost any violent protest on her part would have been preferable to this constant soft evasion of hers, which was gradually, imperceptibly dividing heart from heart.

They were in a bare attic room at the very top of one of the huge newly-built hotels which during the last twenty years have invaded all the high places of Switzerland. The August which had been so hot in England had been rainy and broken in Switzerland. But it had been followed by a warm and mellow September, and the favourite hotels below a certain height were still full. When the Elsmeres arrived at Les Avants, this scantily furnished garret, out of which some servants had been hurried to make room for them, was all that could be found. They, however, liked it for its space and its view. They looked sideways from their windows on to the upper end of the lake, three thousand feet below them. Opposite, across the blue water, rose a grandiose rampart of mountains, the stage on which from morn till night the sun went through a long transformation scene of beauty. The water was marked every now and then by passing boats and steamers—tiny specks which served to measure the vastness of all around them. To right and left, spurs of green mountains shut out alike the lower lake and the icy splendours of the 'Valais depths profound.'[7] What made the charm of the narrow prospect was, first, the sense it produced in the spectator of hanging dizzily above the lake, with infinite air below him, and, then, the magical effects of dawn and evening, when wreaths of mist would blot out the valley and the lake, and leave the eye of the watcher face to face across the fathomless abyss with the majestic mountain mass, and its attendant retinue of clouds, as though they and he were alone in the universe.

It was a peaceful September night. From the open window beside him Robert could see a world of high moonlight, limited and invaded on all sides by sharp black masses of shade. A few rare lights glimmered on the spreading alp below, and every now and then a breath of music came to them wafted from a military band playing a mile or two away. They had been climbing most of the afternoon, and Catherine was lying down, her brown hair loose about her, the thin oval of her face and clear line of brow just visible in the dim candlelight.

Suddenly he stretched out his hand for his Greek Testament, which was always near him, though there had been no common reading since that bitter day of his confession to her. The mark still lay in the well-worn volume at the point reached in their last reading at Murewell. He opened upon it, and began the eleventh chapter of St. John.

Catherine trembled when she saw him take up the book. He began without preface, treating the passage before him in his usual way,—that is to say, taking verse after verse in the Greek, translating and commenting. She never

---

7   From the final stanza of Matthew Arnold's "Obermann Once More."

spoke all through, and at last he closed the little Testament, and bent towards her, his look full of feeling.

'Catherine! can't you let me—will you never let me tell you, now, how that story—how the old things—affect me, from the new point of view? You always stop me when I try. I believe you think of me as having thrown it all away. Would it not comfort you sometimes, if you knew that although much of the Gospels, this very raising of Lazarus, for instance, seem to me no longer true in the historical sense, still they are always full to me of an ideal, a poetical truth? Lazarus may not have died and come to life, may never have existed; but still to me, now as always, love for Jesus of Nazareth is "resurrection" and "life"?'

He spoke with the most painful diffidence, the most wistful tenderness.

There was a pause. Then Catherine said, in a rigid constrained voice,—

'If the Gospels are not true in fact, as history, as reality, I cannot see how they are true at all, or of any value.'

The next minute she rose, and, going to the little wooden dressing-table, she began to brush out and plait for the night her straight silky veil of hair. As she passed him Robert saw her face pale and set.

He sat quiet another moment or two, and then he went towards her and took her in his arms.

'Catherine,' he said to her, his lips trembling, 'am I never to speak my mind to you any more? Do you mean always to hold me at arm's length—to refuse always to hear what I have to say in defence of the change which has cost us both so much?'

She hesitated, trying hard to restrain herself. But it was of no use. She broke into tears—quiet but most bitter tears.

'Robert, I cannot! Oh! you must see I cannot. It is not because I am hard, but because I am weak. How can I stand up against you? I dare not—I dare not. If you were not yourself—not my husband——'

Her voice dropped. Robert guessed that at the bottom of her resistance there was an intolerable fear of what love might do with her if she once gave it an opening. He felt himself cruel, brutal, and yet an urgent sense of all that was at stake drove him on.

'I would not press or worry you, God knows!' he said, almost piteously, kissing her forehead as she lay against him. 'But remember, Catherine, I cannot put these things aside. I once thought I could—that I could fall back on my historical work, and leave religious matters alone as far as criticism was concerned. But I cannot. They fill my mind more and more. I feel more and more impelled to search them out, and to put my conclusions about them into shape. And all the time this is going on, are you and I to remain strangers to one another in all that concerns our truest life—are we, Catherine?'

He spoke in a low voice of intense feeling. She turned her face and pressed her lips to his hand. Both had the scene in the wood-path after her flight and return in their minds, and both were filled with a despairing sense of the difficulty of living, not through great crises, but through the detail of every day.

'Could you not work at other things?' she whispered.

He was silent, looking straight before him into the moonlit shimmer and white spectral hazes of the valley, his arms still round her.

'No!' he burst out at last; 'not till I have satisfied myself. I feel it burning within me, like a command from God, to work out the problem, to make it clearer to myself—and to others,' he added deliberately.

Her heart sank within her. The last words called up before her a dismal future of controversy and publicity, in which at every step she would be condemning her husband.

'And all this time, all these years, perhaps,' he went on—before, in her perplexity, she could find words,—'is my wife never going to let me speak freely to her? Am I to act, think, judge, without her knowledge? Is she to know less of me than a friend, less even than the public for whom I write or speak?'

It seemed intolerable to him, all the more that every moment they stood there together it was being impressed upon him that in fact this was what she meant, what she had contemplated from the beginning.

'Robert, I cannot defend myself against you,' she cried, again clinging to him. 'Oh, think for me! You know what I feel; that I dare not risk what is not mine!'

He kissed her again, and then moved away from her to the window. It began to be plain to him that his effort was merely futile, and had better not have been made. But his heart was very sore.

'Do you ever ask yourself,' he said presently, looking steadily into the night—'no, I don't think you can, Catherine—what part the reasoning faculty, that faculty which marks us out from the animal, was meant to play in life? Did God give it to us simply that you might trample upon it and ignore it, both in yourself and me?'

She had dropped into a chair, and sat with clasped hands, her hair falling about her white dressing-gown, and framing the nobly-featured face blanched by the moonlight. She did not attempt a reply, but the melancholy of an invincible resolution, which was, so to speak, not her own doing, but rather was like a necessity imposed upon her from outside, breathed through her silence.

He turned and looked at her. She raised her arms, and the gesture reminded him for a moment of the Donatello figure in the Murewell library—
the same delicate austere beauty, the same tenderness, the same underlying
reserve. He took her outstretched hands and held them against his breast. His
hotly-beating heart told him that he was perfectly right, and that to accept
the barriers she was setting up would impoverish all their future life together.
But he could not struggle with the woman on whom he had already inflicted
so severe a practical trial. Moreover, he felt strangely as he stood there the
danger of rousing in her those illimitable possibilities of the religious temper,
the dread of which had once before risen spectre-like in his heart.

So once more he yielded. She rewarded him with all the charm, all the
delightfulness, of which under the circumstances she was mistress. They wandered up the Rhone valley, through the St. Gothard, and spent a fortnight
between Como and Lugano. During these days her one thought was to revive
and refresh him, and he let her tend him, and lent himself to the various
heroic futilities by which she would try—as part of her nursing mission—to
make the future look less empty and their distress less real. Of course under
all this delicate give and take both suffered; both felt that the promise of
their marriage had failed them, and that they had come dismally down to a
second best. But after all they were young, and the autumn was beautiful—
and though they hurt each other, they were alone together and constantly,
passionately, interested in each other. Italy, too, softened all things—even
Catherine's English tone and temper. As long as the delicious luxury of the
Italian autumn, with all its primitive pagan suggestiveness, was still round
them; as long as they were still among the cities of the Lombard plain—that
battle-ground and highway of nations, which roused all Robert's historical
enthusiasm, and set him reading, discussing, thinking, in his old impetuous
way, about something else than minute problems of Christian evidence,—the
new-born friction between them was necessarily reduced to a minimum.

But with their return home, with their plunge into London life, the difficulties of the situation began to define themselves more sharply. In after years,
one of Catherine's dreariest memories was the memory of their first instalment in the Bedford Square house. Robert's anxiety to make it pleasant and
homelike was pitiful to watch. He had none of the modern passion for uphol-
stery, and probably the vaguest notions of what was æsthetically correct. But
during their furnishing days he was never tired of wandering about in search
of pretty things—a rug, a screen, an engraving—which might brighten the
rooms in which Catherine was to live. He would put everything in its place

with a restless eagerness, and then Catherine would be called in, and would play her part bravely. She would smile and ask questions, and admire, and then when Robert had gone, she would move slowly to the window and look out at the great mass of the British Museum frowning beyond the little dingy strip of garden, with a sick longing in her heart for the Murewell cornfield, the wood-path, the village, the free air-bathed spaces of heath and common. Oh! this huge London, with its unfathomable poverty and its heartless wealth— how it oppressed and bewildered her! Its mere grime and squalor, its murky poisoned atmosphere, were a perpetual trial to the countrywoman brought up amid the dash of mountain streams and the scents of mountain pastures. She drooped physically for a time, as did the child.

But morally? With Catherine everything really depended on the moral state. She could have followed Robert to a London living with a joy and hope which would have completely deadened all these repulsions of the senses now so active in her. But without this inner glow, in the presence of the profound spiritual difference circumstance had developed between her and the man she loved, everything was a burden. Even her religion, though she clung to it with an ever-increasing tenacity, failed at this period to bring her much comfort. Every night it seemed to her that the day had been one long and dreary struggle to make something out of nothing; and in the morning the night, too, seemed to have been alive with conflict—*All Thy waves and Thy storms have gone over me!*[8]

Robert guessed it all, and whatever remorseful love could do to soften such a strain and burden he tried to do. He encouraged her to find work among the poor; he tried in the tenderest ways to interest her in the great spectacle of London life which was already, in spite of yearning and regret, beginning to fascinate and absorb himself. But their standards were now so different that she was constantly shrinking from what attracted him, or painfully judging what was to him merely curious and interesting. He was really more and more oppressed by her intellectual limitations, though never consciously would he have allowed himself to admit them, and she was more and more bewildered by what constantly seemed to her a breaking up of principle, a relaxation of moral fibre.

And the work among the poor was difficult. Robert instinctively felt that for him to offer his services in charitable work to the narrow Evangelical, whose church Catherine had joined, would have been merely to invite rebuff. So that even in the love and care of the unfortunate they were separated. For he had not yet found a sphere of work, and, if he had, Catherine's invincible

---

8   Psalms 42.7.

impulse in these matters was always to attach herself to the authorities and powers that be. He could only acquiesce when she suggested applying to Mr. Clarendon for some charitable occupation for herself.

After her letter to him, Catherine had an interview with the vicar at his home. She was puzzled by the start and sudden pause for recollection with which he received her name, the tone of compassion which crept into his talk with her, the pitying look and grasp of the hand with which he dismissed her. Then, as she walked home, it flashed upon her that she had seen a copy, some weeks old, of the *Record* lying on the good man's table, the very copy which contained Robert's name among the list of men who during the last ten years had thrown up the Anglican ministry. The delicate face flushed miserably from brow to chin. Pitied for being Robert's wife! Oh, monstrous!—incredible!

Meanwhile Robert, man-like, in spite of all the griefs and sorenesses of the position, had immeasurably the best of it. In the first place such incessant activity of mind as his is in itself both tonic and narcotic. It was constantly generating in him fresh purposes and hopes, constantly deadening regret, and pushing the old things out of sight. He was full of many projects, literary and social, but they were all in truth the fruits of one long experimental process, the passionate attempt of the reason to justify to itself the God in whom the heart believed. Abstract thought, as Mr. Grey saw, had had comparatively little to do with Elsmere's relinquishment of the Church of England. But as soon as the Christian bases of faith were overthrown, that faith had naturally to find for itself other supports and attachments. For faith itself—in God and a spiritual order—had been so wrought into the nature by years of reverent and adoring living that nothing could destroy it. With Elsmere, as with all men of religious temperament, belief in Christianity and faith in God had not at the outset been a matter of reasoning at all, but of sympathy, feeling, association, daily experience. Then the intellect had broken in, and destroyed or transformed the belief in Christianity. But after the crash, *faith* emerged as strong as ever, only craving and eager to make a fresh peace, a fresh compact with the reason.

Elsmere had heard Grey say long ago in one of the few moments of real intimacy he had enjoyed with him at Oxford, 'My interest in philosophy springs solely from the chance it offers me of knowing something more of God!' Driven by the same thirst he too threw himself into the same quest, pushing his way laboriously through the philosophical borderlands of science, through the ethical speculation of the day, through the history of man's moral and religious past. And while on the one hand the intellect was able to contribute an ever stronger support to the faith which was the man, on the other the sphere in him of a patient ignorance which abstains from all attempts at knowing what man cannot know, and substitutes trust for either knowledge or despair, was perpetually widening. 'I take my stand on conscience and the moral life!' was the upshot of it all. 'In them I find my God! As for all these various problems, ethical and scientific, which you press upon me, my pessimist friend, I, too, am bewildered; I, too, have no explanation to offer. But I trust and wait. In spite of them—beyond them—I have abundantly enough for faith—for hope—for action!'

We may quote a passage or two from some letters of his written at this time to that young Armitstead who had taken his place at Murewell, and was still there till Mowbray Elsmere should appoint a new man. Armitstead had been a college friend of Elsmere's. He was a High Churchman of a singularly gentle and delicate type, and the manner in which he had received Elsmere's story on the day of his arrival at Murewell had permanently endeared him to the teller of it. At the same time the defection from Christianity of a man who at Oxford had been to him the object of much hero-worship, and, since Oxford, an example of pastoral efficiency, had painfully affected young Armitstead, and he began a correspondence with Robert which was in many ways a relief to both. In Switzerland and Italy, when his wife's gentle inexorable silence became too oppressive to him, Robert would pour himself out in letters to Armitstead, and the correspondence did not altogether cease with his return to London. To the squire during the same period Elsmere also wrote frequently, but rarely or never on religious matters.

On one occasion Armitstead had been pressing the favourite Christian dilemma—Christianity or nothing. Inside Christianity, light and certainty; outside it, chaos. 'If it were not for the Gospels and the Church I should be a Positivist to-morrow.[9] Your Theism is a mere arbitrary hypothesis, at the mercy of any rival philosophical theory. How, regarding our position as precarious, you should come to regard your own as stable, is to me incomprehensible!'

'What I conceive to be the vital difference between Theism and Christianity,' wrote Elsmere in reply, 'is that as an explanation of things *Theism can never be disproved.* At the worst it must always remain in the position of an alternative hypothesis, which the hostile man of science cannot destroy, though he is under no obligation to adopt it. Broadly speaking, it is not the

---

9 Positivism, the philosophy of science and society originated by French thinker Auguste Comte (1798–1857). Comte posited that societies evolved beyond orthodox religious faith to ultimately arrive at a mode of organization based on individual liberties and empirical truth. His "religion of humanity," a secularized devotion to a canon of great men and women, influenced such authors as Herbert Spencer and George Eliot.

facts which are in dispute, but the inference to be drawn from them.

'Now, considering the enormous complication of the facts, the Theistic inference will, to put it at the lowest, always have its place, always command respect. The man of science may not adopt it, but by no advance of science that I, at any rate, can foresee, can it be driven out of the field.

'Christianity is in a totally different position. Its grounds are not philosophical but literary and historical. It rests not upon all fact, but upon a special group of facts. It is, and will always remain, a great literary and historical problem, a *question of documents and testimony*. Hence, the Christian explanation is vulnerable in a way in which the Theistic explanation can never be vulnerable. The contention, at any rate, of persons in my position is: That to the man who has had the special training required, and in whom this training has not been neutralised by any overwhelming bias of temperament, it can be as clearly demonstrated that the miraculous Christian story rests on a tissue of mistake, as it can be demonstrated that the Isidorian Decretals were a forgery, or the correspondence of Paul and Seneca a pious fraud, or that the mediæval belief in witchcraft was the product of physical ignorance and superstition.'[10]

'You say,' he wrote again, in another connection, to Armitstead from Milan, 'you say you think my later letters have been far too aggressive and positive. I, too, am astonished at myself. I do not know my own mood, it is so clear, so sharp, so combative. Is it the spectacle of Italy, I wonder—of a country practically without religion—the spectacle in fact of Latin Europe as a whole, and the practical Atheism in which it is ingulfed?[11] My dear friend, the problem of the world at this moment is—*how to find a religion?*—some great conception which shall be once more capable, as the old were capable, of welding societies, and keeping man's brutish elements in check. Surely Christianity of the traditional sort is failing everywhere—less obviously with us, and in Teutonic Europe generally, but egregiously, notoriously, in all the Catholic countries. We talk complacently of the decline of Buddhism. But what have we to say of the decline of Christianity? And yet this last is infinitely more striking and more tragic, inasmuch as it affects a more important section of mankind. I, at any rate, am not one of those who would seek to minimise the results of this decline for human life, nor can I bring myself to believe that Positivism or "evolutional morality" will ever satisfy the race.

---

10 The Isidorian Decretals are a collection of forged papal letters and other significant documents, originating in the ninth century; the forged correspondence between Paul and Seneca the Younger, by which Seneca was supposedly converted to Christianity, dates to at least the fourth century.

11 After the *Risorgimento*, the movement for national unification. One of the movement's outcomes was that the Pope lost his temporal powers in the Italian state.

'In the period of social struggle which undeniably lies before us, both in the old and the new world, are we then to witness a war of classes, unsoftened by the ideal hopes, the ideal law, of faith? It looks like it. What does the artisan class, what does the town democracy throughout Europe, care any longer for Christian checks or Christian sanctions as they have been taught to understand them? Superstition, in certain parts of rural Europe, there is in plenty, but wherever you get intelligence and therefore movement, you get at once either indifference to, or a passionate break with, Christianity. And consider what it means, what it will mean, this Atheism of the great democracies which are to be our masters! The world has never seen anything like it; such spiritual anarchy and poverty combined with such material power and resource. Every society—Christian and non-Christian—has always till now had its ideal, of greater or less ethical value, its appeal to something beyond man. Has Christianity brought us to this: that the Christian nations are to be the first in the world's history to try the experiment of a life without faith— that life which you and I, at any rate, are agreed in thinking a life worthy only of the brute?

'Oh forgive me! These things must hurt you—they would have hurt me in old days—but they burn within me, and you bid me speak out. What if it be God Himself who is driving His painful lesson home to me, to you, to the world? What does it mean, this gradual growth of what we call infidelity, of criticism and science on the one hand, this gradual death of the old traditions on the other? *Sin*, you answer, *the enmity of the human mind against God, the momentary triumph of Satan.* And so you acquiesce, heavy-hearted, in God's present defeat, looking for vengeance and requital hereafter. Well, I am not so ready to believe in man's capacity to rebel against his Maker! Where you see ruin and sin, I see the urgent process of Divine education, God's steady ineluctable command "to put away childish things," the pressure of His spirit on ours towards new ways of worship and new forms of love!'

And after a while, it was with these 'new ways of worship and new forms of love' that the mind began to be perpetually occupied. The break with the old things was no sooner complete than the eager soul, incapable then, as always, of resting in negation or opposition, pressed passionately forward to a new synthesis, not only speculative, but practical. Before it rose perpetually the haunting vision of another palace of faith—another church or company of the faithful, which was to become the shelter of human aspiration amid the desolation and anarchy caused by the crashing of the old! How many men and women must have gone through the same strait as itself—how many must be watching with it through the darkness for the rising of a new City of God!

One afternoon, close upon Christmas, he found himself in Parliament Square, on his way towards Westminster Bridge and the Embankment. The beauty of a sunset sky behind the Abbey arrested him, and he stood leaning over the railings beside the Peel statue to look.

The day before he had passed the same spot with a German friend. His companion—a man of influence and mark in his own country, who had been brought up, however, in England, and knew it well—had stopped before the Abbey and had said to him with emphasis: 'I never find myself in this particular spot of London without a sense of emotion and reverence. Other people feel that in treading the Forum of Rome they are at the centre of human things. I am more thrilled by Westminster than Rome; your venerable Abbey is to me the symbol of a nationality to which the modern world owes obligations it can never repay. You are rooted deep in the past; you have also a future of infinite expansiveness stretching before you. Among European nations at this moment you alone have freedom in the true sense, you alone have religion. I would give a year of life to know what you will have made of your freedom and your religion two hundred years hence!'

As Robert recalled the words, the Abbey lay before him, wrapped in the bluish haze of the winter afternoon. Only the towers rose out of the mist, gray and black against the red bands of cloud. A pair of pigeons circled round them, as careless and free in flight as though they were alone with the towers and the sunset. Below, the streets were full of people; the omnibuses rolled to and fro; the lamps were just lit; lines of straggling figures, dark in the half light, were crossing the street here and there. And to all the human rush and swirl below, the quiet of the Abbey and the infinite red distances of sky gave a peculiar pathos and significance.

Robert filled his eye and sense, and then walked quickly away towards the Embankment. Carrying the poetry and grandeur of England's past with him, he turned his face eastward to the great new-made London on the other side of St. Paul's, the London of the democracy, of the nineteenth century, and of the future. He was wrestling with himself, a prey to one of those critical moments of life, when circumstance seems once more to restore to us the power of choice, of distributing a Yes or a No among the great solicitations which meet the human spirit on its path from silence to silence. The thought of his friend's reverence, and of his own personal debt towards the country to whose long travail of centuries he owed all his own joys and faculties, was hot within him.

'Here and here did England help me—how can I help England,—say!'[12]

Ah! that vast chaotic London south and east of the great church! He already knew something of it. A Liberal clergyman there, settled in the very blackest, busiest heart of it, had already made him welcome on Mr. Grey's introduction. He had gone with this good man on several occasions through some little fraction of that teeming world, now so hidden and peaceful between the murky river mists and the cleaner light-filled grays of the sky. He had heard much, and pondered a good deal, the quick mind caught at once by the differences, some tragic, some merely curious and stimulating, between the monotonous life of his own rural folk, and the mad rush, the voracious hurry, the bewildering appearances and disappearances, the sudden ingulfments, of working London.

Moreover, he had spent a Sunday or two wandering among the East End churches. There, rather than among the streets and courts outside, as it had seemed to him, lay the tragedy of the city. Such emptiness, such desertion, such a hopeless breach between the great craving need outside and the boon offered it within! Here and there, indeed, a patch of bright coloured success, as it claimed to be, where the primitive tendency of man towards the organised excitement of religious ritual, visible in all nations and civilisations, had been appealed to with more energy and more results than usual. But in general, blank failure, or rather obvious want of success—as the devoted men now beating the void there were themselves the first to admit, with pain and patient submission to the inscrutable Will of God.

But is it not time we assured ourselves, he was always asking, whether God is still in truth behind the offer man is perpetually making to his brother man on His behalf? He was behind it once, and it had efficacy, had power. But now—what if all these processes of so-called destruction and decay were but the mere workings of that divine plastic force which is for ever moulding human society? What if these beautiful venerable things which had fallen from him, as from thousands of his fellows, represented, in the present stage of the world's history, not the props, but the hindrances, of man?

And if all these large things were true, as he believed, what should be the individual's part in this transition England? Surely, at the least, a part of plain sincerity of act and speech—a correspondence as perfect as could be reached between the inner faith and the outer word and deed. So much, at the least, was clearly required of him!

---

12 Robert Browning, "Home-Thoughts, from the Sea," l. 5.

'Do not imagine,' he said to himself, as though with a fierce dread of possible self-delusion, 'that it is in you to play any great, any commanding part. Shun the thought of it, if it *were* possible! But let me do what is given me to do! Here, in this human wilderness, may I spend whatever of time or energy or faculty may be mine, in the faithful attempt to help forward the new House of Faith that is to be, though my utmost efforts should but succeed in laying some obscure stone in still unseen foundations! Let me try and hand on to some other human soul, or souls, before I die, the truth which has freed, and which is now sustaining, my own heart. Can any man do more? Is not every man who feels any certainty in him whatever bound to do as much? What matter if the wise folk scoff, if even at times, and in a certain sense, one seems to one's self ridiculous—absurdly lonely and powerless! All great changes are preceded by numbers of sporadic, and as the bystander thinks, impotent efforts. But while the individual effort sinks, drowned perhaps in mockery, the general movement quickens, gathers force we know not how, and—

> 'While the tired wave vainly breaking,
>   Seems here no painful inch to gain,
> Far back through creeks and inlets making,
>   Comes silent, flooding in the main!'[13]

Darkness sank over the river; all the gray and purple distance with its dim edge of spires and domes against the sky, all the vague intervening blacknesses of street, or bridge, or railway station were starred and patterned with lights. The vastness, the beauty of the city filled him with a sense of mysterious attraction, and as he walked on with his face uplifted to it, it was as though he took his life in his hand and flung it afresh into the human gulf.

'What does it matter if one's work be raw and uncomely! All that lies outside the great organised traditions of an age must always look so. Let me bear my witness bravely, not spending life in speech, but not undervaluing speech—above all, not being ashamed or afraid of it, because other wise people may prefer a policy of silence. A man has but the one puny life, the one tiny spark of faith. Better be venturesome with both for God's sake, than over-cautious, over-thrifty. And—to his own Master he standeth or falleth!'[14]

Plans of work of all kinds, literary and practical, thoughts of preaching in some bare hidden room to men and women orphaned and stranded like

---

13   Slight misquotation from Arthur Hugh Clough, "Say Not the Struggle Naught Availeth," ll. 9-12.
14   Romans 14.4.

himself, began to crowd upon him. The old clerical instinct in him winced at some of them. Robert had nothing of the sectary about him by nature; he was always too deeply and easily affected by the great historic existences about him. But when the Oxford man or the ex-official of one of the most venerable and decorous of societies protested, the believer, or, if you will, the enthusiast, put the protest by.

And so the dream gathered substance and stayed with him, till at last he found himself at his own door. As he closed it behind him, Catherine came out into the pretty old hall from the dining-room.

'Robert, have you walked all the way?'

'Yes. I came along the Embankment. Such a beautiful evening!'

He slipped his arm inside hers, and they mounted the stairs together. She glanced at him wistfully. She was perfectly aware that these months were to him months of incessant travail of spirit, and she caught at this moment the old strenuous look of eye and brow she knew so well. A year ago, and every thought of his mind had been open to her—and now—she herself had shut them out—but her heart sank within her.

She turned and kissed him. He bent his head fondly over her. But inwardly all the ardour of his mood collapsed at the touch of her. For the protests of a world in arms can be withstood with joy, but the protest that steals into your heart, that takes love's garb and uses love's ways—*there* is the difficulty!

CHAPTER XXXIII

But Robert was some time in finding his opening, in realising any fraction of his dream. At first he tried work under the Broad Church vicar to whom Grey had introduced him. He undertook some rent-collecting, and some evening lectures on elementary science to boys and men. But after a while he began to feel his position false and unsatisfactory. In truth, his opinions were in the main identical with those of the vicar under whom he was acting. But Mr. Vernon was a Broad Churchman, belonged to the Church Reform movement, and thought it absolutely necessary to 'keep things going,' and by a policy of prudent silence and gradual expansion from within, to save the great 'plant' of the Establishment from falling wholesale into the hands of the High Churchmen. In consequence he was involved, as Robert held, in endless contradictions and practical falsities of speech and action. His large church was attended by a handful of some fifty to a hundred persons. Vernon could not preach what he did believe, and would not preach, more than was absolutely necessary, what he did not believe. He was hard-working and kind-hearted, but the perpetual divorce between thought and action, which his position made inevitable, was constantly blunting and weakening all he did. His whole life, indeed, was one long waste of power, simply for lack of an elementary frankness.

But if these became Robert's views as to Vernon, Vernon's feeling towards Elsmere after six weeks' acquaintance was not less decided. He was constitutionally timid, and he probably divined in his new helper a man of no ordinary calibre, whose influence might very well turn out some day to be of the 'incalculably diffusive' kind.[15] He grew uncomfortable, begged Elsmere to beware of any 'direct religious teaching,' talked in warm praise of a 'policy of omissions,' and in equally warm denunciation of 'anything like a policy of attack.' In short, it became plain that two men so much alike, and yet so different, could not long co-operate.

However, just as the fact was being brought home to Elsmere, a friendly chance intervened.

Hugh Flaxman, the Leyburns' new acquaintance and Lady Helen's brother, had been drawn to Elsmere at first sight; and a meeting or two, now at Lady Charlotte's, now at the Leyburns', had led both men far on the way to a friendship. Of Hugh Flaxman himself more hereafter. At present all that need be recorded is that it was at Mr. Flaxman's house, overlooking St. James's Park, Robert first met a man who was to give him the opening for which he was looking.

Mr. Flaxman was fond of breakfast parties *à la* Rogers,[16] and on the first occasion when Robert could be induced to attend one of these functions, he saw opposite to him what he supposed to be a lad of twenty, a young slip of a fellow, whose sallies of fun and invincible good humour attracted him greatly.

Sparkling brown eyes, full lips rich in humour and pugnacity, 'lockës crull as they were layde in presse,' the same look of 'wonderly' activity too, in spite of his short stature and dainty make, as Chaucer lends his squire[17]—the type was so fresh and pleasing that Robert was more and more held by it, especially when he discovered to his bewilderment that the supposed stripling must be from his talk a man quite as old as himself, an official besides, filling what was clearly some important place in the world. He took his full share in

---

15 From George Eliot's closing account of Dorothea Brooke's life in *Middlemarch*, "Finale."

16 Samuel Rogers (1763–1855), poet, host, and raconteur, now best remembered not for his poetry but for the posthumously published *Recollections of the Table-Talk of Samuel Rogers* (1856), edited by William Sharpe.

17 The squire in the General Prologue of the *Canterbury Tales*.

the politics and literature started at the table, and presently, when conversation fell on the proposed municipality for London, said things to which the whole party listened. Robert's curiosity was aroused, and after breakfast he questioned his host and was promptly introduced to 'Mr. Murray Edwardes.'

Whereupon it turned out that this baby-faced sage was filling a post, in the work of which perhaps few people in London could have taken so much interest as Robert Elsmere.

Fifty years before, a wealthy merchant who had been one of the chief pillars of London Unitarianism had made his will and died. His great warehouses lay in one of the Eastern riverside districts of the city, and in his will he endeavoured to do something according to his lights for the place in which he had amassed his money. He left a fairly large bequest wherewith to build and endow a Unitarian chapel and found certain Unitarian charities, in the heart of what was even then one of the densest and most poverty-stricken of London parishes. For a long time, however, chapel and charities seemed likely to rank as one of the idle freaks of religious wealth and nothing more. Unitarianism of the old sort is perhaps the most illogical creed that exists, and certainly it has never been the creed of the poor. In old days it required the presence of a certain arid stratum of the middle classes to live and thrive at all. This stratum was not to be found in R——, which rejoiced instead in the most squalid types of poverty and crime, types wherewith the mild shrivelled Unitarian minister had about as much power of grappling as a Poet Laureate with a Trafalgar Square Socialist.[18]

Soon after the erection of the chapel, there arose that shaking of the dry bones of religious England which we call the Tractarian movement. For many years the new force left R—— quite undisturbed. The parish church droned away, the Unitarian minister preached decorously to empty benches, knowing nothing of the agitations outside. At last, however, towards the end of the old minister's life, a powerful church of the new type, staffed by friends and pupils of Pusey, rose in the centre of R——, and the little Unitarian chapel was for a time more snuffed out than ever, a fate which this time it shared dismally with the parish church. As generally happened, however, in those days, the proceedings at this new and splendid St. Wilfrid's were not long in stirring up the Protestantism of the British rough,—the said Protestantism being always one of the finest excuses for brickbats of which the modern cockney is master. The parish lapsed into a state of private war—hectic clergy heading exasperated processions or intoning defiant Litanies on the one side,—mobs,

---

18   A very topical allusion to the Trafalgar Square Riots (1886 and 1887), in which working-class socialists clashed with the police.

rotten eggs, dead cats, and blatant Protestant orators on the other.[19]

The war went on practically for years, and while it was still raging the minister of the Unitarian chapel died, and the authorities concerned chose in his place a young fellow, the son of a Bristol minister, a Cambridge man besides, as chance would have it, of brilliant attainments, and unusually commended from many quarters, even including some Church ones of the Liberal kind. This curly-haired youth, as he was then in reality, and as to his own quaint vexation he went on seeming to be up to quite middle age, had the wit to perceive at the moment of his entry on the troubled scene that behind all the mere brutal opposition to the new church, and in contrast with the sheer indifference of three-fourths of the district, there was a small party consisting of an aristocracy of the artisans, whose protest against the Puseyite doings was of a much quieter sterner sort, and amongst whom the uproar had mainly roused a certain crude power of thinking. He threw himself upon this element, which he rather divined than discovered, and it responded. He preached a simple creed, drove it home by pure and generous living; he lectured, taught, brought down workers from the West End, and before he had been five years in harness had not only made himself a power in R——, but was beginning to be heard of and watched with no small interest by many outsiders.

This was the man on whom Robert had now stumbled. Before they had talked twenty minutes each was fascinated by the other. They said good-bye to their host, and wandered out together into St. James's Park, where the trees were white with frost and an orange sun was struggling through the fog. Here Murray Edwardes poured out the whole story of his ministry to attentive ears. Robert listened eagerly. Unitarianism was not a familiar subject of thought to him. He had never dreamt of joining the Unitarians, and was indeed long ago convinced that in the beliefs of a Channing no one once fairly started on the critical road could rationally stop.[20] That common thinness and aridity, too, of the Unitarian temper had weighed with him. But here, in the person of Murray Edwardes, it was as though he saw something old and threadbare revivified. The young man's creed, as he presented it, had grace, persuasiveness, even unction; and there was something in his tone of mind which was like a fresh wind blowing over the fevered places of the other's heart.

They talked long and earnestly, Edwardes describing his own work, and

---

19 An accurate description of some of the heated excesses of anti-Ritualist protests, which saw churches (and their clergymen) come under violent assault, sometimes for weeks on end.

20 William Ellery Channing (1780–1842), American Unitarian theologian, influential on Unitarianism's development on both sides of the Atlantic.

the changes creeping over the modern Unitarian body, Elsmere saying little, asking much.

At last the young man looked at Elsmere with eyes of bright decision.

'You cannot work with the Church!' he said—'it is impossible. You will only wear yourself out in efforts to restrain what you could do infinitely more good, as things stand now, by pouring out. Come to us!—I will put you in the way. You shall be hampered by no pledges of any sort. Come and take the direction of some of my workers. We have all got our hands more than full. Your knowledge, your experience, would be invaluable. There is no other opening like it in England just now for men of your way of thinking and mine. Come! Who knows what we may be putting our hands to—what fruit may grow from the smallest seed?'

The two men stopped beside the lightly frozen water. Robert gathered that in this soul, too, there had risen the same large intoxicating dream of a reorganised Christendom, a new wide-spreading shelter of faith for discouraged browbeaten man, as in his own. 'I will!' he said briefly, after a pause, his own look kindling—'it is the opening I have been pining for. I will give you all I can, and bless you for the chance.'

That evening Robert got home late after a busy day full of various engagements. Mary, after some waiting up for 'Fader,' had just been carried protesting, red lips pouting, and fat legs kicking, off to bed. Catherine was straightening the room, which had been thrown into confusion by the child's romps.

It was with an effort—for he knew it would be a shock to her—that he began to talk to her about the breakfast-party at Mr. Flaxman's, and his talk with Murray Edwardes. But he had made it a rule with himself to tell her everything that he was doing or meant to do. She would not let him tell her what he was thinking. But as much openness as there could be between them, there should be.

Catherine listened—still moving about the while—the thin beautiful lips becoming more and more compressed. Yes, it was hard to her, very hard; the people among whom she had been brought up, her father especially, would have held out the hand of fellowship to any body of Christian people, but not to the Unitarian. No real barrier of feeling divided them from any orthodox Dissenter, but the gulf between them and the Unitarian had been dug very deep by various forces—forces of thought originally, of strong habit and prejudice in the course of time.

'He is going to work with them now,' she thought bitterly; 'soon he will be one of them—perhaps a Unitarian minister himself.'

And for the life of her, as he told his tale, she could find nothing but embarrassed monosyllables, and still more embarrassed silences, wherewith to answer him. Till at last he too fell silent, feeling once more the sting of a now habitual discomfort.

Presently, however, Catherine came to sit down beside him. She laid her head against his knee, saying nothing, but gathering his hand closely in both her own.

Poor woman's heart! One moment in rebellion, the next a suppliant. He bent down quickly and kissed her.

'Would you like,' he said presently, after both had sat silent a while in the firelight, 'would you care to go to Madame de Netteville's to-night?'

'By all means,' said Catherine with a sort of eagerness. 'It *was* Friday she asked us for, wasn't it? We will be quick over dinner, and I will go and dress.'

In that last ten minutes which Robert had spent with the squire in his bedroom, on the Monday afternoon, when they were to have walked, Mr. Wendover had drily recommended Elsmere to cultivate Madame de Netteville.[21] He sat propped up in his chair, white, gaunt, and cynical, and this remark of his was almost the only reference he would allow to the Elsmere move.

'You had better go there,' he said huskily, 'it will do you good. She gets the first-rate people and she makes them talk, which Lady Charlotte can't. Too many fools at Lady Charlotte's; she waters the wine too much.'

And he had persisted with the subject—using it, as Elsmere thought, as a means of warding off other conversation. He would not ask Elsmere's plans, and he would not allow a word about himself.

There had been a heart attack, old Meyrick thought, coupled with signs of nervous strain and excitement. It was the last ailment which evidently troubled the doctor most. But, behind the physical breakdown, there was to Robert's sense something else, a spiritual something, infinitely forlorn and piteous, which revealed itself wholly against the elder man's' will, and filled the younger with a dumb helpless rush of sympathy. Since his departure Robert had made the keeping up of his correspondence with the squire a binding obligation, and he was to-night chiefly anxious to go to Madame de Netteville's that he might write an account of it to Murewell.

Still the squire's talk, and his own glimpse of her at Murewell, had made him curious to see more of the woman herself. The squire's ways of describing her were always half approving, half sarcastic. Robert sometimes imagined that he himself had been at one time more under her spell than he cared to

---

21 'to have walked, Mr. Wendover': period corrected to comma as per *SE* and *W*.

confess. If so, it must have been when she was still in Paris, the young English widow of a man of old French family, rich, fascinating, distinguished, and the centre of a small *salon*, admission to which was one of the social blue ribbons of Paris.

Since the war of 1870[22] Madame de Netteville had fixed her headquarters in London, and it was to her house in Hans Place that the squire wrote to her about the Elsmeres. She owed Roger Wendover debts of various kinds, and she had an encouraging memory of the young clergyman on the terrace at Murewell. So she promptly left her cards, together with the intimation that she was at home always on Friday evenings.

'I have never seen the wife,' she meditated, as her delicate jewelled hand drew up the window of the brougham in front of the Elsmeres' lodgings. 'But if she is the ordinary country clergyman's spouse, the squire of course will have given the young man a hint.'

But whether from oblivion, or from some instinct of grim humour towards Catherine, whom he had always vaguely disliked, the squire said not one word about his wife to Robert in the course of their talk of Madame de Netteville.

Catherine took pains with her dress, sorely wishing to do Robert credit. She put on one of the gowns she had taken to Murewell when she married. It was black, simply made, and had been a favourite with both of them in the old surroundings.

So they drove off to Madame de Netteville's. Catherine's heart was beating faster than usual as she mounted the twisting stairs of the luxurious little house. All these new social experiences were a trial to her. But she had the vaguest, most unsuspicious ideas of what she was to see in this particular house.

A long low room was thrown open to them. Unlike most English rooms, it was barely though richly furnished. A Persian carpet, of a self-coloured grayish blue, threw the gilt French chairs and the various figures sitting upon them into delicate relief. The walls were painted white, and had a few French mirrors and girandoles upon them, half a dozen fine French portraits, too, here and there, let into the wall in oval frames.[23] The subdued light came from the white sides of the room, and seemed to be there solely for social purposes. You could hardly have read or written in the room, but you could see a beautiful woman in a beautiful dress there, and you could talk there, either *tête-à-tête*, or to the assembled company, to perfection, so cunningly

22 The Franco-Prussian War.
23 Girandoles are decorative, intricately-designed candlesticks.

was it all devised.

When the Elsmeres entered, there were about a dozen people present—ten gentlemen and two ladies. One of the ladies, Madame de Netteville, was lying back in the corner of a velvet divan placed against the wall, a screen between her and a splendid fire that threw its blaze out into the room. The other, a slim woman with closely curled fair hair, and a neck abnormally long and white, sat near her, and the circle of men was talking indiscriminately to both.

As the footman announced Mr. and Mrs. Elsmere, there was a general stir of surprise. The men looked round; Madame de Netteville half rose with a puzzled look. It was more than a month since she had dropped her invitation. Then a flash, not altogether of pleasure, passed over her face, and she said a few hasty words to the woman near her, advancing the moment afterwards to give her hand to Catherine.

'This is very kind of you, Mrs. Elsmere, to remember me so soon. I had imagined you were hardly settled enough yet to give me the pleasure of seeing you.'

But the eyes fixed on Catherine, eyes which took in everything, were not cordial, for all their smile.

Catherine, looking up at her, was overpowered by her excessive manner, and by the woman's look of conscious sarcastic strength, struggling through all the outer softness of beauty and exquisite dress.

'Mr. Elsmere, you will find this room almost as hot, I am afraid, as that afternoon on which we met last. Let me introduce you to Count Wielandt—Mr. Elsmere. Mrs. Elsmere, will you come over here, beside Lady Aubrey Willert.'

Robert found himself bowing to a young diplomatist, who seemed to him to look at him very much as he himself might have scrutinised an inhabitant of New Guinea. Lady Aubrey made an imperceptible movement of the head as Catherine was presented to her, and Madame de Netteville, smiling and biting her lip a little, fell back into her seat.

There was a faint odour of smoke in the room. As Catherine sat down, a young exquisite a few yards from her threw the end of a cigarette into the fire with a little sharp decided gesture. Lady Aubrey also pushed away a cigarette case which lay beside her hand.

Everybody there had the air more or less of an *habitué* of the house; and when the conversation began again, the Elsmeres found it very hard, in spite of certain perfunctory efforts on the part of Madame de Netteville, to take any share in it.

'Well, I believe the story about Desforêts is true,' said the fair-haired young Apollo, who had thrown away his cigarette, lolling back in his chair.

Catherine started, the little scene with Rose and Langham in the English rectory garden flashing incongruously back upon her.

'If you get it from the *Ferret*, my dear Evershed,' said the ex-Tory minister, Lord Rupert, 'you may put it down as a safe lie. As for me, I believe she has a much shrewder eye to the main chance.'

'What do you mean?' said the other, raising astonished eyebrows.

'Well, it doesn't *pay*, you know, to write yourself down a fiend—not quite.'

'What—you think it will affect her audiences? Well, that is a good joke!' and the young man laughed immoderately, joined by several of the other guests.

'I don't imagine it will make any difference to you, my good friend,' returned Lord Rupert imperturbably; 'but the British public haven't got your nerve. They *may* take it awkwardly—I don't say they will—when a woman who has turned her own young sister out of doors at night, in St. Petersburg, so that ultimately as a consequence the girl dies, comes to ask them to clap her touching impersonations of injured virtue.'

'What has one to do with an actress's private life, my dear Lord Rupert?' asked Madame de Netteville, her voice slipping with a smooth clearness into the conversation, her eyes darting light from under straight black brows.

'What indeed!' said the young man who had begun the conversation with a disagreeable enigmatical smile, stretching out his hand for another cigarette, and drawing it back with a look under his drooped eyelids—a look of cold impertinent scrutiny—at Catherine Elsmere.

'Ah! well—I don't want to be obtrusively moral—Heaven forbid! But there is such a thing as destroying the illusion to such an extent that you injure your pocket. Desforêts is doing it—doing it actually in Paris too.'

There was a ripple of laughter.

'Paris and illusions—*O mon Dieu!*' groaned young Evershed, when he had done laughing, laying meditative hands on his knees and gazing into the fire.

'I tell you I have seen it,' said Lord Rupert, waxing combative, and slapping the leg he was nursing with emphasis. 'The last time I went to see Desforêts in Paris the theatre was crammed, and the house—theatrically speaking—*ice*. They received her in dead silence—they gave her not one single recall—and they only gave her a clap, that I can remember, at those two or three points in the play where clap they positively must or burst. They go to see her—but they loathe her—and they let her know it.'

'Bah!' said his opponent, 'it is only because they are tired of her. Her vagaries don't amuse them any longer—they know them by heart. And—by George! she has some pretty rivals too, now!' he added reflectively,—'not to speak of the Bernhardt.'[24]

'Well, the Parisians *can* be shocked,' said Count Wielandt in excellent English, bending forward so as to get a good view of his hostess. 'They are just now especially shocked by the condition of English morals!'

The twinkle in his eye was irresistible. The men, understanding his reference to the avidity with which certain English aristocratic scandals had been lately seized upon by the French papers, laughed out—so did Lady Aubrey. Madame de Netteville contented herself with a smile.

'They profess to be shocked, too, by Renan's last book,' said the editor from the other side of the room.

'Dear me!' said Lady Aubrey, with meditative scorn, fanning herself lightly the while, her thin but extraordinarily graceful head and neck thrown out against the golden brocade of the cushion behind her.

'Oh! what so many of them feel in Renan's case, of course,' said Madame de Netteville, 'is that every book he writes now gives a fresh opening to the enemy to blaspheme. Your eminent freethinker can't afford just yet, in the present state of the world, to make himself socially ridiculous. The cause suffers.'

'Just my feeling,' said young Evershed calmly. 'Though I mayn't care a rap about him personally, I prefer that a man on my own front bench shouldn't make a public ass of himself if he can help it—not for his sake, of course, but for mine!'

Robert looked at Catherine. She sat upright by the side of Lady Aubrey; her face, of which the beauty to-night seemed lost in rigidity, pale and stiff. With a contraction of heart he plunged himself into the conversation. On his road home that evening he had found an important foreign telegram posted up at the small literary club to which he had belonged since Oxford days. He made a remark about it now to Count Wielandt; and the diplomatist, turning rather unwillingly to face his questioner, recognised that the remark was a shrewd one.

Presently the young man's frank intelligence had told. On his way to and from the Holy Land three years before Robert had seen something of the East, and it so happened that he remembered the name of Count Wielandt

24 Sarah Bernhardt (1844–1923), legendary French actress known for her tragic roles.

as one of the foreign secretaries of legation present at an official party given by the English Ambassador at Constantinople, which he and his mother had attended on their return journey, in virtue of a family connection with the Ambassador. All that he could glean from memory he made quick use of now, urged at first by the remorseful wish to make this new world into which he had brought Catherine less difficult than he knew it must have been during the last quarter of an hour.

But after a while he found himself leading the talk of a section of the room, and getting excitement and pleasure out of the talk itself. Ever since that Eastern journey he had kept an eye on the subjects which had interested him then, reading in his rapid voracious way all that came across him at Murewell, especially in the squire's foreign newspapers and reviews, and storing it when read in a remarkable memory.

Catherine, after the failure of some conversational attempts between her and Madame de Netteville, fell to watching her husband with a start of strangeness and surprise. She had scarcely seen him at Oxford among his equals; and she had very rarely been present at his talks with the squire. In some ways, and owing to the instinctive reserves set up between them for so long, her intellectual knowledge of him was very imperfect. His ease, his re-source, among these men of the world, for whom—independent of all else—she felt a countrywoman's dislike, filled her with a kind of bewilderment.

'Are you new to London?' Lady Aubrey asked her presently, in that tone of absolute detachment from the person addressed which certain women manage to perfection. She, too, had been watching the husband, and the sight had impressed her with a momentary curiosity to know what the stiff, handsome, dowdily-dressed wife was made of.

'We have been two months here,' said Catherine, her large gray eyes taking in her companion's very bare shoulders, the costly fantastic dress, and the diamonds flashing against the white skin.

'In what part?'

'In Bedford Square.'

Lady Aubrey was silent. She had no ideas on the subject of Bedford Square at command.

'We are very central,' said Catherine, feeling desperately that she was doing Robert no credit at all, and anxious to talk if only something could be found to talk about.

'Oh yes, you are near the theatres,' said the other indifferently.

This was hardly an aspect of the matter which had yet occurred to Catherine. A flash of bitterness ran through her. Had they left their Murewell life to be 'near the theatres,' and kept at arm's length by supercilious great ladies?

'We are very far from the Park,' she answered with an effort. 'I wish we weren't, for my little girl's sake.'

'Oh, you have a little girl! How old?'

'Sixteen months.'

'Too young to be a nuisance yet. Mine are just old enough to be in everybody's way. Children are out of place in London. I always want to leave mine in the country, but my husband objects,' said Lady Aubrey coolly. There was a certain piquancy in saying frank things to this stiff Madonna-faced woman.

Madame de Netteville, meanwhile, was keeping up a conversation in an undertone with young Evershed, who had come to sit on a stool beside her, and was gazing up at her with eyes of which the expression was perfectly understood by several persons present. The handsome, dissipated, ill-conditioned youth had been her slave and shadow for the last two years. His devotion now no longer amused her, and she was endeavouring to get rid of it and of him. But the process was a difficult one, and took both time and *finesse*.

She kept her eye, notwithstanding, on the new-comers whom the squire's introduction had brought to her that night. When the Elsmeres rose to go, she said good-bye to Catherine with an excessive politeness, under which her poor guest, conscious of her own *gaucherie* during the evening, felt the touch of satire she was perhaps meant to feel. But when Catherine was well ahead Madame de Netteville gave Robert one of her most brilliant smiles.

'Friday evening, Mr. Elsmere; always Fridays. You will remember?'

The *naïveté* of Robert's social view, and the mobility of his temper, made him easily responsive. He had just enjoyed half an hour's brilliant talk with two or three of the keenest and most accomplished men in Europe. Catherine had slipped out of his sight meanwhile, and the impression of their *entrée* had been effaced. He made Madame de Netteville, therefore, a cordial smiling reply before his tall slender form disappeared after that of his wife.

'Agreeable—rather an acquisition!' said Madame de Netteville to Lady Aubrey, with a light motion of the head towards Robert's retreating figure. 'But the wife! Good heavens! I owe Roger Wendover a grudge. I think he might have made it plain to those good people that I don't want strange women at my Friday evenings.'

Lady Aubrey laughed. 'No doubt she is a genius, or a saint, in mufti. She might be handsome too if some one would dress her.'

Madame de Netteville shrugged her shoulders. 'Oh! life is not long enough to penetrate that kind of person,' she said.

Meanwhile the 'person' was driving homeward very sad and ill at ease. She was vexed that she had not done better, and yet she was wounded by Robert's enjoyment. The Puritan in her blood was all aflame. As she sat looking into the motley lamplit night, she could have 'testified' like any prophetess of old.

Robert meanwhile, his hand slipped into hers, was thinking of Wielandt's talk, and of some racy stories of Berlin celebrities told by a young *attaché* who had joined their group. His lips were lightly smiling, his brow serene.

But as he helped her down from the cab, and they stood in the hall together, he noticed the pale discomposure of her looks. Instantly the familiar dread and pain returned upon him.

'Did you like it, Catherine?' he asked her, with something like timidity, as they stood together by their bedroom fire.

She sank into a low chair and sat a moment staring at the blaze. He was startled by her look of suffering, and, kneeling, he put his arms tenderly round her.

'Oh, Robert, Robert!' she cried, falling on his neck.

'What is it?' he asked, kissing her hair.

'I seem all at sea,' she said in a choked voice, her face hidden,—'the old landmarks swallowed up! I am always judging and condemning,—always protesting. What am I that I should judge? But how—how—can I help it?'

She drew herself away from him, once more looking into the fire with drawn brows.

'Darling, the world is full of difference. Men and women take life in different ways. Don't be so sure yours is the only right one.'

He spoke with a moved gentleness, taking her hand the while.

'"*This* is the way, walk ye in it!"' she said presently, with strong, almost stern emphasis. 'Oh, those women, and that talk! Hateful!'

He rose and looked down on her from the mantelpiece. Within him was a movement of impatience, repressed almost at once by the thought of that long night at Murewell, when he had vowed to himself to 'make amends'!

And if that memory had not intervened she would still have disarmed him wholly.

'Listen!' she said to him suddenly, her eyes kindling with a strange childish pleasure. 'Do you hear the wind, the west wind? Do you remember how it used to shake the house, how it used to come sweeping through the trees in the wood-path? It must be trying the study window now, blowing the vine against it.'

A yearning passion breathed through every feature. It seemed to him she saw nothing before her. Her longing soul was back in the old haunts, surrounded by the old loved forms and sounds. It went to his heart. He tried to soothe her with the tenderest words remorseful love could find. But the conflict of feeling—grief, rebellion, doubt, self-judgment—would not be soothed, and long after she had made him leave her and he had fallen asleep, she knelt on, a white and rigid figure in the dying firelight, the wind shaking the old house, the eternal murmur of London booming outside.

CHAPTER XXXIV

Meanwhile, as if to complete the circle of pain with which poor Catherine's life was compassed, it began to be plain to her that, in spite of the hard and mocking tone Rose generally adopted with regard to him, Edward Langham was constantly at the house in Lerwick Gardens, and that it was impossible he should be there so much unless in some way or other Rose encouraged it.

The idea of such a marriage—nay, of such a friendship—was naturally as repugnant as ever to her. It had been one of the bitterest moments of a bitter time when, at their first meeting after the crisis in her life, Langham, conscious of a sudden movement of pity for a woman he disliked, had pressed the hand she held out to him in a way which clearly showed her what was in his mind, and had then passed on to chat and smoke with Robert in the study, leaving her behind to realise the gulf that lay between the present and that visit of his to Murewell, when Robert and she had felt in unison towards him, his opinions, and his conduct to Rose, as towards everything else of importance in their life.

Now it seemed to her Robert must necessarily look at the matter differently, and she could not make up her mind to talk to him about it. In reality, his objections had never had the same basis as hers, and he would have given her as strong a support as ever, if she had asked for it. But she held her peace, and he, absorbed in other things, took no notice. Besides, he knew Langham too well. He had never been able to take Catherine's alarms seriously.

An attentive onlooker, however, would have admitted that this time, at any rate, they had their justification. Why Langham was so much in the Leyburns' drawing-room during these winter months was a question that several people asked—himself not least. He had not only pretended to forget Rose Leyburn during the eighteen months which had passed since their first acquaintance at Murewell—he had for all practical purposes forgotten her. It is only a small proportion of men and women who are capable of passion on the great scale at all; and certainly, as we have tried to show, Langham was not among them. He had had a passing moment of excitement at Murewell, soon put down, and followed by a week of extremely pleasant sensations, which, like most of his pleasures, had ended in reaction and self-abhorrence. He had left Murewell remorseful, melancholy, and ill at ease, but conscious, certainly, of a great relief that he and Rose Leyburn were not likely to meet again for long.

Then his settlement in London had absorbed him, as all such matters absorb men who have become the slaves of their own solitary habits, and in the joy of his new freedom, and the fresh zest for learning it had aroused in him, the beautiful unmanageable child who had disturbed his peace at Murewell was not likely to be more, but less, remembered. When he stumbled across her unexpectedly in the National Gallery, his determining impulse had been merely one of flight.

However, as he had written to Robert towards the beginning of his London residence, there was no doubt that his migration had made him for the time much more human, observant, and accessible. Oxford had become to him an oppression and a nightmare, and as soon as he had turned his back on it his mental lungs seemed once more to fill with air. He took his modest part in the life of the capital; happy in the obscurity afforded him by the crowd; rejoicing in the thought that his life and his affairs were once more his own, and the academical yoke had been slipped for ever.

It was in this mood of greater cheerfulness and energy that his fresh sight of Rose found him. For the moment, he was perhaps more susceptible than he ever could have been before to her young perfections, her beauty, her brilliancy, her provoking stimulating ways. Certainly, from that first afternoon onwards he became more and more restless to watch her, to be near her, to see what she made of herself and her gifts. In general, though it was certainly owing to her that he came so much, she took small notice of him. He regarded, or chose to regard, himself as a mere 'item'—something systematically overlooked and forgotten in the bustle of her days and nights. He saw that she thought badly of him, that the friendship he might have had was now proudly refused him, that their first week together had left a deep impression of resentment and hostility in her mind. And all the same he came; and she asked him! And sometimes, after an hour when she had been more difficult or more satirical than usual, ending notwithstanding with a little change of tone, a careless 'You will find us next Wednesday as usual; So-and-so is coming to play,' Langham would walk home in a state of feeling he did not care to analyse, but which certainly quickened the pace of life a good deal. She would not let him try his luck at friendship again, but in the strangest slightest ways did she not make him suspect every now and then that he *was* in some sort important to her, that he sometimes preoccupied her against her will; that her will, indeed, sometimes escaped her, and failed to control her manner to him?

It was not only his relations to the beauty, however, his interest in her career, or his perpetual consciousness of Mrs. Elsmere's cold dislike and disapproval of his presence in her mother's drawing-room, that accounted for Langham's heightened mental temperature this winter. The existence and the proceedings of Mr. Hugh Flaxman had a very considerable share in it.

'Tell me about Mr. Langham,' said Mr. Flaxman once to Agnes Leyburn, in the early days of his acquaintance with the family; 'is he an old friend?'

'Of Robert's,' replied Agnes, her cheerful impenetrable look fixed upon the speaker. 'My sister met him once for a week in the country at the Elsmeres'. My mother and I have been only just introduced to him.'

Hugh Flaxman pondered the information a little.

'Does he strike you as—well—what shall we say?—unusual?'

His smile struck one out of her.

'Even Robert might admit that,' she said demurely.

'Is Elsmere so attached to him? I own I was provoked just now by his tone about Elsmere. I was remarking on the evident physical and mental strain your brother-in-law had gone through, and he said with a *nonchalance* I cannot convey: "Yes, it is astonishing Elsmere should have ventured it. I confess I often wonder whether it was worth while." "Why?" said I, perhaps a little hotly. Well, he didn't know—wouldn't say. But I gathered that, according to him, Elsmere is still swathed in such an unconscionable amount of religion that the few rags and patches he has got rid of are hardly worth the discomfort of the change. It seemed to me the tone of the very cool spectator, rather than the friend. However—does your sister like him?'

'I don't know,' said Agnes, looking her questioner full in the face.

Hugh Flaxman's fair complexion flushed a little. He got up to go.

He is one of the most extraordinarily handsome persons I ever saw,' he remarked as he buttoned up his coat. 'Don't you think so?'

'Yes,' said Agnes dubiously, 'if he didn't stoop, and if he didn't in general look half-asleep.'

Hugh Flaxman departed more puzzled than ever as to the reason for the constant attendance of this uncomfortable anti-social person at the Leyburns' house. Being himself a man of very subtle and fastidious tastes, he could imagine that so original a suitor, with such eyes, such an intellectual reputation so well sustained by scantiness of speech and the most picturesque capacity for silence, *might* have attractions for a romantic and wilful girl. But where were the signs of it? Rose rarely talked to him, and was always ready to make him the target of a sub-acid raillery. Agnes was clearly indifferent to him, and Mrs. Leyburn equally clearly afraid of him. Mrs. Elsmere, too, seemed to dislike him, and yet there he was, week after week. Flaxman could not make it out.

Then he tried to explore the man himself. He started various topics with him—University reform, politics, music. In vain. In his most characteristic Oxford days Langham had never assumed a more wholesale ignorance of all subjects in heaven and earth, and never stuck more pertinaciously to the flattest forms of commonplace. Flaxman walked away at last boiling over. The man of parts masquerading as the fool is perhaps at least as exasperating as the fool playing at wisdom.

However, he was not the only person irritated. After one of these fragments of conversation Langham also walked rapidly home in a state of most irrational petulance, his hands thrust with energy into the pockets of his overcoat.

'No, my successful aristocrat, you shall not have everything your own way so easily with me or with *her!* You may break me, but you shall not play upon me. And as for her, I will see it out—I will see it out!'

And he stiffened himself as he walked, feeling life electric all about him, and a strange new force tingling in every vein.

Meanwhile, however, Mr. Flaxman was certainly having a good deal of his own way. Since the moment when his aunt, Lady Charlotte, had introduced him to Miss Leyburn—watching him the while with a half-smile which soon broadened into one of sly triumph—Hugh Flaxman had persuaded himself that country houses are intolerable even in the shooting season, and that London is the only place of residence during the winter for the man who aspires to govern his life on principles of reason. Through his influence and that of his aunt, Rose and Agnes—Mrs. Leyburn never went out—were being carried into all the high life that London can supply in November and January. Wealthy, high-born, and popular, he was gradually devoting his advantages in the freest way to Rose's service. He was an excellent musical amateur, and he was always proud to play with her; he had a fine country house, and the little rooms on Campden Hill were almost always filled with flowers from his gardens; he had a famous musical library, and its treasures were lavished on the girl violinist; he had a singularly wide circle of friends, and with his whimsical energy he was soon inclined to make kindness to the two sisters the one test of a friend's goodwill.

He was clearly touched by Rose; and what was to prevent his making an impression on her? To her sex he had always been singularly attractive. Like his sister, he had all sorts of bright impulses and audacities flashing and darting about him. He had a certain *hauteur* with men, and could play the aristocrat when he pleased, for all his philosophical radicalism. But with women he was the most delightful mixture of deference and high spirits. He loved the grace of them, the daintiness of their dress, the softness of their voices. He would have done anything to please them, anything to save them pain. At twenty-five, when he was still 'Citizen Flaxman' to his college friends, and in the first fervours of a poetic defiance of prejudice and convention, he had married a gamekeeper's pretty daughter. She had died with her child—died, almost, poor thing! of happiness and excitement—of the over-greatness of Heaven's boon to her. Flaxman had adored her, and death had tenderly embalmed a sentiment to which life might possibly have been less kind. Since then he had lived in music, letters, and society, refusing out of a certain fastidiousness to enter politics, but welcomed and considered, wherever he went, tall, good-looking, distinguished, one of the most agreeable and courted of men, and perhaps the richest *parti* in London.

Still, in spite of it all, Langham held his ground—Langham would see it out! And indeed Flaxman's footing with the beauty was by no means clear—least of all to himself. She evidently liked him, but she bantered him a good deal; she would not be the least subdued or dazzled by his birth and wealth, or by those of his friends; and if she allowed him to provide her with pleasures, she would hardly ever take his advice, or knowingly consult his tastes.

Meanwhile she tormented them both a good deal by the artistic acquaint-ance she gathered about her. Mrs. Pierson's world, as we have said, contained a good many dubious odds and ends, and she had handed them all over to Rose. The Leyburns' growing intimacy with Mr. Flaxman and his circle, and through them with the finer types of the artistic life, would naturally and by degrees have carried them away somewhat from this earlier circle if Rose would have allowed it. But she clung persistently to its most unpromising specimens, partly out of a natural generosity of feeling, but partly also for the sake of that opposition her soul loved, her poor prickly soul, full under all her gaiety and indifference of the most desperate doubt and soreness,—opposi-tion to Catherine, opposition to Mr. Flaxman, but, above all, opposition to Langham.

Flaxman could often avenge himself on her—or rather on the more ob-noxious members of her following—by dint of a faculty for light and stinging repartee which would send her, flushed and biting her lip, to have her laugh out in private. But Langham for a long time was defenceless. Many of her friends in his opinion were simply pathological curiosities—their vanity was so frenzied, their sensibilities so morbidly developed. He felt a doctor's interest in them coupled with more than a doctor's scepticism as to all they had to say about themselves. But Rose would invite them, would assume a *quasi*-intimacy with them; and Langham as well as everybody else had to put up with it.

Even the trodden worm, however—— And there came a time when the concentration of a good many different lines of feeling in Langham's mind betrayed itself at last in a sharp and sudden openness. It began to seem to him that she was specially bent often on tormenting *him* by these caprices of hers, and he vowed to himself finally, with an outburst of irritation due in reality to a hundred causes, that he would assert himself, that he would make an effort at any rate to save her from her own follies.

One afternoon, at a crowded musical party, to which he had come much against his will, and only in obedience to a compulsion he dared not analyse, she asked him in passing if he would kindly find Mr. MacFadden, a bass singer, whose name stood next on the programme, and who was not to be seen in the drawing-room.

Langham searched the dining-room and the hall, and at last found Mr. MacFadden—a fair, flabby, unwholesome youth—in the little study or cloak-room, in a state of collapse, flanked by whisky and water, and attended by two frightened maids, who handed over their charge to Langham and fled.

Then it appeared that the great man had been offended by a change in the programme, which hurt his vanity, had withdrawn from the drawing-room on the brink of hysterics, had called for spirits, which had been provided for him with great difficulty by Mrs. Leyburn's maids, and was there drinking himself into a state of rage and rampant dignity which would soon have shown itself in a melodramatic return to the drawing-room, and a public refusal to sing at all in a house where art had been outraged in his person.

Some of the old disciplinary instincts of the Oxford tutor awoke in Langham at the sight of the creature, and, with a prompt sternness which amazed himself, and nearly set MacFadden whimpering, he got rid of the man, shut the hall door on him, and went back to the drawing-room.

'Well?' said Rose in anxiety, coming up to him.

'I have sent him away,' he said briefly, an eye of unusual quickness and brightness looking down upon her; 'he was in no condition to sing. He chose to be offended, apparently, because he was put out of his turn, and has been giving the servants trouble.'

Rose flushed deeply, and drew herself up with a look half trouble, half defiance, at Langham.

'I trust you will not ask him again,' he said, with the same decision. 'And if I might say so there are one or two people still here whom I should like to see you exclude at the same time.'

They had withdrawn into the bow window out of earshot of the rest of the room. Langham's look turned significantly towards a group near the piano. It contained one or two men whom he regarded as belonging to a low type; men who, if it suited their purpose, would be quite ready to tell or invent malicious stories of the girl they were now flattering, and whose standards and instincts represented a coarser world than Rose in reality knew anything about.

Her eyes followed his.

'I know,' she said petulantly, 'that you dislike artists. They are not your world. They are mine.'

'I dislike artists? What nonsense, too! To me personally these men's ways don't matter in the least. They go their road and I mine. But I deeply resent any danger of discomfort and annoyance to you!'

He still stood frowning, a glow of indignant energy showing itself in his attitude, his glance. She could not know that he was at that moment vividly realising the drunken scene that might have taken place in her presence if he had not succeeded in getting that man safely out of the house. But she felt that he was angry, and mostly angry with her, and there was something so piquant and unexpected in his anger!

'I am afraid,' she said, with a queer sudden submissiveness, 'you have been going through something very disagreeable. I am very sorry. Is it my fault?' she added, with a whimsical flash of eye, half fun, half serious.

He could hardly believe his ears.

'Yes, it is your fault, I think!' he answered her, amazed at his own boldness. 'Not that *I* was annoyed—Heavens! what does that matter?—but that you and your mother and sister were very near an unpleasant scene. You will not take advice, Miss Leyburn,—you will take your own way in spite of what any one else can say or hint to you, and some day you will expose yourself to annoyance when there is no one near to protect you!'

'Well, if so, it won't be for want of a mentor,' she said, dropping him a mock curtsey. But her lip trembled under its smile, and her tone had not lost its gentleness.

At this moment Mr. Flaxman, who had gradually established himself as the joint leader of these musical afternoons, came forward to summon Rose to a quartette. He looked from one to the other, a little surprise penetrating through his suavity of manner.

'Am I interrupting you?'

'Not at all,' said Rose; then, turning back to Langham, she said in a hurried whisper: 'Don't say anything about the wretched man; it would make mamma nervous. He shan't come here again.'

Mr. Flaxman waited till the whisper was over, and then led her off, with a change of manner which she immediately perceived, and which lasted for the rest of the evening.

Langham went home, and sat brooding over the fire. Her voice had not been so kind, her look so womanly, for months. Had she been reading *Shirley*, and would she have liked him to play Louis Moore? He went into a fit of silent convulsive laughter as the idea occurred to him.

Some secret instinct made him keep away from her for a time. At last, one Friday afternoon, as he emerged from the Museum, where he had been collating the MSS. of some obscure Alexandrian, the old craving returned with added strength, and he turned involuntarily westward.

An acquaintance of his, recently made in the course of work at the Museum, a young Russian professor, ran after him, and walked with him. Presently they passed a poster on the wall, which contained in enormous letters the announcement of Madame Desforêts's approaching visit to London, a list of plays, and the dates of performances.

The young Russian suddenly stopped and stood pointing at the advertisement, with shaking derisive finger, his eyes aflame, the whole man quivering with what looked like antagonism and hate.

Then he broke into a fierce flood of French. Langham listened till they had passed Piccadilly, passed the Park, and till the young *savant* turned southwards towards his Brompton lodgings.

Then Langham slowly climbed Campden Hill, meditating. His thoughts were an odd mixture of the things he had just heard, and of a scene at Murewell long ago when a girl had denounced him for 'calumny.'

At the door of Lerwick Gardens he was informed that Mrs. Leyburn was upstairs with an attack of bronchitis. But the servant thought the young ladies were at home. Would he come in? He stood irresolute a moment, then went in on a pretext of 'inquiry.'

The maid threw open the drawing-room door, and there was Rose sitting well into the fire—for it was a raw February afternoon—with a book.

She received him with all her old hard brightness. He was, indeed, instantly sorry that he had made his way in. Tyrant! was she displeased because he had slipped his chain for rather longer than usual?

However, he sat down, delivered his book, and they talked first about her mother's illness. They had been anxious, she said, but the doctor, who had just taken his departure, had now completely reassured them.

'Then you will be able probably after all to put in an appearance at Lady Charlotte's this evening?' he asked her.

The omnivorous Lady Charlotte of course had made acquaintance with him in the Leyburns' drawing-room, as she did with everybody who crossed her path, and three days before he had received a card from her for this evening.

'Oh yes! But I have had to miss a rehearsal this afternoon. That concert at Searle House is becoming a great nuisance.'

'It will be a brilliant affair, I suppose. Princes on one side of you—and Albani on the other. I see they have given you the most conspicuous part as violinist.'

'Yes,' she said with a little satirical tightening of the lip. 'Yes—I suppose I ought to be much flattered.'

'Of course,' he said, smiling, but embarrassed. 'To many people you must be at this moment one of the most enviable persons in the world. A delightful art—and every opportunity to make it tell!'

There was a pause. She looked into the fire.

'I don't know whether it is a delightful art,' she said presently, stifling a little yawn. 'I believe I am getting very tired of London. Sometimes I think I shouldn't be very sorry to find myself suddenly spirited back to Burwood!'

Langham gave vent to some incredulous interjection. He had apparently surprised her in a fit of *ennui* which was rare with her.

'Oh no, not yet!' she said suddenly, with a return of animation. 'Madame Desforêts comes next week, and I am to see her.' She drew herself up and turned a beaming face upon him. Was there a shaft of mischief in her eye? He could not tell. The firelight was perplexing.

'You are to see her?' he said slowly. 'Is she coming here?'

'I hope so. Mrs. Pierson is to bring her. I want mamma to have the amusement of seeing her. My artistic friends are a kind of tonic to her—they excite her so much. She regards them as a sort of show—much as you do, in fact, only in a more charitable fashion.'

But he took no notice of what she was saying.

'Madame Desforêts is coming here?' he sharply repeated, bending forward, a curious accent in his tone.

'Yes!' she replied, with apparent surprise. Then with a careless smile: 'Oh, I remember when we were at Murewell, you were exercised that we should know her. Well, Mr. Langham, I told you then that you were only echoing unworthy gossip. I am in the same mind still. I have seen her, and you haven't. To me she is the greatest actress in the world, and an ill-used woman to boot!'

Her tone had warmed with every sentence. It struck him that she had wilfully brought up the topic—that it gave her pleasure to quarrel with him.

He put down his hat deliberately, got up, and stood with his back to the fire. She looked up at him curiously. But the dark regular face was almost hidden from her.

'It is strange,' he said slowly, 'very strange—that you should have told me this at this moment! Miss Leyburn, a great deal of the truth about Madame Desforêts I could neither tell, nor could you hear. There are charges against her proved in open court, again and again, which I could not even mention in your presence. But one thing I can speak of. Do you know the story of the sister at St. Petersburg?'

'I know no stories against Madame Desforêts,' said Rose loftily, her quickened breath responding to the energy of his tone. 'I have always chosen not to know them.'

'The newspapers were full of this particular story just before Christmas. I should have thought it must have reached you.'

'I did not see it,' she replied stiffly; 'and I cannot see what good purpose is to be served by your repeating it to me, Mr. Langham.'

Langham could have smiled at her petulance, if he had not for once been determined and in earnest.

'You will let me tell it, I hope?' he said quietly. 'I will tell it so that it shall not offend your ears. As it happens, I myself thought it incredible at the time. But, by an odd coincidence, it has just this afternoon been repeated to me by a man who was an eyewitness of part of it.'

Rose was silent. Her attitude was *hauteur* itself, but she made no further active opposition.

'Three months ago,' he began, speaking with some difficulty, but still with a suppressed force of feeling which amazed his hearer, 'Madame Desforêts was acting in St. Petersburg. She had with her a large company, and amongst them her own young sister, Elise Romey, a girl of eighteen. This girl had been always kept away from Madame Desforêts by her parents, who had never been sufficiently consoled by their eldest daughter's artistic success for the infamy of her life.'

Rose started indignantly. Langham gave her no time to speak.

'Elise Romey, however, had developed a passion for the stage. Her parents were respectable—and you know young girls in France are brought up

strictly. She knew next to nothing of her sister's escapades. But she knew that
she was held to be the greatest actress in Europe—the photographs in the
shops told her that she was beautiful. She conceived a romantic passion for
the woman whom she had last seen when she was a child of five, and actuated
partly by this hungry affection, partly by her own longing wish to become an
actress, she escaped from home and joined Madame Desforêts in the South
of France. Madame Desforêts seems at first to have been pleased to have her.
The girl's adoration pleased her vanity. Her presence with her gave her new
opportunities of posing. I believe,' and Langham gave a little dry laugh, 'they
were photographed together at Marseilles with their arms round each other's
necks, and the photograph had an immense success. However, on the way to
St. Petersburg, difficulties arose. Elise was pretty, in a *blonde* childish way, and
she caught the attention of the *jeune premier* of the company, a man'—the
speaker became somewhat embarrassed—'whom Madame Desforêts seems
to have regarded as her particular property. There were scenes at different
towns on the journey. Elise became frightened—wanted to go home. But the
elder sister, having begun tormenting her, seems to have determined to keep
her hold on her, as a cat keeps and tortures a mouse—mainly for the sake of
annoying the man of whom she was jealous. They arrived at St. Petersburg in
the depth of winter. The girl was worn out with travelling, unhappy, and ill.
One night in Madame Desforêts's apartment there was a supper party, and
after it a horrible quarrel. No one exactly knows what happened. But towards
twelve o'clock that night Madame Desforêts turned her young sister in evening dress, a light shawl round her, out into the snowy streets of St. Petersburg,
barred the door behind her, and revolver in hand dared the wretched man
who had caused the *fracas* to follow her.'

Rose sat immovable. She had grown pale, but the firelight was not
revealing.

Langham turned away from her towards the blaze, holding out his hands
to it mechanically.

'The poor child,' he said, after a pause, in a lower voice, 'wandered about
for some hours. It was a frightful night—the great capital was quite strange
to her. She was insulted—fled this way and that—grew benumbed with cold
and terror, and was found unconscious in the early morning under the arch-
way of a house some two miles from her sister's lodgings.'

There was a dead silence. Then Rose drew a long quivering breath.

'I do not believe it!' she said passionately. 'I cannot believe it!'

'It was amply proved at the time,' said Langham drily, 'though of course
Madame Desforêts tried to put her own colour on it. But I told you I had

private information. On one of the floors of the house where Elise Romey was picked up, lived a young university professor. He is editing an important Greek text, and has lately had business at the Museum. I made friends with him there. He walked home with me this afternoon, saw the announcement of Madame Desforêts's coming, and poured out the story. He and his wife nursed the unfortunate girl with devotion. She lived just a week, and died of inflammation of the lungs. I never in my life heard anything so pitiful as his description of her delirium, her terror, her appeals, her shivering misery of cold.'

There was a pause.

'She is not a woman,' he said presently, between his teeth. 'She is a wild beast.'

Still there was silence, and still he held out his hand to the flame which Rose too was staring at. At last he turned round.

'I have told you a shocking story,' he said hurriedly. 'Perhaps I ought not to have done it. But, as you sat there talking so lightly, so gaily, it suddenly became to me utterly intolerable that that woman should ever sit here in this room—talk to you—call you by your name—laugh with you—touch your hand! Not even your wilfulness shall carry you so far—you *shall* not do it!'

He hardly knew what he said. He was driven on by a passionate sense of physical repulsion to the notion of any contact between her pure fair youth and something malodorous and corrupt. And there was besides a wild unique excitement in claiming for once to stay—to control her.

Rose lifted her head slowly. The fire was bright. He saw the tears in her eyes, tears of intolerable pity for another girl's awful story. But through the tears something gleamed—a kind of exultation—the exultation which the magician feels when he has called spirits from the vasty deep, and after long doubt and difficult invocation they rise at last before his eyes.

'I will never see her again,' she said in a low wavering voice, but she too was hardly conscious of her own words. Their looks were on each other; the ruddy capricious light touched her glowing cheeks, her straight-lined grace, her white hand. Suddenly from the gulf of another's misery into which they had both been looking there had sprung up, by the strange contrariety of human things, a heat and intoxication of feeling, wrapping them round, blotting out the rest of the world from them like a golden mist. 'Be always thus!' her parted lips, her liquid eyes were saying to him. His breath seemed to fail him; he was lost in bewilderment.

There were sounds outside—Catherine's voice. He roused himself with a supreme effort.

'To-night—at Lady Charlotte's?'

'To-night,' she said, and held out her hand.

A sudden madness seized him—he stooped—his lips touched it—it was hastily drawn away, and the door opened.

CHAPTER XXXV

'In the first place, my dear aunt,' said Mr. Flaxman, throwing himself back in his chair in front of Lady Charlotte's drawing-room fire, 'you may spare your admonitions, because it is becoming more and more clear to me that, whatever my sentiments may be, Miss Leyburn never gives a serious thought to me.'

He turned to look at his companion over his shoulder. His tone and manner were perfectly gay, and Lady Charlotte was puzzled by him.

'Stuff and nonsense!' replied the lady with her usual emphasis; 'I never flatter you, Hugh, and I don't mean to begin now, but it would be mere folly not to recognise that you have advantages which must tell on the mind of any girl in Miss Leyburn's position.'

Hugh Flaxman rose, and, standing before the fire with his hands in his pockets, made what seemed to be a close inspection of his irreproachable trouser-knees.

'I am sorry for your theory, Aunt Charlotte,' he said, still stooping, 'but Miss Leyburn doesn't care twopence about my advantages.'

'Very proper of you to say so,' returned Lady Charlotte sharply; 'the remark, however, my good sir, does more credit to your heart than your head.'

'In the next place,' he went on undisturbed, 'why you should have done your best this whole winter to throw Miss Leyburn and me together, if you meant in the end to oppose my marrying her, I don't quite see.'

He looked up smiling. Lady Charlotte reddened ever so slightly.

'You know my weaknesses,' she said presently, with an effrontery which delighted her nephew. 'She is my latest novelty, she excites me, I can't do without her. As to you, I can't remember that you wanted much encouragement, but, I acknowledge, after all these years of resistance—resistance to my most legitimate efforts to dispose of you—there was a certain piquancy in seeing you caught at last!'

'Upon my word!' he said, throwing back his head with a not very cordial laugh, in which, however, his aunt joined. She was sitting opposite to him, her powerful loosely-gloved hands crossed over the rich velvet of her dress, her fair large face and grayish hair surmounted by a mighty cap, as vigorous, shrewd, and individual a type of English middle age as could be found. The room behind her and the second and third drawing-rooms were brilliantly lighted. Mr. Wynnstay was enjoying a cigar in peace in the smoking-room, while his wife and nephew were awaiting the arrival of the evening's guests upstairs.

Lady Charlotte's mind had been evidently much perturbed by the conversation with her nephew of which we are merely describing the latter half. She was labouring under an uncomfortable sense of being hoist with her own petard—an uncomfortable memory of a certain warning of her husband's, delivered at Murewell.

'And now,' said Mr. Flaxman, 'having confessed in so many words that you have done your best to bring me up to the fence, will you kindly recapitulate the arguments why in your opinion I should not jump it?'

'Society, amusement, flirtation, are one thing,' she replied with judicial imperativeness, 'marriage is another. In these democratic days we must know everybody; we should only marry our equals.'

The instant, however, the words were out of her mouth, she regretted them. Mr. Flaxman's expression changed.

'I do not agree with you,' he said calmly, 'and you know I do not. You could not, I imagine, have relied much upon *that* argument.'

'Good gracious, Hugh!' cried Lady Charlotte crossly; 'you talk as if I were really the old campaigner some people suppose me to be. I have been amusing myself—I have liked to see you amused. And it is only the last few weeks since you have begun to devote yourself so tremendously, that I have come to take the thing seriously at all. I confess, if you like, that I have got you into the scrape—now I want to get you out of it! I am not thin-skinned, but I hate family unpleasantnesses—and you know what the duke will say.'

'The duke be—translated!' said Flaxman coolly. 'Nothing of what you have said or could say on this point, my dear aunt, has the smallest weight with me. But Providence has been kinder to you and the duke than you deserve. Miss Leyburn does not care for me, and she does care—or I am very much mistaken—for somebody else.'

He pronounced the words deliberately, watching their effect upon her.

'What, that Oxford nonentity, Mr. Langham, the Elsmeres' friend? Ridiculous! What attraction could a man of that type have for a girl of hers?'

'I am not bound to supply an answer to that question,' replied her nephew. 'However, he is not a nonentity. Far from it! Ten years ago, when I was leaving Cambridge, he was certainly one of the most distinguished of the young Oxford tutors.

'Another instance of what university reputation is worth!' said Lady Charlotte scornfully. It was clear that even in the case of a beauty whom she thought it beneath him to marry, she was not pleased to see her nephew ousted by the *force majeure* of a rival—and that a rival whom she regarded as an utter nobody, having neither marketable eccentricity, nor family, nor social brilliance to recommend him.

Flaxman understood her perplexity and watched her with critical amused eyes.

'I should like to know,' he said presently, with a curious slowness and suavity, 'I should greatly like to know why you asked him here to-night?'

'You know perfectly well that I should ask anybody—a convict, a crossing-sweeper—if I happened to be half an hour in the same room with him!'

Flaxman laughed.

'Well, it may be convenient to-night,' he said reflectively. 'What are we to do—some thought-reading?'

'Yes. It isn't a crush. I have only asked about thirty or forty people. Mr. Denman is to manage it.'

She mentioned an amateur thought-reader greatly in request at the moment.

Flaxman cogitated for a while and then propounded a little plan to his aunt, to which she, after some demur, agreed.

'I want to make a few notes,' he said drily, when it was arranged; 'I should be glad to satisfy myself.'

When the Misses Leyburn were announced, Rose, though the younger, came in first. She always took the lead by a sort of natural right, and Agnes never dreamt of protesting. To-night the sisters were in white. Some soft creamy stuff was folded and draped about Rose's slim shapely figure in such a way as to bring out all its charming roundness and grace. Her neck and arms bore the challenge of the dress victoriously. Her red-gold hair gleamed in the light of Lady Charlotte's innumerable candles. A knot of dusky blue feathers on her shoulder, and a Japanese fan of the same colour, gave just that touch of purpose and art which the spectator seems to claim as the tribute answering to his praise in the dress of a young girl. She moved with perfect self-possession, distributing a few smiling looks to the people she knew as she advanced towards Lady Charlotte. Any one with a discerning eye could have seen that she was in that stage of youth when a beautiful woman is like a statue to which the master is giving the finishing touches. Life, the sculptor, had been at work upon her, refining here, softening there, planing away awkwardness, emphasising grace, disengaging as it were, week by week, and month by month, all the beauty of which the original conception was capable. And the process is one attended always by a glow and sparkle, a kind of effluence of youth and pleasure, which makes beauty more beautiful and grace more graceful.

The little murmur and rustle of persons turning to look, which had already begun to mark her entrance into a room, surrounded Rose as she walked up to Lady Charlotte. Mr. Flaxman, who had been standing absently silent, woke up directly she appeared, and went to greet her before his aunt.

'You failed us at rehearsal,' he said with smiling reproach; 'we were all at sixes and sevens.'

'I had a sick mother, unfortunately, who kept me at home. Lady Charlotte, Catherine couldn't come. Agnes and I are alone in the world. Will you chaperon us?'

'I don't know whether I will accept the responsibility to-night—in that new gown,' replied Lady Charlotte grimly, putting up her eyeglass to look at it and the wearer. Rose bore the scrutiny with a light smiling silence, even though she knew Mr. Flaxman was looking too.

'On the contrary,' she said, 'one always feels so particularly good and prim in a new frock.'

'Really? I should have thought it one of Satan's likeliest moments,' said Flaxman, laughing—his eyes, however, the while saying quite other things to her, as they finished their inspection of her dress.

Lady Charlotte threw a sharp glance first at him and then at Rose's smiling ease, before she hurried off to other guests.

'I have made a muddle as usual,' she said to herself in disgust, 'perhaps even a worse one than I thought!'

Whatever might be Hugh Flaxman's state of mind, however, he never showed greater self-possession than on this particular evening.

A few minutes after Rose's entry he introduced her for the first time to his sister Lady Helen. The Varleys had only just come up to town for the opening of Parliament, and Lady Helen had come to-night to Martin Street, all ardour to see Hugh's new adoration, and the girl whom all the world was beginning to talk about—both as a beauty and as an artist. She rushed at Rose, if any word so violent can be applied to anything so light and airy as Lady Helen's movements, caught the girl's hands in both hers, and, gazing up at her with undisguised admiration, said to her the prettiest, daintiest, most effusive things possible. Rose—who with all her lithe shapeliness, looked over-tall and even a trifle stiff beside the tiny bird-like Lady Helen—took the advances of Hugh Flaxman's sister with a pretty flush of flattered pride. She looked down at the small radiant creature with soft and friendly eyes, and Hugh Flaxman stood by, so far well pleased.

Then he went off to fetch Mr. Denman, the hero of the evening, to be introduced to her. While he was away, Agnes, who was behind her sister, saw Rose's eyes wandering from Lady Helen to the door, restlessly searching and then returning.

Presently through the growing crowd round the entrance Agnes spied a well-known form emerging.

'Mr. Langham! But Rose never told me he was to be here to-night, and how *dreadful* he looks!'

Agnes was so startled that her eyes followed Langham closely across the room. Rose had seen him at once; and they had greeted each other across the crowd. Agnes was absorbed, trying to analyse what had struck her so. The face was always melancholy, always pale, but to-night it was ghastly, and from the whiteness of cheek and brow, the eyes, the jet-black hair stood out in intense and disagreeable relief. She would have remarked on it to Rose, but that Rose's attention was claimed by the young thought-reader, Mr. Denman, whom Mr. Flaxman had brought up. Mr. Denman was a fair-haired young Hercules, whose tremulous agitated manner contrasted oddly with his athlete's looks. Among other magnetisms he was clearly open to the magnetism of women, and he stayed talking to Rose, staring furtively at her the while from under his heavy lids,—much longer than the girl thought fair.

'Have you seen any experiments in the working of this new force before?' he asked her, with a solemnity which sat oddly on his commonplace bearded face.

'Oh yes!' she said flippantly. 'We have tried it sometimes. It is very good fun.'

He drew himself up. 'Not *fun*,' he said impressively, 'not fun. Thought-reading wants seriousness; the most tremendous things depend upon it. If established it will revolutionise our whole views of life. Even a Huxley could not deny that!'

She studied him with mocking eyes. 'Do you imagine this party to-night looks very serious?'

His face fell.

'One can seldom get people to take it scientifically,' he admitted, sighing. Rose, impatiently, thought him a most preposterous young man. Why was he not cricketing or shooting or exploring, or using the muscles Nature had given him so amply, to some decent practical purpose, instead of making a business out of ruining his own nerves and other people's night after night in hot drawing-rooms? And when would he go away?

'Come, Mr. Denman,' said Flaxman, laying hands upon him; 'the audience is about collected, I think. Ah, there you are!' and he gave Langham a cool greeting. 'Have you seen anything yet of these fashionable dealings with the devil?'

'Nothing. Are you a believer?'

Flaxman shrugged his shoulders. 'I never refuse an experiment of any kind,' he added with an odd change of voice. 'Come, Denman.'

And the two went off. Langham came to a stand beside Rose, while old Lord Rupert, as jovial as ever, and bubbling over with gossip about the Queen's Speech, appropriated Lady Helen, who was the darling of all elderly men.

They did not speak. Rose sent him a ray from eyes full of a new divine shyness. He smiled gently in answer to it, and full of her own young emotion, and of the effort to conceal it from all the world, she noticed none of that change which had struck Agnes.

And all the while, if she could have penetrated the man's silence! An hour before this moment Langham had vowed that nothing should take him to Lady Charlotte's that night. And yet here he was, riveted to her side, alive like any normal human being to every detail of her loveliness, shaken to his inmost being by the intoxicating message of her look, of the transformation which had passed in an instant over the teasing difficult creature of the last few months.

At Murewell his chagrin had been *not* to feel, *not* to struggle, to have been cheated out of experience. Well, here *is* the experience in good earnest! And Langham is wrestling with it for dear life. And how little the exquisite child beside him knows of it, or of the man on whom she is spending her first wilful passion! She stands strangely exulting in her own strange victory over a life, a heart, which had defied and eluded her. The world throbs and thrills about her, the crowd beside her is all unreal, the air is full of whisper, of romance.

The thought-reading followed its usual course. A murder and its detection were given in dumb show. Then it was the turn of card-guessing, bank-note-finding, and the various other forms of telepathic hide and seek. Mr. Flaxman superintended them all, his restless eye wandering every other minute to the farther drawing-room in which the lights had been lowered, catching there always the same patch of black and white,—Rose's dress and the dark form beside her.

'Are you convinced? Do you believe?' said Rose, merrily looking up at her companion.

'In telepathy? Well—so far—I have not got beyond the delicacy and perfection of Mr. Denman's—muscular sensation. So much I am sure of!'

'Oh, but your scepticism is ridiculous!' she said gaily. 'We *know* that
some people have an extraordinary power over others.'

'Yes, that certainly we know!' he answered, his voice dropping, an odd
strained note in it. 'I grant you that.'

She trembled deliciously. Her eyelids fell. They stood together, conscious
only of each other.

'Now,' said Mr. Denman, advancing to the doorway between the two
drawing-rooms, 'I have done all I can—I am exhausted. But let me beg of you
all to go on with some experiments amongst yourselves. Every fresh discovery
of this power in a new individual is a gain to science. I believe about one in
ten has some share of it. Mr. Flaxman and I will arrange everything, if any
one will volunteer?'

The audience broke up into groups, laughing, chatting, suggesting this
and that. Presently Lady Charlotte's loud dictatorial voice made itself heard,
as she stood eyeglass in hand looking round the circle of her guests.

'Somebody must venture—we are losing time.'

Then the eyeglass stopped at Rose, who was now sitting tall and radiant
on the sofa, her blue fan across her white knees. 'Miss Leyburn—you are always public-spirited—will you be victimised for the good of science?'

The girl got up with a smile.

'And Mr. Langham—will you see what you can do with Miss Leyburn?
Hugh—we all choose her task, don't we—then Mr. Langham wills?'

Flaxman came up to explain. Langham had turned to Rose—a wild fury
with Lady Charlotte and the whole affair sweeping through him. But there
was no time to demur; that judicial eye was on them; the large figure and
towering cap bent towards him. Refusal was impossible.

'Command me!' he said with a sudden straightening of the form and a
flush on the pale cheek. 'I am afraid Miss Leyburn will find me a very bad
partner.'

'Well, now then!' said Flaxman; 'Miss Leyburn, will you please go down
into the library while we settle what you are to do!'

She went, and he held the door open for her. But she passed out unconscious of him—rosy, confused, her eyes bent on the ground.

'Now, then, what shall Miss Leyburn do?' asked Lady Charlotte in the
same loud emphatic tone.

'If I might suggest something quite different from anything that has been
yet tried,' said Mr. Flaxman, 'suppose we require Miss Leyburn to kiss the

hand of the little marble statue of Hope in the far drawing-room. What do you say, Langham?'

'What you please!' said Langham, moving up to him. A glance passed between the two men. In Langham's there was a hardly sane antagonism and resentment, in Flaxman's an excited intelligence.

'Now then,' said Flaxman coolly, 'fix your mind steadily on what Miss Leyburn is to do—you must take her hand—but except in thought, you must carefully follow and not lead her. Shall I call her?'

Langham abruptly assented. He had a passionate sense of being watched—tricked. Why were he and she to be made a spectacle for this man and his friends! A mad irrational indignation surged through him.

Then she was led in blindfolded, one hand stretched out feeling the air in front of her. The circle of people drew back. Mr. Flaxman and Mr. Denman prepared, note-book in hand, to watch the experiment. Langham moved desperately forward.

But the instant her soft trembling hand touched his, as though by enchantment, the surrounding scene, the faces, the lights, were blotted out from him. He forgot his anger, he forgot everything but her and this thing she was to do. He had her in his grasp—he was the man, the master—and what enchanting readiness to yield in the swaying pliant form! In the distance far away gleamed the statue of Hope, a child on tiptoe, one outstretched arm just visible from where he stood.

There was a moment's silent expectation. Every eye was riveted on the two figures—on the dark handsome man—on the blindfolded girl.

At last Rose began to move gently forward. It was a strange wavering motion. The breath came quickly through her slightly parted lips; her bright colour was ebbing. She was conscious of nothing but the grasp in which her hand was held—otherwise her mind seemed a blank. Her state during the next few seconds was not unlike the state of some one under the partial influence of an anæsthetic; a benumbing grip was laid on all her faculties; and she knew nothing of how she moved or where she was going.

Suddenly the trance cleared away. It might have lasted half an hour or five seconds, for all she knew. But she was standing beside a small marble statue in the farthest drawing-room, and her lips had on them a slight sense of chill, as though they had just been laid to something cold.

She pulled off the handkerchief from her eyes. Above her was Langham's face, a marvellous glow and animation in every line of it.

'Have I done it?' she asked in a tremulous whisper.

For the moment her self-control was gone. She was still bewildered.

He nodded, smiling.

'I am so glad,' she said, still in the same quick whisper, gazing at him. There was the most adorable *abandon* in her whole look and attitude. He could but just restrain himself from taking her in his arms, and for one bright flashing instant each saw nothing but the other.

The heavy curtain which had partially hidden the door of the little old-fashioned powder-closet as they approached it, and through which they had swept without heeding, was drawn back with a rattle.

'She has done it! Hurrah!' cried Mr. Flaxman. 'What a rush that last was, Miss Leyburn! You left us all behind.'

Rose turned to him, still dazed, drawing her hand across her eyes. A rush? She had known nothing about it!

Mr. Flaxman turned and walked back, apparently to report to his aunt, who, with Lady Helen, had been watching the experiment from the main drawing-room. His face was a curious mixture of gravity and the keenest excitement. The gravity was mostly sharp compunction. He had satisfied a passionate curiosity, but in the doing of it he had outraged certain instincts of breeding and refinement which were now revenging themselves.

'Did she do it exactly?' said Lady Helen eagerly.

'Exactly,' he said, standing still.

Lady Charlotte looked at him significantly. But he would not see her look.

'Lady Charlotte, where is my sister?' said Rose, coming up from the back room, looking now nearly as white as her dress.

It appeared that Agnes had just been carried off by a lady who lived on Campden Hill close to the Leyburns, and who had been obliged to go at the beginning of the last experiment. Agnes, torn between her interest in what was going on and her desire to get back to her mother, had at last hurriedly accepted this Mrs. Sherwood's offer of a seat in her carriage, imagining that her sister would want to stay a good deal later, and relying on Lady Charlotte's promise that she should be safely put into a hansom.

'I must go,' said Rose, putting her hand to her head. 'How tiring this is! How long did it take, Mr. Flaxman?'

'Exactly three minutes,' he said, his gaze fixed upon her with an expression that only Lady Helen noticed.

'So little! Good-night, Lady Charlotte!' and giving her hand first to her hostess then to Mr. Flaxman's bewildered sister, she moved away into the crowd.

'Hugh, of course you are going down with her?' exclaimed Lady Charlotte under her breath. 'You must. I promised to see her safely off the premises.'

He stood immovable. Lady Helen with a reproachful look made a step forward, but he caught her arm.

'Don't spoil sport,' he said, in a tone which, amid the hum of discussion caused by the experiment, was heard only by his aunt and sister.

They looked at him—the one amazed, the other grimly observant—and caught a slight significant motion of the head towards Langham's distant figure.

Langham came up and made his farewells. As he turned his back, Lady Helen's large astonished eyes followed him to the door.

'Oh, Hugh!' was all she could say as they came back to her brother.

'Never mind, Nellie,' he whispered, touched by the bewildered sympathy of her look; 'I will tell you all about it to-morrow. I have not been behaving well, and am not particularly pleased with myself. But for her it is all right. Poor, pretty little thing!'

And he walked away into the thick of the conversation.

Downstairs the hall was already full of people waiting for their carriages. Langham, hurrying down, saw Rose coming out of the cloak-room, muffled up in brown furs, a pale child-like fatigue in her looks which set his heart beating faster than ever.

'Miss Leyburn, how are you going home?'

'Will you ask for a hansom, please?'

'Take my arm,' he said, and she clung to him through the crush till they reached the door.

Nothing but private carriages were in sight. The street seemed blocked, a noisy tumult of horses and footmen and shouting men with lanterns. Which of them suggested, 'Shall we walk a few steps?' At any rate, here they were, out in the wind and the darkness, every step carrying them farther away from that moving patch of noise and light behind.

'We shall find a cab at once in Park Lane,' he said. 'Are you warm?'

'Perfectly.'

A fur hood fitted round her face, to which the colour was coming back. She held her cloak tightly round her, and her little feet, fairly well shod, slipped in and out on the dry frosty pavement.

Suddenly they passed a huge unfinished house, the building of which was being pushed on by electric light. The great walls, ivory white in the glare, rose into the purply-blue of the starry February sky, and as they passed within the power of the lamps, each saw with noonday distinctness every line and feature in the other's face. They swept on—the night, with its alternations of flame and shadow, an unreal and enchanted world about them. A space of darkness succeeded the space of daylight. Behind them in the distance was the sound of hammers and workmen's voices; before them the dim trees of the park. Not a human being was in sight. London seemed to exist to be the mere dark friendly shelter of this wandering of theirs.

A blast of wind blew her cloak out of her grasp. But before she could close it again, an arm was flung around her. She could not speak or move, she stood passive, conscious only of the strangeness of the wintry wind, and of this warm breast against which her cheek was laid.

'Oh, stay there!' a voice said close to her ear. 'Rest there—pale tired child—pale tired little child!'

That moment seemed to last an eternity. He held her close, cherishing and protecting her from the cold—not kissing her—till at length she looked up with bright eyes, shining through happy tears.

'Are you sure at last?' she said, strangely enough, speaking out of the far depths of her own thought to his.

'Sure!' he said, his expression changing. 'What can I be sure of? I am sure that I am not worth your loving, sure that I am poor, insignificant, obscure, that if you give yourself to me you will be miserably throwing yourself away!'

She looked at him, still smiling, a white sorceress weaving spells about him in the darkness. He drew her lightly gloved hand through his arm, holding the fragile fingers close in his, and they moved on.

'Do you know,' he repeated—a tone of intense melancholy replacing the tone of passion,—'how little I have to give you?'

'I know,' she answered, her face turned shyly away from him, her words coming from under the fur hood which had fallen forward a little. 'I know that—that—you are not rich, that you distrust yourself, that——'

'Oh, hush,' he said, and his voice was full of pain. 'You know so little; let me paint myself. I have lived alone, for myself, in myself, till sometimes there seems to be hardly anything left in me to love or be loved; nothing but a brain, a machine that exists only for certain selfish ends. My habits are the tyrants of years; and at Murewell, though I loved you there, they were strong enough to carry me away from you. There is something paralysing in me, which is always forbidding me to feel, to will. Sometimes I think it is an actual physical disability—the horror that is in me of change, of movement, of effort. Can you bear with me? Can you be poor? Can you live a life of monotony? Oh, impossible!' he broke out, almost putting her hand away from him. 'You, who ought to be a queen of this world, for whom everything bright and brilliant is waiting if you will but stretch out your hand to it. It is a crime—an infamy—that I should be speaking to you like this!'

Rose raised her head. A passing light shone upon her. She was trembling and pale again, but her eyes were unchanged.

'No, no,' she said wistfully; 'not if you love me.'

He hung above her, an agony of feeling in the fine rigid face, of which the beautiful features and surfaces were already worn and blanched by the life of thought. What possessed him was not so much distrust of circumstance as doubt, hideous doubt, of himself, of this very passion beating within him. She saw nothing, meanwhile, but the self-depreciation which she knew so well in him, and against which her love in its rash ignorance and generosity cried out.

'You will not say you love me!' she cried, with hurrying breath. 'But I know—I know—you do.'

Then her courage sinking, ashamed, blushing, once more turning away from him—'At least, if you don't, I am very—very—unhappy.'

The soft words flew through his blood. For an instant he felt himself saved, like Faust,—saved by the surpassing moral beauty of one moment's impression. That she should need him, that his life should matter to hers! They were passing the garden wall of a great house. In the deepest shadow of it, he stooped suddenly and kissed her.

CHAPTER XXXVI

Langham parted with Rose at the corner of Martin Street. She would not let him take her any farther.

'I will say nothing,' she whispered to him, as he put her into a passing hansom, wrapping her cloak warmly round her, 'till I see you again. To-morrow?'

'To-morrow morning,' he said, waving his hand to her, and in another instant he was facing the north wind alone.

He walked on fast towards Beaumont Street, but by the time he reached his destination midnight had struck. He made his way into his room where the fire was still smouldering, and striking a light, sank into his large reading chair, beside which the volumes used in the afternoon lay littered on the floor.

He was suddenly penetrated with the cold of the night, and hung shivering over the few embers which still glowed. What had happened to him? In this room, in this chair, the self-forgetting excitement of that walk, scarcely half an hour old, seems to him already long passed—incredible almost.

And yet the brain was still full of images, the mind still full of a hundred new impressions. That fair head against his breast, those soft confiding words, those yielding lips. Ah! it is the poor, silent, insignificant student that has conquered. It is he, not the successful man of the world, that has held that young and beautiful girl in his arms, and heard from her the sweetest and humblest confession of love. Fate can have neither wit nor conscience to have ordained it so; but fate has so ordained it. Langham takes note of his victory, takes dismal note also that the satisfaction of it has already half departed.

So the great moment has come and gone! The one supreme experience which life and his own will had so far rigidly denied him, is his. He has felt the torturing thrill of passion—he has evoked such an answer as all men might envy him,—and fresh from Rose's kiss, from Rose's beauty, the strange maimed soul falls to a pitiless analysis of his passion, her response! One moment he is at her feet in a voiceless trance of gratitude and tenderness; the next—is nothing what it promises to be?—and has the boon already, now that he has it in his grasp, lost some of its beauty, just as the sea-shell drawn out of the water, where its lovely iridescence tempted eye and hand, loses half its fairy charm?

The night wore on. Outside an occasional cab or cart would rattle over the stones of the street, an occasional voice or step would penetrate the thin walls of the house, bringing a shock of sound into that silent upper room. Nothing caught Langham's ear. He was absorbed in the dialogue which was to decide his life.

Opposite to him, as it seemed, there sat a spectral reproduction of himself, his true self, with whom he held a long and ghastly argument.

'But I love her!—I love her! A little courage—a little effort—and I too can achieve what other men achieve. I have gifts, great gifts. Mere contact with her, the mere necessities of the situation, will drive me back to life, teach me how to live normally, like other men. I have not forced her love—it has been a free gift. Who can blame me if I take it, if I cling to it, as the man freezing in a crevasse clutches the rope thrown to him?'

To which the pale spectre self said scornfully—

'*Courage* and *effort* may as well be dropped out of your vocabulary. They are words that you have no use for. Replace them by two others—*habit* and *character*. Slave as you are of habit, of the character you have woven for yourself out of years of deliberate living—what wild unreason to imagine that love can unmake, can recreate! What you are, you are to all eternity. Bear your own burden, but for God's sake beguile no other human creature into trusting you with theirs!'

'But she loves me! Impossible that I should crush and tear so kind, so warm a heart! Poor child—poor child! I have played on her pity. I have won all she had to give. And now to throw her gift back in her face—oh monstrous—oh inhuman!' and the cold drops stood on his forehead.

But the other self was inexorable. 'You have acted as you were bound to act—as any man may be expected to act in whom will and manhood and true human kindness are dying out, poisoned by despair and the tyranny of the critical habit. But at least do not add another crime to the first. What in God's name have you to offer a creature of such claims, such ambitions? You are poor—you must go back to Oxford—you must take up the work your soul loathes—grow more soured, more embittered—maintain a useless degrading struggle, till her youth is done, her beauty wasted, and till you yourself have lost every shred of decency and dignity, even that decorous outward life in which you can still wrap yourself from the world! Think of the little house—the children—the money difficulties—she, spiritually starved, every illusion gone,—you incapable soon of love, incapable even of pity, conscious only of a dull rage with her, yourself, the world! Bow the neck—submit—refuse that long agony for yourself and her, while there is still time. *Kismet—Kismet!*'

And spread out before Langham's shrinking soul there lay a whole dismal Hogarthian series, image leading to image, calamity to calamity, till in the last scene of all the maddened inward sight perceived two figures, two gray and withered figures, far apart, gazing at each other with cold and sunken eyes across dark rivers of sordid irremediable regret.[25]

The hours passed away, and in the end, the spectre self, a cold and bloodless conqueror, slipped back into the soul which remorse and terror, love and pity, a last impulse of hope, a last stirring of manhood, had been alike powerless to save.

The February dawn was just beginning when he dragged himself to a table and wrote.

Then for hours afterwards he sat sunk in his chair, the stupor of fatigue broken every now and then by a flash of curious introspection. It was a base thing which he had done—it was also a strange thing psychologically; and at intervals he tried to understand it, to track it to its causes.

At nine o'clock he crept out into the frosty daylight, found a commissionaire who was accustomed to do errands for him, and sent him with a letter to Lerwick Gardens.

On his way back he passed a gunsmith's, and stood looking fascinated at

---

25 William Hogarth (1697-1764), painter best known for his satirical representations of contemporary English life. The narrator is thinking of *Marriage à-la-mode* (1743-45), a narrative sequence of six paintings in which a venal marriage goes disastrously wrong.

the shining barrels. Then he moved away, shaking his head, his eyes gleaming as though the spectacle of himself had long ago passed the bounds of tragedy—become farcical even.

'I should only stand a month—arguing—with my finger on the trigger.'

In the little hall his landlady met him, gave a start at the sight of him, and asked him if he ailed and if she could do anything for him. He gave her a sharp answer and went upstairs, where she heard him dragging books and boxes about as though he were packing.

A little later Rose was standing at the dining-room window of No. 27, looking on to a few trees bedecked with rime which stood outside. The ground and roofs were white, a promise of sun was struggling through the fog. So far everything in these unfrequented Campden Hill roads was clean, crisp, enlivening, and the sparkle in Rose's mood answered to that of Nature.

Breakfast had just been cleared away. Agnes was upstairs with Mrs. Leyburn. Catherine, who was staying in the house for a day or two, was in a chair by the fire reading some letters forwarded to her from Bedford Square.

He would appear some time in the morning, she supposed. With an expression half rueful, half amused, she fell to imagining his interview with Catherine, with her mother. Poor Catherine! Rose feels herself happy enough to allow herself a good honest pang of remorse for much of her behaviour to Catherine this winter; how thorny she has been, how unkind often, to this sad changed sister. And now this will be a fresh blow! 'But afterwards, when she has got over it,—when she knows that it makes me happy,—that nothing else would make me happy,—then she will be reconciled, and she and I perhaps will make friends, all over again, from the beginning. I won't be angry or hard over it—poor Cathie!'

And with regard to Mr. Flaxman. As she stands there waiting idly for what destiny may send her, she puts herself through a little light catechism about this other friend of hers. He had behaved somewhat oddly towards her of late; she begins now to remember that her exit from Lady Charlotte's house the night before had been a very different matter from the royally attended leave-takings, presided over by Mr. Flaxman, which generally befell her there. Had he understood? With a little toss of her head she said to herself that she did not care if it was so. 'I have never encouraged Mr. Flaxman to think I was going to marry him.'

But of course Mr. Flaxman will consider she has done badly for herself. So will Lady Charlotte and all her outer world. They will say she is dismally throwing herself away, and her mother, no doubt influenced by the clamour, will take up very much the same line.

What matter! The girl's spirit seemed to rise against all the world. There was a sort of romantic exaltation in her sacrifice of herself, a jubilant looking forward to remonstrance, a wilful determination to overcome it. That she was about to do the last thing she could have been expected to do, gave her pleasure. Almost all artistic faculty goes with a love of surprise and caprice in life. Rose had her full share of the artistic love for the impossible and the difficult.

Besides—success! To make a man hope and love, and live again—*that* shall be her success. She leaned against the window, her eyes filling, her heart very soft.

Suddenly she saw a commissionaire coming up the little flagged passage to the door. He gave in a note, and immediately afterwards the dining-room door opened.

'A letter for you, Miss,' said the maid.

Rose took it—glanced at the handwriting. A bright flush—a surreptitious glance at Catherine who sat absorbed in a wandering letter from Mrs. Darcy. Then the girl carried her prize to the window and opened it.

Catherine read on, gathering up the Murewell names and details as some famished gleaner might gather up the scattered ears on a plundered field. At last something in the silence of the room, and of the other inmate in it, struck her.

'Rose,' she said, looking up, 'was that some one brought you a note?'

The girl turned with a start—a letter fell to the ground. She made a faint ineffectual effort to pick it up, and sank into a chair.

'Rose—darling!' cried Catherine, springing up, 'are you ill?'

Rose looked at her with a perfectly colourless fixed face, made a feeble negative sign, and then laying her arms on the breakfast-table in front of her, let her head fall upon them.

Catherine stood over her aghast. 'My darling—what is it? Come and lie down—take this water.'

She put some close to her sister's hand, but Rose pushed it away. 'Don't talk to me,' she said with difficulty.

Catherine knelt beside her in helpless pain and perplexity, her cheek resting against her sister's shoulder as a mute sign of sympathy. What could be the matter? Presently her gaze travelled from Rose to the letter on the floor. It lay with the address uppermost, and she at once recognised Langham's handwriting. But before she could combine any rational ideas with this quick perception, Rose had partially mastered herself. She raised her head slowly and grasped her sister's arm.

'I was startled,' she said, a forced smile on her white lips. 'Last night

Mr. Langham asked me to marry him—I expected him here this morning to consult with mamma and you. That letter is to inform me that—he made a mistake—and he is very sorry! So am I! It is so—so—bewildering!'

She got up restlessly and went to the fire as though shivering with cold. Catherine thought she hardly knew what she was saying. The elder sister followed her, and throwing an arm round her, pressed the slim irresponsive figure close. Her eyes were bright with anger, her lips quivering.

'That he should *dare*!' she cried. 'Rose—my poor little Rose.'

'Don't blame him!' said Rose, crouching down before the fire, while Catherine fell into the armchair again. 'It doesn't seem to count, from you— you have always been so ready to blame him!'

Her brow contracted; she looked frowning into the fire, her still colourless mouth working painfully.

Catherine was cut to the heart. 'Oh, Rose!' she said, holding out her hands, 'I will blame no one, dear. I seem hard—but I love you so. Oh, tell me—you would have told me everything once!'

There was the most painful yearning in her tone. Rose lifted a listless right hand and put it into her sister's outstretched palms. But she made no answer, till suddenly, with a smothered cry, she fell towards Catherine.

'Catherine! I cannot bear it. I said I loved him—he kissed me—I could kill myself and him.'

Catherine never forgot the mingled tragedy and domesticity of the hour that followed—the little familiar morning sounds in and about the house, maids running up and down stairs, tradesmen calling, bells ringing,—and here, at her feet, a spectacle of moral and mental struggle which she only half understood, but which wrung her inmost heart. Two strains of feeling seemed to be present in Rose—a sense of shock, of wounded pride, of intolerable humiliation, and a strange intervening passion of pity, not for herself but for Langham, which seemed to have been stirred in her by his letter. But though the elder questioned, and the younger seemed to answer, Catherine could hardly piece the story together, nor could she find the answer to the question filling her own indignant heart, 'Does she love him?'

At last Rose got up from her crouching position by the fire and stood, a white ghost of herself, pushing back the bright encroaching hair from eyes that were dry and feverish.

'If I could only be angry—downright angry,' she said, more to herself than Catherine, 'it would do one good.'

'Give others leave to be angry for you!' cried Catherine.

'Don't!' said Rose, almost fiercely, drawing herself away. 'You don't know.

It is a fate. Why did we ever meet? You may read his letter; you must—
you misjudge him—you always have. No, no'—and she nervously crushed
the letter in her hand—'not yet. But you shall read it some time—you and
Robert too. Married people always tell one another. It is due to him, perhaps
due to me too,' and a hot flush transfigured her paleness for an instant. 'Oh,
my head! Why does one's mind affect one's body like this? It shall not—it is
humiliating! "Miss Leyburn has been jilted and cannot see visitors,"—that
is the kind of thing. Catherine, when you have finished that document, will
you kindly come and hear me practise my last Raff—I am going. Good-bye.'

She moved to the door, but Catherine had only just time to catch her, or
she would have fallen over a chair from sudden giddiness.

'Miserable!' she said, dashing a tear from her eyes, 'I must go and lie
down then in the proper missish fashion. Mind, on your peril, Catherine, not
a word to any one but Robert. I shall tell Agnes. And Robert is not to speak
to me! No, don't come—I will go alone.'

And warning her sister back, she groped her way upstairs. Inside her
room, when she had locked the door, she stood a moment upright with the
letter in her hand,—the blotted incoherent scrawl, where Langham had for
once forgotten to be literary, where every pitiable half-finished sentence
pleaded with her—even in the first smart of her wrong—for pardon, for compassion, as towards something maimed and paralysed from birth, unworthy
even of her contempt. Then the tears began to rain over her cheeks.

'I was not good enough—I was not good enough—God would not let
me!'

And she fell on her knees beside the bed, the little bit of paper crushed in
her hands against her lips. Not good enough for what? *To save?*

How lightly she had dreamed of healing, redeeming, changing! And the
task is refused her. It is not so much the cry of personal desire that shakes
her as she kneels and weeps, nor is it mere wounded woman's pride. It is a
strange stern sense of law. Had she been other than she is—more loving, less
self-absorbed, loftier in motive—he could not have loved her so, have left
her so. Deep undeveloped forces of character stir within her. She feels herself
judged,—and with a righteous judgment—issuing inexorably from the facts
of life and circumstance.

Meanwhile Catherine was shut up downstairs with Robert, who had
come over early to see how the household fared.

Robert listened to the whole luckless story with astonishment and dismay. This particular possibility of mischief had gone out of his mind for some

time. He had been busy in his East End work. Catherine had been silent. Over how many matters they would once have discussed with open heart was she silent now?

'I ought to have been warned,' he said with quick decision, 'if you knew this was going on. I am the only man among you, and I understand Langham better than the rest of you. I might have looked after the poor child a little.'

Catherine accepted the reproach mutely as one little smart the more. However, what had she known? She had seen nothing unusual of late, nothing to make her think a crisis was approaching. Nay, she had flattered herself that Mr. Flaxman, whom she liked, was gaining ground.

Meanwhile Robert stood pondering anxiously what could be done. Could anything be done?

'I must go and see him,' he said presently. 'Yes, dearest, I must. Impossible the thing should be left so! I am his old friend,—almost her guardian. You say she is in great trouble—why, it may shadow her whole life! No—he must explain things to us—he is bound to—he shall. It may be something comparatively trivial in the way after all—money or prospects or something of the sort. You have not seen the letter, you say? It is the last marriage in the world one could have desired for her—but if she loves him, Catherine, if she loves him——'

He turned to her—appealing, remonstrating. Catherine stood pale and rigid. Incredible that he should think it right to intermeddle—to take the smallest step towards reversing so plain a declaration of God's will! She could not sympathise—she would not consent. Robert watched her in painful indecision. He knew that she thought him indifferent to her true reason for finding some comfort even in her sister's trouble—that he seemed to her mindful only of the passing human misery, indifferent to the eternal risk.

They stood sadly looking at one another. Then he snatched up his hat.

'I must go,' he said in a low voice; 'it is right.'

And he went—stepping, however, with the best intentions in the world, into a blunder.

Catherine sat painfully struggling with herself after he had left her. Then some one came into the room—some one with pale looks and flashing eyes. It was Agnes.

'She just let me in to tell me, and put me out again,' said the girl—her whole, even, cheerful self one flame of scorn and wrath. 'What are such creatures made for, Catherine—why do they exist?'

Meanwhile, Robert had trudged off through the frosty morning streets to Langham's lodgings. His mood was very hot by the time he reached his destination, and he climbed the staircase to Langham's room in some excitement. When he tried to open the door after the answer to his knock bidding him enter, he found something barring the way. 'Wait a little,' said the voice inside, 'I will move the case.'

With difficulty the obstacle was removed and the door opened. Seeing his visitor, Langham stood for a moment in sombre astonishment. The room was littered with books and packing-cases with which he had been busy.

'Come in,' he said, not offering to shake hands.

Robert shut the door, and, picking his way among the books, stood leaning on the back of the chair Langham pointed out to him. Langham paused opposite to him, his waving jet-black hair falling forward over the marble pale face which had been Robert's young ideal of manly beauty.

The two men were only six years distant in age, but so strong is old association that Robert's feeling towards his friend had always remained in many respects the feeling of the undergraduate towards the don. His sense of it now filled him with a curious awkwardness.

'I know why you are come,' said Langham slowly, after a scrutiny of his visitor.

'I am here by a mere accident,' said the other, thinking perfect frankness best. 'My wife was present when her sister received your letter. Rose gave her leave to tell me. I had gone up to ask after them all, and came on to you,—of course on my own responsibility entirely! Rose knows nothing of my coming—nothing of what I have to say.'

He paused, struck against his will by the looks of the man before him. Whatever he had done during the past twenty-four hours he had clearly had the grace to suffer in the doing of it.

'You can have nothing to say!' said Langham, leaning against the chimney piece and facing him with black, darkly-burning eyes. 'You know me.'

Never had Robert seen him under this aspect. All the despair, all the bitterness hidden under the languid student's exterior of every day, had, as it were, risen to the surface. He stood at bay, against his friend, against himself.

'No!' exclaimed Robert stoutly, 'I do not know you in the sense you mean. I do not know you as the man who could beguile a girl on to a confession of love, and then tell her that for you marriage was too great a burden to be faced!'

Langham started, and then closed his lips in an iron silence. Robert repented him a little. Langham's strange individuality always impressed him against his will.

'I did not come simply to reproach you, Langham,' he went on, 'though

I confess to being very hot! I came to try and find out—for myself only, mind—whether what prevents you from following up what I understand happened last night is really a matter of feeling, or a matter of outward circumstance. If, upon reflection, you find that your feeling for Rose is not what you imagined it to be, I shall have my own opinion about your conduct—but I shall be the first to acquiesce in what you have done this morning. If, on the other hand, you are simply afraid of yourself in harness, and afraid of the responsibilities of practical married life, I cannot help begging you to talk the matter over with me, and let us face it together. Whether Rose would ever, under any circumstances, get over the shock of this morning I have not the remotest idea. But'—and he hesitated—'it seems the feeling you appealed to yesterday has been of long growth. You know perfectly well what havoc a thing of this kind *may* make in a girl's life. I don't say it will. But, at any rate, it is all so desperately serious I could not hold my hand. I am doing what is no doubt wholly unconventional; but I am your friend and her brother; I brought you together, and I ask you to take me into counsel. If you had but done it before!'

There was a moment's dead silence.

'You cannot pretend to believe,' said Langham at last, with the same sombre self-containedness, 'that a marriage with me would be for your sister-in-law's happiness?'

'I don't know what to believe!' cried Robert. 'No,' he added frankly, 'no; when I saw you first attracted by Rose at Murewell I disliked the idea heartily; I was glad to see you separated; *à priori*, I never thought you suited to each other. But reasoning that holds good when a thing is wholly in the air looks very different when a man has committed himself and another, as you have done.'

Langham surveyed him for a moment, then shook his hair impatiently from his eyes and rose from his bending position by the fire.

'Elsmere, there is nothing to be said! I have behaved as vilely as you please. I have forfeited your friendship. But I should be an even greater fiend and weakling than you think me if, in cold blood, I could let your sister run the risk of marrying me. I could not trust myself—you may think of the statement as you like—I should make her *miserable*. Last night I had not parted from her an hour before I was utterly and irrevocably sure of it. My habits are my masters. I believe,' he added slowly, his eyes fixed weirdly on something beyond Robert, 'I could even grow to *hate* what came between me and them!'

Was it the last word of the man's life? It struck Robert with a kind of shiver.

'Pray heaven,' he said with a groan, getting up to go, 'you may not have made her miserable already!'

'Did it hurt her so much?' asked Langham almost inaudibly, turning away, Robert's tone meanwhile calling up a new and scorching image in the subtle brain tissue.

'I have not seen her,' said Robert abruptly; 'but when I came in I found my wife—who has no light tears—weeping for her sister.'

His voice dropped as though what he were saying were in truth too pitiful and too intimate for speech.

Langham said no more. His face had become a marble mask again.

'Good-bye!' said Robert, taking up his hat with a dismal sense of having got foolishly through a fool's errand. 'As I said to you before, what Rose's feeling is at this moment I cannot even guess. Very likely she would be the first to repudiate half of what I have been saying. And I see that you will not talk to me—you will not take me into your confidence and speak to me not only as her brother but as your friend. And—and—are you going? What does this mean?'

He looked interrogatively at the open packing-cases.

'I am going back to Oxford,' said the other briefly. 'I cannot stay in these rooms, in these streets.'

Robert was sore perplexed. What real—nay, what terrible suffering—in the face and manner, and yet how futile, how needless! He felt himself wrestling with something intangible and phantom-like, wholly unsubstantial, and yet endowed with a ghastly indefinite power over human life.

'It is very hard,' he said hurriedly, moving nearer, 'that our old friendship should be crossed like this. Do trust me a little! You are always undervaluing yourself. Why not take a friend into council sometimes when you sit in judgment on yourself and your possibilities? Your own perceptions are all warped!'

Langham, looking at him, thought his smile one of the most beautiful and one of the most irrelevant things he had ever seen.

'I will write to you, Elsmere,' he said, holding out his hand, 'speech is impossible to me. I never had any words except through my pen.'

Robert gave it up. In another minute Langham was left alone.

But he did no more packing for hours. He spent the middle of the day sitting dumb and immovable in his chair. Imagination was at work again more feverishly than ever. He was tortured by a fixed image of Rose, suffering and paling.

And after a certain number of hours he could no more bear the incubus of this thought than he could put up with the flat prospects of married life the night before. He was all at sea, barely sane, in fact. His life had been so long purely intellectual that this sudden strain of passion and fierce practical interests seemed to unhinge him, to destroy his mental balance.

He bethought him. This afternoon he knew she had a last rehearsal at Searle House. Afterwards her custom was to come back from St. James's Park to High Street, Kensington, and walk up the hill to her own home. He knew it, for on two occasions after these rehearsals he had been at Lerwick Gardens, waiting for her, with Agnes and Mrs. Leyburn. Would she go this afternoon? A subtle instinct told him that she would.

It was nearly six o'clock that evening when Rose, stepping out from the High Street station, crossed the main road and passed into the darkness of one of the streets leading up the hill. She had forced herself to go, and she would go alone. But as she toiled along she felt weary and bruised all over. She carried with her a heart of lead—a sense of utter soreness—a longing to hide herself from eyes and tongues. The only thing that dwelt softly in the shaken mind was a sort of inconsequent memory of Mr. Flaxman's manner at the rehearsal. Had she looked so ill? She flushed hotly at the thought, and then realised again, with a sense of childish comfort, the kind look and voice, the delicate care shown in shielding her from any unnecessary exertion, the brotherly grasp of the hand with which he had put her into the cab that took her to the Underground.

Suddenly, where the road made a dark turn to the right, she saw a man standing. As she came nearer she saw that it was Langham.

'You!' she cried, stopping.

He came up to her. There was a light over the doorway of a large detached house not far off, which threw a certain illumination over him, though it left her in shadow. He said nothing, but he held out both his hands mutely. She fancied rather than saw the pale emotion of his look.

'What?' she said, after a pause. 'You think to-night is last night! You and I have nothing to say to each other, Mr. Langham.'

'I have everything to say,' he answered, under his breath; 'I have committed a crime—a villainy.'

'And it is not pleasant to you?' she said, quivering. 'I am sorry—I cannot help you. But you are wrong—it was no crime—it was necessary and profitable, like the doses of one's childhood! Oh! I might have guessed you would do this! No, Mr. Langham, I am in no danger of an interesting decline. I have just played my *concerto* very fairly. I shall not disgrace myself at the concert to-morrow night. You may be at peace—I have learnt several things to-day that have been salutary—very salutary.'

She paused. He walked beside her while she pelted him,—unresisting, helplessly silent.

'Don't come any farther,' she said resolutely after a minute, turning to face him. 'Let us be quits! I was a temptingly easy prey. I bear no malice. And do not let me break your friendship with Robert; that began before this foolish business—it should outlast it. Very likely *we* shall be friends again, like ordinary people, some day. I do not imagine your wound is very deep, and——'

But no! Her lips closed; not even for pride's sake, and retort's sake, will she desecrate the past, belittle her own first love.

She held out her hand. It was very dark. He could see nothing among her furs but the gleaming whiteness of her face. The whole personality seemed centred in the voice—the half-mocking vibrating voice. He took her hand and dropped it instantly.

'You do not understand,' he said hopelessly—feeling as though every phrase he uttered, or could utter, were equally fatuous, equally shameful. 'Thank heaven, you never will understand.'

'I think I do,' she said with a change of tone, and paused. He raised his eyes involuntarily, met hers, and stood bewildered. What *was* the expression in them? It was yearning—but not the yearning of passion. 'If things had been different—if one could change the self—if the past were nobler!'—was that the cry of them? A painful humility—a boundless pity—the rise of some moral wave within her he could neither measure nor explain—these were some of the impressions which passed from her to him. A fresh gulf opened between them, and he saw her transformed on the farther side, with, as it were, a loftier gesture, a nobler stature, than had ever yet been hers.

He bent forward quickly, caught her hands, held them for an instant to his lips in a convulsive grasp, dropped them, and was gone.

He gained his own room again. There lay the medley of his books, his only friends, his real passion. Why had he ever tampered with any other?

'*It was not love—not love!*' he said to himself, with an accent of infinite relief as he sank into his chair. '*Her* smart will heal.'

BOOK VI - NEW OPENINGS

CHAPTER XXXVII

Ten days after Langham's return to Oxford Elsmere received a characteristic letter from him, asking whether their friendship was to be considered as still existing or at an end. The calm and even proud melancholy of the letter showed a considerable subsidence of that state of half-frenzied irritation and discomfort in which Elsmere had last seen him. The writer, indeed, was clearly settling down into another period of pessimistic quietism such as that which had followed upon his first young efforts at self-assertion years before. But this second period bore the marks of an even profounder depression of all the vital forces than the first, and as Elsmere, with a deep sigh, half-angry, half-relenting, put down the letter, he felt the conviction that no fresh influence from outside would ever again be allowed to penetrate the solitude of Langham's life. In comparison with the man who had just addressed him, the tutor of his undergraduate recollections was a vigorous and sociable human being.

The relenting grew upon him, and he wrote a sensible affectionate letter in return. Whatever had been his natural feelings of resentment, he said, he could not realise, now that the crisis was past, that he cared less about his old friend. 'As far as we two are concerned, let us forget it all. I could hardly say this, you will easily imagine, if I thought that you had done serious or irreparable harm. But both my wife and I agree now in thinking that by a pure accident, as it were, and to her own surprise, Rose has escaped either. It will be some time, no doubt, before she will admit it. A girl is not so easily disloyal to her past. But to us it is tolerably clear. At any rate, I send you our opinion for what it is worth, believing that it will and must be welcome to you.'

Rose, however, was not so long in admitting it. One marked result of that new vulnerableness of soul produced in her by the shock of that February morning was a great softening towards Catherine. Whatever might have been Catherine's intense relief when Robert returned from his abortive mission, she never afterwards let a disparaging word towards Langham escape her lips to Rose. She was tenderness and sympathy itself, and Rose, in her curious reaction against her old self, and against the noisy world of flattery and excitement in which she had been living, turned to Catherine as she had never done since she was a tiny child. She would spend hours in a corner of the Bedford Square drawing-room, pretending to read, or play with little Mary, in reality recovering, like some bruised and trodden plant, under the healing influence of thought and silence.

One day, when they were alone in the firelight, she startled Catherine by saying with one of her old odd smiles—

'Do you know, Cathie, how I always see myself nowadays? It is a sort of hallucination. I see a girl at the foot of a precipice. She has had a fall, and she is sitting up, feeling all her limbs. And, to her great astonishment, there is no bone broken!'

And she held herself back from Catherine's knee lest her sister should attempt to caress her, her eyes bright and calm. Nor would she allow an answer, drowning all that Catherine might have said in a sudden rush after the child, who was wandering round them in search of a playfellow.

In truth, Rose Leyburn's girlish passion for Edward Langham had been a kind of accident unrelated to the main forces of character. He had crossed her path in a moment of discontent, of aimless revolt and longing, when she was but fresh emerged from the cramping conditions of her childhood and trembling on the brink of new and unknown activities. His intellectual prestige, his melancholy, his personal beauty, his very strangenesses and weaknesses, had made a deep impression on the girl's immature romantic sense. His resistance had increased the charm, and the interval of angry resentful separation had done nothing to weaken it. As to the months in London, they had been one long duel between herself and him—a duel which had all the fascination of difficulty and uncertainty, but in which pride and caprice had dealt and sustained a large proportion of the blows. Then, after a moment of intoxicating victory, Langham's endangered habits and threatened individuality had asserted themselves once for all. And from the whole long struggle—passion, exultation, and crushing defeat—it often seemed to her that she had gained neither joy nor irreparable grief, but a new birth of character, a soul!

It may be easily imagined that Hugh Flaxman felt a peculiarly keen interest in Langham's disappearance. On the afternoon of the Searle House rehearsal he had awaited Rose's coming in a state of extraordinary irritation. He expected a blushing *fiancée*, in a fool's paradise, asking by manner, if not by word, for his congratulations, and taking a decent feminine pleasure perhaps in the pang she might suspect in him. And he had already taken *his* pleasure in the planning of some double-edged congratulations.

Then up the steps of the concert platform there came a pale tired girl, who seemed specially to avoid his look, who found a quiet corner and said hardly a word to anybody till her turn came to play.

His revulsion of feeling was complete. After her piece he made his way up to her, and was her watchful unobtrusive guardian for the rest of the afternoon.

He walked home after he had put her into her cab in a whirl of impatient conjecture.

'As compared to last night, she looks this afternoon as if she had had an illness! What on earth has that philandering ass been about? If he did not propose to her last night, he ought to be shot—and if he did, *à fortiori*, for clearly she is *miserable*. But what a brave child! How she played her part! I wonder whether she thinks that *I* saw nothing, like all the rest! Poor little cold hand!'

Next day in the street he met Elsmere, turned and walked with him, and by dint of leading the conversation a little discovered that Langham had left London.

Gone! But not without a crisis—that was evident. During the din of preparations for the Searle House concert, and during the meetings which it entailed, now at the Varleys', now at the house of some other connection of his—for the concert was the work of his friends, and given in the town house of his decrepit great-uncle, Lord Daniel—he had many opportunities of observing Rose. And he felt a soft indefinable change in her which kept him in a perpetual answering vibration of sympathy and curiosity. She seemed to him for the moment to have lost her passionate relish for living, that relish which had always been so marked with her. Her bubble of social pleasure was pricked. She did everything she had to do, and did it admirably. But all through she was to his fancy absent and *distraite*, pursuing through the tumult of which she was often the central figure some inner meditations of which neither he nor any one else knew anything. Some eclipse had passed over the girl's light self-satisfied temper; some searching thrill of experience had gone through the whole nature. She had suffered, and she was quietly fighting down her suffering without a word to anybody.

Flaxman's guesses as to what had happened came often very near the truth, and the mixture of indignation and relief with which he received his own conjectures amused himself.

'To think,' he said to himself once with a long breath, 'that that creature was never at a public school, and will go to his death without any one of the kickings due to him!'

Then his very next impulse, perhaps, would be an impulse of gratitude towards this same 'creature,' towards the man who had released a prize he had had the tardy sense to see was not meant for him. *Free* again—to be loved, to be won! There was the fact of facts after all.

His own future policy, however, gave him much anxious thought. Clearly at present the one thing to be done was to keep his own ambitions carefully out of sight. He had the skill to see that she was in a state of reaction, of moral and mental fatigue. What she mutely seemed to ask of her friends was not to be made to feel.

He took his cue accordingly. He talked to his sister. He kept Lady Charlotte in order. After all her eager expectation on Hugh's behalf, Lady Helen had been dumfoundered by the sudden emergence of Langham at Lady Charlotte's party for their common discomfiture. Who was the man?— why, what did it all mean? Hugh had the most provoking way of giving you half his confidence. To tell you he was seriously in love, and to omit to add the trifling item that the girl in question was probably on the point of engaging herself to somebody else! Lady Helen made believe to be angry, and it was not till she had reduced Hugh to a whimsical penitence and a full confession of all he knew or suspected, that she consented, with as much loftiness as the physique of an elf allowed her, to be his good friend again, and to play those cards for him which at the moment he could not play for himself.

So in the cheeriest daintiest way Rose was made much of by both brother and sister. Lady Helen chatted of gowns and music and people, whisked Rose and Agnes off to this party and that, brought fruit and flowers to Mrs. Leyburn, made pretty deferential love to Catherine, and generally, to Mrs. Pierson's disgust, became the girls' chief chaperon in a fast-filling London. Meanwhile, Mr. Flaxman was always there to befriend or amuse his sister's *protégées*—always there, but never in the way. He was bantering, sympathetic, critical, laudatory, what you will; but all the time he preserved a delicate distance between himself and Rose, a bright nonchalance and impersonality of tone towards her which made his companionship a perpetual tonic. And, between them, he and Helen coerced Lady Charlotte. A few inconvenient inquiries after Rose's health, a few unexplained stares and 'humphs' and grunts, a few irrelevant disquisitions on her nephew's merits of head and heart, were all she was able to allow herself. And yet she was inwardly seething with a mass of sentiments, to which it would have been pleasant to give expression—anger with Rose for having been so blind and so presumptuous as to prefer some one else to Hugh; anger with Hugh for his persistent disregard of her advice and the duke's feelings; and a burning desire to know the precise why and wherefore of Langham's disappearance. She was too lofty to become Rose's aunt without a struggle, but she was not too lofty to feel the hungriest interest in her love affairs.

But, as we have said, the person who for the time profited most by Rose's shaken mood was Catherine. The girl coming over, restless under her own smart, would fall to watching the trial of the woman and the wife, and would often perforce forget herself and her smaller woes in the pity of it. She stayed in Bedford Square once for a week, and then for the first time she realised the profound change which had passed over the Elsmeres' life. As much tenderness between husband and wife as ever—perhaps more expression of it even than before, as though from an instinctive craving to hide the separateness below from each other and from the world. But Robert went his way, Catherine hers. Their spheres of work lay far apart; their interests were diverging fast; and though Robert at any rate was perpetually resisting, all sorts of fresh invading silences were always coming in to limit talk, and increase the number of sore points which each avoided. Robert was hard at work in the East End under Murray Edwardes's auspices.[1] He was already known to certain circles as a seceder from the Church who was likely to become both powerful and popular. Two articles of his in the *Nineteenth Century*, on disputed points of Biblical criticism, had distinctly made their mark, and several of the veterans of philosophical debate had already taken friendly and flattering notice of the new writer.[2] Meanwhile Catherine was teaching in Mr. Clarendon's Sunday school, and attending his prayer-meetings. The more expansive Robert's energies became, the more she suffered, and the more the small daily opportunities for friction multiplied. Soon she could hardly bear to hear him talk about his work, and she never opened the number of the *Nineteenth Century* which contained his papers. Nor had he the heart to ask her to read them.

Murray Edwardes had received Elsmere, on his first appearance in R——, with a cordiality and a helpfulness of the most self-effacing kind. Robert had begun with assuring his new friend that he saw no chance, at any rate for the present, of his formally joining the Unitarians.

'I have not the heart to pledge myself again just yet! And I own I look rather for a combination from many sides than for the development of any now existing sect. But supposing,' he added, smiling, 'supposing I do in time set up a congregation and a service of my own, is there really room for you and me? Should I not be infringing on a work I respect a great deal too much for anything of the sort?'

Edwardes laughed the notion to scorn.

The parish, as a whole, contained 20,000 persons. The existing churches,

---

1   One of the most impoverished and crime-ridden areas of London, soon to be the site of the Whitechapel Murders (1888).

2   Extremely prestigious monthly journal, founded in 1877. William Gladstone's review of *Robert Elsmere*, along with Ward's rejoinder, appeared there.

which, with the exception of St. Wilfrid's, were miserably attended, provided accommodation at the outside for 3000. His own chapel held 400, and was about half full.

'You and I may drop our lives here,' he said, his pleasant friendliness darkened for a moment by the look of melancholy which London work seems to develop even in the most buoyant of men, 'and only a few hundred persons, at the most, be ever the wiser. Begin with us—then make your own circle.'

And he forthwith carried off his visitor to the point from which, as it seemed to him, Elsmere's work might start, viz. a lecture-room half a mile from his own chapel, where two helpers of his had just established an independent venture.

Murray Edwardes had at the time an interesting and miscellaneous staff of lay-curates. He asked no questions as to religious opinions, but in general the men who volunteered under him—civil servants, a young doctor, a briefless barrister or two—were men who had drifted from received beliefs, and found a pleasure and freedom in working for and with him they could hardly have found elsewhere. The two who had planted their outpost in what seemed to them a particularly promising corner of the district were men of whom Edwardes knew personally little. 'I have really not much concern with what they do,' he explained to Elsmere, 'except that they get a small share of our funds. But I know they want help, and if they will take you in, I think you will make something of it.'

After a tramp through the muddy winter streets, they came upon a new block of warehouses, in the lower windows of which some bills announced a night-school for boys and men. Here, to judge from the commotion round the doors, a lively scene was going on. Outside, a gang of young roughs were hammering at the doors, and shrieking witticisms through the keyhole. Inside, as soon as Murray Edwardes and Elsmere, by dint of good humour and strong shoulders, had succeeded in shoving their way through and shutting the door behind them, they found a still more animated performance in progress. The schoolroom was in almost total darkness; the pupils, some twenty in number, were racing about, like so many shadowy demons, pelting each other and their teachers with the 'dips' which, as the buildings were new, and not yet fitted for gas, had been provided to light them through their three R's. In the middle stood the two philanthropists they were in search of, freely bedaubed with tallow, one employed in boxing a boy's ears, the other in saving a huge inkbottle whereon some enterprising spirit had just laid hands by way of varying the rebel ammunition. Murray Edwardes, who was in his element, went to the rescue at once, helped by Robert. The boy-minister, as he looked, had been, in fact, 'bow' of the Cambridge eight, and possessed muscles which men twice his size might have envied.[3] In three minutes he had put a couple of ringleaders into the street by the scruff of the neck, relit a lamp which had been turned out, and got the rest of the rioters in hand. Elsmere backed him ably, and in a very short time they had cleared the premises.

Then the four looked at each other, and Edwardes went off into a shout of laughter.

'My dear Wardlaw, my condolences to your coat! But I don't believe if I were a rough myself I could resist "dips." Let me introduce a friend—Mr. Elsmere—and if you will have him, a recruit for your work. It seems to me another pair of arms will hardly come amiss to you!'

The short red-haired man addressed shook hands with Elsmere, scrutinising him from under bushy eyebrows. He was panting and beplastered with tallow, but the inner man was evidently quite unruffled, and Elsmere liked the shrewd Scotch face and gray eyes.

'It isn't only a pair of arms we want,' he remarked drily, 'but a bit of science behind them. Mr. Elsmere, I observed, can use his.'

Then he turned to a tall affected-looking youth with a large nose and long fair hair, who stood gasping with his hands upon his sides, his eyes, full of a moody wrath, fixed on the wreck and disarray of the schoolroom.

'Well, Mackay, have they knocked the wind out of you? My friend and helper—Mr. Elsmere. Come and sit down, won't you, a minute. They've left us the chairs, I perceive, and there's a spark or two of fire. Do you smoke? Will you light up?'

The four men sat on chatting some time, and then Wardlaw and Elsmere walked home together. It had been all arranged. Mackay, a curious morbid fellow, who had thrown himself into Unitarianism and charity mainly out of opposition to an orthodox and *bourgeois* family, and who had a great idea of his own social powers, was somewhat grudging and ungracious through it all. But Elsmere's proposals were much too good to be refused. He offered to bring to the undertaking his time, his clergyman's experience, and as much money as might be wanted. Wardlaw listened to him cautiously for an hour, took stock of the whole man physically and morally, and finally said, as he very quietly and deliberately knocked the ashes out of his pipe,—

'All right, I'm your man, Mr. Elsmere. If Mackay agrees, I vote we make you captain of this venture.'

'Nothing of the sort,' said Elsmere. 'In London I am a novice; I come to learn, not to lead.'

Wardlaw shook his head with a little shrewd smile. Mackay faintly

---

3   The rower seated nearest the boat's bow.   Edwardes was part of Cambridge University's boat-racing crew.

endorsed his companion's offer, and the party broke up.

That was in January. In two months from that time, by the natural force of things, Elsmere, in spite of diffidence and his own most sincere wish to avoid a premature leadership, had become the head and heart of the Elgood Street undertaking, which had already assumed much larger proportions. Wardlaw was giving him silent approval and invaluable help, while young Mackay was in the first uncomfortable stages of a hero-worship which promised to be exceedingly good for him.

CHAPTER XXXVIII

There were one or two curious points connected with the beginnings of Elsmere's venture in North R——, one of which may just be noticed here. Wardlaw, his predecessor and colleague, had speculatively little or nothing in common with Elsmere or Murray Edwardes. He was a devoted and orthodox Comtist, for whom Edwardes had provided an outlet for the philanthropic passion, as he had for many others belonging to far stranger and remoter faiths.

By profession he was a barrister, with a small and struggling practice. On this practice, however, he had married, and his wife, who had been a doctor's daughter and a national schoolmistress, had the same ardours as himself. They lived in one of the dismal little squares near the Goswell Road, and had two children. The wife, as a Positivist mother is bound to do, tended and taught her children entirely herself. She might have been seen any day wheeling their perambulator through the dreary streets of a dreary region; she was their Providence, their deity, the representative to them of all tenderness and all authority. But when her work with them was done, she would throw herself into charity organisation cases, into efforts for the protection of workhouse servants, into the homeliest acts of ministry towards the sick, till her dowdy little figure and her face, which but for the stress of London, of labour, and of poverty, would have had a blunt fresh-coloured dairymaid's charm, became symbols of a divine and sacred helpfulness in the eyes of hundreds of straining men and women.

The husband also, after a day spent in chambers, would give his evenings to teaching or committee work. They never allowed themselves to breathe even to each other that life might have brighter things to show them than the neighbourhood of the Goswell Road. There was a certain narrowness in their devotion; they had their bitternesses and ignorances like other people; but the more Robert knew of them the more profound became his admiration for that potent spirit of social help which in our generation Comtism has done so much to develop, even among those of us who are but moderately influenced by Comte's philosophy, and can make nothing of the religion of Humanity.

Wardlaw has no large part in the story of Elsmere's work in North R——. In spite of Robert's efforts, and against his will, the man of meaner gifts and commoner clay was eclipsed by that brilliant and persuasive something in Elsmere which a kind genius had infused into him at birth. And we shall see that in time Robert's energies took a direction which Wardlaw could not follow with any heartiness. But at the beginning Elsmere owed him much, and it was a debt he was never tired of honouring.

In the first place, Wardlaw's choice of the Elgood Street room as a fresh centre for civilising effort had been extremely shrewd. The district lying about it, as Robert soon came to know, contained a number of promising elements.

Close by the dingy street which sheltered their schoolroom rose the great pile of a new factory of artistic pottery, a rival on the north side of the river to Doulton's immense works on the south.[4] The old winding streets near it, and the blocks of workmen's dwellings recently erected under its shadow, were largely occupied by the workers in its innumerable floors, and among these workers was a large proportion of skilled artisans, men often of a considerable amount of cultivation, earning high wages, and maintaining a high standard of comfort. A great many of them, trained in the art school which Murray Edwardes had been largely instrumental in establishing within easy distance of their houses, were men of genuine artistic gifts and accomplishment, and as the development of one faculty tends on the whole to set others working, when Robert, after a few weeks' work in the place, set up a popular historical lecture once a fortnight, announcing the fact by a blue and white poster in the schoolroom windows, it was the potters who provided him with his first hearers.

The rest of the parish was divided between a population of dock labourers, settled there to supply the needs of the great dock which ran up into the south-eastern corner of it, two or three huge breweries, and a colony of watchmakers, an offshoot of Clerkenwell, who lived together in two or three streets, and showed the same peculiarities of race and specialised training to be noticed in the more northerly settlement from which they had been thrown off like a swarm from a hive.[5] Outside these well-defined trades there

---

4   Royal Doulton, a leading pottery.

5   From the eighteenth century onward, the country's watchmakers congregated in Clerkenwell.

was, of course, a warehouse population, and a mass of heterogeneous cadging and catering which went on chiefly in the riverside streets at the other side of the parish from Elgood Street, in the neighbourhood of St. Wilfrid's.

St. Wilfrid's at this moment seemed to Robert to be doing a very successful work among the lowest strata of the parish. From them at one end of the scale, and from the innumerable clerks and superintendents who during the daytime crowded the vast warehouses of which the district was full, its Lenten congregations, now in full activity, were chiefly drawn.

The Protestant opposition, which had shown itself so brutally and persistently in old days, was now, so far as outward manifestations went, all but extinct. The cassocked monk-like clergy might preach and 'process' in the open air as much as they pleased. The populace, where it was not indifferent, was friendly, and devoted living had borne its natural fruits.

A small incident, which need not be recorded, recalled to Elsmere's mind—after he had been working some six weeks in the district—the forgotten unwelcome fact that St. Wilfrid's was the very church where Newcome, first as senior curate and then as vicar, had spent those ten wonderful years into which Elsmere at Murewell had been never tired of inquiring. The thought of Newcome was a very sore thought. Elsmere had written to him announcing his resignation of his living immediately after his interview with the bishop. The letter had remained unanswered, and it was by now tolerably clear that the silence of its recipient meant a withdrawal from all friendly relations with the writer. Elsmere's affectionate sensitive nature took such things hardly, especially as he knew that Newcome's life was becoming increasingly difficult and embittered. And it gave him now a fresh pang to imagine how Newcome would receive the news of his quondam friend's 'infidel propaganda,' established on the very ground where he himself had all but died for those beliefs Elsmere had thrown over.

But Robert was learning a certain hardness in this London life which was not without its uses to character. Hitherto he had always swum with the stream, cheered by the support of all the great and prevailing English traditions. Here, he and his few friends were fighting a solitary fight apart from the organised system of English religion and English philanthropy. All the elements of culture and religion already existing in the place were against them. The clergy of St. Wilfrid's passed them with cold averted eyes; the old and *fainéant*[6] rector of the parish church very soon let it be known what he thought as to the taste of Elsmere's intrusion on his parish, or as to the eternal chances of those who might take either him or Edwardes as guides in matters

---

6   Lazy.

religious. His enmity did Elgood Street no harm, and the pretensions of the
Church, in this Babel of 20,000 souls, to cover the whole field, bore clearly no
relation at all to the facts. But every little incident in this new struggle of his
life cost Elsmere more perhaps than it would have cost other men. No part of
it came easily to him. Only a high Utopian vision drove him on from day to
day, bracing him to act and judge, if need be, alone and for himself, approved
only by conscience and the inward voice.

> 'Tasks in hours of insight willed
> Can be in hours of gloom fulfilled;'[7]

and it was that moment by the river which worked in him through all the
prosaic and perplexing details of this new attempt to carry enthusiasm into
life.

It was soon plain to him that in this teeming section of London the
chance of the religious reformer lay entirely among the *upper working class*.
In London, at any rate, all that is most prosperous and intelligent among the
working class holds itself aloof—broadly speaking—from all existing spiritual
agencies, whether of Church or Dissent.

Upon the genuine London artisan the Church has practically no hold
whatever; and Dissent has nothing like the hold which it has on similar material in the great towns of the North. Towards religion in general the prevailing
attitude is one of indifference tinged with hostility. 'Eight hundred thousand
people in South London, of whom the enormous proportion belong to the
working class, and among them, Church and Dissent nowhere—*Christianity
not in possession.*' Such is the estimate of an Evangelical of our day;[8] and similar laments come from all parts of the capital. The Londoner is on the whole
more conceited, more prejudiced, more given over to crude theorising, than
his North-country brother, the mill-hand, whose mere position, as one of a
homogeneous and tolerably constant body, subjects him to a continuous discipline of intercourse and discussion. Our popular religion, broadly speaking,
means nothing to him. He is sharp enough to see through its contradictions
and absurdities; he has no dread of losing what he never valued; his sense of
antiquity, of history, is *nil*; and his life supplies him with excitement enough
without the stimulants of 'other-worldliness.' Religion has been on the whole
irrationally presented to him, and the result on his part has been an irrational
breach with the whole moral and religious order of ideas.

But the race is quick-witted and imaginative. The Greek cities which

---

7   Matthew Arnold, "Morality," ll. 5-6.
8   Anthony Thorold (1826–95), the Bishop of Rochester.

welcomed and spread Christianity carried within them much the same elements as are supplied by certain sections of the London working class—elements of restlessness, of sensibility, of passion. The mere intermingling of races, which a modern capital shares with those old towns of Asia Minor, predisposes the mind to a greater openness and receptiveness, whether for good or evil.

As the weeks passed on, and after the first inevitable despondency produced by strange surroundings and an unwonted isolation had begun to wear off, Robert often found himself filled with a strange flame and ardour of hope! But his first steps had nothing to do with religion. He made himself quickly felt in the night-school, and as soon as he possibly could he hired a large room at the back of their existing room, on the same floor, where, on the recreation evenings, he might begin the story-telling, which had been so great a success at Murewell. The story-telling struck the neighbourhood as a great novelty. At first only a few youths straggled in from the front room, where dominoes and draughts and the illustrated papers held seductive sway. The next night the number was increased, and by the fourth or fifth evening the room was so well filled both by boys and a large contingent of artisans, that it seemed well to appoint a special evening in the week for story-telling, or the recreation room would have been deserted.

In these performances Elsmere's aim had always been twofold—the rousing of moral sympathy and the awakening of the imaginative power pure and simple. He ranged the whole world for stories. Sometimes it would be merely some feature of London life itself—the history of a great fire, for instance, and its hairbreadth escapes; a collision in the river; a string of instances as true and homely and realistic as they could be made of the way in which the poor help one another. Sometimes it would be stories illustrating the dangers and difficulties of particular trades—a colliery explosion and the daring of the rescuers; incidents from the life of the great Northern ironworks, or from that of the Lancashire factories; or stories of English country life and its humours, given sometimes in dialect—Devonshire, or Yorkshire, or Cumberland—for which he had a special gift. Or, again, he would take the sea and its terrors—the immortal story of the *Birkenhead*; the deadly plunge of the *Captain*;[9] the records of the lifeboats, or the fascinating story of the ships of science, exploring step by step, through miles of water, the past, the inhabitants, the hills and valleys of that underworld, that vast Atlantic bed, in which Mont Blanc might be buried without showing even his topmost

9   The HMS *Birkenhead* was shipwrecked off the coast of South Africa in 1852; the HMS *Captain* near Spain in 1870. The latter was especially disastrous, with only a handful of survivors.

snowfield above the plain of waves. Then at other times it would be the simple frolic and fancy of fiction—fairy tale and legend, Greek myth or Icelandic
saga, episodes from Walter Scott, from Cooper, from Dumas; to be followed
perhaps on the next evening by the terse and vigorous biography of some man
of the people—of Stephenson or Cobden, of Thomas Cooper or John Bright,
or even of Thomas Carlyle.[10]

One evening, some weeks after it had begun, Hugh Flaxman, hearing
from Rose of the success of the experiment, went down to hear his new acquaintance tell the story of Monte Cristo's escape from the Château d'If.[11] He
started an hour earlier than was necessary, and with an admirable impartiality
he spent that hour at St. Wilfrid's hearing vespers. Flaxman had a passion
for intellectual or social novelty; and this passion was beguiling him into a
close observation of Elsmere. At the same time he was crossed and complicated by all sorts of fastidious conservative fibres, and when his friends talked
rationalism, it often gave him a vehement pleasure to maintain that a good
Catholic or Ritualist service was worth all their arguments, and would outlast them. His taste drew him to the Church, so did a love of opposition to
current 'isms.' Bishops counted on him for subscriptions, and High Church
divines sent him their pamphlets. He never refused the subscriptions, but it
should be added that with equal regularity *he* dropped the pamphlets into
his waste-paper basket. Altogether a not very decipherable person in religious
matters—as Rose had already discovered.

The change from the dim and perfumed spaces of St. Wilfrid's to the
bare warehouse room with its packed rows of listeners was striking enough.
Here were no bowed figures, no *recueillement*.[12] In the blaze of crude light
every eager eye was fixed upon the slight elastic figure on the platform, each
change in the expressive face, each gesture of the long arms and thin flexible
hands, finding its response in the laughter, the attentive silence, the frowning
suspense of the audience. At one point a band of young roughs at the back

---

10 Sir Walter Scott (1771–1832), pioneer of the modern historical novel, includ-
ing *Waverley* and *Ivanhoe*; James Fenimore Cooper (1789–1851), prolific American
novelist whose works include *The Last of the Mohicans* and *The Pioneers*; Alexandre
Dumas (1802–1870), French historical novelist, author of *The Three Musketeers*;
George Stephenson (1781–1848), engineer famed for his work on the British railway system; Richard Cobden (1804–1865), Radical politician and campaigner with
John Bright against the protectionist Corn Laws; Thomas Cooper (1805–1892),
Chartist and author; John Bright (1811–1889), Radical politician; Thomas Carlyle
(1795–1881), man of letters whose works influenced Victorian philosophies of self-
development and work.
11 From Dumas' *The Count of Monte Cristo* (1844).
12 "Meditation, contemplation" (Collins).

made a disturbance, but their neighbours had the offenders quelled and out in a twinkling, and the room cried out for a repetition of the sentences which had been lost in the noise. When Dantes, opening his knife with his teeth, managed to cut the strings of the sack, a gasp of relief ran through the crowd; when at last he reached *terra firma* there was a ringing cheer.

'What is he, d'ye know?' Flaxman heard a mechanic ask his neighbour, as Robert paused for a moment to get breath, the man jerking a grimy thumb in the story-teller's direction meanwhile. 'Seems like a parson somehow. But he ain't a parson.'

'Not he,' said the other laconically. 'Knows better. Most of 'em as comes down 'ere stuffs all they have to say as full of goody-goody as an egg's full of meat. If he wur that sort you wouldn't catch *me* here. Never heard him say anything in the "dear brethren" sort of style, and I've been 'ere most o' these evenings and to his lectures besides.'

'Perhaps he's one of your d—d sly ones,' said the first speaker dubiously. 'Means to shovel it in by and by.'

'Well, I don't know as I couldn't stand it if he did,' returned his companion. 'He'd let other fellers have their say, anyhow.'

Flaxman looked curiously at the speaker. He was a young man, a gasfitter—to judge by the contents of the basket he seemed to have brought in with him on his way from work—with eyes like live birds', and small emaciated features. During the story Flaxman had noticed the man's thin begrimed hand, as it rested on the bench in front of him, trembling with excitement.

Another project of Robert's, started as soon as he had felt his way a little in the district, was the scientific Sunday school. This was the direct result of a paragraph in Huxley's Lay Sermons, where the hint of such a school was first thrown out.[13] However, since the introduction of science teaching into the Board schools, the novelty and necessity of such a supplement to a child's ordinary education is not what it was.[14] Robert set it up mainly for the sake of drawing the boys out of the streets in the afternoons, and providing them with some other food for fancy and delight than larking and smoking and penny dreadfuls.[15] A little simple chemical and electrical experiment went

---

13 Thomas Henry Huxley (1825–1895), scientist, inventor of the word "agnostic," and supporter of Darwin; *Lay Sermons, Addresses, and Reviews* (1871). The suggestion appears in "Scientific Education: Notes of an After-Dinner Speech."

14 That is, the schools under the supervision of local School Boards, as provided for by the Education Act (1870).

15 Cheap, wildly sensational literature, enormously popular and therefore the bugbear of many moralizers and social reformers. One of the most famous examples is *The String of Pearls* (1846–47), the story of murderous barber Sweeney Todd.

down greatly; so did a botany class, to which Elsmere would come armed with two stores of flowers, one to be picked to pieces, the other to be distributed according to memory and attention. A year before he had had a number of large coloured plates of tropical fruit and flowers prepared for him by a Kew assistant. These he would often set up on a large screen, or put up on the walls, till the dingy schoolroom became a bower of superb blossom and luxuriant leaf, a glow of red and purple and orange. And then—still by the help of pictures—he would take his class on a tour through strange lands, talking to them of China or Egypt or South America, till they followed him up the Amazon, or into the pyramids or through the Pampas, or into the mysterious buried cities of Mexico, as the children of Hamelin followed the magic of the Pied Piper.

Hardly any of those who came to him, adults or children, while almost all of the artisan class, were of the poorest class. He knew it, and had laid his plans for such a result. Such work as he had at heart has no chance with the lowest in the social scale, in its beginnings. It must have something to work upon, and must penetrate downwards. He only can receive who already hath—there is no profounder axiom.

And meanwhile the months passed on, and he was still brooding, still waiting. At last the spark fell.

There, in the next street but one to Elgood Street, rose the famous Workmen's Club of North R———.[16] It had been started by a former Liberal clergyman of the parish, whose main object, however, had been to train the workmen to manage it for themselves. His training had been, in fact, too successful. Not only was it now wholly managed by artisans, but it had come to be a centre of active, nay, brutal, opposition to the Church and faith which had originally fostered it. In organic connection with it was a large debating hall, in which the most notorious secularist lecturers held forth every Sunday evening; and next door to it, under its shadow and patronage, was a little dingy shop filled to overflowing with the coarsest free-thinking publications, Colonel Ingersoll's books occupying the place of honour in the window and the *Freethinker* placard flaunting at the door.[17] Inside there was still more

16 Workmen's clubs were part of the movement for working-class moral and intellectual improvement that included the Mechanics' Institutes and the coffee-house with which Robert has already been affiliated. Nevertheless, they were controversial precisely because they sometimes encouraged freethought, as seen here, and were also denounced for selling alcohol.

17 Robert Ingersoll (1833–1899), American agnostic, political speaker, and Attorney General of Illinois. He commented positively on *Robert Elsmere* in "Criticism of 'Robert Elsmere,' 'John Ward, Preacher,' and 'An African Farm,'" rpt. in *The Works of Robert G. Ingersoll: Volume XI, Miscellany* (New York: Dresden Publishing Co., 1909),

highly seasoned literature even than the *Freethinker* to be had. There was in particular a small halfpenny paper which was understood to be in some sense the special organ of the North R—— Club; which was at any rate published close by, and edited by one of the workmen founders of the club. This unsavoury sheet began to be more and more defiantly advertised through the parish as Lent drew on towards Passion week, and the exertions of St. Wilfrid's and of the other churches, which were being spurred on by the Ritualists' success, became more apparent. Soon it seemed to Robert that every bit of hoarding and every waste wall was filled with the announcement:—

'Read *Faith and Fools*. Enormous success. Our *Comic Life of Christ* now nearly completed.[18] Quite the best thing of its kind going. Woodcut this week—Transfiguration.'

His heart grew fierce within him. One night in Passion week he left the night-school about ten o'clock. His way led him past the club, which was brilliantly lit up, and evidently in full activity. Round the door there was a knot of workmen lounging. It was a mild moonlit April night, and the air was pleasant. Several of them had copies of *Faith and Fools*, and were showing the week's woodcut to those about them, with chuckles and spirts of laughter.

Robert caught a few words as he hurried past them, and stirred by a sudden impulse turned into the shop beyond, and asked for the paper. The woman handed it to him, and gave him his change with a business-like *sang-froid*, which struck on his tired nerves almost more painfully than the laughing brutality of the men he had just passed.

Directly he found himself in another street he opened the paper under a lamp-post. It contained a caricature of the Crucifixion, the scroll emanating from Mary Magdalene's mouth, in particular, containing obscenities which cannot be quoted here.

Robert thrust it into his pocket and strode on, every nerve quivering.

'This is Wednesday in Passion week,' he said to himself. 'The day after to-morrow is Good Friday!'

He walked fast in a north-westerly direction, and soon found himself within the City, where the streets were long since empty and silent. But he noticed nothing around him. His thoughts were in the distant East, among the flat roofs and white walls of Nazareth, the olives of Bethany, the steep streets and rocky ramparts of Jerusalem. He had seen them with the bodily

---

409-18. *The Freethinker* (1881-), still-extant atheist periodical (see www.freethinker. co.uk).

18 Inspired by George William Foote's *Comic Life of Christ*, published in *The Freethinker* in 1882, which led to Foote being successfully prosecuted for blasphemy the following year.

eye, and the fact had enormously quickened his historical perception. The child of Nazareth, the moralist and teacher of Capernaum and Gennesaret, the strenuous seer and martyr of the later Jerusalem preaching—all these various images sprang into throbbing poetic life within him. That anything in human shape should be found capable of dragging this life and this death through the mire of a hideous and befouling laughter! Who was responsible? To what cause could one trace such a temper of mind towards such an object—present and militant as that temper is in all the crowded centres of working life throughout modern Europe? The toiler of the world as he matures may be made to love Socrates or Buddha or Marcus Aurelius.[19] It would seem often as though he could not be made to love Jesus! Is it the Nemesis that ultimately discovers and avenges the sublimest, the least conscious departure from simplicity and verity?—is it the last and most terrible illustration of a great axiom: '*Faith has a judge—in truth*'?[20]

He went home and lay awake half the night pondering. If he could but pour out his heart! But though Catherine, the wife of his heart, of his youth, is there, close beside him, doubt and struggle and perplexity are alike frozen on his lips. He cannot speak without sympathy, and she will not hear except under a moral compulsion which he shrinks more and more painfully from exercising.

The next night was a story-telling night. He spent it in telling the legend of St. Francis.[21] When it was over he asked the audience to wait a moment, and there and then—with the tender imaginative Franciscan atmosphere, as it were, still about them—he delivered a short and vigorous protest in the name of decency, good feeling, and common sense, against the idiotic profanities with which the whole immediate neighbourhood seemed to be reeking. It was the first time he had approached any religious matter directly. A knot of workmen sitting together at the back of the room looked at each other with a significant grimace or two.

When Robert ceased speaking one of them, an elderly watchmaker, got up and made a dry and cynical little speech, nothing moving but the thin lips in the shrivelled mahogany face. Robert knew the man well. He was a Genevese by birth, Calvinist by blood, revolutionist by development. He complained that Mr. Elsmere had taken his audience by surprise; that a good many of those present understood the remarks he had just made as an attack upon an institution in which many of them were deeply interested; and that he invited Mr. Elsmere to a more thorough discussion of the matter, in a place

---

19 Marcus Aurelius (121–180 CE), Roman Emperor and author of the *Meditations*.
20 *Amiel's Journal*, 304.
21 St. Francis of Assisi (d. 1226).

where he could be both heard and answered.

The room applauded with some signs of suppressed excitement. Most of the men there were accustomed to disputation of the sort which any Sunday visitor to Victoria Park may hear going on there week after week.[22] Elsmere had made a vivid impression; and the prospect of a fight with him had an unusual piquancy.

Robert sprang up. 'When you will,' he said. 'I am ready to stand by what I have just said in the face of you all, if you care to hear it.'

Place and particulars were hastily arranged, subject to the approval of the club committee, and Elsmere's audience separated in a glow of curiosity and expectation.

'Didn't I tell ye?' the gasfitter's snarling friend said to him. 'Scratch him and you find the parson. These upper-class folk, when they come among us poor ones, always seem to me just hunting for souls, as those Injuns he was talking about last week hunt for scalps. They can't get to heaven without a certain number of 'em slung about 'em.'

'Wait a bit!' said the gasfitter, his quick dark eyes betraying a certain raised inner temperature.

Next morning the North R—— Club was placarded with announcements that on Easter Eve next Robert Elsmere, Esq., would deliver a lecture in the Debating Hall on 'The Claim of Jesus upon Modern Life'; to be followed, as usual, by general discussion.

CHAPTER XXXIX

It was the afternoon of Good Friday. Catherine had been to church at St. Paul's, and Robert, though not without some inward struggle, had accompanied her. Their midday meal was over, and Robert had been devoting himself to Mary, who had been tottering round the room in his wake, clutching one finger tight with her chubby hand. In particular, he had been coaxing her into friendship with a wooden Japanese dragon which wound itself in awful yet most seductive coils round the cabinet at the end of the room. It was Mary's weekly task to embrace this horror, and the performance went by the name of 'kissing the Jabberwock.'[23] It had been triumphantly achieved, and, as the reward of bravery, Mary was being carried round the room on her father's

---

22 Popular working-class gathering-place in the East End, famed for its wide variety of radical speakers.

23 The monster from Lewis Carroll's "Jabberwocky" in *Through the Looking-Glass* (1872).

shoulder, holding on mercilessly to his curls, her shining blue eyes darting scorn at the defeated monster.

At last Robert deposited her on the rug beside a fascinating farmyard which lay there spread out for her, and stood looking, not at the child, but at his wife.

'Catherine, I feel so much as Mary did three minutes ago!'

She looked up startled. The tone was light, but the sadness, the emotion of the eyes, contradicted it.

'I want courage,' he went on—'courage to tell you something that may hurt you. And yet I ought to tell it.'

Her face took the shrinking expression which was so painful to him. But she waited quietly for what he had to say.

'You know, I think,' he said, looking away from her to the gray Museum outside, 'that my work in R—— hasn't been religious as yet at all. Oh, of course, I have said things here and there, but I haven't delivered myself in any way. Now there has come an opening.'

And he described to her—while she shivered a little and drew herself together—the provocations which were leading him into a tussle with the North R—— Club.

'They have given me a very civil invitation. They are the sort of men after all whom it pays to get hold of, if one can. Among their fellows, they are the men who think. One longs to help them to think to a little more purpose.'

'What have you to give them, Robert?' asked Catherine after a pause, her eyes bent on the child's stocking she was knitting. Her heart was full enough already, poor soul. Oh, the bitterness of this Passion week! He had been at her side often in church, but through all his tender silence and consideration she had divined the constant struggle in him between love and intellectual honesty, and it had filled her with a dumb irritation and misery indescribable. Do what she would, wrestle with herself as she would, there was constantly emerging in her now a note of anger, not with Robert, but, as it were, with those malign forces of which he was the prey.

'What have I to give them?' he repeated sadly. 'Very little, Catherine, as it seems to me to-night. But come and see.'

His tone had a melancholy which went to her heart. In reality he was in that state of depression which often precedes a great effort. But she was startled by his suggestion.

'Come with you, Robert? To the meeting of a secularist club!'

'Why not? I shall be there to protest against outrage to what both you and I hold dear. And the men are decent fellows. There will be no disturbance.'

'What are you going to do?' she asked in a low voice.

'I have been trying to think it out,' he said with difficulty. 'I want simply, if I can, to transfer to their minds that image of Jesus of Nazareth which thought, and love, and reading have left upon my own. I want to make them realise for themselves the historical character, so far as it can be realised—to make them see for themselves the real figure, as it went in and out amongst men—so far as our eyes can now discern it.'

The words came quicker towards the end, while the voice sank—took the vibrating characteristic note the wife knew so well.

'How can that help them?' she said abruptly. 'Your historical Christ, Robert, will never win souls. If he was God, every word you speak will insult him. If he was man, he was not a good man!'

'Come and see,' was all he said, holding out his hand to her. It was in some sort a renewal of the scene at Les Avants, the inevitable renewal of an offer he felt bound to make, and she felt bound to resist.

She let her knitting fall and placed her hand in his. The baby on the rug was alternately caressing and scourging a woolly baa-lamb, which was the fetish of her childish worship. Her broken incessant baby-talk, and the ringing kisses with which she atoned to the baa-lamb for each successive outrage, made a running accompaniment to the moved undertones of the parents.

'Don't ask me, Robert, don't ask me! Do you want me to come and sit thinking of last year's Easter Eve?'

'Heaven knows I was miserable enough last Easter Eve,' he said slowly.

'And now,' she exclaimed, looking at him with a sudden agitation of every feature, 'now you are not miserable? You are quite confident and sure? You are going to devote your life to attacking the few remnants of faith that still remain in the world?'

Never in her married life had she spoken to him with this accent of bitterness and hostility. He started and withdrew his hand, and there was a silence.

'I held once a wife in my arms,' he said presently with a voice hardly audible, 'who said to me that she would never persecute her husband. But what is persecution if it is not the determination not to understand?'

She buried her face in her hands. 'I could not understand,' she said sombrely.

'And rather than try,' he insisted, 'you will go on believing that I am a man without faith, seeking only to destroy.'

'I know you think you have faith,' she answered, 'but how can it seem faith to me? "He that will not confess Me before men, him will I also deny before My Father which is in heaven."[24] Your unbelief seems to me more dangerous than these horrible things which shock you. For you can make it attractive, you can make it loved, as you once made the faith of Christ loved.'

He was silent. She raised her face presently, whereon were the traces of some of those quiet difficult tears which were characteristic of her, and went softly out of the room.

He stood a while leaning against the mantelpiece, deaf to little Mary's clamour, and to her occasional clutches at his knees, as she tried to raise herself on her tiny tottering feet. A sense as though of some fresh disaster was upon him. His heart was sinking, sinking within him. And yet none knew better than he that there was nothing fresh. It was merely that the scene had recalled to him anew some of those unpalatable truths which the optimist is always much too ready to forget.

Heredity, the moulding force of circumstance, the iron hold of the past upon the present—a man like Elsmere realises the working of these things in other men's lives with a singular subtlety and clearness, and is for ever overlooking them, running his head against them, in his own.

He turned and laid his arms on the chimneypiece, burying his head on them. Suddenly he felt a touch on his knee, and, looking down, saw Mary peering up, her masses of dark hair streaming back from the straining little face, the grave open mouth, and alarmed eyes.

'Fader, tiss! fader, tiss!' she said imperatively.

He lifted her up and covered the little brown cheeks with kisses. But the touch of the child only woke in him a fresh dread—the like of something he had often divined of late in Catherine. Was she actually afraid now that he might feel himself bound in future to take her child spiritually from her? The suspicion of such a fear in her woke in him a fresh anguish; it seemed a measure of the distance they had travelled from that old perfect unity.

'She thinks I could even become in time her tyrant and torturer,' he said to himself with measureless pain, 'and who knows—who can answer for himself? Oh, the puzzle of living!'

When she came back into the room, pale and quiet, Catherine said nothing, and Robert went to his letters. But after a while she opened his study door.

'Robert, will you tell me what your stories are to be next week, and let me put out the pictures?'

It was the first time she had made any such offer. He sprang up with a flash in his gray eyes, and brought her a slip of paper with a list. She took it

24 Matthew 10.33.

without looking at him. But he caught her in his arms, and for a moment in that embrace the soreness of both hearts passed away.

But if Catherine would not go, Elsmere was not left on this critical occasion without auditors from his own immediate circle. On the evening of Good Friday Flaxman had found his way to Bedford Square, and, as Catherine was out, was shown into Elsmere's study.

'I have come,' he announced, 'to try and persuade you and Mrs. Elsmere to go down with me to Greenlaws to-morrow. My Easter party has come to grief, and it would be a real charity on your part to come and resuscitate it. Do! You look abominably fagged, and as if some country would do you good.'

'But I thought——' began Robert, taken aback.

'You thought,' repeated Flaxman coolly, 'that your two sisters-in-law were going down there with Lady Helen, to meet some musical folk. Well, they are not coming. Miss Leyburn thinks your mother-in-law not very well to-day, and doesn't like to come. And your younger sister prefers also to stay in town. Helen is much disappointed, so am I. But——' And he shrugged his shoulders.

Robert found it difficult to make a suitable remark. His sisters-in-law were certainly inscrutable young women. This Easter party at Greenlaws, Mr. Flaxman's country house, had been planned, he knew, for weeks.[25] And certainly nothing could be very wrong with Mrs. Leyburn, or Catherine would have been warned.

'I am afraid your plans must be greatly put out,' he said, with some embarrassment.

'Of course they are,' replied Flaxman, with a dry smile. He stood opposite Elsmere, his hands in his pockets.

'Will you have a confidence?' the bright eyes seemed to say. 'I am quite ready. Claim it if you like.'

But Elsmere had no intention of claiming it. The position of all Rose's kindred, indeed, at the present moment was not easy. None of them had the least knowledge of Rose's mind. Had she forgotten Langham? Had she lost her heart afresh to Flaxman? No one knew. Flaxman's absorption in her was clear enough. But his love-making, if it was such, was not of an ordinary kind, and did not always explain itself. And, moreover, his wealth and social position were elements in the situation calculated to make people like the Elsmeres particularly diffident and discreet. Impossible for them, much as

---

25 "Greenlaws, Mr. Flaxman's country house,": second comma restored as per *SE* and *W*.

they liked him, to make any of the advances!

No, Robert wanted no confidences. He was not prepared to take the responsibility of them. So, letting Rose alone, he took up his visitor's invitation to themselves, and explained the engagement for Easter Eve, which tied them to London.

'Whew!' said Hugh Flaxman, 'but that will be a shindy worth seeing. I must come!'

'Nonsense!' said Robert, smiling. 'Go down to Greenlaws, and go to church. That will be much more in your line.'

'As for church,' said Flaxman meditatively, 'if I put off my party altogether, and stay in town, there will be this further advantage, that, after hearing you on Saturday night, I can, with a blameless impartiality, spend the following day in St. Andrew's, Well Street.[26] Yes! I telegraph to Helen—she knows my ways—and I come down to protect you against an atheistical mob to-morrow night!'

Robert tried to dissuade him. He did not want Flaxman. Flaxman's Epicureanism, the easy tolerance with which, now that the effervescence of his youth had subsided, the man harboured and dallied with a dozen contradictory beliefs, were at times peculiarly antipathetic to Elsmere.[27] They were so now, just as heart and soul were nerved to an effort which could not be made at all without the nobler sort of self-confidence.

But Flaxman was determined.

'No,' he said; 'this one day we'll give—to heresy. Don't look so forbidding! In the first place, you won't see me; in the next, if you did, you would feel me as wax in your hands. I am like the man in Sophocles—always the possession of the last speaker![28] One day I am all for the church. A certain number of chances in the hundred there still are, you will admit, that she is in the right of it. And if so, why should I cut myself off from a whole host of beautiful things not to be got outside her? But the next day—*vive* Elsmere and the Revolution! If only Elsmere could persuade me intellectually! But I never yet came across a religious novelty that seemed to me to have a leg of

---

26 An Anglican church.

27 Elsmere uses epicureanism in the modern sense, as of a pleasure-seeker, one with little interest in moral or spiritual absolutes.

28 Sophocles, fifth century BCE Greek tragedian. The reference is to *Oedipus Rex*: "For Oedipus excites himself too much / at every sort of trouble, not conjecturing, / like a man of sense, what will be from what was, / but he is always at the speaker's mercy, / when he speaks terrors." *Oedipus the King*, tr. David Grene, in *The Complete Greek Tragedies: Volume II, Sophocles* (Chicago and London: University of Chicago Press, 1992), ll. 914-18.

logic to stand on!'

He laid his hand on Robert's shoulder, his eyes twinkling with a sudden energy. Robert made no answer. He stood erect, frowning a little, his hands thrust far into the pockets of his light gray coat. He was in no mood to disclose himself to Flaxman. The inner vision was fixed with extraordinary intensity on quite another sort of antagonist, with whom the mind was continuously grappling.

'Ah, well—till to-morrow!' said Flaxman, with a smile, shook hands, and went.

Outside he hailed a cab and drove off to Lady Charlotte's.

He found his aunt and Mr. Wynnstay in the drawing-room alone, one on either side of the fire. Lady Charlotte was reading the latest political biography with an apparent profundity of attention; Mr. Wynnstay was lounging and caressing the cat. But both his aunt's absorption and Mr. Wynnstay's nonchalance seemed to Flaxman overdone. He suspected a domestic breeze.

Lady Charlotte made him effusively welcome. He had come to propose that she should accompany him the following evening to hear Elsmere lecture. 'I advise you to come,' he said. 'Elsmere will deliver his soul, and the amount of soul he has to deliver in these dull days is astounding. A dowdy dress and a veil, of course. I will go down beforehand and see some one on the spot, in case there should be difficulties about getting in. Perhaps Miss Leyburn, too, might like to hear her brother-in-law?'

'*Really*, Hugh,' cried Lady Charlotte impatiently, 'I think you might take your snubbing with dignity. Her refusal this morning to go to Greenlaws was brusqueness itself. To my mind that young person gives herself airs!' And the Duke of Sedbergh's sister drew herself up with a rustle of all her ample frame.

'Yes, I was snubbed,' said Flaxman, unperturbed; 'that, however, is no reason why she shouldn't find it attractive to go to-morrow night.'

'And you will let her see that, just because you couldn't get hold of her, you have given up your Easter party and left your sister in the lurch?'

'I never had excessive notions of dignity,' he replied composedly. 'You may make up any story you please. The real fact is that I want to hear Elsmere.'

'You had better go, my dear!' said her husband sardonically. 'I cannot imagine anything more piquant than an atheistic slum on Easter Eve.'

'Nor can I!' she replied, her combativeness rousing at once. 'Much obliged to you, Hugh. I will borrow my housekeeper's dress, and be ready to leave here at half-past seven.'

Nothing more was said of Rose, but Flaxman knew that she would be asked, and let it alone.

'Will his wife be there?' asked Lady Charlotte.

'Who? Elsmere's? My dear aunt, when you happen to be the orthodox wife of a rising heretic, your husband's opinions are not exactly the spectacular performance they are to you and me. I should think it most unlikely.'

'Oh, she persecutes him, does she?'

'She wouldn't be a woman if she didn't!' observed Mr. Wynnstay, *sotto voce*. The small dark man was lost in a great armchair, his delicate painter's hands playing with the fur of a huge Persian cat. Lady Charlotte threw him an eagle glance, and he subsided—for the moment.

Flaxman, however, was perfectly right. There had been a breeze. It had been just announced to the master of the house by his spouse that certain Socialist celebrities—who might any day be expected to make acquaintance with the police—were coming to dine at his table, to finger his spoons, and mix their diatribes with his champagne, on the following Tuesday. Overt rebellion had never served him yet, and he knew perfectly well that when it came to the point he should smile more or less affably upon these gentry, as he had smiled upon others of the same sort before. But it had not yet come to the point, and his intermediate state was explosive in the extreme.

Mr. Flaxman dexterously continued the subject of the Elsmeres. Dropping his bantering tone, he delivered himself of a very delicate critical analysis of Catherine Elsmere's temperament and position, as in the course of several months his intimacy with her husband had revealed them to him. He did it well, with acuteness and philosophical relish. The situation presented itself to him as an extremely refined and yet tragic phase of the religious difficulty, and it gave him intellectual pleasure to draw it out in words.

Lady Charlotte sat listening, enjoying her nephew's crisp phrases, but also gradually gaining a perception of the human reality behind this word-play of Hugh's. That 'good heart' of hers was touched; the large imperious face began to frown.

'Dear me!' she said, with a little sigh. 'Don't go on, Hugh! I suppose it's because we all of us believe so little that the poor thing's point of view seems to one so unreal. All the same, however,' she added, regaining her usual rôle of magisterial common-sense, 'a woman, in my opinion, ought to go with her husband in religious matters.'

'Provided, of course, she sets him at nought in all others,' put in Mr. Wynnstay, rising and daintily depositing the cat. 'Many men, however, my dear, might be willing to compromise it differently. Granted a certain *modicum* of worldly conformity, they would not be at all indisposed to a conscience clause.'

He lounged out of the room, while Lady Charlotte shrugged her shoulders with a look at her nephew in which there was an irrepressible twinkle. Mr. Flaxman neither heard nor saw. Life would have ceased to be worth having long ago had he ever taken sides in the smallest degree in this *ménage*.

Flaxman walked home again, not particularly satisfied with himself and his manœuvres. Very likely it was quite unwise of him to have devised another meeting between himself and Rose Leyburn so soon. Certainly she had snubbed him—there could be no doubt of that. Nor was he in much perplexity as to the reason. He had been forgetting himself, forgetting his *rôle* and the whole lie of the situation, and if a man will be an idiot he must suffer for it. He had distinctly been put back a move.

The facts were very simple. It was now nearly three months since Langham's disappearance. During that time Rose Leyburn had been, to Flaxman's mind, enchantingly dependent on him. He had played his part so well, and the beautiful high-spirited child had suited herself so naïvely to his acting! Evidently she had said to herself that his age, his former marriage, his relation to Lady Helen, his constant kindness to her and her sister, made it natural that she should trust him, make him her friend, and allow him an intimacy she allowed to no other male friend. And when once the situation had been so defined in her mind, how the girl's true self had come out!—what delightful moments that intimacy had contained for him!

He remembered how on one occasion he had been reading some Browning to her and Helen, in Helen's crowded belittered drawing-room, which seemed all piano and photographs and lilies of the valley. He never could exactly trace the connection between the passage he had been reading and what happened. Probably it was merely Browning's poignant passionate note that had affected her. In spite of all her proud bright reserve, both he and Helen often felt through these weeks that just below this surface there was a heart which quivered at the least touch.

He finished the lines and laid down the book. Lady Helen heard her three-year-old boy crying upstairs, and ran up to see what was the matter. He and Rose were left alone in the scented fire-lit room. And a jet of flame suddenly showed him the girl's face turned away, convulsed with a momentary struggle for self-control. She raised a hand an instant to her eyes, not dreaming evidently that she could be seen in the dimness; and her gloves dropped from her lap.

He moved forward, stooped on one knee, and as she held out her hand for the gloves, he kissed the hand very gently, detaining it afterwards as a brother might. There was not a thought of himself in his mind. Simply he could not bear that so bright a creature should ever be sorry. It seemed to him intolerable, against the nature of things. If he could have procured for her at that moment a coerced and transformed Langham, a Langham fitted to make her happy, he could almost have done it; and, short of such radical consolation, the very least he could do was to go on his knee to her, and comfort her in tender brotherly fashion.

She did not say anything; she let her hand stay a moment, and then she got up, put on her veil, left a quiet message for Lady Helen, and departed. But as he put her into a hansom her whole manner to him was full of a shy shrinking sweetness. And when Rose was shy and shrinking she was adorable.

Well, and now he had never again gone nearly so far as to kiss her hand, and yet because of an indiscreet moment everything was changed between them; she had turned resentful stand-off, nay, as nearly rude as a girl under the restraints of modern manners can manage to be. He almost laughed as he recalled Helen's report of her interview with Rose that morning, in which she had tried to persuade a young person outrageously on her dignity to keep an engagement she had herself spontaneously made.

'I am very sorry, Lady Helen,' Rose had said, her slim figure drawn up so stiffly that the small Lady Helen felt herself totally effaced beside her. 'But I had rather not leave London this week. I think I will stay with mamma and Agnes.'

And nothing Lady Helen could say moved her, or modified her formula of refusal.

'What *have* you been doing, Hugh?' his sister asked him, half dismayed, half provoked.

Flaxman shrugged his shoulders and vowed he had been doing nothing. But, in truth, he knew very well that the day before he had overstepped the line. There had been a little scene between them, a quick passage of speech, a rash look and gesture on his part, which had been quite unpremeditated, but which had nevertheless transformed their relation. Rose had flushed up, had said a few incoherent words, which he had understood to be words of reproach, had left Lady Helen's as quickly as possible, and next morning his Greenlaws party had fallen through.

'Check, certainly,' said Flaxman to himself ruefully, as he pondered these circumstances—'not mate, I hope, if one can but find out how not to be a fool in future.'

And over his solitary fire he meditated far into the night.

Next day, at half-past seven in the evening, he entered Lady Charlotte's drawing-room, gayer, brisker, more alert than ever.

Rose started visibly at the sight of him, and shot a quick glance at the unblushing Lady Charlotte.

'I thought you were at Greenlaws,' she could not help saying to him, as she coldly offered him her hand. *Why* had Lady Charlotte never told her he was to escort them? Her irritation rose anew.

'What can one do,' he said lightly, 'if Elsmere will fix such a performance for Easter Eve? My party was at its last gasp too; it only wanted a telegram to Helen to give it its *coup de grâce.*'

Rose flushed up, but he turned on his heel at once, and began to banter his aunt on the housekeeper's bonnet and veil in which she had a little too obviously disguised herself.

And certainly, in the drive to the East End, Rose had no reason to complain of importunity on his part. Most of the way he was deep in talk with Lady Charlotte as to a certain loan exhibition in the East End, to which he and a good many of his friends were sending pictures; apparently his time and thoughts were entirely occupied with it. Rose, leaning back silent in her corner, was presently seized with a little shock of surprise that there should be so many interests and relations in his life of which she knew nothing. He was talking now as the man of possessions and influence. She saw a glimpse of him as he was in his public aspect, and the kindness, the disinterestedness, the quiet sense, and the humour of his talk insensibly affected her as she sat listening. The mental image of him which had been dominant in her mind altered a little. Nay, she grew a little hot over it. She asked herself scornfully whether she were not as ready as any bread-and-butter miss of her acquaintance to imagine every man she knew in love with her.

Very likely he had meant what he said quite differently, and she—oh! humiliation—had flown into a passion with him for no reasonable cause. Supposing he *had* meant, two days ago, that if they were to go on being friends she must let him be her lover too, it would of course have been unpardonable. How *could* she let any one talk to her of love yet—especially Mr. Flaxman, who guessed, as she was quite sure, what had happened to her? He must despise her to have imagined it. His outburst had filled her with the oddest and most petulant resentment. Were all men self-seeking? Did all men think women shallow and fickle? Could a man and a woman never be honestly and simply friends? If he *had* made love to her, he could not possibly—and there was the sting of it—feel towards her maiden dignity that romantic respect which she herself cherished towards it. For it was incredible that any delicate-minded girl should go through such a crisis as she had gone through, and then fall calmly into another lover's arms a few weeks later as though nothing had happened.

How we all attitudinise to ourselves! The whole of life often seems one long dramatic performance, in which one half of us is for ever posing to the other half.

But had he really made love to her?—had he meant what she had assumed him to mean? The girl lost herself in a torment of memory and conjecture, and meanwhile Mr. Flaxman sat opposite, talking away, and looking certainly as little love-sick as any man can well look. As the lamps flashed into the carriage her attention was often caught by his profile and finely-balanced head, by the hand lying on his knee, or the little gestures, full of life and freedom, with which he met some raid of Lady Charlotte's on his opinions, or opened a corresponding one on hers. There was certainly power in the man, a bright human sort of power, which inevitably attracted her. And that he was good too she had special grounds for knowing.

But what an aristocrat he was after all! What an over-prosperous exclusive set he belonged to! She lashed herself into anger as the other two chatted and sparred, with all these names of wealthy cousins and relations, with their parks and their pedigrees and their pictures! The aunt and nephew were debating how they could best bleed the family, in its various branches, of the art treasures belonging to it for the benefit of the East-Enders; therefore the names were inevitable. But Rose curled her delicate lip over them. And was it the best breeding, she wondered, to leave a third person so ostentatiously outside the conversation?

'Miss Leyburn, why are you coughing?' said Lady Charlotte suddenly.

'There is a great draught,' said Rose, shivering a little.

'So there is!' cried Lady Charlotte. 'Why, we have got both the windows open. Hugh, draw up Miss Leyburn's.'

He moved over to her and drew it up.

'I thought you liked a tornado,' he said to her, smiling. 'Will you have a shawl?—there is one behind me.'

'No, thank you,' she replied rather stiffly, and he was silent—retaining his place opposite to her, however.

'Have we reached Mr. Elsmere's part of the world yet?' asked Lady Charlotte, looking out.

'Yes, we are not far off—the river is to our right. We shall pass St. Wilfrid's soon.'

The coachman turned into a street where an open-air market was going on. The roadway and pavements were swarming; the carriage could barely pick its way through the masses of human beings. Flaming gas-jets threw it all into strong satanic light and shade. At the corner of a dingy alley Rose could see a fight going on; the begrimed ragged children, regardless of the April rain, swooped backwards and forwards under the very hoofs of the horses, or flattened their noses against the windows whenever the horses were forced into a walk.

The young girl-figure in gray, with the gray feathered hat, seemed specially to excite their notice. The glare of the street brought out the lines of the face, the gold of the hair. The Arabs outside made loutishly flattering remarks once or twice, and Rose, colouring, drew back as far as she could into the carriage.[29] Mr. Flaxman seemed not to hear; his aunt, with that obtrusive thirst for information which is so fashionable now among all women of position, was cross-questioning him as to the trades and population of the district, and he was drily responding. In reality his mind was full of a whirl of feeling, of a wild longing to break down a futile barrier and trample on a baffling resistance, to take that beautiful tameless creature in strong coercing arms, scold her, crush her, love her! Why does she make happiness so difficult? What right has she to hold devotion so cheap? He too grows angry. 'She was *not* in love with that spectral creature,' the inner self declares with energy—'I will vow she never was. But she is like all the rest—a slave to the merest forms and trappings of sentiment. Because he *ought* to have loved her, and didn't, because she *fancied* she loved him, and didn't, my love is to be an offence to her! Monstrous—unjust!'

Suddenly they sped past St. Wilfrid's, resplendent with lights, the jewelled windows of the choir rising above the squalid walls and roofs into the rainy darkness, as the mystical chapel of the Graal, with its 'torches glimmering fair,' flashed out of the mountain storm and solitude on to Galahad's seeking eyes.[30]

Rose bent forward involuntarily. 'What angel singing!' she said, dropping the window again to listen to the retreating sounds, her artist's eye kindling. 'Did you hear it? It was the last chorus in the St. Matthew Passion music.'[31]

'I did not distinguish it,' he said—'but their music is famous.'

His tone was distant; there was no friendliness in it. It would have been pleasant to her if he would have taken up her little remark and let bygones be bygones. But he showed no readiness to do so. The subject dropped, and presently he moved back to his former seat and Lady Charlotte and he resumed

---

29 Street children (here, more likely teens).

30 There does not appear to be an exact match for this quotation in any version of the Grail legend, although the appearances of the Grail are often accompanied by a blaze of light.

31 By Johannes Sebastian Bach (1727).

their talk. Rose could not but see that his manner towards her was much changed. She herself had compelled it, but all the same she saw him leave her with a capricious little pang of regret, and afterwards the drive seemed to her more tedious and the dismal streets more dismal than before.

She tried to forget her companions altogether. Oh! what would Robert have to say? She was unhappy, restless. In her trouble lately it had often pleased her to go quite alone to strange churches, where for a moment the burden of the self had seemed lightened. But the old things were not always congenial to her, and there were modern ferments at work in her. No one of her family, unless it were Agnes, suspected what was going on. But in truth the rich crude nature had been touched at last, as Robert's had been long ago in Mr. Grey's lecture-room, by the piercing under-voices of things—the moral message of the world. 'What will he have to say?' she asked herself again feverishly, and as she looked across to Mr. Flaxman she felt a childish wish to be friends again with him, with everybody. Life was too difficult as it was, without quarrels and misunderstandings to make it worse.

CHAPTER XL

A long street of warehouses—and at the end of it the horses slackened.

'I saw the president of the club yesterday,' said Flaxman, looking out. 'He is an old friend of mine—a most intelligent fanatic—met him on a Mansion House Fund committee last winter.[32] He promised we should be looked after. But we shall only get back seats, and you'll have to put up with the smoking. They don't want ladies, and we shall only be there on sufferance.'

The carriage stopped. Mr. Flaxman guided his charges with some difficulty through the crowd about the steps, who inspected them and their vehicle with a frank and not over-friendly curiosity. At the door they found a man who had been sent to look for them, and were immediately taken possession of. He ushered them into the back of a large bare hall, glaringly lit, lined with white brick, and hung at intervals with political portraits and a few cheap engravings of famous men, Jesus of Nazareth taking his turn with Buddha, Socrates, Moses, Shakespeare, and Paul of Tarsus.

'Can't put you any forrarder, I'm afraid,' said their guide, with a shrug of the shoulders. 'The committee don't like strangers coming, and Mr. Collett,

---

32 Mansion House Funds were organized to relieve suffering not only in the British Isles, but across the world; they were so-called because they were under the aegis of the Lord Mayor.

he got hauled over the coals for letting you in this evening.'

It was a new position for Lady Charlotte to be anywhere on sufferance. However, in the presence of three hundred smoking men, who might all of them be political assassins in disguise for anything she knew, she accepted her fate with meekness; and she and Rose settled themselves into their back seat under a rough sort of gallery, glad of their veils, and nearly blinded with the smoke.

The hall was nearly full, and Mr. Flaxman looked curiously round upon its occupants. The majority of them were clearly artisans—a spare, stooping, sharp-featured race. Here and there were a knot of stalwart dock-labourers, strongly marked out in physique from the watchmakers and the potters, or an occasional seaman out of work, ship-steward, boatswain, or what not, generally bronzed, quick-eyed, and comely, save where the film of excess had already deadened colour and expression. Almost every one had a pot of beer before him, standing on long wooden flaps attached to the benches. The room was full of noise, coming apparently from the farther end, where some political bravo seemed to be provoking his neighbours. In their own vicinity the men scattered about were for the most part tugging silently at their pipes, alternately eyeing the clock and the new-comers.

There was a stir of feet round the door.

'There he is,' said Mr. Flaxman, craning round to see, and Robert entered.

He started as he saw them, flashed a smile to Rose, shook his head at Mr. Flaxman, and passed up the room.

'He looks pale and nervous,' said Lady Charlotte grimly, pouncing at once on the unpromising side of things. 'If he breaks down are you prepared, Hugh, to play Elisha?'[33]

Flaxman was far too much interested in the beginnings of the performance to answer.

Robert was standing forward on the platform, the chairman of the meeting at his side, members of the committee sitting behind on either hand. A good many men put down their pipes, and the hubbub of talk ceased. Others smoked on stolidly.

The chairman introduced the lecturer. The subject of the address would be, as they already knew, 'The Claim of Jesus upon Modern Life.' It was not very likely, he imagined, that Mr. Elsmere's opinions would square with those dominant in the club; but, whether or no, he claimed for him, as for everybody, a patient hearing, and the Englishman's privilege of fair play.

The speaker, a cabinetmaker dressed in a decent brown suit, spoke with

---

33 Appointed by God to follow Elijah as prophet.

fluency, and at the same time with that accent of moderation and *savoir faire* which some Englishmen in all classes have obviously inherited from centuries of government by discussion. Lady Charlotte, whose Liberalism was the mere varnish of an essentially aristocratic temper, was conscious of a certain dismay at the culture of the democracy as the man sat down. Mr. Flaxman, glancing to the right, saw a group of men standing, and amongst them a slight sharp-featured thread-paper of a man, with a taller companion, whom he identified as the pair he had noticed on the night of the story-telling. The little gasfitter was clearly all nervous fidget and expectation; the other, large and gaunt in figure, with a square impassive face, and close-shut lips that had a perpetual mocking twist in the corners, stood beside him like some clumsy modern version, in a commoner clay, of Goethe's 'spirit that denies.'[34]

Robert came forward with a roll of papers in his hand.

His first words were hardly audible. Rose felt her colour rising, Lady Charlotte glanced at her nephew, the standing group of men cried, 'Speak up!' The voice in the distance rose at once, braced by the touch of difficulty, and what it said came firmly down to them.

In after days Flaxman could not often be got to talk of the experience of this evening. When he did he would generally say, briefly, that as an *intellectual* effort he had never been inclined to rank this first public utterance very high among Elsmere's performances. The speaker's own emotion had stood somewhat in his way. A man argues better, perhaps, when he feels less.

'I have often heard him put his case, as I thought, more cogently in conversation,' Flaxman would say—though only to his most intimate friends— 'but what I never saw before or since was such an *effect of personality* as he produced that night. From that moment, at any rate, I loved him, and I understood his secret!'

Elsmere began with a few words of courteous thanks to the club for the hearing they had promised him.

Then he passed on to the occasion of his address—the vogue in the district of 'certain newspapers which, I understand, are specially relished and patronised by your association.'

And he laid down on a table beside him the copies of the *Freethinker* and of *Faith and Fools* which he had brought with him, and faced his audience again, his hands on his sides.

'Well! I am not here to-night to attack those newspapers. I want to reach your sympathies if I can in another way. If there is anybody here who takes pleasure in them, who thinks that such writing and such witticisms as he

---

34 Mephistopheles in *Faust*, 1.3.163.

gets purveyed to him in these sheets do really help the cause of truth and intellectual freedom, I shall not attack his position from the front. I shall try to undermine it. I shall aim at rousing in him such a state of feeling as may suddenly convince him that what is injured by writing of this sort is not the orthodox Christian, or the Church, or Jesus of Nazareth, but always and inevitably the man who writes it and the man who loves it! His mind is possessed of an inflaming and hateful image, which drives him to mockery and violence. I want to replace it, if I can, by one of calm, of beauty and tenderness, which may drive him to humility and sympathy. And this, indeed, is the only way in which opinion is ever really altered—by the substitution of one mental picture for another.

'But in the first place,' resumed the speaker, after a moment's pause, changing his note a little, 'a word about myself. I am not here to-night quite in the position of the casual stranger, coming down to your district for the first time. As some of you know, I am endeavouring to make what is practically a settlement among you, asking you working-men to teach me, if you will, what you have to teach as to the wants and prospects of your order, and offering you in return whatever there is in me which may be worth your taking. Well, I imagine I should look at a man who preferred a claim of that sort with some closeness! You may well ask me for "antecedents," and I should like, if I may, to give them to you very shortly.

'Well, then, though I came down to this place under the wing of Mr. Edwardes' (some cheering) 'who is so greatly liked and respected here, I am not a Unitarian, nor am I an English Churchman. A year ago I was the vicar of an English country parish, where I should have been proud, so far as personal happiness went, to spend my life. Last autumn I left it and resigned my orders because I could no longer accept the creed of the English Church.' Unconsciously the thin dignified figure drew itself up, the voice took a certain dryness. All this was distasteful, but the orator's instinct was imperious.

As he spoke about a score of pipes which had till now been active in Flaxman's neighbourhood went down. The silence in the room became suddenly of a perceptibly different quality.

'Since then I have joined no other religious association. But it is not—God forbid!—because there is nothing left me to believe, but because in this transition England it is well for a man who has broken with the old things, to be very *patient*. No good can come of forcing opinion or agreement prematurely. A generation, nay, more, may have to spend itself in mere waiting and preparing for those new leaders and those new forms of corporate action which any great revolution of opinion, such as that we are now living through, has always produced in the past, and will, we are justified in believing, produce again. But the hour and the men will come, and "they also serve who only stand and wait!"'[35]

Voice and look had kindled into fire. The consciousness of his audience was passing from him—the world of ideas was growing clearer.

'So much, then, for personalities of one sort. There are some of another, however, which I must touch upon for a moment. I am to speak to you to-night of the Jesus of history, but not only as an historian.[36] History is good, but religion is better!—and if Jesus of Nazareth concerned me, and, in my belief, concerned you, only as an historical figure, I should not be here to-night.

'But if I am to talk religion to you, and I have begun by telling you I am not this and not that, it seems to me that for mere clearness' sake, for the sake of that round and whole image of thought which I want to present to you, you must let me run through a preliminary confession of faith—as short and simple as I can make it. You must let me describe certain views of the universe and of man's place in it, which make the framework, as it were, into which I shall ask you to fit the picture of Jesus which will come after.'

Robert stood a moment considering. An instant's nervousness, a momentary sign of self-consciousness, would have broken the spell and set the room against him. He showed neither.

'My friends,' he said at last, speaking to the crowded benches of London workmen with the same simplicity he would have used towards his boys at Murewell, 'the man who is addressing you to-night believes in *God*; and in *Conscience*, which is God's witness in the soul; and in *Experience*, which is at once the record and the instrument of man's education at God's hands. He places his whole trust, for life and death, "*in God the Father Almighty*"—in that force at the root of things which is revealed to us whenever a man helps his neighbour, or a mother denies herself for her child; whenever a soldier dies without a murmur for his country, or a sailor puts out in the darkness to rescue the perishing; whenever a workman throws mind and conscience into his work, or a statesman labours not for his own gain but for that of the State! He believes in an Eternal Goodness—and an Eternal Mind—of which Nature and Man are the continuous and the only revelation....'

The room grew absolutely still. And into the silence there fell, one by one, the short terse sentences, in which the seer, the believer, struggled to express what God has been, is, and will ever be to the soul which trusts Him.

---

35 John Milton (1608–1674), "On His Blindness," l. 14.

36 That is, Jesus considered as a man emerging from a specific time and place, whose biography can be reconstructed by empirical historical method, as opposed to the Incarnate God attested to in the New Testament.

In them the whole effort of the speaker was really to restrain, to moderate, to depersonalise the voice of faith. But the intensity of each word burnt it into the hearer as it was spoken. Even Lady Charlotte turned a little pale—the tears stood in her eyes.

Then, from the witness of God in the soul, and in the history of man's moral life, Elsmere turned to the glorification of *Experience*, 'of that unvarying and rational order of the world which has been the appointed instrument of man's training since life and thought began.'

'There,' he said slowly, 'in the unbroken sequences of nature, in the physical history of the world, in the long history of man, physical, intellectual, moral—*there* lies the revelation of God. There is no other, my friends!'

Then, while the room hung on his words, he entered on a brief exposition of the text, '*Miracles do not happen,*' restating Hume's old argument, and adding to it some of the most cogent of those modern arguments drawn from literature, from history, from the comparative study of religions and religious evidence, which were not practically at Hume's disposal, but which are now affecting the popular mind as Hume's reasoning could never have affected it.

'We are now able to show how miracle, or the belief in it, which is the same thing, comes into being. The study of miracle in all nations, and under all conditions, yields everywhere the same results. Miracle may be the child of imagination, of love, nay, of a passionate sincerity, but invariably it lives with ignorance and is withered by knowledge!'

And then, with lightning unexpectedness, he turned upon his audience, as though the ardent soul reacted at once against a strain of mere negation.

'But do not let yourselves imagine for an instant that, because in a rational view of history there is no place for a Resurrection and Ascension, therefore you may profitably allow yourself a mean and miserable mirth of *this* sort over the past!'—and his outstretched hand struck the newspapers beside him with passion, 'Do not imagine for an instant that what is binding, adorable, beautiful in that past is done away with when miracle is given up! No, thank God! We still "live by admiration, hope, and love."[37] God only draws closer, great men become greater, human life more wonderful as miracle disappears. Woe to you if you cannot see it!—it is the testing truth of our day.

'And besides—do you suppose that mere violence, mere invective, and savage mockery ever accomplished anything—nay, what is more to the point, ever *destroyed* anything in human history? No—an idea cannot be killed from without—it can only be supplanted, transformed, by another idea, and that one of equal virtue and magic. Strange paradox! In the moral world you

---

37 William Wordsworth, *The Excursion*, 4.763.

cannot pull down except by gentleness—you cannot revolutionise except by sympathy. Jesus only superseded Judaism by absorbing and recreating all that was best in it. There are no inexplicable gaps and breaks in the story of humanity. The religion of to-day, with all its faults and mistakes, will go on unshaken so long as there is nothing else of equal loveliness and potency to put in its place. The Jesus of the churches will remain paramount so long as the man of to-day imagines himself dispensed by any increase of knowledge from loving the Jesus of history.

'But *why*? you will ask me. What does the Jesus of history matter to me?'

And so he was brought to the place of great men in the development of mankind—to the part played in the human story by those lives in which men have seen all their noblest thoughts of God, of duty, and of law embodied, realised before them with a shining and incomparable beauty.

' ... You think—because it is becoming plain to the modern eye that the ignorant love of his first followers wreathed his life in legend, that therefore you can escape from Jesus of Nazareth, you can put him aside as though he had never been? Folly! Do what you will, you cannot escape him. His life and death underlie our institutions as the alphabet underlies our literature. Just as the lives of Buddha and of Mohammed are wrought ineffaceably into the civilisation of Africa and Asia, so the life of Jesus is wrought ineffaceably into the higher civilisation, the nobler social conceptions of Europe. It is wrought into your being and into mine. We are what we are to-night, as Englishmen and as citizens, largely because a Galilean peasant was born and grew to manhood, and preached, and loved, and died. And you think that a fact so tremendous can be just scoffed away—that we can get rid of it, and of our share in it, by a ribald paragraph and a caricature!

'No. Your hatred and your ridicule are powerless. And thank God they are powerless. There is no wanton waste in the moral world, any more than in the material. There is only fruitful change and beneficent transformation. Granted that the true story of Jesus of Nazareth was from the beginning obscured by error and mistake; granted that those errors and mistakes which were once the strength of Christianity are now its weakness, and by the slow march and sentence of time are now threatening, unless we can clear them away, to lessen the hold of Jesus on the love and remembrance of man. What then? The fact is merely a call to you and me, who recognise it, to go back to the roots of things, to reconceive the Christ, to bring him afresh into our lives, to make the life so freely given for man minister again in new ways to man's new needs. Every great religion is, in truth, a concentration of great ideas, capable, as all ideas are, of infinite expansion and adaptation. And woe to our human weakness if it loose its hold one instant before it must on any of those rare and precious possessions which have helped it in the past, and may again inspire it in the future!

'*To reconceive the Christ!* It is the special task of our age, though in some sort and degree it has been the ever-recurring task of Europe since the beginning.'

He paused, and then very simply, and so as to be understood by those who heard him, he gave a rapid sketch of that great operation worked by the best intellect of Europe during the last half-century—broadly speaking—on the facts and documents of primitive Christianity. From all sides and by the help of every conceivable instrument those facts have been investigated, and now at last the great result—'the revivified reconceived truth'—seems ready to emerge! Much may still be known—much can never be known; but if we will, we may now discern the true features of Jesus of Nazareth, as no generation but our own has been able to discern them, since those who had seen and handled passed away.

'Let me try, however feebly, and draw it afresh for you, that life of lives, that story of stories, as the labour of our own age in particular has patiently revealed it to us. Come back with me through the centuries; let us try and see the Christ of Galilee and the Christ of Jerusalem as he was, before a credulous love and Jewish tradition and Greek subtlety had at once dimmed and glorified the truth. Ah! do what we will, it is so scanty and poor, this knowledge of ours, compared with all that we yearn to know—but, such as it is, let me, very humbly and very tentatively, endeavour to put it before you.'

At this point Flaxman's attention was suddenly distracted by a stir round the door of entrance on his left hand. Looking round, he saw a Ritualist priest, in cassock and cloak, disputing in hurried undertones with the men about the door. At last he gained his point apparently, for the men, with half-angry, half-quizzing looks at each other, allowed him to come in, and he found a seat. Flaxman was greatly struck by the face—by its ascetic beauty, the stern and yet delicate whiteness and emaciation of it. He sat with both hands resting on the stick he held in front of him, intently listening, the perspiration of physical weakness on his brow and round his finely curved mouth. Clearly he could hardly see the lecturer, for the room had become inconveniently crowded, and the men about him were mostly standing.

'One of the St. Wilfrid's priests, I suppose,' Flaxman said to himself. 'What on earth is he doing *dans cette galère*? Are we to have a disputation? That would be dramatic.'

He had no attention, however, to spare, and the intruder was promptly

forgotten. When he turned back to the platform he found that Robert, with
Mackay's help, had hung on a screen to his right, four or five large drawings
of Nazareth, of the Lake of Gennesaret, of Jerusalem, and the Temple of
Herod, of the ruins of that synagogue on the probable site of Capernaum in
which conceivably Jesus may have stood. They were bold and striking, and
filled the bare hall at once with suggestions of the East. He had used them
often at Murewell. Then, adopting a somewhat different tone, he plunged
into the life of Jesus. He brought to it all his trained historical power, all his
story-telling faculty, all his sympathy with the needs of feeling. And bit by
bit, as the quick nervous sentences issued and struck, each like the touch of
a chisel, the majestic figure emerged, set against its natural background, instinct with some fraction at least of the magic of reality, most human, most
persuasive, most tragic. He brought out the great words of the new faith,
to which, whatever may be their literal origin, Jesus, and Jesus only, gave
currency and immortal force. He dwelt on the magic, the permanence, the
expansiveness, of the young Nazarene's central conception—the spiritualised,
universalised 'Kingdom of God.' Elsmere's thought, indeed, knew nothing
of a perfect man, as it knew nothing of an incarnate God; he shrank from
nothing that he believed true; but every limitation, every reserve he allowed
himself, did but make the whole more poignantly real, and the claim of Jesus
more penetrating.

'The world has grown since Jesus preached in Galilee and Judæa. We cannot learn the *whole* of God's lesson from him now—nay, we could not then!
But all that is most essential to man—all that saves the soul, all that purifies
the heart—that he has still for you and me, as he had it for the men and
women of his own time.'

Then he came to the last scenes. His voice sank a little; his notes dropped
from his hand; and the silence grew oppressive. The dramatic force, the tender passionate insight, the fearless modernness with which the story was
told, made it almost unbearable. Those listening saw the trial, the streets of
Jerusalem, that desolate place outside the northern gate; they were spectators
of the torture, they heard the last cry. No one present had ever so seen, so
heard before. Rose had hidden her face. Flaxman for the first time forgot to
watch the audience; the men had forgotten each other; and for the first time
that night, in many a cold embittered heart, there was born that love of the
Son of Man which Nathaniel felt, and John, and Mary of Bethany, and which
has in it now, as then, the promise of the future.

"'*He laid him in a tomb which had been hewn out of a rock, and he rolled
a stone against the door of the tomb.*" The ashes of Jesus of Nazareth mingled

with the earth of Palestine—[38]

> '"Far hence he lies
>   In the lorn Syrian town,
> And on his grave, with shining eyes,
>   The Syrian stars look down."'[39]

He stopped. The melancholy cadence of the verse died away. Then a gleam broke over the pale exhausted face—a gleam of extraordinary sweetness.

'And in the days and weeks that followed the devout and passionate fancy of a few mourning Galileans begat the exquisite fable of the Resurrection. How natural—and amid all its falseness—how true, is that naïve and contradictory story! The rapidity with which it spread is a measure of many things. It is, above all, a measure of the greatness of Jesus, of the force with which he had drawn to himself the hearts and imaginations of men....

'And now, my friends, what of all this? If these things I have been saying to you are true, what is the upshot of them for you and me? Simply this, as I conceive it—that instead of wasting your time, and degrading your souls, by indulgence in such grime as this'—and he pointed to the newspapers—'it is your urgent business and mine—at this moment—to do our very *utmost* to bring this life of Jesus, our precious invaluable possession as a people, back into some real and cogent relation with our modern lives and beliefs and hopes. Do not answer me that such an effort is a mere dream and futility, conceived in the vague, apart from reality—that men must have something to worship, and that if they cannot worship Jesus they will not trouble to love him. Is the world desolate with God still in it, and does it rest merely with us to love or not to love? Love and revere *something* we must, if we are to be men and not beasts. At all times and in all nations, as I have tried to show you, man has helped himself by the constant and passionate memory of those great ones of his race who have spoken to him most audibly of God and of eternal hope. And for us Europeans and Englishmen, as I have also tried to show you, history and inheritance have decided. If we turn away from the true Jesus of Nazareth because he has been disfigured and misrepresented by the Churches, we turn away from that in which our weak wills and desponding souls are meant to find their most obvious and natural help and inspiration—from that symbol of the Divine, which, of necessity, means most to *us*. No! give him back your hearts—be ashamed that you have ever forgotten your debt to him! Let combination and brotherhood do for the newer and

---

38 Mark 15.46.
39 Matthew Arnold, "Obermann Once More" (1867), ll. 173–76.

simpler faith what they did once for the old—let them give it a practical
shape, a practical grip on human life....Then we too shall have our Easter!—
we too shall have the right to say, *He is not here, he is risen.* [40] Not here—in legend, in miracle, in the beautiful outworn forms and crystallisations of older
thought. *He is risen*—in a wiser reverence and a more reasonable love; risen in
new forms of social help inspired by his memory, called afresh by his name!
Risen—if you and your children will it—in a church or company of the
faithful, over the gates of which two sayings of man's past, into which man's
present has breathed new meanings, shall be written:—

> *'In Thee, O Eternal, have I put my trust.'*[41]
> and—
> *'This do in remembrance of Me.'*[42]

The rest was soon over. The audience woke from the trance in which
it had been held with a sudden burst of talk and movement. In the midst
of it, and as the majority of the audience were filing out into the adjoining
rooms, the gasfitter's tall companion Andrews mounted the platform, while
the gasfitter himself, with an impatient shrug, pushed his way into the out-
going crowd. Andrews went slowly and deliberately to work, dealing out his
long cantankerous sentences with a nasal *sangfroid* which seemed to change
in a moment the whole aspect and temperature of things. He remarked that
Mr. Elsmere had talked of what great scholars had done to clear up this matter of Christ and Christianity. Well, he was free to maintain that old Tom
Paine was as good a scholar as any of 'em, and most of them in that hall
knew what *he* thought about it.[43] Tom Paine hadn't anything to say against
Jesus Christ, and he hadn't. He was a workman and a fine sort of man, and
if he'd been alive now he'd have been a Socialist, 'as most of us are,' and he'd
have made it hot for the rich loafers, and the sweaters, and the middlemen,
'as we'd like to make it hot for 'em.' But as for those people who got up the
Church—Mythologists Tom Paine called 'em—and the miracles, and made
an uncommonly good thing out of it, pecuniarily speaking, he didn't see what
they'd got to do with keeping up, or mending, or preserving *their* precious bit
of work. The world had found 'em out, and serve 'em right.

And he wound up with a fierce denunciation of priests, not without a

---

40 Luke 24.6.
41 Psalms 71.1.
42 1 Corinthians 11.24.
43 Thomas Paine (1737–1809), Anglo-American radical, here being singled out for
his attack on orthodox religion, *The Age of Reason* (1794–1807).

harsh savour and eloquence, which was much clapped by the small knot of workmen amongst whom he had been standing.

Then there followed a Socialist—an eager, ugly, black-bearded little fellow, who preached the absolute necessity of doing without 'any cultus whatsoever,' threw scorn on both the Christians and the Positivists for refusing so to deny themselves, and appealed earnestly to his group of hearers 'to help in bringing religion back from heaven to earth, where it belongs.' Mr. Elsmere's new church, if he ever got it, would only be a fresh instrument in the hands of the *bourgeoisie*. And when the people had got their rights and brought down the capitalists, they were not going to be such fools as put their necks under the heel of what were called 'the educated classes.' The people who wrote the newspapers Mr. Elsmere objected to, knew quite enough for the working-man—and people should not be too smooth-spoken; what the working class wanted beyond everything just now was *grit*.

A few other short speeches followed, mostly of the common Secularist type, in defence of the newspapers attacked. But the defence, on the whole, was shuffling and curiously half-hearted. Robert, sitting by with his head on his hand, felt that there, at any rate, his onslaught had told.

He said a few words in reply, in a low husky voice, without a trace of his former passion, and the meeting broke up. The room had quickly filled when it was known that he was up again; and as he descended the steps of the platform, after shaking hands with the chairman, the hundreds present broke into a sudden burst of cheering. Lady Charlotte pressed forward to him through the crowd, offering to take him home. 'Come with us, Mr. Elsmere: you look like a ghost.' But he shook his head, smiling. 'No, thank you, Lady Charlotte—I must have some air,' and he took her out on his arm, while Flaxman followed with Rose.

It once occurred to Flaxman to look round for the priest he had seen come in. But there were no signs of him. 'I had an idea he would have spoken,' he thought. 'Just as well, perhaps. We should have had a row.'

Lady Charlotte threw herself back in the carriage as they drove off, with a long breath, and the inward reflection, 'So his wife wouldn't come and hear him! Must be a woman with a character that—a Strafford in petticoats!'[44]

Robert turned up the street to the City, the tall slight figure seeming to shrink together as he walked. After his passionate effort, indescribable

---

44 Thomas Wentworth, 1st Earl of Strafford (1593–1641), executed by bill of attainder after Parliament's attempt to impeach him for his conduct as Lord Deputy of Ireland failed.

depression had overtaken him.

'Words—words!' he said to himself, striking out his hands in a kind of feverish protest, as he strode along, against his own powerlessness, against that weight of the present and the actual which seems to the enthusiast alternately light as air, or heavy as the mass of Ætna on the breast of Enceladus.[45]

Suddenly, at the corner of a street, a man's figure in a long black robe stopped him and laid a hand on his arm.

'Newcome!' cried Robert, standing still.

'I was there,' said the other, bending forward and looking close into his eyes. 'I heard almost all. I went to confront, to denounce you!'

By the light of a lamp not far off Robert caught the attenuated whiteness and sharpness of the well-known face, to which weeks of fasting and mystical excitement had given a kind of unearthly remoteness. He gathered himself together with an inward groan. He felt as though there were no force in him at that moment wherewith to meet reproaches, to beat down fanaticism. The pressure on nerve and strength seemed unbearable.

Newcome, watching him with eagle eye, saw the sudden shrinking and hesitation. He had often in old days felt the same sense of power over the man who yet, in what seemed his weakness, had always escaped him in the end.

'I went to denounce,' he continued, in a strange tense voice, 'and the Lord refused it to me. He kept me watching for you here. These words are not mine I speak. I waited patiently in that room till the Lord should deliver His enemy into my hand. My wrath was hot against the deserter that could not even desert in silence—hot against his dupes. Then suddenly words came to me—they have come to me before, they burn up the very heart and marrow in me—"*Who is he that saith, and it cometh to pass, and the Lord commandeth it not?*"[46] There they were in my ears, written on the walls—the air——'

The hand dropped from Robert's arm. A dull look of defeat, of regret, darkened the gleaming eyes. They were standing in a quiet deserted street, but through a side opening the lights, the noise, the turbulence of the open-air market came drifting to them through the rainy atmosphere which blurred and magnified everything.

'Ay, after days and nights in His most blessed sanctuary,' Newcome resumed slowly, 'I came by His commission, as I thought, to fight His battle with a traitor! And at the last moment His strength, which was in me, went from me. I sat there dumb; His hand was heavy upon me. His will be done!'

---

45 In Greek mythology, Enceladus was either buried under Mount Aetna after being killed by one of the gods, or died after Athena hurled the mountain *at* him.
46 Lamentations 3.37.

The voice sank; the priest drew his thin shaking hand across his eyes, as though the awe of a mysterious struggle were still upon him. Then he turned again to Elsmere, his face softening, radiating.

'Elsmere, take the sign, the message! I thought it was given to me to declare the Lord's wrath. Instead, He sends you once more by me, even now—even fresh from this new defiance of His mercy, the tender offer of His grace! He lies at rest to-night, my brother'—what sweetness in the low vibrating tones!—'after all the anguish. Let me draw you down on your knees beside Him. It is you, you, who have helped to drive in the nails, to embitter the agony! It is you who in His loneliness have been robbing Him of the souls that should be His! It is you who have been doing your utmost to make His Cross and Passion of no effect. Oh, let it break your heart to think of it! Watch by Him to-night, my friend, my brother, and to-morrow let the risen Lord reclaim His own!'

Never had Robert seen any mortal face so persuasively beautiful; never surely did saint or ascetic plead with a more penetrating gentleness. After the storm of those opening words the change was magical. The tears stood in Elsmere's eyes. But his quick insight, in spite of himself, divined the subtle natural facts behind the outburst, the strained physical state, the irritable brain—all the consequences of a long defiance of physical and mental law. The priest repelled him, the man drew him like a magnet.

'What can I say to you, Newcome?' he cried despairingly. 'Let me say nothing, dear old friend! I am tired out; so, I expect, are you. I know what this week has been to you. Walk with me a little. Leave these great things alone. We cannot agree. Be content—God knows! Tell me about the old place and the people. I long for news of them.'

A sort of shudder passed through his companion. Newcome stood wrestling with himself. It was like the slow departure of a possessing force. Then he sombrely assented, and they turned towards the City. But his answers, as Robert questioned him, were sharp and mechanical, and presently it became evident that the demands of the ordinary talk to which Elsmere rigorously held him were more than he could bear.

As they reached St. Paul's, towering into the watery moonlight of the clouded sky, he stopped abruptly and said good-night.

'You came to me in the spirit of war,' said Robert, with some emotion, as he held his hand; 'give me instead the grasp of peace!'

The spell of his manner, his presence, prevailed at last. A melancholy quivering smile dawned on the priest's delicate lip.

'God bless you—God restore you!' he said sadly, and was gone.

CHAPTER XLI

A week later Elsmere was startled to find himself detained, after his story-telling, by a trio of workmen, asking on behalf of some thirty or forty members
of the North R—— Club that he would give them a course of lectures on the
New Testament. One of them was the gasfitter Charles Richards; another was
the watchmaker Lestrange, who had originally challenged Robert to deliver
himself; and the third was a tough old Scotchman of sixty with a philosophical turn, under whose spoutings of Hume and Locke, of Reid and Dugald
Stewart, delivered in the shrillest of cracked voices, the Club had writhed
many an impatient half-hour on debating nights.[47] He had an unexpected
artistic gift, a kind of 'sport' as compared with the rest of his character, which
made him a valued designer in the pottery works; but his real interests were
speculative and argumentative, concerned with 'common nawtions and the
praimary elements of reason,' and the appearance of Robert in the district
seemed to offer him at last a foeman worthy of his steel. Elsmere shrewdly
suspected that the last two looked forward to any teaching he might give
mostly as a new and favourable exercising ground for their own wits; but he
took the risk, gladly accepted the invitation, and fixed Sunday afternoons for
a weekly New Testament lecture.

His first lecture, which he prepared with great care, was delivered to
thirty-seven men a fortnight later. It was on the political and social state of
Palestine and the East at the time of Christ's birth; and Robert, who was as
fervent a believer in 'large maps' as Lord Salisbury, had prepared a goodly
store of them for the occasion, together with a number of drawings and photographs which formed part of the collection he had been gradually making
since his own visit to the Holy Land.[48] There was nothing he laid more stress
on than these helps to the eye and imagination in dealing with the Bible. He
was accustomed to maintain in his arguments with Hugh Flaxman that the
orthodox traditional teaching of Christianity would become impossible as

---

47 Stewart (1753–1828) was a Scottish philosopher, associated with the "common
sense" school.

48 Robert Gascoyne-Cecil, Marquess of Salisbury (1830–1903), Conservative
Prime Minister at the end of *Robert Elsmere*'s time frame. His quip about maps ("If
the noble lord would only use a larger map") was part of a rejoinder to a speech about
Russia making potential incursions into India.

soon as it should be the habit to make a free and modern use of history and geography and social material in connection with the Gospels. Nothing tends so much, he would say, to break down the irrational barrier which men have raised about this particular tract of historical space, nothing helps so much to let in the light and air of scientific thought upon it, and therefore nothing prepares the way so effectively for a series of new conceptions.

By a kind of natural selection Richards became Elsmere's chief helper and adjutant in the Sunday lectures,—with regard to all such matters as beating up recruits, keeping guard over portfolios, handing round maps and photographs, etc.,—supplanting in this function the jealous and sensitive Mackay, who, after his original opposition, had now arrived at regarding Robert as his own particular property, and the lecturer's quick smile of thanks for services rendered as his own especial right. The bright, quicksilvery, irascible little workman, however, was irresistible and had his way. He had taken a passion for Robert as for a being of another order and another world. In the discussions which generally followed the lecture he showed a receptiveness, an intelligence, which were in reality a matter not of the mind but of the heart. He loved, therefore he understood. At the club he stood for Elsmere with a quivering spasmodic eloquence, as against Andrews and the Secularists. One thing only puzzled Robert. Among all the little fellow's sallies and indiscretions, which were not infrequent, no reference to his home life was ever included. Here he kept even Robert absolutely at arm's length. Robert knew that he was married and had children, nothing more.

The old Scotchman, Macdonald, came out after the first lecture somewhat crestfallen.

'Not the sort of stooff I'd expected!' he said, with a shade of perplexity on the rugged face. 'He doosn't talk eneuf in the *aa*bstract for me.'

But he went again, and the second lecture, on the origin of the Gospels, got hold of him, especially as it supplied him with a whole armoury of new arguments in support of Hume's doctrine of conscience, and in defiance of 'that blatin' creetur, Reid.' The thesis with which Robert, drawing on some of the stores supplied him by the squire's book, began his account—*i.e.* the gradual growth within the limits of history of man's capacity for telling the exact truth—fitted in, to the Scotchman's thinking, so providentially with his own favourite experimental doctrines as against the 'intueetion' folks, 'who will have it that a babby's got as moch mind as Mr. Gladstone, ef it only knew it!' that afterwards he never missed a lecture.

Lestrange was more difficult. He had the inherited temperament of the Genevese *frondeur*, which made Geneva the headquarters of Calvinism in the sixteenth century, and bids fair to make her the headquarters of continental radicalism in the nineteenth. Robert never felt his wits so much stretched and sharpened as when after the lecture Lestrange was putting questions and objections with an acrid subtlety and persistence worthy of a descendant of that burgher class which first built up the Calvinistic system and then produced the destroyer of it in Rousseau. Robert bore his heckling, however, with great patience and adroitness. He had need of all he knew, as Murray Edwardes had warned him. But luckily he knew a great deal; his thought was clearing and settling month by month, and whatever he may have lost at any moment by the turn of an argument, he recovered immediately afterwards by the force of personality, and of a single-mindedness in which there was never a trace of personal grasping.

Week by week the lecture became more absorbing to him, the men more pliant, his hold on them firmer. His disinterestedness, his brightness and resource, perhaps, too, the signs about him of a light and frail physical organisation, the novelty of his position, the inventiveness of his method, gave him little by little an immense power in the place. After the first two lectures Murray Edwardes became his constant and enthusiastic hearer on Sunday afternoons, and, catching some of Robert's ways and spirit, he gradually brought his own chapel and teaching more and more into line with the Elgood Street undertaking. So that the venture of the two men began to take ever larger proportions; and, kindled by the growing interest and feeling about him, dreams began to rise in Elsmere's mind which as yet he hardly dared to cherish; which came and went, however, weaving a substance for themselves out of each successive incident and effort.

Meanwhile he was at work on an average three evenings in the week besides the Sunday. In West End drawing-rooms his personal gift had begun to tell no less than in this crowded, squalid East; and as his aims became known, other men, finding the thoughts of their own hearts revealed in him, or touched with that social compunction which is one of the notes of our time, came down and became his helpers. Of all the social projects of which that Elgood Street room became the centre, Elsmere was, in some sense, the life and inspiration. But it was not these projects themselves which made this period of his life remarkable. London at the present moment, if it be honeycombed with vice and misery, is also honeycombed with the labour of an ever-expanding charity. Week by week men and women of like gifts and energies with Elsmere spend themselves, as he did, in the constant effort to serve and to alleviate. What *was* noticeable, what *was* remarkable in this work of his, was the spirit, the religious passion which, radiating from him, began after a while, to kindle the whole body of men about him. It was from his Sunday lectures and his talks with the children, boys and girls, who came in after the lecture to spend a happy hour and a half with him on Sunday afternoons, that in later years hundreds of men and women will date the beginnings of a new absorbing life. There came a time, indeed, when, instead of meeting criticism by argument, Robert was able simply to point to accomplished facts. 'You ask me,' he would say in effect, 'to prove to you that men can love, can make a new and fruitful use, for daily life and conduct, of a merely human Christ. Go amongst our men, talk to our children, and satisfy yourself. A little while ago scores of these men either hated the very name of Christianity or were entirely indifferent to it. To scores of them now the name of the teacher of Nazareth, the victim of Jerusalem, is dear and sacred; his life, his death, his words, are becoming once more a constant source of moral effort and spiritual hope. See for yourself!'

However, we are anticipating. Let us go back to May.

One beautiful morning Robert was sitting working in his study, his windows open to the breezy blue sky and the budding plane-trees outside, when the door was thrown open and 'Mr. Wendover' was announced.

The squire entered; but what a shrunken and aged squire! The gait was feeble, the bearing had lost all its old erectness, the bronzed strength of the face had given place to a waxen and ominous pallor. Robert, springing up with joy to meet the great gust of Murewell air which seemed to blow about him with the mention of the squire's name, was struck, arrested. He guided his guest to a chair with an almost filial carefulness.

'I don't believe, Squire,' he exclaimed, 'you ought to be doing this—wandering about London by yourself!'

But the squire, as silent and angular as ever when anything personal to himself was concerned, would take no notice of the implied anxiety and sympathy. He grasped his umbrella between his knees with a pair of brown twisted hands, and, sitting very upright, looked critically round the room. Robert, studying the dwindled figure, remembered with a pang the saying of another Oxford scholar, *à propos* of the death of a young man of extraordinary promise, '*What learning has perished with him! How vain seems all toil to acquire!*'—and the words, as they passed through his mind, seemed to him to ring another death-knell.[49]

But after the first painful impression he could not help losing himself in

---

49 Mark Pattison on the death of Richard Robinson (1844–70). See Thomas Wright, *The Life of Walter Pater*, 2 vols. (New York: G. P. Putnam's Sons, 1907), 1. 242.

the pleasure of the familiar face, the Murewell associations.

'How is the village, and the Institute? And what sort of man is my successor—the man, I mean, who came after Armitstead?'

'I had him once to dinner,' said the squire briefly; 'he made a false quantity, and asked me to subscribe to the Church Missionary Society. I haven't seen him since. He and the village have been at loggerheads about the Institute, I believe. He wanted to turn out the Dissenters.[50] Bateson came to me, and we circumvented him, of course. But the man's an ass. Don't talk of him!'

Robert sighed a long sigh. Was all his work undone? It wrung his heart to remember the opening of the Institute, the ardour of his boys. He asked a few questions about individuals, but soon gave it up as hopeless. The squire neither knew nor cared.

'And Mrs. Darcy?'

'My sister had tea in her thirtieth summer-house last Sunday,' remarked the squire grimly. 'She wished me to communicate the fact to you and Mrs. Elsmere. Also, that the worst novel of the century will be out in a fortnight, and she trusts to you to see it well reviewed in all the leading journals.'

Robert laughed, but it was not very easy to laugh. There was a sort of ghastly undercurrent in the squire's sarcasms that effectually deprived them of anything mirthful.

'And your book?'

'Is in abeyance. I shall bequeath you the manuscript in my will, to do what you like with.'

'Squire!'

'Quite true! If you had stayed, I should have finished it, I suppose. But after a certain age the toil of spinning cobwebs entirely out of his own brain becomes too much for a man.'

It was the first thing of the sort that iron mouth had ever said to him. Elsmere was painfully touched.

'You must not—you shall not give it up,' he urged. 'Publish the first part alone, and ask me for any help you please.'

The squire shook his head.

'Let it be. Your paper in the *Nineteenth Century* showed me that the best thing I can do is to hand on my materials to you. Though I am not sure that when you have got them you will make the best use of them. You and Grey between you call yourselves Liberals, and imagine yourselves reformers, and all the while you are doing nothing but playing into the hands of the Blacks. All this theistic philosophy of yours only means so much grist to their mill

---

50 "Dissenters": as per *SE* and *W.* Lowercase changes the text's meaning.

in the end.'

'They don't see it in that light themselves,' said Robert, smiling.

'No,' returned the squire, 'because most men are puzzle-heads. Why,' he added, looking darkly at Robert, while the great head fell forward on his breast in the familiar Murewell attitude, 'why can't you do your work and let the preaching alone?'

'Because,' said Robert, 'the preaching seems to me my work. There is the great difference between us, Squire. You look upon knowledge as an end in itself. It may be so. But to me knowledge has always been valuable first and foremost for its bearing on life.'

'Fatal twist that,' returned the squire harshly. 'Yes, I know; it was always in you. Well, are you happy? does this new crusade of yours give you pleasure?'

'Happiness,' replied Robert, leaning against the chimneypiece and speaking in a low voice, 'is always relative. No one knows it better than you. Life is full of oppositions. But the work takes my whole heart and all my energies.'

The squire looked at him in disapproving silence for a while.

'You will bury your life in it miserably,' he said at last; 'it will be a toil of Sisyphus leaving no trace behind it; whereas such a book as you might write, if you gave your life to it, might live and work, and harry the enemy when you are gone.'[51]

Robert forbore the natural retort.

The squire went round his library, making remarks, with all the caustic shrewdness natural to him, on the new volumes that Robert had acquired since their walks and talks together.

'The Germans,' he said at last, putting back a book into the shelves with a new accent of distaste and weariness, 'are beginning to founder in the sea of their own learning. Sometimes I think I will read no more German. It is a nation of learned fools, none of whom ever sees an inch beyond his own professorial nose.'

Then he stayed to luncheon, and Catherine, moved by many feelings— perhaps in subtle striving against her own passionate sense of wrong at this man's hands—was kind to him, and talked and smiled, indeed, so much that the squire for the first time in his life took individual notice of her, and as he parted with Elsmere in the hall made the remark that Mrs. Elsmere seemed to like London, to which Robert, busy in an opportune search for his guest's coat, made no reply.

'When are you coming to Murewell?' the squire said to him abruptly,

---

51 In Greek mythology, Sisyphus' punishment in Hades was to eternally roll a stone up a hill; it rolled down again as soon as he neared the top.

as he stood at the door muffled up as though it were December. 'There are a good many points in that last article you want talking to about. Come next month with Mrs. Elsmere.'

Robert drew a long breath, inspired by many feelings.

'I will come, but not yet. I must get broken in here more thoroughly first. Murewell touches me too deeply, and my wife. You are going abroad in the summer, you say. Let me come to you in the autumn.'

The squire said nothing, and went his way, leaning heavily on his stick, across the square. Robert felt himself a brute to let him go, and almost ran after him.

That evening Robert was disquieted by the receipt of a note from a young fellow of St. Anselm's, an intimate friend and occasional secretary of Grey. Grey, the writer said, had received Robert's last letter, was deeply interested in his account of his work, and begged him to write again. He would have written, but that he was himself in the doctor's hands, suffering from various ills, probably connected with an attack of malarial fever which had befallen him in Rome the year before.

Catherine found him poring over the letter, and, as it seemed to her, op-pressed by an anxiety out of all proportion to the news itself.

'They are not really troubled, I think,' she said, kneeling down beside him, and laying her cheek against his. 'He will soon get over it, Robert.'

But, alas! this mood, the tender characteristic mood of the old Catherine, was becoming rarer and rarer with her. As the spring expanded, as the sun and the leaves came back, poor Catherine's temper had only grown more wintry and more rigid. Her life was full of moments of acute suffering. Never, for instance, did she forget the evening of Robert's lecture to the club. All the time he was away she had sat brooding by herself in the drawing-room, divining with a bitter clairvoyance all that scene in which he was taking part, her being shaken with a tempest of misery and repulsion. And together with that torturing image of a glaring room in which her husband, once Christ's loyal minister, was employing all his powers of mind and speech to make it easier for ignorant men to desert and fight against the Lord who bought them, there mingled a hundred memories of her father which were now her constant companions. In proportion as Robert and she became more divided, her dead father resumed a ghostly hold upon her. There were days when she went about rigid and silent, in reality living altogether in the past, among the gray farms, the crags, and the stony ways of the mountains.

At such times her mind would be full of pictures of her father's minis-trations—his talks with the shepherds on the hills, with the women at their doors, his pale dreamer's face beside some wild deathbed, shining with the Divine message, the 'visions' which to her awestruck childish sense would often seem to hold him in their silent walks among the misty hills.

Robert, taught by many small indications, came to recognise these states of feeling in her with a dismal clearness, and to shrink more and more sensitively while they lasted from any collision with her. He kept his work, his friends, his engagements to himself, talking resolutely of other things, she trying to do the same, but with less success, as her nature was less pliant than his.

Then there would come moments when the inward preoccupation would give way, and that strong need of loving, which was, after all, the basis of Catherine's character, would break hungrily through, and the wife of their early married days would reappear, though still only with limitations. A certain nervous physical dread of any approach to a particular range of subjects with her husband was always present in her. Nay, through all these months it gradually increased in morbid strength. Shock had produced it; perhaps shock alone could loosen the stifling pressure of it. But still every now and then her mood was brighter, more caressing, and the area of common mundane interests seemed suddenly to broaden for them.

Robert did not always make a wise use of these happier times; he was incessantly possessed with his old idea that if she only *would* allow herself some very ordinary intercourse with his world, her mood would become less strained, his occupations and his friends would cease to be such bugbears to her, and, for his comfort and hers, she might ultimately be able to sympathise with certain sides at any rate of his work.

So again and again, when her manner no longer threw him back on himself, he made efforts and experiments. But he managed them far less cleverly than he would have managed anybody else's affairs, as generally happens. For instance, at a period when he was feeling more enthusiasm than usual for his colleague Wardlaw, and when Catherine was more accessible than usual, it suddenly occurred to him to make an effort to bring them together. Brought face to face, each *must* recognise the nobleness of the other. He felt boyishly confident of it. So he made it a point, tenderly but insistently, that Catherine should ask Wardlaw and his wife to come and see them. And Catherine, driven obscurely by a longing to yield in something, which recurred, and often terrified herself, yielded in this.

The Wardlaws, who in general never went into society, were asked to a quiet dinner in Bedford Square, and came. Then, of course, it appeared that Robert, with the idealist's blindness, had forgotten a hundred small differences of temperament and training which must make it impossible for

Catherine, in a state of tension, to see the hero in James Wardlaw. It was an unlucky dinner. James Wardlaw, with all his heroisms and virtues, had long ago dropped most of those delicate intuitions and divinations, which make the charm of life in society, along the rough paths of a strenuous philanthropy. He had no tact, and, like most saints, he drew a certain amount of inspiration from a contented ignorance of his neighbour's point of view. Also, he was not a man who made much of women, and he held strong views as to the subordination of wives. It never occurred to him that Robert might have a Dissenter in his own household, and as, in spite of their speculative differences, he had always been accustomed to talk freely with Robert, he now talked freely to Robert plus his wife, assuming, as every good Comtist does, that the husband is the wife's pope.

Moreover, a solitary eccentric life, far from the society of his equals, had developed in him a good many crude Jacobinisms.[52] His experience of London clergymen, for instance, had not been particularly favourable, and he had a store of anecdotes on the subject which Robert had heard before, but which now, repeated in Catherine's presence, seemed to have lost every shred of humour they once possessed. Poor Elsmere tried with all his might to divert the stream, but it showed a tormenting tendency to recur to the same channel. And meanwhile the little spectacled wife, dressed in a high home-made cashmere, sat looking at her husband with a benevolent and smiling admiration. *She* kept all her eloquence for the poor.

After dinner things grew worse. Mrs. Wardlaw had recently presented her husband with a third infant, and the ardent pair had taken advantage of the visit to London of an eminent French Comtist to have it baptized with full Comtist rites. Wardlaw stood astride on the rug, giving the assembled company a minute account of the ceremony observed, while his wife threw in gentle explanatory interjections. The manner of both showed a certain exasperating confidence, if not in the active sympathy, at least in the impartial curiosity of their audience, and in the importance to modern religious history of the incident itself. Catherine's silence grew deeper and deeper; the conversation fell entirely to Robert. At last Robert, by main force, as it were, got Wardlaw off into politics, but the new Irish Coercion Bill was hardly introduced before the irrepressible being turned to Catherine, and said to her with smiling obtuseness—

'I don't believe I've seen you at one of your husband's Sunday addresses yet, Mrs. Elsmere? And it isn't so far from this part of the world either.'

---

52 The Jacobins were the leading party in the French Revolution, and later, under the sway of Robespierre, the guiding force in the Reign of Terror.

Catherine slowly raised her beautiful large eyes upon him. Robert, looking at her with a qualm, saw an expression he was learning to dread flash across the face.

'I have my Sunday school at that time, Mr. Wardlaw. I am a Churchwoman.'

The tone had a touch of *hauteur* Robert had hardly ever heard from his wife before. It effectually stopped all further conversation. Wardlaw fell into silence, reflecting that he had been a fool. His wife, with a timid flush, drew out her knitting, and stuck to it for the twenty minutes that remained. Catherine immediately did her best to talk, to be pleasant; but the discomfort of the little party was too great. It broke up at ten, and the Wardlaws departed.

Catherine stood on the rug while Elsmere went with his guests to the door, waiting restlessly for her husband's return. Robert, however, came back to her, tired, wounded, and out of spirits, feeling that the attempt had been wholly unsuccessful, and shrinking from any further talk about it. He at once sat down to some letters for the late post. Catherine lingered a little, watching him, longing miserably, like any girl of eighteen, to throw herself on his neck and reproach him for their unhappiness, his friends—she knew not what! He all the time was intimately conscious of her presence, of her pale beauty, which now at twenty-nine, in spite of its severity, had a subtler finish and attraction than ever, of the restless little movements so unlike herself, which she made from time to time. But neither spoke except upon indifferent things. Once more the difficult conditions of their lives seemed too obvious, too oppressive. Both were ultimately conquered by the same sore impulse to let speech alone.

CHAPTER XLII

And after this little scene, through the busy exciting weeks of the season which followed, Robert, taxed to the utmost on all sides, yielded to the impulse of silence more and more.

Society was another difficulty between them. Robert delighted in it so far as his East End life allowed him to have it. No one was ever more ready to take other men and women at their own valuation than he. Nothing was so easy to him as to believe in other people's goodness, or cleverness, or superhuman achievement. On the other hand, London is kind to such men as Robert Elsmere. His talk, his writing, were becoming known and relished; and even the most rigid of the old school found it difficult to be angry with him. His knowledge of the poor and of social questions attracted the men of action; his growing historical reputation drew the attention of the men of thought.[53] Most people wished to know him and to talk to him, and Catherine, smiled upon for his sake, and assumed to be his chief disciple, felt herself more and more bewildered and antagonistic as the season rushed on.

For what pleasure could she get out of these dinners and these evenings, which supplied Robert with so much intellectual stimulus? With her all the moral nerves were jarring and out of tune. At any time Richard Leyburn's daughter would have found it hard to tolerate a society where everything is an open question and all confessions of faith are more or less bad taste. But now, when there was no refuge to fall back upon in Robert's arms, no certainty of his sympathy—nay, a certainty that, however tender and pitiful he might be, he would still think her wrong and mistaken! She went here and there obediently because he wished; but her youth seemed to be ebbing, the old Murewell gaiety entirely left her, and people in general wondered why Elsmere should have married a wife older than himself, and apparently so unsuited to him in temperament.

Especially was she tried at Madame de Netteville's. For Robert's sake she tried for a time to put aside her first impression and to bear Madame de Netteville's evenings—little dreaming, poor thing, all the time that Madame de Netteville thought her presence at the famous 'Fridays' an incubus only to be put up with because the husband was becoming socially an indispensable.

But after two or three Fridays Catherine's endurance failed her. On the last occasion she found herself late in the evening hemmed in behind Madame de Netteville and a distinguished African explorer, who was the lion of the evening. Eugénie de Netteville had forgotten her silent neighbour, and presently, with some biting little phrase or other, she asked the great man his opinion on a burning topic of the day, the results of Church Missions in Africa. The great man laughed, shrugged his shoulders, and ran lightly through a string of stories in which both missionaries and converts played parts which were either grotesque or worse. Madame de Netteville thought the stories amusing, and as one ceased she provoked another, her black eyes full of a dry laughter, her white hand lazily plying her great ostrich fan.

Suddenly a figure rose behind them.

'Oh, Mrs. Elsmere!' said Madame de Netteville, starting, and then coolly recovering herself, 'I had no idea you were there all alone. I am afraid our conversation has been disagreeable to you. I am afraid you are a friend of missions!'

---

53 "men of action": as per *SE* and *W*.

And her glance, turning from Catherine to her companion, made a little malicious signal to him which only he detected, as though bidding him take note of a curiosity.

'Yes, I care for them, I wish for their success,' said Catherine, one hand, which trembled slightly, resting on the table beside her, her great gray eyes fixed on Madame de Netteville. 'No Christian has any right to do otherwise.'

Poor brave goaded soul! She had a vague idea of 'bearing testimony' as her father would have borne it in like circumstances. But she turned very pale. Even to her the word 'Christian' sounded like a bombshell in that room. The great traveller looked up astounded. He saw a tall woman in white with a beautiful head, a delicate face, a something indescribably noble and unusual in her whole look and attitude. She looked like a Quaker prophetess—like Dinah Morris in society—like—but his comparisons failed him.[54] How did such a being come *there*? He was amazed; but he was a man of taste, and Madame de Netteville caught a certain æsthetic approbation in his look.

She rose, her expression hard and bright as usual.

'May one Christian pronounce for all?' she said with a scornful affectation of meekness. 'Mrs. Elsmere, please find some chair more comfortable than that ottoman; and Mr. Ansdale, will you come and be introduced to Lady Aubrey?'

After her guests had gone Madame de Netteville came back to the fire flushed and frowning. It seemed to her that in that strange little encounter she had suffered, and she never forgot or forgave the smallest social discomfiture.

'Can I put up with that again?' she asked herself with a contemptuous hardening of the lip. 'I suppose I must if *he* cannot be got without her. But I have an instinct that it is over—that she will not appear here again. Daudet might make use of her.[55] I can't. What a specimen! A boy and girl match, I suppose. What else could have induced that poor wretch to cut his throat in such fashion? He, of all men!'

And Eugénie de Netteville stood thinking—not, apparently, of the puritanical wife; the dangerous softness which overspread the face could have had no connection with Catherine.

Madame de Netteville's instinct was just. Catherine Elsmere never appeared again in her drawing-room.

But, with a little sad confession of her own invincible distaste, the wife pressed the husband to go without her. She urged it at a bitter moment, when

---

54 Dinah Morris is the Methodist woman preacher in George Eliot's *Adam Bede* (1859).

55 Alphonse Daudet (1840–1897), French novelist and short story writer, author of *Lettres de Mon Moulin* (1869).

it was clear to her that their lives must of necessity, even in outward matters, be more separate than before. Elsmere resisted for a time; then, lured one evening towards the end of February by the prospect conveyed in a note from Madame de Netteville, wherein Catherine was mentioned in the most scrupulously civil terms, of meeting one of the most eminent of French critics, he went, and thenceforward went often. He had, so far, no particular liking for the hostess; he hated some of her *habitués*; but there was no doubt that in some ways she made an admirable holder of a *salon*, and that round about her there was a subtle mixture of elements, a liberty of discussion and comment, to be found nowhere else. And how bracing and refreshing was that free play of equal mind to the man weary sometimes of his leader's *rôle* and weary of himself!

As to the *woman*, his social *naïveté*, which was extraordinary, but in a man of his type most natural, made him accept her exactly as he found her. If there were two or three people in Paris or London who knew or suspected incidents of Madame de Netteville's young married days which made her reception at some of the strictest English houses a matter of cynical amusement to them, not the remotest inkling of their knowledge was ever likely to reach Elsmere. He was not a man who attracted scandals. Nor was it anybody's interest to spread them. Madame de Netteville's position in London society was obviously excellent. If she had peculiarities of manner and speech they were easily supposed to be French. Meanwhile she was undeniably rich and distinguished, and gifted with a most remarkable power of protecting herself and her neighbours from boredom. At the same time, though Elsmere was, in truth, more interested in her friends than in her, he could not possibly be insensible to the consideration shown for him in her drawing-room. Madame de Netteville allowed herself plenty of jests with her intimates as to the young reformer's social simplicity, his dreams, his optimisms. But those intimates were the first to notice that as soon as he entered the room those optimisms of his were adroitly respected. She had various delicate contrivances for giving him the lead; she exercised a kind of *surveillance* over the topics introduced; or in conversation with him she would play that most seductive part of the cynic shamed out of cynicism by the neighbourhood of the enthusiast.

Presently she began to claim a practical interest in his Elgood Street work. Her offers were made with a curious mixture of sympathy and mockery. Elsmere could not take her seriously. But neither could he refuse to accept her money, if she chose to spend it on a library for Elgood Street, or to consult with her about the choice of books. This whim of hers created a certain friendly bond between them which was not present before. And on Elsmere's side it was strengthened when, one evening, in a corner of her inner drawing-room, Madame de Netteville suddenly, but very quietly, told him the story of her life—her English youth, her elderly French husband, the death of her only child, and her flight as a young widow to England during the war of 1870. She told the story of the child, as it seemed to Elsmere, with a deliberate avoidance of emotion, nay, even with a certain hardness. But it touched him profoundly. And everything else that she said, though she professed no great regret for her husband, or for the break-up of her French life, and though everything was reticent and measured, deepened the impression of a real forlornness behind all the outward brilliance and social importance. He began to feel a deep and kindly pity for her, coupled with an earnest wish that he could help her to make her life more adequate and satisfying. And all this he showed in the look of his frank gray eyes, in the cordial grasp of the hand with which he said good-bye to her.

Madame de Netteville's gaze followed him out of the room—the tall boyish figure, the nobly carried head. The riddle of her flushed cheek and sparkling eye was hard to read. But there were one or two persons living who could have read it, and who could have warned you that the *true* story of Eugénie de Netteville's life was written, not in her literary studies or her social triumphs, but in various recurrent outbreaks of unbridled impulse—the secret, and in one or two cases the shameful landmarks of her past. And, as persons of experience, they could also have warned you that the cold intriguer, always mistress of herself, only exists in fiction, and that a certain poisoned and fevered interest in the religious leader, the young and pious priest, as such, is common enough among the corrupter women of all societies.

Towards the end of May she asked Elsmere to dine 'en petit comité, a gentlemen's dinner—except for my cousin, Lady Aubrey Willert'—to meet an eminent Liberal Catholic, a friend of Montalembert's youth.[56]

It was a week or two after the failure of the Wardlaw experiment. Do what each would, the sore silence between the husband and wife was growing, was swallowing up more of life.

'Shall I go, Catherine?' he asked, handing her the note.

'It would interest you,' she said gently, giving it back to him scrupulously, as though she had nothing to do with it.

He knelt down before her, and put his arms round her, looking at her with eyes which had a dumb and yet fiery appeal written in them. His heart was hungry for that old clinging dependence, that willing weakness of love, her youth had yielded him so gladly, instead of this silent strength of antagonism. The memory of her Murewell self flashed miserably through him as

---

56 Charles de Montalembert (1810–70), French Catholic scholar and politician, known for his associations with the more liberal "Gallican" wing of the Church.

he knelt there, of her delicate penitence towards him after her first sight of Newcome, of their night walks during the Mile End epidemic. Did he hold now in his arms only the ghost and shadow of that Murewell Catherine?

She must have read the reproach, the yearning of his look, for she gave a little shiver, as though bracing herself with a kind of agony to resist.

'Let me go, Robert!' she said gently, kissing him on the forehead and drawing back. 'I hear Mary calling, and nurse is out.'

The days went on and the date of Madame de Netteville's dinner-party had come round. About seven o'clock that evening Catherine sat with the child in the drawing-room, expecting Robert. He had gone off early in the afternoon to the East End with Hugh Flaxman to take part in a committee of workmen organised for the establishment of a choral union in R——, the scheme of which had been Flaxman's chief contribution so far to the Elgood Street undertaking.

It seemed to her as she sat there working, the windows open on to the bit of garden, where the trees were already withered and begrimed, that the air without and her heart within were alike stifling and heavy with storm. *Something* must put an end to this oppression, this misery! She did not know herself. Her whole inner being seemed to her lessened and degraded by this silent struggle, this fever of the soul, which made impossible all those serenities and sweetnesses of thought in which her nature had always lived of old. The fight into which fate had forced her was destroying her. She was drooping like a plant cut off from all that nourishes its life.

And yet she never conceived it possible that she should relinquish that fight. Nay, at times there sprang up in her now a dangerous and despairing foresight of even worse things in store. In the middle of her suffering she already began to feel at moments the ascetic's terrible sense of compensation. What, after all, is the Christian life but warfare? '*I came not to send peace, but a sword!*'[57]

Yes, in these June days Elsmere's happiness was perhaps nearer wreck than it had ever been. All strong natures grow restless under such a pressure as was now weighing on Catherine. Shock and outburst become inevitable.

So she sat alone this hot afternoon, haunted by presentiments, by vague terror for herself and him; while the child tottered about her, cooing, shouting, kissing, and all impulsively, with a ceaseless energy, like her father.

The outer door opened, and she heard Robert's step, and apparently Mr. Flaxman's also. There was a hurried subdued word or two in the hall, and the two entered the room where she was sitting.

---

57 Matthew 10.34.

Robert came, pressing back the hair from his eyes with a gesture which with him was the invariable accompaniment of mental trouble. Catherine sprang up.

'Robert, you look so tired! and how late you are!' Then as she came nearer to him: 'And your coat—*torn—blood*!'

'There is nothing wrong with *me*, dear,' he said hastily, taking her hands— 'nothing! But it has been an awful afternoon. Flaxman will tell you. I must go to this place, I suppose, though I hate the thought of it! Flaxman, will you tell her all about it?' And, loosing his hold, he went heavily out of the room and upstairs.

'It has been an accident,' said Flaxman gently, coming forward, 'to one of the men of his class. May we sit down, Mrs. Elsmere? Your husband and I have gone through a good deal these last two hours.'

He sat down with a long breath, evidently trying to regain his ordinary even manner. His clothes, too, were covered with dust, and his hand shook. Catherine stood before him in consternation, while a nurse came for the child.

'We had just begun our committee at four o'clock,' he said at last, 'though only about half of the men had arrived, when there was a great shouting and commotion outside, and a man rushed in calling for Elsmere. We ran out, found a great crowd, a huge brewer's dray standing in the street, and a man run over. Your husband pushed his way in. I followed, and, to my horror, I found him kneeling by—Charles Richards!'

'Charles Richards?' Catherine repeated vacantly.

Flaxman looked up at her, as though puzzled; then a flash of astonishment passed over his face.

'Elsmere has never told you of Charles Richards, the little gasfitter, who has been his right hand for the past three months?'

'No—never,' she said slowly.

Again he looked astonished; then he went on sadly: 'All this spring he has been your husband's shadow—I never saw such devotion. We found him lying in the middle of the road. He had only just left work, a man said who had been with him, and was running to the meeting. He slipped and fell, crossing the street, which was muddy from last night's rain. The dray swung round the corner—the driver was drunk or careless—and they went right over him. One foot was a sickening sight. Your husband and I luckily knew how to lift him for the best. We sent off for doctors. His home was in the next street, as it happened—nearer than any hospital; so we carried him there. The neighbours were round the door.'

Then he stopped himself.

'Shall I tell you the whole story?' he said kindly; 'it has been a tragedy! I won't give you details if you had rather not.'

'Oh no!' she said hurriedly; 'no—tell me.'

And she forgot to feel any wonder that Flaxman, in his chivalry, should treat her as though she were a girl with nerves.

'Well, it was the surroundings that were so ghastly. When we got to the house an old woman rushed at me—"His wife's in there, but ye'll not find her in her senses; she's been at it from eight o'clock this morning. We've took the children away." I didn't know what she meant exactly till we got into the little front room. There, such a spectacle! A young woman on a chair by the fire sleeping heavily, dead drunk; the breakfast things on the table, the sun blazing in on the dust and the dirt, and on the woman's face. I wanted to carry him into the room on the other side—he was unconscious; but a doctor had come up with us, and made us put him down on a bed there was in the corner. Then we got some brandy and poured it down. The doctor examined him, looked at his foot, threw something over it. "Nothing to be done," he said—"internal injuries—he can't live half an hour." The next minute the poor fellow opened his eyes. They had pulled away the bed from the wall. Your husband was on the farther side, kneeling. When he opened his eyes, clearly the first thing he saw was his wife. He half sprang up—Elsmere caught him—and gave a horrible cry—indescribably horrible. "*At it again, at it again! My God!*" Then he fell back fainting. They got the wife out of the room between them—a perfect log—you could hear her heavy breathing from the kitchen opposite. We gave him more brandy and he came to again. He looked up in your husband's face. "She hasn't broke out for two months," he said, so piteously, "two months—and now—I'm done—I'm done—and she'll just go straight to the devil!" And it comes out, so the neighbours told us, that for two years or more he had been patiently trying to reclaim this woman, without a word of complaint to anybody, though his life must have been a dog's life. And now, on his deathbed, what seemed to be breaking his heart was, not that he was dying, but that his task was snatched from him!'

Flaxman paused, and looked away out of window. He told his story with difficulty.

'Your husband tried to comfort him—promised that the wife and children should be his special care, that everything that could be done to save and protect them should be done. And the poor little fellow looked up at him, with the tears running down his cheeks, and—and—blessed him. "I cared about nothing," he said, "when you came. You've been—God—to me—I've seen Him—in you." Then he asked us to say something. Your husband said verse after verse of the Psalms, of the Gospels, of St. Paul. His eyes grew filmy, but he seemed every now and then to struggle back to life, and as soon as he caught Elsmere's face his look lightened. Towards the last he said something we none of us caught; but your husband thought it was a line from Emily Brontë's "Hymn," which he said to them last Sunday in lecture.'[58]

He looked up at her interrogatively, but there was no response in her face.

'I asked him about it,' the speaker went on, 'as we came home. He said Grey of St. Anselm's once quoted it to him, and he has had a love for it ever since.'

'Did he die while you were there?' asked Catherine presently after a silence. Her voice was dull and quiet. He thought her a strange woman. .

'No,' said Flaxman, almost sharply; 'but by now it must be over. The last sign of consciousness was a murmur of his children's names. They brought them in, but his hands had to be guided to them. A few minutes after it seemed to me that he was really gone, though he still breathed. The doctor was certain there would be no more consciousness. We stayed nearly another hour. Then his brother came, and some other relations, and we left him. Oh, it is over now!'

Hugh Flaxman sat looking out into the dingy bit of London garden. Penetrated with pity as he was, he felt the presence of Elsmere's pale, silent, unsympathetic wife an oppression. How could she receive such a story in such a way?

The door opened and Robert came in hurriedly.

'Good-night, Catherine—he has told you?'

He stood by her, his hand on her shoulder, wistfully looking at her, the face full of signs of what he had gone through.

'Yes, it was terrible!' she said, with an effort.

His face fell. He kissed her on the forehead and went away.

When he was gone, Flaxman suddenly got up and leant against the open French window, looking keenly down on his companion. A new idea had stirred in him.

And presently, after more talk of the incident of the afternoon, and when he had recovered his usual manner, he slipped gradually into the subject of his own experiences in North R—— during the last six months. He assumed all through that she knew as much as there was to be known of Elsmere's work, and that she was as much interested as the normal wife is in her husband's doings. His tact, his delicacy, never failed him for a moment. But he spoke of his own impressions, of matters within his personal knowledge. And since the Easter sermon he had been much on Elsmere's track; he had been filled

---

58 De Ryals (610n518.31) and Ashton (584) suggest "No Coward Soul."

with curiosity about him.

Catherine sat a little way from him, her blue dress lying in long folds about her, her head bent, her long fingers crossed on her lap. Sometimes she gave him a startled look, sometimes she shaded her eyes, while her other hand played silently with her watch-chain. Flaxman, watching her closely, however little he might seem to do so, was struck by her austere and delicate beauty as he had never been before.

She hardly spoke all through, but he felt that she listened without resistance, nay, at last that she listened with a kind of hunger. He went from story to story, from scene to scene, without any excitement, in his most ordinary manner, making his reserves now and then, expressing his own opinion when it occurred to him, and not always favourably. But gradually the whole picture emerged, began to live before them. At last he hurriedly looked at his watch.

'What a time I have kept you! It has been a relief to talk to you.'

'You have not had dinner!' she said, looking up at him with a sudden nervous bewilderment which touched him and subtly changed his impression of her.

'No matter. I will get some at home. Good-night!'

When he was gone she carried the child up to bed; her supper was brought to her solitary in the dining-room; and afterwards in the drawing-room, where a soft twilight was fading into a soft and starlit night, she mechanically brought out some work for Mary, and sat bending over it by the window. After about an hour she looked up straight before her, threw her work down, and slipped on to the floor, her head resting on the chair.

The shock, the storm, had come. There for hours lay Catherine Elsmere weeping her heart away, wrestling with herself, with memory, with God. It was the greatest moral upheaval she had ever known—greater even than that which had convulsed her life at Murewell.

CHAPTER XLIII

Robert, tired and sick at heart, felt himself in no mood this evening for a dinner-party in which conversation would be treated more or less as a fine art. Liberal Catholicism had lost its charm; his sympathetic interest in Montalembert, Lacordaire, Lamennais, had to be quickened, pumped up again as it were, by great efforts, which were constantly relaxed within him as he sped westwards by the recurrent memory of that miserable room, the group of men, the bleeding hand, the white dying face.[59]

In Madame de Netteville's drawing-room he found a small number of people assembled. M. de Quérouelle, a middle-sized, round-headed old gentleman of a familiar French type; Lady Aubrey, thinner, more lath-like than ever, clad in some sumptuous mingling of dark red and silver; Lord Rupert, beaming under the recent introduction of a Land Purchase Bill for Ireland, by which he saw his way at last to wash his hands of 'a beastly set of tenants';[60] Mr. Wharncliffe, a young private secretary with a waxed moustache, six feet of height, and a general air of superlativeness which demanded and secured attention; a famous journalist, whose smiling self-repressive look assured you that he carried with him the secrets of several empires; and one Sir John Headlam, a little black-haired Jewish-looking man with a limp—an ex-Colonial Governor, who had made himself accepted in London as an amusing fellow, but who was at least as much disliked by one half of society as he was popular with the other.

'Purely for talk, you see, not for show!' said Madame de Netteville to Robert, with a little smiling nod round her circle as they stood waiting for the commencement of dinner.

'I shall hardly do my part,' he said with a little sigh. 'I have just come from a very different scene.'

She looked at him with inquiring eyes.

'A terrible accident in the East End,' he said briefly. 'We won't talk of it. I only mention it to propitiate you beforehand. Those things are not forgotten at once.'

She said no more, but, seeing that he was indeed out of heart, physically and mentally, she showed the most subtle consideration for him at dinner. M. de Quérouelle was made to talk. His hostess wound him up and set him going, tune after tune. He played them all, and, by dint of long practice, to perfection, in the French way. A visit of his youth to the island grave of Chateaubriand; his early memories, as a poetical aspirant, of the magnificent flatteries by which Victor Hugo made himself the god of young romantic Paris; his talks with Montalembert in the days of *L'Avenir*; his memories of Lamennais's sombre figure, of Maurice de Guérin's feverish ethereal charm; his account of the opposition *salons* under the Empire—they had all been elaborated in the course of years, till every word fitted and each point led to

---

59 Jean-Baptiste Henri Lacordaire (1802–1861), liberal Catholic priest; Hugues Felicité Robert de Lammenais (1782–1854), Catholic priest who ultimately abandoned orthodox Christianity.

60 Purchase of Land (Ireland) Act 1885, which made it possible for tenants to take out what we would now call a one hundred percent mortgage to buy land.

the next with the 'inevitableness' of true art.[61] Robert, at first silent and *distrait*, found it impossible after a while not to listen with interest. He admired the skill, too, of Madame de Netteville's second in the duet, the finish, the alternate sparkle and melancholy of it; and at last he too was drawn in, and found himself listened to with great benevolence by the Frenchman, who had been informed about him, and regarded him indulgently, as one more curious specimen of English religious provincialisms. The journalist, Mr. Addlestone, who had won a European reputation for wisdom by a great scantiness of speech in society, coupled with the look of Minerva's owl, attached himself to them; while Lady Aubrey, Sir John Headlam, Lord Rupert, and Mr. Wharncliffe made a noisier and more dashing party at the other end.

'Are you still in your old quarters, Lady Aubrey?' asked Sir John Headlam, turning his old roguish face upon her. 'That house of Nell Gwynne's, wasn't it, in Meade Street?'[62]

'Oh dear no! We could only get it up to May this year, and then they made us turn out for the season, for the first time for ten years. There is a tiresome young heir who has married a wife and wants to live in it. I could have left a train of gunpowder and a slow match behind, I was so cross!'

'Ah—"Reculer pour mieux *faire* sauter!"' said Sir John, mincing out his pun as though he loved it.[63]

'Not bad, Sir John,' she said, looking at him calmly, 'but you have way to make up. You were so dull the last time you took me in to dinner, that positively——'

'You began to wonder to what I owed my paragraph in the *Société de Londres*,' he rejoined, smiling, though a close observer might have seen an angry flash in his little eyes. 'My dear Lady Aubrey, it was simply because I had not seen you for six weeks. My education had been neglected. I get my art and my literature from you. The last time but one we met, you gave me the cream of three new French novels and all the dramatic scandal of the period. I have lived on it for weeks. By the way, have you read the *Princesse de——* ?'

He looked at her audaciously. The book had affronted even Paris.

'I haven't,' she said, adjusting her bracelets, while she flashed a rapier-glance at him, 'but if I had, I should say precisely the same. Lord Rupert, will

61 *L'Avenir* (1830-32), a polemical Catholic newspaper published by the trio of Montalembert, Lacordaire, and Lammenais; ended after being formally denounced by the Vatican. Maurice de Guérin (1810-39),   French author influenced by Lammenais.

62 Famed actress (1650–1687) and mistress of Charles II.

63 The usual saying is without the "faire," and means "Back up in order to better jump forward." With "faire," it now means "to better make somebody jump forward."

you kindly keep Sir John in order?'

Lord Rupert plunged in with the gallant floundering motion character-istic of him, while Mr. Wharncliffe followed like a modern gunboat behind a three-decker. That young man was a delusion. The casual spectator, to borrow a famous Cambridge *mot*, invariably assumed that all 'the time he could spare from neglecting his duties he must spend in adorning his person.'[64] Not at all! The *tenue* of a dandy was never more cleverly used to mask the schemes of a Disraeli or the hard ambition of a Talleyrand than in Master Frederick Wharncliffe, who was in reality going up the ladder hand over hand, and meant very soon to be on the top rungs.[65]

It was a curious party, typical of the house, and of a certain stratum of London. When, every now and then, in the pauses of their own conversation, Elsmere caught something of the chatter going on at the other end of the table, or when the party became fused into one for a while under the genial influence of a good story or the exhilaration of a personal skirmish, the whole scene—the dainty oval room, the lights, the servants, the exquisite fruit and flowers, the gleaming silver, the tapestried walls—would seem to him for an instant like a mirage, a dream, yet with something glittering and arid about it which a dream never has.

The hard self-confidence of these people—did it belong to the same world as that humbling, that heavenly self-abandonment which had shone on him that afternoon from Charles Richards's begrimed and blood-stained face? '*Blessed are the poor in spirit*,' he said to himself once with an inward groan.[66] 'Why am I here? Why am I not at home with Catherine?'

But Madame de Netteville was pleasant to him. He had never seen her so womanly, never felt more grateful for her delicate social skill. As she talked to him, or to the Frenchman, of literature, or politics, or famous folk, flashing her beautiful eyes from one to the other, Sir John Headlam would, every now and then, turn his odd puckered face observantly towards the farther end of the table.

'By Jove!' he said afterwards to Wharncliffe as they walked away from the door together, 'she was inimitable to-night; she has more *rôles* than Desforêts!' Sir John and his hostess were very old friends.

---

64 Based on a complaint by William Hepworth Thompson, the Master of Trinity College, Cambridge, about classicist Sir Richard Jebb: "What time he can spare from the adornment of his person he devotes to the neglect of his duties."

65 Benjamin Disraeli (1804–1881), two-time Conservative Prime Minister and rival of William Gladstone; Charles Maurice de Talleyrand-Périgord (1754–1838), powerful French diplomat who served several governments in succession.

66 Matthew 5.3.

Upstairs smoking began, Lady Aubrey and Madame de Netteville joining in. M. de Quérouelle, having talked the best of his *répertoire* at dinner, was now inclined for amusement, and had discovered that Lady Aubrey could amuse him, and was, moreover, *une belle personne*. Madame de Netteville was obliged to give some time to Lord Rupert. The other men stood chatting politics and the latest news, till Robert, conscious of a complete failure of social energy, began to look at his watch. Instantly Madame de Netteville glided up to him.

'Mr. Elsmere, you have talked no business to me, and I must know how my affairs in Elgood Street are getting on. Come into my little writing-room.' And she led him into a tiny panelled room at the far end of the drawing-room and shut off from it by a heavy curtain, which she now left half-drawn.

'The latest?' said Fred Wharncliffe to Lady Aubrey, raising his eyebrows with the slightest motion of the head towards the writing-room.

'I suppose so,' she said indifferently; 'she is East-Ending for a change. We all do it nowadays. It is like Dizzy's young man who "liked bad wine, he was so bored with good."'[67]

Meanwhile, Madame de Netteville was leaning against the open window of the fantastic little room, with Robert beside her.

'You look as if you had had a strain,' she said to him abruptly, after they had talked business for a few minutes. 'What has been the matter?'

He told her Richards's story, very shortly. It would have been impossible to him to give more than the driest outline of it in that room. His companion listened gravely. She was an epicure in all things, especially in moral sensation, and she liked his moments of reserve and strong self-control. They made his general expansiveness more distinguished.

Presently there was a pause, which she broke by saying—

'I was at your lecture last Sunday—you didn't see me!'

'Were you? Ah! I remember a person in black, and veiled, who puzzled me. I don't think we want you there, Madame de Netteville.'

His look was pleasant, but his tone had some decision in it.

'Why not? Is it only the artisans who have souls? A reformer should refuse no one.'

'You have your own opportunities,' he said quietly; 'I think the men prefer to have it to themselves for the present. Some of them are dreadfully in earnest.'

'Oh, I don't pretend to be in earnest,' she said with a little wave of her

---

67   Benjamin Disraeli's novel *Sybil* (1845): "'I rather like bad wine,' said Mr. Mountchesney, 'one gets so bored with good wine'" (ch. 1).

hand; 'or, at any rate, I know better than to talk of earnestness to *you.*'

'Why to me?' he asked, smiling.

'Oh, because you and your like have your fixed ideas of the upper class and the lower. One social type fills up your horizon. You are not interested in any other, and, indeed, you know nothing of any other.'

She looked at him defiantly. Everything about her to-night was splendid and regal—her dress of black and white brocade, the diamonds at her throat, the carriage of her head, nay, the marks of experience and living on the dark subtle face.

'Perhaps not,' he replied: 'it is enough for one life to try and make out where the English working class is tending to.'

'You are quite wrong, utterly wrong. The man who keeps his eye only on the lower class will achieve nothing. What can the idealist do without the men of action—the men who can take his beliefs and make them enter by violence into existing institutions? And the men of action are to be found with *us.*'

'It hardly looks just now as if the upper class was to go on enjoying a monopoly of them,' he said, smiling.

'Then appearances are deceptive. The populace supplies mass and weight—nothing else. What *you* want is to touch the leaders, the men and women whose voices carry, and then your populace would follow hard enough. For instance,'—and she dropped her aggressive tone and spoke with a smiling kindness,—'come down next Saturday to my little Surrey cottage; you shall see some of these men and women there, and I will make you confess when you go away that you have profited your workmen more by deserting them than by staying with them. Will you come?'

'My Sundays are too precious to me just now, Madame de Netteville. Besides, my firm conviction is that the upper class can produce a Brook Farm, but nothing more.[68] The religious movement of the future will want a vast effusion of feeling and passion to carry it into action, and feeling and passion are only to be generated in sufficient volume among the masses, where the vested interests of all kinds are less tremendous. You upper-class folk have your part, of course. Woe betide you if you shirk it—but——'

'Oh, let us leave it alone,' she said with a little shrug. 'I know you would give us all the work and refuse us all the profits. We are to starve for your workman, to give him our hearts and purses and everything we have, not that we may hoodwink him—which might be worth doing—but that he may rule

---

68 The unsuccessful Massachusetts utopian community, which operated from 1841–1847.

us. It is too much!'

'Very well,' he said drily, his colour rising. 'Very well, let it be too much.'

And, dropping his lounging attitude, he stood erect, and she saw that he meant to be going. Her look swept over him from head to foot—over the worn face with its look of sensitive refinement and spiritual force, the active frame, the delicate but most characteristic hand. Never had any man so attracted her for years; never had she found it so difficult to gain a hold. Eugénie de Netteville, *poseuse*, schemer, woman of the world that she was, was losing command of herself.

'What did you really mean by "worldliness" and the "world" in your lecture last Sunday?' she asked him suddenly, with a little accent of scorn. 'I thought your diatribes absurd. What you religious people call the "world" is really only the average opinion of sensible people which neither you nor your kind could do without for a day.'

He smiled, half amused by her provocative tone, and defended himself not very seriously. But she threw all her strength into the argument, and he forgot that he had meant to go at once. When she chose she could talk admirably, and she chose now. She had the most aggressive ways of attacking, and then, in the same breath, the most subtle and softening ways of yielding and, as it were, of asking pardon. Directly her antagonist turned upon her he found himself disarmed he knew not how. The disputant disappeared, and he felt the woman, restless, melancholy, sympathetic, hungry for friendship and esteem, yet too proud to make any direct bid for either. It was impossible not to be interested and touched.

Such at least was the woman whom Robert Elsmere felt. Whether in his hours of intimacy with her, twelve months before, young Alfred Evershed had received the same impression may be doubted. In all things Eugénie de Netteville was an artist.

Suddenly the curtain dividing them from the larger drawing-room was drawn back, and Sir John Headlam stood in the doorway. He had the glittering amused eyes of a malicious child as he looked at them.

'Very sorry, madame,' he began in his high cracked voice, 'but Wharncliffe and I are off to the New Club to see Desforêts. They have got her there to-night.'

'Go,' she said, waving her hand to him, 'I don't envy you. She is not what she was.'

'No, there is only one person,' he said, bowing with grotesque little airs of gallantry, 'for whom time stands still.'

Madame de Netteville looked at him with smiling half-contemptuous serenity. He bowed again, this time with ironical emphasis, and disappeared.

'Perhaps I had better go back and send them off,' she said, rising. 'But you and I have not had our talk out yet.'

She led the way into the drawing-room. Lady Aubrey was lying back on the velvet sofa, a little green paroquet that was accustomed to wander tamely about the room perching on her hand. She was holding the field against Lord Rupert and Mr. Addlestone in a three-cornered duel of wits, while M. de Quérouelle sat by, his plump hands on his knees, applauding.

They all rose as their hostess came in.

'My dear' said Lady Aubrey, 'it is disgracefully early, but my country before pleasure. It is the Foreign Office to-night, and since James took office I can't with decency absent myself. I had rather be a scullerymaid than a minister's wife. Lord Rupert, I will take you on if you want a lift.'

She touched Madame de Netteville's cheek with her lips, nodding to the other men present, and went out, her fair stag-like head well in the air, 'chaffing' Lord Rupert, who obediently followed her, performing marvellous feats of agility in his desire to keep out of the way of the superb train sweeping behind her. It always seemed as if Lady Aubrey could have had no childhood, as if she must always have had just that voice and those eyes. Tears she could never have shed, not even as a baby over a broken toy. Besides, at no period of her life could she have looked upon a lost possession as anything else than the opportunity for a new one.

The other men took their departure for one reason or another. It was not late, but London was in full swing, and M. de Quérouelle talked with gusto of four 'At homes' still to be grappled with.

As she dismissed Mr. Wharncliffe, Robert too held out his hand.

'No,' she said, with a quick impetuousness, 'no: I want my talk out. It is barely half-past ten, and neither of us wants to be racing about London to-night.'

Elsmere had always a certain lack of social decision, and he lingered rather reluctantly—for another ten minutes, as he supposed.

She threw herself into a low chair. The windows were open to the back of the house, and the roar of Piccadilly and Sloane Street came borne in upon the warm night air. Her superb dark head stood out against a stand of yellow lilies close behind her, and the little paroquet, bright with all the colours of the tropics, perched now on her knee, now on the back of her chair, touched every now and then by quick unsteady fingers.

Then an incident followed which Elsmere remembered to his dying day with shame and humiliation.

In ten minutes from the time of their being left alone, a woman who was five years his senior had made him what was practically a confession of love—had given him to understand that she knew what were the relations between himself and his wife—and had implored him with the quick breath of an indescribable excitement to see what a woman's sympathy and a woman's unique devotion could do for the causes he had at heart.

The truth broke upon Elsmere very slowly, awakening in him, when at last it was unmistakable, a swift agony of repulsion, which his most friendly biographer can only regard with a kind of grim satisfaction. For after all there is an amount of innocence and absent-mindedness in matters of daily human life, which is not only *niaiserie*,[69] but comes very near to moral wrong. In this crowded world a man has no business to walk about with his eyes always on the stars. His stumbles may have too many consequences. A harsh but a salutary truth! If Elsmere needed it, it was bitterly taught him during a terrible half-hour. When the half-coherent enigmatical sentences, to which he listened at first with a perplexed surprise, began gradually to define themselves; when he found a woman roused and tragically beautiful between him and escape; when no determination on his part not to understand; when nothing he could say availed to protect her from herself; when they were at last face to face with a confession and an appeal which were a disgrace to both—then at last Elsmere paid 'in one minute glad life's arrears,'—the natural penalty of an optimism, a boundless faith in human nature, with which life, as we know it, is inconsistent.[70]

How he met the softness, the grace, the seduction of a woman who was an expert in all the arts of fascination he never knew. In memory afterwards it was all a ghastly mirage to him. The low voice, the splendid dress, the scented room came back to him, and a confused memory of his own futile struggle to ward off what she was bent on saying—little else. He had been maladroit, he thought, had lost his presence of mind. Any man of the world of his acquaintance, he believed, trampling on himself, would have done better.

But when the softness and the grace were all lost in smart and humiliation, when the Madame de Netteville of ordinary life disappeared, and something took her place which was like a coarse and malignant underself suddenly brought into the light of day—from that point onwards, in after days, he remembered it all.

'...I know,' cried Eugénie de Netteville at last, standing at bay before him, her hands locked before her, her white lips quivering, when her cup of shame

---

69   "Silliness" (Collins).
70   A slight misquotation of Robert Browning's "Prospice" (1864), l. 19.

was full, and her one impulse left was to strike the man who had humiliated her—'I know that you and your puritanical wife are miserable—*miserable*. What is the use of denying facts that all the world can see, that you have taken pains,' and she laid a fierce deliberate emphasis on each word, 'all the world shall see? There—let your wife's ignorance and bigotry, and your own obvious relation to her, be my excuse, if I wanted any; but,' and she shrugged her white shoulders passionately, 'I want *none*! I am not responsible to your petty codes. Nature and feeling are enough for me. I saw you wanting sympathy and affection——'

'My wife!' cried Robert, hearing nothing but that one word. And then, his glance sweeping over the woman before him, he made a stern step forward.

'Let me go, Madame de Netteville, let me go, or I shall forget that you are a woman and I a man, and that in some way I cannot understand my own blindness and folly——'

'Must have led to this most undesirable scene,' she said with mocking suddenness, throwing herself, however, effectually in his way. Then a change came over her, and erect, ghastly white, with frowning brow and shaking limbs, a baffled and smarting woman from whom every restraint had fallen away, let loose upon him a torrent of gall and bitterness which he could not have cut short without actual violence.

He stood proudly enduring it, waiting for the moment when what seemed to him an outbreak of mania should have spent itself. But suddenly he caught Catherine's name coupled with some contemptuous epithet or other, and his self-control failed him. With flashing eyes he went close up to her and took her wrists in a grip of iron.

'You shall not,' he said, beside himself, 'you shall not! What have I done—what has she done—that you should allow yourself such words? My poor wife!'

A passionate flood of self-reproachful love was on his lips. He choked it back. It was desecration that *her* name should be mentioned in that room. But he dropped the hand he held. The fierceness died out of his eyes. His companion stood beside him panting, breathless, afraid.

'Thank God,' he said slowly, 'thank God for yourself and me that I *love* my wife! I am not worthy of her—doubly unworthy, since it has been possible for any human being to suspect for one instant that I was ungrateful for the blessing of her love, that I could ever forget and dishonour her! But worthy or not—— No!—no matter! Madame de Netteville, let me go, and forget that such a person exists.'

She looked at him steadily for a moment, at the stern manliness of the face which seemed in this half-hour to have grown older, at the attitude with its mingled dignity and appeal. In that second she realised what she had done and what she had forfeited; she measured the gulf between herself and the man before her. But she did not flinch. Still holding him, as it were, with menacing defiant eyes, she moved aside, she waved her hand with a contemptuous gesture of dismissal. He bowed, passed her, and the door shut.

For nearly an hour afterwards Elsmere wandered blindly and aimlessly through the darkness and silence of the park.

The sensitive optimist nature was all unhinged, felt itself wrestling in the grip of dark implacable things, upheld by a single thread above that moral abyss which yawns beneath us all, into which the individual life sinks so easily to ruin and nothingness. At such moments a man realises within himself, within the circle of consciousness, the germs of all things hideous and vile. '*Save for the grace of God,*' he says to himself, shuddering, 'save only for the grace of God——'

Contempt for himself, loathing for life and its possibilities, as he had just beheld them; moral tumult, pity, remorse, a stinging self-reproach—all these things wrestled within him. What, preach to others, and stumble himself into such mire as this? Talk loudly of love and faith, and make it possible all the time that a fellow human creature should think you capable at a pinch of the worst treason against both?

Elsmere dived to the very depths of his own soul that night. Was it all the natural consequence of a loosened bond, of a wretched relaxation of effort— a wretched acquiescence in something second best? Had love been cooling? Had it simply ceased to take the trouble love must take to maintain itself? And had this horror been the subtle inevitable Nemesis?

All at once, under the trees of the park, Elsmere stopped for a moment in the darkness, and bared his head, with the passionate reverential action of a devotee before his saint. The lurid image which had been pursuing him gave way, and in its place came the image of a new-made mother, her child close within her sheltering arm. Ah! it was all plain to him now. The moral tempest had done its work.

One task of all tasks had been set him from the beginning—to keep his wife's love! If she had slipped away from him, to the injury and moral lessening of both, on his cowardice, on his clumsiness, be the blame! Above all, on his fatal power of absorbing himself in a hundred outside interests, controversy, literature, society. Even his work seemed to have lost half its sacredness. If there be a canker at the root, no matter how large the show of leaf and blossom overhead, there is but the more to wither! Of what worth is any success, but that which is grounded deep on the rock of personal love and duty?

Oh! let him go back to her!—wrestle with her, open his heart again, try new ways, make new concessions. How faint the sense of *her* trial has been growing within him of late! hers which had once been more terrible to him than his own! He feels the special temptations of his own nature; he throws himself, humbled, convicted, at her feet. The woman, the scene he has left, is effaced, blotted out by the natural intense reaction of remorseful love.

So he sped homewards at last through the noise of Oxford Street, seeing, hearing nothing. He opened his own door, and let himself into the dim, silent house. How the moment recalled to him that other supreme moment of his life at Murewell! No light in the drawing-room. He went upstairs and softly turned the handle of her room.

Inside the room seemed to him nearly dark. But the window was wide open. The free loosely-growing branches of the plane trees made a dark, delicate network against the luminous blue of the night. A cool air came to him laden with an almost rural scent of earth and leaves. By the window sat a white motionless figure. As he closed the door it rose and walked towards him without a word. Instinctively Robert felt that something unknown to him had been passing here. He paused breathless, expectant.

She came to him. She linked her cold trembling fingers round his neck.

'Robert, I have been waiting so long—it was so late! I thought'—and she choked down a sob—'perhaps something has happened to him, we are separated for ever, and I shall never be able to tell him. Robert, Mr. Flaxman talked to me; he opened my eyes; I have been so cruel to you, so hard! I have broken my vow. I don't deserve it; but—*Robert!*——'

She had spoken with extraordinary self-command till the last word, which fell into a smothered cry for pardon. Catherine Elsmere had very little of the soft clingingness which makes the charm of a certain type of woman. Each phrase she had spoken had seemed to take with it a piece of her life. She trembled and tottered in her husband's arms.

He bent over her with half-articulate words of amazement, of passion. He led her to her chair, and, kneeling before her, he tried, so far as the emotion of both would let him, to make her realise what was in his *own* heart, the penitence and longing which had winged his return to her. Without a mention of Madame de Netteville's name, indeed! *That* horror she should never know. But it was to it, as he held his wife, he owed his poignant sense of something half-jeopardised and wholly recovered; it was that consciousness in the background of his mind, ignorant of it as Catherine was then and always, which gave the peculiar epoch-making force to this sacred and critical hour of their lives. But she would hear nothing of his self-blame—nothing. She put her hand across his lips.

'I have seen things as they are, Robert,' she said very simply; 'while I have been sitting here, and downstairs, after Mr. Flaxman left me. You were right—I *would* not understand. And, in a sense, I shall never understand. I cannot change,' and her voice broke into piteousness. 'My Lord is my Lord always; but He is yours too. Oh, I know it, say what you will! *That* is what has been hidden from me; that is what my trouble has taught me; the powerlessness, the worthlessness, of words. *It is the spirit that quickeneth.*[71] I should never have felt it so, but for this fiery furnace of pain. But I have been wandering in strange places, through strange thoughts. God has not one language, but many. I have dared to think He had but one, the one I knew. I have dared'—and she faltered—'to condemn your faith as no faith. Oh! I lay there so long in the dark downstairs, seeing you by that bed; I heard your voice, I crept to your side. Jesus was there, too. Ah, He was—He was! Leave me that comfort! What are you saying? Wrong—you? Unkind? Your wife knows nothing of it. Oh, did you think when you came in just now before dinner that I didn't care, that I had a heart of stone? Did you think I had broken my solemn promise, my vow to you that day at Murewell? So I have, a hundred times over. I made it in ignorance; I had not counted the cost—how could I? It was all so new, so strange. I dare not make it again, the will is so weak, circumstances so strong. But oh! take me back into your life! Hold me there! Remind me always of this night; convict me out of my own mouth! But I *will* learn my lesson; I will learn to hear the two voices, the voice that speaks to you and the voice that speaks to me—I must. It is all plain to me now. It has been appointed me.'

Then she broke down into a kind of weariness, and fell back in her chair, her delicate fingers straying with soft childish touch over his hair.

'But I am past thinking. Let us bury it all, and begin again. Words are nothing.'

Strange ending to a day of torture! As she towered above him in the dimness, white and pure and drooping, her force of nature all dissolved, lost in this new heavenly weakness of love, he thought of the man who passed through the place of sin, and the place of expiation, and saw at last the rosy light creeping along the East, caught the white moving figures, and that sweet distant melody rising through the luminous air, which announced to him the

---

71 John 6.63.

approach of Beatrice and the nearness of those 'shining tablelands whereof our God Himself is moon and sun.'[72] For eternal life, the ideal state, is not something future and distant. Dante knew it when he talked of '*quella que imparadisa la mia mente*.'[73] Paradise is here, visible and tangible by mortal eyes and hands, whenever self is lost in loving, whenever the narrow limits of personality are beaten down by the inrush of the Divine Spirit.

CHAPTER XLIV

The saddest moment in the lives of these two persons whose history we have followed for so long was over and done with. Henceforward to the end Elsmere and his wife were lovers as of old.

But that day and night left even deeper marks on Robert than on Catherine. Afterwards she gradually came to feel, running all through his views of life, a note sterner, deeper, maturer than any present there before. The reasons for it were unknown to her, though sometimes her own tender, ignorant remorse supplied them. But they were hidden deep in Elsmere's memory.

A few days afterwards he was casually told that Madame de Netteville had left England for some time. As a matter of fact he never set eyes on her again. After a while the extravagance of his self-blame abated. He saw things as they were—without morbidness. But a certain boyish carelessness of mood he never afterwards quite recovered. Men and women of all classes, and not only among the poor, became more real and more tragic—moral truths more awful—to him. It was the penalty of a highly-strung nature set with exclusive intensity towards certain spiritual ends.

On the first opportunity after that conversation with Hugh Flaxman which had so deeply affected her, Catherine accompanied Elsmere to his Sunday lecture. He tried a little, tenderly, to dissuade her. But she went, shrinking and yet determined.

She had not heard him speak in public since that last sermon of his in Murewell Church, every detail of which by long brooding had been burnt into her mind. The bare Elgood Street room, the dingy outlook on the high walls of a warehouse opposite, the lines of blanched quick-eyed artisans, the dissent from what she loved, and he had once loved, implied in everything,

---

72 Alfred, Lord Tennyson, "Ode on the Death of the Duke of Wellington" (1852), ll. 216-17.

73 The slight misquotation is from Dante, *Paradiso,* 28.3.

the lecture itself, on the narratives of the Passion; it was all exquisitely painful to her, and, yet, yet she was glad to be there.

Afterwards Wardlaw, with the brusque remark to Elsmere that 'any fool could see he was getting done up,' insisted on taking the children's class. Catherine, too, had been impressed, as she saw Robert raised a little above her in the glare of many windows, with the sudden perception that the worn, exhausted look of the preceding summer had returned upon him. She held out her hand to Wardlaw with a quick, warm word of thanks. He glanced at her curiously. What had brought her there after all?

Then Robert, protesting that he was being ridiculously coddled, and that Wardlaw was much more in want of a holiday than he, was carried off to the Embankment, and the two spent a happy hour wandering westward, Somerset House, the bridges, the Westminster towers rising before them into the haze of the June afternoon. A little fresh breeze came off the river; that, or his wife's hand on his arm, seemed to put new life into Elsmere. And she walked beside him, talking frankly, heart to heart, with flashes of her old sweet gaiety, as she had not talked for months.

Deep in her mystical sense all the time lay the belief in a final restoration, in an all-atoning moment, perhaps at the very end of life, in which the blind would see, the doubter be convinced. And, meanwhile, the blessedness of this peace, this surrender! Surely the air this afternoon was pure and life-giving for them, the bells rang for them, the trees were green for them!

He had need in the week that followed of all that she had given back to him. For Mr. Grey's illness had taken a dangerous and alarming turn. It seemed to be the issue of long ill-health, and the doctors feared that there were no resources of constitution left to carry him through it. Every day some old St. Anselm's friend on the spot wrote to Elsmere, and with each post the news grew more despairing. Since Elsmere had left Oxford he could count on the fingers of one hand the occasions on which he and Grey had met face to face. But for him, as for many another man of our time, Henry Grey's influence was not primarily an influence of personal contact. His mere life, that he was there, on English soil, within a measurable distance, had been to Elsmere in his darkest moments one of his thoughts of refuge. At a time when a religion which can no longer be believed clashes with a scepticism full of danger to conduct, every such witness as Grey to the power of a new and coming truth holds a special place in the hearts of men who can neither accept fairy tales, nor reconcile themselves to a world without faith. The saintly life grows to be a beacon, a witness. Men cling to it as they have always clung to each other, to the visible and the tangible; as the elders of Miletus, though the Way lay before them, clung to the man who had set their feet therein, 'sorrowing most of all that they should see his face no more.'[74]

The accounts grew worse—all friends shut out, no possibility of last words—the whole of Oxford moved and sorrowing. Then at last, on a Friday, came the dreaded expected letter: 'He is gone! He died early this morning, without pain, conscious almost to the end. He mentioned several friends by name, you among them, during the night. The funeral is to be on Tuesday. You will be here, of course.'

Sad and memorable day! By an untoward chance it fell in Commemoration week, and Robert found the familiar streets teeming with life and noise, under a showery uncertain sky, which every now and then would send the bevies of lightly-gowned maidens, with their mothers and attendant squires, skurrying for shelter, and leave the roofs and pavements glistening. He walked up to St. Anselm's—found, as he expected, that the first part of the service was to be in the chapel, the rest in the cemetery, and then mounted the well-known staircase to Langham's rooms. Langham was apparently in his bedroom. Lunch was on the table—the familiar commons, the familiar toast-and-water. There, in a recess, were the same splendid wall maps of Greece he had so often consulted after lecture. There was the little case of coins, with the gold Alexanders he had handled with so much covetous reverence at eighteen. Outside, the irregular quadrangle with its dripping trees stretched before him; the steps of the new Hall, now the shower was over, were crowded with gowned figures. It might have been yesterday that he had stood in that room, blushing with awkward pleasure under Mr. Grey's first salutation.

The bedroom door opened and Langham came in.

'Elsmere! But of course I expected you.'

His voice seemed to Robert curiously changed. There was a flatness in it, an absence of positive cordiality which was new to him in any greeting of Langham's to himself, and had a chilling effect upon him. The face, too, was changed. Tint and expression were both dulled; its marble-like sharpness and finish had coarsened a little, and the figure, which had never possessed the erectness of youth, had now the pinched look and the confirmed stoop of the valetudinarian.

'I did not write to you, Elsmere,' he said immediately, as though in anticipation of what the other would be sure to say; 'I knew nothing but what the bulletins said, and I was told that Cathcart wrote to you. It is many years now since I have seen much of Grey. Sit down and have some lunch. We have

---

74 Acts 20.38.

time, but not too much time.'

Robert took a few mouthfuls. Langham was difficult, talked disconnect-
edly of trifles, and Robert was soon painfully conscious that the old sympathetic bond between them no longer existed. Presently, Langham, as though
with an effort to remember, asked after Catherine, then inquired what he
was doing in the way of writing, and neither of them mentioned the name of
Leyburn. They left the table and sat spasmodically talking, in reality expectant. And at last the sound present already in both minds made itself heard—
the first long solitary stroke of the chapel bell.

Robert covered his eyes.

'Do you remember in this room, Langham, you introduced us first?'

'I remember,' replied the other abruptly. Then, with a half-cynical, half-
melancholy scrutiny of his companion, he said, after a pause, 'What a faculty
of hero-worship you have always had, Elsmere!'

'Do you know anything of the end?' Robert asked him presently, as that
tolling bell seemed to bring the strong feeling beneath more irresistibly to the
surface.

'No, I never asked!' cried Langham, with sudden harsh animation. 'What
purpose could be served? Death should be avoided by the living. We have no
business with it. Do what we will, we cannot rehearse our own parts. And the
sight of other men's performances helps us no more than the sight of a great
actor gives the dramatic gift. All they do for us is to imperil the little nerve,
break through the little calm, we have left.'

Elsmere's hand dropped, and he turned round to him with a flashing
smile.

'Ah—I know it now—you loved him still.'

Langham, who was standing, looked down on him sombrely, yet more
indulgently.

'How much you always made of feeling,' he said after a little pause, 'in a
world where, according to me, our chief object should be not to feel!'

Then he began to hunt for his cap and gown. In another minute the two
made part of the crowd in the front quadrangle, where the rain was sprinkling, and the insistent grief-laden voice of the bell rolled, from pause to
pause, above the gowned figures, spreading thence in wide waves of mourning sound over Oxford.

The chapel service passed over Robert like a solemn pathetic dream. The
lines of undergraduate faces, the Provost's white head, the voice of the chap-
lain reading, the full male unison of the voices replying—how they carried
him back to the day when as a lad from school he had sat on one of the

chancel benches beside his mother, listening for the first time to the subtle simplicity, if one may be allowed the paradox, of the Provost's preaching![75] Just opposite to where he sat now with Langham, Grey had sat that first afternoon; the freshman's curious eyes had been drawn again and again to the dark massive head, the face with its look of reposeful force, of righteous strength. During the lesson from Corinthians, Elsmere's thoughts were irrelevantly busy with all sorts of mundane memories of the dead. What was especially present to him was a series of Liberal election meetings in which Grey had taken a warm part, and in which he himself had helped just before he took Orders. A hundred odd, incongruous details came back to Robert now with poignant force. Grey had been to him at one time primarily the professor, the philosopher, the representative of all that was best in the life of the University; now, fresh from his own grapple with London and its life, what moved him most was the memory of the citizen, the friend and brother of common man, the thinker who had never shirked action in the name of thought, for whom conduct had been from beginning to end the first reality.

The procession through the streets afterwards, which conveyed the body of this great son of modern Oxford to its last resting-place in the citizens' cemetery on the western side of the town, will not soon be forgotten, even in a place which forgets notoriously soon. All the University was there, all the town was there. Side by side with men honourably dear to England, who had carried with them into one or other of the great English careers the memory of the teacher, were men who had known from day to day the cheery modest helper in a hundred local causes; side by side with the youth of Alma Mater went the poor of Oxford; tradesmen and artisans followed or accompanied the group of gowned and venerable figures, representing the Heads of Houses and the Professors, or mingled with the slowly pacing crowd of Masters; while along the route groups of visitors and merrymakers, young men in flannels or girls in light dresses, stood with suddenly grave faces here and there, caught by the general wave of mourning, and wondering what such a spectacle might mean.

Robert, losing sight of Langham as they left the chapel, found his arm grasped by young Cathcart, his correspondent. The man was a junior Fellow who had attached himself to Grey during the two preceding years with especial devotion. Robert had only a slight knowledge of him, but there was something in his voice and grip which made him feel at once infinitely more at home with him at this moment than he had felt with the old friend of his

---

75 "the Provost's white head": capitalization here and below as per *SE* and *W*, in line with usage elsewhere in the novel.

undergraduate years.

They walked down Beaumont Street together. The rain came on again, and the long black crowd stretched before them was lashed by the driving gusts. As they went along, Cathcart told him all he wanted to know.

'The night before the end he was perfectly calm and conscious. I told you he mentioned your name among the friends to whom he sent his good-bye. He thought for everybody. For all those of his house he left the most minute and tender directions. He forgot nothing. And all with such extraordinary simplicity and quietness, like one arranging for a journey! In the evening an old Quaker aunt of his, a North-country woman whom he had been much with as a boy, and to whom he was much attached, was sitting with him. I was there too. She was a beautiful old figure in her white cap and kerchief, and it seemed to please him to lie and look at her. "It'll not be for long, Henry," she said to him once. "I'm seventy-seven this spring. I shall come to you soon." He made no reply, and his silence seemed to disturb her. I don't fancy she had known much of his mind of late years. "You'll not be doubting the Lord's goodness, Henry?" she said to him, with the tears in her eyes. "No," he said, "no, never. Only it seems to be His Will, we should be certain of nothing—but *Himself!* I ask no more." I shall never forget the accent of those words: they were the breath of his inmost life. If ever man was *Gottbetrunken* it was he—and yet not a word beyond what he felt to be true, beyond what the intellect could grasp!'[76]

Twenty minutes later Robert stood by the open grave. The rain beat down on the black concourse of mourners. But there were blue spaces in the drifting sky, and a wavering rainy light played at intervals over the Wytham and Hinksey Hills, and over the butter-cupped river meadows, where the lush hay-grass bent in long lines under the showers. To his left, the Provost, his glistening white head bare to the rain, was reading the rest of the service.

As the coffin was lowered Elsmere bent over the grave. 'My friend, my master,' cried the yearning filial heart, 'oh, give me something of yourself to take back into life, something to brace me through this darkness of our ignorance, something to keep hope alive as you kept it to the end!'

And on the inward ear there rose, with the solemnity of a last message, words which years before he had found marked in a little book of Meditations borrowed from Grey's table—words long treasured and often repeated—

'Amid a world of forgetfulness and decay, in the sight of his own short-comings and limitations, or on the edge of the tomb, he alone who has found his soul in losing it, who in singleness of mind *has lived in order to love and*

---

76 God-drunk.

understand, will find that the God who is near to him as his own conscience has a face of light and love!'[77]

Pressing the phrases into his memory, he listened to the triumphant outbursts of the Christian service.

'Man's hope,' he thought, 'has grown humbler than this. It keeps now a more modest mien in the presence of the Eternal Mystery; but is it in truth less real, less sustaining? Let Grey's trust answer for me.'

He walked away absorbed, till at last in the little squalid street outside the cemetery it occurred to him to look round for Langham. Instead, he found Cathcart, who had just come up with him.

'Is Langham behind?' he asked. 'I want a word with him before I go.'

'Is he here?' asked the other with a change of expression.

'But of course! He was in the chapel. How could you——'

'I thought he would probably go away,' said Cathcart, with some bitterness.[78] 'Grey made many efforts to get him to come and see him before he became so desperately ill. Langham came once. Grey never asked for him again.'

'It is his old horror of expression, I suppose,' said Robert, troubled; 'his dread of being forced to take a line, to face anything certain and irrevocable.[79] I understand. He could not say good-bye to a friend to save his life. There is no shirking that! One must either do it or leave it!'

Cathcart shrugged his shoulders, and drew a masterly little picture of Langham's life in college. He had succeeded by the most adroit devices in completely isolating himself both from the older and the younger men.

'He attends college-meeting sometimes, and contributes a sarcasm or two on the cramming system of the college. He takes a constitutional to Summertown every day on the least frequented side of the road, that he may avoid being spoken to. And as to his ways of living, he and I happen to have the same scout—old Dobson, you remember? And if I would let him, he would tell me tales by the hour. He is the only man in the University who knows anything about it. I gather from what he says that Langham is becoming a complete valetudinarian. Everything must go exactly by rule—his food, his work, the management of his clothes—and any little *contretemps* makes him ill. But the comedy is to watch him when there is anything going on in the place that he thinks may lead to a canvass and to any attempt to influence him for a vote. On these occasions he goes off with automatic regularity to

77 T. H. Green, "The Witness of God," *Works of Thomas Hill Green, Vol. III: Miscellanies and Memoir*, ed. R. L. Nettleship (London: Longmans, Green, and Co., 1888), 246.

78 "said Cathcart, with some bitterness": comma as per *SE* and *W*.

79 "said Robert, troubled": comma as per *SE* and *W*.

an hotel at West Malvern, and only reappears when the *Times* tells him the thing is done with.'

Both laughed. Then Robert sighed. Weaknesses of Langham's sort may be amusing enough to the contemptuous and unconcerned outsider. But the general result of them, whether for the man himself or those whom he affects, is tragic, not comic; and Elsmere had good reason for knowing it.

Later, after a long talk with the Provost, and meetings with various other old friends, he walked down to the station, under a sky clear from rain, and through a town gay with festal preparations. Not a sign now, in these crowded, bustling streets, of that melancholy pageant of the afternoon. The heroic memory had flashed for a moment like something vivid and gleaming in the sight of all, understanding and ignorant. Now it lay committed to a few faithful hearts, there to become one seed among many of a new religious life in England.

On the platform Robert found himself nervously accosted by a tall shabbily-dressed man.

'Elsmere, have you forgotten me?'

He turned and recognised a man whom he had last seen as a St. Anselm's undergraduate—one MacNiell, a handsome rowdy young Irishman, supposed to be clever, and decidedly popular in the college. As he stood looking at him, puzzled by the difference between the old impression and the new, suddenly the man's story flashed across him; he remembered some disgraceful escapade—an expulsion.

'You came for the funeral, of course?' said the other, his face flushing consciously.

'Yes—and you too?'

The man turned away, and something in his silence led Robert to stroll on beside him to the open end of the platform.

'I have lost my only friend,' MacNiell said at last hoarsely. 'He took me up when my own father would have nothing to say to me. He found me work; he wrote to me; for years he stood between me and perdition. I am just going out to a post in New Zealand he got for me, and next week before I sail—I—I—am to be married—and he was to be there. He was so pleased—he had seen her.'

It was one story out of a hundred like it, as Robert knew very well. They talked for a few minutes, then the train loomed in the distance.

'He saved you,' said Robert, holding out his hand, 'and at a dark moment in my own life I owed him everything. There is nothing we can do for him in return but—to remember him! Write to me, if you can or will, from New

Zealand, for his sake.'

A few seconds later the train sped past the bare little cemetery, which lay just beyond the line. Robert bent forward. In the pale yellow glow of the evening he could distinguish the grave, the mound of gravel, the planks, and some figures moving beside it. He strained his eyes till he could see no more, his heart full of veneration, of memory, of prayer. In himself life seemed so restless and combative. Surely he, more than others, had need of the lofty lessons of death!

CHAPTER XLV

In the weeks which followed—weeks often of mental and physical depression, caused by his sense of personal loss and by the influence of an overworked state he could not be got to admit—Elsmere owed much to Hugh Flaxman's cheery sympathetic temper, and became more attached to him than ever, and more ready than ever, should the fates deem it so, to welcome him as a brother-in-law. However, the fates for the moment seemed to have borrowed a leaf from Langham's book, and did not apparently know their own minds. It says volumes for Hugh Flaxman's general capacities as a human being that at this period he should have had any attention to give to a friend, his position as a lover was so dubious and difficult.

After the evening at the Workmen's Club, and as a result of further meditation, he had greatly developed the tactics first adopted on that occasion. He had beaten a masterly retreat, and Rose Leyburn was troubled with him no more.

The result was that a certain brilliant young person was soon sharply conscious of a sudden drop in the pleasures of living. Mr. Flaxman had been the Leyburns' most constant and entertaining visitor. During the whole of May he paid one formal call in Lerwick Gardens, and was then entertained *tête-à-tête* by Mrs. Leyburn, to Rose's intense subsequent annoyance, who knew perfectly well that her mother was incapable of chattering about anything but her daughters.

He still sent flowers, but they came from his head gardener, addressed to Mrs. Leyburn. Agnes put them in water; and Rose never gave them a look. Rose went to Lady Helen's because Lady Helen made her, and was much too engaging a creature to be rebuffed; but, however merry and protracted the teas in those scented rooms might be, Mr. Flaxman's step on the stairs, and Mr. Flaxman's hand on the curtain over the door, till now the feature in the

entertainment most to be counted on, were, generally speaking, conspicuously absent.

He and the Leyburns met, of course; for their list of common friends was
now considerable; but Agnes, reporting matters to Catherine, could only say
that each of these occasions left Rose more irritable, and more inclined to say
biting things as to the foolish ways in which society takes its pleasures.

Rose certainly was irritable, and at times, Agnes thought, depressed. But
as usual she was unapproachable about her own affairs, and the state of her
mind could only be somewhat dolefully gathered from the fact that she was
much less unwilling to go back to Burwood this summer than had ever been
known before.

Meanwhile, Mr. Flaxman left certain other people in no doubt as to his
intentions.

'My dear aunt,' he said calmly to Lady Charlotte, 'I mean to marry Miss
Leyburn if I can at any time persuade her to have me. So much you may take
as fixed, and it will be quite waste of breath on your part to quote dukes to
me. But the other factor in the problem is by no means fixed. Miss Leyburn
won't have me at present, and as for the future I have most salutary qualms.'

'Hugh!' interrupted Lady Charlotte angrily, 'as if you hadn't had the
mothers of London at your feet for years!'

Lady Charlotte was in a most variable frame of mind; one day hoping
devoutly that the Langham affair might prove lasting enough in its effects to
tire Hugh out; the next, outraged that a silly girl should waste a thought on
such a creature, while Hugh was in her way; at one time angry that an insignificant chit of a schoolmaster's daughter should apparently care so little to
be the Duke of Sedbergh's niece, and should even dare to allow herself the
luxury of snubbing a Flaxman; at another, utterly sceptical as to any lasting
obduracy on the chit's part. The girl was clearly anxious not to fall too easily,
but as to final refusal—pshaw! And it made her mad that Hugh would hold
himself so cheap.

Meanwhile, Mr. Flaxman felt himself in no way called upon to answer
that remark of his aunt's we have recorded.

'I have qualms,' he repeated, 'but I mean to do all I know, and you and
Helen must help me.'

Lady Charlotte crossed her hands before her.

'I may be a Liberal and a lion-hunter,' she said firmly, 'but I have still conscience enough left not to aid and abet my nephew in throwing himself away.'

She had nearly slipped in 'again'; but just saved herself.

'Your conscience is all a matter of the Duke,' he told her. 'Well, if you won't help me, then Helen and I will have to arrange it by ourselves.'

But this did not suit Lady Charlotte at all. She had always played the part of earthly providence to this particular nephew, and it was abominable to her that the wretch, having refused for ten years to provide her with a love affair to manage, should now manage one for himself in spite of her.

'You are such an arbitrary creature!' she said fretfully; 'you prance about the world like Don Quixote, and expect me to play Sancho without a murmur.'

'How many drubbings have I brought you yet?' he asked her, laughing.[80] He was really very fond of her. 'It is true there is a point of likeness; I won't take your advice. But then why don't you give me better? It is strange,' he added, musing; 'women talk to us about love as if we were too gross to understand it; and when they come to business, and they're not in it themselves, they show the temper of attorneys.'[81]

'Love!' cried Lady Charlotte nettled. 'Do you mean to tell me, Hugh, that you are really, *seriously* in love with that girl?'

'Well, I only know,' he said, thrusting his hands far into his pockets, 'that unless things mend I shall go out to California in the autumn and try ranching.'

Lady Charlotte burst into an angry laugh. He stood opposite to her, with his orchid in his buttonhole, himself the fine flower of civilisation. Ranching, indeed! However, he had done so many odd things in his life, that, as she knew, it was never quite safe to decline to take him seriously, and he looked at her now so defiantly, his clear greenish eyes so wide open and alert, that her will began to waver under the pressure of his.

'What do you want me to do, sir?'

His glance relaxed at once, and he laughingly explained to her that what he asked of her was to keep the prey in sight.

'I can do nothing for myself at present,' he said; 'I get on her nerves. She was in love with that black-haired, *enfant du siècle*,—or rather, she prefers to assume that she was—and I haven't given her time to forget him. A serious blunder, and I deserve to suffer for it. Very well, then, I retire, and I ask you and Helen to keep watch. Don't let her go. Make yourselves nice to her; and, in fact, spoil me a little now I am on the high road to forty, as you used to spoil me at fourteen.'

Mr. Flaxman sat down by his aunt and kissed her hand, after which Lady Charlotte was as wax before him. 'Thank heaven,' she reflected, 'in ten days

---

80 "he asked her, laughing": comma as per *SE* and *W*.
81 "he added, musing": comma as per *SE* and *W*.

the Duke and all of them go out of town.' Retribution, therefore, for wrong-doing would be tardy, if wrong-doing there must be. She could but ruefully reflect that after all the girl was beautiful and gifted; moreover, if Hugh would force her to befriend him in this criminality, there might be a certain joy in thereby vindicating those Liberal principles of hers, in which a scornful family had always refused to believe. So, being driven into it, she would fain have done it boldly and with a dash. But she could not rid her mind of the Duke, and her performance all through, as a matter of fact, was blundering.

However, she was for the time very gracious to Rose, being in truth really fond of her; and Rose, however high she might hold her little head, could find no excuse for quarrelling either with her or Lady Helen.

Towards the middle of June there was a grand ball given by Lady Fauntleroy at Fauntleroy House, to which the two Miss Leyburns, by Lady Helen's machinations, were invited. It was to be one of the events of the season, and when the cards arrived 'to have the honour of meeting their Royal Highnesses,' etc. etc., Mrs. Leyburn, good soul, gazed at them with eyes which grew a little moist under her spectacles. She wished Richard could have seen the girls dressed, 'just once.' But Rose treated the cards with no sort of tenderness. 'If one could but put them up to auction,' she said flippantly, holding them up, 'how many German opera tickets I should get for nothing! I don't know what Agnes feels. As for me, I have neither nerve enough for the people, nor money enough for the toilette.'

However, with eleven o'clock Lady Helen ran in, a fresh vision of blue and white, to suggest certain dresses for the sisters which had occurred to her in the visions of the night, 'original, adorable,—cost, a mere nothing!'

'My harpy,' she remarked, alluding to her dressmaker,'would ruin you over them, of course. Your maid'—the Leyburns possessed a remarkably clever one—'will make them divinely for twopence-halfpenny. Listen.'

Rose listened; her eye kindled; the maid was summoned; and the invitation accepted in Agnes's neatest hand. Even Catherine was roused during the following ten days to a smiling indulgent interest in the concerns of the workroom.

The evening came, and Lady Helen fetched the sisters in her carriage. The ball was a magnificent affair. The house was one of historical interest and importance, and all that the ingenuity of the present could do to give fresh life and gaiety to the pillared rooms, the carved galleries and stately staircases of the past, had been done. The ball-room, lined with Vandycks and Lelys, glowed softly with electric light; the picture gallery had been banked with flowers and carpeted with red, and the beautiful dresses of the women trailed up and down it, challenging the satins of the Netschers and the Terburgs on the walls.[82]

Rose's card was soon full to overflowing. The young men present were of the smartest, and would not willingly have bowed the knee to a nobody, however pretty. But Lady Helen's devotion, the girl's reputation as a musician, and her little nonchalant disdainful ways, gave her a kind of prestige, which made her, for the time being at any rate, the equal of anybody. Petitioners came and went away empty. Royalty was introduced, and smiled both upon the beauty and the beauty's delicate and becoming dress; and still Rose, though a good deal more flushed and erect than usual, and though flesh and blood could not resist the contagious pleasure which glistened even in the eyes of that sage Agnes, was more than half-inclined to say with the Preacher, that all was vanity.[83]

Presently, as she stood waiting with her hand on her partner's arm before gliding into a waltz, she saw Mr. Flaxman opposite to her, and with him a young *débutante* in white tulle—a thin, pretty, undeveloped creature, whose sharp elbows and timid movements, together with the blushing enjoyment glowing so frankly from her face, pointed her out as the school-girl of sweet seventeen, just emancipated, and trying her wings.

'Ah, there is Lady Florence!' said her partner, a handsome young Hussar. 'This ball is in her honour, you know. She comes out to-night. What, another cousin? Really she keeps too much in the family!'

'Is Mr. Flaxman a cousin?'

The young man replied that he was, and then, in the intervals of waltzing, went on to explain to her the relationships of many of the people present, till the whole gorgeous affair began to seem to Rose a mere family party. Mr. Flaxman was of it. She was not.

'Why am I here?' the little Jacobin said to herself fiercely as she waltzed; 'it is foolish, unprofitable. I do not belong to them, nor they to me!'

'Miss Leyburn! charmed to see you!' cried Lady Charlotte, stopping her; and then, in a loud whisper in her ear, 'Never saw you look better. Your taste, or Helen's, that dress? The roses—exquisite!'

Rose dropped her a little mock curtsey and whirled on again.

'*Lady Florences* are always well dressed,' thought the child angrily; 'and who notices it?'

---

82 Sir Anthony van Dyck (1599–1641), Sir Peter Lely (1618–1680), Caspar Netscher (1639–1684) and Gerard Terburg (1617–1681), all leading Dutch painters of the seventeenth century; van Dyck and Lely dominated English court painting during the period.

83 Ecclesiastes 1.2.

Another turn brought them against Mr. Flaxman and his partner. Mr. Flaxman came at once to greet her with smiling courtesy.

'I have a Cambridge friend to introduce to you—a beautiful youth. Shall I find you by Helen? Now, Lady Florence, patience a moment. That corner is too crowded. How good that last turn was!'

And bending with a sort of kind chivalry over his partner, who looked at him with the eyes of a joyous excited child, he led her away. Five minutes later Rose, standing flushed by Lady Helen, saw him coming again towards her, ushering a tall blue-eyed youth, whom he introduced to her as 'Lord Waynflete.' The handsome boy looked at her with a boy's open admiration, and beguiled her of a supper dance, while a group standing near, a mother and three daughters, stood watching with cold eyes and expressions which said plainly to the initiated that mere beauty was receiving a ridiculous amount of attention.

'I wouldn't have given it him, but it is *rude*—it is *bad manners*, not even to ask!' the supposed victress was saying to herself, with quivering lips, her eyes following not the Trinity freshman, who was their latest captive, but an older man's well-knit figure, and a head on which the fair hair was already growing scantily, receding a little from the fine intellectual brows.

An hour later she was again standing by Lady Helen, waiting for a partner, when she saw two persons crossing the room, which was just beginning to fill again for dancing, towards them. One was Mr. Flaxman, the other was a small wrinkled old man, who leant upon his arm, displaying the ribbon of the Garter as he walked.[84]

'Dear me,' said Lady Helen, a little fluttered, 'here is my uncle Sedbergh. I thought they had left town.'

The pair approached, and the old Duke bowed over his niece's hand with the manners of a past generation.

'I made Hugh give me an arm,' he said quaveringly. 'These floors are homicidal. If I come down on them I shall bring an action.'

'I thought you had all left town?' said Lady Helen.

'Who can make plans with a Government in power pledged to every sort of villainy and public plunder?' said the old man testily. 'I suppose Varley's there to-night, helping to vote away my property and Fauntleroy's.'

'Some of his own too, if you please!' said Lady Helen, smiling.[85] 'Yes, I suppose he is waiting for the division, or he would be here.'

'I wonder why Providence blessed *me* with such a Radical crew of

---

84 A Companion of the Order of the Garter, an honor conferred by the monarch.
85 "Lady Helen, smiling": comma as per *SE* and *W*.

relations?' remarked the Duke. 'Hugh is a regular Communist. I never heard such arguments in my life. And as for any idea of standing by his order——'

The old man shook his bald head and shrugged his small shoulders with almost French vivacity. He had been handsome once, and delicately featured, but now the left eye drooped, and the face had a strong look of peevishness and ill-health.

'Uncle,' interposed Lady Helen, 'let me introduce you to my two great friends, Miss Leyburn, Miss Rose Leyburn.'

The Duke bowed, looked at them through a pair of sharp eyes, seemed to cogitate inwardly whether such a name had ever been known to him, and turned to his nephew.

'Get me out of this, Hugh, and I shall be obliged to you. Young people may risk it, but if *I* broke I shouldn't mend.'

And still grumbling audibly about the floor, he hobbled off towards the picture gallery. Mr. Flaxman had only time for a smiling backward glance at Rose.

'Have you given my pretty boy a dance?'

'Yes,' she said, but with as much stiffness as she might have shown to his uncle.

'That's over,' said Lady Helen with relief. 'My uncle hardly meets any of us now without a spar. He has never forgiven my father for going over to the Liberals. And then he thinks we none of us consult him enough. No more we do—except Aunt Charlotte. *She's* afraid of him!'

'Lady Charlotte afraid!' echoed Rose.

'Odd, isn't it? The Duke avenges a good many victims on her, if they only knew!'

Lady Helen was called away, and Rose was left standing, wondering what had happened to her partner.

Opposite, Mr. Flaxman was pushing through a doorway, and Lady Florence was again on his arm. At the same time she became conscious of a morsel of chaperons' conversation such as, by the kind contrivances of fate, a girl is tolerably sure to hear under similar circumstances.

The *débutante's* good looks, Hugh Flaxman's apparent susceptibility to them, the possibility of results, and the satisfactory disposition of the family goods and chattels that would be brought about by such a match, the opportunity it would offer the man, too, of rehabilitating himself socially after his first matrimonial escapade—Rose caught fragments of all these topics as they were discussed by two old ladies, presumably also of the family 'ring,' who gossiped behind her with more gusto than discretion. Highmindedness, of course, told her to move away; something else held her fast, till her partner came up for her.

Then she floated away into the whirlwind of waltzers. But as she moved round the room on her partner's arm, her delicate half-scornful grace attracting look after look, the soul within was all aflame—aflame against the serried ranks and phalanxes of this unfamiliar, hostile world! She had just been reading Trevelyan's *Life of Fox* aloud to her mother, who liked occasionally to flavour her knitting with literature, and she began now to revolve a passage from it, describing the upper class of the last century, which had struck that morning on her quick retentive memory: "'*A few thousand people who thought that the world was made for them*"—did it not run so?—"*and that all outside their own fraternity were unworthy of notice or criticism, bestowed upon each other an amount of attention quite inconceivable.... Within the charmed precincts there prevailed an easy and natural mode of intercourse, in some respects singularly delightful.*"[86] Such, for instance, as the Duke of Sedbergh was master of! Well, it was worth while, perhaps, to have gained an experience, even at the expense of certain illusions, as to the manners of dukes, and—and—as to the constancy of friends. But never again—never again!' said the impetuous inner voice. 'I have my world—they theirs!'

But why so strong a flood of bitterness against our poor upper class, so well intentioned for all its occasional lack of lucidity, should have arisen in so young a breast it is a little difficult for the most conscientious biographer to explain. She had partners to her heart's desire; young Lord Waynflete used his utmost arts upon her to persuade her that at least half a dozen numbers of the regular programme were extras and therefore at his disposal; and when royalty supped, it was graciously pleased to ordain that Lady Helen and her two companions should sup behind the same folding-doors as itself, while beyond these doors surged the inferior crowd of persons who had been specially invited to 'meet their Royal Highnesses,' and had so far been held worthy neither to dance nor to eat in the same room with them. But in vain. Rose still felt herself, for all her laughing outward *insouciance*, a poor, bruised, helpless chattel, trodden under the heel of a world which was intolerably powerful, rich, and self-satisfied, the odious product of 'family arrangements.'

Mr. Flaxman sat far away at the same royal table as herself. Beside him was the thin tall *débutante*. 'She is like one of the Gainsborough princesses,' thought Rose, studying her with involuntary admiration. 'Of course it is all plain. He will get everything he wants, and a Lady Florence into the bargain.

---

86 George Otto Trevelyan (1838–1928), Liberal politician, author of *The Early History of Charles James Fox* (1880). The quotation appears in ch. 3.

Radical, indeed! What nonsense!'

Then it startled her to find that the eyes of Lady Florence's neighbour were, as it seemed, on herself; or was he merely nodding to Lady Helen?— and she began immediately to give a smiling attention to the man on her left.

An hour later she and Agnes and Lady Helen were descending the great staircase on their way to their carriage. The morning light was flooding through the chinks of the carefully veiled windows; Lady Helen was yawning behind her tiny white hand, her eyes nearly asleep. But the two sisters, who had not been up till three, on four preceding nights, like their chaperon, were still almost as fresh as the flowers massed in the hall below.

'Ah, there is Hugh!' cried Lady Helen. 'How I hope he has found the carriage!'

At that moment Rose slipped on a spray of gardenia, which had dropped from the bouquet of some predecessor. To prevent herself from falling downstairs, she caught hold of the stem of a brazen chandelier fixed in the balustrade. It saved her, but she gave her arm a most painful wrench, and leant limp and white against the railing of the stairs. Lady Helen turned at Agnes's exclamation, but before she could speak, as it seemed, Mr. Flaxman, who had been standing talking just below them, was on the stairs.

'You have hurt your arm? Don't speak—take mine. Let me get you downstairs out of the crush.'

She was too far gone to resist, and when she was mistress of herself again she found herself in the library with some water in her hand which Mr. Flaxman had just put there.

'Is it the playing hand?' said Lady Helen anxiously.

'No,' said Rose, trying to laugh; 'the bowing elbow.' And she raised it, but with a contortion of pain.

'Don't raise it,' he said peremptorily. 'We will have a doctor here in a moment, and have it bandaged.'

He disappeared. Rose tried to sit up, seized with a frantic longing to disobey him, and get off before he returned. Stinging the girl's mind was the sense that it might all perfectly well seem to him a planned appeal to his pity.

'Agnes, help me up,' she said with a little involuntary groan; 'I shall be better at home.'

But both Lady Helen and Agnes laughed her to scorn, and she lay back once more overwhelmed by fatigue and faintness. A few more minutes, and a doctor appeared, caught by good luck in the next street. He pronounced it a severe muscular strain, but nothing more; applied a lotion and improvised a sling. Rose consulted him anxiously as to the interference with her playing.

'A week,' he said; 'no more, if you are careful.'

Her pale face brightened. Her art had seemed specially dear to her of late.

'Hugh!' called Lady Helen, going to the door. '*Now* we are ready for the carriage.'

Rose leaning on Agnes walked out into the hall. They found him there waiting.

'The carriage is here,' he said, bending towards her with a look and tone which so stirred the fluttered nerves, that the sense of faintness stole back upon her. 'Let me take you to it.'

'Thank you,' she said coldly, but by a superhuman effort; 'my sister's help is quite enough.'

He followed them with Lady Helen. At the carriage door the sisters hesitated a moment. Rose was helpless without a right hand. A little imperative movement from behind displaced Agnes, and Rose felt herself hoisted in by a strong arm. She sank into the farther corner. The glow of the dawn caught her white delicate features, the curls on her temples, all the silken confusion of her dress. Hugh Flaxman put in Agnes and his sister, said something to Agnes about coming to inquire, and raised his hat. Rose caught the quick force and intensity of his eyes, and then closed her own, lost in a languid swoon of pain, memory, and resentful wonder.

Flaxman walked away down Park Lane through the chill morning quietness, the gathering light striking over the houses beside him on to the misty stretches of the Park. His hat was over his eyes, his hands thrust into his pockets; a close observer would have noticed a certain trembling of the lips. It was but a few seconds since her young warm beauty had been for an instant in his arms; his whole being was shaken by it, and by that last look of hers. 'Have I gone too far?' he asked himself anxiously. 'Is it divinely true—*already*—that she resents being left to herself? Oh, little rebel! You tried your best not to let me see. But you *were* angry, you were! Now, then, how to proceed? She is all fire, all character; I rejoice in it. She will give me trouble; so much the better. Poor little hurt thing! the fight is only beginning; but I will make her do penance some day for all that loftiness to-night.'

If these reflections betray to the reader a certain masterful note of confidence in Mr. Flaxman's mind, he will perhaps find small cause to regret that Rose *did* give him a great deal of trouble.

Nothing could have been more 'salutary,' to use his own word, than the dance she led him during the next three weeks. She provoked him indeed at moments so much that he was a hundred times on the point of trying to seize his kingdom of heaven by violence, of throwing himself upon her with a tempest shock of reproach and appeal. But some secret instinct restrained him. She was wilful, she was capricious; she had a real and powerful distraction in her art. He must be patient and risk nothing.

He suspected, too, what was the truth—that Lady Charlotte was doing harm. Rose, indeed, had grown so touchily sensitive that she found offence in almost every word of Lady Charlotte's about her nephew. Why should the apparently casual remarks of the aunt bear so constantly on the subject of the nephew's social importance? Rose vowed to herself that she needed no reminder of that station whereunto it had pleased God to call her, and that Lady Charlotte might spare herself all those anxieties and reluctances which the girl's quick sense detected, in spite of the invitations so freely showered on Lerwick Gardens.

The end of it all was that Hugh Flaxman found himself again driven into a corner. At the bottom of him was still a confidence that would not yield. Was it possible that he had ever given her some tiny involuntary glimpse of it, and that but for that glimpse she would have let him make his peace much more easily? At any rate, now he felt himself at the end of his resources.

'I must change the venue,' he said to himself; 'decidedly I must change the venue.'

So by the end of June he had accepted an invitation to fish in Norway with a friend, and was gone. Rose received the news with a callousness which made even Lady Helen want to shake her.

On the eve of his journey, however, Hugh Flaxman had at last confessed himself to Catherine and Robert. His obvious plight made any further scruples on their part futile, and what they had they gave him in the way of sympathy. Also Robert, gathering that he already knew much, and without betraying any confidence of Rose's, gave him a hint or two on the subject of Langham. But more not the friendliest mortal could do for him, and Flaxman went off into exile announcing to a mocking Elsmere that he should sit pensive on the banks of Norwegian rivers till fortune had had time to change.

BOOK VII - GAIN AND LOSS[1]

CHAPTER XLVI

A hot July had well begun, but still Elsmere was toiling on in Elgood Street, and could not persuade himself to think of a holiday. Catherine and the child he had driven away more than once, but the claims upon himself were becoming so absorbing he did not know how to go even for a few weeks. There were certain individuals in particular who depended on him from day to day. One was Charles Richards's widow. The poor desperate creature had put herself abjectly into Elsmere's hands. He had sent her to an asylum, where she had been kindly and skilfully treated, and after six weeks' abstinence she had just returned to her children, and was being watched by himself and a competent woman neighbour, whom he had succeeded in interesting in the case.

Another was a young 'secret springer,' to use the mysterious terms of the trade—Robson by name—whom Elsmere had originally known as a clever workman belonging to the watchmaking colony, and a diligent attendant from the beginning on the Sunday lectures. He was now too ill to leave his lodgings, and his sickly pessimist personality had established a special hold on Robert. He was dying of tumour in the throat, and had become a torment to himself and a disgust to others. There was a spark of wayward genius in him, however, which enabled him to bear his ills with a mixture of savage humour and clear-eyed despair. In general outlook he was much akin to the author of the *City of Dreadful Night*, whose poems he read; the loathsome spectacles of London had filled him with a kind of sombre energy of revolt against all that is.[2] And now that he could only work intermittently, he would sit brooding for hours, startling the fellow-workmen who came in to see him with ghastly Heine-like jokes on his own hideous disease, living no one exactly knew how, though it was supposed on supplies sent him by a shopkeeper uncle in the country, and constantly on the verge, as all his acquaintances felt, of some

---

1   An inversion of John Henry Newman's conversion novel *Loss and Gain* (1848).
2   James Thomson (1834–1882), whose *City of Dreadful Night* (1874) evokes a speaker wandering through a miserable London where no spiritual comfort is at hand.

ingenious expedient or other for putting an end to himself and his troubles.[3] He was unmarried, and a misogynist to boot. No woman willingly went near him, and he tended himself. How Robert had gained any hold upon him no one could guess. But from the moment when Elsmere, struck in the lecture-room by the pallid ugly face and swathed neck, began regularly to go and see him, the elder man felt instinctively that virtue had gone out of him,[4] and that in some subtle way yet another life had become pitifully, silently depend-ent on his own stock of strength and comfort.

His lecturing and teaching work also was becoming more and more the instrument of far-reaching change, and therefore more and more difficult to leave. The thoughts of God, the image of Jesus, which were active and fruitful in his own mind, had been gradually passing from the one into the many, and Robert watched the sacred transforming emotion, once nurtured at his own heart, now working among the crowd of men and women his fiery speech had gathered round him, with a trembling joy, a humble prostration of the soul before the Eternal Truth, no words can fitly describe. With an ever-increasing detachment of mind from the objects of self and sense, he felt himself a tool in the Great Workman's hand. 'Accomplish Thy purposes in me,' was the cry of his whole heart and life; 'use me to the utmost; spend every faculty I have, O "Thou who mouldest men"!'[5]

But in the end his work itself drove him away. A certain memorable Saturday evening brought it about. It had been his custom of late to spend an occasional evening hour after his night-school work in the North R——— Club, of which he was now by invitation a member. Here, in one of the in-ner rooms, he would stand against the mantelpiece chatting, smoking often with the men. Everything came up in turn to be discussed; and Robert was at least as ready to learn from the practical workers about him as to teach. But in general these informal talks and debates became the supplement of the Sunday lectures. Here he met Andrews and the Secularist crew face to face; here he grappled in Socratic fashion with objections and difficulties, throwing into the task all his charm and all his knowledge, a man at once of no preten-sions and of unfailing natural dignity. Nothing, so far, had served his cause and his influence so well as these moments of free discursive intercourse. The mere orator, the mere talker, indeed, would never have gained any permanent hold; but the life behind gave weight to every acute or eloquent word, and

---

3   Although struck down by a mysterious debilitating illness in 1848, Heine still managed some extremely dark humor about his eventually fatal condition.

4   Mark 5.30.

5   A slight misquotation from the penultimate stanza of Robert Browning, "Rabbi Ben Ezra" (1864).

importance even to those mere sallies of a boyish enthusiasm which were still common enough in him.

He had already visited the club once during the week preceding this Saturday. On both occasions there was much talk of the growing popularity and efficiency of the Elgood Street work, of the numbers attending the lectures, the story-telling, the Sunday school, and of the way in which the attractions of it had spread into other quarters of the parish, exciting there, especially among the clergy of St. Wilfrid's, an anxious and critical attention. The conversation on Saturday night, however, took a turn of its own. Robert felt in it a new and curious note of *responsibility*. The men present were evidently beginning to regard the work as *their* work also, and its success as their interest. It was perfectly natural, for not only had most of them been his supporters and hearers from the beginning, but some of them were now actually teaching in the night-school or helping in the various branches of the large and overflowing boys' club. He listened to them for a while in his favourite attitude, leaning against the mantelpiece, throwing in a word or two now and then as to how this or that part of the work might be amended or expanded. Then suddenly a kind of inspiration seemed to pass from them to him. Bending forward as the talk dropped a moment, he asked them, with an accent more emphatic than usual, whether in view of this collaboration of theirs, which was becoming more valuable to him and his original helpers every week, it was not time for a new departure.

'Suppose I drop my dictatorship,' he said, 'suppose we set up parliamentary government, are you ready to take your share? Are you ready to combine, to commit yourselves? Are you ready for an effort to turn this work into something lasting and organic?'

The men gathered round him smoked on in silence for a minute. Old Macdonald, who had been sitting contentedly puffing away in a corner peculiarly his own, and dedicated to the glorification—in broad Berwickshire—of the experimental philosophers, laid down his pipe and put on his spectacles, that he might grasp the situation better. Then Lestrange, in a dry cautious way, asked Elsmere to explain himself further.

Robert began to pace up and down, talking out his thought, his eye kindling.

But in a minute or two he stopped abruptly, with one of those striking rapid gestures characteristic of him.

'But no mere social and educational body, mind you!' and his bright commanding look swept round the circle. 'A good thing surely, "yet is there better than it."[6] The real difficulty of every social effort—you know it and I know it—lies, not in the planning of the work, but in the kindling of will and passion enough to carry it *through*. And that can only be done by religion—by faith.'

He went back to his old leaning attitude, his hands behind him. The men gazed at him—at the slim figure, the transparent changing face—with a kind of fascination, but were still silent, till Macdonald said slowly, taking off his glasses again and clearing his throat—

'You'll be aboot starrtin' a new church, I'm thinkin', Misther Elsmere?'

'If you like,' said Robert impetuously. 'I have no fear of the great words. You can do nothing by despising the past and its products; you can also do nothing by being too much afraid of them, by letting them choke and stifle your own life. Let the new wine have its new bottles if it must, and never mind words.[7] Be content to be a new "sect," "conventicle," or what not, so long as you feel that you are *something* with a life and purpose of its own, in this tangle of a world.'

Again he paused with knit brows, thinking. Lestrange sat with his elbows on his knees studying him, the spare gray hair brushed back tightly from the bony face, on the lips the slightest Voltairean smile. Perhaps it was the coolness of his look which insensibly influenced Robert's next words.

'However, I don't imagine we should call ourselves a church! Something much humbler will do, if you choose ever to make anything of these suggestions of mine. "Association," "society," "brotherhood," what you will! But always, if I can persuade you, with something in the name, and everything in the body itself, to show that for the members of it life rests still, as all life worth having has everywhere rested on *trust* and *memory*!—*trust* in the God of experience and history; *memory* of that God's work in man, by which alone we know Him and can approach Him. Well, of that work—I have tried to prove it to you a thousand times—Jesus of Nazareth has become to *us*, by the evolution of circumstance, the most moving, the most efficacious of all types and epitomes. We have made our protest—we are daily making it—in the face of society, against the fictions and overgrowths which at the present time are excluding him more and more from human love. But now, suppose we turn our backs on negation, and have done with mere denial! Suppose we throw all our energies into the practical building of a new house of faith, the gathering and organising of a new Company of Jesus!'

Other men had been stealing in while he was speaking. The little room

---

6   Arthur Hugh Clough, "Hope Evermore and Believe!", l. 24.

7   Variant of Luke 5.38, Mark 2.22, or Matthew 9.17.

was nearly full. It was strange, the contrast between the squalid modernness of the scene, with its incongruous sights and sounds, the Club-room, painted in various hideous shades of cinnamon and green, the smoke, the lines and groups of working-men in every sort of working dress, the occasional rumbling of huge waggons past the window, the click of glasses and cups in the refreshment bar outside, and this stir of spiritual passion which any competent observer might have felt sweeping through the little crowd as Robert spoke, connecting what was passing there with all that is sacred and beautiful in the history of the world.

After another silence a young fellow, in a shabby velvet coat, stood up. He was commonly known among his fellow-potters as 'the hartist,' because of his long hair, his little affectations of dress, and his æsthetic susceptibilities generally. The wits of the Club made him their target, but the teasing of him that went on was more or less tempered by the knowledge that in his own queer way he had brought up and educated two young sisters almost from infancy, and that his sweetheart had been killed before his eyes a year before in a railway accident.

'I dun know,' he said in a high treble voice, 'I dun know whether I speak for anybody but myself—very likely not; but what I *do* know,' and he raised his right hand and shook it with a gesture of curious felicity, 'is this—what Mr. Elsmere starts I'll join; where he goes I'll go; what's good enough for him's good enough for me. He's put a new heart and a new stomach into me, and what I've got he shall have, whenever it pleases 'im to call for it! So if he wants to run a new thing against or alongside the old uns, and he wants me to help him with it—I don't know as I'm very clear what he's driving at, nor what good I can do 'im—but when Tom Wheeler's asked for he'll be there!'

A deep murmur, rising almost into a shout of assent ran through the little assembly. Robert bent forward, his eye glistening, a moved acknowledgment in his look and gesture. But in reality a pang ran through the fiery soul. It was 'the personal estimate,' after all, that was shaping their future and his, and the idealist was up in arms for his idea, sublimely jealous lest any mere personal fancy should usurp its power and place.

A certain amount of desultory debate followed as to the possible outlines of a possible organisation, and as to the observances which might be devised to mark its religious character. As it flowed on the atmosphere grew more and more electric. A new passion, though still timid and awestruck, seemed to shine from the looks of the men standing or sitting round the central figure. Even Lestrange lost his smile under the pressure of that strange subdued expectancy about him; and when Robert walked homeward, about midnight, there weighed upon him an almost awful sense of crisis, of an expanding future.

He let himself in softly and went into his study. There he sank into a chair and fainted. He was probably not unconscious very long, but after he had struggled back to his senses, and was lying stretched on the sofa among the books with which it was littered, the solitary candle in the big room throwing weird shadows about him, a moment of black depression overtook him. It was desolate and terrible, like a prescience of death. How was it he had come to feel so ill? Suddenly, as he looked back over the preceding weeks, the physical weakness and disturbance which had marked them, and which he had struggled through, paying as little heed as possible, took shape, spectre-like, in his mind.

And at the same moment a passionate rebellion against weakness and disablement arose in him. He sat up dizzily, his head in his hands.

'Rest—strength,' he said to himself, with strong inner resolve, 'for the work's sake!'

He dragged himself up to bed and said nothing to Catherine till the morning. Then, with boyish brightness, he asked her to take him and the babe off without delay to the Norman coast, vowing that he would lounge and idle for six whole weeks if she would let him. Shocked by his looks, she gradually got from him the story of the night before. As he told it, his swoon was a mere untoward incident and hindrance in a spiritual drama, the thrill of which, while he described it, passed even to her. The contrast, however, between the strong hopes she felt pulsing through him, and his air of fragility and exhaustion, seemed to melt the heart within her, and make her whole being, she hardly knew why, one sensitive dread. She sat beside him, her head laid against his shoulder, oppressed by a strange and desolate sense of her comparatively small share in this ardent life. In spite of his tenderness and devotion, she felt often as though he were no longer hers—as though a craving hungry world, whose needs were all dark and unintelligible to her, were asking him from her, claiming to use as roughly and prodigally as it pleased the quick mind and delicate frame.

As to the schemes developing round him, she could not take them in whether for protest or sympathy. She could think only of where to go, what doctor to consult, how she could persuade him to stay away long enough.

There was little surprise in Elgood Street when Elsmere announced that he must go off for a while. He so announced it that everybody who heard him understood that his temporary withdrawal was to be the mere preparation for a great effort—the vigil before the tourney; and the eager friendliness with which he was met sent him off in good heart.

Three or four days later he, Catherine and Mary were at Petites Dalles, a little place on the Norman coast, near Fécamp, with which he had first made acquaintance years before, when he was at Oxford.

Here all that in London had been oppressive in the August heat suffered 'a sea change,' and became so much matter for physical delight. It was fiercely hot indeed. Every morning, between five and six o'clock, Catherine would stand by the little white-veiled window, in the dewy silence, to watch the eastern shadows spreading sharply already into a blazing world of sun, and see the tall poplar just outside shooting into a quivering changeless depth of blue. Then, as early as possible, they would sally forth before the glare became unbearable. The first event of the day was always Mary's bathe, which gradually became a spectacle for the whole beach, so ingenious were the blandishments of the father who wooed her into the warm sandy shallows, and so beguiling the glee and pluck of the two-year-old English *bébé*. By eleven the heat out of doors grew intolerable, and they would stroll back—father and mother and trailing child—past the hotels on the *plage*, along the irregular village lane, to the little house where they had established themselves, with Mary's nurse and a French *bonne* to look after them; would find the green wooden shutters drawn close; the *déjeuner* waiting for them in the cool bare room; and the scent of the coffee penetrating from the kitchen, where the two maids kept up a dumb but perpetual warfare.[8] Then afterwards Mary, emerging from her sun-bonnet, would be tumbled into her white bed upstairs, and lie, a flushed image of sleep, till the patter of her little feet on the boards which alone separated one storey from the other, warned mother and nurse that an imp of mischief was let loose again. Meanwhile Robert, in the carpetless *salon*, would lie back in the rickety armchair which was its only luxury, lazily dozing and dreaming, Balzac, perhaps, in his hand, but quite another *comédie humaine* unrolling itself vaguely meanwhile in the contriving optimist mind.[9]

Petites Dalles was not fashionable yet, though it aspired to be; but it could boast of a deputy, and a senator, and a professor of the Collège de France, as good as any at Étretat, a tired journalist or two, and a sprinkling of Rouen men of business. Robert soon made friends among them, *more suo*, by dint of a rough-and-ready French, spoken with the most unblushing accent imaginable, and lounged along the sands through many an amusing and

---

8   Beach ... maid ... lunch.

9   Honoré de Balzac (1799–1850), French realist novelist, many of whose works belonged to his chronicle of nineteenth-century France, *La Comédie Humaine*.

sociable hour with one or other of his new acquaintances.

But by the evening husband and wife would leave the crowded beach, and mount by some tortuous dusty way on to the high plateau through which was cleft far below the wooded fissure of the village. Here they seemed to have climbed the beanstalk into a new world. The rich Normandy country lay all round them—the cornfields, the hedgeless tracts of white-flowered lucerne or crimson clover, dotted by the orchard trees which make one vast garden of the land as one sees it from a height. On the fringe of the cliff, where the soil became too thin and barren even for French cultivation, there was a wild belt, half heather, half tangled grass and flower-growth, which the English pair loved for their own special reasons. Bathed in light, cooled by the evening wind, the patches of heather glowing, the tall grasses swaying in the breeze, there were moments when its wide, careless, dusty beauty reminded them poignantly, and yet most sweetly, of the home of their first unclouded happiness, of the Surrey commons and wildernesses.

One evening they were sitting in the warm dusk by the edge of a little dip of heather sheltered by a tuft of broom, when suddenly they heard the purring sound of the night-jar, and immediately after the bird itself lurched past them, and as it disappeared into the darkness they caught several times the characteristic click of the wing.

Catherine raised her hand and laid it on Robert's. The sudden tears dropped on to her cheeks.

'Did you hear it, Robert?'

He drew her to him. These involuntary signs of an abiding pain in her always smote him to the heart.

'I am not unhappy, Robert,' she said at last, raising her head. 'No; if you will only get well and strong. I have submitted. It is not for myself, but——'

For what then? Merely the touchingness of mortal things as such?—of youth, of hope, of memory?

Choking down a sob, she looked seaward over the curling flame-coloured waves, while he held her hand close and tenderly. No—she was not unhappy. Something, indeed, had gone for ever out of that early joy. Her life had been caught and nipped in the great inexorable wheel of things. It would go in some sense maimed to the end. But the bitter self-torturing of that first endless year was over. Love, and her husband, and the thousand subtle forces of a changing world had conquered. She would live and die steadfast to the old faiths. But her present mind and its outlook was no more the mind of her early married life than the Christian philosophy of to-day is the Christian philosophy of the Middle Ages. She was not conscious of change, but change there was.

She had, in fact, undergone that dissociation of the moral judgment from a special series of religious formulæ which is the crucial, the epoch-making fact of our day. 'Unbelief,' says the orthodox preacher, 'is sin, and implies it': and while he speaks, the saint in the unbeliever gently smiles down his argument, and suddenly, in the rebel of yesterday men see the rightful heir of to-morrow.

CHAPTER XLVII

Meanwhile the Leyburns were at Burwood again. Rose's summer, indeed, was much varied by visits to country houses—many of them belonging to friends and acquaintances of the Flaxman family—by concerts, and the demands of several new and exciting artistic friendships. But she was seldom loth to come back to the little bare valley and the gray-walled house. Even the rain which poured down in August, quite unabashed by any consciousness of fine weather elsewhere, was not as intolerable to her as in past days.

The girl was not herself; there was visible in her not only that general softening and deepening of character which had been the consequence of her trouble in the spring, but a painful *ennui* she could hardly disguise, a longing for she knew not what. She was beginning to take the homage paid to her gift and her beauty with a quiet dignity, which was in no sense false modesty, but implied a certain clearness of vision, curious and disquieting in so young and dazzling a creature. And when she came home from her travels she would develop a taste for long walks, breasting the mountains in rain or sun, penetrating to their austerest solitudes alone, as though haunted by that profound saying of Obermann, 'Man is not made for enjoyment only—*la tristesse fait aussi partie de ses vastes besoins.*'[10]

What, indeed, was it that ailed her? In her lonely moments, especially in those moments among the high fells, beside some little tarn or streamlet, while the sheets of mist swept by her, or the great clouds dappled the spreading sides of the hills, she thought often of Langham—of that first thrill of passion which had passed through her, delusive and abortive, like one of those first thrills of spring which bring out the buds, only to provide victims for the frost. Now with her again 'a moral east wind was blowing.'[11] The passion was

---

10 Not in *Obermann*, actually, but Senancour's *Libres Méditations d'un Solitaire Inconnu* (Paris: P. Mongie Aîné, 1819), 262-63.

11 "Moral east wind" was a common turn of phrase. (Cf. Mr. Jarndyce in Charles Dickens' *Bleak House*, grumbling about the East Wind.) Ward may be thinking of Matthew Arnold's comment about Thomas Gray in the essay "Thomas Gray": "A sort of spiritual east wind was at that time blowing; neither Butler nor Gray could flower."

gone. The thought of Langham still roused in her a pity that seemed to strain at her heartstrings. But was it really she, really this very Rose, who had rested for that one intoxicating instant on his breast? She felt a sort of bitter shame over her own shallowness of feeling. She must surely be a poor creature, else how could such a thing have befallen her and have left so little trace behind?

And then, her hand dabbling in the water, her face raised to the blind friendly mountains, she would go dreaming far afield. Little vignettes of London would come and go on the inner retina; smiles and sighs would follow one another.

'*How kind he was that time! how amusing this!*'

Or, '*How provoking he was that afternoon! how cold that evening!*'

Nothing else—the pronoun remained ambiguous.

'I want a friend!' she said to herself once as she was sitting far up in the bosom of High Fell, 'I want a friend badly. Yet my lover deserts me, and I send away my friend!'

One afternoon Mrs. Thornburgh, the vicar, and Rose were wandering round the churchyard together, enjoying a break of sunny weather after days of rain. Mrs. Thornburgh's personal accent, so to speak, had grown perhaps a little more defined, a little more emphatic even, than when we first knew her. The vicar, on the other hand, was a trifle grayer, a trifle more submissive, as though on the whole, in the long conjugal contest of life, he was getting clearly worsted as the years went on. But the performance through which his wife was now taking him tried him exceptionally, and she only kept him to it with difficulty. She had had an attack of bronchitis in the spring, and was still somewhat delicate—a fact which to his mind gave her an unfair advantage of him. For she would make use of it to keep constantly before him ideas which he disliked, and in which he considered she took a morbid and unbecoming pleasure. The vicar was of opinion that when his latter end overtook him he should meet it on the whole as courageously as other men. But he was altogether averse to dwelling upon it, or the adjuncts of it, beforehand. Mrs. Thornburgh, however, since her illness had awoke to that inquisitive affectionate interest in these very adjuncts which many women feel. And it was extremely disagreeable to the vicar.

At the present moment she was engaged in choosing the precise spots in the little churchyard where it seemed to her it would be pleasant to rest. There was one corner in particular which attracted her, and she stood now looking at it with measuring eyes and dissatisfied mouth.

'William, I wish you would come here and help me!'

The vicar took no notice, but went on talking to Rose.

'William!' imperatively.

The vicar turned unwillingly.

'You know, William, if you wouldn't mind lying with your feet *that* way, there would be just room for me. But, of course, if you *will* have them the other way——' The shoulders in the old black silk mantle went up, and the gray curls shook dubiously.

The vicar's countenance showed plainly that he thought the remark worse than irrelevant.

'My dear,' he said crossly, 'I am not thinking of those things, nor do I wish to think of them. Everything has its time and place. It is close on tea, and Miss Rose says she must be going home.'

Mrs. Thornburgh again shook her head, this time with a disapproving sigh.

'You talk, William,' she said severely, 'as if you were a young man, instead of being turned sixty-six last birthday.'

And again she measured the spaces with her eye, checking the results aloud. But the vicar was obdurately deaf. He strolled on with Rose, who was chattering to him about a visit to Manchester, and the little church gate clicked behind them. Hearing it, Mrs. Thornburgh relaxed her measurements. They were only really interesting to her after all when the vicar was by. She hurried after them as fast as her short squat figure would allow, and stopped midway to make an exclamation.

'A carriage!' she said, shading her eyes with a very plump hand, 'stopping at Greybarns!'

The one road of the valley was visible from the churchyard, winding along the bottom of the shallow green trough, for at least two miles. Greybarns was a farmhouse just beyond Burwood, about half a mile away.

Mrs. Thornburgh moved on, her matronly face aglow with interest.

'Mary Jenkinson taken ill!' she said. 'Of course, that's Doctor Baker! Well, it's to be hoped it won't be twins *this* time. But, as I told her last Sunday, "It's constitutional, my dear." I knew a woman who had three pairs! Five o'clock now. Well, about *seven* it'll be worth while sending to inquire.'

When she overtook the vicar and his companion, she began to whisper certain particulars into the ear that was not on Rose's side. The vicar, who, like Uncle Toby, was possessed of a fine natural modesty, would have preferred that his wife should refrain from whispering on these topics in Rose's presence.[12] But he submitted lest opposition should provoke her into still more

---

12 From Laurence Sterne's *The Life and Adventures of Tristram Shandy, Gentleman* (1759–67). Uncle Toby has "a most extreme and unparalleled modesty of

audible improprieties; and Rose walked on a step or two in front of the pair, her eyes twinkling a little. At the vicarage gate she was let off without the customary final gossip. Mrs. Thornburgh was so much occupied in the fate hanging over Mary Jenkinson that she, for once, forgot to catechise Rose as to any marriageable young men she might have come across in a recent visit to a great country-house of the neighbourhood; an operation which formed the invariable pendant to any of Rose's absences.

So, with a smiling nod to them both, the girl turned homewards. As she did so she became aware of a man's figure walking along the space of road between Greybarns and Burwood, the western light behind it.

Dr. Baker? But even granting that Mrs. Jenkinson had brought him five miles on a false alarm, in the provoking manner of matrons, the shortest professional visit could not be over in this time.

She looked again, shading her eyes. She was nearing the gate of Burwood, and involuntarily slackened step. The man who was approaching, catching sight of the slim girlish figure in the broad hat and pink and white cotton dress, hurried up. The colour rushed to Rose's cheek. In another minute she and Hugh Flaxman were face to face.

She could not hide her astonishment.

'Why are you not in Scotland?' she said after she had given him her hand. 'Lady Helen told me last week she expected you in Ross-shire.'

Directly the words left her mouth she felt she had given him an opening. And why had Nature plagued her with this trick of blushing?

'Because I am here!' he said smiling, his keen dancing eyes looking down upon her. He was bronzed as she had never seen him. And never had he seemed to bring with him such an atmosphere of cool pleasant strength. 'I have slain so much since the first of July that I can slay no more. I am not like other men. The Nimrod in me is easily gorged, and goes to sleep after a while.[13] So this is Burwood?

He had caught her just on the little sweep leading to the gate, and now his eye swept quickly over the modest old house, with its trim garden, its overgrown porch and open casement windows. She dared not ask him again why he was there. In the properest manner she invited him 'to come in and see mamma.'

'I hope Mrs. Leyburn is better than she was in town? I shall be delighted to see her. But must you go in so soon? I left my carriage half a mile below, and have been revelling in the sun and air. I am loth to go indoors yet awhile.

---

nature" (ch. 21).

13 The "mighty one," "the mighty hunter before the Lord," Genesis 10.8-9.

Are you busy? Would it trouble you to put me in the way to the head of the valley? Then, if you will allow me, I will present myself later.'

Rose thought his request as little in the ordinary line of things as his appearance. But she turned and walked beside him, pointing out the crags at the head, the great sweep of High Fell, and the pass over to Ullswater, with as much *sangfroid* as she was mistress of.

He, on his side, informed her that on his way to Scotland he had bethought himself that he had never seen the Lakes, that he had stopped at Whinborough, was bent on walking over the High Fell pass to Ullswater, and making his way thence to Ambleside, Grasmere, and Keswick.

'But you are much too late to-day to get to Ullswater?' cried Rose incautiously.

'Certainly. You see my hotel,' and he pointed, smiling, to a white farmhouse standing just at the bend of the valley, where the road turned towards Whinborough. 'I persuaded the good woman there to give me a bed for the night, took my carriage a little farther, then, knowing I had friends in these parts, I came on to explore.'

Rose angrily felt her flush getting deeper and deeper.

'You are the first tourist,' she said coolly, 'who has ever stayed in Whindale.'

'Tourist! I repudiate the name. I am a worshipper at the shrine of Wordsworth and Nature. Helen and I long ago defined a tourist as a being with straps. I defy you to discover a strap about me, and I left my Murray in the railway carriage.'[14]

He looked at her laughing. She laughed too. The infection of his strong sunny presence was irresistible. In London it had been so easy to stand on her dignity, to remember whenever he was friendly that the night before he had been distant. In these green solitudes it was not easy to be anything but natural—the child of the moment!

'You are neither more practical nor more economical than when I saw you last,' she said demurely. 'When did you leave Norway?'

They wandered on past the vicarage talking fast. Mr. Flaxman, who had been joined for a time, on his fishing tour, by Lord Waynflete, was giving her an amusing account of the susceptibility to titles shown by the primitive democrats of Norway. As they passed a gap in the vicarage hedge, laughing and chatting. Rose became aware of a window and a gray head hastily withdrawn. Mr. Flaxman was puzzled by the merry flash, instantly suppressed, that shot across her face.

14　One of the Murray Handbooks, early tourist guides published by the firm of John Murray.

Presently they reached the hamlet of High Close, and the house where Mary Backhouse died, and where her father and the poor bedridden Jim still lived. They mounted the path behind it, and plunged into the hazel plantation which had sheltered Robert and Catherine on a memorable night. But when they were through it, Rose turned to the right along a scrambling path leading to the top of the first great shoulder of High Fell. It was a steep climb, though a short one, and it seemed to Rose that when she had once let him help her over a rock her hand was never her own again. He kept it an almost constant prisoner on one pretext or another till they were at the top.

Then she sank down on a rock out of breath. He stood beside her, lifting his brown wideawake from his brow. The air below had been warm and relaxing. Here it played upon them both with a delicious life-giving freshness. He looked round on the great hollow bosom of the fell, the crags buttressing it on either hand, the winding greenness of the valley, the white sparkle of the river.

'It reminds me a little of Norway. The same austere and frugal beauty— the same bare valley floors. But no pines, no peaks, no fiords!'

'No!' said Rose scornfully, 'we are not Norway, and we are not Switzerland. To prevent disappointment, I may at once inform you that we have no glaciers, and that there is perhaps only one place in the district where a man who was not an idiot could succeed in killing himself.'

He looked at her, calmly smiling.

'You are angry,' he said, 'because I make comparisons. You are wholly on a wrong scent. I never saw a scene in the world that pleased me half as much as this bare valley, that gray roof'—and he pointed to Burwood among its trees—'and this knoll of rocky ground.'

His look travelled back to her, and her eyes sank beneath it. He threw himself down on the short grass beside her.

'It rained this morning,' she still had the spirit to murmur under her breath.

He took not the smallest heed.

'Do you know,' he said—and his voice dropped—'can you guess at all why I am here to-day?'

'You had never seen the Lakes,' she repeated in a prim voice, her eyes still cast down, the corners of her mouth twitching. 'You stopped at Whinborough, intending to take the pass over to Ullswater, thence to make your way to Ambleside and Keswick—or was it to Keswick and Ambleside?'

She looked up innocently. But the flashing glance she met abashed her again.

'*Taquine!*' he said, 'but you shall not laugh me out of countenance.[15] If I said all that to you just now, may I be forgiven. One purpose, one only, brought me from Norway, forbade me to go to Scotland, drew me to Whinborough, guided me up your valley—the purpose of seeing your face!'

It could not be said at that precise moment that he had attained it. Rather she seemed bent on hiding that face quite away from him. It seemed to him an age before, drawn by the magnetism of his look, her hands dropped, and she faced him, crimson, her breath fluttering a little. Then she would have spoken, but he would not let her. Very tenderly and quietly his hand possessed itself of hers as he knelt beside her.

'I have been in exile for two months—you sent me. I saw that I troubled you in London. You thought I was pursuing you—pressing you. Your manner said "Go!" and I went. But do you think that for one day, or hour, or moment I have thought of anything else in those Norway woods but of you and of this blessed moment when I should be at your feet, as I am now?'

She trembled. Her hand seemed to leap in his. His gaze melted, enwrapped her. He bent forward. In another moment her silence would have so answered for her that his covetous arms would have stolen about her for good and all. But suddenly a kind of shiver ran through her—a shiver which was half memory, half shame. She drew back violently, covering her eyes with her hand.

'Oh no, no!' she cried, and her other hand struggled to get free, 'don't, don't talk to me so—I have a—a—confession.'

He watched her, his lips trembling a little, a smile of the most exquisite indulgence and understanding dawning in his eyes. Was she going to confess to him what he knew so well already? If he could only force her to say it on his breast.

But she held him at arm's length.

'You remember—you remember Mr. Langham?'

'Remember him!' echoed Mr. Flaxman fervently.

'That thought-reading night at Lady Charlotte's, on the way home, he spoke to me. I said I loved him. I *did* love him; I let him kiss me!'

Her flush had quite faded. He could hardly tell whether she was yielding or defiant as the words burst from her.

An expression, half trouble, half compunction, came into his face.

'I knew,' he said very low; 'or rather, I guessed.' And for an instant it occurred to him to unburden himself, to ask her pardon for that espionage of his. But no, no; not till he had her safe. 'I guessed, I mean, that there had

---

15 Tease.

been something grave between you. I saw you were sad. I would have given the world to comfort you.'

Her lip quivered childishly.

'I said I loved him that night. The next morning he wrote to me that it could never be.'

He looked at her a moment embarrassed. The conversation was not easy. Then the smile broke once more.

'And you have forgotten him as he deserved. If I were not sure of that I could wish him all the tortures of the *Inferno*! As it is, I cannot think of him; I cannot let you think of him. Sweet, do you know that ever since I first saw you the one thought of my days, the dream of my nights, the purpose of my whole life, has been to win you? There was another in the field; I knew it. I stood by and waited. He failed you—I knew he must in some form or other. Then I was hasty, and you resented it. Little tyrant, you made yourself a Rose with many thorns! But, tell me, tell me, it is all over—your pain, my waiting. Make yourself sweet to me! unfold to me at last?'

An instant she wavered. His bliss was almost in his grasp. Then she sprang up, and Flaxman found himself standing by her, rebuffed and surprised.

'No, no!' she cried, holding out her hands to him though all the time. 'Oh, it is too soon! I should despise myself, I do despise myself. It tortures me that I can change and forget so easily; it ought to torture you. Oh, don't ask me yet to—to——'

'To be my wife,' he said calmly, his cheek a little flushed, his eye meeting hers with a passion in it that strove so hard for self-control it was almost sternness.

'Not yet!' she pleaded, and then, after a moment's hesitation, she broke into the most appealing smiles, though the tears were in her eyes, hurrying out the broken, beseeching words. 'I want a friend so much—a real friend. Since Catherine left I have had no one. I have been running riot. Take me in hand. Write to me, scold me, advise me, I will be your pupil, I will tell you everything. You seem to me so fearfully wise, so much older. Oh, don't be vexed. And—and—in six months——'

She turned away, rosy as her name. He held her still, so rigidly, that her hands were almost hurt. The shadow of the hat fell over her eyes; the delicate outlines of the neck and shoulders in the pretty pale dress were defined against the green hill background. He studied her deliberately, a hundred different expressions sweeping across his face. A debate of the most feverish interest was going on within him. Her seriousness at the moment, the chances of the future, her character, his own—all these knotty points entered into it, had to be weighed and decided with lightning rapidity. But Hugh Flaxman was born under a lucky star, and the natal charm held good.

At last he gave a long breath; he stooped and kissed her hands.

'So be it. For six months I will be your guardian, your friend, your teasing implacable censor. At the end of that time I will be—well, never mind what. I give you fair warning.'

He released her. Rose clasped her hands before her and stood drooping. Now that she had gained her point, all her bright mocking independence seemed to have vanished. She might have been in reality the tremulous timid child she seemed. His spirits rose; he began to like the rôle she had assigned to him. The touch of unexpectedness, in all she said and did, acted with exhilarating force on his fastidious romantic sense.

'Now, then,' he said, picking up her gloves from the grass, 'you have given me my rights; I will begin to exercise them at once. I must take you home, the clouds are coming up again, and on the way will you kindly give me a full, true, and minute account of these two months during which you have been so dangerously left to your own devices?'

She hesitated, and began to speak with difficulty, her eyes on the ground. But by the time they were in the main Shanmoor path again, and she was not so weakly dependent on his physical aid, her spirits too returned. Pacing along with her hands behind her, she began by degrees to throw into her accounts of her various visits and performances plenty of her natural malice.

And after a bit, as that strange storm of feeling which had assailed her on the mountain-top abated something of its bewildering force, certain old grievances began to raise very lively heads in her. The smart of Lady Fauntleroy's ball was still there; she had not yet forgiven him all those relations; and the teasing image of Lady Florence woke up in her.

'It seems to me,' he said at last drily, as he opened a gate for her not far from Burwood, 'that you have been making yourself agreeable to a vast number of people. In my new capacity of censor I should like to warn you that there is nothing so bad for the character as universal popularity.'

'*I* have not got a thousand and one important cousins!' she exclaimed, her lip curling. 'If I want to please, I must take pains, else "nobody minds me."'

He looked at her attentively, his handsome face aglow with animation.

'What can you mean by that?' he said slowly.

But she was quite silent, her head well in air.

'Cousins?' he repeated. 'Cousins? And clearly meant as a taunt at me! Now when did you see my cousins? I grant that I possess a monstrous and indefensible number. I have it. You think that at Lady Fauntleroy's ball I devoted myself too much to my family, and too little to——'

'Not at all!' cried Rose hastily, adding, with charming incoherence, while she twisted a sprig of honeysuckle in her restless fingers, '*Some* cousins of course are pretty.'

He paused an instant: then a light broke over his face, and his burst of quiet laughter was infinitely pleasant to hear. Rose got redder and redder. She realised dimly that she was hardly maintaining the spirit of their contract, and that he was studying her with eyes inconveniently bright and penetrating.

'Shall I quote to you,' he said, 'a sentence of Sterne's? If it violate our contract I must plead extenuating circumstances. Sterne is admonishing a young friend as to his manners in society: "You are in love," he says. "*Tant mieux.* But do not imagine that the fact bestows on you a licence to behave like a bear towards all the rest of the world. *Affection may surely conduct thee through an avenue of women to her who possesses thy heart without tearing the flounces of any of their petticoats*"—not even those of little cousins of seventeen![16] I say this, you will observe, in the capacity you have assigned me. In another capacity I venture to think I could justify myself still better.'

'My guardian and director,' cried Rose, 'must not begin his functions by misleading and sophistical quotations from the classics!'

He did not answer for a moment. They were at the gate of Burwood, under a thick screen of wild cherry trees. The gate was half open, and his hand was on it.

'And my pupil,' he said, bending to her, 'must not begin by challenging the prisoner whose hands she has bound, or he will not answer for the consequences!'

His words were threatening, but his voice, his fine expressive face, were infinitely sweet. By a kind of fascination she never afterwards understood, Rose for answer startled him and herself. She bent her head; she laid her lips on the hand which held the gate, and then she was through it in an instant. He followed her in vain. He never overtook her till at the drawing-room door she paused with amazing dignity.

'Mamma,' she said, throwing it open, 'here is Mr. Flaxman. He is come from Norway, and is on his way to Ullswater. I will go and speak to Margaret about tea.'

---

16 One of the letters forged by William Combe. See *Original Letters of Laurence Sterne* (1788; New York and London: Garland Publishing, 1975), 201.

CHAPTER XLVIII

After the little incident recorded at the end of the preceding chapter, Hugh Flaxman may be forgiven if, as he walked home along the valley that night towards the farmhouse where he had established himself, he entertained a very comfortable scepticism as to the permanence of that curious contract into which Rose had just forced him. However, he was quite mistaken. Rose's maiden dignity avenged itself abundantly on Hugh Flaxman for the injuries it had received at the hands of Langham. The restraints, the anomalies, the hairsplittings of the situation delighted her ingenuous youth. 'I am free—he is free. We will be friends for six months. Possibly we may not suit one another at all. If we do—*then*——'

In the thrill of that *then* lay, of course, the whole attraction of the position.

So that next morning Hugh Flaxman saw the comedy was to be scrupulously kept up. It required a tolerably strong masculine certainty at the bottom of him to enable him to resign himself once more to his part. But he achieved it, and being himself a modern of the moderns, a lover of half-shades and refinements of all sorts, he began very soon to enjoy it, and to play it with an increasing cleverness and perfection.

How Rose got through Agnes's cross-questioning on the matter history sayeth not. Of one thing, however, a conscientious historian may be sure, namely, that Agnes succeeded in knowing as much as she wanted to know. Mrs. Leyburn was a little puzzled by the erratic lines of Mr. Flaxman's journeys. It was, as she said, curious that a man should start on a tour through the Lakes from Long Whindale.

But she took everything naïvely as it came, and as she was told. Nothing with her ever passed through any changing crucible of thought. It required no planning to elude her. Her mind was like a stretch of wet sand, on which all impressions are equally easy to make and equally fugitive. He liked them all, she supposed, in spite of the comparative scantiness of his later visits to Lerwick Gardens, or he would not have come out of his way to see them. But as nobody suggested anything else to her, her mind worked no further, and she was as easily beguiled after his appearance as before it by the intricacies of some new knitting.

Things of course might have been different if Mrs. Thornburgh had interfered again; but, as we know, poor Catherine's sorrows had raised a whole odd host of misgivings in the mind of the vicar's wife. She prowled nervously round Mrs. Leyburn, filled with contempt for her placidity; but she did not attack her. She spent herself, indeed, on Rose and Agnes, but long practice had made them adepts in the art of baffling her; and when Mr. Flaxman went to tea at the vicarage in their company, in spite of an absorbing desire to get at the truth, which caused her to forget a new cap, and let fall a plate of tea-cakes, she was obliged to confess crossly to the vicar afterwards that 'no one could tell what a man like that was after. She supposed his manners were very aristocratic, but for her part she liked plain people.'

On the last morning of Mr. Flaxman's stay in the valley he entered the Burwood drive about eleven o'clock, and Rose came down the steps to meet him. For a moment he flattered himself that her disturbed looks were due to the nearness of their farewells.

'There is something wrong,' he said, softly detaining her hand a moment—so much, at least, was in his right.

'Robert is ill. There has been an accident at Petites Dalles. He has been in bed for a week. They hope to get home in a few days. Catherine writes bravely, but she is evidently very low.'

Hugh Flaxman's face fell. Certain letters he had received from Elsmere in July had lain heavy on his mind ever since, so pitiful was the half-conscious revelation in them of an incessant physical struggle. An accident! Elsmere was in no state for accidents. What miserable ill-luck!

Rose read him Catherine's account. It appeared that on a certain stormy day a swimmer had been observed in difficulties among the rocks skirting the northern side of the Petites Dalles bay. The old *baigneur* of the place, owner of the still primitive *établissement des bains*, without stopping to strip, or even to take off his heavy boots, went out to the man in danger with a plank.[17] The man took the plank and was safe. Then to the people watching, it became evident that the *baigneur* himself was in peril. He became unaccountably feeble in the water, and the cry rose that he was sinking. Robert, who happened to be bathing near, ran off to the spot, jumped in, and swam out. By this time the old man had drifted some way. Robert succeeded, however, in bringing him in, and then, amid an excited crowd, headed by the *baigneur's* wailing family, they carried the unconscious form on to the higher beach. Elsmere was certain life was not extinct, and sent off for a doctor. Meanwhile no one seemed to have any common sense, or any knowledge of how to proceed, but himself. For two hours he stayed on the beach in his dripping bathing-clothes,

---

17 The bath-house owner ... the bath-house.

a cold wind blowing, trying every device known to him: rubbing, hot bottles, artificial respiration. In vain. The man was too old and too bloodless. Directly after the doctor arrived he breathed his last, amid the wild and passionate grief of wife and children.

Robert, with a cloak flung about him, still stayed to talk to the doctor, to carry one of the *baigneur's* sobbing grandchildren to its mother in the village. Then, at last, Catherine got hold of him, and he submitted to be taken home, shivering, and deeply depressed by the failure of his efforts. A violent gastric and lung chill declared itself almost immediately, and for three days he had been anxiously ill. Catherine, miserable, distrusting the local doctor, and not knowing how to get hold of a better one, had never left him night or day. 'I had not the heart to write even to you,' she wrote to her mother. 'I could think of nothing but trying one thing after another. Now he has been in bed eight days, and is much better. He talks of getting up to-morrow, and declares he must go home next week. I have tried to persuade him to stay here another fortnight, but the thought of his work distresses him so much that I hardly dare urge it. I cannot say how I dread the journey. He is not fit for it in any way.'

Rose folded up the letter, her face softened to a most womanly gravity. Hugh Flaxman paused a moment outside the door, his hands on his sides, considering.

'I shall not go on to Scotland,' he said; 'Mrs. Elsmere must not be left. I will go off there at once.'

In Rose's soberly-sweet looks as he left her, Hugh Flaxman saw for an instant, with the stirring of a joy as profound as it was delicate, not the fanciful enchantress of the day before, but his wife that was to be. And yet she held him to his bargain. All that his lips touched as he said good-bye was the little bunch of yellow briar roses she gave him from her belt.

Thirty hours later he was descending the long hill from Sassetôt to Petites Dalles. It was the 1st of September. A chilly west wind blew up the dust before him and stirred the parched leafage of the valley. He knocked at the door, of which the woodwork was all peeled and blistered by the sun. Catherine herself opened it.

'This is kind—this is like yourself!' she said, after a first stare of amazement, when he had explained himself. 'He is in there, much better.'

Robert looked up, stupefied, as Hugh Flaxman entered. But he sprang up with his old brightness.

'Well, this *is* friendship! What on earth brings you here, old fellow? Why aren't you in the stubbles celebrating St. Partridge?'

Hugh Flaxman said what he had to say very shortly, but so as to make Robert's eyes gleam, and to bring his thin hand with a sort of caressing touch upon Flaxman's shoulder.

'I shan't try to thank you—Catherine can if she likes. How relieved she will be about that bothering journey of ours! However, I am really ever so much better. It was very sharp while it lasted; and the doctor no great shakes. But there never was such a woman as my wife; she pulled me through! And now then, sir, just kindly confess yourself a little more plainly. What brought you and my sisters-in-law together? You need not try and persuade *me* that Long Whindale is the natural gate of the Lakes, or the route intended by Heaven from London to Scotland, though I have no doubt you tried that little fiction on them.'

Hugh Flaxman laughed, and sat down very deliberately.

'I am glad to see that illness has not robbed you of that perspicacity for which you are so remarkable, Elsmere. Well, the day before yesterday I asked your sister Rose to marry me. She——'

'Go on, man,' cried Robert, exasperated by his pause.

'I don't know how to put it,' said Flaxman calmly. 'For six months we are to be rather more than friends, and a good deal less than *fiancés*. I am to be allowed to write to her. You may imagine how seductive it is to one of the worst and laziest letter-writers in the three kingdoms that his fortunes in love should be made to depend on his correspondence. I may scold her *if* she gives me occasion. And in six months, as one says to a publisher, "the agreement will be open to revision."'

Robert stared.

'And you are not engaged?'

'Not as I understand it,' replied Flaxman. 'Decidedly not!' he added with energy, remembering that very platonic farewell.

Robert sat with his hands on his knees, ruminating.

'A fantastic thing, the modern young woman! Still I think I can understand. There may have been more than mere caprice in it.'

His eye met his friend's significantly.

'I suppose so,' said Flaxman quietly. Not even for Robert's benefit was he going to reveal any details of that scene on High Fell. 'Never mind, old fellow, I am content. And, indeed, *faute de mieux*, I should be content with anything that brought me nearer to her, were it but by the thousandth of an inch.'

Robert grasped his hand affectionately.

'Catherine,' he called through the door, 'never mind the supper; let it burn. Flaxman brings news.'

Catherine listened to the story with amazement. Certainly her ways would never have been as her sister's.

'Are we supposed to know?' she asked, very naturally.

'She never forbade me to tell,' said Flaxman, smiling.[18] 'I think, however, if I were you, I should say nothing about it—yet. I told her it was part of our bargain that *she* should explain my letters to Mrs. Leyburn. I gave her free leave to invent any fairy tale she pleased, but it was to be *her* invention, not mine.'

Neither Robert nor Catherine were very well pleased. But there was something reassuring as well as comic in the stoicism with which Flaxman took his position. And clearly the matter must be left to manage itself.

Next morning the weather had improved. Robert, his hand on Flaxman's arm, got down to the beach. Flaxman watched him critically, did not like some of his symptoms, but thought on the whole he must be recovering at the normal rate, considering how severe the attack had been.

'What do you think of him?' Catherine asked him next day, with all her soul in her eyes. They had left Robert established in a sunny nook, and were strolling on along the sands.

'I think you must get him home, call in a first-rate doctor, and keep him quiet,' said Flaxman. 'He will be all right presently.'

'How *can* we keep him quiet?' said Catherine, with a momentary despair in her fine pale face. 'All day long and all night long he is thinking of his work. It is like something fiery burning the heart out of him.'

Flaxman felt the truth of the remark during the four days of calm autumn weather he spent with them before the return journey. Robert would talk to him for hours, now on the sands, with the gray infinity of sea before them, now pacing the bounds of their little room till fatigue made him drop heavily into his long chair; and the burden of it all was the religious future of the working-class. He described the scene in the Club, and brought out the dreams swarming in his mind, presenting them for Flaxman's criticism, and dealing with them himself, with that startling mixture of acute common-sense and eloquent passion which had always made him so effective as an initiator. Flaxman listened dubiously at first, as he generally listened to Elsmere, and then was carried away, not by the beliefs, but by the man. *He* found his pleasure in dallying with the magnificent *possibility* of the Church; doubt with him applied to all propositions, whether positive or negative; and he had the dislike of the aristocrat and the cosmopolitan for the provincialisms of religious dissent. Political dissent or social reform was another matter. Since the

---

18 "Flaxman, smiling": comma as per *SE* and *W*.

Revolution, every generous child of the century has been open to the fascina-tion of political or social Utopias. But religion! *What—what is truth?* Why not let the old things alone?

However, it was through the social passion, once so real in him, and still living, in spite of disillusion and self-mockery, that Robert caught him, had in fact been slowly gaining possession of him all these months.

'Well,' said Flaxman one day, 'suppose I grant you that Christianity of the old sort shows strong signs of exhaustion, even in England, and in spite of the Church expansion we hear so much about; and suppose I believe with you that things will go badly without religion—what then? Who can have a religion for the asking?'

'But who can have it without? *Seek*, that you may find. Experiment; try new combinations. If a thing is going that humanity can't do without, and you and I believe it, what duty is more urgent for us than the effort to replace it?'

Flaxman shrugged his shoulders.

'What will you gain? A new sect?'

'Possibly. But what we *stand* to gain is a new social bond,' was the flash-ing answer—'a new compelling force in man and in society. Can you deny that the world wants it? What are you economists and sociologists of the new type always pining for? Why, for that diminution of the self in man which is to enable the individual to see the *world's* ends clearly, and to care not only for his own but for his neighbour's interest, which is to make the rich devote themselves to the poor, and the poor bear with the rich. If man only *would*, he *could*, you say, solve all the problems which oppress him. It is man's will which is eternally defective, eternally inadequate. Well, the great religions of the world are the stimulants by which the power at the root of things has worked upon this sluggish instrument of human destiny. Without religion you cannot make the will equal to its tasks. Our present religion fails us; we must, we will have another!'

He rose and began to pace along the sands, now gently glowing in the warm September evening, Flaxman beside him.

A new religion! Of all words, the most tremendous! Flaxman pitifully weighed against it the fraction of force fretting and surging in the thin elastic frame beside him. He knew well, however—few better—that the outburst was not a mere dream and emptiness. There was experience behind it—a burning, driving experience of actual fact.

Presently Robert said, with a change of tone, 'I must have that whole block of warehouses, Flaxman.'

'Must you?' said Flaxman, relieved by the drop from speculation to the practical. 'Why?'

'Look here!' And sitting down again on a sand-hill overgrown with wild grasses and mats of sea-thistle, the poor pale reformer began to draw out the details of his scheme on its material side. Three floors of rooms brightly furnished, well lit and warmed; a large hall for the Sunday lectures, concerts, entertainments, and story-telling; rooms for the boys' club; two rooms for women and girls, reached by a separate entrance; a library and reading-room open to both sexes, well stored with books, and made beautiful by pictures; three or four smaller rooms to serve as committee rooms and for the purposes of the Naturalist Club which had been started in May on the Murewell plan; and, if possible, a gymnasium.

'*Money!*' he said, drawing up with a laugh in mid-career. 'There's the rub, of course. But I shall manage it.'

To judge from the past, Flaxman thought it extremely likely that he would. He studied the cabalistic lines Elsmere's stick had made in the sand for a minute or two; then he said drily, 'I will take the first expense; and draw on me afterwards up to five hundred a year, for the first four years.'

Robert turned upon him and grasped his hand.

'I do not thank you,' he said quietly, after a moment's pause; 'the work itself will do that.'

Again they strolled on, talking, plunging into details, till Flaxman's pulse beat as fast as Robert's; so full of infectious hope and energy was the whole being of the man before him.

'I can take in the women and girls now,' Robert said once. 'Catherine has promised to superintend it all.'

Then suddenly something struck the mobile mind, and he stood an instant looking at his companion. It was the first time he had mentioned Catherine's name in connection with the North R—— work. Flaxman could not mistake the emotion, the unspoken thanks in those eyes. He turned away, nervously knocking off the ashes of his cigar. But the two men understood each other.

CHAPTER XLIX

Two days later they were in London again. Robert was a great deal better, and beginning to kick against invalid restraints. All men have their pet irrationalities. Elsmere's irrationality was an aversion to doctors, from the point of view of his own ailments. He had an unbounded admiration for them as a class, and would have nothing to say to them as individuals that he could possibly help. Flaxman was sarcastic; Catherine looked imploring in vain. He vowed that he was treating himself with a skill any professional might envy, and went his way. And for a time the stimulus of London and of his work seemed to act favourably upon him. After his first welcome at the Club he came home with bright eye and vigorous step, declaring that he was another man.

Flaxman established himself in St. James's Place. Town was deserted; the partridges at Greenlaws clamoured to be shot; the head-keeper wrote letters which would have melted the heart of a stone. Flaxman replied recklessly that any decent fellow in the neighbourhood was welcome to shoot his birds—a reply which almost brought upon him the resignation of the outraged keeper by return of post. Lady Charlotte wrote and remonstrated with him for neglecting a landowner's duties, inquiring at the same time what he meant to do with regard to 'that young lady.' To which Flaxman replied calmly that he had just come back from the Lakes, where he had done, not indeed all that he meant to do, but still something. Miss Leyburn and he were not engaged, but he was on probation for six months, and found London the best place for getting through it.

'So far,' he said, 'I am getting on well, and developing an amount of energy especially in the matter of correspondence, which alone ought to commend the arrangement to the relations of an idle man. But we must be left "to dream our dream unto ourselves alone." One word from anybody belonging to me to anybody belonging to her on the subject, and—— But threats are puerile. *For the present*, dear aunt, I am your devoted nephew,

HUGH FLAXMAN.'

'*On probation!*'

Flaxman chuckled as he sent off the letter.

He stayed because he was too restless to be anywhere else, and because he loved the Elsmeres for Rose's sake and his own. He thought moreover that a cool-headed friend with an eye for something else in the world than religious reform might be useful just then to Elsmere, and he was determined at the same time to see what the reformer meant to be at.

In the first place, Robert's attention was directed to getting possession of the whole block of buildings, in which the existing school and lecture-rooms took up only the lowest floor. This was a matter of some difficulty, for the floors above were employed in warehousing goods belonging to various minor import trades, and were held on tenures of different lengths. However, by dint of some money and much skill, the requisite clearances were effected during September and part of October. By the end of that month all but the top floor, the tenant of which refused to be dislodged, fell into Elsmere's hands.

Meanwhile, at a meeting held every Sunday after lecture—a meeting composed mainly of artisans of the district, but including also Robert's helpers from the West, and a small sprinkling of persons interested in the man and his work from all parts—the details of 'The New Brotherhood of Christ' were being hammered out. Catherine was generally present, sitting a little apart, with a look which Flaxman, who now knew her well, was always trying to decipher afresh—a sort of sweet aloofness, as though the spirit behind it saw, down the vistas of the future, ends and solutions which gave it courage to endure the present. Murray Edwardes too was always there. It often struck Flaxman afterwards that in Robert's attitude towards Edwardes at this time, in his constant desire to bring him forward, to associate him with himself as much as possible in the government and formation of the infant society, there was a half-conscious prescience of a truth that as yet none knew, not even the tender wife, the watchful friend.

The meetings were of extraordinary interest. The men, the great majority of whom had been disciplined and moulded for months by contact with Elsmere's teaching and Elsmere's thought, showed a responsiveness, a receptivity, even a power of initiation which often struck Flaxman with wonder. Were these the men he had seen in the Club-hall on the night of Robert's address—sour, stolid, brutalised, hostile to all things in heaven and earth?

'And we go on prating that the age of saints is over, the rôle of the individual lessening day by day! Fool! go and *be* a saint, go and give yourself to ideas; go and *live* the life hid with Christ in God, and see,'—so would run the quick comment of the observer.

But incessant as was the reciprocity, the interchange and play of feeling between Robert and the wide following growing up around him, it was plain to Flaxman that although he never moved a step without carrying his world with him, he was never at the mercy of his world. Nothing was ever really left to chance. Through all these strange debates, which began rawly and clumsily enough, and grew every week more and more absorbing to all concerned, Flaxman was convinced that hardly any rule or formula of the new society was ultimately adopted which had not been for long in Robert's mind—thought out and brought into final shape, perhaps, on the Petites Dalles sands. It was an unobtrusive art, his art of government, but a most effective one.

At any moment, as Flaxman often felt, at any rate in the early meetings, the discussions as to the religious practices which were to bind together the new association might have passed the line, and become puerile or grotesque. At any moment the jarring characters and ambitions of the men Elsmere had to deal with might have dispersed that delicate atmosphere of moral sympathy and passion in which the whole new birth seemed to have been conceived, and upon the maintenance of which its fruition and development depended. But as soon as Elsmere appeared, difficulties vanished, enthusiasm sprang up again. The rules of the new society came simply and naturally into being, steeped and haloed, as it were, from the beginning, in the passion and genius of one great heart. The fastidious critical instinct in Flaxman was silenced no less than the sour, half-educated analysis of such a man as Lestrange.

In the same way all personal jars seemed to melt away beside him. There were some painful things connected with the new departure. Wardlaw, for instance, a conscientious Comtist, refusing stoutly to admit anything more than 'an unknowable reality behind phenomena,' was distressed and affronted by the strongly religious bent Elsmere was giving to the work he had begun. Lestrange, who was a man of great though raw ability, who almost always spoke at the meetings, and whom Robert was bent on attaching to the society, had times when the things he was half inclined to worship one day he was much more inclined to burn the next in the sight of all men, and when the smallest failure of temper on Robert's part might have entailed a disagreeable scene, and the possible formation of a harassing left wing.

But Robert's manner to Wardlaw was that of a grateful younger brother. It was clear that the Comtist could not formally join the Brotherhood. But all the share and influence that could be secured him in the practical working of it was secured him. And what was more, Robert succeeded in infusing his own delicacy, his own compunctions on the subject, into the men and youths who had profited in the past by Wardlaw's rough self-devotion. So that if, through much that went on now, he could only be a spectator, at least he was not allowed to feel himself an alien or forgotten.

As to Lestrange, against a man who was as ready to laugh as to preach, and into whose ardent soul nature had infused a saving sense of the whimsical in life and character, cynicism and vanity seemed to have no case. Robert's quick temper had been wonderfully disciplined by life since his Oxford days. He had now very little of that stiff-neckedness, so fatal to the average reformer, which makes a man insist on all or nothing from his followers. He took what each man had to give. Nay, he made it almost seem as though the grudging support of Lestrange, or the critical half-patronising approval of the young barrister from the West who came down to listen to him, and made a favour of teaching in his night-school, were as precious to him as was the whole-hearted, the self-abandoning veneration, which the majority of those about him had begun to show towards the man in whom, as Charles Richards said, they had 'seen God.'

At last by the middle of November the whole great building, with the exception of the top floor, was cleared and ready for use. Robert felt the same joy in it, in its clean paint, the half-filled shelves in the library, the pictures standing against the walls ready to be hung, the rolls of bright-coloured matting ready to be laid down, as he had felt in the Murewell Institute. He and Flaxman, helped by a voluntary army of men, worked at it from morning till night. Only Catherine could ever persuade him to remember that he was not yet physically himself.

Then came the day when the building was formally opened, when the gilt letters over the door, 'The New Brotherhood of Christ,' shone out into the dingy street, and when the first enrolment of names in the book of the Brotherhood took place.

For two hours a continuous stream of human beings surrounded the little table beside which Elsmere stood, inscribing their names, and receiving from him the silver badge, bearing the head of Christ, which was to be the outward and conspicuous sign of membership. Men came of all sorts: the intelligent well-paid artisan, the pallid clerk or small accountant, stalwart warehousemen, huge carters and draymen, the boy attached to each by the laws of the profession often straggling lumpishly behind his master. Women were there: wives who came because their lords came, or because Mr. Elsmere had been 'that good' to them that anything they could do to oblige him 'they would, and welcome'; prim pupil-teachers, holding themselves with straight superior shoulders; children, who came trooping in, grinned up into Robert's face and retreated again with red cheeks, the silver badge tight clasped in hands which not even much scrubbing could make passable.

Flaxman stood and watched it from the side. It was an extraordinary scene: the crowd, the slight figure on the platform, the two great inscriptions, which represented the only 'articles' of the new faith, gleaming from the freshly coloured walls—

'In Thee, O Eternal, have I put my trust;'
'This do in remembrance of Me;'

—the recesses on either side of the hall lined with white marble, and destined, the one to hold the names of the living members of the Brotherhood, the other to commemorate those who had passed away (empty this last save for the one poor name of 'Charles Richards'); the copies of Giotto's Paduan Virtues—Faith, Fortitude, Charity, and the like[19]—which broke the long wall at intervals.[20] The cynic in the onlooker tried to assert itself against the feeling with which the air seemed overcharged. In vain.

'Whatever comes of it,' Flaxman said to himself with strong involuntary conviction, 'whether he fails or no, the spirit that is moving here is the same spirit that spread the Church, the spirit that sent out Benedictine and Franciscan into the world, that fired the children of Luther, or Calvin, or George Fox; the spirit of devotion, through a man, to an idea; through one much-loved, much-trusted soul to some eternal verity, newly caught, newly conceived, behind it.[21] There is no approaching the idea for the masses except through the human life; there is no lasting power for the man except as the slave of the idea!'

A week later he wrote to his aunt as follows. He could not write to her of Rose, he did not care to write of himself, and he knew that Elsmere's club address had left a mark even on her restless and overcrowded mind. Moreover, he himself was absorbed.

'We are in the full stream of religion-making. I watch it with a fascination you at a distance cannot possibly understand, even when my judgment demurs, and my intelligence protests that the thing cannot live without Elsmere, and that Elsmere's life is a frail one. After the ceremony of enrolment which I described to you yesterday the Council of the New Brotherhood was chosen by popular election, and Elsmere gave an address. Two-thirds of the council, I should think, are working-men, the rest of the upper class; Elsmere, of course, president.

'Since then the first religious service under the new constitution has been held. The service is extremely simple, and the basis of the whole is "new bottles for the new wine." The opening prayer is recited by everybody present standing. It is rather an act of adoration and faith than a prayer, properly so called. It represents, in fact, the placing of the soul in the presence of God. The mortal turns to the eternal; the ignorant and imperfect look away from themselves to the knowledge and perfection of the All-Holy. It is Elsmere's drawing up, I imagine—at any rate it is essentially modern, expressing the

---

19 Allegorical virtues capitalized as per *SE*.

20 Fourteenth-century allegorical frescoes in the Cappella Scrovegni, Padua. Giotto di Bondone (c. 1266–1337), Italian Renaissance painter.

21 Martin Luther (1483–1546), German monk who sparked the Protestant Reformation; John Calvin (1509–1564), one of the Reformation's dominant theologians; George Fox (1624–1691), founder of the Society of Friends.

modern spirit, answering to modern need, as I imagine the first Christian prayers expressed the spirit and answered to the need of an earlier day.

'Then follows some passage from the life of Christ. Elsmere reads it and expounds it, in the first place, as a lecturer might expound a passage of Tacitus, historically and critically. His explanation of miracle, his efforts to make his audience realise the germs of miraculous belief which each man carries with him in the constitution and inherited furniture of his mind, are some of the most ingenious—perhaps the most convincing—I have ever heard. My heart and my head have never been very much at one, as you know, on this matter of the marvellous element in religion.

'But then when the critic has done, the poet and the believer begins. Whether he has got hold of the true Christ is another matter; but that the Christ he preaches moves the human heart as much as—and in the case of the London artisan, more than—the current orthodox presentation of him, I begin to have ocular demonstration.

'I was present, for instance, at his children's Sunday class the other day. He had brought them up to the story of the Crucifixion, reading from the Revised Version, and amplifying wherever the sense required it.[22] Suddenly a little girl laid her head on the desk before her, and with choking sobs implored him not to go on. The whole class seemed ready to do the same. The pure human pity of the story—the contrast between the innocence and the pain of the sufferer—seemed to be more than they could bear. And there was no comforting sense of a jugglery by which the suffering was not real after all, and the sufferer not man but God.

'He took one of them upon his knee and tried to console them. But there is something piercingly penetrating and austere even in the consolations of this new faith. He did but remind the children of the burden of gratitude laid upon them. "Would you let him suffer so much in vain? His suffering has made you and me happier and better to-day, at this moment, than we could have been without Jesus. You will understand how, and why, more clearly when you grow up. Let us in return keep him in our hearts always, and obey his words! It is all you can do for his sake, just as all you could do for a mother who died would be to follow her wishes and sacredly keep her memory."

'That was about the gist of it. It was a strange little scene, wonderfully suggestive and pathetic.

'But a few more words about the Sunday service. After the address came

---

22 The Revised Version of the Bible (1881–94), one of the publishing sensations of the nineteenth century, is a corrected and modernized revision of the King James Version.

a hymn. There are only seven hymns in the little service book, gathered out of the finest we have. It is supposed that in a short time they will become so familiar to the members of the Brotherhood that they will be sung readily by heart. The singing of them in the public service alternates with an equal number of psalms. And both psalms and hymns are meant to be recited or sung constantly in the homes of the members, and to become part of the everyday life of the Brotherhood. They have been most carefully chosen, and a sort of ritual importance has been attached to them from the beginning. Each day in the week has its particular hymn or psalm.

'Then the whole wound up with another short prayer, also repeated standing, a commendation of the individual, the Brotherhood, the nation, the world, to God. The phrases of it are terse and grand. One can see at once that it has laid hold of the popular sense, the popular memory. The Lord's Prayer followed. Then, after a silent pause of "recollection," Elsmere dismissed them.

'"*Go in peace, in the love of God, and in the memory of His servant, Jesus.*"

'I looked carefully at the men as they were tramping out. Some of them were among the Secularist speakers you and I heard at the club in April. In my wonder, I thought of a saying of Vinet's: "*C'est pour la religion que le peuple a le plus de talent; c'est en religion qu'il montre le plus d'esprit.*"[23]

In a later letter he wrote—

'I have not yet described to you what is perhaps the most characteristic, the most binding practice of the New Brotherhood. It is that which has raised most angry comment, cries of "profanity," "wanton insult," and what not. I came upon it yesterday in an interesting way. I was working with Elsmere at the arrangement of the library, which is now becoming a most fascinating place, under the management of a librarian chosen from the neighbourhood, when he asked me to go and take a message to a carpenter who has been giving us voluntary help in the evenings after his day's work. He thought that as it was the dinner hour, and the man worked in the dock close by, I might find him at home. I went off to the model lodging-house where I was told to look for him, mounted the common stairs, and knocked at his door. Nobody seemed to hear me, and as the door was ajar I pushed it open.

'Inside was a curious sight.

'The table was spread with the midday meal. Round the table stood four children, the eldest about fourteen, and the youngest six or seven. At one

---

23 Alexandre Vinet (1797–1847), Protestant theologian. "It is for religion that the people have the most talent; it is in religion that they show the most spirit." The quotation appears in J.-F. Astié's *Esprit d'Alexandre Vinet: Pensées et Réflexions* (Lausanne: A. Delafontaine, 1861), 1:75.

end of it stood the carpenter himself in his working apron, a brawny Saxon, bowed a little by his trade. Before him was a plate of bread, and his horny hands were resting on it. The street was noisy; they had not heard my knock; and as I pushed open the door there was an old coat hanging over the corner of it which concealed me.

'Something in the attitudes of all concerned reminded me, kept me where I was, silent.

'The father lifted his right hand.

'"The Master said, '*This do in remembrance of Me!*'"

'The children stooped for a moment in silence, then the youngest said slowly, in a little softened cockney voice that touched me extraordinarily,—

'"*Jesus, we remember Thee always!*"

'It was the appointed response. As she spoke I recollected the child perfectly at Elsmere's class. I also remembered that she had no mother; that her mother had died of cancer in June, visited and comforted to the end by Elsmere and his wife.

'Well, the great question of course remains—is there a sufficient strength of *feeling* and *conviction* behind these things? If so, after all, everything was new once, and Christianity was but modified Judaism.'

'December 22.

'I believe I shall soon be as deep in this matter as Elsmere. In Elgood Street great preparations are going on for Christmas. But it will be a new sort of Christmas. We shall hear very little, it seems, of angels and shepherds, and a great deal of the humble childhood of a little Jewish boy whose genius grown to maturity transformed the Western world. To see Elsmere, with his boys and girls about him, trying to make them feel themselves the heirs and fellows of the Nazarene child, to make them understand something of the lessons that child must have learnt, the sights he must have seen, and the thoughts that must have come to him, is a spectacle of which I will not miss more than I can help. Don't imagine, however, that I am converted exactly!— but only that I am more interested and stimulated than I have been for years. And don't expect me for Christmas. I shall stay here.'

'New Year's Day.

'I am writing from the library of the New Brotherhood. The amount of activity, social, educational, religious, of which this great building promises to be the centre is already astonishing. Everything, of course including the constitution of the infant society, is as yet purely tentative and experimental.

But for a scheme so young, things are falling into working order with wonderful rapidity. Each department is worked by committees under the central council. Elsmere, of course, is *ex-officio* chairman of a large proportion; Wardlaw, Mackay, I, and a few other fellows "run" the rest for the present. But each committee contains working-men; and it is the object of everybody concerned to make the workman element more and more real and efficient. What with the "tax" on the members which was fixed by a general meeting, and the contributions from outside, the society already commands a fair income. But Elsmere is anxious not to attempt too much at once, and will go slowly and train his workers.

'Music, it seems, is to be a great feature in the future. I have my own projects as to this part of the business, which, however, I forbid you to guess at.

'By the rules of the Brotherhood, every member is bound to some work in connection with it during the year, but little or much, as he or she is able. And every meeting, every undertaking of whatever kind, opens with the special "word" or formula of the society, "This do in remembrance of Me."'

'January 6.

'Besides the Sunday lectures, Elsmere is pegging away on Saturday evenings at "The History of the Moral Life in Man." It is a remarkable course, and very largely attended by people of all sorts. He tries to make it an exposition of the leading principles of the new movement, of "that continuous and only revelation of God in life and nature," which is in reality the basis of his whole thought. By the way, the letters that are pouring in upon him from all parts are extraordinary. They show an amount and degree of interest in ideas of the kind which are surprising to a Laodicean like me. But he is not surprised—says he always expected it—and that there are thousands who only want a rallying-point.

'His personal effect, the love that is felt for him, the passion and energy of the nature—never has our generation seen anything to equal it. As you perceive, I am reduced to taking it all seriously, and don't know what to make of him or myself.

'*She*, poor soul! is now always with him, comes down with him day after day, and works away. She no more believes in his *ideas*, I think, than she ever did; but all her antagonism is gone. In the midst of the stir about him her face often haunts me. It has changed lately; she is no longer a young woman, but so refined, so spiritual!

'But he is ailing and fragile. *There* is the one cloud on a scene that fills me with increasing wonder and reverence.'

CHAPTER L

One cold Sunday afternoon in January, Flaxman, descending the steps of the New Brotherhood, was overtaken by a young Dr. Edmondson, an able young physician, just set up for himself as a consultant, who had only lately attached himself to Elsmere, and was now helping him with eagerness to organise a dispensary. Young Edmondson and Flaxman exchanged a few words on Elsmere's lecture, and then the doctor said abruptly,—

'I don't like his looks nor his voice. How long has he been hoarse like that?'

'More or less for the last month. He is very much worried by it himself, and talks of clergyman's throat. He had a touch of it, it appears, once in the country.'

'Clergyman's throat?' Edmondson shook his head dubiously. 'It may be. I wish he would let me overhaul him.'

'I wish he would!' said Flaxman devoutly. 'I will see what I can do. I will get hold of Mrs. Elsmere.'

Meanwhile Robert and Catherine had driven home together. As they entered the study she caught his hands, a suppressed and exquisite passion gleaming in her face.

'You did not explain Him! You never will!'

He stood, held by her, his gaze meeting hers. Then in an instant his face changed, blanched before her—he seemed to gasp for breath—she was only just able to save him from falling. It was apparently another swoon of exhaustion. As she knelt beside him on the floor, having done for him all she could, watching his return to consciousness, Catherine's look would have terrified any of those who loved her. There are some natures which are never blind, never taken blissfully unawares, and which taste calamity and grief to the very dregs.

'Robert, to-morrow you *will* see a doctor?' she implored him when at last he was safely in bed—white, but smiling.

He nodded.

'Send for Edmondson. What I mind most is this hoarseness,' he said, in a voice that was little more than a tremulous whisper.

Catherine hardly closed her eyes all night. The room, the house, seemed to her stifling, oppressive, like a grave. And, by ill luck, with the morning came a long expected letter, not indeed from the squire, but about the squire. Robert had been for some time expecting a summons to Murewell. The squire had written to him last in October from Clarens, on the Lake of Geneva. Since then weeks had passed without bringing Elsmere any news of him at all. Meanwhile the growth of the New Brotherhood had absorbed its founder, so that the inquiries which should have been sent to Murewell had been postponed. The letter which reached him now was from old Meyrick. 'The squire has had another bad attack, and is *much* weaker. But his mind is clear again, and he greatly desires to see you. If you can, come to-morrow.'

'*His mind is clear again!*' Horrified by the words and by the images they called up, remorseful also for his own long silence, Robert sprang up from bed, where the letter had been brought to him, and presently appeared downstairs, where Catherine, believing him safely captive for the morning, was going through some household business.

'I *must* go, I *must* go!' he said as he handed her the letter. 'Meyrick puts it cautiously, but it may be the end!'

Catherine looked at him in despair.

'Robert, you are like a ghost yourself, and I have sent for Dr. Edmondson.'

'Put him off till the day after to-morrow. Dear little wife, listen; my voice is ever so much better. Murewell air will do me good.' She turned away to hide the tears in her eyes. Then she tried fresh persuasions, but it was useless. His look was glowing and restless. She saw he felt it a call impossible to disobey. A telegram was sent to Edmondson, and Robert drove off to Waterloo.

Out of the fog of London it was a mild, sunny winter's day. Robert breathed more freely with every mile. His eyes took note of every landmark in the familiar journey with a thirsty eagerness. It was a year and a half since he had travelled it. He forgot his weakness, the exhausting pressure and publicity of his new work. The past possessed him, thrust out the present. Surely he had been up to London for the day and was going back to Catherine!

At the station he hailed an old friend among the cabmen.

'Take me to the corner of the Murewell lane, Tom. Then you may drive on my bag to the Hall, and I shall walk over the common.'

The man urged on his tottering old steed with a will. In the streets of the little town Robert saw several acquaintances who stopped and stared at the apparition. Were the houses, the people real, or was it all a hallucination—his flight and his return, so unthought of yesterday, so easy and swift to-day?

By the time they were out on the wild ground between the market town and Murewell, Robert's spirits were as buoyant as thistle-down. He and the driver kept up an incessant gossip over the neighbourhood, and he jumped down from the carriage as the man stopped with the alacrity of a boy.

'Go on, Tom; see if I am not there as soon as you.'

'Looks most uncommon bad,' the man muttered to himself as his horse shambled off. 'Seems as spry as a lark all the same.'

Why, the gorse was out, positively out in January! and the thrushes were singing as though it were March. Robert stopped opposite a bush covered with timid half-opened blooms, and thought he had seen nothing so beautiful since he had last trodden that road in spring. Presently he was in the same cart-track he had crossed on the night of his confession to Catherine; he lingered beside the same solitary fir on the brink of the ridge. A winter world lay before him; soft brown woodland, or reddish heath and fern, struck sideways by the sun, clothing the earth's bareness everywhere—curling mists—blue points of distant hill—a gray luminous depth of sky.

The eyes were moist, the lips moved. There in the place of his old anguish he stood and blessed God!—not for any personal happiness, but simply for that communication of Himself which may make every hour of common living a revelation.

Twenty minutes later, leaving the park gate to his left, he hurried up the lane leading to the vicarage. One look! he might not be able to leave the squire later. The gate of the wood-path was ajar. Surely just inside it he should find Catherine in her garden hat, the white-frocked child dragging behind her! And there was the square stone house, the brown cornfield, the red-brown woods! Why, what had the man been doing with the study? White blinds showed it was a bedroom now. Vandal! Besides, how could the boys have free access except to that ground-floor room? And all that pretty stretch of grass under the acacia had been cut up into stiff little lozenge-shaped beds, filled, he supposed, in summer with the properest geraniums. He should never dare to tell that to Catherine.

He stood and watched the little significant signs of change in this realm, which had been once his own, with a dissatisfied mouth, his undermind filled the while with tempestuous yearning and affection. In that upper room he had lain through that agonised night of crisis; the dawn-twitterings of the summer birds seemed to be still in his ears. And there, in the distance, was the blue wreath of smoke hanging over Mile End. Ah! the new cottages must be warm this winter. The children did not lie in the wet any longer—thank God! Was there time just to run down to Irwin's cottage, to have a look at the Institute?

He had been standing on the farther side of the road from the rectory that he might not seem to be spying out the land and his successor's ways too closely. Suddenly he found himself clinging to a gate near him that led into a field. He was shaken by a horrible struggle for breath. The self seemed to be foundering in a stifling sea, and fought like a drowning thing. When the moment passed, he looked round him bewildered, drawing his hand across his eyes. The world had grown black—the sun seemed to be scarcely shining. Were those the sounds of children's voices on the hill, the rumbling of a cart—or was it all sight and sound alike, mirage and delirium?

With difficulty, leaning on his stick as though he were a man of seventy, he groped his way back to the Park. There he sank down, still gasping, among the roots of one of the great cedars near the gate. After a while the attack passed off and he found himself able to walk on. But the joy, the leaping pulse of half an hour ago, were gone from his veins. Was that the river—the house? He looked at them with dull eyes. All the light was lowered. A veil seemed to lie between him and the familiar things.

However, by the time he reached the door of the Hall will and nature had reasserted themselves, and he knew where he was and what he had to do.

Vincent flung the door open with his old lordly air.

'Why, sir! *Mr.* Elsmere!'

The butler's voice began on a note of joyful surprise, sliding at once into one of alarm. He stood and stared at this ghost of the old rector.

Elsmere grasped his hand, and asked him to take him into the dining-room and give him some wine before announcing him. Vincent ministered to him with a long face, pressing all the alcoholic resources of the Hall upon him in turn. The squire was much better, he declared, and had been carried down to the library.

'But, lor, sir, there ain't much to be said for your looks neither—seems as if London didn't suit you, sir.'

Elsmere explained feebly that he had been suffering from his throat, and had overtired himself by walking over the common. Then, recognising from a distorted vision of himself in a Venetian mirror hanging by that something of his natural colour had returned to him, he rose and bade Vincent announce him.

'And Mrs. Darcy?' he asked, as they stepped out into the hall again.

'Oh, Mrs. Darcy, sir, she's very well,' said the man, but, as it seemed to Robert, with something of an embarrassed air.

He followed Vincent down the long passage—haunted by old memories, by the old sickening sense of mental anguish—to the curtained door. Vincent ushered him in. There was a stir of feet, and a voice, but at first he saw nothing. The room was very much darkened. Then Meyrick emerged into distinctness.

'Squire, here *is* Mr. Elsmere! Well, Mr. Elsmere, sir, I'm sure we're very much obliged to you for meeting the squire's wishes so promptly. You'll find him poorly, Mr. Elsmere, but mending—oh yes, mending, sir—no doubt of it.'

Elsmere began to perceive a figure by the fire. A bony hand was advanced to him out of the gloom.

'That'll do, Meyrick. You won't be wanted till the evening.'

The imperious note in the voice struck Robert with a sudden sense of relief. After all, the squire was still capable of trampling on Meyrick.

In another minute the door had closed on the old doctor, and the two men were alone. Robert was beginning to get used to the dim light. Out of it the squire's face gleamed almost as whitely as the tortured marble of the Medusa just above their heads.

'It's some inflammation in the eyes,' the squire explained briefly, 'that's made Meyrick set up all this d—d business of blinds and shutters. I don't mean to stand it much longer. The eyes are better, and I prefer to see my way out of the world, if possible.'

'But you are recovering?' Robert said, laying his hand affectionately on the old man's knee.

'I have added to my knowledge,' said the squire drily. 'Like Heine, I am qualified to give lectures in heaven on the ignorance of doctors on earth.[24] And I am not in bed, which I was last week. For Heaven's sake don't ask questions. If there is a loathsome subject on earth it is the subject of the human body. Well, I suppose my message to you dragged you away from a thousand things you had rather be doing. What are you so hoarse for? Neglecting yourself as usual, for the sake of "the people," who wouldn't even subscribe to bury you? Have you been working up the Apocrypha as I recommended you last time we met?'

Robert smiled.

'For the last four months, Squire, I have been doing two things with neither of which had you much sympathy in old days—holiday-making and "slumming."'

'Oh, I remember,' interrupted the squire hastily. 'I was low last week, and

---

24 The phrasing of this anecdote is very close to Matthew Arnold's: "'But,' said he to some one who found him thus engaged, 'what good this reading is to do me I don't know, except that it will qualify me to give lectures in heaven on the ignorance of doctors on earth about diseases of the spinal marrow.'" "Heinrich Heine," *The Cornhill Magazine* 8 (1863): 240.

read the Church papers by way of a counter-irritant. You have been starting a new religion, I see. A new religion! *Humph!*'

The great head fell forward, and through the dusk Robert caught the sarcastic gleam of the eyes.

'You are hardly the man to deny,' he said, undisturbed, 'that the old ones *laissent à désirer*.'[25]

'Because there are old abuses, is that any reason why you should go and set up a brand-new one—an ugly anachronism besides,' retorted the squire. 'However, you and I have no common ground—never had. I say *know*, you say *feel*. Where is the difference, after all, between you and any charlatan of the lot? Well, how is Madame de Netteville?'

'I have not seen her for six months,' Robert replied, with equal abruptness.

The squire laughed a little under his breath.

'What did you think of her?'

'Very much what you told me to think—intellectually,' replied Robert, facing him, but flushing with the readiness of physical delicacy.

'Well, I certainly never told you to think anything—*morally*,' said the squire. 'The word moral has no relation to her. Whom did you see there?'

The catechism was naturally most distasteful to its object, but Elsmere went through with it, the squire watching him for a while with an expression which had a spark of malice in it. It is not unlikely that some gossip of the Lady Aubrey sort had reached him. Elsmere had always seemed to him oppressively good. The idea that Madame de Netteville had tried her arts upon him was not without its piquancy.

But while Robert was answering a question he was aware of a subtle change in the squire's attitude—a relaxation of his own sense of tension. After a minute he bent forward, peering through the darkness. The squire's head had fallen back, his mouth was slightly open, and the breath came lightly, quiveringly through. The cynic of a moment ago had dropped suddenly into a sleep of more than childish weakness and defencelessness.

Robert remained bending forward, gazing at the man who had once meant so much to him.

Strange white face, sunk in the great chair! Behind it glimmered the Donatello figure, and the divine Hermes, a glorious shape in the dusk, looking scorn on human decrepitude. All round spread the dim walls of books. The life they had nourished was dropping into the abyss out of ken—they remained. Sixty years of effort and slavery to end so—a river lost in the sands!

Old Meyrick stole in again, and stood looking at the sleeping squire.

---

25 Leave something to be desired.

'A bad sign! a bad sign!' he said, and shook his head mournfully.

After he had made an effort to take some food which Vincent pressed upon him, Robert, conscious of a stronger physical *malaise* than had ever yet tormented him, was crossing the hall again, when he suddenly saw Mrs. Darcy at the door of a room which opened into the hall. He went up to her with a warm greeting.

'Are you going in to the squire? Let us go together.'

She looked at him with no surprise, as though she had seen him the day before, and as he spoke she retreated a step into the room behind her, a curious film, so it seemed to him, darkening her small gray eyes.

'The squire is not here. He is gone away. Have you seen my white mice? Oh, they are such darlings! Only, one of them is ill, and they won't let me have the doctor.'

Her voice sank into the most pitiful plaintiveness. She stood in the middle of the room, pointing with an elfish finger to a large cage of white mice which stood in the window. The room seemed full besides of other creatures. Robert stood rooted, looking at the tiny withered figure in the black dress, its snowy hair and diminutive face swathed in lace, with a perplexity into which there slipped an involuntary shiver. Suddenly he became aware of a woman by the fire, a decent, strong-looking body in gray, who rose as his look turned to her. Their eyes met; her expression and the little jerk of her head towards Mrs. Darcy, who was now standing by the cage coaxing the mice with the weirdest gestures, were enough. Robert turned, and went out sick at heart. The careful exquisite beauty of the great hall struck him as something mocking and anti-human.

No one else in the house said a word to him of Mrs. Darcy. In the evening the squire talked much at intervals, but in another key. He insisted on a certain amount of light, and, leaning on Robert's arm, went feebly round the bookshelves. He took out one of the volumes of the Fathers that Newman had given him.

'When I think of the hours I wasted over this barbarous rubbish,' he said, his blanched fingers turning the leaves vindictively, 'and of the other hours I maundered away in services and self-examination! Thank Heaven, however, the germ of revolt and sanity was always there. And when once I got to it, I learnt my lesson pretty quick.'

Robert paused, his kind inquiring eyes looking down on the shrunken squire.

'Oh, not one *you* have any chance of learning, my good friend,' said the other aggressively. 'And after all it's simple. *Go to your grave with your eyes open*—that's all. But men don't learn it, somehow. Newman was incapable—so are you. All the religions are nothing but so many vulgar anæsthetics, which only the few have courage to refuse.'

'Do you want me to contradict you?' said Robert, smiling; 'I am quite ready.'

The squire took no notice. Presently, when he was in his chair again, he said abruptly, pointing to a mahogany bureau in the window, 'The book is all there—both parts, first and second. Publish it if you please. If not, throw it into the fire. Both are equally indifferent to me. It has done its work; it has helped me through half a century of living.'

'It shall be to me a sacred trust,' said Elsmere with emotion. 'Of course if you don't publish it, I shall publish it.'

'As you please. Well, then, if you have nothing more rational to tell me about, tell me of this ridiculous Brotherhood of yours.'

Robert, so adjured, began to talk, but with difficulty. The words would not flow, and it was almost a relief when in the middle that strange creeping sleep overtook the squire again.

Meyrick, who was staying in the house, and who had been coming in and out through the evening, eyeing Elsmere, now that there was more light on the scene, with almost as much anxiety and misgiving as the squire, was summoned. The squire was put into his carrying-chair. Vincent and a male attendant appeared, and he was borne to his room, Meyrick peremptorily refusing to allow Robert to lend so much as a finger to the performance. They took him up the library stairs, through the empty book-rooms and that dreary room which had been his father's, and so into his own. By the time they set him down he was quite awake and conscious again.

'It can't be said that I follow my own precepts,' he said to Robert grimly as they put him down. 'Not much of the open eye about this. I shall sleep myself into the unknown as sweetly as any saint in the calendar.'

Robert was going when the squire called him back.

'You'll stay to-morrow, Elsmere?'

'Of course, if you wish it.'

The wrinkled eyes fixed him intently.

'Why did you ever go?'

'As I told you before, Squire, because there was nothing else for an honest man to do.'

The squire turned round with a frown.

'What the deuce are you dawdling about, Benson? Give me my stick and get me out of this.'

By midnight all was still in the vast pile of Murewell. Outside, the night was slightly frosty. A clear moon shone over the sloping reaches of the park; the trees shone silverly in the cold light, their black shadows cast along the grass. Robert found himself quartered in the Stuart room, where James II. had slept, and where the tartan hangings of the ponderous carved bed, and the rose and thistle reliefs of the walls and ceilings, untouched for two hundred years, bore witness to the loyal preparations made by some bygone Wendover. He was mortally tired, but by way of distracting his thoughts a little from the squire, and that other tragedy which the great house sheltered somewhere in its walls, he took from his coat-pocket a French *Anthologie* which had been Catherine's birthday gift to him, and read a little before he fell asleep.

Then he slept profoundly—the sleep of exhaustion. Suddenly he found himself sitting up in bed, his heart beating to suffocation, strange noises in his ears.

A cry 'Help!' resounded through the wide empty galleries.

He flung on his dressing-gown, and ran out in the direction of the squire's room.

The hideous cries and scuffling grew more apparent as he reached it. At that moment Benson, the man who had helped to carry the squire, ran up.

'My God, sir!' he said, deadly white, 'another attack!'

The squire's room was empty, but the door into the lumber-room adjoining it was open, and the stifled sounds came through it.

They rushed in and found Meyrick struggling in the grip of a white figure, that seemed to have the face of a fiend and the grip of a tiger. Those old bloodshot eyes—those wrinkled hands on the throat of the doctor—horrible!

They released poor Meyrick, who staggered bleeding into the squire's room. Then Robert and Benson got the squire back by main force. The whole face was convulsed, the poor shrunken limbs rigid as iron. Meyrick, who was sitting gasping, by a superhuman effort of will mastered himself enough to give directions for a strong opiate. Benson managed to control the madman while Robert found it. Then between them they got it swallowed.

But nature had been too quick for them. Before the opiate could have had time to work, the squire shrank together like a puppet of which the threads are loosened, and fell heavily sideways out of his captors' hands on to the bed. They laid him there, tenderly covering him from the January cold. The swollen eyelids fell, leaving just a thread of white visible underneath, the clenched hands slowly relaxed; the loud breathing seemed to be the breathing of death.

Meyrick, whose wound on the head had been hastily bound up, threw himself beside the bed. The night-light beyond cast a grotesque shadow of him on the wall, emphasising, as though in mockery, the long straight back, the ragged whiskers, the strange ends and horns of the bandage. But the passion in the old face was as purely tragic as any that ever spoke through the lips of an Antigone or a Gloucester.[26]

'The last—the last!' he said, choked, the tears falling down his lined cheeks on to the squire's hand. 'He can never rally from this. And I was fool enough to think yesterday I had pulled him through!'

Again a long gaze of inarticulate grief; then he looked up at Robert.

'He wouldn't have Benson to-night. I slept in the next room with the door ajar. A few minutes ago I heard him moving. I was up in an instant, and found him standing by that door, peering through, bare-footed, a wind like ice coming up. He looked at me, frowning, all in a flame. "*My father,*" he said—"*my father*—he went that way—what do *you* want here? Keep back!" I threw myself on him; he had something sharp which scratched me on the temple; I got that away from him, but it was his hands'—and the old man shuddered. 'I thought they would have done for me before any one could hear, and that then he would kill himself as his father did.'

Again he hung over the figure on the bed—his own withered hand stroking that of the squire with a yearning affection.

'When was the last attack?' asked Robert sadly.

'A month ago, sir, just after they got back. Ah, Mr. Elsmere, he suffered. And he's been so lonely. No one to cheer him, no one to please him with his food—to put his cushions right—to coax him up a bit, and that—and his poor sister too, always there before his eyes. Of course he would stand to it he liked to be alone. But I'll never believe men are made so unlike one to the other. The Almighty meant a man to have a wife or a child about him when he comes to the last. He missed you, sir, when you went away. Not that he'd say a word, but he moped. His books didn't seem to please him, nor anything else. I've just broke my heart over him this last year.'

There was silence a moment in the big room, hung round with the shapes of bygone Wendovers. The opiate had taken effect. The squire's countenance was no longer convulsed. The great brow was calm; a more than common dignity and peace spoke from the long peaked face. Robert bent over him. The madman, the cynic, had passed away: the dying scholar and thinker lay before him.

---

26 Antigone, daughter of Oedipus in Greek mythology, central figure of Sophocles' *Antigone*, who resists Creon's order that her brother receive no burial; the Earl of Gloucester, betrayed by his illegitimate son Edmund in Shakespeare's *King Lear*.

'Will he rally?' he asked, under his breath.

Meyrick shook his head.

'I doubt it. It has exhausted all the strength he had left. The heart is failing rapidly. I think he will sleep away. And, Mr. Elsmere, you go—go and sleep. Benson and I'll watch. Oh, my scratch is nothing, sir. I'm used to a rough-and-tumble life. But you go. If there's a change we'll wake you.'

Elsmere bent down and kissed the squire's forehead tenderly, as a son might have done. By this time he himself could hardly stand. He crept away to his own room, his nerves still quivering with the terror of that sudden waking, the horror of that struggle.

It was impossible to sleep. The moon was at the full outside. He drew back the curtains, made up the fire, and, wrapping himself in a fur coat which Flaxman had lately forced upon him, sat where he could see the moonlit park, and still be within the range of the blaze.

As the excitement passed away a reaction of feverish weakness set in. The strangest whirlwind of thoughts fled through him in the darkness, suggested very often by the figures on the seventeenth-century tapestry which lined the walls. Were those the trees in the wood-path? Surely that was Catherine's figure, trailing—and that dome—strange! Was he still walking in Grey's funeral procession, the Oxford buildings looking sadly down? Death here! Death there! Death everywhere, yawning under life from the beginning! The veil which hides the common abyss, in sight of which men could not always hold themselves and live, is rent asunder, and he looks shuddering into it.

Then the image changed, and in its stead, that old familiar image of the river of Death took possession of him. He stood himself on the brink; on the other side were Grey and the squire. But he felt no pang of separation, of pain; for he himself was just about to cross and join them! And during a strange brief lull of feeling the mind harboured image and expectation alike with perfect calm.

Then the fever-spell broke—the brain cleared—and he was terribly himself again. Whence came it—this fresh inexorable consciousness? He tried to repel it, to forget himself, to cling blindly, without thought, to God's love and Catherine's. But the anguish mounted fast. On the one hand, this fast-growing certainty, urging and penetrating through every nerve and fibre of the shaken frame; on the other, the ideal fabric of his efforts and his dreams, the New Jerusalem of a regenerate faith; the poor, the loving, and the simple walking therein!

'*My God! my God! no time, no future!*'

In his misery he moved to the uncovered window, and stood looking through it, seeing and not seeing. Outside, the river, just filmed with ice, shone under the moon; over it bent the trees, laden with hoar-frost. Was that a heron, rising for an instant, beyond the bridge, in the unearthly blue?

And quietly—heavily—like an irrevocable sentence, there came, breathed to him as it were from that winter cold and loneliness, words that he had read an hour or two before, in the little red book beside his hand—words in which the gayest of French poets has fixed, as though by accident, the most tragic of all human cries—

'Quittez le long espoir, et les vastes pensées.'[27]

He sank on his knees, wrestling with himself and with the bitter longing for life, and the same words rang through him, deafening every cry but their own.

'*Quittez—quittez—le long espoir et les vastes pensées!*'

CHAPTER LI

There is little more to tell. The man who had lived so fast was no long time dying. The eager soul was swift in this as in all else.

The day after Elsmere's return from Murewell, where he left the squire still alive (the telegram announcing the death reached Bedford Square a few hours after Robert's arrival), Edmondson came up to see him and examine him. He discovered tubercular disease of the larynx, which begins with slight hoarseness and weakness, and develops into one of the most rapid forms of phthisis. In his opinion it had been originally set up by the effects of the chill at Petites Dalles acting upon a constitution never strong, and at that moment peculiarly susceptible to mischief. And of course the speaking and preaching of the last four months had done enormous harm.

It was with great outward composure that Elsmere received his *arrêt de mort* at the hands of the young doctor, who announced the result of his examination with a hesitating lip and a voice which struggled in vain to preserve its professional calm.[28] He knew too much of medicine himself to be deceived by Edmondson's optimist remarks as to the possible effect of a warm climate like Algiers on his condition. He sat down, resting his head on his hands a

---

27 Jean de la Fontaine, "Le vieillard et les trois jeunes hommes." "Give up excessive hope and grand dreams."

28 *arrêt de mort*: death sentence.

moment; then, wringing Edmondson's hand, he went out feebly to find his wife.

Catherine had been waiting in the dining-room, her whole soul one dry tense misery. She stood looking out of the window taking curious heed of a Jewish wedding that was going on in the square, of the preposterous bouquets of the coachman and the gaping circle of errand-boys. How pinched the bride looked in the north wind!

When the door opened and Catherine saw her husband come in—her young husband, to whom she had been married not yet four years—with that indescribable look in the eyes which seemed to divine and confirm all those terrors which had been shaking her during her agonised waiting, there followed a moment between them which words cannot render. When it ended—that half-articulate convulsion of love and anguish—she found herself sitting on the sofa beside him, his head on her breast, his hand clasping hers.

'Do you wish me to go, Catherine?' he asked her gently,—'to Algiers?'

Her eyes implored for her.

'Then I will,' he said, but with a long sigh. 'It will only prolong it two months,' he thought; 'and does one not owe it to the people for whom one has tried to live, to make a brave end among them? Ah, no! no! those two months are *hers!*'

So, without any outward resistance, he let the necessary preparations be made. It wrung his heart to go, but he could not wring hers by staying.

After his interview with Robert, and his further interview with Catherine, to whom he gave the most minute recommendations and directions, with a reverent gentleness which seemed to make the true state of the case more ghastly plain to the wife than ever, Edmondson went off to Flaxman.

Flaxman heard his news with horror.

'A *bad* case, you say—advanced?'

'A bad case!' Edmondson repeated gloomily. 'He has been fighting against it too long under that absurd delusion of clergyman's throat. If only men would not insist upon being their own doctors! And, of course, that going down to Murewell the other day was madness. I shall go with him to Algiers, and probably stay a week or two. To think of that life, that career, cut short! This is a queer sort of world!'

When Flaxman went over to Bedford Square in the afternoon, he went like a man going himself to execution. In the hall he met Catherine.

'You have seen Dr. Edmondson?' she asked, pale and still, except for a little nervous quivering of the lip.

He stooped and kissed her hand.

'Yes. He says he goes with you to Algiers. I will come after if you will have me. The climate may do wonders.'

She looked at him with the most heart-rending of smiles.

'Will you go in to Robert? He is in the study.'

He went, in trepidation, and found Robert lying tucked up on the sofa, apparently reading.

'Don't—don't, old fellow,' he said affectionately, as Flaxman almost broke down. 'It comes to all of us sooner or later. Whenever it comes we think it too soon. I believe I have been sure of it for some time. We are such strange creatures! It has been so present to me lately that life was too good to last. You remember the sort of feeling one used to have as a child about some treat in the distance—that it was too much joy—that something was sure to come between you and it? Well, in a sense, I have had my joy, the first-fruits of it at least.'

But as he threw his arms behind his head, leaning back on them, Flaxman saw the eyes darken and the naïve boyish mouth contract, and knew that under all these brave words there was a heart which hungered.

'How strange!' Robert went on reflectively; 'yesterday I was travelling, walking like other men, a member of society. To-day I am an invalid; in the true sense, a man no longer. The world has done with me; a barrier I shall never recross has sprung up between me and it.—Flaxman, to-night is the story-telling. Will you read to them? I have the book here prepared—some scenes from David Copperfield.[29] And you will tell them?'

A hard task, but Flaxman undertook it. Never did he forget the scene. Some ominous rumour had spread, and the New Brotherhood was besieged. Impossible to give the reading. A hall full of strained upturned faced listened to Flaxman's announcement, and to Elsmere's messages of cheer and exhortation, and then a wild wave of grief spread through the place. The street outside was blocked, men looking dismally into each other's eyes, women weeping, children sobbing for sympathy, all feeling themselves at once shelterless and forsaken. When Elsmere heard the news of it, he turned on his face, and asked even Catherine to leave him for a while.

The preparations were pushed on. The New Brotherhood had just become the subject of an animated discussion in the press, and London was touched by the news of its young founder's breakdown. Catherine found herself besieged by offers of help of various kinds. One offer Flaxman persuaded her to accept. It was the loan of a villa at El Biar, on the hill above Algiers, belonging to a connection of his own. A resident on the spot was to take all

---

29 Autobiographical novel (1849–50) by Charles Dickens.

trouble off their hands; they were to find servants ready for them, and every comfort.

Catherine made every arrangement, met every kindness, with a self-reliant calm that never failed. But it seemed to Flaxman that her heart was broken—that half of her, in feeling, was already on the other side of this horror which stared them all in the face. Was it his perception of it which stirred Robert after a while to a greater hopefulness of speech, a constant bright dwelling on the flowery sunshine for which they were about to exchange the fog and cold of London? The momentary revival of energy was more pitiful to Flaxman than his first quiet resignation.

He himself wrote every day to Rose. Strange love-letters! in which the feeling that could not be avowed ran as a fiery under-current through all the sad brotherly record of the invalid's doings and prospects. There was deep trouble in Long Whindale. Mrs. Leyburn was tearful and hysterical, and wished to rush off to town to see Catherine. Agnes wrote in distress that her mother was quite unfit to travel, showing her own inner conviction, too, that the poor thing would only be an extra burden on the Elsmeres if the journey were achieved. Rose wrote asking to be allowed to go with them to Algiers; and after a little consultation it was so arranged, Mrs. Leyburn being tenderly persuaded, Robert himself writing, to stay where she was.

The morning after the interview with Edmondson, Robert sent for Murray Edwardes. They were closeted together for nearly an hour. Edwardes came out with the look of one who has been lifted into 'heavenly places.'[30]

'I thank God,' he said to Catherine, with deep emotion, 'that I ever knew him. I pray that I may be found worthy to carry out my pledges to him.'

When Catherine went into the study she found Robert gazing into the fire with dreamy eyes. He started and looked up to her with a smile.

'Murray Edwardes has promised himself heart and soul to the work. If necessary, he will give up his chapel to carry it on. But we hope it will be possible to work them together. What a brick he is! What a blessed chance it was that took me to that breakfast party at Flaxman's!'

The rest of the time before departure he spent almost entirely in consultation and arrangement with Edwardes. It was terrible how rapidly worse he seemed to grow directly the situation had declared itself, and the determination *not* to be ill had been perforce overthrown. But his struggle against breathlessness and weakness, and all the other symptoms of his state during these last days, was heroic. On the last day of all, by his own persistent wish, a certain number of members of the Brotherhood came to say good-bye to

---

30 Ephesians 1.3.

him. They came in one by one, Macdonald first. The old Scotchman, from the height of his sixty years of tough weather-beaten manhood, looked down on Robert with a fatherly concern.

'Eh, Mister Elsmere, but it's a fine place yur gawin' tu, they say. Ye'll do weel there, sir—ye'll do weel. And as for the wark, sir, we'll keep it oop—we'll not let the Deil mak' hay o' it, if we knaws it—the auld leer!' he added, with a phraseology which did more honour to the Calvinism of his blood than the philosophy of his training.

Lestrange came in, with a pale sharp face, and said little in his ten minutes. But Robert divined in him a sort of repressed curiosity and excitement akin to that of Voltaire turning his feverish eyes towards *le grand secret*. 'You, who preached to us that consciousness, and God, and the soul are the only realities—are you so sure of it now you are dying, as you were in health? Are your courage, your certainty, what they were?' These were the sort of questions that seemed to underlie the man's spoken words.

There was something trying in it, but Robert did his best to put aside his consciousness of it. He thanked him for his help in the past, and implored him to stand by the young society and Mr. Edwardes.

'I shall hardly come back, Lestrange. But what does one man matter? One soldier falls, another presses forward.'

The watchmaker rose, then paused a moment, a flush passing over him.

'We can't stand without you!' he said abruptly; then, seeing Robert's look of distress, he seemed to cast about for something reassuring to say, but could find nothing. Robert at last held out his hand with a smile, and he went. He left Elsmere struggling with a pang of horrible depression. In reality there was no man who worked harder at the New Brotherhood during the months that followed than Lestrange. He worked under perpetual protest from the *frondeur* within him, but something stung him on—on—till a habit had been formed which promises to be the joy and salvation of his later life. Was it the haunting memory of that thin figure—the hand clinging to the chair—the white appealing look?

Others came and went, till Catherine trembled for the consequences. She herself took in Mrs. Richards and her children, comforting the sobbing creatures afterwards with a calmness born of her own despair. Robson, in the last stage himself, sent him a grimly characteristic message. 'I shall solve the riddle, sir, before you. The doctor gives me three days. For the first time in my life, I shall know what you are still guessing at. May the blessing of one who never blessed thing or creature before he saw you go with you!'

After it all Robert sank on the sofa with a groan.

'No more!' he said hoarsely—'no more! Now for air—the sea! To-morrow, wife, to-morrow! *Cras ingens iterabimus æquor.*[31] Ah me! I leave *my* new Salamis behind!'

But on that last evening he insisted on writing letters to Langham and Newcome.

'I will spare Langham the sight of me' he said, smiling sadly. 'And I will spare myself the sight of Newcome—I could not bear it, I think! But I must say good-bye—for I love them both.'

Next day, two hours after the Elsmeres had left for Dover, a cab drove up to their house in Bedford Square, and Newcome descended from it. 'Gone, sir, two hours ago,' said the housemaid, and the priest turned away with an involuntary gesture of despair. To his dying day the passionate heart bore the burden of that 'too late,' believing that even at the eleventh hour Elsmere would have been granted to his prayers. He might even have followed them, but that a great retreat for clergy he was just on the point of conducting made it impossible.

Flaxman went down with them to Dover. Rose, in the midst of all her new and womanly care for her sister and Robert, was very sweet to him. In any other circumstances, he told himself, he could easily have broken down the flimsy barrier between them, but in those last twenty-four hours he could press no claim of his own.

When the steamer cast loose, the girl, hanging over the side, stood watching the tall figure on the pier against the gray January sky. Catherine caught her look and attitude, and could have cried aloud in her own gnawing pain.

Flaxman got a cheery letter from Edmondson describing their arrival. Their journey had gone well; even the odious passage from Marseilles had been tolerable; little Mary had proved a model traveller; the villa was luxurious, the weather good.

'I have got rooms close by them in the Vice-Consul's cottage,' wrote Edmondson. 'Imagine, within sixty hours of leaving London in a January fog, finding yourself tramping over wild marigolds and mignonette, under a sky and through an air as balmy as those of an English June—when an English June behaves itself. Elsmere's room overlooks the bay, the great plain of the Metidja dotted with villages, and the grand range of the Djurjura, backed by snowy summits one can hardly tell from the clouds. His spirits are marvellous. He is plunged in the history of Algiers, raving about one Fromentin,

---

31 Horace, Ode 1.7.32. "Tomorrow we will be back on the vast ocean." Salamis (on the island of Cyprus) here refers to the same Ode, which praises Teucer, the city's founder.

learning Spanish even![32] The wonderful purity and warmth of the air seem to have relieved the larynx greatly. He breathes and speaks much more easily than when we left London. I sometimes feel when I look at him as though in this as in all else he were unlike the common sons of men—as though to *him* it might be possible to subdue even this fell disease.'

Elsmere himself wrote—

"'I had not heard the half"[33]—O Flaxman! An enchanted land—air, sun, warmth, roses, orange blossom, new potatoes, green peas, veiled Eastern beauties, domed mosques and preaching Mahdis[34]—everything that feeds the outer and the inner man. To throw the window open at waking to the depth of sunlit air between us and the curve of the bay, is for the moment heaven! One's soul seems to escape one, to pour itself into the luminous blue of the morning. I am better—I breathe again.

'Mary flourishes exceedingly. She lives mostly on oranges, and has been adopted by sixty nuns who inhabit the convent over the way, and sell us the most delicious butter and cream. I imagine, if she were a trifle older, her mother would hardly view the proceedings of these dear berosaried women with so much equanimity.

'As for Rose, she writes more letters than Clarissa, and receives more than an editor of the *Times*.[35] I have the strongest views, as you know, as to the vanity of letter-writing. There was a time when you shared them, but there are circumstances and conjunctures, alas! in which no man can be sure of his friend or his friend's principles. Kind friend, good fellow, go often to Elgood Street. Tell me everything about everybody. It is possible, after all, that I may live to come back to them.'

But a week later, alas! the letters fell into a very different strain. The weather had changed, had turned indeed damp and rainy, the natives of course declaring that such gloom and storm in January had never been known before. Edmondson wrote in discouragement. Elsmere had had a touch of cold, had been confined to bed, and almost speechless. His letter was full of medical detail, from which Flaxman gathered that, in spite of the rally of the first ten days, it was clear that the disease was attacking constantly fresh tissue. 'He is very depressed too,' said Edmondson; 'I have never seen him so yet. He sits and looks at us in the evening sometimes with eyes that wring one's heart. It

---

32 Eugène Fromentin (1820–76), French artist and author; famous for his paintings and accounts of Arab life in Algeria.

33 1 Kings 10.7.

34 In Islam, the Mahdi is a messianic figure destined to rule on earth for a period of time until the Day of Judgment.

35 The eponymous heroine of Samuel Richardson's lengthy epistolary novel (1748).

is as though, after having for a moment allowed himself to hope, he found it a doubly hard task to submit.'

Ah, that depression! It was the last eclipse through which a radiant soul was called to pass; but while it lasted it was black indeed. The implacable reality, obscured at first by the emotion and excitement of farewells, and then by a brief spring of hope and returning vigour, showed itself now in all its stern nakedness—sat down, as it were, eye to eye with Elsmere—immovable, ineluctable. There were certain features of the disease itself which were specially trying to such a nature. The long silences it enforced were so unlike him, seemed already to withdraw him so pitifully from their yearning grasp! In these dark days he would sit crouching over the wood fire in the little *salon*, or lie drawn to the window looking out on the rainstorms bowing the ilexes or scattering the meshes of clematis, silent, almost always gentle, but turning sometimes on Catherine, or on Mary playing at his feet, eyes which, as Edmondson said, 'wrung the heart.'

But in reality, under the husband's depression, and under the wife's inexhaustible devotion, a combat was going on, which reached no third person, but was throughout poignant and tragic to the highest degree. Catherine was making her last effort, Robert his last stand. As we know, ever since that passionate submission of the wife which had thrown her morally at her husband's feet, there had lingered at the bottom of her heart one last supreme hope. All persons of the older Christian type attribute a special importance to the moment of death. While the man of science looks forward to his last hour as a moment of certain intellectual weakness, and calmly warns his friends beforehand that he is to be judged by the utterances of health and not by those of physical collapse, the Christian believes that on the confines of eternity the veil of flesh shrouding the soul grows thin and transparent, and that the glories and the truths of Heaven are visible with a special clearness and authority to the dying. It was for this moment, either in herself or in him, that Catherine's unconquerable faith had been patiently and dumbly waiting. Either she would go first, and death would wing her poor last words to him with a magic and power not their own; or, when he came to leave her, the veil of doubt would fall away perforce from a spirit as pure as it was humble, and the eternal light, the light of the Crucified, shine through.

Probably, if there had been no breach in Robert's serenity, Catherine's poor last effort would have been much feebler, briefer, more hesitating. But when she saw him plunged for a short space in mortal discouragement, in a sombreness that as the days went on had its points and crests of feverish irritation, her anguished pity came to the help of her creed. Robert felt himself besieged, driven within the citadel, her being urging, grappling with his. In little half-articulate words and ways, in her attempts to draw him back to some of their old religious books and prayers, in those kneeling vigils he often found her maintaining at night beside him, he felt a persistent attack which nearly—in his weakness—overthrew him.

For 'reason and thought grow tired like muscles and nerves.'[36] Some of the greatest and most daring thinkers of the world have felt this pitiful longing to be at one with those who love them, at whatever cost, before the last farewell. And the simpler Christian faith has still to create around it those venerable associations and habits which buttress individual feebleness and diminish the individual effort.

One early February morning, just before dawn, Robert stretched out his hand for his wife and found her kneeling beside him. The dim mingled light showed him her face vaguely—her clasped hands, her eyes. He looked at her in silence, she at him; there seemed to be a strange shock as of battle between them. Then he drew her head down to him.

'Catherine,' he said to her in a feeble intense whisper, 'would you leave me without comfort, without help, at the end?'

'Oh, my beloved!' she cried, under her breath, throwing her arms round him, 'if you would but stretch out your hand to the true comfort—the true help—the Lamb of God sacrificed for us!'

He stroked her hair tenderly.

'My weakness might yield—my true best self never. I know Whom I have believed. Oh, my darling, be content. Your misery, your prayers hold me back from God—from that truth and that trust which can alone be honestly mine. Submit, my wife! Leave me in God's hands.'

She raised her head. His eyes were bright with fever, his lips trembling, his whole look heavenly. She bowed herself again with a quiet burst of tears, and an indescribable self-abasement. They had had their last struggle, and once more he had conquered! Afterwards the cloud lifted from him. Depression and irritation disappeared. It seemed to her often as though he lay already on the breast of God; even her wifely love grew timid and awestruck.

Yet he did not talk much of immortality, of reunion. It was like a scrupulous child that dares not take for granted more than its father has allowed it to know. At the same time, it was plain to those about him that the only realities to him in a world of shadows were God—love—the soul.

One day he suddenly caught Catherine's hands, drew her face to him, and studied it with his glowing and hollow eyes, as though he would draw it

---

36 *Amiel's Journal*, 14.

into his soul.

'He made it,' he said hoarsely, as he let her go—'this love—this yearning. And in life He only makes us yearn that He may satisfy. He cannot lead us to the end and disappoint the craving He Himself set in us. No, no—could you—could I—do it? And He, the source of love, of justice——'

Flaxman arrived a few days afterwards. Edmondson had started for London the night before, leaving Elsmere better again, able to drive and even walk a little, and well looked after by a local doctor of ability. As Flaxman, tramping up behind his carriage, climbed the long hill to El Biar, he saw the whole marvellous place in a white light of beauty—the bay, the city, the mountains, oliveyard and orange-grove, drawn in pale tints on luminous air. Suddenly, at the entrance of a steep and narrow lane, he noticed a slight figure standing—a parasol against the sun.

'We thought you would like to be shown the short cut up the hill,' said Rose's voice, strangely demure and shy. 'The man can drive round.'

A grip of the hand, a word to the driver, and they were alone in the high-walled lane, which was really the old road up the hill, before the French brought zigzags and civilisation. She gave him news of Robert—better than he had expected. Under the influence of one of the natural reactions that wait on illness, the girl's tone was cheerful, and Flaxman's spirits rose. They talked of the splendour of the day, the discomforts of the steamer, the picturesque-ness of the landing—of anything and everything but the hidden something which was responsible for the dancing brightness in his eyes, the occasional swift veiling of her own.

Then, at an angle of the lane, where a little spring ran cool and brown into a moss-grown trough, where the blue broke joyously through the gray cloud of olive-wood, where not a sight or sound was to be heard of all the busy life which hides and nestles along the hill, he stopped, his hands seizing hers.

'How long?' he said, flushing, his light overcoat falling back from his strong, well-made frame; 'from August to February—how long?'

No more! It was most natural, nay, inevitable. For the moment death stood aside and love asserted itself. But this is no place to chronicle what it said.

And he had hardly asked, and she had hardly yielded, before the same misgiving, the same shrinking, seized on the lovers themselves. They sped up the hill, they crept into the house, far apart. It was agreed that neither of them should say a word.

But, with that extraordinarily quick perception that sometimes goes with such a state as his, Elsmere had guessed the position of things before he and Flaxman had been half an hour together. He took a boyish pleasure in making his friend confess himself, and, when Flaxman left him, at once sent for Catherine and told her.

Catherine, coming out afterwards, met Flaxman in the little tiled hall. How she had aged and blanched! She stood a moment opposite to him, in her plain long dress with its white collar and cuffs, her face working a little.

'We are so glad!' she said, but almost with a sob—'God bless you!'

And, wringing his hand, she passed away from him, hiding her eyes, but without a sound. When they met again she was quite self-contained and bright, talking much both with him and Rose about the future.

And one little word of Rose's must be recorded here, for those who have followed her through these four years. It was at night, when Robert, with smiles, had driven them out of doors to look at the moon over the bay, from the terrace just beyond the windows. They had been sitting on the balustrade talking of Elsmere. In this nearness to death, Rose had lost her mocking ways; but she was shy and difficult, and Flaxman felt it all very strange, and did not venture to woo her much.

When, all at once, he felt her hand steal trembling, a little white suppliant, into his, and her face against his shoulder.

'You won't—you won't ever be angry with me for making you wait like that? It was impertinent—it was like a child playing tricks!'

Flaxman was deeply shocked by the change in Robert. He was terribly emaciated. They could only talk at rare intervals in the day, and it was clear that his nights were often one long struggle for breath. But his spirits were extraordinarily even, and his days occupied to a point Flaxman could hardly have believed. He would creep downstairs at eleven, read his English letters (among them always some from Elgood Street), write his answers to them—those difficult scrawls are among the treasured archives of a society which is fast gathering to itself some of the best life in England—then often fall asleep with fatigue. After food there would come a short drive, or, if the day was very warm, an hour or two of sitting outside, generally his best time for talking. He had a wheeled chair in which Flaxman would take him across to the convent garden—a dream of beauty. Overhead an orange canopy—leaf and blossom and golden fruit all in simultaneous perfection; underneath a revel of every imaginable flower—narcissus and anemones, geraniums and clematis; and all about, hedges of monthly roses, dark red and pale alternately, making a roseleaf carpet under their feet. Through the tree-trunks shone the white sun-warmed convent, and far beyond were glimpses of downward-trending valleys edged by twinkling sea.

Here, sensitive and receptive to his last hour, Elsmere drank in beauty and delight; talking, too, whenever it was possible to him, of all things in heaven and earth. Then, when he came home, he would have out his books and fall to some old critical problem—his worn and scored Greek Testament always beside him, the quick eye making its way through some new monograph or other, the parched lips opening every now and then to call Flaxman's attention to some fresh light on an obscure point—only to relinquish the effort again and again with an unfailing patience.

But though he would begin as ardently as ever, he could not keep his attention fixed to these things very long. Then it would be the turn of his favourite poets—Wordsworth, Tennyson, Virgil. Virgil perhaps most frequently. Flaxman would read the Æneid aloud to him, Robert following the passages he loved best in a whisper, his hand resting the while in Catherine's. And then Mary would be brought in, and he would lie watching her while she played.

'I have had a letter,' he said to Flaxman one afternoon, 'from a Broad Church clergyman in the Midlands, who imagines me to be still militant in London, protesting against the "absurd and wasteful isolation" of the New Brotherhood. He asks me why instead of leaving the Church I did not join the Church Reform Union, why I did not attempt to widen the Church from within, and why we in Elgood Street are not now in organic connection with the new Broad Church settlement in East London.[37] I believe I have written him rather a sharp letter; I could not help it. It was borne in on me to tell him that it is all owing to him and his brethren that we are in the muddle we are in to-day. Miracle is to our time what the law was to the early Christians. We *must* make up our minds about it one way or the other. And if we decide to throw it over as Paul threw over the law, then we must *fight* as he did. There is no help in subterfuge, no help in anything but a perfect sincerity. We must come out of it. The ground must be cleared; then may come the re-building. Religion itself, the peace of generations to come, is at stake. If we could wait indefinitely while the Church widened, well and good. But we have but the one life, the one chance of saying the word or playing the part assigned us.'

On another occasion, in the convent garden, he broke out with—

---

37 The Church Reform Union, founded in 1870, was intended to ward off disestablishment by reconstructing the Church of England on more liberal Protestant principles (including greater empowerment for laymen). T. H. Green belonged to it.

'I often lie here, Flaxman, wondering at the way in which men become the slaves of some metaphysical word—*personality*, or *intelligence*, or what not! What meaning can they have as applied to *God?* Herbert Spencer is quite right.[38] We no sooner attempt to define what we mean by a Personal God than we lose ourselves in labyrinths of language and logic. But why attempt it at all? I like that French saying, *"Quand on me demande ce que c'est que Dieu, je l'ignore; quand on ne me le demande pas, je le sais très-bien!"*[39] No, we cannot realise Him in words—we can only live in Him, and die to Him!'

On another occasion, he said, speaking to Catherine of the squire and of Meyrick's account of his last year of life—

'How selfish one is, *always*—when one least thinks it! How could I have forgotten him so completely as I did during all that New Brotherhood time? Where, what is he now? Ah! if somewhere, somehow, one could——'

He did not finish the sentence, but the painful yearning of his look finished it for him.

But the days passed on, and the voice grew rarer, the strength feebler. By the beginning of March all coming downstairs was over. He was entirely confined to his room, almost to his bed. Then there came a horrible week, when no narcotics took effect, when every night was a wrestle for life, which it seemed must be the last. They had a good nurse, but Flaxman and Catherine mostly shared the watching between them.

One morning he had just dropped into a fevered sleep. Catherine was sitting by the window gazing out into a dawn-world of sun which reminded her of the summer sunrises at Petites Dalles. She looked the shadow of herself. Spiritually, too, she was the shadow of herself. Her life was no longer her own: she lived in him—in every look of those eyes—in every movement of that wasted frame.

As she sat there, her Bible on her knee, her strained unseeing gaze resting on the garden and the sea, a sort of hallucination took possession of her. It seemed to her that she saw the form of the Son of man passing over the misty slope in front of her, that the dim majestic figure turned and beckoned. In her half-dream she fell on her knees. 'Master!' she cried in agony, 'I cannot leave him! Call me not! My life is here. I have no heart—it beats in his.'

And the figure passed on, the beckoning hand dropping at its side. She followed it with a sort of anguish, but it seemed to her as though mind and body were alike incapable of moving—that she would not if she could. Then

38 As he argues in "Religion: A Retrospect and Prospect," *The Nineteenth Century* 15 (Jan. 1884): 1-12, esp. 7–8.
39 When someone asks me what God is, I don't know the answer to the question; when no-one asks me, I know the answer quite well!

suddenly a sound from behind startled her. She turned, her trance shaken off in an instant, and saw Robert sitting up in bed.

For a moment her lover, her husband, of the early days was before her— as she ran to him. But he did not see her.

An ecstasy of joy was on his face; the whole man bent forward listening. '*The child's cry!—thank God! Oh! Meyrick—Catherine—thank God!*'

And she knew that he stood again on the stairs at Murewell in that September night which gave them their first-born, and that he thanked God because her pain was over.

An instant's strained looking, and, sinking back into her arms, he gave two or three gasping breaths, and died.

Five days later Flaxman and Rose brought Catherine home. It was supposed that she would return to her mother at Burwood. Instead, she settled down again in London, and not one of those whom Robert Elsmere had loved was forgotten by his widow. Every Sunday morning, with her child beside her, she worshipped in the old ways; every Sunday afternoon saw her black-veiled figure sitting motionless in a corner of the Elgood Street Hall. In the week she gave all her time and money to the various works of charity which he had started. But she held her peace. Many were grateful to her; some loved her; none understood her. She lived for one hope only; and the years passed all too slowly.

The New Brotherhood still exists, and grows. There are many who imagined that as it had been raised out of the earth by Elsmere's genius, so it would sink with him. Not so! He would have fought the struggle to victory with surpassing force, with a brilliancy and rapidity none after him could rival. But the struggle was not his. His effort was but a fraction of the effort of the race. In that effort, and in the Divine force behind it, is our trust, as was his.

> 'Others, I doubt not, if not we,
> The issue of our toils shall see;
> And (they forgotten and unknown)
> Young children gather as their own
> The harvest that the dead had sown.'[40]

THE END

---

40 The conclusion of Arthur Hugh Clough's "Come, Poet, Come."

APPENDIX A - PREFACE TO WESTMORELAND EDITION

Ward supplied new prefaces for the novels published in Smith, Elder's collected Library Edition (also known as the Westmoreland Edition), beginning with *Robert Elsmere* in 1911. In these excerpts, she explains the novel's genesis, discusses its relevance to contemporary religious debates, and identifies the real-life inspirations for several of the characters. By this point, Ward had become more interested in the Modernist movement within the Roman Catholic Church as a model for Anglican reform, and her references to it here anticipate *The Case of Richard Meynell* (1911).

INTRODUCTION

I

After twenty-one years 'Robert Elsmere' is now to be reissued as the first instalment of this collected edition. During these years, something, probably, not very far short of a million copies of the work have been distributed in the English-speaking countries, and translations of it have appeared in most foreign languages. Its enemies and its friends agree in attributing to it a certain wide popular influence. It has been much written about, and a good deal preached against. Its circulation is still quite steady; and two years ago—if these details may be allowed me—fifty thousand copies of a new cheap edition were sold in a fortnight, and a hundred thousand within the year. Fifteen years after its publication, M. Brunetière, [1]the editor of the *Revue des Deux Mondes*, and, at the moment, the most important literary supporter of French Catholicism, began a negotiation with me for the appearance of a French translation of the whole or part of the book in the *Revue*; and when I asked him in astonishment how it could possibly suit him to entertain such a project, he replied that whereas in 1888 the ideas expressed in 'Robert Elsmere'

---

1 Ferdinand Brunetière (1849-1906), French editor and literary scholar. At the time that Ward was writing this introduction, Brunetière would no longer have been in sympathy with her views, as he had become a strictly orthodox Catholic.

could have had no interest for the public of the *Revue*, there was now so much affinity between them and the problems and debates which Modernism had been forcing on French Catholicism that —always supposing its length could be got over—it had become worth his while to publish it. Its length could not be got over, and the project fell through. But the incident gave the writer of the story a very keen pleasure. For it seemed to show that, with all its many faults, 'Robert Elsmere' had yet possessed a certain representative and pioneering character; and that to some extent at least the generation in which it appeared had spoken through it.

If then it had, or still has, this touch of representative significance, it will perhaps not be thought unseemly on my part if now, looking back twenty-one years, I try to trace some of the half-forgotten circumstances and influences that produced the book. In truth these circumstances and influences—or their natural successors—are still at work in this new century as they were in that which has just closed. 'Modernism' is indeed a far more widespread and active force to-day throughout educated Europe than it was thirty years ago. If in the Church of England, at the present moment, Liberal thought has fewer distinguished and eloquent voices — voices that have the ear of England — than was the case a generation ago, Liberal influence is none the less diffusive, because it has won so many victories that the field of controversy is both changed and narrowed; while the emergence of Modernism in Roman Catholicism is a phenomenon so striking, and represents an advance of critical and historical thought so far-reaching and decisive, that it rightly holds the attention of Europe. If Modernism wins and maintains its right of citizenship within Catholicism, the steady advance of the new Christianity throughout Europe, Catholic or Protestant, is assured; although, for centuries to come, the new and the old may still live and interact side by side. And what is worth notice is that 'Modernism,' in its Catholic form, is a movement starting not from the laity, but from the clergy; it is affecting the central teachings and the accredited teachers of the Church; and its followers are so certain of their ground that they have no idea of leaving the communion they love, and spend their whole energies in reforming it from within. Twenty years ago, in endeavouring to trace the effect of critical thought on an Anglican clergyman, it seemed to me that an honest man in Elsmere's position could only depart and renounce. Fogazzaro, in 'Il Santo,'[2] has with great beauty and force pleaded just the opposite thesis. The Santo does not carry his Modernist denials and affirmations out of the Church; it is the passionate aim of his

---

2 Antonio Fogazarro (1842-1911), Italian novelist and poet; his novel *Il Santo*, the final volume of a trilogy, appeared in 1905.

life of sacrifice and love to naturalise them within it. And the religious novel which still remains to be written for ourselves will take the same ground. The Modernist Anglican parson of the future will not go; the struggle will arise and develop and be fought out within the Church; and only then, through the kindling of that fire, will the Church of England renew its youth, and regain its hold upon the nation.

But in the last third of the nineteenth century the process of thought involved was still so crude and incomplete that it certainly appeared as if there were nothing for an Elsmere but to go. Let me try and show through a little autobiography how the situation worked.

'Robert Elsmere' was begun some time in 1885, finished at the very end of 1887, and published in February, 1888. But if I try to trace back some of the causes which led to its composition, I find myself once more in the heart of that Oxford life, of which some aspects and forces find expression in the early part of the book. From 1872 to 1881, my early married years were spent in the beautiful city to which I came, a child of fourteen, with my parents in 1865, there to find, as I grew up, friends and influences and surroundings which strengthened whatever tendencies to a literary life were natural to one of my name and family tradition. My husband and I married in 1872, and our three children were born before 1880. In the free intervals which the cares of home left me, I got through a good deal of reading and writing of a rather various kind, concerned now with English, now with French, now with Spanish literature; and articles by me appeared in *Macmillan's*, the *Saturday Review,* and the *Fortnightly.* But in 1879 all this was merged in a task which occupied me for nearly two years, and was in truth the only piece of serious and consecutive *training,* in both writing and thinking, to which, so far as those years of youth are concerned, I can look back. Dr. Wace, now Dean of Canterbury, came to Oxford to beat up contributors for the second and succeeding volumes of 'The Dictionary of Christian Biography.' The first volume — since amended —was thought inadequate and imperfect. It was the ambition of the new editor to secure some historical recruits from Oxford who might help him with the later volumes, especially in the obscurer fields and side-paths connected with the incursion of the northern races into Europe and the break-up of the Roman Empire. Among other additions to his staff, he found in Mr. Arthur Dyke Acland, then historical lecturer at Christchurch and bursar of the College, and afterwards a member of Mr. Gladstone's last Cabinet, a student ready to help him with the Ostrogoths; from Mr. T. R. Buchanan, Fellow of All Souls, and lately Under Secretary for India, he obtained a similar promise with regard to the Franks; and he came to me, on the ground, I imagine, of some articles on Spanish Chronicles contributed by me to the *Saturday Review,* for the West-Goths and Spanish Christianity generally, up to 800 A.D.[3]

Mr. Acland and Mr. Buchanan were soon carried off by politics into wider fields where Franks and Ostrogoths were but as ghosts vanishing at cockcrow. But for me, the two years of labour among the documents of the early Spanish Church and the West-Gothic Kingdom, aided at every step by German criticism and research, were the determining years of life. Practically, I have described them and their effect on the mind in 'Robert Elsmere. ' Robert, in the leisure of a country parsonage, sets himself to study the origins of modern France, as the infant state gradually emerged from the wreck or the transformation of the Roman polity. In the chapter describing the Squire's library, Elsmere, for the benefit of Langham, sketches 'the sort of book he thought might be written on the rise of modern society in Gaul, dwelling first on the outward spectacle of the blood-stained Frankish world as it was, say, in the days of Gregory the Great, on its savage kings, its fiendish women, its bishops and its saints; and then, on the conflict of ideas going on behind all the fierce incoherence of the Empire's decay, the struggle of Roman order and of German freedom, of Roman luxury with German hardness; above all, the war of orthodoxy and heresy with its widespread political complications.' His ambition is 'to grasp and analyse that strange sense which haunts the student of Rome's decline, as it once overshadowed the infancy of Europe, — as of a slowly departing majesty, a great presence just withdrawn and still incalculably potent.' Langham listens to the historical ambitions of his companion, and when Robert has developed them, he interposes with the remark: 'There is one thing that doesn't seem to have troubled you yet. You will come to it! It makes almost the chief interest — it is indeed the dominant problem — of history. History depends on *testimony.* What is the nature and the value of testimony at given times? In other words, did the man of the third century understand, or report, or interpret facts in the same way as the man of the sixteenth or the nineteenth? And if not, what are the differences, and what are the deductions to be drawn from them, if any?'

Langham, in fact, asks his friend if, in approaching history, he has ever reflected on the psychology of testimony. Robert replies that he is as yet a beginner. He has been making a general survey of the ground; he must now go to work, inch by inch, and find out what the ground is made of. The point

3 Henry Wace (1836-1924), Protestant clergyman, Dean of Canterbury, and historian; Sir Arthur Dyke Acland (1847-1926), clergyman, politician, cabinet member for education; Thomas Ryburn Buchanan (1846-1911), lawyer and politician, Under-Secretary for India from 1908-9.

is of course enormously important. 'I should think it is,' said Langham to himself, as he rose: 'the whole of orthodox Christianity is in it, for instance!'

It was to this conclusion that two years of historical work, dealing at first hand with the chronicles and councils, the treatises and biographies of Spain during the four centuries before Charles the Great, had led the mind of the writer who tried to express herself in 'Robert Elsmere.' The astonishment awakened in Elsmere, as his task develops by those strange processes of mind current in the historians of certain periods, processes which are often more significant and illuminating than the facts which the historians are trying to relate, was in truth my own astonishment. After some fourteen years spent at Oxford in a more or less continuous though always desultory study of English poetry, French *belles-lettres,* and what one may call the general literature of modern religion, the *Acta* of Spanish Councils, and the chronicles and hagiography of the West-Gothic Kingdom, —studied with a certain intensity, — produced in me, beside the immediate historical result, a kind of far-reaching stir and rumination, if one may so put it, which gradually affected the whole mind. And it was this stir and rumination which, six years later, I endeavoured to reproduce in 'Robert Elsmere.'

There were of course other elements in the matter. There was the stimulus of that literary atmosphere supplied by Oxford itself, with its perpetual appeal to the past, and the poetry of the past. And beside the atmosphere of literature, there was the atmosphere of religious controversy, then far more evident and tangible at Oxford than it is to-day. For us young married people of the early seventies the influence of the great Liberal reaction which had followed the Tractarian Movement was still a living and combative force. Christ Church, from which in my day the harsh and, to us, mysterious figure of Pusey emerged occasionally, to deliver a Jeremiah-like word of warning or appeal from the University pulpit, was the headquarters of orthodoxy; Balliol, with Jowett for its Master, represented the Liberal camp. Through the famous Bamptons and his University sermons generally, still more perhaps through an unseen and very able management of affairs, Dr. Liddon had become the champion and leader of the Church forces; while at Balliol, the Master, and still more the beloved tutor and professor, Thomas Hill Green, stood for a constructive Liberalism, the results of which in English religious thought at the present day are, I venture to think, of far greater importance than anything which can be traced to the winning personality and the oratorical gift of Liddon. Then, a stone's throw off, Mark Pattison, at Lincoln College, the sarcastic and often bitter exponent of a type of learning which despised the idealism of Balliol hardly less than the ecclesiasticism of Christ Church, wielded a power, of limited range indeed, but, on those who felt it, of penetrating effect. In the picture of the Squire in 'Robert Elsmere' those who knew Mark Pattison may have recognised a few of his more obvious traits:

'Mr. Wendover was a man of middle height and loose bony frame, of which all the lower half had a thin and shrunken look. But the shoulders, which had the scholar's stoop, and the head, were massive and squarely outlined. The head was specially remarkable for its great breadth and comparative flatness above the eyes, and for the way in which the head itself dwarfed the face, which, as contrasted with the large angularity of the skull, was somewhat pinched and drawn. The hair was reddish grey, the eyes small, but deep-set under firm brows, and the thin-lipped wrinkled mouth, the long nose and chin, produced an effect of hard sarcastic strength.'

Such, as I look back, was the outer aspect of Mark Pattison, one of the friends of my youth to whom I have most cause to be grateful. I saw him thus, in the winter evenings, when, as a girl of nineteen, I would sometimes find myself in his library at Lincoln; 'the Rector' on one side of the fire, myself on the other, the cat and the cheerful blaze between. He looked thus as he talked of men and books and University affairs, with a frankness he showed much more readily to women than to men, and to the young rather than to his own contemporaries. He was always interested in the young girl-students of Oxford. He tried to help them, and set a standard before them; and when afterwards that bitter but most impressive fragment of autobiography appeared — one of the 'documents' of University life in the nineteenth century which no after historian will neglect — there were some of us who read it with no mere intellectual interest, but with a sharp pang at heart that our true friend should have suffered so much and so barrenly.

For the rest, 'the Rector' suggested the Squire only so far as outward aspect, a few personal traits, and the two main facts of great learning and a general impatience of fools are concerned. It is difficult to imagine Pattison as a country squire, or in any other setting indeed than college walls; but if he had ever found himself a great landowner, he would not have allowed himself to be managed by his agent; and there would have been no insanitary cottages on his estates.

To return, however, to the Oxford of thirty years ago. In addition to Christ Church, Balliol, and Lincoln, with the literary and philosophical culture for which they stood, there was, of course, Science, camped around the University Museum, in the background. As far as my own personal recollection goes, the men of science entered but little into the struggle of ideas that was going on. The main Darwinian battle had been won long before 1870; science was quietly verifying and exploring along the new lines; it was in literature, history, and theology that evolutionary conceptions were most visibly and dramatically at work. The ever-advancing study of comparative religion, and of the earliest documents and primitive history of Christianity — there lay in truth the chief interest of these years for many minds. When they began, 'Ecce Homo' had just been published; Baur's 'St. Paul,' the 'Vie de Jesus,' and Strauss's 'Neues Leben Jesu' were comparatively new books. Before my husband and I left Oxford in 1881, all Renan's 'Origines' had appeared, so had 'Literature and Dogma' and 'Supernatural Religion'; while Germany had seen the rise of that richer and more varied theological school of which Harnack has now become throughout Europe the chief representative. Before 1888, the year of 'Robert Elsmere,' this later German school, built on the foundations provided by Strauss and Baur, was at its height, it had captured the great majority of the German universities, and in the Dialogue on 'The New Reformation,' published in January, 1889, which I have reprinted at the end of the second volume of this edition, the effect of its development on English minds may be seen, I think, with some clearness.

Under the constant pressure of this advancing force, which we now see fully developed in 'Modernism,' the orthodoxy of Oxford, in my youth, showed itself naturally impatient and ill at ease. The University pulpit was filled with men endeavouring to fit a not very exacting science to a very grudging orthodoxy. It was not the great debate itself that we heard there, but rather its weakened echoes. Yet the great debate was all round us, and the heat of it was in the Oxford air. It was in the spring of 1881 that the Reverend John Wordsworth, Fellow and Tutor of Brasenose College, as he then was—now the Bishop of Salisbury— preached the Bampton Lectures in St. Mary's. A personal recollection with regard to the first of those Lectures may be given here, as it was in fact to the indignant reaction excited by that sermon in the mind of one of Dr. Wordsworth's hearers that 'Robert Elsmere' may ultimately be traced.

The syllabus of the Lecture had been circulated beforehand. It contained the following: 'The present unsettlement in religion. — Its relation to the move-ment of civilisation. — Sense of injustice often felt in a time of transition.— Book of Job. — Christ, however, connects unbelief and sin. — Moral causes of unbelief, (1) Prejudice; (2) Severe claims of religion; (3) Intellectual faults, especially indolence, coldness, recklessness, pride, and avarice.' These headings were developed in the sermon itself with a good deal of vigour and rigour. I remember gazing from those dim pews under the gallery, where the Masters' wives sit, at the fine ascetic face of the preacher, with its strong likeness to his great-uncle, the poet of English pantheism; and seeing beside it and around it, in imagination, the forms of those, his colleagues and contemporaries, the patient scholars and thinkers of the Liberal host, whom he was in truth — though perhaps not consciously — attacking. My heart burned within me; and it sprang into my mind that the only way to show England what was in truth going on in its midst, was to try and express it concretely, — in terms of actual life and conduct. Who and what were the persons who had either provoked the present unsettlement of religion, or were suffering under its effects? What was their history? How had their thoughts and doubts come to be? and what was the effect of them on conduct?

It was from this protesting impulse, constantly cherished and strengthened, that, a few years later, 'Robert Elsmere' took its beginning. It found immediate expression, however, in a pamphlet called 'Unbelief and Sin — a Protest addressed to those who attended the Bampton Lecture of Sunday, March 6.' I wrote it rapidly; it was printed, and put up for sale in the windows of a well-known bookseller's shop in the High Street. Then an incident, not without its touch of comedy, put a speedy end to its existence. I was then quite inexperienced in the details of publication, and I had not noticed that — no doubt with a shrewd eye to their large clerical *clientele* — the firm of booksellers concerned had omitted to give any printer's name on the pamphlet. It had only been in the window a few hours, and had been so far selling rapidly, when a well-known High Churchman walked in and asked to look at it. It was handed to him; he turned it over and asked to see one of the partners. The partner appeared; it was pointed out to him that to publish the pamphlet without a printer's name was an illegal act; that it must be at once withdrawn or penalties might be exacted. The frightened booksellers withdrew the pamphlet, and the incident closed — apparently — with a few letters in the *Guardian*. But, as I have already said, the crude pamphlet thus easily suppressed contained the germ of the later book. In it I tried to sketch two types of character, A and B, the one carried by history and criticism into 'unbelief,'— the other gradually stifling in himself the instincts and powers of the free mind; and I endeavoured to show that what the Bampton Lecturer had denounced as 'unbelief' was simply a 'particular way of judging' a series of documents and events belonging to history like any other documents and events; and that 'the Christian problem was first and foremost a literary problem,' and must be handled as such. As to the analysis of the phenomena of unbelief given by the preacher himself, the little pamphlet asked indignantly, 'Is this all that a religious teacher at the centre of English intellectual activity, whose business it is to make a study of religious thought and of the religious life in man, can tell us about that great movement of the human mind against the traditional Christian theology, which is to many of us the most important fact of our day and age? Does he see no further, does he understand no more than this?'

The note of emotion and complaint in this passage is of the date. The fight was hotter then than now; the older orthodoxy weighed upon England and on the minds of us all, like that consciousness of the Empire on the minds of Goth and Frank — a presence just withdrawn, or withdrawing, and 'still incalculably potent.' The certainties of what Dr. Wordsworth called 'unbelief' are much more certain now than then; and the attitude of the 'believer' towards them has fundamentally changed. Both sides have grown calmer to-day — the one in assertion, the other in denial; and between and beneath the two, the history and criticism, which in 1881 were still in the main a severing and disintegrating force, are now building unseen — perchance — the foundations of a larger unity. The 'unbelief' of the eighties must needs depart and go into exile. 'Robert Elsmere' expresses this point of view. Our empty churches and the ever diminishing hold of the Christian tradition in its older forms are the result of that situation. But Christianity, as a spirit and a life, is imperishable; the loom of Time has woven steadily in these twenty years; and there will be a new birth for the Church of England, and a new subject for the 'Dichtung' of the future, whenever English 'Modernism' is at last so sure of itself that instead of going out, it claims resolutely to stay within, and, at the cost perhaps of some decisive conflict, to make good its right and its citizenship within the Church of our fathers.

Meanwhile — beside the grave of George Tyrrell,[4] and envious of the new forces in Catholicism — we wait still for the signs of that greater future.

[...]

IV

Of the characters and composition of the book I have not myself very much to say. In Catherine I tried to embody influences and modes of thought well known to my own youth, though, for the purposes of the story, they had to be embodied in a personality narrower and severer on the intellectual side than any of those dear friends and kinswomen of my own, faithful and self-denying children of the national Church, whose lives and faith inspired the

4 George Tyrrell (1861-1909), prominent and extremely controversial Modernist theologian.

portrait of Catherine. Those whose memory goes back thirty or forty years, who are acquainted, moreover, with the Anglican memoirs and biographies of the mid-nineteenth century, will recognise very easily the sources whence she was drawn; nor, amid the weakened barriers and diffusive debates of our own day, is the type yet as rare as many people suppose. Nothing changes so slowly, in any nation, as the main types of its religious life. The ideas on which they ultimately rest may have been transformed or cast aside in the general march of the world's thought, but though, for the moment, 'the brains be out' the type survives; until perhaps, in the course of years, the flood of a changed and transfigured thought flows back into the old moulds and channels, and the type itself, through all differences, enters upon a new and vigorous life. I have often thought with regard to the Catherines of the world, *plus ça change, plus c'est la même chose!*

In Henry Grey I was of course thinking of the noblest and most persuasive master of philosophic thought in modern Oxford, Thomas Hill Green. The fragment of a Balliol sermon, in the first volume, is taken, as all editions of the book have pointed out, from one of the 'Lay Sermons,' delivered by Mr. Green, as a college tutor, and published after his death. But the character of Grey is in no sense a portrait of T. H. Green. Reality suggested many points in the description, as I was at some pains to admit; but I was writing a novel and not a biographical study, and 'Grey,' after the first few pages, plays a role and function wholly relative to the story and conditioned by it. His conversation with Elsmere at the moment of crisis reproduces ideas which are to be found in Mr. Green's writings, but does so in a style and setting which have nothing to do with the living figure. I desired with all my heart to pay a tribute to an influence and a personality which had meant so much to Oxford and to me; but the world of imagination has its own laws and paths, and Grey walks in them; too happy, in his creator's eyes, if at any point he calls to mind that infinitely richer and more potent life that Oxford knew, thirty years ago, as 'Green of Balliol.'

Langham owes his being entirely to the fact that in 1885, three years before the appearance of 'Robert Elsmere,' I had published a translation of Amiel's 'Journal Intime.' All those who felt with me the spell of that most pathetic and beautiful of the spiritual autobiographies of our day will remember the tragic passages in which Amiel dwells on the 'impossibility of willing,' the paralysis indeed of will power, and the lack of any effective interest in practical life and affairs, which wrecked his own career and quenched his own happiness. It was that impotence and that paralysis of the practical will, under the constant pressure of speculative thought, which, clothed in Oxford conditions and circumstances, I tried to realise anew in the character of Langham. Some of the phrases in the description of him are taken or paraphrased from the 'Journal Intime.' And yet, of course, Langham is no more Amiel than Grey is T. H. Green; as soon as he enters the little world of the novel, action and reaction begin; he shapes others and is shaped by them; and that final barrenness into which he falls has small relation indeed to the sad beauty, the tremulous hope, the dignity and renunciation which make Amiel's last pages so dear to many.

Elsmere himself is a figure of pure imagination, inspired and coloured, as all such figures are, by the actual human experience amid which he was conceived. Of the origins of the Squire I have said as much as I know, and it would not interest the readers of these pages if I were to try and unravel for them the threads and shreds of reality which went to the weaving of the minor groups and the general background of the story. And of the story itself it is not for me, even at this distance of time, to attempt any general criticism. Its faults are patent. It is the work of one who, in spite of — or perhaps because of — her long immersion in a learned and literary society was in many respects younger than her years, with much of the inexperience, much also of the courageous optimism of youth. From a purely literary point of view the book wants irony and detachment; it is not sufficiently objective and disinterested. Here and there I have been tempted to rewrite a scene which a wider experience of life since it was written might have enabled me to improve. But in the end I have changed little or nothing. The omission of a few paragraphs, the correction of a few redundancies and repetitions —my revision has only amounted to this. For the book belonged to a particular moment both in my own life and in the life of my generation. Whatever merit it has is a merit first and foremost of sincerity, of correspondence to something really felt and seen, the communication of a burning and still recent impression. The feeling of to-day would express itself in other ways and through other methods; but the feeling of yesterday has its own rights, and, if one may so speak, its own sacredness. And is there not a kind of responsibility, also, to those who shared it with us? It was thus the book was written; it was thus it was welcomed, and by many whose eyes are now closed for ever; and for whatever span of life it may still command, it shall go out with the same dress and aspect as at first. The voices of hope and doubt that speak through it are still breathing over England and Europe, though they speak with other accents and a changed emphasis. Perhaps time and strength may yet be left me in which to try and interpret them afresh.

APPENDIX B - THE HISTORY OF DAVID GRIEVE

Ward's first novel after *Robert Elsmere* was *The History of David Grieve* (1891), a *bildungsroman* which tells the story of a young man's journey from orphaned farm boy to intellectual bookseller; the counterpart to his tale is that of his uncanny sister Louie, whose greed and sexual adventurousness ultimately lead to her death. (David's own sexual adventurousness, needless to say, does not.) Although David does not share Robert's crisis of faith—he is a freethinker practically from the beginning—the first excerpt below suggests Ward's ongoing interest in fictional narrative as a route to moral and spiritual development. In the second, David's expression of mature belief still owes much to *Robert Elsmere's* Idealism.

'D' yo think as theer's onybody in Haworth as would lend me a seet o' yan o' Miss Brontë's tales for an hour?' he said, reddening furiously, as they stopped at the sexton's gate.

'Why, to be sure, mon,' said the sexton cheerily, pleased with the little opening for intelligent patronage. 'Coom your ways in, and we'll see if we can't oblige yo. I 've got a tidy lot o' books in my parlour, an I can give yo "Shirley," I know.'

David went into the stone-built cottage with his guide, and was shown in the little musty front room a bookcase full of books which made his eyes gleam with desire. The half-curbed joy and eagerness he showed so touched the sexton that, after inquiring as to the lad's belongings, and remembering that in his time he had enjoyed many a pipe and 'glass o' yell' with 'owd Reuben Grieve' at the 'Brown Bess,' the worthy man actually lent him indefinitely three precious volumes — 'Shirley,' 'Benjamin Franklin's Autobiography,' and 'Nicholas Nickleby.'

David ran off hugging them, and thenceforward he bore patiently enough with the days of driving and tramping which remained, for the sake of the long evenings when in some lonely corner of moor and wood he lay full length on the grass revelling in one or other of his new possessions. He had a voracious way of tearing out the heart of a book first of all, and then beginning it again with a different and a tamer curiosity, lingering, tasting, and digesting. By the time he and Reuben reached home he had rushed through all three books, and his mind was full of them.

'Shirley' and 'Nicholas Nickleby' were the first novels of modern life he had ever laid hands on, and before he had finished them he felt them in his veins like new wine. The real world had been to him for months something sickeningly narrow and empty, from which at times he had escaped with passion into a distant dream-life of poetry and history. Now the walls of this real world were suddenly pushed back as it were on all sides, and there was an inrush of crowd, excitement, and delight. Human beings like those he heard of or talked with every day — factory hands and mill-owners, parsons, squires, lads and lasses — the Yorkes, and Robert Moore, Squeers, Smike, Kate Nickleby and Newman Noggs, came by, looked him in the eyes, made him take sides, compare himself with them, join in their fights and hatreds, pity and exult with them. Here was something more disturbing, personal, and stimulating than that mere imaginative relief he had been getting out of 'Paradise Lost,' or the scenes of the 'Jewish Wars'!

By a natural transition the mental tumult thus roused led to a more intense self-consciousness than any he had yet known. In measuring himself with the world of 'Shirley' or of Dickens, he began to realise the problem of his own life with a singular keenness and clearness. Then — last of all — the record of Franklin's life — of the steady rise of the ill-treated printers' devil to knowledge and power — filled him with an urging and concentrating ambition, and set his thoughts, endowed with a new heat and nimbleness, to the practical unravelling of a practical case.

[...]

'David!' she broke out, 'what is it you believe? You know Dora thinks you believe nothing.'

'Does she?' he said, with evident shrinking. 'No, I don't think she does.'

Lucy instinctively moved her chair closer to him, and laid her head against his knee.

'Yes, she does. But I don't mind about that. I just wish you'd tell me why you believe in God, when you won't go to church, and when you think Jesus was just — just a man.'

She drew her breath quickly. She was making a first voyage of discovery in her husband's deepest mind, and she was astonished at her own venturesomeness.

He put out a hand and touched her hair.

'I can't read Nature and life any other way,' he said at last, after a silence. 'There seems to me something in myself, and in other human beings, which is beyond Nature — which, instead of being made by Nature, is the condition of our knowing there is a Nature at all. This something — reason, conscious-ness, soul, call it what you will — unites us to the world; for everywhere in the world reason is at home, and gradually finds itself; it makes us aware of a great order in which we move; it breaks down the barriers of sense between us and the absolute consciousness, the eternal life — "not ourselves," yet in us and akin to us! — whence, if there is any validity in human logic, that order must spring. And so, in its most perfect work, it carries us to God — it bids us claim our sonship — it gives us hope of immortality!'

His voice had the vibrating intensity of prayer. Lucy hardly understood what he said at all, but the tears came into her eyes as she sat hiding them against his knee.

'But what makes you think God is good — that He cares anything about us?' she said softly.

'Well — I look back on human life, and I ask what reason — which is the Divine Life communicated to us, striving to fulfil itself in us — has done, what light it throws upon its "great Original." And then I see that it has gradually expressed itself in law, in knowledge, in love; that it has gradually learnt, under the pressure of something which is itself and not itself, that to be gained life must be lost; that beauty, truth, love, are the *realities* which abide. Goodness has slowly proved itself in the world, — is every day proving itself, — like a light broadening in darkness! — to be that to which reason tends, in which it realises itself. And, if so, goodness here, imperfect and struggling as we see it always, must be the mere shadow and hint of that goodness which is in God! — and the utmost we can conceive of human tenderness, holiness, truth, though it tell us all we know, can yet suggest to us only the minutest fraction of what must be the Divine tenderness, — holiness, — truth.'

There was a silence.

'But this,' he added after a bit, 'is not to be *proved* by argument, though argument is necessary and inevitable, the mind being what it is. It can only be proved by living, — by taking it into our hearts, — by every little victory we gain over the evil self.'

The fire burnt quietly beside them. Everything was still in the house. Noth-ing stirred but their own hearts. At last Lucy looked up quickly.

'I am glad,' she said, with a kind of sob—'glad you think God loves us, and, if Sandy and I were to die, you would find us again.'

APPENDIX C - THE CASE OF RICHARD MEYNELL

The Case of Richard Meynell (1911) tracks the effects of Robert Elsmere's work into the next generation. However, by this point, Ward had rejected Robert's solution to his own crisis: no longer was it best for religious liberals to leave the church. Instead, they needed to remain within the precincts of orthodox Anglicanism, the better to reform it from inside. But in *The Case of Richard Meynell*, the Church of England is not in a mood to cooperate, and Richard is put on trial for heresy. The following is taken from Richard's sermon, "The Two Christianities," delivered after Richard loses his case but before he loses his position (which has not yet happened at novel's end); Ward intends it to model what Modernist Christianity, the historically-based religion of the future, might look like.

'...Why are we here, my friends? For what purpose is this great demonstration, this moving rite in which we have joined this day? One-sixth at least of this congregation stands here under a sentence of ecclesiastical death. A few weeks perhaps, and this mighty church will know its white-haired Bishop no more. Bishop and Chapter will have been driven out; and we, the rank and file, whose only desire is to cling to the Church in which we were baptized and bred, will find ourselves exiles and homeless.

'What is our crime? This only,—that God has spoken in our consciences, and we have not been able to resist Him. Nor dare we desert our posts in the national Church, till force drive us out. Why? Because there is something infinitely greater at stake than any reproach that can be hurled at us on the ground of broken pledges—pledges made too early, given in ignorance and good faith, and broken now, solemnly, in the face of God and this people— for a greater good. What does our personal consistency—which, mind you, is a very different thing from personal honesty!—matter? We are as sensitive as any man who attacks us on the point of personal honour. But we are constrained of God; we bear in our hands the cause of our brethren, the cause of half the nation; and we can no other. Ask yourselves what we have to gain by it. Nay!—With expulsion and exile in sight—with years perhaps of the wilderness before us—we stand here for the liberties of Christ's Church!—its liberties of growth and life. . . .

'My friends, what is the life either of intellect or spirit but the response of man to the communication of God? Age by age, man's consciousness cuts deeper into the vast mystery that surrounds us; absorbs, transmutes, translates ever more of truth, into conceptions he can use, and language he can understand.

'From this endless process arise science—and history—and philosophy. But just as science, and history, and philosophy, change with this ever-living and growing advance, so religion—man's ideas of God and his own soul.

'Within the last hundred years man's knowledge of the physical world has broadened beyond the utmost dreams of our fathers. But of far greater importance to man is his knowledge of himself. There too, the century of which we are now the heirs has lifted the veil—for us first among living men—from secrets hitherto unknown. History has come into being.

'What is HISTORY? Simply the power—depending upon a thousand laborious processes—of constructing a magic lens within the mind which allows us to look deep into the past, to see its life and colour and movement again, as no generation but our own has yet been able to see it. We hold our breath sometimes, as for a brief moment perhaps we catch its very gesture, its very habit as it lived, the very tone of its voices. It has been a new and marvellous gift of our God to us; and it has transformed or is transforming Christianity.

'Like science, this new discipline of the human mind is divine, and authoritative. It lessens the distance between our human thought and the thought of God, because in the familiar phrase, it enables us to "think, in some sort, His thoughts after Him." Like science it marches slowly on its way; through many mistakes; through hypothesis and rectification; through daring vision and laborious proof; to an ever-broadening certainty. History has taken hold of the Christian tradition. History has worked upon it with an amazing tenderness, and patience and reverence. And at the end of a hundred years what do we see?—that half of Christendom, at least, which we in this church represent?

'We see a Christ stripped of Jewish legend, and Greek speculation, and medieval scholasticism; moving simply and divinely among the ways of his Jewish world, a man among men. We can watch, dimly indeed by comparison with our living scrutiny of living men, but still more clearly than any generation of Christendom since the disappearance of the first has been able to watch, the rise of His thoughts, the nature of His environment, the sequence of His acts, the original significance, the immediate interpretation, the subsequent influence of his death. We know much more of Jesus of Nazareth than the fathers of Nicæa knew; probably than St. Paul knew; certainly than

Irenæus or Clement knew.[1]

'But that is only half the truth; only half of what history has to tell. On the one side we have to do with the recovered fact: on the other with its working through two thousand years upon the world.

'*There*, for the Modernist, lies revelation!—in the unfolding of the Christian idea, through the successive stages of human thought and imagination it has traversed, down to the burst of revelation in the present day. Yet we are only now at the beginning of an immense development. The content of the Christian idea of love—love, self-renouncing, self-fulfilling—is infinite, inexhaustible, like that of beauty, or of truth. Why? At this moment, I am only concerned to give you the Christian answer, which is the answer of a reasonable faith. Because, like the streams springing for ever from "the pure founts of Cephisus," to nourish the swelling plains below,2 these governing ideas of our life—tested by life, confirmed by life—have their source in the very being of God, sharers in His Eternity, His Ever-Fruitfulness. . . .

'But even so, you have not exhausted the wealth of Christianity. For to the potency of the Christian idea, is added the magic of an incomparable embodiment in human life. The story of Jesus bears the idea which it enshrines eternally through the world. It is to the idea as the vessel of the Grail.

'... Do these conceptions make us love our Master less? Ask your own hearts? There must be many in this crowded church that have known sorrow—intolerable anguish and disappointment — gnawing self-reproach— during the past year, or months, or weeks ; many that have watched sufferings which no philosophic optimism can explain, and catastrophes that leave men dumb. Some among them will have been driven back upon their faith—driven to the foot of the Cross. Through all intellectual difference, has not the natural language of their fathers been also their language? Is there anything in their changed opinions which has cut them off from that sacrifice

'Renewed in every pulse,

That on the tedious Cross

Told the long hours of death, as, one by one,

---

1 St. Irenæus (second century CE) and, given what Meynell is implying, more likely St. Clement of Alexandria (second and third centuries CE) than Pope Clement I (first century CE), all Church fathers.

2 From Sophocles' *Oedipus at Colonus*: "Nor fail the wandering springs/that feed the streams of Cephisus,/but daily and ever the river/with his pure waters gives increase/over the swelling bosom of the land." *Oedipus at Colonus*, tr. David Grene, in *The Complete Greek Tragedies: Vol. II, Sophocles* (Chicago: University of Chicago Press, 1992), 112.

The life-strings of that tender heart gave way?[3]

'Is there anything in this new compelling knowledge that need—that does—divide *us*—whose consciences dare not refuse it—from the immortal triumph of that death? In our sharpest straits, are we not comforted and cleansed and sustained by the same thoughts, the same visions that have always sustained and comforted the Christian? No!—the sons of tradition and dogma have no monopoly in the exaltation, the living passion of the Cross! We, too, watching that steadfastness grow steadfast; bowed before that innocent suffering, grow patient; drinking in the wonder of that faith, amid utter defeat, learn to submit and go forward. In us too, as we behold,—Hope "masters Agony!"[4]—and we follow, for a space at least, with our Master, into the heavenly house, and still our sore hearts before our God.'

---

3 John Keble, "Tuesday before Easter," from *The Christian Year*, ll. 39-42.
4 Keble, "Tuesday before Easter," l. 53.

APPENDIX D - GLADSTONE'S RESPONSE TO ROBERT ELSMERE

In her memoirs, *A Writer's Recollections* (1918), Ward reprints a letter in which she describes a stimulating but heated debate with W. E. Gladstone over *Robert Elsmere*: "The new lines of criticism are not familiar to him, and they really press him hard [...] But there is a sense, I think, that question and answer don't fit, and with it ever increasing interest and—sometimes—irritation" (238). Although Gladstone, then Prime Minister, initially waffled about writing the review, he ultimately produced what was by far the most influential critical assessment of the novel as both literature and theology. Most notably, Gladstone criticizes the novel for proposing a new religion without invoking any of the authority (sacramental, Scriptural, or otherwise) upon which the old rests. The review appeared in the May 1888 issue of *The Nineteenth Century*, the prestigious monthly in which Robert Elsmere also "publishes"; the journal printed Ward's rejoinder to Gladstone, a dialogue called "The New Reformation," in March 1889.

[Gladstone's original page references have been silently deleted]

"ROBERT ELSMERE" AND THE BATTLE OF BELIEF

Human nature, when aggrieved, is apt and quick in devising compensations. The increasing seriousness and strain of our present life may have had the effect of bringing about the large preference, which I understand to be exhibited in local public libraries, for works of fiction. This is the first expedient of revenge. But it is only a link in a chain. The next step is, that the writers of what might be grave books, *in esse* or *in posse*, have endeavored with some success to circumvent the multitude. Those who have systems or hypotheses to recommend in philosophy, conduct, or religion induct them into the costume of romance. Such was the second expedient of nature, the counterstroke of her revenge. When this was done in "Télémaque," "Rasselas," or "Cœlebs," it was not without literary effect.[1] Even the last of these three appears to have been successful with its own generation. It would now be deemed intolerably

---

1 Archbishop François de Salignac de la Mothe-Fénelon, *Les Aventures de Télémaque* (1699); Samuel Johnson, *The History of Rasselas, Prince of Abissinia* (1759); Hannah More, *Cœlebs in Search of a Wife* (1809).

dull. But a dull book is easily renounced. The more didactic fictions of the
present day, so far as I know them, are not dull. We take them up, however,
and we find that, when we meant to go to play, we have gone to school. The
romance is a gospel of some philosophy, or of some religion; and requires sustained thought on many or some of the deepest subjects, as the only rational
alternative to placing ourselves at the mercy of our author. We find that he
has put upon us what is not indeed a treatise, but more formidable than if
it were. For a treatise must nowhere beg the question it seeks to decide, but
must carry its reader onward by reasoning patiently from step to step. But
the writer of the romance, under the convenient necessity which his form
imposes, skips in thought, over undefined distances, from stage to stage, as
a bee from flower to flower. A creed may (as here) be accepted in a sentence,
and then abandoned in a page. But we, the common herd of readers, if we are
to deal with the consequences, to accept or repel the influence of the book,
must, as in a problem of mathematics, supply the missing steps. Thus, in
perusing as we ought a propagandist romance, we must terribly increase the
pace; and it is the pace that kills.

Among the works to which the preceding remarks might apply, the most
remarkable within my knowledge is "Robert Elsmere." It is indeed remarkable
in many respects. It is a novel of nearly twice the length, and much more than
twice the matter, of ordinary novels. It dispenses almost entirely, in the con-
struction of what must still be called its plot, with the aid of incident in the
ordinary sense. We have indeed near the close a solitary individual crushed by
a wagon, but this catastrophe has no relation to the plot, and its only purpose
is to exhibit a good deathbed in illustration of the great missionary idea of
the piece. The *nexus* of the structure is to be found wholly in the workings of
character. The assumption and the surrender of a rectory are the most salient
events, and they are simple results of what the actor has thought right. And
yet the great, nay, paramount function of character-drawing, the projection
upon the canvas of human beings endowed with the true forces of nature and
vitality, does not appear to be by any means the master-gift of the authoress.
In the mass of matter which she has prodigally expended there might obviously be retrenchment; for there are certain laws of dimension which apply to
a novel, and which separate it from an epic. In the extraordinary number of
personages brought upon the stage in one portion or other of the book, there
are some which are elaborated with greater pains and more detail, than their
relative importance seems to warrant. "Robert Elsmere" is hard reading, and
requires toil and effort. Yet, if it be difficult to persist, it is impossible to stop.
The prisoner on the treadmill must work severely to perform his task; but if

he stops he at once receives a blow which brings him to his senses. Here, as there, it is human infirmity which shrinks; but here, as not there, the propelling motive is within. Deliberate judgment and deep interest alike rebuke a fainting reader. The strength of the book, overbearing every obstacle, seems to lie in an extraordinary wealth of diction, never separated from thought; in a close and searching faculty of social observation; in generous appreciation of what is morally good, impartially[2] exhibited in all directions: above all, in the sense of mission with which the writer is evidently possessed, and in the earnestness and persistency of purpose with which through every page and line it is pursued. The book is eminently an offspring of the time, and will probably make a deep or at least a very sensible impression; not, however, among mere novel-readers, but among those who share, in whatever sense, the deeper thought of the period.

[...]

If there be truth in this novel and interesting suggestion, we cannot wonder at finding the result exhibited in "Robert Elsmere," for never was a book written with greater persistency and intensity of purpose. Every page of its principal narrative is adapted and addressed by Mrs. Ward to the final aim which is bone of her bone and flesh of her flesh. This aim is to expel the preternatural element from Christianity, to destroy its dogmatic structure, yet to keep intact the moral and spiritual results. The Brotherhood presented to us with such sanguine hopefulness is a "Christian" brotherhood, but with a Christianity emptied of that which Christians believe to be the soul and springhead of its life. For Christianity, in the established Christian sense, is the presentation to us not of abstract dogmas for acceptance, but of a living and a Divine Person, to whom they are to be united by a vital incorporation. It is the reunion to God of a nature severed from God by sin, and the process is one, not of teaching lessons, but of imparting a new life, with its ordained equipment of gifts and powers.

It is, I apprehend, a complete mistake to suppose, as appears to be the supposition of this remarkable book, that all which has to be done with Scripture, in order to effect the desired transformation of religion, is to eliminate from it the miraculous element. Tremendous as is the sweeping process which extrudes the Resurrection, there is much else, which is in no sense miracu-

---

2 Mrs Ward has given evidence of this impartiality in her Dedication to the memory of two friends, of whom one, Mrs. Alfred Lyttelton, lived and died unshaken in belief. The other is more or less made known in the pages of the work. [original footnote]

lous, to extrude along with it. The Procession of Palms, for example, is indeed profoundly significant, but it is in no way miraculous. Yet, in any consistent history of a Robert Elsmere's Christ, there could be no Procession of Palms. Unless it be the healing of the ear of Malchus, there is not a miraculous event between the commencement of the Passion and the Crucifixion itself. Yet the notes of a superhuman majesty overspread the whole. We talk of all religions as essentially one; but what religion presents to its votaries such a tale as this? Bishop Temple, in his sermons at Rugby, has been among the later teachers who have shown how the whole behavior of our Lord, in this extremity of His abasement, seems more than ever to transcend all human limits, and to exhibit without arguing His Divinity. The parables, again, are not less refractory than the miracles, and must disappear along with them: for what parables are there which are not built upon the idea of His unique and transcendent office? The Gospel of Saint John has much less of miracle than the Synoptics; but it must of course descend from its pedestal, in all that is most its own. And what is gained by all this condemnation, until we get rid of the Baptismal formula? It is a question not of excision from the gospels, but of tearing them into shreds. Far be it from me to deny that the parts which remain, or which remain legible, are vital parts; but this is no more than to say that there may remain vital organs of a man, after the man himself has been cut in pieces.

[...]

In a concise but striking notice in the *Times*[3] it is placed in the category of "clever attacks upon revealed religion." It certainly offers us a substitute for revealed religion; and possibly the thought of the book might be indicated in these words: "The Christianity accepted in England is a good thing; but come with me, and I will show you a better."

It may, I think, be fairly described as a devout attempt, made in good faith, to simplify the difficult mission of religion in the world by discarding the supposed lumber of the Christian theology, while retaining and applying, in their undiminished breadth of scope, the whole personal, social, and spiritual morality which has now, as matter of fact, entered into the patrimony of Christendom; and, since Christendom is the dominant power of the world, into the patrimony of the race. It is impossible indeed to conceive a more religious life than the later life of Robert Elsmere, in his sense of the word religion. And that sense is far above the sense in which religion is held, or practically ap-

---

3 *Times*, April 7, 1888. [original footnote]

plied, by great multitudes of Christians. It is, however, a new form of religion. The question is, can it be actually and beneficially substituted for the old one? It abolishes of course the whole authority of Scripture. It abolishes also Church, priesthood or ministry, sacraments, and the whole established machinery which trains the Christian as a member of a religious society. These have been regarded by fifty generations of men as wings of the soul. It is still required by Mrs. Ward to fly, and to fly as high as ever; but it is to fly without wings. For baptism, we have a badge of silver, and inscription in a book. For the Eucharist there is at an ordinary meal a recital of the fragment, "This do in remembrance of Me." The children respond, "Jesus, we remember Thee always." It is hard to say that prayer is retained. In the Elgood Street service "it is rather an act of adoration and faith, than a prayer properly so called," and it appears that memory and trust are the instruments on which the individual is to depend, for maintaining his communion with God. It would be curious to know how the New Brotherhood is to deal with the great mystery of marriage, perhaps the truest touchstone of religious revolution.

It must be obvious to every reader that in the great duel between the old faith and the new, as it is fought in "Robert Elsmere," there is a great inequality in the distribution of the arms. Reasoning is the weapon of the new scheme; emotion the sole resource of the old. Neither Catherine nor Newcome have a word to say beyond the expression of feeling; and it is when he has adopted the negative side that the hero himself is fully introduced to the faculty of argument. This is a singular arrangement, especially in the case of a writer who takes a generous view of the Christianity that she only desires to supplant by an improved device. The explanation may be simple. There are abundant signs in the book that the negative speculatists have been consulted if not ransacked; but there is nowhere a sign that the authoress has made herself acquainted with the Christian apologists, old or recent; or has weighed the evidences derivable from the Christian history; or has taken measure of the relation in which the doctrines of grace have historically stood to the production of the noblest, purest, and greatest characters of the Christian ages. If such be the case, she has skipped lightly (to put it no higher) over vast mental spaces of literature and learning relevant to the case, and has given sentence in the cause without hearing the evidence.

Victorian Secrets

Helbeck of Bannisdale

by Mary Augusta Ward

edited by Beth Sutton-Ramspeck

Written when the New Woman novel was at the height of its popularity, *Helbeck of Bannisdale* depicts the tension between a heroine's desire for independence and her love for a man who prefers wifely submission. After her father's death, Laura Fountain struggles with the legacy of his agnosticism and her growing affection for Catholic ascetic Alan Helbeck. She must decide whether love can triumph over religious scruples. Mary Ward's powerful novel captures the drama and conflict of the late nineteenth-century debates surrounding faith, doubt, and a woman's place in society.

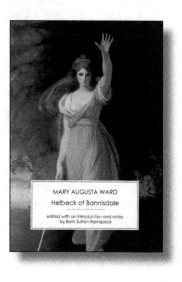

MARY AUGUSTA WARD

Helbeck of Bannisdale

edited with an introduction and notes
by Beth Sutton-Ramspeck

This scholarly edition, edited by Beth Sutton-Ramspeck, includes:

* Critical introduction
* Author biography
* Select bibliography
* Ward's introduction to the Westmoreland Edition
* Dr James Begg's 'The Blight of Popery'
* Extract from Thomas Henry Huxley's 'Agnosticism and Christianity'
* Extract from Alys Whithall Pearsall Smith's 'A Reply from the Daughters'
* Glossary of regional terms, words and phrases used in the text

ISBN: 978-1-906469-59-7
Available in paperback, EPUB, and Kindle editions.

www.victoriansecrets.co.uk